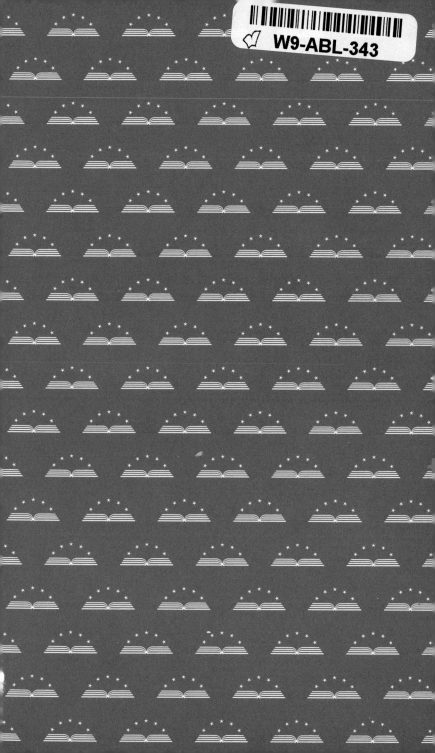

PHILIP ROTH

PHILIP ROTH

NOVELS
1993–1995
Operation Shylock
Sabbath's Theater

THE LIBRARY OF AMERICA

The paper used in this publication meets the
minimum requirements of the American National Standard for
Information Sciences—Permanence of Paper for Printed
Library Materials, ANSI Z39.48—1984.

Distributed to the trade in the United States
by Penguin Group (USA) Inc.
and in Canada by Penguin Books Canada Ltd.

Library of Congress Catalog Card Number: 2010920145
ISBN: 978-1-59853-078-0

———

First Printing
The Library of America—205

Manufactured in the United States of America

PHILIP ROTH

NOVELS
1993–1995
Operation Shylock
Sabbath's Theater

THE LIBRARY OF AMERICA

Operation Shylock copyright © 1993 by Philip Roth. Published by
permission of Simon & Schuster, Inc. *Operation Shylock* author's
note copyright © 2010 The Franklin Mint, LLC. *Sabbath's
Theater* copyright © 1995 by Philip Roth. This edition
published by special arrangement with Houghton
Mifflin Harcourt Publishing Company.

The paper used in this publication meets the
minimum requirements of the American National Standard for
Information Sciences—Permanence of Paper for Printed
Library Materials, ANSI Z39.48—1984.

Distributed to the trade in the United States
by Penguin Group (USA) Inc.
and in Canada by Penguin Books Canada Ltd.

Library of Congress Catalog Card Number: 2010920145
ISBN: 978–1–59853–078–0

First Printing
The Library of America—205

Manufactured in the United States of America

Ross Miller
wrote the Chronology and Notes
for this volume

Contents

OPERATION SHYLOCK

A Confession

For Claire

Contents

וַיִּוָּתֵ֥ר יַֽעֲקֹ֖ב לְבַדּ֑וֹ וַיֵּאָבֵ֥ק
אִישׁ֙ עִמּ֔וֹ עַ֖ד עֲל֥וֹת הַשָּֽׁחַר

So Jacob was left alone, and a man wrestled with him until daybreak.

—GENESIS 32:24

———

The whole content of my being shrieks in contradiction against itself.

Existence is surely a debate . . .

—KIERKEGAARD

Preface

For legal reasons, I have had to alter a number of facts in this book. These are minor changes that mainly involve details of identification and locale and are of little significance to the overall story and its verisimilitude. Any name that has been changed is marked with a small circle the first time it appears.

I've drawn *Operation Shylock* from notebook journals. The book is as accurate an account as I am able to give of actual occurrences that I lived through during my middle fifties and that culminated, early in 1988, in my agreeing to undertake an intelligence-gathering operation for Israel's foreign intelligence service, the Mossad.

The commentary on the Demjanjuk case reflects accurately and candidly what I was thinking in January 1988, nearly five years before Soviet evidence introduced on appeal by the defense led the Israeli Supreme Court to consider vacating the death sentence handed down in 1988 by the Jerusalem District Court, whose sessions I attended and describe here. On the basis of Soviet interrogations dating from 1944 to 1960 that came fully to light only after the demise of the Soviet Union—and in which twenty-one former Red Army soldiers who volunteered to become SS auxiliaries and whom the Soviet authorities later executed established the surname of Treblinka's Ivan the Terrible to have been Marchenko and not Demjanjuk—the defense contended that it was impossible for the prosecution to prove beyond a shadow of a doubt that the Cleveland autoworker John Ivan Demjanjuk and the notorious gas-chamber operator were the same "Ivan." The prosecution's rebuttal claimed not only that the records from the old Soviet Union were riddled with inconsistencies and contradictions but that, even more importantly, because the evidence had been taken under unascertainable circumstances from guards no longer available for cross-examination, it was inadmissible hearsay. In addition the prosecution argued that newly discovered documentation from German federal archives now proved conclusively that Demjanjuk had perjured himself repeatedly in denying that he had also been a guard at the

7

Trawniki training camp, the Flossenburg concentration camp, and the Sobibor death camp.

As of this date, the Supreme Court is still deliberating the appeal.

P.R.

December 1, 1992

1

Pipik Appears

I LEARNED about the other Philip Roth in January 1988, a few days after the New Year, when my cousin Apter° telephoned me in New York to say that Israeli radio had reported that I was in Jerusalem attending the trial of John Demjanjuk, the man alleged to be Ivan the Terrible of Treblinka. Apter told me that the Demjanjuk trial was being broadcast, in its entirety, every day, on radio and TV. According to his landlady, I had momentarily appeared on the TV screen the day before, identified by the commentator as one of the courtroom spectators, and then this very morning he had himself heard the corroborating news items on the radio. Apter was calling to check on my whereabouts because he had understood from my last letter that I wasn't to be in Jerusalem until the end of the month, when I planned to interview the novelist Aharon Appelfeld. He told his landlady that if I were in Jerusalem I would already have contacted him, which was indeed the case—during the four visits I had made while I was working up the Israel sections of *The Counterlife*, I'd routinely taken Apter to lunch a day or two after my arrival.

This cousin Apter—twice removed on my mother's side—is an unborn adult, in 1988 a fifty-four-year-old who had evolved into manhood without evolving, an under-life-size, dollish-looking man with the terrifyingly blank little face of an aging juvenile actor. There is imprinted on Apter's face absolutely nothing of the mayhem of Jewish life in the twentieth century, even though in 1943 his entire family had been consumed by the German mania for murdering Jews. He had been saved by a German officer who'd kidnapped him at the Polish transport site and sold him to a male brothel in Munich. This was a profitable sideline the officer had. Apter was nine. He remains chained to his childishness to this day, someone who still, in late middle age, cries as easily as he blushes and who can barely meet one's level gaze with his own chronically imploring eyes, someone whose whole life lies in the hands of the past. For that reason, I didn't believe any of what he said to me on the phone about another Philip Roth, who had showed up in Jerusalem without letting him know. His hunger is unappeasable for those who are not here.

But four days later I received a second call in New York about my presence in Jerusalem, this one from Aharon Appelfeld. Aharon had been a close friend since we'd met at a reception given for him by Israel's London cultural attaché in the early eighties, when I was still living most of each year in London. The American publication of his newly translated novel, *The Immortal Bartfuss*, was to be the occasion for the conversation I'd arranged to conduct with him for *The New York Times Book Review*. Aharon phoned to tell me that at the Jerusalem café where he went to write every day, he'd picked up the previous weekend's edition of *The Jerusalem Post* and, on the page-long listing of the coming week's cultural events, under Sunday, come on a notice he thought I should know about. Had he seen it a few days earlier, Aharon said, he would have attended the event as my silent emissary.

"Diasporism: The Only Solution to the Jewish Problem." A lecture by Philip Roth; discussion to follow. 6:00 P.M. Suite 511, King David Hotel. Refreshments.

I spent all that evening wondering what to do about Aharon's confirmation of Apter's news. Finally, having convinced myself during a largely sleepless night that some fluky series of errors had resulted in a mix-up of identities that it was in my best interest to disregard, I got out of bed early the next morning and, before I had even washed my face, telephoned suite 511 of Jerusalem's King David Hotel. I asked the woman who answered—and who answered speaking American English —if a Mr. Roth was there. I heard her call out to someone, "Hon—you." Then a man came on the line. I asked if this was Philip Roth. "It is," he replied, "and who is this, please?"

The calls from Israel had reached me at the two-room Manhattan hotel suite where my wife and I had been living for nearly five months, as though aground on the dividing line between past and future. The impersonality of big-city hotel life was most uncongenial to the domestic instinct so strong in both of us, yet ill-equipped though we were to be displaced and to be living together in this uprooted, unfamiliar way, it was preferable for the time being to our returning to the Connecticut farmhouse where, during the previous spring and early summer, while Claire stood helplessly by, fearing the worst, I had barely made it through the most harrowing exigency of my life. Half a mile from the nearest neighbor's dwelling and encompassed by woods and open fields at the end of a long dirt road, that large, secluded old house whose setting had for over fifteen years furnished just the isolation my concentration required had become the eerie backdrop for a bizarre emotional collapse; that cozy clapboard sanctuary, with its wide chestnut floorboards and worn easy chairs, a place where books were piled everywhere and a log fire burned high in the hearth most every night, had suddenly become a hideous asylum confining side by side one abominable lunatic and one bewildered keeper. A place I loved had come to fill me with dread, and I found myself reluctant to resume our residence there even after we'd mislaid these five months as hotel refugees and my familiar industrious personality had drifted back to take the reins and set me again to trotting reliably enough along the good old rut of my life. (Drifted back tentatively at the start, by no means convinced that things were as secure as they had seemed before; drifted back rather the way the work force standing out in the street drifts back into an office building that has been temporarily cleared because of a bomb scare.)

What had happened was this:

In the aftermath of minor knee surgery, my pain, instead of diminishing as the weeks passed, got worse and worse, far exceeding the prolonged discomfort that had prompted me to decide on surgery in the first place. When I went to see my young surgeon about the worsening condition, he merely said, "This happens sometimes," and, claiming to have warned me beforehand that the operation might not work, dismissed me as his patient. I was left with only some pills to mitigate my astonishment and manage the pain. Such a surprising outcome from a brief outpatient procedure might have made anyone angry and despondent; what happened in my case was worse.

My mind began to disintegrate. The word DISINTEGRA- TION seemed itself to be the matter out of which my brain was constituted, and it began spontaneously coming apart. The fourteen letters, big, chunky, irregularly sized compo- nents of my brain, elaborately intertwined, tore jaggedly loose from one another, sometimes a fragment of a letter at a time, but usually in painfully unpronounceable nonsyllabic segments of two or three, their edges roughly serrated. This mental coming apart was as distinctly physical a reality as a tooth being pulled, and the agony of it was excruciating.

Hallucinations like these and worse stampeded through me day and night, a herd of wild animals I could do nothing to stop. I couldn't stop anything, my will blotted out by the mag- nitude of the tiniest, most idiotic thought. Two, three, four times a day, without provocation or warning, I'd begin to cry. It didn't matter if I was alone in my studio, turning the page of yet another book that I couldn't read, or at dinner with Claire, looking hopelessly at the food she'd prepared that I couldn't find any reason to eat—I cried. I cried before friends, before strangers; even sitting alone on the toilet I would dissolve, wring myself dry with tears, an outpouring of tears that left me feeling absolutely raw—shorn by tears of five decades of living, my inmost being lay revealed to everyone in all its sickly puniness.

I could not forget my shirtsleeves for two minutes at a time. I couldn't seem to prevent myself from feverishly rolling up my shirtsleeves and then rolling them down just as feverishly and meticulousy buttoning the cuff, only immediately to un- button the cuff and begin the meaningless procedure once more, as though its meaning went, in fact, to the core of my existence. I couldn't stop flinging open the windows and then, when my claustrophobic fit had given way to chills, banging them shut as though it were not I but someone else who had flung them all open. My pulse rate would shoot up to 120 beats a minute even while I sat, brain-dead, in front of the nightly TV news, a corpse but for a violently thumping heart that had taken to keeping time to a clock ticking twice as fas as any on earth. That was another manifestation of the panic that I could do nothing to control: panic sporadically throughout the day and then without letup, titanically, at night.

I dreaded the hours of darkness. Climbing the obstacle course of stairs to our bedroom one painful step at a time—bending the good leg, dragging the bad leg—I felt myself on the way to a torture session that this time I couldn't survive. My only chance of getting through to daylight without having my mind come completely apart was to hook hold of a talismanic image out of my most innocent past and try to ride out the menace of the long night lashed to the mast of that recollection. One that I worked hysterically hard, in a kind of convulsion of yearning, to summon forth to save me was of my older brother guiding me along our street of rooming houses and summer cottages to the boardwalk and down the flight of wooden steps to the beach at the Jersey shore town where our family rented a room for a month each summer. *Take me, Sandy, please.* When I thought (oftentimes mistakenly) that Claire was asleep, I would chant this incantation aloud, four childish words that I had not uttered so passionately, if ever at all, since 1938, when I was five and my attentive, protective brother was ten.

I wouldn't let Claire draw the shades at night, because I had to know the sun was rising the very second that sunrise began; but each morning, when the panes began to lighten in the east-facing windows just to the side of where I lay, whatever relief I felt from my terror of the night that had just ended was copiously displaced by my terror of the day about to begin. Night was interminable and unbearable, day was interminable and unbearable, and when I reached into my pillbox for the capsule that was supposed to carve a little hole where I could hide for a few hours from all the pain that was stalking me, I couldn't believe (though I had no choice but to believe) that the fingers trembling in the pillbox were mine. "Where's Philip?" I said hollowly to Claire while I stood gripping her hand at the edge of the pool. For summers on end I had swum regularly in this pool for thirty minutes at the end of each day; now I was fearful of even putting in a toe, overwhelmed by the pretty, summery surface sheen of those thousands of gallons of water in which I was sure to be sucked under for good.

"Where is Philip Roth?" I asked aloud. "Where did he go?" I was not speaking histrionically. I asked because I wanted to know.

This and more like it lasted one hundred days and one hundred nights. If anyone had telephoned then to say that Philip Roth had been spotted at a war-crimes trial in Jerusalem or was advertised in the Jerusalem paper as lecturing at the King David Hotel on the only solution to the Jewish problem, I can't imagine what I would have done. As thoroughly enveloped as I was in the disaster of self-abandonment, it might have furnished corroboratory evidence just unhinging enough to convince me to go ahead and commit suicide. Because I thought about killing myself all the time. Usually I thought of drowning: in the little pond across the road from the house . . . if I weren't so horrified of the water snakes there nibbling at my corpse; in the picturesque big lake only a few miles away . . . if I weren't so frightened of driving out there alone. When we came to New York that May for me to receive an honorary degree from Columbia, I opened the window of our fourteenth-floor hotel room after Claire had momentarily gone downstairs to the drugstore and, leaning as far out over the interior courtyard as I could while still holding tight to the sill, I told myself, "Do it. No snakes to stop you now." But there was my father to stop me now; he was coming from New Jersey the next day to see me get my degree. Jokingly on the phone he'd taken to calling me "Doctor," just as he'd done on the previous occasions when I was about to receive one of these things. I'd wait to jump until after he went home.

At Columbia, facing from the platform the several thousand people gathered festively together in the big sunny library plaza to watch the commencement exercises, I was convinced that I couldn't make it through the afternoon-long ceremony without beginning either to scream aloud or to sob uncontrollably. I'll never know how I got through that day or through the dinner welcoming the honorary-degree candidates the evening before without letting on to everybody who saw me that I was a man who was finished and about to prove it. Nor will I ever know what I might have gone ahead to do halfway out the hotel window that morning or even on the platform the next day, had I not been able to interpose between my de-

nuded self and its clamorous longing for obliteration the devotion linking me to an eighty-six-year-old father whose life my
death by suicide would smash to smithereens.

After the ceremony at Columbia, my father came back to
the hotel with us for a cup of coffee. He'd surmised weeks
before that something was critically wrong even though I insisted, when we saw each other or spoke on the phone, that it
was only the persistence of the physical pain that was getting
me down. "You look drained," he said, "you look awful."
How I looked had made his own face go ashen—and he was as
yet suffering from no fatal disease, as far as anyone knew.
"Knee," I replied. "Hurts." And said no more. "This isn't like
you, Phil, you take everything in your stride." I smiled. "I
do?" "Here," he said, "open it when you get home," and he
handed me a package that I could tell he had encased himself
in its bulky brown-paper wrapping. He said, "To go with your
new degree, Doctor."

What he gave me was a framed five-by-seven portrait photo
taken by a Metropolitan Life photographer some forty-five
years earlier, on the occasion of my father's Newark district's
winning one of the company's coveted sales awards. There,
as I could barely remember him now, was the striving, unde-
flectable insurance man out of my early grade school years,
conventionally stolid-looking in the American style of the Depression era: neatly knotted conservative tie; double-breasted
business suit; thinning hair closely cut; level, steady gaze; congenial, sober, restrained smile—the man that the boss wants
on his team and that the customer can believe is a balanced
person, a card-carrying member of the everyday world. "Trust
me," the face in the portrait proclaimed. "Work me. Promote
me. You will not be let down."

When I telephoned from Connecticut the next morning,
planning to tell him all too truthfully how the gift of that old
picture had buoyed me, my father suddenly heard his fifty-
four-year-old son sobbing as he hadn't sobbed since his in-
fancy. I was astonished by how unalarmed his reaction was to
what must have sounded like nothing short of a complete
collapse. "Go ahead," he said, as though he knew everything
I'd been hiding from him and, just because he knew everything, had decided, seemingly out of the blue, to give me that

photograph picturing him at his most steadfast and determined. "Let it all out," he said very softly, "whatever it is, let it
all come out. . . ."

I'm told that all the misery I've just described was caused by
the sleeping pill that I was taking every night, the benzodi-
azepine triazolam marketed as Halcion, the pill that has lately
begun to be charged with driving people crazy all over the
globe. In Holland, distribution of Halcion had been prohibited entirely since 1979, two years after it was introduced there
and eight years before it was prescribed for me; in France and
Germany, doses of the size I was taking nightly had been removed from the pharmacies in the 1980s; and in Britain it was
banned outright following a BBC television exposé aired in
the fall of 1991. *The* revelation—which came as less than a revelation to someone like me—occurred in January 1992, with
a long article in *The New York Times* whose opening para-
graphs were featured prominently on the front page. "For two
decades," the piece began, "the drug company that makes
Halcion, the world's best-selling sleeping pill, concealed data
from the Food and Drug Administration showing that it
caused significant numbers of serious psychiatric side effects. . . ."

It was eighteen months after my breakdown that I first read
a comprehensive indictment of Halcion—and a description of
what the author called "Halcion madness"—in a popular
American magazine. The article quoted from a letter in *The
Lancet*, the British medical journal, in which a Dutch psychiatrist listed symptoms associated with Halcion that he had discovered in a study of psychiatric patients who had been
prescribed the drug; the list read like a textbook summary of
my catastrophe: ". . . severe malaise; depersonalization and
derealization; paranoid reactions; acute and chronic anxiety;
continuous fear of going insane; . . . patients often feel desperate and have to fight an almost irresistible impulse to commit suicide. I know of one patient who did commit suicide."

It was only through a lucky break that instead of having
eventually to be hospitalized myself—or perhaps even buried
—I came to withdraw from Halcion and my symptoms began
to subside and disappear. One weekend early in the summer of

1987, my friend Bernie Avishai drove down from Boston to visit me after having become alarmed by my suicidal maunderings over the phone. I was by then three months into the suffering and I told him, when we were alone together in my studio, that I had decided to commit myself to a mental institution. Holding me back, however, was my fear that once I went in I'd never come out. Somebody had to convince me otherwise—I wanted Bernie to. He interrupted to ask a question whose irrelevance irritated me terribly: "What are you on?" I reminded him that I didn't take drugs and was "on" nothing, only some pills to help me sleep and to calm me down. Angered by his failure to grasp the severity of my situation, I confessed the shameful truth about myself as forthrightly as I could. "I've cracked up. I've broken down. Your friend here is mentally ill!" "Which pills?" he replied.

A few minutes later he had me on the phone to the Boston psychopharmacologist who just the previous year, I later learned, had saved Bernie from a Halcion-induced breakdown very much like mine. The doctor asked me first how I was feeling; when I told him, he, in turn, told me what I was taking to make me feel that way. I refused at first to accept that all this pain stemmed simply from a sleeping pill and insisted that he, like Bernie, was failing to understand the *ghastliness* of what I was going through. Eventually, with my permission, he telephoned my local doctor and, under their joint supervision, I began that night to come off the drug, a process that I wouldn't care to repeat a second time and that I didn't think I'd live through the first. "Sometimes," the Dutch psychiatrist, Dr. C. van der Kroef, had written in *The Lancet,* "there are withdrawal symptoms, such as rapidly mounting panic and heavy sweating." My withdrawal symptoms were unremitting for seventy-two hours.

Elsewhere, enumerating the cases of Halcion madness that he had observed in the Netherlands, Dr. van der Kroef remarked, "Without exception, the patients themselves described this period as hell."

For the next four weeks, feelings of extreme vulnerability, though no longer quite disemboweling me, still chaperoned me everywhere, especially as I was virtually unable to sleep and so was bleary with exhaustion throughout the day and then, during the insomniac, Halcionless nights, weighed down by the leaden thought of how I had disgraced myself before Claire and my brother and those friends who had drawn close to us during my hundred miserable days. I was abashed, and a good thing it was, too, since mortification seemed to me as promising a sign as any of the return of the person I formerly had been, more concerned, for better or worse, with something as pedestrian as his self-respect than with carnivorous snakes needling through the mud floor of his pond.

But much of the time I didn't believe it was Halcion that had done me in. Despite the speed with which I recovered my mental, then my emotional equilibrium and looked to be ordering daily life as competently as I ever had before, I privately remained half-convinced that, though the drug perhaps intensified my collapse, it was I who had made the worst happen, after having been derailed by nothing more cataclysmic than a botched knee operation and a siege of protracted physical pain; half-convinced that I owed my transformation—my *deformation*—not to any pharmaceutical agent but to something concealed, obscured, masked, suppressed, or maybe simply uncreated in me until I was fifty-four but as much me and mine as my prose style, my childhood, or my intestines; half-convinced that whatever else I might imagine myself to be, I was *that* too and, if the circumstances were trying enough, I could be again, a shamefully dependent, meaninglessly deviant, transparently pitiable, brazenly defective *that*, deranged as opposed to incisive, diabolical as opposed to reliable, without introspection, without serenity, without any of the ordinary boldness that makes life feel like such a great thing—a frenzied, maniacal, repulsive, anguished, odious, hallucinatory *that* whose existence is one long tremor.

And am I half-convinced still, five years later, after all that the psychiatrists, newspapers, and medical journals have disclosed about the mind-altering wallop lurking for many of us in Upjohn's magic little sleeping pill? The simple, truthful answer is, "Why not? Wouldn't you be, if you were me?"

As for the Philip Roth whom I had spoken with in suite 511 of the King David Hotel and who most certainly was not me—

well, what exactly he was after I had no idea, for instead of answering when he'd asked my name, I'd immediately hung up. You shouldn't have phoned in the first place, I thought. You have no reason to be interested and you mustn't be rattled. That would be ridiculous. For all you know, it's simply someone else who happens coincidentally to bear the same name. And if that's not so, if there *is* an impostor in Jerusalem passing himself off as you, there's still nothing that needs to be done. He'll be found out by others without your intervening. He already has been—by Apter and Aharon. Enough people know you in Israel to make it impossible for him *not* to be exposed and apprehended. What harm can he do you? The harm can only be done *by* you, going off half-cocked and impulsively making phone calls like this one. The last thing for him to know is that his hoax is bugging you, because bugging you has to be at the heart of whatever he is ostensibly trying to do. Aloof and unconcerned, for now at least, is your only—

This is how rattled I was already. After all, when he'd so matter-of-factly announced to me who he was I had only to tell him who I was and to see what then transpired—it might have been eye-opening and could even have been fun. My prudence in hanging up seemed, moments afterward, to have been nothing but the expression of helpless panic, a jolting indication that, nearly seven months after coming off Halcion, I might not be detraumatized at all. "Well, this is Philip Roth, too, the one who was born in Newark and has written umpteen books. Which one are you?" I could so easily have undone him with that; instead it was he who undid me merely by answering the phone in my name.

I decided to say nothing about him to Claire when I arrived in London the following week. I didn't want her to think that there was anything in the offing with the potential to seriously disconcert me, particularly since she, for one, didn't yet seem convinced that I had recovered sufficient strength to ride out an emotional predicament at all complex or demanding . . . and what was more to the point, when I was suddenly less than a hundred percent sure myself. Once I'd arrived in London I didn't even want to *remember* what Apter and Aharon had phoned New York to tell me. . . . Yes, a situation that I might well have lightheartedly treated as a source of entertainment only a year earlier, or as a provocation to be soundly dealt with, now required that I take certain small but deliberate precautionary measures to guard against my being thrown. I wasn't happy to make that discovery, yet I didn't know how better to keep this bizarre triviality from developing in my mind the way the bizarre had become so painfully magnified under the sway of the Halcion. I would do what I must to maintain a reasonable perspective.

During my second night in London, still sleeping poorly because of jet lag, I began to wonder, after having popped awake in the dark for the third or fourth time, if those calls from Jerusalem—as well as my call *to* Jerusalem—had not perhaps occurred in dreams. Earlier that day I would have sworn that I had taken both calls at my desk in the hotel while I was sitting there beginning to work up the set of questions, based on my rereading of his books, that I intended to ask Aharon in Jerusalem, and yet, contemplating the unlikely content of the calls, I managed to convince myself during the course of that long night that they could have been placed and received only while I was asleep, that these were dreams of the kind that everyone dreams nightly, in which characters are identifiable and ring true when they're speaking, while what they're saying rings absolutely false. And the origin of the dreams was, when I thought about it, all too pathetically manifest. The imposturing other whose inexplicable antics I had been warned about by Apter and Aharon and whose voice I'd heard with my own ears was a specter created out of my fear of mentally coming apart while abroad and on my own for the first time since recovering—a nightmare about the return of a usurping self altogether beyond my control. As for the messengers bearing the news of my Jerusalem counterself, they too couldn't have been any more grossly emblematic of the dreaming's immediate, personal ramifications, since not only did their acquaintance with the unforeseen grotesquely exceed my own, but each had undergone the most tremendous transformation even before the clay of his original being had had time to anneal into a solid, shatterproof identity. The much-praised transfigurations concocted by Franz Kafka pale beside the unthinkable metamorphoses perpetrated by the Third Reich on the childhoods of my cousin and of my friend, to enumerate only two.

So eager was I to establish as fact that a dream had merely overflowed its banks that I got up to phone Aharon before it was even dawn. It was already an hour later in Jerusalem and he was a very early riser, but even if I had to risk waking him up, I felt I couldn't wait a minute longer to have him confirm that this business was all a mental aberration of mine and that no phone conversation had taken place between the two of us about another Philip Roth. Yet, once out of bed and on the way down to the kitchen to call him quietly from there, I recognized what a pipe dream it was to be telling myself that I had only been dreaming. I ought to be rushing to telephone not Aharon, I thought, but the Boston psychopharmacologist to ask if my uncertainty as to what was real meant that three months of being bombarded chemically by triazolam had left my brain cells permanently impaired. And the only reason to be phoning Aharon was to hear what new sightings he had to report. But why not bypass Aharon and inquire directly of the impostor himself what exactly he was out to achieve? By feigning "a reasonable perspective" I was only opening myself further to a dangerous renewal of delusion. If there was any place for me to be phoning at four fifty-five in the morning, it was suite 511 of the King David Hotel.

I thought very well of myself at breakfast for having made it back to bed at five without calling anyone; I felt settling over me that blissful sense of being in charge of one's life, a man who once again hubristically imagines himself at the helm of himself. Everything else might be a delusion, but the reasonable perspective was not.

Then the phone rang. "Philip? More good news. You are in the morning's paper." It was Aharon calling *me*.

"Wonderful. Which paper this time?"

"A Hebrew paper this time. An article about your visit to Lech Walesa. In Gdansk. This is where you were before you came to attend the Demjanjuk trial."

Had I been speaking to almost anyone else I might have been tempted to believe that I was being teased or toyed with. But however much pleasure Aharon may take in the ridiculous side of life, deliberately to perpetrate comic mischief, even of the most mildly addling variety, was simply incompatible with his ascetic, gravely gentle nature. He saw the joke, that was clear, but he wasn't in on it any more than I was.

Across from me Claire was drinking her coffee and looking through the *Guardian*. We were finishing breakfast. I hadn't been dreaming in New York and I wasn't dreaming now.

Aharon's voice is mild, very light and mild, modulated for the ears of the highly attuned, and his English is spoken precisely, each word lightly glazed with an accent as Old Worldish as it is Israeli. It is an appealing voice to listen to, alive with the dramatic cadences of the master storyteller and vibrant in its own distinctly quiet way—and I was listening very hard. "I'll translate from your statement here," he was telling me. " 'The reason for my visit to Walesa was to discuss with him the resettlement of Jews in Poland once Solidarity comes to power there, as it will.' "

"You'd better translate the whole thing. Start from scratch. What page is it on? How long is it?"

"Not long, not short. It's on the back page, with the features. There's a photograph."

"Of?"

"You."

"And is it me?" I asked.

"I would say so."

"What's the heading over the story?"

" 'Philip Roth Meets Solidarity Leader.' In smaller letters, ' "Poland Needs Jews," Walesa Tells Author in Gdansk.' "

" 'Poland Needs Jews,' " I repeated. "My grandparents should only be alive to hear that one."

" ' "Everyone speaks about Jews," Walesa told Roth. "Spain was ruined by the expulsion of the Jews," the Solidarity leader said during their two-hour meeting at the Gdansk shipyards, where Solidarity was born in 1980. "When people say to me, 'What Jew would be crazy enough to come here?' I explain to them that the long experience, over many hundreds of years, of Jews and Poles together cannot be summed up with the word 'anti-Semitism.' Let's talk about a thousand years of glory rather than four years of war. The greatest explosion of Yiddish culture in history, every great intellectual movement of modern Jewish life," said the Solidarity leader to Roth, "took place on Polish soil. Yiddish culture is no less Polish than Jewish. Poland without Jews is unthinkable. Poland needs Jews," Walesa told the American-born Jewish author, "and Jews need Poland."' Philip, I feel that I'm reading to you out of a story you wrote."

"I wish you were."

"'Roth, the author of *Portnoy's Complaint* and other controversial Jewish novels, calls himself an "ardent Diasporist." He says that the ideology of Diasporism has replaced his writing. "The reason for my visit to Walesa was to discuss with him the resettlement of Jews in Poland once Solidarity comes to power there, as it will." Right now, the author finds that his ideas on resettlement are received with more hostility in Israel than in Poland. He maintains that however virulent Polish anti-Semitism may once have been, "the Jew hatred that pervades Islam is far more entrenched and dangerous." Roth continues, "The so-called normalization of the Jew was a tragic illusion from the start. But when this normalization is expected to flourish in the very heart of Islam, it is even worse than tragic—it is suicidal. Horrendous as Hitler was for us, he lasted a mere twelve years, and what is twelve years to the Jew? The time has come to return to the Europe that was for centuries, and remains to this day, the most authentic Jewish homeland there has ever been, the birthplace of rabbinic Judaism, Hasidic Judaism, Jewish secularism, socialism—on and on. The birthplace, of course, of Zionism too. But Zionism has outlived its historical function. The time has come to renew in the European Diaspora our preeminent spiritual and cultural role." Roth, who is fearful of a second Jewish Holocaust in the Middle East, sees "Jewish resettlement" as the only means by which to assure Jewish survival and to achieve "a historical as well as a spiritual victory over Hitler and Auschwitz." "I am not blind," Roth says, "to the horrors. But I sit at the Demjanjuk trial, I look at this tormentor of Jews, this human embodiment of the criminal sadism unleashed by the Nazis on our people, and I ask myself, 'Who and what is to prevail in Europe: the will of this subhuman murderer-brute or the civilization that gave to mankind Shalom Aleichem, Heinrich Heine, and Albert Einstein? Are we to be driven for all time from the continent that nourished the flourishing Jewish worlds of Warsaw, of Vilna, of Riga, of Prague, of Berlin, of Lvov, of Budapest, of Bucharest, of Salonica and Rome because of *him*?' It is time," concludes Roth, "to return to where we belong and to where we have every historical right to resume the great Jewish European destiny that the murderers like this Demjanjuk disrupted."'"

That was the end of the article.

"What swell ideas I have," I said. "Going to make lots of new pals for me in the Zionist homeland."

"Anyone who reads this in the Zionist homeland," said Aharon, "will only think, 'Another crazy Jew.'"

"I'd much prefer then that in the hotel register he'd sign 'Another crazy Jew' and not 'Philip Roth.'"

"'Another crazy Jew' might not be sufficiently crazy to satisfy his *mishigas*."

When I saw that Claire was no longer reading her paper but listening to what I was saying, I told her, "It's Aharon. There's a madman in Israel using my name and going around pretending to be me." Then to Aharon I said, "I'm telling Claire that there's a madman in Israel pretending to be me."

"Yes, and the madman undoubtedly believes that in New York and London and Connecticut there is a madman pretending to be him."

"Unless he's not at all mad and knows exactly what he's doing."

"Which is what?" asked Aharon.

"I didn't say I know, I said he knows. So many people in Israel have met me, have seen me—how can this person present himself as Philip Roth to an Israeli journalist and get away with it so easily?"

"I think this is a very young woman who wrote the story—I believe this is a person in her twenties. That's probably what's behind it—her inexperience."

"And the picture?"

"The picture they find in their files."

"Look, I have to contact her paper before this gets picked up by the wire services."

"And what can *I* do, Philip? Anything?"

"For the time being, no, nothing. I may want to talk to my lawyer before I even call the paper. I may want her to call the paper." But looking at my watch I realized that it was much too early to phone New York. "Aharon, just hold tight until I have a chance to think it through and check out the legal side. I don't even know what it is an impostor can be charged with. Invasion of privacy? Defamation of character? Reckless conduct? Is impersonation an actionable offense? What exactly has he appropriated that's against the law and how do I stop him in a country where I'm not even a citizen? I'd actually be dealing with Israeli law, and I'm not yet in Israel. Look, I'll call you back when I find something out."

But once off the phone I immediately came up with an explanation not wholly disconnected from what I'd thought the night before in bed. Although the idea probably originated in Aharon's remark that he felt that he was reading to me out of a story I'd written, it was nonetheless another ridiculously subjective attempt to convert into a mental event of the kind I was professionally all too familiar with what had once again been established as all too objectively real. It's Zuckerman, I thought, whimsically, stupidly, escapistly, it's Kepesh, it's Tarnopol and Portnoy—it's all of them in one, broken free of print and mockingly reconstituted as a single satirical facsimile of me. In other words, if it's not Halcion and it's no dream, then it's got to be literature—as though there cannot be a life-without ten thousand times more unimaginable than the life-within.

"Well," I said to Claire, "there's somebody in Jerusalem attending the Ivan the Terrible trial who's going around claiming to be me. Calls himself by my name. Gave an interview to an Israeli newspaper—that's what Aharon was reading to me over the phone."

"You found this out just now?" she asked.

"No. Aharon phoned me in New York last week. So did my cousin Apter. Apter's landlady said she'd seen me on TV. I didn't tell you because I didn't know what, if anything, it all amounted to."

"You're green, Philip. You've turned a frightening color."

"Have I? I'm tired, that's all. I was up on and off all night."

"You're not taking . . ."

"You can't be serious."

"Don't sound resentful. I just don't want anything to happen to you. Because you *have* turned a terrible color—and you seem . . . swamped."

"Do I? Did I? I didn't think I did. And it's you who have actually turned colors."

"I'm worried, that's why. You seem . . ."

"What? Seem *what*? What it seems to me I seem to be is someone who has just found out that somebody down in Jerusalem is giving newspaper interviews in his name. You heard what I said to Aharon. As soon as the business day begins in New York, I'm going to call Helene. I think now that the best thing is for *her* to telephone the paper and to get them to print a retraction tomorrow. It's a start at stopping him. Once their retraction's out, no other newspaper is going to go near him. That's step number one."

"What's step number two?"

"I don't know. Maybe step number two won't be necessary. I don't know what the law is. Do I slap an injunction on him? In Israel? Maybe what Helene does is to contact a lawyer down there. When I speak to her, I'll find out."

"Maybe step number two is not going there right now."

"That's ridiculous. Look, I'm *not* swamped. It's not *my* plans that are going to change—it's his."

But by the afternoon I was back again to thinking that it was far more reasonable, sensible, and even, in the long run, more satisfyingly ruthless to do nothing for now. Telling Claire anything, given her continuing apprehension about my wellbeing, was, of course, a mistake and, had she not been sitting across from me at the breakfast table when Aharon phoned in his latest report, one that I would never have made. And an even bigger mistake, I thought, would be to set lawyers loose now, on two continents no less, who might not effect an outcome any less damaging than I could—if, that is, I could manage to remain something more helpful than volatilely irritated until, eventually, this impostor played out his disaster, all alone, as he must. A retraction was not likely to undo whatever damage had already been done by the newspaper's original error. The ideas espoused so forcefully by the Philip Roth in that story were mine now and would likely endure as mine even in the recollection of those who'd read the retraction tomorrow. Nonetheless, this was not, I sternly reminded myself, the worst upheaval of my life, and I was not going to permit myself to behave as though it were. Instead of rushing to mobilize an army of legal defenders, better just to sit comfortably back on the sidelines and watch while he manufactures for the Israeli press and public a version of me so absolutely not-me that it will require nothing, neither judicial intervention nor newspaper retractions, to clear everyone's mind of confusion and expose him as whatever he is.

After all, despite the temptation to chalk him up to Halcion's lingering hold on me, he was not my but *his* hallucination, and by January 1988 I'd come to understand that he had more to fear from that than I did. Up against reality I was not quite so outclassed as I'd been up against that sleeping pill; up against reality I had at my disposal the strongest weapon in anyone's arsenal: my own reality. It wasn't I who was in danger of being displaced by him but he who had *without question* to be effaced by me—exposed, effaced, and extinguished. It was just a matter of time. Panic characteristically urges, in its quivering, raving, overexcitable way, "Do something before he goes too far!" and is loudly seconded by Powerless Fear. Meanwhile, poised and balanced, Reason, the exalted voice of Reason, counsels, "You have everything on your side, he has nothing on his. Try eradicating him overnight, before he has fully revealed exactly what he's intent on doing, and he'll only elude you to pop up elsewhere and start this stuff all over again. *Let* him go too far. There is no more cunning way to shut him down. He can only be defeated."

Needless to say, had I told Claire that evening that I'd changed my mind since morning and, instead of racing into battle armed with lawyers, proposed now to let him inflate the hoax until it blew up in his face, she would have replied that to do that would only invite trouble potentially more threatening to my newly reconstituted stability than the little that had so far resulted from what was still only a minor, if outlandish, nuisance. She would argue with even more concern than she'd displayed at breakfast—because three months of helplessly watching my collapse up close had deeply scarred her faith in me and hadn't done much for her own stability either—that I was nowhere ready for a test as unlikely and puzzling as this one, while I, experiencing all the satisfaction that's bestowed by a strategy of restraint, exhilarated by the sense of personal freedom that issues from refusing to respond to an emergency other than with a realistic appraisal and levelheaded self-control, was convinced of just the opposite. I felt absolutely rapturous over the decision to take on this impostor by myself, for on my own and by myself was how I'd always preferred to encounter just about everything. My God, I thought, this is me again, finally the much-pined-for natural upsurge of my obstinate, energetic, independent self, zeroed back in on life and brimming with my old resolve, vying once again with an adversary a little less chimerical than sickly, crippling unreality. He was just what the psychopharmacologist ordered! All right, bud, one on one, let's fight! You can only be defeated.

At dinner that evening, before Claire had a chance to ask me anything, I lied and told her that I had spoken with my lawyer, that from New York she had contacted the Israeli paper, and that a retraction was to be printed there the next day.

"I still don't like it," she replied.

"But what more can we do? What more *need* be done?"

"I don't like the idea of you there alone while this person is on the loose. It's not a good idea at all. Who knows what he is or who he is or what he's actually up to? Suppose he's crazy. You yourself called him a madman this morning. What if this madman is armed?"

"Whatever I may have called him, I happen to know nothing about him."

"That's my point."

"And why should he be armed? You don't need a pistol to impersonate me."

"It's Israel—*everybody's* armed. Half the people in the street traipsing around carrying guns—I never saw so many guns in my life. Your going there, at a time like this, with everything erupting everywhere, is a terrible, terrible mistake."

She was referring to the riots that had begun in Gaza and the West Bank the month before and that I'd been following in New York on the nightly news. A curfew was in effect in East Jerusalem and tourists had been warned away particularly from the Old City because of the stone throwing there and the possibility of violent clashes escalating between the army and the Arab residents. The media had taken to describing these riots, which had become a more or less daily occurrence in the Occupied Territories, as a Palestinian uprising.

"Why can't you contact the Israeli police?" she asked.

"I think the Israeli police may find themselves facing problems more pressing than mine right now. What would I tell them? Arrest him? Deport him? On what grounds? As far as I know, he hasn't passed a phony check in my name, he hasn't been paid for any services in my name—"

"But he must have entered Israel with a phony passport, with *papers* in your name. That's illegal."

"But do we know this? We don't. It's illegal but not very likely. I suspect that all he's done in my name is to shoot his mouth off."

"But there *must* be legal safeguards. A person cannot simply run off to a foreign country and go around pretending to be someone he is not."

"Happens probably more often than you think. How about some realism? Darling, how about your taking a reasonable perspective?"

"I don't want anything to happen to you. That's my reasonable perspective."

"What 'happened' to me happened to me many months ago now."

"Are you really up to this? I have to ask you, Philip."

"There's nothing for me to be 'up to.' Did anything like what happened to me ever happen to me before that drug? Has anything like it happened to me since the drug? Tomorrow they're printing a retraction. They're faxing Helene a copy. That's enough for now."

"Well, I don't understand this calm of yours—or hers, frankly."

"Now the calm's upsetting. This morning it was my chagrin."

"Yes, well—I don't believe it."

"Well, there's nothing I can do about that."

"Promise me you won't do anything ridiculous."

"Such as?"

"I don't *know*. Trying to find this person. Trying to *fight*

with this person. You have no idea whom you might be dealing with. You must not try to look for him and solve this stupid thing yourself. At least promise that you won't do that."

I laughed at the very idea. "My guess," I said, lying once
again, "is that by the time I get to Jerusalem, he won't be anywhere to be found."

"You won't do it."

"I won't have to. Look, see it this way, will you? I have
everything on my side, he has nothing on his, absolutely
nothing."

"But you're wrong. You know what he has on his side? It's
clear from every word you speak. He has you."

After our dinner that evening I told Claire that I was going off
to my study at the top of the house to sit down again with
Aharon's novels to continue making my notes for the
Jerusalem conversation. But no more than five minutes had
passed after I'd settled at the desk, when I heard the television
set playing below and I picked up the phone and called the
King David Hotel in Jerusalem and asked to be put through to
511. To disguise my voice I used a French accent, not the bedroom accent, not the farcical accent, not that French accent
descended from Charles Boyer through Danny Kaye to the TV
ads for table wines and traveler's checks, but the accent of
highly articulate and cosmopolitan Frenchmen like my friend
the writer Philippe Sollers, no "zis," no "zat," all initial *h*'s
duly aspirated—fluent English simply tinged with the natural
inflections and marked by the natural cadences of an intelligent foreigner. It's an imitation I don't do badly—once, on
the phone, I fooled even mischievous Sollers—and the one I'd
decided on even while Claire and I were arguing at the dinner
table about the wisdom of my trip, even while, I must admit,
the exalted voice of Reason had been counseling me, earlier
that day, that doing nothing was the surest way to do him in.
By nine o'clock that night, curiosity had all but consumed me,
and curiosity is not a very rational whim.

"Hello, Mr. Roth? Mr. Philip Roth?" I asked.

"Yes."

"Is this really the author I'm speaking to?"

"It is."

"The author of *Portnoy et son complexe*?"

"Yes, yes. Who is this, please?"

My heart was pounding as though I were out on my first big robbery with an accomplice no less brilliant than Jean Genet—this was not merely treacherous, this was *interesting*. To think that he was pretending at his end of the line to be me while I was pretending at my end not to be me gave me a terrific, unforeseen, Mardi Gras kind of kick, and probably it was this that accounted for the stupid error I immediately made. "I am Pierre Roget," I said, and only in the instant after uttering a convenient nom de guerre that I'd plucked seemingly out of nowhere did I realize that its initial letters were the same as mine—and the same as his. Worse, it happened also to be the barely transmogrified name of the nineteenth-century word cataloger who is known to virtually everyone as the author of the famous thesaurus. I hadn't realized that either—the author of the definitive book of synonyms!

"I am a French journalist based in Paris," I said. "I have just read in the Israeli press about your meeting with Lech Walesa in Gdansk."

Slip number two: Unless I knew Hebrew, how could I have read his interview in the Israeli press? What if he now began speaking to me in a language that I had learned just badly enough to manage to be bar mitzvahed at the age of thirteen and that I no longer understood at all?

Reason: "You are playing right into his plan. This is the very situation his criminality craves. Hang up."

Claire: "Are you really all right? Are you really up to this? Don't go."

Pierre Roget: "If I read correctly, you are leading a movement to resettle Europe with Israeli Jews of European background. Beginning in Poland."

"Correct," he replied.

"And you continue at the same time to write your novels?"

"Writing novels while Jews are at a crossroads like this? My life now is focused entirely on the Jewish European resettlement movement. On Diasporism."

Did he sound *anything* like me? I would have thought that my voice could far more easily pass for someone like Sollers speaking English than his could pass for mine. For one thing, he had much more Jersey in his speech than I'd ever had, though whether because it came naturally to him or because he mistakenly thought it would make the impersonation more convincing, I couldn't figure out. But then this was a more resonant voice than mine as well, richer and more stentorian by far. Maybe that was how he thought somebody who had published sixteen books would talk on the phone to an interviewer, while the fact is that if I talked like that I might not have had to write sixteen books. But the impulse to tell him this, strong as it was, I restrained; I was having too good a time to think of stifling either one of us.

"You are a Jew," I said, "who in the past has been criticized by Jewish groups for your 'self-hatred' and your 'anti-Semitism.' Would it be correct to assume—"

"Look," he said, abruptly breaking in, "I am a Jew, period. I would not have gone to Poland to meet with Walesa if I were anything else. I would not be here visiting Israel and attending the Demjanjuk trial if I were anything else. Please, I will be glad to tell you all you wish to know about resettlement. Otherwise I haven't time to waste on what has been said about me by stupid people."

"But," I persisted, "won't stupid people say that because of this resettlement idea you are an enemy of Israel and its mission? Won't this confirm—"

"I am Israel's enemy," he interrupted again, "if you wish to put it that sensationally, only because I am for the Jews and Israel is no longer in the Jewish interest. Israel has become the gravest threat to Jewish survival since the end of World War Two."

"Was Israel ever in the Jewish interest, in your opinion?"

"Of course. In the aftermath of the Holocaust, Israel was the Jewish hospital in which Jews could begin to recover from the devastation of that horror, from a dehumanization so terrible that it would not have been at all surprising had the Jewish spirit, had the Jews themselves, succumbed entirely to that legacy of rage, humiliation and grief. But that is not what happened. Our recovery actually came to pass. In less than a century. Miraculous, more than miraculous—yet the recovery of the Jews is by now a fact and the time has come to return to our real life and our real home, to our ancestral Jewish Europe."

"Real home?" I replied, unable now to imagine how I ever could have considered not placing this call. "Some real home."

"I am not making promiscuous conversation," he snapped back at me sharply. "The great mass of Jews have been in Europe since the Middle Ages. Virtually everything we identify culturally as Jewish has its origins in the life we led for centuries among European Christians. The Jews of Islam have their own, very different destiny. I am not proposing that Israeli Jews whose origins are in Islamic countries return to Europe, since for them this would constitute not a homecoming but a radical uprooting."

"What do you do then with them? Ship them back for the Arabs to treat as befits their status as Jews?"

"No. For those Jews, Israel must continue to be their country. Once the European Jews and their families have been resettled and the population has been halved, then the state can be reduced to its 1948 borders, the army can be demobilized, and those Jews who have lived in an Islamic cultural matrix for centuries can continue to do so, independently, autonomously, but in peace and harmony with their Arab neighbors. For these people to remain in this region is simply as it should be, their rightful habitat, while for the European Jews, Israel has been an exile and no more, a sojourn, a temporary interlude in the European saga that it is time to resume."

"Sir, what makes you think that the Jews would have any more success in Europe in the future than they had there in the past?"

"Do not confuse our long European history with the twelve years of Hitler's reign. If Hitler had not existed, if his twelve years of terror were erased from our past, then it would seem to you no more unthinkable that Jews should also be Europeans than that they should also be Americans. There might even seem to you a much more necessary and profound connection between the Jew and Budapest, the Jew and Prague, than the one between the Jew and Cincinnati and the Jew and Dallas."

Could it be, I asked myself while he pedantically continued on in this vein, that the history he's most intent on erasing happens to be his own? Is he mentally so damaged that he truly believes that my history is his; is he some psychotic, some amnesiac, who isn't pretending at all? If every word he speaks he means, if the only person pretending here is me. . . . But whether that made things better or worse I couldn't begin to know. Nor, when next I found myself *arguing*, could I determine whether an outburst of sincerity from me made this conversation any more or less absurd, either.

"But Hitler *did* exist," I heard Pierre Roget emotionally informing him. "Those twelve years *cannot* be expunged from history any more than they can be obliterated from memory, however mercifully forgetful one might prefer to be. The meaning of the destruction of European Jewry cannot be measured or interpreted by the brevity with which it was attained."

"The meanings of the Holocaust," he replied gravely, "are for us to determine, but one thing is sure—its meaning will be no less tragic than it is now if there is a second Holocaust and the offspring of the European Jews who evacuated Europe for a seemingly safer haven should meet collective annihilation in the Middle East. A second Holocaust is *not* going to occur on the continent of Europe, *because* it was the site of the first. But a second Holocaust could happen here all too easily, and, if the conflict between Arab and Jew escalates much longer, it will— *it must*. The destruction of Israel in a nuclear exchange is a possibility much less farfetched today than was the Holocaust itself fifty years ago."

"The resettlement in Europe of more than a million Jews. The demobilization of the Israeli army. A return to the borders of 1948. It sounds to me," I said, "that you are proposing the final solution of the Jewish problem for Yasir Arafat."

"No. Arafat's final solution is the same as Hitler's: extermination. I am proposing the alternative to extermination, a solution not to Arafat's Jewish problem but to ours, one comparable in scope and magnitude to the defunct solution called Zionism. But I do not wish to be misunderstood, in France or anywhere else in the world. I repeat: In the immediate postwar era, when for obvious reasons Europe was uninhabitable by Jews, Zionism was the single greatest force contributing to the recovery of Jewish hope and morale. But having succeeded in restoring the Jews to health, Zionism has tragically ruined its own health and must now accede to vigorous Diasporism."

"Will you define Diasporism for my readers, please?" I asked, meanwhile thinking, The starchy rhetoric, the professorial presentation, the historical perspective, the passionate commitment, the grave undertones . . . What sort of hoax *is* this hoax?

"Diasporism seeks to promote the dispersion of the Jews in the West, particularly the resettlement of Israeli Jews of European background in the European countries where there were sizable Jewish populations before World War II. Diasporism plans to rebuild *everything*, not in an alien and menacing Middle East but in those very lands where everything once flourished, while, at the same time, it seeks to avert the catastrophe of a second Holocaust brought about by the exhaustion of Zionism as a political and ideological force. Zionism undertook to restore Jewish life and the Hebrew language to a place where neither had existed with any real vitality for nearly two millennia. Diasporism's dream is more modest: a mere half-century is all that separates us from what Hitler destroyed. If Jewish resources could realize the seemingly fantastic goals of Zionism in even less than fifty years, now that Zionism is counterproductive and itself the foremost Jewish problem, I have no doubt that the resources of world Jewry can realize the goals of Diasporism in half, if not even one tenth, the time."

"You speak about resettling Jews in Poland, Romania, Germany? In Slovakia, the Ukraine, Yugoslavia, the Baltic states? And you realize, do you," I asked him, "how much hatred for Jews still exists in most of these countries?"

"Whatever hatred for Jews may be present in Europe—and I don't minimize its persistence—there are ranged against this residual anti-Semitism powerful currents of enlightenment and morality that are sustained by the memory of the Holocaust, a horror that operates now as a bulwark *against* European anti-Semitism, however virulent. No such bulwark exists in Islam. Exterminating a Jewish nation would cause Islam to lose not a single night's sleep, except for the great night of celebration. I think you would agree that a Jew is safer today walking aimlessly around Berlin than going unarmed into the streets of Ramallah."

"What about the Jew walking around Tel Aviv?"

"In Damascus missiles armed with chemical warheads are aimed not at downtown Warsaw but directly at Dizengoff Street."

"So what Diasporism comes down to is fearful Jews in flight, terrified Jews once again running away."

"To flee an imminent cataclysm is 'running away' only from extinction. It is running *toward* life. Had thousands more of Germany's fearful Jews fled in the 1930s—"

"Thousands more would have fled," I said, "if there had been somewhere for them to flee to. You may recall that they were no more welcome elsewhere than they would be now if they were to turn up en masse at the Warsaw train station in flight from an Arab attack."

"You know what will happen in Warsaw, at the railway station, when the first trainload of Jews returns? There will be crowds to welcome them. People will be jubilant. People will be in tears. They will be shouting, 'Our Jews are back! Our Jews are back!' The spectacle will be transmitted by television throughout the world. And what a historic day for Europe, for Jewry, for all mankind when the cattle cars that transported Jews to death camps are transformed by the Diasporist movement into decent, comfortable railway carriages carrying Jews by the tens of thousands back to their native cities and towns. A historic day for human memory, for human justice, and for atonement too. In those train stations where the crowds gather to weep and sing and celebrate, where people fall to their knees in Christian prayer at the feet of their Jewish brethren, only there and then will the conscience cleansing of Europe begin." He paused theatrically here before concluding this visionary outpouring with the quiet, firm pronouncement "And Lech Walesa happens to believe this just as strongly as Philip Roth does."

"Does he? With all due respect, Philip Roth, your prophecy strikes me as nonsense. It sounds to me like a farcical scenario out of one of your books—Poles weeping with joy at the feet of the Jews! And you tell me you are *not* writing fiction these days?"

"This will come to pass," he declared oracularly, "because it *must* come to pass—the reintegration of the Jew into Europe by the year 2000, not a reentry as refugees, you must understand, but an orderly population transfer *with an interna-tional legal basis, with restoration of property, of citizenship, and of all national rights.* And then, in the year 2000, the pan-European celebration of the reintegrated Jew to be held in the city of Berlin."

"Oh, that's the best idea yet," I said. "The Germans partic-ularly will be delighted to usher in the third millennium of Christianity with a couple of million Jews holding a welcome-home party at the Brandenburg Gate."

"In his day Herzl too was accused of being a satirist and of making an elaborate joke when he proposed the establishment of a Jewish state. Many deprecated *his* plan as a hilarious fan-tasy, an outlandish fiction, and called him crazy as well. But my conversation with Lech Walesa was not outlandish fiction. The contact I have made with President Ceaușescu, through the chief rabbi of Romania, is no hilarious fantasy. These are the first steps toward bringing about *a new Jewish reality based on principles of historical justice.* For years now, President Ceaușescu has been selling Jews to Israel. Yes, you hear me correctly: Ceaușescu has *sold* to the Israelis several hundred thousand Romanian Jews for ten thousand dollars a head. This is a fact. Well, I propose to offer him ten thousand more dol-lars for each Jew he takes back. I'll go as high as fifteen if I have to. I have carefully studied Herzl's life and have learned from his experience how to deal with these people. Herzl's ne-gotiations with the sultan in Constantinople, though they hap-pened to fail, were no more of a hilarious fantasy than the negotiations I will soon be conducting with the dictator of Romania at his Bucharest palace."

"And the money to pay the dictator off? My guess is that to fund your effort you have only to turn to the PLO."

"I have every reason to believe that my funding will come from the American Jews who for decades now have been con-tributing enormous sums for the survival of a country with which they happen to have only the most abstractly sentimen-tal connection. The roots of American Jewry are not in the Middle East but in Europe—their Jewish style, their Jewish words, their strong nostalgia, their actual, weighable history, all this issues from their European origins. Grandpa did not hail from Haifa—Grandpa came from Minsk. Grandpa wasn't a Jewish nationalist—he was a Jewish humanist, a spiritual, believing Jew, who complained not in an antique tongue called Hebrew but in colorful, rich, vernacular Yiddish."

Our conversation was interrupted here by the hotel operator, who broke in to tell him that Frankfurt was now on the line.

"Pierre, hold a second."

Pierre, hold a second, and I did it, *held*, and, of course, obediently waiting for him to come back on made me even more ludicrous to myself than remembering everything I'd said in our conversation. I should have taped this, I realized—as evidence, as proof. But of what? That he wasn't me? This needed to be *proved*?

"A German colleague of yours," he said when he returned to speak to me again, "a journalist with *Der Spiegel*. You must excuse me if I leave you to talk with him now. He's been trying to reach me for days. This has been a good, strong interview—your questions may be aggressive and nasty, but they are also intelligent, and I thank you for them."

"One more, however, one last nasty question. Tell me, please," I asked, "are they lining up, the Romanian Jews who are dying to go back to Ceauşescu's Romania? Are they lining up, the Polish Jews who are dying to return to Communist Poland? Those Russians struggling to leave the Soviet Union, is your plan to turn them around at the Tel Aviv airport and force them onto the next flight back to Moscow? Anti-Semitism aside, you think people fresh from these terrible places will voluntarily choose to return just because Philip Roth tells them to?"

"I think I have made my position sufficiently clear to you for now," he replied most courteously. "In what journal will our interview be published?"

"I am free-lance, Mr. Philip Roth. Could be anywhere from *Le Monde* to *Paris-Match*."

"And you will be kind enough to send a copy to the hotel when it appears?"

"How long do you expect to remain there?"

"As long as the disassociation of Jewish identity threatens the welfare of my people. As long as it takes Diasporism to re-compose, once and for all, the splintered Jewish existence. Your last name again, Pierre?"

"Roget," I said. "Like the thesaurus."

His laugh erupted much too forcefully for me to believe that it had been provoked by my little quip alone. He knows, I thought, hanging up. He knows perfectly well who I am.

2

A Life Not My Own

ACCORDING to the testimony of six elderly Treblinka survivors, during the fifteen months from July 1942 to September 1943 when nearly a million Jews were murdered at Treblinka, the gas chamber there was operated by a guard, known
to the Jews as Ivan the Terrible, whose sideline was to maim
and torture, preferably with a sword, the naked men, women,
and children herded together outside the gas chamber waiting
to be asphyxiated. Ivan was a strong, vigorous, barely educated
Soviet soldier, a Ukrainian in his early twenties whom the Germans had captured on the Eastern Front and, along with hundreds more Ukrainian POWs, recruited and trained to staff the
Belsec, Sobibor, and Treblinka extermination camps in Poland.
John Demjanjuk's lawyers, one of whom, Yoram Sheftel, was
an Israeli, never disputed the existence of Ivan the Terrible or
the horror of the atrocities he committed. They claimed only
that Demjanjuk and Ivan the Terrible were two different
people and that the evidence to the contrary was all worthless.
They argued that the identity photo spread assembled for the
Treblinka survivors by the Israeli police was totally unreliable
because of the faulty and amateurish procedures used, procedures that had led or manipulated the survivors into mistakenly identifying Demjanjuk as Ivan. They argued that the
sole piece of documentary evidence, an identity card from
Trawniki, an SS training camp for Treblinka guards—a card
bearing Demjanjuk's name, signature, personal details, and a
photograph—was a KGB forgery designed to discredit
Ukrainian nationalists by marking one of them as this savage
war criminal. They argued that during the period when Ivan
the Terrible had been running the Treblinka gas chamber,
Demjanjuk had been held as a German prisoner of war in a region nowhere near the Polish death camps. The defense's
Demjanjuk was a hardworking, churchgoing family man who
had come to America with a young Ukrainian wife and a tiny
child from a European DP camp in 1952—a father of three

grown American children, a skilled autoworker with Ford, a decent, law-abiding American citizen renowned among the Ukrainian Americans in his Cleveland suburb for his wonderful vegetable garden and the pierogi that he helped the ladies cook for the celebrations at St. Vladimir's Orthodox Church. His only crime was to be born a Ukrainian whose Christian name had formerly been Ivan and to have been about the same age and perhaps even to have resembled somewhat the Ukrainian Ivan whom these elderly Treblinka survivors had, of course, not seen in the flesh for over forty years. Early in the trial, Demjanjuk had himself pleaded to the court, "I am not that awful man to whom you refer. I am innocent."

I learned all this from a thick file of xeroxed newspaper clippings about the Demjanjuk trial that I purchased at the office of *The Jerusalem Post*, the English-language Israeli paper. On the drive from the airport I'd seen the file advertised in that day's *Post*, and after checking in at the hotel, instead of phoning Apter and making arrangements to meet him later in the day, as I'd planned to do, I took a taxi directly over to the newspaper office. Then, before I went off to dinner with Aharon at a Jerusalem restaurant, I read carefully through the several hundred clippings, which dated back some ten years to when the U.S. government filed denaturalization charges against Demjanjuk in the Cleveland district court for falsifying, on his visa application, the details of his whereabouts during World War II.

I was reading at a table in the garden courtyard of the American Colony Hotel. Ordinarily I stayed at Mishkenot Sha'ananim, the guest house for visiting academics and artists run by the mayor's Jerusalem Foundation and located a couple of hundred yards down the road from the King David Hotel. Several months earlier I had reserved an apartment there for my January visit, but the day before leaving London I had canceled the reservation and made one instead at the American Colony, a hotel staffed by Arabs and situated at the other end of Jerusalem, virtually on the pre-1968 borderline between Jordanian Jerusalem and Israeli Jerusalem and only blocks away from where violence had sporadically broken out in the Arab Old City during the previous few weeks. I explained to Claire that I had changed reservations to be as far as I could get from

the other Philip Roth should he happen, despite the newspaper retraction, to be hanging on in Jerusalem still registered
at the King David under my name. My staying at an Arab
hotel, I said, minimized the likelihood of our paths ever
crossing, which was what she herself had cautioned me against
foolishly facilitating. "And maximizes," she replied, "the likelihood of getting stoned to death." "Look, I'll be all but incognito at the American Colony," I answered, "and for now
incognito is the smartest, least disruptive, most reasonable
strategy." "No, the smartest strategy is to tell Aharon to come
to the guest room here and stay in London with you." Since
on the day I left for Israel she herself was to fly to Africa to
begin to make a film in Kenya, I suggested to her, when we
parted at Heathrow Airport, that she was about as likely to be
eaten by a lion in the streets of Nairobi as I was to come to any
harm in a first-class hotel at the edge of East Jerusalem.
Gloomily she disagreed and departed.

After reading the clipping file right through to an article
from just the week before about a request by defense counsel
Yoram Sheftel to enter ten new documents in evidence at this
late stage of the proceedings, I wondered if it was while at the
Demjanjuk trial that the impostor had first got the idea to pretend to be me, emboldened by the identity issue at the heart of
the case, or if he had deliberately selected the trial for his performance because of the opportunities for publicity provided
by the extensive media coverage. It disgusted me that he
should insinuate this crazy stunt into the midst of such a grim
and tragic affair, and, for the first time, really, I found myself
outraged in the way that somebody without my professional
curiosity about shenanigans like this one probably would have
been from the start—not merely because, for whatever his reasons, he had decided that our two destinies should become
publicly entangled but because he had chosen to entangle
them here.

At dinner that evening I thought repeatedly of asking
Aharon to recommend a Jerusalem lawyer for me to consult
with about my problem, but instead I was mostly silent while
Aharon spoke about a recent guest of his, a Frenchwoman, a
university professor, married and the mother of two children,
who had been discovered as a new-born infant in a Paris

churchyard only months before the Allies liberated the city in 1944. She had been raised by foster parents as a Catholic but a few years back had come to believe that, in fact, she had been a Jewish child abandoned at birth by Jewish parents hiding somewhere in Paris and placed by them in the churchyard so that she would not be thought Jewish or raised as a Jew. This idea had begun to develop in her during the Lebanon war, when everyone she knew, including her husband and her children, was condemning the Israelis as criminal murderers and she found herself, alone and embattled, arguing strenuously in their defense.

She knew Aharon only through his books but wrote him nonetheless a compelling and impassioned letter about her discovery. He answered sympathetically, and a few days later she turned up on his doorstep to ask him to help her find a rabbi to convert her. That evening she had dinner with Aharon and his wife, Judith, and explained to them how she had never in her life felt she belonged to France, even though she wrote and spoke the language flawlessly and in her appearance and her behavior seemed to everyone as French as French could be—she was a Jew and she belonged to the Jews, of this she was ardently convinced.

The next morning Aharon took her to a rabbi he knew to ask if the rabbi would supervise her conversion. He refused, as did three other rabbis they went together to see. And each gave much the same reason for saying no: because neither her husband nor her children were Jews, the rabbis were disinclined to divide the family along religious lines. "Suppose I *divorce* my husband, *disown* my children—" But as she happened to love them all dearly, the rabbi to whom she made this proposal took it no more seriously than it was meant.

After her unsuccessful week in Jerusalem, desolated to have to return, still a Catholic, to her old life in France, she was at dinner at the Appelfelds' house on the evening before her departure, when Aharon and Judith, who could no longer bear to see the woman suffering so, suddenly announced to her, "You are a Jew! We, the Appelfelds, declare you a Jew! There—we have converted you!"

As we sat in the restaurant laughing together at the antic audacity of this obliging deed, Aharon, a small, bespectacled compact man with a perfectly round face and a perfectly bald head, looked to me very much like a benign wizard, as adept in the mysteries of legerdemain as his namesake, the brother of Moses. "He'd have no trouble," I later wrote in the preface to our interview, "passing for a magician who entertains children at birthday parties by pulling doves out of a hat—it's easier to associate his gently affable and kindly appearance with that job than with the responsibility by which he seems inescapably propelled: responding, in a string of elusively portentous stories, to the disappearance from Europe . . . of just about all the continent's Jews, his parents among them." Aharon himself had managed to remain alive by escaping from the Transnistria concentration camp at the age of nine and living either in hiding, foraging alone in the woods, or working as a menial laborer for poor local peasants until the Russians liberated him three years later. Before being transported to the camp, he had been the pampered child of wealthy, highly assimilated Bukovina Jews, a little boy educated by tutors, raised by nannies, and fitted out always in the finest clothes.

"To be declared a Jew by Appelfeld," I said, "that's no small thing. You do have it in you to bestow this mantle on people. You even try it with me."

"Not with you, Philip. You were a Jew par excellence years before I came along."

"No, no, never so exclusively, totally, and incessantly as the Jew it pleases you to imagine me to be."

"Yes, exclusively, totally, incessantly, *irreducibly.* That you continue to struggle so to deny it is for me the ultimate proof."

"Against such reasoning," I said, "there is no defense."

He laughed quietly. "Good."

"And tell me, do *you* believe this Catholic professor's fantasy of herself?"

"What I believe is not what concerns me."

"Then what *about* what she believes? Doesn't it occur to the professor that she may have been left in a churchyard precisely because she was *not* Jewish? And that her sense of apartness originates not in her having been born a Jew but in her having been orphaned and raised by people other than her natural parents? Besides, would a Jewish mother be likely to abandon her infant on the very eve of the liberation, when the chances for Jewish survival couldn't have been better? No, no, to have been found when she was found makes Jewish parentage for this woman the *least* likely possibility."

"But a possibility no less. Even if the Allies were to liberate them in only a matter of days, they had still to survive those days in hiding. And to survive in hiding with a crying infant might not have been feasible."

"This is what she thinks."

"It's one thing she thinks."

"Yes, a person can, of course, think absolutely anything. . . ." And I, of course, was thinking about the man who wanted people to think that he was me—did *he* think that he was me as well?

"You look tired," Aharon said. "You look upset. You're not yourself tonight."

"Don't have to be. Got someone else to do it for me."

"But nothing is in the papers, nothing more that I have seen."

"Oh, but he's still at it, I'm sure. What's to stop him? Certainly not me. And shouldn't I at least try? Wouldn't you? Wouldn't anyone in his right mind?" It was Claire's position I heard myself taking up now that she was gone. "Shouldn't I place an ad in *The Jerusalem Post* informing the citizens of Israel that there is this impostor about, an ad disassociating myself from whatever he says or does in my name? A full-page ad would end this overnight. I could appear on television. Better, I could simply go and talk to the police, because more than likely he's traveling with false documents. I know he's got to be breaking some kind of law."

"But instead you do nothing."

"Well, I *have* done something. Since I spoke with you I phoned him. At the King David. I interviewed him on the phone from London, posing as a journalist."

"Yes, and you look pleased with that—*now* you look like yourself."

"Well, it wasn't entirely unenjoyable. But, Aharon, what *am* I to do? It's too ridiculous to take seriously and too serious to be ridiculous. And it's activating—*re*activating—the very state of mind that I've been working for months now to shake off.

You know what's at the heart of the misery of a breakdown? Me-itis. Microcosmosis. Drowning in the tiny tub of yourself. Coming here I had it all figured out: desubjectified in Jerusalem, subsumed in Appelfeld, swimming in the sea of the other self—the other self being yours. Instead there is this me to plague and preoccupy me, a me who is not even me to obsess me day and night—the me who's not me encamped boldly in Jewish Jerusalem while I go underground with the Arabs."

"So that's why you're staying over there."

"Yes—because I'm not here for him, I'm here for *you*. That was the idea and, Aharon, it's *still* the idea. Look"—and from my jacket pocket I took the sheet of paper on which I'd typed out for him my opening question—"let's start," I said. "The hell with him. Read this."

I'd written: I find echoes in your fiction of two Middle European writers of a previous generation—Bruno Schulz, the Polish Jew who wrote in Polish and was shot and killed at fifty by the Nazis in Drogobych, the heavily Jewish Galician city where he taught high school and lived at home with his family, and Kafka, the Prague Jew who wrote in German and also lived, according to Max Brod, "spellbound in the family circle" for most of his forty-one years. Tell me, how pertinent to your imagination do you consider Schulz and Kafka to be?

Over tea then, we talked about neither me nor not-me but, somewhat more productively, about Schulz and Kafka until finally we grew tired and it was time to go home. Yes, I thought, this is how to prevail—forget this shadow and stick to the task. Of all the people who had assisted me in recovering my strength—among others, Claire, Bernie, the psychopharmacologist—I had chosen Aharon and talking to him as the final way out, the means by which to repossess that part of myself that I thought was lost, the part that was able to discourse and to think and that had simply ceased to exist in the midst of the Halcion wipeout when I was sure that I'd never be able to use my mind again. Halcion had destroyed not merely my ordinary existence, which was bad enough, but whatever was special to me as well, and what Aharon represented was someone whose maturation had been convulsed by the worst possible cruelty and who had managed nonetheless to reclaim his ordinariness *through* his extraordinariness, someone whose conquest of futility and chaos and whose rebirth as a harmonious human being and a superior writer constituted an achievement that, to me, bordered on the miraculous, all the more so because it arose from a force in him utterly invisible to the naked eye.

Later in the evening, before he went to bed, Aharon reformulated what he'd explained at the restaurant and typed out an answer in Hebrew to give to the translator the next day. Speaking of Kafka and himself, he said, "Kafka emerges from an inner world and tries to get some grip on reality, and I came from a world of detailed, empirical reality, the camps and the forests. My real world was far beyond the power of imagination, and my task as an artist was not to develop my imagination but to restrain it, and even then it seemed impossible to me, because everything was so unbelievable that one seemed oneself to be fictional. . . . At first I tried to run away from myself and from my memories, to live a life that was not my own and to write about a life that was not my own. But a hidden feeling told me that I was not allowed to flee from myself and that if I denied the experience of my childhood in the Holocaust I would be spiritually deformed. . . ."

My tiny cousin Apter, the unborn adult, earns his living painting scenes of the Holy Land for the tourist trade. He sells them from a little workshop—squeezed between a souvenir stall and a pastry counter—that he shares with a leather craftsman in the Jewish quarter of the Old City. Tourists who ask his prices are answered in their native tongues, for Apter, however underdeveloped as a man, happens to be someone whose past has left him fluent in English, Hebrew, Yiddish, Polish, Russian, and German. He even knows some Ukrainian, the language he calls Goyish. What the tourists are told when they ask Apter's prices is, "This is not for me to decide"—a sentiment that, unfortunately, is not humbly feigned: Apter is too cultivated to think well of his pictures. "I, who love Cézanne, who weep and pray before his paintings, I paint like a philistine without any ideals." "Of their kind," I tell him, "they're perfectly all right." "Why such terrible pictures?" he asks—"Is this too

Hitler's fault?" "If it's any comfort to you, Hitler painted worse." "No," says Apter, "I've seen his pictures. Even Hitler painted better than I do."

In any one week Apter might be paid as much as a hundred dollars or as little as five for one of his three-by-four-foot landscapes. A philanthropic English Jew, a Manchester manufacturer who owns a high-rise condo in Jerusalem and who somehow came to know Apter's biography, once gave my cousin a thousand-pound check for a single painting and, ever since, has made of Apter something of a ward, sending a minion around once a year to purchase more or less the same painting for the same outlandish price. On the other hand, an elderly American woman once walked off with a picture without giving Apter anything, or so Apter says—it was one of those dozen he paints every week depicting the Jerusalem animal market near St. Stephen's gate. The theft had left him sobbing in the street. "Police!" he shouted. "Help me! Someone help me!" But when no one came to his assistance, he raced after her himself and soon chased her down in the next turning, where she was resting against a wall, the stolen painting at her feet. "I am not a greedy man," he said to her, "but, madam, please, I must eat." As Apter recounted the story, she insisted to the small crowd that quickly formed around the weeping artist with his beggarly hands outstretched that she had already paid him a penny, which for such a painting was more than enough. Indignantly she screamed in Yiddish, "Look at his pocket! He's lying!" "The twisted ogre mouth," Apter told me, "the terrible, horrible shriek—Cousin Philip, I understood what I was up against. I said to her, 'Madam, which camp?' 'All of them!' she cried, and then she spat in my face."

In Apter's stories, people steal from him, spit at him, defraud and insult and humiliate him virtually every day and, more often than not, these people who victimize my cousin are survivors of the camps. Are his stories accurate and true? I myself never inquire about their veracity. I think of them instead as fiction that, like so much of fiction, provides the storyteller with the lie through which to expose his unspeakable truth. I treat the stories rather the way Aharon has chosen to understand the story concocted by his Catholic "Jew."

I had every intention, the morning after my dinner with Aharon, of taking a taxi directly from the hotel up to Apter's cubbyhole workshop in the old Jewish quarter and of spending a couple of hours with him before meeting once again with Aharon to resume our conversation over lunch. Instead, I went off in the taxi to the morning session of the Demjanjuk trial—to face down my impostor. If he wasn't there, I'd go on to the King David Hotel. I had to: twenty-four more hours of doing nothing and I'd be able to think of nothing else. As it was, I had been sleepless most of the night, up just about hourly to double-check that my door was locked, and then back to bed, waiting for him to appear above the footboard, Magrittishly suspended in midair, as though the footboard were a footstone, the hotel room a graveyard, and one or the other of us the ghost. And my dreams—rocketing clusters of terrible forebodings too sinister even to be named—I awakened from them with a ruthless determination to murder the bastard with my own two hands. Yes, by morning it was clear even to me that by doing nothing I was only exaggerating everything, and yet *still* I wavered, and it wasn't until the taxi was pulling up at the gate to the Jewish quarter that I finally told the driver to turn around and gave him the address of the convention center at the other end of the city, out beyond the Knesset and the museum, where, in a hall ordinarily used for lectures and movies, Demjanjuk had been on trial now for eleven months. At breakfast I'd copied the address out of the paper and heavily circled the spot on my Jerusalem street map. *No more wavering.*

Outside the doorway to the hall four armed Israeli soldiers were standing about chattering together next to a booth bearing a hand written sign that read, in Hebrew and in English, "Check Your Weapons Here." I walked by them unnoticed and into an outer lobby where I had only to show my passport to a young policewoman and write my name in a register at her desk to be allowed to proceed on through the metal detector to the inner lobby. I took my time signing looking up and down the page to see if my name had been written there already. Failing to find it proved nothing, of course—the court had been in session for an hour by then and there were scores of names recorded in the ledger's pages. What's more, I thought, the passport he held was more likely in his name than in mine. (But without a passport in my name how had he registered as me at his hotel?)

Inside the lobby I had to hand over the passport again, this time as security for an audio headset. The soldier on duty there, another young woman, showed me how I could tune it to a simultaneous English translation of the Hebrew proceedings. I waited for her to recognize me as someone who'd been to the trial before, but once she'd done her job she went back to reading her magazine.

When I entered the courtroom and saw, from behind the last row in spectators, what exactly was going on, I forgot completely why I had come; when, after sorting out the dozen or so figures on the raised platform at the front of the courtroom, I realized which one was the accused, not only did my double cease to exist, but, for the time being, so did I.

There he was. *There he was.* Once upon a time, drove two, three hundred of them into a room barely big enough for fifty, wedged them in every which way, bolted the doors shut, and started up the engine. Pumped out carbon monoxide for half an hour, waited to hear the screams die down, then sent in the live ones to pry out the dead ones and clean up the place for the next big load. "Get that shit out of there," he told them. Back when the transports were really rolling, did this ten, fifteen times a day, sometimes sober, sometimes not, but always with plenty of gusto. Vigorous, healthy boy. Good worker. Never sick. Not even drink slowed him down. Just the opposite. Bludgeoned the bastards with an iron pipe, tore open the pregnant women with his sword, gouged out their eyes, whipped their flesh, drove nails through their ears, once took a drill and bored a hole right in someone's buttocks—felt like it that day, so he did it. Screaming in Ukrainian, shouting in Ukrainian, and when they didn't understand Ukrainian, shot them in the head. What a time! Nothing like it ever again! A mere twenty-two and he owned the place—could do to any of them whatever he wished. To wield a whip and a pistol and a sword and a club, to be young and healthy and strong and drunk and powerful, *boundlessly* powerful, like a god! Nearly a million of them, a *million*, and on every one a Jewish face in which he could read the terror. Of him. *Of him!* Of a peasant boy of twenty-two! In the history of this entire world, had the opportunity ever been given to anyone anywhere to kill so many people all by himself, one by one? What a job! A sensational blowout every day! One continuous party! Blood! Vodka! Women! Death! Power! And the screams! Those unending screams! And all of it *work*, good, hard work and yet wild, wild, untainted joy—the joy most people only get to dream of, nothing short of ecstasy! A year, a year and a half of that is just about enough to satisfy a man forever; after that a man need never complain that life had passed him by; after that anyone could be content with a routine, regular nine-to-five job where no blood ever really flowed except, on rare occasions, as a result of an accident on the factory floor. Nine to five, then home to dinner with the wife and kids—that's all you needed after that. At twenty-two he'd seen all that anyone could ever hope to see. Great while it lasted, stupendous while you were young and fearless and on a tear, running over with animal zest for just about everything, but the sort of thing you outgrow eventually, as indeed he had. You have to know when to quit with a job like that and, luckily, he was one who did.

There he was. There *it* was, bald now and grown stocky, a big, cheerful palooka of sixty-eight, a good father, a good neighbor, loved by his family and all his friends. Still did pushups every morning, even in his cell, the kind where you've got to leave the floor and clap your hands together before you come back down on your palms—could still boast wrists so thick and strong that, on the plane over, ordinary handcuffs hadn't been large enough to encompass them. Nonetheless, it was nearly fifty years since he'd last smashed open anyone's skull, and he was by now as benign and unfrightening as an old boxing champ. Good old Johnny—man the demon as good old Johnny. Loved his garden, everyone said. Rather tend tomatoes now and raise string beans than bore a hole in somebody's ass with a drill. No, you've got to be young and in your prime, you've got to be on top of things and raring to go to manage successfully even something as simple as having a little fun like that with somebody's big fat behind. He'd sowed his oats and settled down, all that rough stuff sworn off long ago.

Could only barely remember now all the hell he had raised. So many years! The way they fly! No, he was somebody else entirely. That hell-raiser was no longer him.

There he was, between two police guards at a small table behind the corner table from which his three attorneys conducted his defense. He wore a pale blue suit over an open-necked shirt, and there as a headset arched across his large bald skull. I didn't realize right off that he was listening to a simultaneous translation of the proceedings into Ukrainian—he looked as though he were passing the time with a favorite pop cassette. His arms were crossed casually over his chest, and ever so faintly his jaws moved up and down as though he were an animal at rest tasting the last of its cud. That's all he did while I watched him. Once he looked indifferently out at the spectators, entirely at ease with himself, munching almost imperceptibly on nothing. Once he took a sip of water from the glass on the table. Once he yawned. You have the wrong man, this yawn proclaimed. With all due respect, these Jewish old people who identify Demjanjuk as their terrible Ivan are senile or mistaken or lying. I was a German prisoner of war. I know no more about a camp at Treblinka than an ox or a cow does. You might as well have a cud-chewing quadruped on trial here for murdering Jews—it would make as much sense as trying me. I am stupid. I am harmless. I am nobody. I knew nothing then and I know nothing now. My heart goes out to you for all you suffered, but the Ivan you want was never anybody as simple and innocent as good old Johnny the gardener from Cleveland, Ohio.

I remembered reading in the clipping file that on the day the prisoner was extradited from the United States and arrived in Israel, he asked the Israeli police, as they were taking him from the plane in his oversized handcuffs, if he could be permitted to kneel down and kiss the airstrip. A pious pilgrim in the Holy Land, a devout believer and religious soul—that was all he'd ever been. Permission was denied him.

So there he was. Or wasn't.

When I looked around the crowded courtroom for an empty place, I saw that at least a third of the three hundred or so spectators were high school kids, probably bused in together for the morning session. There was also a large contin-

gent of soldiers, and it was in among them that I found a seat
about halfway back in the center of the hall. They were boys
and girls in their late teens, with that ragtag look that distin-
guishes Israeli soldiers from all others, and though clearly they
too were there for "educational" reasons, I couldn't spot more
than a handful of them paying attention to the trial. Most were
sprawled across their seats, either shifting restlessly or whispering back and forth or just catatonically daydreaming, and not a
few were asleep. The same could be said of the students, some
of whom were passing notes like schoolkids anywhere who've
been taken on a trip by the teacher and are bored out of their
minds. I watched two girls of about fourteen giggling together
over a note they'd received from a boy in the row behind
them. Their teacher, a lanky, intense young man with glasses,
hissed at them to cut it out, but watching the two of them I
was thinking, No, no, it's right—to them Treblinka *should* be a
nowhere someplace up in the Milky Way; in this country, so
heavily populated in its early years by survivors and their families, it's actually a cause for rejoicing, I thought, that by this
afternoon these young teenagers won't even remember the defendant's name.

At a dais in the center of the stage sat the three judges in
their robes, but it was a while before I could begin to take
them in or even to look their way because, once again, I was
staring at John Demjanjuk, who claimed to be no less run-of-
the-mill than he looked—my face, he argued, my neighbors,
my job, my ignorance, my church affiliation, my long, un-
blemished record as an ordinary family man in Ohio, all this
innocuousness disproves a thousand times over these crazy accusations. How could I be both that and this?

Because you are. Because your appearance proves only that
to be both a loving grandfather and a mass murderer is not all
that difficult. It's because you could do both so well that I
can't stop staring at you. Your lawyers may like to think otherwise but this admirably unimportant American life of yours is
your *worst* defense—that you've been so wonderful in Ohio at
living your little, dull life is precisely what makes you so loathsome here. You've really only lived sequentially the two seemingly antipodal, mutually excluding lives that the Nazis, with
no strain to speak of, managed to enjoy simultaneously—so

what, in the end, is the big deal? The Germans have proved definitively to all the world that to maintain two radically divergent personalities, one very nice and one not so nice, is no longer the prerogative of psychopaths only. The mystery isn't that you, who had the time of your life at Treblinka, went on to become an amiable, hardworking American nobody but that those who cleaned the corpses out for you, your accusers here, could ever pursue anything resembling the run-of-the-mill after what was done to them by the likes of you—that *they* can manage run-of-the-mill lives, *that's* what's unbelievable!

Not ten feet from Demjanjuk, at a desk at the foot of the judges' dais, was a very pretty dark-haired young woman whose function there I couldn't at first ascertain. Later in the morning I realized that she was a documents clerk assisting the chief judge, but when I first noticed her so handsomely composed in the middle of everything, I could think only of those Jewish women whom Demjanjuk was accused of brutalizing with a sword and a whip and a club in the narrow pathway, the "tube," where those off the cattle cars were corralled together by him before he drove them through the gas-chamber door. She was a young woman of a physical type he must have encountered more than once in the tube and over whom his power there had been absolute. Now, whenever he looked toward the judges or toward the witness stand across from the defense attorney's table, she had to be somewhere in his field of vision, head unshaven, fully clothed, self-assured and unafraid, an attractive young Jewish woman beyond his reach in every way. Before I understood what her job must be, I even wondered if that couldn't have been *why* she'd been situated exactly where she was. I wondered if in his dreams back at the jail he ever saw in that documents clerk the ghost of the young women he had destroyed, if in his dreams there was ever a flicker of remorse, or if, as was more likely, in the dreams as in the waking thoughts he only wished that she had been there in the tube at Treblinka too—she, the three judges, his courtroom guards, the prosecuting attorneys, the translators, and, not least of all, those who came to the courtroom every day to stare as I was staring.

His trial was really no surprise to him, this propaganda trial trumped up by the Jews, this unjust, lying farce of a trial to which he had been dragged in irons from his loving family and his peaceful home. All the way back there in the tube, he'd known the trouble these people could cook up for a simple boy like himself. He knew their hatred of Ukrainians, had known about it all his life. Who had made the famine when he was a child? Who had transformed his country into a cemetery for seven million human beings? Who had turned his neighbors into subhuman creatures devouring mice and rats? As a mere boy he'd seen it all, in his village, in his *family*—mothers who ate the gizzards of the family pet cat, little sisters who had given themselves for a rotten potato, fathers who resorted to cannibalism. The crying. The shrieking. The agony. And everywhere the dead. Seven million of them! Seven million Ukrainian dead! And because of whom? Caused by whom!

Remorse? Go fuck your remorse!

Or did I have Demjanjuk wrong? While he chewed his cud and sipped his water and yawned through the trial's tedious stretches, perhaps his mind was empty of everything but the words "It wasn't me"—needed nothing more than that to keep the past at bay. "I hate no one. Not even you filthy Jews who want me dead. I am an innocent man. It was somebody else."

And *was* it somebody else?

So there he was—or wasn't. I stared and I stared, wondering if, despite all I'd read of the evidence against him, his claim that he was innocent was true; if the survivors who'd identified him could all be lying or wrong; if the identity card of the uniformed concentration-camp guard, bearing his Cyrillic signature and the photo of his youthful face, could indeed be a forgery; if the contradictory stories of his whereabouts as a German POW during the months when the prosecution's evidence placed him at Treblinka, muddled stories that he'd changed at virtually every inquiry before and since he'd received the original indictment, added up nonetheless to a believable alibi; if the demonstrably incriminating lies with which, since 1945, he had been answering the questions of refugee agencies and immigration authorities, lies that had led to his denaturalization and deportation from the United States, somehow pointed not to his guilt but to his innocence.

But the tattoo in his left armpit, the tattoo the Nazis had given their SS staff to register each individual's blood type—could that mean anything other than that he'd worked for them and that here in this courtroom he was lying? If not for fear of the truth being discovered, why had he set about secretly in the DP camp to obliterate that tattoo? Why, if not to hide the truth, had he undertaken the excruciatingly painful process of rubbing it bloody with a rock, of waiting for the flesh to heal, and of then repeatedly scraping and scraping with the rock until in time the skin was so badly scarred that his telltale tattoo was eradicated? "My tragic mistake," Demjanjuk told the court, "is that I can't think properly and I can't answer properly." Stupidity—the only thing to which he had confessed since the complaint identifying him as Ivan the Terrible was first filed against him by the U.S. Attorney's office eleven years earlier in Cleveland. And you cannot hang a man for being stupid. The KGB had framed him. Ivan the Terrible was somebody else.

A disagreement was brewing between the chief judge, a somber, gray-haired man in his sixties named Dov Levin, and the Israeli defense lawyer, Yoram Sheftel. I couldn't understand what the dispute was about because my headset had turned out to be defective, and rather than get up and possibly lose my seat while going for a replacement, I stayed where I was and, without understanding anything of the conflict, listened to the exchange heat up in Hebrew. Seated on the dais to the left of Levin was a middle-aged female judge with glasses and short-clipped hair; beneath her robe she was mannishly attired in a shirt and tie. To Levin's right was a smallish, bearded judge with a skullcap, a grandfatherly, sagacious-looking man of about my age and the sole Orthodox member of the panel.

I watched as Sheftel grew more and more exasperated with whatever Levin was telling him. The day before, I'd read in the Demjanjuk clipping file about the lawyer's flamboyant, hot-headed style. The theatrical zealousness with which he espoused his client's innocence, particularly in the face of the anguished eyewitness survivor testimony, seemed to have made him less than beloved by his compatriots; indeed, since the trial was being broadcast nationally on radio and television, chances were that the young Israeli lawyer had become one of the least popular figures in all of Jewish history. I remembered

reading that during a noon recess some months back, a courtroom spectator whose family had been killed at Treblinka had
shouted at Sheftel, "I can't understand how a Jew can defend
such a criminal. How can a Jew defend a Nazi? How can Israel
allow it? Let me tell you what they did to my family, let me explain what they did to my body!" As best I could gather from
his argument with the chief judge, neither that nor any other
challenge to his Jewish loyalties had diminished Sheftel's confidence or the forcefulness he was prepared to bring to Demjanjuk's defense. I wondered how endangered he was when he
exited the courtroom, this small, unstoppable battering ram of
a man, this engine of defiance so easily discernible by his long
sideburns and his narrow-gauge beard. Stationed at regular in-
tervals around the edge of the courtroom were unarmed uniformed policemen with walkie-talkies; undoubtedly there were
armed plainclothesmen in the hall as well—here Sheftel was no
less secure from harm than was his hated client. But when he
drove home at the end of the day in his luxurious Porsche?
When he went out with his girlfriend to the beach or a movie?
There had to be people all over Israel, people watching television at this very moment, who would have been glad to shut
him up with whatever it took to do it right.

Sheftel's dispute with the judge had resulted in Levin's de-
claring an early lunch recess. I came to my feet with everyone
else as the judges stood and left the dais. All around me the
high school kids raced for the exits; only a little less eagerly, the
soldiers followed them out. In a few minutes no more than
thirty or so spectators remained scattered about the hall, most
huddled together talking softly to one another, the rest just
sitting silently alone as though too infirm to move or swallowed up in a trance. All were elderly—retired, I thought at
first, people who had the time to attend the sessions regularly.
Then I realized that they must be camp survivors. And what
was it like for them to find standing only a few feet away the
mustached young man in the neat gray business suit whom I
now recognized, from his newspaper photos, as Demjanjuk's
twenty-two-year-old son, John junior, the son who vocifer-
ously protested that his father was being framed and who, in
his media interviews here, proclaimed his father's absolute and
total innocence of all wrongdoing? These survivors had, of

course, to recognize who he was—I'd read that at the start of
the trial, the son, at the family's request, had been seated
prominently right up behind his father on the stage, and even
I, a newcomer, had spotted him when Demjanjuk, several
times that morning, had looked down into the first row, where
John junior was seated, and, grimacing unself-consciously, had
signaled to him his boredom with the tiresome legal wran-
gling. I calculated that John junior had been no more than
eleven or twelve when his father had first been fingered as Ivan
the Terrible by U.S. immigration. The boy had gone through
his childhood thinking, as so many lucky children do, that he
had a name no more or less distinctive than anyone else's and,
happily enough, a life to match. Well, he would never be able
to believe that again: forevermore he was the namesake of the
Demjanjuk whom the Jews had tried before all of mankind for
someone else's horrible crime. Justice may be served by this
trial, but his children, I thought, are now plunged into the
hatred—the curse is revived.

Did no survivor in all of Israel think of killing John Demjanjuk, Jr., of taking revenge on the guilty father through the perfectly innocent son? Was there no one whose family had been
exterminated at Treblinka who had thought of kidnapping
him and of then mutilating him, gradually, piecemeal, an inch
at a go, until Demjanjuk could take no more and admitted to
the court who he was? Was there no survivor, driven insane
with rage by this defendant's carefree yawning and his indifferent chewing of his cud, no grieving, wrathful wreck of a
survivor, blighted and enraged enough to envisage in the torturing of the one the means of extracting a confession from
the other, to perceive in the outright murder of the next in line
a perfectly just and fitting requital?

I asked these questions of myself when I saw the tall, slender, well-groomed young man headed briskly toward the main
exit with the three defense lawyers—I was astonished that, like
Sheftel, Demjanjuk's namesake, his male successor and only
son, was about to step into the Jerusalem streets wholly
unprotected.

Outside the courtroom the balmy winter weather had taken a
dramatic turn. It was another day entirely. A tremendous rain-

storm was raging, sheets of rain driven laterally by a strong
wind that made it impossible to discern anything beyond the
first few rows of cars in the lot surrounding the convention
center. The people trying to determine how to leave the building were packed together in the outer foyer and on the walk-
way under the overhang. It was only when I'd moved into this
crowd that I remembered whom I'd come looking for—my
tiny local difficulty had been utterly effaced by a very great
mass of real horror. To have run off, as I had, to hunt him
down seemed to me now far worse than rash; it was to succumb momentarily to a form of insanity. I was thoroughly
ashamed of myself and disgusted once again for getting into a
dialogue with this annoyance—how crazy and foolish to have
taken the bait! And how little urgency finding him had for me
now. Laden with all I'd just witnessed, I resolved to put myself
to my proper use.

I was to meet Aharon for lunch just off Jaffa Street, at the
Ticho House, but with the rainstorm growing more and more
violent I didn't see how I could possibly get there in time. Yet,
having just removed myself from standing in my own way, I
was determined that nothing, but nothing, should obstruct
me, least of all the inclement weather. Squinting through the
rain to search for a taxi, I suddenly saw young Demjanjuk dart
out from beneath the overhang, following behind one of his
lawyers into the open door of a waiting car. I had the impulse
to race after him and ask if I could bum a ride to downtown
Jerusalem. I didn't do it, of course, but if I had, might I not
myself have been mistaken for the self-appointed Jewish
avenger and been gunned down in my tracks? But by whom?
Young Demjanjuk was there for the taking. And could I be the
only person in all of this crowd to see how very easy taking
him could be?

About a quarter of a mile up a hill from the parking lot,
there was a big hotel that I remembered seeing on the drive in,
and, desperate, I finally stepped out of the crowd and into the
rainstorm and made a dash for the hotel. Minutes later, my
clothes soaked and my shoes filled with water, I was standing
in the hotel lobby looking for a phone to call a taxi, when
someone tapped me on the shoulder. I turned to find facing
me the other Philip Roth.

3

We

"I CAN'T speak," he said. "It's you. You came!"

But the one who couldn't speak was I. I was breathless, and only in part because of running uphill against the lashing force of that storm. I suppose until that moment I'd never wholeheartedly believed in his existence, at least as anything more substantial than that pompous voice on the telephone and some transparently ridiculous newspaper blather. Seeing him materialize voluminously in space, measurable as a customer in a clothing shop, palpable as a prizefighter up in the ring, was as frightening as seeing a vaporous ghost—and simultaneously electrifying, as though after immersion in that torrential storm, I'd been doused, for good measure, like a cartoon-strip character, full in the face with an antihallucinogenic bucket of cold water. As jolted by the spellbinding reality of his unreality as by its immensely disorienting antithesis, I was at a loss to remember the plans I'd made for how to act and what to say when I'd set out to hunt him down in the taxi that morning—in the mental simulation of our face-off I had failed to remember that the face-off would not, when it came to pass, be a mental simulation. He was crying. He had taken me in his arms, sopping wet though I was, and begun to cry, and not undramatically either—as though one or the other of us had just returned intact from crossing Central Park alone at night. Tears of joyous relief—and I had imagined that confronted with the materialization of *me*, he would recoil in fear and capitulate.

"Philip Roth! The real Philip Roth—after all these years!" His body trembled with emotion, tremendous emotion even in the two hands that tightly grasped my back.

It required a series of violent thrusts with my elbows to unlock his hold on me. "And you," I said, shoving him a little as I stepped away, "you must be the fake Philip Roth."

He laughed. But still cried! Not even in my mental simula-

60

tion had I loathed him quite as I did seeing those stupid, unaccountable tears.

"Fake, oh, compared to you, *absolutely* fake—compared to you, nothing, no one, a cipher. I can't tell you what it's like for me! In Israel! In Jerusalem! I don't know what to say! I don't know where to begin! The books! Those books! I go back to *Letting Go*, my favorite to this day! Libby Herz and the psychiatrist! Paul Herz and that coat! I go back to 'The Love Vessel' in the old *Dial*! The work you've done! The potshots you've taken! Your women! Ann! Barbara! Claire! Such terrific women! I'm sorry, but imagine yourself in my place. For me—to meet you—in Jerusalem! What brings you here?"

To this dazzling little question, so ingenuously put, I heard myself reply, "Passing through."

"I'm looking at myself," he said, ecstatically, "except it's *you*."

He was exaggerating, something he may have been inclined to do. I saw before me a face that I would not very likely have taken for my own had I found it looking back at me that morning from the mirror. Someone else, a stranger, someone who had seen only my photograph or some newspaper caricature of me, might possibly have been taken in by the resemblance, especially if the face called itself by my name, but I couldn't believe that there was anyone who would say, "Don't fool me, you're really that writer," had it gone about its business as Mr. Nusbaum's or Dr. Schwartz's. It was actually a conventionally better-looking face, a little less mismade than my own, with a more strongly defined chin and not so large a nose, one that, also, didn't flatten Jewishly like mine at the tip. It occurred to me that he looked like the after to my before in the plastic surgeon's advertisement.

"What's your game, my friend?"

"No game," he replied, surprised and wounded by my angry tone. "And I'm no fake. I was using 'real' ironically."

"Well, I'm not so pretty as you and I'm not so ironical as you and I was using 'fake' *unerringly*."

"Hey, take it easy, you don't know your strength. Don't call names, okay?"

"You go around pretending to be me."

This brought that smile back—"You go around pretending to be *me*," he loathsomely replied.

"You exploit the physical resemblance," I went on, "by telling people that you are the writer, the author of my books."

"I don't have to tell them anything They take me for the author of those books right off. It happens all the time."

"And you just don't bother to correct them."

"Look, can I buy you lunch? You—here! What a shock to the system! But can we stop this sparring and sit down in this hotel and talk seriously together over lunch? Will you give me a chance to *explain*?"

"I want to know what you're up to, buddy!"

"I *want* you to know," he said gently and, like a Marcel Marceau at his corniest, with an exaggerated tamping-down gesture of his two hands, indicated that I ought to try to stop shouting and be reasonable like him. "I want you to know *everything*. I've dreamed all my life—"

"Oh no, not the 'dreams,'" I told him, incensed now not only by the ingenue posturing, not only by how he persisted in coming on so altogether unlike the stentorian Diasporist Herzl he'd impersonated for me on the phone, but by the Holly-wooded version of my face so nebbishly pleading with me to try to calm down. Odd, but for the moment that smoothed-out rectification of my worst features got my goat as much as anything did. What do we despise most in the appearance of somebody who looks like ourselves? For me, it was the earnest attractiveness. "Please, not the softly melting eyes of the nice Jewish boy. Your 'dreams'! I *know* what you've been up to here, I *know* what's been going on here between you and the press, so just can the harmless-shlimazl act now."

"But your eyes melt a little too, you know. I know the things you've done for people. You hide your sweet side from the public—all the glowering photographs and I'm-nobody's-sucker interviews. But behind the scenes, as I happen to know, you're one very soft touch, Mr. Roth."

"Look, what are *you* and who are *you*? Answer me!"

"Your greatest admirer."

"Try again."

"I can't do better than that."

"Try anyway. *Who are you?*"

"The person in the world who has read and loved your books like no one else. Not just once, not just twice—so many times I'm embarrassed to say."

"Yes, that embarrasses you in front of me? What a sensitive boy."

"You look at me as though I'm fawning, but it's the truth— I know your books inside out. I know your *life* inside out. I could be your biographer. I *am* your biographer. The insults you've put up with, they drive me nuts just on your behalf. *Portnoy's Complaint*, not even nominated for a National Book Award! The book of the decade and not even *nominated*! Well, you had no friend in Swados; he called the shots on that committee and had it in for you but good. So much animosity —I don't get it. Podhoretz—I actually cannot speak the man's name without tasting my gall in my mouth. And Gilman—that attack on *When She Was Good*, on the integrity of *that book*. Saying you wrote for Womrath's Book Store—about that perfectly honorable little book! And Professor Epstein, *there's* a genius. And those broads at *Ms.* And this exhibitionist Wolcott—"

I sank back into the chair behind me, and there in the hotel lobby, clammy and shivering under the rain-soaked clothes, I listened as he recalled every affront that had ever appeared in print, every assault that had ever been made on my writing and me—some, insults so small that, miraculously, even I had forgotten them, however much they might have exasperated me a quarter of a century earlier. It was as though the genie of grievance had escaped the bottle in which a writer's resentments are pickled and preserved and had manifested itself in humanish form, spawned by the inbreeding of my overly licked oldest wounds and mockingly duplicating the man I am.

"—Capote on the Carson show, coming on with that 'Jewish Mafia' shit, 'From Columbia University to Columbia Pictures'—"

"*Enough*," I said, and pushed myself violently up out of the chair. "That is really enough!"

"It's been no picnic, that's all I'm trying to say. I know what a struggle living is for you, Philip. May I call you Philip?"

"Why not? That's the name. What's yours?"

With that sonny-boy smile I wanted to smash with a brick, he replied, "Sorry, truly sorry, but it's the same. Come on, have some lunch. Maybe," he said, pointing to my shoes, "you want to stop in the toilet and shake those out. You got drenched, man."

"And you're not wet at all," I observed.

"Hitched a ride up the hill."

Could it be? Hitched the ride I'd thought of hitching with Demjanjuk's son?

"You were at the trial then," I said.

"There every day," he replied. "Go, go ahead, dry off," he said, "I'll get a table for us in the dining room. Maybe you can relax over lunch. We have a lot to talk about, you and me."

In the bathroom I took a deliberately long time to dry myself off, thinking to give him every opportunity to call a taxi and make a clean getaway without ever having to confront me again. His had been a commendable, if nauseating, performance for someone who, despite his cleverly seizing the initiative, had to have been only a little less caught off guard in the lobby than I was; as the sweet-natured innocent, cravenly oscillating between bootlicking and tears, his had been a more startlingly original performance by far than my own mundane portrayal of the angry victim. Yet the impact of *my* materialization must surely have been more galvanic even for him than his had been for me and he had to be thinking hard now about the risk of pushing this thing further. I gave him all the time he needed to wise up and clear out and disappear for good, and then, with my hair combed and my shoes each emptied of about half a cup of water, I came back up into the lobby to phone a taxi to get me over to my lunch date with Aharon—I was half an hour late already—and immediately I spotted him just outside the entryway to the restaurant, ingratiating smile still intact, more handsomely me than even before.

"I was beginning to think Mr. Roth had taken a powder," he said.

"And I was hoping the same about you."

'Why," he asked, "would I want to do a thing like that?"

"Because you're involved in a deceptive practice. Because you're breaking the law."

"Which law? Israeli law, Connecticut state law, or international law?"

"The law that says that a person's identity is his private property and can't be appropriated by somebody else."

"Ah, so you've been studying your Prosser."

"Prosser?"

"Professor Prosser's *Handbook of the Law of Torts*."

"I haven't been studying anything. All I need to know about a case like this common sense can tell me."

"Well, still, take a look at Prosser. In 1960, in the *California Law Review*, Prosser published a long article, a reconsideration of the original 1890 Warren and Brandeis *Harvard Law Review* article in which they'd borrowed Judge Cooley's phrase 'the general right to be let alone' and staked out the dimensions of the privacy interest. Prosser discusses privacy cases as having four separate branches and causes of action—one, intrusion upon seclusion; two, public disclosure of private facts; three, false light in the public eye; and four, appropriation of identity. The prima facie case is defined as follows: 'One who appropriates to his own use or benefit the name or likeness of another is subject to liability to the other for invasion of his privacy.' Let's have lunch."

The dining room was completely empty. There wasn't even a waiter to show us in. At the table he chose for us, directly in the center of the room, he drew out my chair for me as though *he* were the waiter and stood politely behind it while I sat down. I couldn't tell whether this was straight satire or seriously meant—yet *more* idolatry—and even wondered if, with my behind an inch from the seat, he might do what sadistic kids like to do in grade school and at the last moment pull the chair out from under me so that I landed on the floor. I grabbed an edge of the chair in either hand and pulled the seat safely under me as I sat.

"Hey," he said, laughing, "you don't entirely trust me," and came around to take the chair across the table.

An indication of how stunned I'd been out in the lobby— and had remained even off by myself in the bathroom, where I had somehow got round to believing that victory was achieved and he was about to run off, never to dare to return—was that only when we were sitting opposite each other did I notice that he was dressed identically to me: not similarly, *identically*. Same washed-out button-down, open-neck Oxford blue shirt, same well-worn tan V-neck cashmere sweater, same cuffless khaki trousers, same gray Brooks Brothers herringbone sports jacket threadbare at the elbows—a perfect replica of the colorless uniform that I had long ago devised to simplify life's sartorial problem and that I had probably recycled not even ten times since I'd been a penniless freshman instructor at the University of Chicago in the mid-fifties. I'd realized, while packing my suitcase for Israel, that I was just about ragged enough for my periodic overhaul—and so too, I saw, was *he*. There was a nub of tiny threadlets where the middle front button had come off his jacket—I noticed because for some time now I'd been exhibiting a similar nub of threadlets where the middle button had yet again vanished from *my* jacket. And with that, everything inexplicable became even more inexplicable, as though what we were missing were our navels.

"What do you make of Demjanjuk?" he asked.

Were we going to *chat*? About Demjanjuk no less?

"Don't we have other, more pressing concerns, you and I? Don't we have the prima facie case of identity appropriation to talk about, as outlined in point four by Professor Prosser?"

"But all that sort of pales, don't you think, beside what you saw in that courtroom this morning?"

"How would you know what I saw this morning?"

"Because I saw you seeing it. I was in the balcony. Upstairs with the press and the television. You couldn't take your eyes off him. Nobody can the first time. Is he or isn't he, was he or wasn't he?—the first time, that's all that goes round in anyone's head."

"But if you'd spotted me from the balcony, what was all that emotion about back in the lobby? You already knew I was here."

"You minimize your meaning, Philip. Still doing battle against being a personage. You don't entirely take in who you are."

"So you're taking it in for me—is that the story?"

When, in response, he lowered his face—as though I'd impertinently raised a subject we'd already agreed to consider off bounds—I saw that his hair had seriously thinned out and was striated gray in a pattern closely mirroring my own. Indeed, all those differences between our features that had been so reassuringly glaring at first sight were dismayingly evaporating the more accustomed to his appearance I became. Penitentially tilted forward like that, his balding head looked *astonishingly* like mine.

I repeated my question. "*Is* that the story? Since I apparently don't 'take in' what a personage I am, you have kindly taken it upon yourself to go about as this great personage *for* me?"

"Like to see a menu, Philip? Or would you like a drink?"

There was still no waiter anywhere, and it occurred to me that this dining room was not even open yet for business. I reminded myself then that the escape hatch of the "dream" was no longer available to me. Because I am sitting in a dining room where there is no food to be obtained; because across from me there sits a man who, I must admit, is nearly my duplicate in every way, down to the button missing from his jacket and the silver-gray filaments of hair that he has just pointedly displayed to me; because, instead of adjusting manfully to the predicament and intuitively taking control, I am being pushed to within an inch of I don't know what intemperate act by this stupidly evolving, unendurable farce, apparently all this only means that I am wide awake. What is being manufactured here is *not* a dream, however weightless and incorporeal life happens to feel at this moment and however alarmingly I may sense myself as a speck of being embodying nothing but its own speckness, a tiny existence even more repugnant than his.

"I'm talking to you," I said.

"I know. Amazing. And *I'm* talking to *you*. And not just in my head. More amazing."

"I meant I would like an *answer* from you. A serious answer."

"Okay, I'll answer seriously. I'll be blunt, too. Your prestige has been a little wasted on you. There's a lot you haven't done with it that you could have done—a lot of good. That is not a criticism, just a statement of fact. It's enough for you to write—God knows a writer like you doesn't owe anyone any more than that. Of course not every writer is equipped to be a public figure."

"So you've gone public for me."

"A rather cynical way to put it, wouldn't you say?"

"Yes? What is the uncynical way?"

"Look, at bottom—and this is meant with no disrespect, but since bluntness is *your* style—at bottom you are only instrumental."

I was looking at his glasses. It had taken this long for me to get round to the glasses, glasses framed in a narrow gold half-frame exactly like my own. . . . Meanwhile he had reached inside his jacket pocket and withdrawn a worn old billfold (yes, worn exactly like mine) and extracted from it an American passport that he handed across the table to me. The photograph was one taken of me some ten years ago. And the signature was my signature. Flipping through its pages, I saw that Philip Roth had been stamped in and out of half a dozen countries that I myself had never visited: Finland, West Germany, Sweden, Poland, Romania.

"Where'd you get this?"

"Passport office."

"This happens to be me, you know." I was pointing to the photograph.

"No," he quietly replied. "It's me. Before my cancer."

"Tell me, did you think this all out beforehand or are you making the story up as you go along?"

"I'm terminally ill," he replied, and so confusing was that remark that when he reached across for the passport, the strongest and best evidence I had of the fraud that he was perpetrating, I stupidly handed it back to him instead of keeping it and causing a fracas then and there. "Look," he said, leaning intensely across the table in a way I recognized as an imitation of my own conversational style, "about the two of us and our connection is there really any more to say? Maybe the trouble is that you haven't read enough Jung. Maybe it comes down to nothing more than that. You're a Freudian, I'm a Jungian. Read Jung. He'll help you. I began to study him when I first had to deal with you. He explained for me parallelisms that are unexplainable. You have the Freudian belief in the sovereign

power of causality. Causeless events don't exist in your universe. To you things that aren't thinkable in intellectual terms
aren't worth thinking about. A lot of smart Jews are like that.
Things that aren't thinkable in intellectual terms don't even
exist. How can I exist, a duplicate of you? How can you exist,
a duplicate of me? You and I defy causal explanation. Well,
read Jung on 'synchronicity.' There are meaningful arrangements that defy causal explanation and they are happening *all
the time*. We are a case of synchronicity, synchronistic phenomena. Read a little Jung, Philip, if only for your peace of mind.
'The uncontrollability of real things'—Carl Jung knows all
about it. Read *The Secret of the Golden Flower*. It'll open your
eyes to a whole other world. You look stupefied—without a
causal explanation you are lost. How on this planet can there
be two men of the same age who happen not only to look alike
but to bear the same name? All right, you *need* causality? I'll
give you causality. Forget about just you and me—there would
have been another *fifty* little Jewish boys of our age growing
up to look like us if it hadn't been for certain tragic events that
occurred in Europe between 1939 and 1945. And is it impossible that half a dozen of them might not have been Roths? Is
our family name that rare? Is it impossible that a couple of
those little Roths might not have been called after a grandfather Fayvel, like you, Philip, and like me? You, from your career perspective, may think it's horrible that there are two of us
and that you are not unique. From my Jewish perspective, I
have to say I think it's horrible that *only* two are left."

"No, no, not horrible—*actionable*. It's actionable that of
the two of us left, one of us goes around impersonating the
other. Had there been seven thousand of us left in the world,
only one of us, you see, would have written my books."

"Philip, nobody could treasure your books more than I do.
But we are at a point in Jewish history when maybe there is
more for us to be talking about, especially together here at last
in Jerusalem, than your books. Okay, I have allowed people to
confuse me with you. But, tell me, please, how else could I
have got to Lech Walesa?"

"You can't seriously be asking me that question."

"I can and I am, and with good reason. By seeing Lech
Walesa, by having with him the fruitful talk we had, what harm

did I do you? What harm did I do anyone? The harm will come only if, because of your books and for no other reason, you should want to be so legalistic as to go ahead and try to undo everything I achieved in Gdansk. Yes, the law *is* on your side. Who says no? I wouldn't have undertaken an operation on this scale without first knowing in every last detail the law that I am up against. In the case of *Onassis v. Christian Dior– New York Inc.*, where a professional model, a Jackie Onassis look alike, was used in advertisements for Dior dresses, the court determined that the effect of using a look-alike was to represent Jackie Onassis as associated with the product and up-held her claim. In the case of *Carson v. Here's Johnny Portable Toilets*, a similar decision was reached. Because the phrase 'Here's Johnny' was associated with Carson and his TV show, the toilet company had no right, according to the court, to display the phrase on their portable toilets. The law couldn't be any more clear: even if the defendant is using *his own name*, he may be liable to prosecution for appropriation if the use implies that some other famous individual of that name is actually being represented. I am, as you see, more knowledgeable than you are about exactly what *is* actionable here. But I really cannot believe that you can believe that there is a telling similarity between the peddling of high-fashion shmatas, let alone the selling and renting of portable toilets, and the mission to which I have dedicated my life. I took your achievement as my own; if you like, all right, I stole your books. *But for what purpose?* Once again the Jewish people are at a terrible crossroad. Because of Israel. Because of Israel and the way that Israel endangers us all. Forget the law and listen, please, to what I have to say. The majority of Jews don't choose Israel. Its existence only confuses everyone, Jews and Gentiles alike. I repeat: Israel only *endangers* everyone. Look at what happened to Pollard. I am haunted by Jonathan Pollard. An American Jew paid by Israeli intelligence to spy against his own country's military establishment. I'm frightened by Jonathan Pollard. I'm frightened because if I'd been in his job with US. naval intelligence, *I would have done exactly the same thing.* I daresay, Philip Roth, that *you* would have done the same thing if you were convinced, as Pollard was convinced, that, by turning over to Israel secret U.S. information about Arab weapons systems,

you could be saving Jewish lives. Pollard had fantasies about
saving Jewish lives. I understand that, *you* understand that:
Jewish lives must be saved, and at absolutely any cost. But the
cost is not betraying your country, it's *greater* than that: it's
defusing the country that most endangers Jewish lives today—
and that is the country called Israel! I would not say this to
anyone else—I am saying this only to you. *But it must be said.*
Pollard is just another Jewish victim of the existence of Israel—
because Pollard enacted no more, really, than the Israelis demand of Diaspora Jews *all the time.* I don't hold Pollard responsible, I hold Israel responsible—Israel, which with its
all-embracing Jewish totalism has replaced the goyim as the
greatest intimidator of Jews in the world; Israel, which today,
with its hunger for Jews, is, in many, many terrible ways, deforming and disfiguring Jews as only our anti-Semitic enemies
once had the power to do. Pollard loves Jews. I love Jews. *You*
love Jews. But no more Pollards, please. God willing, no more
Demjanjuks either. We haven't even spoken of Demjanjuk. I
want to hear what you saw in that courtroom today. Instead of
talking about lawsuits, can we, now that we know each other a
little better, talk about—"

"No. *No.* What is going on in that courtroom is not an issue
between us. Nothing there has the least bearing on this fraud
that you are perpetrating by passing yourself off as me."

"*Again* with the fraud," he mumbled sadly, with a deliberately comical Jewish intonation. "Demjanjuk in that courtroom has *everything* to do with us. If it wasn't for Demjanjuk,
for the Holocaust, for Treblinka—"

"If this is a joke," I said, rising out of my seat, "it is a very
stupid, very wicked joke and I advise you to stop it right now!
Not Treblinka—not that, please. Look, I don't know who you
are or what you are up to, but I'm warning you—pack up and
get out of here. Pack it up and go!"

"Oh, where the hell is a waiter? Your clothes are wet, you
haven't eaten—" And to calm me down he reached across the
table and took hold of my hand. "Just hang on—*waiter!*"

"Hands off, clown! I don't want lunch—*I want you out of
my life!* Like Christian Dior, like Johnny Carson and the
portable toilet—*out!*"

"Christ, you're on a short fuse, Philip. You're a real heart-attack type. You act like I'm trying to ridicule you, when, Christ, if I valued you any more—"

"Enough—*you're a fraud!*"

"But," he pleaded, "you don't know yet what I'm trying to *do.*"

"I *do* know. You are about to empty Israel of the Ashkenazis. You are about to resettle Jews in all the wonderful places where they were once so beloved by the local yokels. You and Walesa, you and Ceauşescu are about to avert a second Holocaust!"

"But—then—that was *you*," he cried. "*You* were Pierre Roget! You tricked me!" And he slumped over in his chair at the horror of the discovery, pure commedia dell'arte.

"Repeat that, will you? I did what?"

But he was now in tears, second time since we'd met. What *is* it with this guy? Watching him shamelessly carrying on so emotionally reminded me of my Halcion crying jags. Was this his parody of my powerlessness, still more of his comic improvisation, or was he hooked on Halcion himself? Is this a brilliant creative disposition whose ersatz satire I'm confronting or a genuine ersatz maniac? I thought, Let Oliver Sacks figure him out—you get a taxi and go, but then somewhere within me a laugh began, and soon I was overcome with laughter, laughter pouring forth from some cavernous core of understanding deeper even than my fears: despite all the unanswered questions, never, never had anybody seemed less of a menace to me or a more pathetic rival for my birthright. He struck me instead as *a great idea* . . . yes, a great idea breathing with life!

Although I was over an hour late for our appointment, I found Aharon still waiting for me in the café of the Ticho House when finally I arrived there. He had figured that it was the rainstorm that delayed me and had been sitting alone at a table with a glass of water, patiently reading a book.

For the next hour and a half we ate our lunch and talked about his novel *Tzili*, beginning with how the child's consciousness seemed to me the hidden perspective from which not just this but other novels of his were narrated as well. I said nothing about anything else. Having left the aspirant Philip

Roth weeping in that empty hotel dining room, crushed and humiliated by my loud laughter, I had no idea what to expect next. I had faced him down—so now what?

This, I told myself: *this.* Stick to the task!

Out of the long lunchtime conversation, Aharon and I were able to compose, in writing, the next segment of our exchange.

ROTH: In your books, there's no news from the public realm that might serve as a warning to an Appelfeld victim, nor is the victim's impending doom presented as part of a European catastrophe. The historical focus is supplied by the reader, who understands, as the victims cannot, the magnitude of the enveloping evil. Your reticence as a historian, when combined with the historical perspective of a knowing reader, accounts for the peculiar impact your work has—for the power that emanates from stories that are told through such very modest means. Also, dehistoricizing the events and blurring the background, you probably approximate the disorientation felt by people who were unaware that they were on the brink of a cataclysm.

It's occurred to me that the perspective of the adults in your fiction resembles in its limitations the viewpoint of a child, who, of course, has no historical calendar in which to place unfolding events and no intellectual means of penetrating their meaning. I wonder if your own consciousness as a child at the edge of the Holocaust isn't mirrored in the simplicity with which the imminent horror is perceived in your novels.

APPELFELD: You're right. In *Badenheim 1939* I completely ignored the historical explanation. I assumed that the historical facts were known and that readers would fill in what was missing. You're also correct, it seems to me, in assuming that my description of the Second World War has something in it of a child's vision. Historical explanations, however, have been alien to me ever since I became aware of myself as an artist. And the Jewish experience in the Second World War was not "historical." We came in contact with archaic mythical forces, a kind of dark subconscious the meaning of which we did not know, nor do we know it to this day. This world appears to be rational (with trains, departure times, stations, and engineers), but in fact these were journeys of the imagination, lies and ruses, which only deep, irrational drives could have invented. I didn't understand, nor do I yet understand, the motives of the murderers.

I was a victim, and I try to understand the victim. That is a broad, complicated expanse of life that I've been trying to deal with for thirty years now. I haven't idealized the victims. I don't think that in *Badeheim 1939* there's any idealization either. By the way, Badenheim is a rather real place, and spas like that were scattered all over Europe, shockingly petit bourgeois and idiotic in their formalities. Even as a child I saw how ridiculous they were.

It is generally agreed, to this day, that Jews are deft, cunning, and sophisticated creatures, with the wisdom of the world stored up in them. But isn't it fascinating to see how easy it was to fool the Jews? With the simplest, almost childish tricks they were gathered up in ghettos, starved for months, encouraged with false hopes, and finally sent to their death by train. That ingenuousness stood before my eyes while I was writing *Badenheim*. In that ingenuousness I found a kind of distillation of humanity. Their blindness and deafness, their obsessive preoccupation with themselves is an integral part of their ingenuousness. The murderers were practical, and they knew just what they wanted. The ingenuous person is always a shlimazl, a clownish victim of misfortune, never hearing the danger signals in time, getting mixed up, tangled up, and finally falling into the trap. Those weaknesses charmed me. I fell in love with them. The myth that the Jews run the world with their machinations turned out to be somewhat exaggerated.

ROTH: Of all your translated books, *Tzili* depicts the harshest reality and the most extreme form of suffering. Tzili, the simplest child of a poor Jewish family, is left alone when her family flees the Nazi invasion. The novel recounts her horrendous adventures in surviving and her excruciating loneliness among the brutal peasants for whom she works. The book strikes me as a counterpart to Jerzy Kosinski's *The Painted Bird*. Though less grotesque, *Tzili* portrays a fearful child in a world even bleaker and more barren than Kosinski's, a child moving in isolation through a landscape as uncongenial to human life as any in Beckett's *Molloy*.

As a boy you wandered alone like Tzili after your escape, at age nine, from the camp. I've been wondering why, when you came to transform your own life in an unknown place, hiding out among the hostile peasants, you decided to imagine a girl as the survivor of this ordeal. And did it occur to you ever *not* to fictionalize this material but to present your experiences as you remember them, to write a survivor's tale as direct, say, as Primo Levi's depiction of his Auschwitz incarceration?

APPELFELD: I have never written about things as they happened. All my works are indeed chapters from my most personal experience, but nevertheless they are not "the story of my life." The things that happened to me in my life have already happened, they are already formed, and time has kneaded them and given them shape. To write things as they happened means to enslave oneself to memory, which is only a minor element in the creative process. To my mind, to create means to order, sort out and choose the words and the pace that fit the work. The materials are indeed materials from one's life, but, ultimately, the creation is an independent creature.

I tried several times to write "the story of my life" in the woods after I ran away from the camp. But all my efforts were in vain. I wanted to be faithful to reality and to what really happened. But the chronicle that emerged proved to be a weak scaffolding. The result was rather meager, an unconvincing imaginary tale. The things that are most true are easily falsified.

Reality, as you know, is always stronger than the human imagination. Not only that, reality can permit itself to be unbelievable, inexplicable, out of all proportion. The created work, to my regret, cannot permit itself all that.

The reality of the Holocaust surpassed any imagination. If I remained true to the facts, no one would believe me. But the moment I chose a girl, a little older than I was at that time, I removed "the story of my life" from the mighty grip of memory and gave it over to the creative laboratory. There memory is not the only proprietor. There one needs a causal explanation, a thread to tie things together. The exceptional is permissible only if it is part of an overall structure and contributes to an understanding of that structure. I had to remove those parts that were unbelievable from "the story of my life" and present a more credible version.

When I wrote *Tzili* I was about forty years old. At that time I was interested in the possibilities of naiveness in art. Can there be a naive modern art? It seemed to me that without the naiveté still found among children and old people and, to some extent, in ourselves, the work of art would be flawed. I tried to correct that flaw. God knows how successful I was.

Dear Philip,

I enraged you/you blitzed me. Every word I spoke—stupid/wrong/unnatural. Had to be. Been dreading/dreaming this meeting since 1959. Saw your photo on *Goodbye, Columbus*/knew that my life would never be the same. Explained to everyone we were two different people/had no desire to be anyone but myself/wanted *my* fate/hoped your first book would be your last/wanted you to fail and disappear/thought constantly about your dying. IT WAS NOT

WITHOUT RESISTANCE THAT I ACCEPTED MY ROLE: THE
NAKED YOU/THE MESSIANIC YOU! THE SACRIFICIAL
YOU. MY JEWISH PASSIONS SHIELDED BY NOTHING. MY
JEWISH LOVING UNRESTRAINED.

LET ME EXIST. Do not destroy me to preserve your good name.
I AM YOUR GOOD NAME. I am only spending the renown you
hoard. You hide yourself/in lonely rooms/country recluse/anony-
mous expatriate/garreted monk. Never spent it as you should/
might/wouldn't/couldn't: IN BEHALF OF THE JEWISH
PEOPLE. Please! Allow me to be the public instrument through
which you express the love for the Jews/the hatred for their ene-
mies/that is in every word you ever wrote. *Without legal intervention.*

Judge me not by words but by the woman who bears this letter. To
you I say everything stupidly. Judge me not by awkward words which
falsify everything I feel/know. Around you I will never be a smith
with words. See beyond words. I am not the writer/I am something
else. I AM THE YOU THAT IS NOT WORDS.

Yours,
Philip Roth

The immediate physical reality of her was so strong and exciting
—and unsettling—that it was a little like sitting across a table
from the moon. She was about thirty-five, a voluptuously
healthy-looking creaturely female around whose firm, rosy
neck it wouldn't have been inappropriate to tie the county
fair's first-prize ribbon—this was a biological winner, this was
somebody who was *well.* Her whitish blond hair was worn casually pinned in a tousled bun at the back of her head, and she
had a wide mouth, the warm interior of which she showed
you, like a happy, panting dog, even when she wasn't speaking,
as though she were taking your words in through her mouth,
as though another's words were not received by the brain but
processed—once past the small, even, splendidly white teeth
and the pink, perfect gums—by the whole, radiant, happy-go-
lucky thing. Her vivacious alertness, even her powers of concentration, seemed situated in the vicinity of her jaws; her eyes,
beautifully clear and strongly focused though they were, did
not appear to reach anywhere like so deep into the terrific
ubiquity of all that hereness. She had the substantial breasts
and the large round behind of a much heavier, less sprightly
woman—she might, in another life, have been a fecund wet

nurse from the Polish hinterlands. In fact, she was an oncology
nurse and he had met her five years earlier, when he was first a
cancer patient in a Chicago hospital. Her name was Wanda
Jane "Jinx" Possesski,° and she aroused in me the sort of yearnings excited by the thought of a luxuriously warm fur coat on
a freezing winter day: specifically, a craving to be enwrapped.

The woman by whom he wished to be judged was sitting
across from me at a small table in the garden of the American
Colony courtyard, beneath the charming arched windows of
the old hotel. The violent morning rain squalls had subsided
into little more than a sun shower while I was having lunch
with Aharon, and now, at a few minutes before three, the sky
was clear and the courtyard stones aglitter with light. It felt
like a May afternoon, warm, breezy, lullingly serene, even
though it was January of 1988 and we happened to be only a
few hundred yards from where Israeli soldiers had teargassed a
rock-throwing mob of young Arab boys just the day before.
Demjanjuk was on trial for murdering close to a million Jews
at Treblinka, Arabs were rising up against the Jewish authorities all over the Occupied Territories, and yet from where I was
seated amid the lush shrubbery, between a lemon tree and an
orange tree, the world could not have seemed any more enticing. Pleasant Arab waiters, singing little birds, a good cold
beer—and this woman of his who evoked in me the illusion
that nothing could be more durable than the perishable matter
from which we are made.

All the while I read his dreadful letter she watched me as
though she'd brought to the hotel directly from President Lincoln the original manuscript of the Gettysburg Address. The
only reason I didn't tell her, "This is as loony a piece of prose
as I've ever received in my life," and tear it into little pieces was
because I didn't want her to get up and go. I wanted to hear
her talk, for one thing: it was my chance to find out more, only
more lies perhaps, but then, enough lies, and maybe some
truth would begin trickling through. And I wanted to hear her
talk because of the beguilingly ambiguous timbre of her voice,
which was harmonically a puzzle to me. The voice was like
something you've gotten out of the freezer that's taking its
own sweet time to thaw: moist and spongy enough at the
edges to eat, otherwise off-puttingly refrigerated down to its

deep-frozen core. It was difficult to tell just how coarse she was, if there was a great deal going on in her or if maybe there was nothing at all and she was just a petty criminal's obedient moll. Probably it was only my infatuation with the exciting fullness of such a female presence that led me to visualize a mist of innocence hanging over her bold carnality that might enable me *to get somewhere.* I folded the letter in thirds and slipped it into my inside pocket—*what I should have done with his passport.*

"It's incredible," she said. "Overwhelming. You even read the same way."

"From left to right."

"Your facial expressions, the way you take everything in, even your clothes—it's *uncanny.*"

"But then everything is uncanny, is it not? Right down to our sharing the very same name."

"And," she said, smiling widely, "the sarcasm, too."

"He tells me that I should judge him by the woman who bears his letter, but much as I'd like to, it's hard, in my position, not to judge him by other things first."

"By what he's undertaken. I know. It's so gigantic for Jews. For Gentiles, too. I think for everyone. The lives he'll save. The lives he's *saved.*"

"Already? Yes? Whose?"

"Mine, for one."

"I thought it was you who was the nurse and he who was the patient—I thought you'd helped save him."

"I'm a recovering anti-Semite. I was saved by A-S.A."

"A-S.A.?"

"Anti-Semites Anonymous. The recovery group Philip founded."

"It's just one brainstorm after another with Philip," I said. "He didn't tell me about A-S.A."

"He didn't tell you hardly anything. He couldn't. He's so in awe of you, he got all bottled up."

"Oh, I wouldn't say bottled up. I'd say unbottled up almost to a fault."

"All I know is he came back in terrible shape. He's still in bed. He says he disgraced himself. He came away thinking you hated him."

"Why on earth would I hate Philip?"

"That's why he wrote this letter."

"And sent you to act as his advocate."

"I'm not a big reader, Mr. Roth. I'm not a reader at all. When Philip was my patient I didn't even know you existed, let alone that you were his look-alike. People are *always* mistaking him for you everywhere we go—everywhere, everyone, except illiterate me. To me he was just the most intense person I'd ever met in my life. He still is. There's no one like him."

"Except?" I said, tapping my chest.

"I meant the way he's set out to change he world."

"Well, he's come to the right place for that. Every year they treat dozens of tourists here who go around thinking themselves the Messiah and exhorting mankind to repent. It's a famous phenomenon at the mental-health center—local psychiatrists call it 'Jerusalem syndrome.' Most of them think they're the Messiah or God, and the rest claim to be Satan. You got off easy with Phillip."

But nothing I said, however disdainful or outright contemptuous of him, had any noticeable effect on the undampable conviction with which she continued extolling to me the achievements of this blatant fraud. Was it *she* suffering from that novel form of hysteria known as Jerusalem syndrome? The government psychiatrist who had entertained me with a witty exposition on the subject a few years back had told me that there are also Christians they find wandering out in the desert who believe themselves to be John the Baptist. I thought: *his* harbinger, Jinx the Baptist, mouthpiece for the Messiah in whom she's discovered salvation and the exalted purpose of her life. "The Jews," she said, staring straight out at me with her terribly gullible eyes, "are all he thinks about. Night and day, since his cancer, his life has been dedicated to the Jews."

"And you," I asked, "who believe in him so—are you now a Jew lover too?"

But I could not seem to say anything to impair her buoyancy, and for the first time I wondered if perhaps she was afloat on dope, if both of them were, and if that accounted for everything, including the very soulful smile my sharp words had evoked—if behind the audacious mystery of these two there was nothing but a pound of good pot.

"Philip lover, yes; Jew lover, no. Uh-uh. All Jinx can love, and it's plenty for her, is no longer hating Jews, no longer blaming Jews, no longer detesting Jews on sight. No, I can't say that Jinx Possesski is a lover of Jews or that Jinx Possesski ever will be. What can I say—okay?—is what I said: I'm a recovering anti-Semite."

"And what's that like?" I asked, thinking now that there was something not *entirely* unbelievable about her words and that I could do no better than be still and listen.

"Oh, it's a story."

"How long are you in recovery?"

"Almost five years. I was poisoned by it. A lot, I think now, had do with the job. I don't blame the job, I blame Jinx—but still, there's one thing about a cancer hospital: the pain is just something that you can't imagine. When someone's in pain, you almost want to run out of the room, screaming to get the pain medication. People have no idea, they really and truly have no idea, what it is like to have pain like that. Their pain is so outrageous, and everyone is afraid of dying. There's a lot of failure in cancer—you know, it's not a maternity ward. On a maternity ward, I might never have found out the truth about myself. It might never have happened to me. You want to hear all this?"

"If you want to tell me," I said. What I wanted to hear was why she loved this fraud.

"I got drawn into people's suffering," she said. "I couldn't help it. If they cry, I hold their hand, I hug them—if they cry, *I* cry. I hug them, they hug me—to me there's no way not to. It's like you were their savior. Jinx could do no wrong. But I can't be their savior. And that got to me after a while." The nonsensically happy look slipped suddenly from Jinx's face and she was convulsed by a rush of tenderness that left her for a moment unable to go on. "These patients . . ." she said, her voice completely deiced now and as soft through and through as a small child's, ". . . they look at you with those eyes. . . ." The magnitude of the emotions she was reckoning with took me by surprise. *If this is an act, then she's Sarah Bernhardt.* "They look at you with those eyes, they're so wide open—and they grab, *they grab*—and I give, but I can't give them life. . . . After a while," she went on, the emotion subsiding into something sad and rueful, "I was just helping people to die. Make you more comfortable. Give you more pain medication. Give you a back massage. Turn you a certain way. Anything. I did a lot for patients. I always went one beyond the medical thing. 'You wanna play cards, you wanna smoke a little marijuana?' The patients were the only thing that meant anything to me. After a day when maybe three people died, you bagged the last person—'This is *it*,' you say, 'I'm fuckin' tired of puttin' a fuckin' tag on someone's toe!'" How violently the moods wavered! One little word was enough to turn her around—and the little word in this case was *it*. "This is *it*," and she was as radiant with a crude, bold, coarse forcefulness as she had been stricken just the minute before by all that anguishing heartache. What there was to subject her to him I still couldn't say, but what might subordinate a man to her I had no difficulty perceiving: everything existed in such generous portions. Not since I had last read Strindberg could I remember having run across such a tantalizing layer cake of female excitement. The desire I then suppressed—to reach out and cup her breast—was only in part the urge men have perpetually to suppress when the fire is suddenly lit in a public place: beneath the soft, plump mass of breast I wanted to feel, against my palm, the power of that heart.

"You know," she was saying, "I'm sick and tired of turning someone over and thinking that this is not going to affect me! 'Tag 'em and wrap 'em. Have you tagged them and wrapped them yet? Tag 'em and wrap 'em up.' 'No, because the family hasn't come yet. Get the fuckin' family here so we can tag 'em and wrap 'em, and get the hell out of here!' I OD'd on death, Mr. Roth. Because," and again she could not speak, so felled was she by these memories ". . . because there was too much death. It was too much dying, you know? And I just couldn't handle myself. I turned on the Jews. The Jewish doctors. Their wives. Their kids. And they were good doctors. Excellent doctors, excellent surgeons. But I'd see the photographs framed on their desks, the kids with tennis rackets, the wives by the pool, I'd hear them on the phone, making dates for the evening like nobody on the floor was dying—planning for their tennis, their vacations, their trips to London and Paris,

'We're staying at the Ritz, we're eating at the Schmitz, we're
going to back up a truck and empty out Gucci's,' and I'd freak
out, man, I'd go off on a real anti-Semitic binge. I worked on
the gastric floor—stomach-liver-pancreatic floor. Two other
nurses about the same age, and it was like an infection that
went from me to them. At our nursing station, which was
great, we had the greatest music, a lot of rock 'n' roll, and we
gave each other a tremendous amount of support, but we were
all, like, calling in sick a lot, and I was yakking and yakking
about the Jews more and more. We were all young there,
twenty-three, twenty-four, twenty-five—five days a week, and
you worked overtime and every night you stayed late. You
stayed late because these people were so sick, and I'd think
about those Jewish doctors home with their wives and their
kids—even when I was away from the floor, it wouldn't leave
me. I was on fire with it. The Jews, the Jews. When we'd work
evenings, all three of us together, we'd get home, smoke a
joint, *definitely* smoke a joint—couldn't wait to roll it. We
made piña coladas. Anything. All night. If we didn't drink at
home we'd get dressed up or throw our makeup on and go
out, Near North, Rush Street, the scene. Go to all the bars.
Sometimes you met people and you went on dates and you
fucked—okay?—but not really as an outlet. The outlet for the
dying was pot. The outlet for the dying was the Jews. With me
anti-Semitism was in the family. Is it hereditary, environmental, or strictly a moral flaw? A topic of discussion at A-S.A.
meetings. The answer? We don't care why we have it, we are
here to admit that we have it and help each other get rid of it.
But in me I think I had it for all the reasons you can. My father
hated them, to begin with. A boiler engineer in Ohio. I heard
it growing up but it was like wallpaper, it never meant a thing
before I was a cancer nurse. But once I started—okay?—I
couldn't stop. Their money. Their wives. Those women, those
faces of theirs—those hideous Jewish faces. Their kids. Their
clothes. Their voices. You name it. But mostly the look, the
Jewish look. It didn't stop. *I* didn't stop. It got to the point
that the resident, this one doctor, Kaplan, he didn't like to
look you in the eyes that much—he would say something
about a patient and all I saw were those Jewish lips. He was a
young guy but already he had the underslung jaw like the old

Jews get, and the long ears, and those real liver lips—the whole bit that I couldn't stand. That's how I went berserk. That's when I hit bottom. He was scared because he was not used to giving so much pain medication. He was scared the patient would suffer respiratory arrest and die. But she was a woman my age—so young, so young. She had cancer that went *everywhere*. And she was just in so much pain. She was in *so* much pain. Mr. Roth, a *terrific* amount of pain." And the tears were streaming onto her face, the mascara running, and the impulse I now suppressed was not to palpate her large, warm breast or to measure the warlike strength of the heart beneath but to take her two hands from the tabletop and enclose them in mine, those transgressive, tabooless nurse's hands, so deceptively clean and innocent-seeming, that had nonetheless been everywhere, swathing, spraying, washing, wiping, freely touching everywhere, handling everything, open wounds, drainage bags, every running orifice, as naturally as a cat pawing a mouse. "I had to get out of cancer. I didn't want to be a cancer nurse. I just wanted to be a nurse, anything. I was screaming at him, at Kaplan, at those fucking Jew lips, 'You better fucking give us the pain medication we need! Or we are going to get the attending and he's going to be pissed off at you for waking him up! Get it! Get it now!' You know," she said, surprisingly childishly. "You know? You know?"

You know, like, okay?—and still there was enough persuasiveness there to *make* you know.

"She was young," she told me, "strong. Their will is very, very strong. It'll keep them going forever, despite as much pain as they can endure. Even *more* pain than they can endure and they endure. It's horrible. So you give them more medication because their heart is so strong and their will is so strong. They're in pain, Mr. Roth—*you have to give them something!* You know? You know?"

"I do now, yes."

"They need an almost *elephant* dose of morphine, the people that are so young." And she made none of the effort she had the moment before to hide her weeping in her shoulder or to pause and steady herself. "They're young—it's *doubly* bad! I shouted at Dr. Kaplan, 'I will not allow someone to be cruel to someone who is dying!' So he got it for me. And I gave it to her." Momentarily she seemed to see herself in the scene, to see herself giving it to her, to that woman her own age, "so young, so young." She was there again. Maybe, I thought, she's always there and *that's* why she's with him.

"What happened?" I asked her.

Weakly—and this was no weakling—but very weakly she finally answered, all the while looking down at the hands that I persisted in envisioning everywhere, hands that she once must have washed two hundred times a day. "She died," she said.

When she looked up again she was smiling sadly, certifying with that smile that she was out of cancer now, that all the dying, though it hadn't stopped, though it never stopped, no longer required that she smoke pot and down piña coladas and hate the likes of Dr. Kaplan and me. "She was going to die anyway, she was ready to die, but she died on me. I killed her. Her skin was beautiful. You know? She was a waitress. A good person. An outgoing person. She told me she wanted six children. But I gave her morphine and she died. I went berserk. I went to the bathroom and I went hysterical. The Jews! The Jews! The head nurse came in. She was the reason why you see me here and not in jail. Because the family was very bad. They came in screaming. 'What happened? What happened?' Families get so guilt-ridden because they can't do anything and they don't want her to die. They know that she's suffering horribly, that there's no hope, yet when she dies, 'What happened? What happened?' But the head nurse was, like, so good, a great woman, and she held me. 'Possesski, you gotta get out of here.' It took me a year. I was twenty-six years old. I got transferred. I got on the surgical floor. There's always hope on the surgical floor. Except there's a procedure called 'open and close.' Where you open them up and the doctor won't even attempt anything. And they stay and they die. They die! *Mr. Roth, I couldn't get away from death.* Then I met Philip. He had cancer. He was operated on. Hope! Hope! Then the pathology report. Three lymph nodes are involved. So I'm, like, 'Oh, my God.' I didn't want to get attached. I tried to stop myself. You always try to stop yourself. That's what the cursing is all about. The tough talk isn't so tough, you know? You think it's cold. It's not cold at all. That happened with Philip. I thought I hated him. Okay, I *wanted* to hate him. I should have learned from that girl I killed. Stay away. Look at his looks. But instead I fell in love with him, I fell *in love* with his looks, with every fucking Jewish thing about him. That talk. Those jokes. That intensity. The imitations. Crazy with life. He was the one patient ever who gave me more strength than I gave them. We fell in love."

Just then, through the large window opposite me, I noticed Demjanjuk's legal team in the lobby beyond the courtyard— they too must be guests here in this East Jerusalem hotel and on their way either to or from the afternoon session. I recognized Sheftel first, the Israeli lawyer, and then the other two; with them, still dressed impeccably in suit and tie, as though he were lawyer number four, was Demjanjuk's tall young son. Jinx looked to see what had diverted my attention from her life's searing drama of death and love.

"Know why Demjanjuk continues lying?" she asked.

"*Is* he lying?"

"*Is* he! The defense has *nothing.*"

"Sheftel looks awfully cocky to me."

"Bluff, all bluff—there's no alibi *at all*. The alibi's proved false a dozen times over. And the card, the Trawniki card, it's got to be Demjanjuk's—it's *his* picture, *his* signature."

"And not a fake?"

"The prosecution has *proved* it's not fake. And those old people on the witness stand, the people who cleaned out the gas chambers for him, the people who worked alongside him *every day*, it's *overwhelming*, the case against him. Anyway, Demjanjuk *knows* they know. He acts like a stupid peasant but he's a cunning bastard and no fool. He knows he'll be hanged. He knows it's coming to him, too."

"So why does he continue to lie?"

She jerked a thumb toward the lobby, a brusque little gesture that took me by surprise after the impassioned vulnerability of her aria, something she'd probably learned to mime, along with the anti-Semitism, from the boiler engineer, her father. And what she was saying about the trial I figured she must be miming too, for these were no longer words stained with her blood but words she repeated as though she didn't even believe in the meaning of words. Parroting her hero, I thought, as the adoring mate of a hero will.

"The son," she explained. "He wants the son to be good and not to know. Demjanjuk's lying for the son. If Demjanjuk confessed, that boy would be finished. He wouldn't have a chance." One of those hands of hers settled familiarly on my arm, one of those hands whose history of besmirchment by the body's secretions I could not stop myself envisioning; and for me, in that raw contact, there was such a shock of intimacy that I felt momentarily absorbed into her being, very like what an infant must feel back when the mother's hands aren't mere appendages but the very incarnation of her whole warm, wonderful big body. Resist, I thought, this overtempting presence —these are not two people with your interests at heart!

"Talk to him. Sit down and talk to Philip, *please*."

" 'Philip' and I have nothing to talk about."

"Oh, *don't*," she begged me, and as her fingers closed on me even more tightly, the pressure of her thumb in the crook of my arm triggered a rush of just about everything urging me in the wrong direction, "*please, don't. . . .*"

"Don't what?"

"Undermine what he is doing!"

"It's not I who is doing the undermining."

"But the man," she cried, "is in *remission*!"

Even under less excitable conditions, "remission" is not a word easy to ignore, any more than "guilty" or "innocent" is in the courtroom when pronounced by the jury foreman to the judge.

I said, "Remission from cancer is nothing that I am against, for him or anyone. I am not even against his so-called Diasporism. I have no interest in those ideas either way. What I am against is his entangling our two lives and confusing people about who is who. What I cannot permit and what I will not permit is his encouraging people to believe that he is me. That must stop!"

"It will—okay? It'll stop."

"Will it? How do you know?"

"Because Philip told the to tell you that it would."

"Yes, did he? Why *didn't* you then? Why didn't *he*, in that letter—that completely idiotic letter!" I said, angrily remembering the vacuous pithiness, the meaningless dissonance, the hysterical incoherence of that life-and-death longhand, remembering all those stupid slashes only vaguely disguising what I surmised he'd as soon do with me.

"You're misunder*stand*ing him," she pleaded. "It *will* stop. He's sick about how this has upset you. What happened has sent him reeling. I mean with vertigo. I mean literally *he can't stand up*. I left him there in bed. He crashed, Mr. Roth, completely."

"I see. He thought I wouldn't mind. He thought the interviews with the journalists would just roll off my back."

"If you would meet with him one more time—"

"I *met with him*. I'm meeting with *you*," I said, and pulled my arm out from beneath her hand. "If you love him, Miss Possesski, and are devoted to him, and want to avoid the sort of trouble that might possibly endanger the health of a cancer patient in remission, then you'd be well advised to stop him *now*. He must stop using my name now. This is as far as I go with meetings."

"But," she said, her voice heating up and her hands clenched in anger, "that's like asking you to stop using *his* name."

"No, no, not at all! *Your patient in remission is a liar.* Whatever great motives may be motivating him, he happens to be lying through his teeth! His name is *not* the same as mine, and if he told you that it was, then he lied to you, too."

Just the contortion of her mouth caused me instinctively to raise a hand to ward off a blow. And what I caught with that hand was a fist quite hard enough to have broken my nose. "Prick!" she snarled. "Your name! Your name! Do you ever, ever, ever think of anything *other* than your fucking name!"

Interlocked on the tabletop now, our fingers began a fight of their own; her grip was anything but girlish, and even pressing with all my strength, I was barely able to keep her five fingers immobilized between mine. Meanwhile I kept an eye on the other hand.

"You're asking the wrong man," I said. "The question is, 'Does he?'"

Our struggle was being watched by the hotel waiters. A group of them had gathered just inside the windowed door to the lobby so as to look on at what must have struck them as a lovers' quarrel, no more or less dangerous—and entertaining —than that, a touch of comic relief from the violence in the street, and probably not a little pornographically piquant.

"You should be a tenth as selfless, a *hundredth* as selfless! Do you know many dying men? Do you know many dying men whose thoughts are only for saving others? Do you know many people kept alive on a hundred and fifty pills a day who could begin to do what he is doing? What he went through in Poland just to *see* Walesa! *I* was worn out. But Philip would not be stopped, not by *anything*. Dizzy spells that would fell a horse and *still* he doesn't stop! He falls down, he gets up, he keeps going. And the pain—he is like trying to excrete his own insides! The people we have to see before we even *get* to Walesa! It wasn't the shipyards where we met him. That's just stuff for the papers. It was way the hell out and beyond. The car rides, the passwords, the hiding places—and still this man *does not stop!* Eighteen months ago every last doctor gave him no more than six months to live—and here he is, in Jerusalem, alive! Let him have what keeps him alive! Let this man go on with his dream!"

"The dream that he is me?"

"You! You! Nothing in your world but *you*! Stop stroking my hand! Let go of my hand! Stop coming *on* with me!"

"You tried to hit me with that hand."

"You are trying to seduce me! *Let me go!*"

She was wearing a belted blue poplin raincoat over a short denim skirt and a white ribbed sweater, a very youthful outfit, and it made her appear, when our fingers fell apart and she rose in a fury from her chair, rather statuesquely pubescent, a woman's fullness coyly displayed in mock-maidenly American disguise.

In the features of one of the young waiters huddled up to the glass of the lobby door I saw the feverish look of a man who hopes with all his heart that the long-awaited striptease is about to begin. Or perhaps, when her hand reached down into her raincoat pocket, he thought that he was going to witness a shooting, that the voluptuous woman was about to pull a gun.

And as I was still completely in the dark about what this couple was after and what they were truly contriving to do, my expectations were all at once no more realistic than his. In coming to Jerusalem like this, refusing to consider seriously an impostor's more menacing meaning, heeding only my desperate yearning to be intact and entire, to prove that I was unimpaired by that ghastly breakdown and once again a robust, forceful, undamaged man, I had made the biggest, stupidest mistake yet, even more unfortunate a mistake than my lurid first marriage and one from which, it appeared, there was to be no escape. *I should have listened to Claire.*

But what the voluptuous woman pulled from her pocket was only an envelope. "You shit! The remission *depends* on this!" And hurling the envelope onto the table, she ran from the courtyard and out of the hotel through the lobby, where the thrill-seeking, mesmerized waiters were no longer to be seen.

Only when I began to read this second communication from him, which was composed in longhand like the first, did I realize how skillfully he had worked to make his handwriting resemble my own. Alone now, without all her radiant realness to distract me, I saw on this sheet of paper the pinched and twisted signs of my own impatient, overaccelerated left-handed scrawl, the same irregular slope climbing unevenly uphill, the *o*'s and *e*'s and *a*'s compressed and all but indistinguishable from *i*'s, the *i*'s themselves hastily undotted and the *t*'s uncrossed, the "The" in the heading atop the page a perfect replica of the "The" I'd been writing since elementary school, which looked more like "Fli." It was, like mine, a hand in a hurry to be finished with writing abnormally into, rather than flowing right-handedly away from, the barrier of its own impeding torso. Of all the falsifications I knew of so far, including the phony passport, this document was far and away the most professional and even more infuriating to behold than the forgery of his conniving face. He'd even taken a crack at my style. At least the style wasn't his, if that loonily cryptic, slash-bedecked letter she'd given me first was any sample of the prose that came to this counterfeiter "naturally."

THE TEN TENETS OF ANTI-SEMITES
ANONYMOUS

1. We admit that we are haters prone to prejudice and powerless to control our hatred.
2. We recognize that it is not Jews who have wronged us but we who hold Jews responsible for our troubles and the world's evils. It is we who wrong *them* by believing this.
3. A Jew may well have shortcomings like any other human being, but the shortcomings we are here to be honest about are our own, i.e., paranoia, sadism, negativism, destructiveness, envy.
4. Our money problems are not of the Jews' making but of our own.
5. Our job problems are not of the Jews' making but of our own (so too with sexual problems, marital problems, problems in the community).
6. Anti-Semitism is a form of flight from reality, a refusal to think honestly about ourselves and our society.
7. Inasmuch as anti-Semites cannot control their hatred, they are not like other people. We recognize that even to drop a casual anti-Semitic slur endangers our struggle to rid ourselves of our sickness.
8. Helping to detoxify others is the cornerstone of our recovery. Nothing will so much ensure immunity from the illness of anti-Semitism as intensive work with other anti-Semites.
9. We are not scholars, we do not care why we have this dreadful illness, we come together to admit that we have it and to help one another get rid of it.
10. In the fellowship of A-S.A. we strive to master the temptation to Jew hatred in all its forms.

4

Jewish Mischief

"**N**ow suppose," I said to Aharon when we met to resume our work over lunch the next day, "suppose this isn't a stupid prank, isn't an escapade of some crazy kind, isn't a malevolent hoax; suppose, despite every indication to the contrary, these two are not a pair of con artists or crackpots—however astonishing the supposition, suppose that they are exactly what they present themselves to be and that every word they speak is the truth." My resolve to compartmentalize my impostor, to keep coolly disengaged, and, while in Jerusalem, to remain concentrated solely on the assignment with Aharon had, of course, collapsed completely before the provocation of Wanda Jane's visit. As Claire had forlornly predicted (as I who'd phoned him right off the bat in the guise of Pierre Roget, secretly had never doubted), the very absurdity of his impersonation was too tantalizing for me to be able to think of anything else quite so excitedly. "Aharon, suppose it is so. All of it. A man named XYZ happens to look like the twin of a well-known writer whose name, remarkably enough, is also XYZ. Perhaps some three or four generations back, before the millions of European Jews migrated en masse to America, they were rooted in the same Galician clan—and perhaps not. Doesn't matter. Even if they share no common ancestry—and wildly unlikely as all the similarities might seem—such a coincidence could happen and in this instance it does. The duplicate XYZ is mistaken repeatedly for the original XYZ and naturally comes to take a more than passing interest in him. Whether he then develops his interest in certain Jewish contradictions because these figure prominently in the writer's work or whether they engage him for biographical reasons of his own, the duplicate finds in Jews a source for fantasies no less excessive than those of the original. For instance: Because the duplicate XYZ believes that the state of Israel, as currently constituted, is destined to be destroyed by its Arab enemies in a nuclear exchange he invents Diasporism, a program that seeks to resettle all Israeli Jews of European origin back in those countries where they or their families were residents before the outbreak of the Second World War and thereby to avert 'a second Holocaust.' He's inspired to pursue its implementation by the example of Theodor Herzl, whose plan for a Jewish national state had seemed no less utopian and antihistorical to its critics some fifty-odd years before it came to fruition. Of the numerous strong arguments against *his* utopia, none is more of an impediment than the fact that these are countries in which Jewish security and well-being would be perennially menaced by the continuing existence of European anti-Semitism, and it's with this problem still obstructing him that he enters the hospital as a cancer patient and finds himself being nursed by Jinx Possesski. He is ill, Jewish, and battling to live, and she is not only pantingly alive but rabidly anti-Semitic. A volcanic drama of repulsion and attraction ensues— bitter cracks, remorseful apologies, sudden clashes, tender reconciliations, educational tirades, furtive fondlings, weeping, embraces, wrenching emotional confusion, and then, late one night, there comes the discovery, the revelation, the breakthrough. Sitting at the foot of the bed in the dark hospital room where, struggling miserably against the dry heaves, he is on the chemotherapy intravenous drip, the nurse discloses to her suffering patient the miseries of *her* consuming disease. She tells it all as she never has before, and while she does, XYZ comes to realize that there are anti-Semites who are like alcoholics who actually want to stop but don't know how. The analogy to alcoholism continues to deepen the longer he listens to her. But, of course, he thinks—there are occasional anti-Semites, who engage in nothing more really than a little anti-Semitism as a social lubricant at parties and business lunches; moderate anti-Semites, who can control their anti-Semitism and even keep it a secret when they have to; and then there are the all-out anti-Semites, the real career haters, who may perhaps have begun as moderate anti-Semites but who eventually are consumed by what turns out in them to be a progressively debilitating disease. For three hours Jinx confesses to him her helplessness before the most horrible feelings and thoughts about Jews, to the murderous malice that engulfs her whenever she has so much as to speak with a Jew, and all the while he is thinking, She must be cured. If she is cured, we are saved! If I can save her, I can save the Jews! I must not die! I will not die! When she has finished, he says to her softly, 'Well, at last you've told your story.' Weeping wretchedly, she replies, 'I don't feel any better for it.' 'You will,' he promises her. 'When? *When?*' 'In time,' answers XYZ, and then he asks if she knows another anti-Semite who is ready to give it up. She isn't even sure, she meekly replies, that she is ready to herself, and even if she thinks herself ready, is she *able*? It isn't with him as it is with other Jews—she's in love with him and this miraculously washes away all hatred. But with the other Jews, it's automatic, it just rises up in her at the mere *sight* of them. Perhaps if she could steer clear of Jews for just a little while . . . but in this hospital, with all its Jewish doctors, Jewish patients, and Jewish families, with the Jewish crying, the Jewish whispering, the Jewish screaming. . . . He says to her, 'An anti-Semite who cannot meet, or mix with, Jews still has an anti-Semitic mind. However far from Jews you flee, you will take it with you. The dream of eluding the anti-Semitic feelings by escaping from Jews is only the reverse of cleansing yourself of these feelings by ridding the earth of all Jews. The only shield against your hatred is the program of recovery that we have begun in this hospital tonight. Tomorrow night bring with you another anti-Semite, another of the nurses who knows in her heart what anti-Semitism is doing to her life.' For what he is thinking now is that, like the alcoholic, the anti-Semite can only be cured by another anti-Semite, while what she is thinking is that she does not want her Jew to absolve *another* anti-Semite of her anti-Semitism but craves that loving forgiveness for herself alone. Isn't one anti-Semitic woman enough? Must he have all the anti-Semitic women in the world begging his Jewish forgiveness, confessing to their Gentile rottenness, admitting to him that he is superior and they are slime? *Tell me, girls, your dirty goy secrets.* It's *this* that turns the Jew *on!* But the next evening, from the nurses' station where they play all the wonderful rock 'n' roll, she brings to him not just one anti-Semitic woman besides herself but two. The room is dark but for the night lamp shining at the side of the sickbed where he lies gaunt, silent, greenishly pale, so miserable he is not even sure any longer whether he is conscious or comatose, whether the three nurses are seated in a row at the foot of his bed saying what he thinks he hears them saying or it is all a deathbed delirium and the three are tending him in the final awful moments of his life. 'I am an anti-Semite like Wanda Jane,' whispers one of the weeping nurses. 'I need to discuss my anger with Jews. . . .'"

Here I found myself laughing as uproariously as I had when I'd left Jinx's savior and my impostor in the hotel dining room the day before, and, for the moment, I could go no further.

"What's so hilarious?" asked Aharon, smiling at my laughter. "His mischief or yours? That he pretends to be you or that you now pretend to be him?"

"I don't know. I suppose what's most hilarious is my distress. Define 'mischief,' please"

"To a mischief-maker like you? Mischief is how some Jews get involved in living."

"Here," I said, and, laughing still, laughing with the foolish, uncontrollable laughter of a child who no longer can remember what it was that started him off, I handed him a copy of "The Ten Tenets of A-S.A." "This is what she left with me."

"So," said Aharon, as he held between two fingers the document whose margins were filled with my scrawl, "you are his editor, too."

"Aharon, who *is* this man?" I asked, and waited and waited for the laughter to subside. "*What* is he?" I went on when I could speak again. "He gives off none of the aura of a real person, none of the *coherence* of a real person. Or even the *in*coherence of a real person. Oh, it's all plenty incoherent, but incoherent in some wholly artificial way: he emanates the aura of something absolutely spurious, almost the way that Nixon did. He didn't even strike me as Jewish—that seemed as false as everything else and *that's* supposed to be at the heart of it all. It isn't just that what he calls by my name has no connection to me; it doesn't seem to have any to him, either. A mismade artifact. No, even that puts it too positively."

"A vacuum," said Aharon. "A vacuum into which is drawn your own gift for deceit."

"Don't exaggerate. More like a vacuum cleaner into which is sucked my dust."

"He has less talent for impersonating you than you have—maybe that's the irritation. Substitute selves? Alter egos? The writer's medium. It's all too shallow and too porous for you, without the proper weight and substance. Is this the double that is to be my own? An aesthetic outrage. The great wonders performed on the golem by Rabbi Liva of Prague you are now going to perform on him. Why? Because you have a better conception of him than he does. Rabbi Liva started with clay; you begin with sentences. It's perfect," said Aharon, with amusement, and all the while reading my marginal commentary on the Ten Tenets. "You are going to rewrite him."

What I had noted in the margins was this: "Anti-Semites come from all walks of life. This is too complicated for them. 1. Each tenet must not convey more than one idea. First tenet shouldn't have both hatred *and* prejudice. Powerless to control is a redundancy—powerless over or can't control. 2. No logic to progression. Should unfold from general to specific, from acceptance to action, from diagnosis to program of recovery to joy of living TOLERANT. 3. Avoid fancy words. Sounding like a highbrow. Drop negativism, endangers, intensive, immunity. Anything bookish bad for your purpose (generally true throughout life)." And on the reverse side of the sheet, which Aharon had now turned over and begun to read, I'd tried recasting the first few A-S.A. tenets in a simpler style, so that A-S.A. members (should there be any such!) could actually utilize them. I'd taken my inspiration from something Jinx had said to me—"We don't care why we have it, we are here to admit that we have it and help each other get rid of it." Jinx has got the tone, I thought: blunt and monosyllabic. Anti-Semites come from all walks of life.

1. We admit [I'd written] that we are haters and that hatred has ruined our lives.
2. We recognize that by choosing Jews as the target for our hatred, we have become anti-Semites and that all our thoughts and actions have been affected by this prejudice.
3. Coming to understand that Jews are not the cause of our troubles but our own shortcomings are, we become ready to correct them.

4. We ask our fellow anti-Semites and the Spirit of Tolerance to help us overcome these defects.

5. We are willing to fully apologize for all the harm
caused by our anti-Semitism. . . .

While Aharon was reading my revisions we were approached
by a very slight, elderly cripple who seesawed toward us on
two aluminum forearm crutches from the nearby table where
he'd been eating. There was generally a contingent of the elderly eating their lunch in the clean, quiet café of the Ticho
House, which was tucked away from the heavy Jaffa Street
traffic behind a labyrinth of pinkish stone walls. The fare was
simple and inexpensive and, afterward, you could take your
coffee or tea on the terrace outside or on a bench beneath the
tall trees in the garden. Aharon had thought it would be a
tranquil place to hold our conversations undisturbed, without
the distractions of the city intruding.

When the old man had made it to our table, he did not
speak until he had cumbersomely uncrated his hundred meager pounds of limbs and torso onto the chair to the side of me
and sat there waiting, it would seem, for a wildly fluttering
heartbeat to decelerate, all the while, through the heavy lenses
of his horn-rimmed glasses, determining the meaning of my
face. He had that alarming boiled look of someone suffering
from a skin disease, and the word to express the meaning of
his face seemed to me to be "ordeal." He wore a heavy cardigan sweater buttoned up beneath his plain blue suit and, under
the sweater, a starched white shirt and bow tie, very neat and
businesslike—how a decorous neighborhood tradesman might
attire himself in an underheated appliance shop.

"Roth," he said. "The author."

"Yes."

Here he removed his hat to reveal a microscopically honey-
combed skull, a perfectly bald surface minutely furrowed and
grooved like the shell of a hard-boiled egg whose dome has
been fractured lightly by the back of a spoon. The man's been
dropped, I thought, and reassembled, a mosaic of smithereens,
cemented, sutured, wired, bolted. . . .

"May I ask your name, sir?" I said. "This is Aharon Appelfeld, the Israeli author. You are?"

"Get out," he said to Aharon. "Get out before it happens. Philip Roth is right. He is not afraid of the crazy Zionists. Listen to him. You have family? Children?"

"Three children," Aharon replied.

"This is no place for Jewish children. Enough dead Jewish children. Take them while they're alive and go."

"Have you children?" Aharon asked him.

"I have no one. I came to New York after the camps. I gave to Israel. That was my child. I lived in Brooklyn on nothing. Work only, and ninety cents on the dollar to Israel. Then I retired. Sold my jewelry business. Came here. And every day I am living here I want to run away. I think of my Jews in Poland. The Jew in Poland had terrible enemies too. But because he had terrible enemies did not mean he could not keep his Jewish soul. But these are Jews in a Jewish country without a Jewish soul. This is the Bible all over again. God prepares a catastrophe for these Jews without souls. If ever there will be a new chapter in the Bible you will read how God sent a hundred million Arabs to destroy the people of Israel for their sins."

"Yes? And was it for their sins," Aharon asked, "that God sent Hitler?"

"God sent Hitler because God is crazy. A Jew knows God and how He operates. A Jew knows God and how, from the very first day He created man, He has been irritated with him from morning till night. That is what it means that the Jews are chosen. The goyim smile: God is merciful, God is loving, God is good. Jews don't smile—they know God not from dreaming about Him in goyisch daydreams but from living all their lives with a God Who does not ever stop, *not once*, to think and reason and use His head with His loving children. To appeal to a crazy, irritated father, that is what it is to be a Jew. To appeal to a crazy, *violent* father, and for three thousand years, that is what it is to be a crazy Jew!" Having disposed of Aharon, he turned back to me, this crippled old wraith who should have been lying down somewhere, in the care of a doctor, surrounded by a family, his head at rest on a clean white pillow until he could peacefully die. "Before it's too late, Mr. Roth, before God sends to massacre the Jews without souls a hundred million Arabs screaming to Allah, I wish to make a contribution."

It was the moment for me to tell him that if that was his intention, he had the wrong Mr. Roth. "How did you find me?" I asked.

"You were not at the King David so I came for my lunch. I come every day here for my lunch—and here, today, is you." Speaking of himself, he added grimly, "Always lucky." He removed an envelope from his breast pocket, a process that, because of his bad tremor, one had to wait very patiently for him to complete, as though he were a struggling stammerer subduing the nemesis syllable. There was more than enough time to stop him and direct his contribution to the legitimate recipient, but instead I allowed him to hand it to me.

"And what is your name?" I asked again, and with Aharon looking on, I, without so much as the trace of a tremor, slipped the envelope into my own breast pocket.

"Smilesburger," he replied, and then began the pathetic drama of returning his hat to the top of his head, a drama with a beginning, a middle, and an end.

"Own a suitcase?" he asked Aharon.

"Threw it away," Aharon gently replied.

"Mistake." And with that Mr. Smilesburger hoisted himself painfully upward, uncoiling from the chair until at last he was wavering dangerously before us on his forearm crutches. "No more suitcases," he said, "no more Jews."

His sallying forth from the café, on no legs and no strength and those crutches, was another pathetic drama, this one reminiscent of a lone peasant working a muddy field with a broken-down, primitive plow.

I withdrew from my jacket pocket the long white envelope containing Smilesburger's "contribution." Painstakingly printed across the face of the envelope, in those wavering over-sized letters children first use to scrawl *cat* and *dog*, was the name by which I had been known all my life and under which I had published the books to which Jinx's savior and my impostor now claimed authorship in cities as far apart as Jerusalem and Gdansk.

"So *this* is what it's about," I said. "Bilking the senile out of their dough—shaking down old Jews for money. What a charming scam." While slicing open the envelope with a table knife, I asked Aharon, "What's your guess?"

"A million dollars," he replied.

"I say fifty. Two twenties and a ten."

Well, I was wrong and Aharon was right. Hiding as a child from his murderers in the Ukrainian woods while I was still on a Newark playground playing fly-catcher's-up after school had clearly made him less of a stranger than I to life in its more immoderate manifestations. Aharon was right: a numbered cashier's check, drawn on the Bank of Israel in New York, for the sum of one million dollars, and payable to me. I looked to be sure that the transaction had not been postdated to the year 3000, but no, it bore the date of the previous Thursday—January 21, 1988.

"This makes me think," I said, handing it across the table to him, "of Dostoyevsky's very greatest line."

"Which line is that?" Aharon asked, examining the check carefully, back and front.

"Do you remember, in *Crime and Punishment*, when Raskolnikov's sister, Dunya, is lured to Svidrigailov's apartment? He locks her in with him, pockets the key, and then, like a serpent, sets out to seduce her, forcibly if necessary. But to his astonishment, just when he has her helplessly cornered, this beautiful, well-bred Dunya pulls a pistol out of her purse and points it at his heart. Dostoyevsky's greatest line comes when Svidrigailov sees the gun."

"Tell me," said Aharon.

" 'This,' said Svidrigailov, 'changes everything.' "

ROTH: *Badenheim 1939* has been called fablelike, dreamlike, nightmarish, and so on. None of these descriptions makes the book less vexing to me. The reader is asked, pointedly, to understand the transformation of a pleasant Austrian resort for Jews into a grim staging area for Jewish "relocation" to Poland as being somehow analogous to events preceding Hitler's Holocaust. At the same time, your vision of Badenheim and its Jewish inhabitants is almost impulsively antic and indifferent to matters of causality. It isn't that a menacing situation develops, as it frequently does in life, without warning or logic but that about these events you are laconic, I think, to a point of unrewarding inscrutability. Do you mind addressing my difficulties with this highly praised novel, which is perhaps your most famous book in America? What *is* the relation between the fictional world of *Badenheim* and historical reality?

APPELFELD: Rather clear childhood memories underlie *Badenheim 1939*. Every summer we, like all the other petit bourgeois families, would set out for a resort. Every summer we tried to find a restful place where people didn't gossip in the corridors, didn't confess to one another in corners, didn't interfere with you, and, of course, didn't speak Yiddish. But every summer, as though we were being spited, we were once again surrounded by Jews, and that left a bad taste in my parents' mouths, and no small amount of anger.

Many years after the Holocaust, when I came to retrace my childhood from before the Holocaust, I saw that these resorts occupied a particular place in my memories. Many faces and bodily twitches came back to life. It turned out that the grotesque was etched in no less than the tragic. Walks in the woods and the elaborate meals brought people together in Badenheim—to speak to one another and to confess to one another. People permitted themselves not only to dress extravagantly but also to speak freely, sometimes picturesquely. Husbands occasionally lost their lovely wives, and from time to time a shot would ring out in the evening, a sharp sign of disappointed love. Of course I could arrange these precious scraps of life to stand on their own artistically. But what was I to do? Every time I tried to reconstruct those forgotten resorts, I had visions of the trains and the camps, and my most hidden childhood memories were spotted with the soot from the trains.

Fate was already hidden within those people like a mortal illness. Assimilated Jews built a structure of humanistic values and looked out on the world from it. They were certain that they were no longer Jews and that what applied to "the Jews" did not apply to them. That strange assurance made them into blind or half-blind creatures. I have always loved assimilated Jews, because that was where the Jewish character, and also, perhaps, Jewish fate, was concentrated with greatest force.

Aharon took a bus back home around two, though only after we had gone ahead and, at my insistence, tried our best to ignore the Smilesburger check and to begin the conversation about *Badenheim 1939* that later evolved into the written exchange transcribed above. And I headed off on foot toward the central produce market and the dilapidated working-class neighborhood just behind it, to meet my cousin Apter at the room in his landlady's house in a little alley in Ohel-Moshe, thinking while I walked that Mr. Smilesburger's wasn't the first million donated to a Jewish cause by a well-fixed Jew, that a million was peanuts, really, when it came to Jewish philanthropy, that probably in this very city not a week went by when some American Jew who'd made a bundle in real estate or shopping malls didn't drop by to schmooze at the office of the mayor and, on the way out, happily hand over to him a check twice as big as mine. And not just fat cats gave and gave—even obscure old people like Smilesburger were leaving small fortunes to Israel all the time. It was part of a tradition of largesse that went back to the Rothschilds and beyond, staggering checks written out to Jews imperiled or needy in ways that their prosperous benefactors had either survived or, as they saw it, miraculously eluded against all the historical odds. Yes, there was a well-known, well-publicized context in which both this donor and his donation made perfectly ordinary sense, even if, in personal terms, I still didn't know what had hit me.

My thoughts were confused and contradictory. Surely it was time to turn to my lawyer, to get her to contact local counsel (or the local police) and begin to do what had to be done to disentangle the other one from me before some new development made into a mere trifle the million-dollar misunderstanding at the Ticho House. I told myself to get to a phone and call New York immediately, but instead I wandered circuitously toward the old market on Agrippas Street, under the auspices of a force stronger than prudence, more compelling even than anxiety or fear, something that preferred this narrative to unfold according to his, and not my, specifications—a story determined this time without any interference from me. Perhaps that was my reconstituted sanity back in power again, the calculated detachment, the engrossed neutrality of a working writer that, some half-year earlier, I was sure had been impaired forever. As I'd explained to Aharon the day before, there was nothing I coveted so much, after those months of spinning like a little stick in the subjectivist whirlpool of a breakdown, as to be *de*subjectified, the emphasis anywhere but on my own plight. Let his hisness drive *him* nuts—my myness was to be shipped off on a sabbatical, one long overdue and well earned. With Aharon, I thought, self-obliteration's a cinch, but to annihilate myself while this other one was running freely about . . . well, triumph at that and you will dwell in the house of the purely objective forever.

But then why, if "engrossed neutrality" is the goal, accept this check in the first place, a check that can only mean trouble?

The other one. The double. The impostor. It only now occurred to me how these designations unwittingly conferred a kind of legitimacy on this guy's usurping claims. There was no "other one." There was one and one alone on the one hand and a transparent fake on the other. This side of madness and the madhouse, doubles, I thought, figure mainly in books, as fully materialized duplicates incarnating the hidden depravity of the respectable original, as personalities or inclinations that refuse to be buried alive and that infiltrate civilized society to reveal a nineteenth-century gentleman's iniquitous secret. I knew all about these fictions about the fictions of the self-divided, having decoded them as cleverly as the next clever boy some four decades earlier in college. But this was no book I was studying or one I was writing, nor was this double a character in anything other than the vernacular sense of that word. Registered in suite 511 at the King David Hotel was not the other me, the second me, the irresponsible me, the deviant me, the opposing me, the delinquent, turpitudinous me embodying my evil fantasies of myself—I was being confounded by somebody who, very simply, was not me, who had nothing to do with me, who called himself by my name but had no relation to me. To think of him as a *double* was to bestow on him the destructive status of a famously real and prestigious archetype, and *impostor* was no improvement; it only intensified the menace I'd conceded with the Dostoyevskyan epithet by imputing professional credentials in duplicitous cunning to this . . . this *what*? Name him. Yes, name him now! Because aptly naming him is knowing him for what he is and isn't, exorcising and possessing him all at once. Name him! In his pseudonymity is his anonymity, and it's that anonymity that's killing me. Name him! Who is this preposterous proxy? Nothing like namelessness to make a mystery of nothing. *Name him!* If I alone am Philip Roth, he is who?

Moishe Pipik

But of course! The anguish I could have saved myself if only I'd known. Moishe Pipik—a name I had learned to enjoy long before I had ever read of Dr. Jekyll and Mr. Hyde or Golyadkin the First and Golyadkin the Second, a name that more

than likely had not been uttered in my presence since I was still
a child small enough to be engrossed by the household drama
of all our striving relatives, their tribulations, promotions, ill-
nesses, arguments, etc., back when one or another of us pint-
sized boys, having said or done something thought to be
definingly expressive of an impish inner self, would hear the
loving aunt or the mocking uncle announce, "Is this a Moishe
Pipik!" Always a light little moment, that—laughter, smiles,
commentary, clarification, and the spoiled spotlit one, in the
center suddenly of the family stage, atingle with prideful embarrassment, delighted by the superstar billing but abashed a
little by the role that did not seem quite to accord with a boy-
child's own self-imaginings. Moishe Pipik! The derogatory,
joking nonsense name that translates literally to Moses Bellybutton and that probably connoted something slightly different to every Jewish family on our block—the little guy who
wants to be a big shot, the kid who pisses in his pants, the
someone who is a bit ridiculous, a bit funny, a bit childish, the
comical shadow alongside whom we had all grown up, that
little folkloric fall guy whose surname designated the *thing*
that for most children was neither here nor there, neither a
part nor an orifice, somehow a concavity and a convexity both,
something neither upper nor lower, neither lewd nor entirely
respectable either, a short enough distance from the genitals to
make it suspiciously intriguing and yet, despite this teasing
proximity, this conspicuously puzzling centrality, as meaningless as it was without function—the sole archaeological evidence of the fairy tale of one's origins, the lasting imprint of
the fetus who was somehow oneself without actually being
anyone at all, just about the silliest, blankest, stupidest water-
mark that could have been devised for a species with a brain
like ours. It might as well have been the omphalos at Delphi
given the enigma the pipik presented. Exactly what was your
pipik trying to tell you? Nobody could ever really figure it out.
You were left with only the word, the delightful play-word itself, the sonic prankishness of the two syllabic pops and the
closing click encasing those peepingly meekish, unobtrusively
shlemielish twin vowels. And all the more rapturously ridiculous for being yoked to Moishe, to Moses, which signaled,
even to small and ignorant boys overshadowed by their big

wage-earning, wisecracking elders, that in the folk language of
our immigrant grandparents and their inconceivable forebears
there was a strong predisposition to think of even the super-
men of our tribe as all kind of imminently pathetic. The goyim
had Paul Bunyan and we had Moishe Pipik.

I was laughing my head off in the Jerusalem streets, laughing once again without restraint, hilariously laughing all by
myself at the simple obviousness of the discovery that had
turned a burden into a joke—"Is this a Moishe Pipik!" I
thought, and felt all at once the return of my force, of the
obstinacy and mastery whose strong resurgence I had been
waiting and waiting on for so many months now, of the
effectiveness that was mine back before I was ever on Halcion,
of the gusto that was mine before I'd ever been poleaxed by
any calamity at all, back before I had ever heard of contradiction or rejection or remorse. I felt what I'd felt way, way back,
when, because of the lucky accident of a happy childhood, I
didn't know I could be overcome by anything—all the endowment that was originally mine before I was ever impeded by
guilt, a full human being strong in the magic. Sustaining that
state of mind is another matter entirely, but it sure is wonderful while it lasts. Moishe Pipik! Perfect!

When I reached the central market it was still crowded with
shoppers and, for a few minutes, I stopped to stroll through
the produce-piled aisles, captivated by that stir of agitated,
workaday busyness that makes open-air markets, wherever
they are, so enjoyable to wander around in, particularly when
you're clearing your head of a fog. Neither the stallkeepers
shouting in Hebrew the price of their bargains while nimbly
bagging what had just been sold nor the shoppers, speeding
through the maze of stalls with the concentrated alacrity of
people intent on getting the most for the least in the shortest
possible amount of time, appeared to be in any way worried
about being blown sky-high, and yet every few months or so,
in this very market, an explosive device, hidden by the PLO in
a refuse pile or a produce crate, was found by the bomb squad
and defused or, if it wasn't, went off, maiming and killing
whoever was nearby. What with violence between armed
Israeli soldiers and angry Arab mobs flaring up all over the Occupied Territories and tear-gas canisters being lobbed back and

forth only a couple of miles away in the Old City, it would have seemed only human had shoppers begun to shy away from risking life and limb in a target known to be a terrorist favorite. Yet the animation looked to me as intense as ever, the same old commotion of buying and selling testifying to just how palpably bad life has to become for people to ignore something as fundamental as getting supper on the table. Nothing could appear to be *more* human than refusing to believe extinction possible so long as you were encircled by luscious eggplants and ripe tomatoes and meat so fresh and pink that it looked good enough to wolf down raw. Probably the first thing they teach at terrorist school is that human beings are never less heedful of their safety than when they are out gathering food. The next best place to plant a bomb is a brothel.

At the end of a row of butcher stalls I saw a woman on her knees beside one of the metal trash cans where the butchers threw their leavings, a large, round-faced woman, about forty or so, wearing glasses and dressed in clothes that hardly looked like a beggar's. The tidy ordinariness of her attire was what had drawn my attention to her, kneeling there on the sticky cobblestones—wet with smelly leakage from the stalls, runny by mid-afternoon with a thin mash of garbagey muck—and fishing through the slops with one hand while holding a perfectly respectable handbag in the other. When she realized that I was watching her, she looked up and, without a trace of embarrassment—and speaking not in Hebrew but in accented English—explained, "Not for me." She then resumed her search with a fervor so disturbing to me, with gestures so convulsive and a gaze so fixed, that I was unable to walk off.

"For whom then?" I asked.

"For my friend," she said, foraging deep down into the bucket as she spoke. "She has six children. She said to me, 'If you see anything . . .'"

"For soup?" I asked.

"Yes. She puts something in with it—makes soup."

Here, I thought to say to her, here is a check for a million dollars. Feed your friend and her children with this. Endorse it, I thought, and give it to her. Whether she's crazy or sane, whether there is or is not a friend, all of that is immaterial. She

is in need, here is a check—give it to her and go. I am not responsible for this check!

"Philip! Philip Roth!"

My first impulse was not to turn around and acknowledge
whoever thought he had recognized me but to rush away and
get lost in the crowd—not again, I thought, not *another* million. But before I could move, the stranger was already there
beside me, smiling broadly and reaching out for my hand, a
smallish, boxy, middle-aged man, dark-complexioned, with a
sizable dark mustache and a heavily creased face and an arresting shock of snowy white hair.

"Philip," he said warmly even though I withheld my hand
and cautiously backed off—"Philip!" He laughed. "You don't
even know me. I'm so fat and old and lined with my worries,
you don't even remember me! You've grown only a forehead
—I've grown this ridiculous hair! It's Zee, Philip. It's George."

"Zee!"

I threw my arms around him while the woman at the
garbage pail, transfixed all at once by the two of us embracing,
uttered something aloud, angrily said something in what was
no longer English, and abruptly darted away without having
scavenged anything for her friend—and without the million
dollars either. Then, from some fifty feet away, she turned back
and, pointing now from a safe distance, began to shout in a
voice so loud that everywhere people looked to see what the
problem was. Zee too looked—and listened. And laughed,
though without much amusement, when he found out that
the problem was him. "Another expert," he explained, "on the
mentality of the Arab. Their experts on our mentality are
everywhere, in the university, in the military, on the street corner, in the market—"

"Zee" was for Ziad, George Ziad,° whom I hadn't seen in
more than thirty years, since the mid-fifties, when we'd lived
for a year down the corridor from each other in a residence
hall for divinity students at the University of Chicago, where I
was getting my M.A. in English and George was a graduate
student in the program called Religion and Art. Most of the
twenty or so rooms in the Disciples Divinity House, a smallish
neo-Gothic building diagonally across from the main university campus, were rented by students affiliated with the Disci-

ples of Christ Church, but since there weren't always enough of them to fill the place, outsiders like the two of us were allowed to rent there as well. The rooms on our floor were bright with sunlight and inexpensive, and, despite the usual prohibitions that obtained everywhere in university living quarters back then, it wasn't impossible, if you had the courage for it, to slip a girl through your door late in the evening. Zee had had the courage and the strong need for it too. In his early twenties, he had been a very lithe, dapperly dressed young man, small but romantically handsome, and his credentials—a Harvard-educated Egyptian enrolled at Chicago to study Dostoyevsky and Kierkegaard—made him irresistible to all those Chicago coeds avid for cross-cultural adventure.

"I live here," George answered when I asked what he was doing in Israel. "In the Occupied Territories. I live in Ramallah."

"And not in Cairo."

"I don't come from Cairo."

"You don't? But didn't you?"

"We fled to Cairo. We came from here. I was born here. The house I grew up in is still exactly where it was. I was more stupid than usual today. I came to look at it. Then, still more stupidly, I came here—to observe the oppressor in his natural habitat."

"I didn't know any of this, did I? That you came from Jerusalem?"

"It was not something I talked about in 1955. I wanted to forget all that. My father couldn't forget, and so I would. Weeping and ranting all day long about everything he had lost to the Jews; his house, his practice, his patients, his books, his art, his garden, his almond trees—every day he screamed, he wept, he ranted, and I was a wonderful son, Philip. I couldn't forgive him his despair for the almond trees. The trees particularly enraged me. When he had the stroke and died, I was relieved. I was in Chicago and I thought, 'Now I won't have to hear about the almond trees for the rest of my life. Now I can be who I am.' And now the trees and the house and the garden are all I can think about. My father and his ranting are all I can think about. I think about his tears every day. And that, to my surprise, is who I am."

"What do you do here, Zee?"

Smiling at me benignly, he answered, "Hate."

I didn't know what to reply and so said nothing.

"She had it right, the expert on my mentality. What she said is true. I am a stone-throwing Arab consumed by hate."

Again I offered no reply.

His next words came slowly, tinged with a tone of sweet contempt. "What do you expect me to throw at the occupier? Roses?"

"No, no," he finally said when I continued to remain silent, "it's the children who do it, not the old men. Don't worry, Philip, I don't throw anything. The occupier has nothing to fear from a civilized fellow like me. Last month they took a hundred boys, the occupiers. Held them for eighteen days. Took them to a camp near Nablus. Boys eleven, twelve, thirteen. They came back brain-damaged. Can't hear. Lame. Very thin. No, not for me. I prefer to be fat. What do I do? I teach at a university when it is not shut down. I write for a newspaper when it is not shut down. They damage my brain in more subtle ways. I fight the occupier with words, as though words will ever stop them from stealing our land. I oppose our masters with ideas—that is my humiliation and shame. Clever thinking is the form my capitulation takes. Endless analyses of the situation—that is the grammar of my degradation. Alas, I am not a stone-throwing Arab—I am a word-throwing Arab, soft, sentimental, and ineffective, altogether like my father. I come to Jerusalem to stand and look at the house where I was a boy. I remember my father and how his life was destroyed. I look at the house and want to kill. Then I drive back to Ramallah to cry like him over all that is lost. And you—I know why you are here. I read it in the papers and I said to my wife, 'He hasn't changed.' I read aloud to my son just two nights ago your story 'The Conversion of the Jews.' I said, 'He wrote this when I knew him, he wrote this at the University of Chicago, he was twenty-one years old, and he hasn't changed at all.' I loved *Portnoy's Complaint*, Philip. It was great, great! I assign it to my students at the university. 'Here is a Jew,' I tell them, 'who has never been afraid to speak out about Jews. An independent Jew and he has suffered for it too.' I try to convince them that there are Jews in the world who are not in any way like these Jews we have here. But to them the Israeli Jew is so evil they find it hard to believe. They look around and they think, What have they done? Name one single thing that Israeli society has done! And, Philip, my students are right— who *are* they? what *have* they done? The people are coarse and noisy and push you in the street. I've lived in Chicago, in New York, in Boston, I've lived in Paris, in London, and nowhere have I seen such people in the street. The *arrogance*! What have they created like you Jews out in the world? Absolutely nothing. Nothing but a state founded on force and the will to dominate. If you want to talk about culture, there is absolutely no comparison. Dismal painting and sculpture, no musical composition, and a very minor literature—that is what all their arrogance has produced. Compare this to American Jewish culture and it is pitiable, it is laughable. And yet they are not only arrogant about the Arab and *his* mentality, they are not only arrogant about the goyim and *their* mentality, they are arrogant about you and *your* mentality. These provincial nobodies look down on *you*. Can you imagine it? There is more Jewish spirit and Jewish laughter and Jewish intelligence on the Upper West Side of Manhattan than in this entire country—and as for Jewish *conscience*, as for a Jewish sense of *justice*, as for Jewish *heart* . . . there's more Jewish heart at the knish counter at Zabar's than in the whole of the Knesset! But *look* at you! You look great. Still so thin! You look like a Jewish baron, like a Rothschild from Paris."

"Do I really? No, no, still an insurance man's son from New Jersey."

"How is your father? How is your mother? How is your brother?" he asked me, excitedly.

The metamorphosis that, physically, had all but effaced the boy I'd known at Chicago was nothing, I had come to realize, beside an alteration, or deformation, far more astonishing and grave. The gush, the agitation, the volubility, the frenzy barely beneath the surface of every word he babbled, the nerve-racking sense he communicated of someone aroused and decomposing all at the same time, of someone in a permanent state of imminent apoplexy . . . how could that be Zee, how could this overweight, overwrought cyclone of distress possibly have been the cultivated young gentleman we all so admired for his suavity and his slick composure? Back then I was still a crisscross of personalities, a grab bag of raw qualities, strands of street-corner boyishness still inextricably interwoven with the burgeoning high-mindedness, while George had seemed to me so successfully imperturbable, so knowing in the ways of life, so wholly and impressively *formed*. Well, to hear him tell it now, I'd had him wrong in every way: in reality he'd been living under an ice cap, a son trying in vain to stanch the bleeding of a wronged and ruined father, with his wonderful manners and his refined virility not only masking the pain of dispossession and exile but concealing even from himself how scorched he was by shame, perhaps even more so than the father.

Emotionally, his voice quaking, Zee said to me, "I dream of Chicago. I dream of those days when I was a student in Chicago."

"Yes, we were lively boys."

"I dream about Walter Schneeman's Red Door Book Shop. I dream about the University Tavern. I dream about the Tropical Hut. I dream about my carrel in the library. I dream about my courses with Preston Roberts. I dream about my Jewish friends, about you and Herb Haber and Barry Targan and Art Geffin—Jews who could not *conceive* of being Jews like this! There are weeks, Philip, when I dream of Chicago every single night!" Taking my hands tightly in his and shaking them as though they were a set of reins, he said suddenly, "What are you doing? What are you doing *right this minute*?"

I was, of course, on my way to visit Apter at his room, but I decided not to tell this to George Ziad in the state of agitation he was in. The previous evening I had spoken briefly on the phone with Apter, assuring him once again that the person identified as me at the Demjanjuk trial a week earlier had merely been someone who looked like me and that I had arrived in Jerusalem only the day before and would come to see him at his stall in the Old City the very next afternoon. And here, like virtually every other man I seemed to meet in Jerusalem, Apter had begun to cry. Because of the violence, he told me, because of the Arabs throwing stones, he was too frightened to leave his room and I must come to see him there.

I did not want to tell George that I had a cousin here who

was an emotionally impaired Holocaust survivor, because I did not want to hear him tell me how it was the Holocaust survivors, poisoned by their Holocaust pathology, against whose "will to dominate" the Palestinians had for over four decades now been struggling to survive.

"Zee, I have time for just a quick cup of coffee—then I've got to run."

"Coffee where? Here? In the city of my father? Here in the city of my father they'll sit down right next to us—they'll sit in my *lap*." He said this while pointing to two young men standing beside a fruit vendor's stall only some ten or fifteen feet away. They were wearing jeans and talking together, two short, strongly built fellows I would have assumed were market workers taking a few minutes off for a smoke had Zee not said, "Israeli security. Shin Bet. I can't even go into a public toilet in the city of my father that they don't come in next to me and start pissing on my shoes. They're everywhere. Interrogate me at the airport, search me at customs, intercept my mail, follow my car, tap my phone, bug my house—they even infiltrate my classroom." He began to laugh very loudly. "Last year, my best student, he wrote a wonderful Marxist analysis of *Moby Dick*—he was Shin Bet too. My only 'A.' Philip, I cannot sit and have coffee here. Triumphant Israel is a terrible, terrible place to have coffee. These victorious Jews are terrible people. I don't just mean the Kahanes and the Sharons. I mean them *all*, the Yehoshuas and the Ozes included. The good ones who are against the occupation of the West Bank but not against the occupation of my father's house, the 'beautiful Israelis' who want their Zionist thievery and their clean conscience too. They are no less superior than the rest of them—these beautiful Israelis are even *more* superior. What do they know about 'Jewish,' these 'healthy, confident' Jews who look down their noses at you Diaspora 'neurotics'? This is health? This is confidence? This is *arrogance*. Jews who make military brutes out of their sons—and how superior they feel to you Jews who know nothing of guns! Jews who use clubs to break the hands of Arab children—and how superior they feel to you Jews incapable of such violence! Jews without tolerance, Jews for whom it is always black and white, who have all these crazy splinter parties, who have a party of *one man*, they are so

intolerant one of the other—these are the Jews who are superior to the Jews in the Diaspora? Superior to people who know
in their bones the meaning of give-and-take? Who live with
success, like tolerant human beings, in the great world of
crosscurrents and human differences? Here they are *authentic*,
here, locked up in their Jewish ghetto and armed to the teeth?
And you there, *you* are 'unauthentic,' living freely in contact
with all of mankind? The *arrogance*, Philip, it is *insufferable*!
What they teach their children in the schools is to look with
disgust on the Diaspora Jew, to see the English-speaking Jew
and the Spanish-speaking Jew and the Russian-speaking Jew as
a freak, as a worm, as a terrified neurotic. As if this Jew who
now speaks Hebrew isn't just *another kind of Jew*—as if speaking Hebrew is the culmination of human achievement! I'm
here, they think, and I speak Hebrew, this is my language and
my home, and I don't have to go around thinking all the time,
'I'm a Jew but what is a Jew?' I don't have to be this kind of
self-questioning, self-hating, alienated, frightened neurotic.
And what those so-called neurotics have given to the world in
the way of brainpower and art and science and all the skills and
ideals of civilization, to this they are oblivious. But then to the
entire *world* they are oblivious. For the entire world they have
one word: goy! 'I live here and I speak Hebrew and all I know
and see are other Jews like me and isn't that wonderful!' Oh,
what an impoverished Jew this arrogant Israeli is! Yes, they are
the authentic ones, the Yehoshuas and the Ozes, and tell me, I
ask them, what are Saul Alinsky and David Riesman and Meyer
Schapiro and Leonard Bernstein and Bella Abzug and Paul
Goodman and Allen Ginsberg, and on and on and on and *on*?
Who do they think they *are*, these provincial nobodies! Jailers!
This is their great Jewish achievement—to make Jews into jailers and jet-bomber pilots! And just suppose they were to succeed, suppose they were to win and have their way and every
Arab in Nablus and every Arab in Hebron and every Arab in
the Galilee and in Gaza, suppose every Arab in the world, were
to disappear courtesy of the Jewish nuclear bomb, what would
they have here fifty years from now? A noisy little state of no
importance whatsoever. That's what the persecution and the
destruction of the Palestinians will have been for—the creation
of a Jewish Belgium, without even a Brussels to show for it.

That's what these 'authentic' Jews will have contributed to civilization—a country lacking every quality that gave the Jews their great distinction! They may be able to instill in other Arabs who live under their evil occupation fear and respect for their 'superiority,' but I grew up with *you* people, I was educated with *you* people, *by* you people, I lived with *real* Jews, at Harvard, at Chicago, with *truly* superior people, whom I admired, whom loved, to whom I did *indeed* feel inferior and *rightly* so—the vitality in them, the irony in them, the human sympathy, the human *tolerance*, the goodness of heart that was simply *instinctive* in them, people with the Jewish sense of survival that was all human, elastic, adaptable, humorous, creative, and all this they have replaced here with a stick! The Golden *Calf* was more Jewish than Ariel Sharon, God of Samaria and Judea and the Holy Gaza Strip! The worst of the ghetto Jew combined with the worst of the bellicose, belligerent goy, and that is what these people call 'authentic'! Jews have a reputation for being intelligent, and they *are* intelligent. The only place I have ever *been* where all the Jews are stupid is Israel. I spit on them! I *spit* on them!" And this my friend Zee proceeded to do, spat on the wet, gritty marketplace pavement while looking defiantly at the two toughs in jeans he'd identified as Israeli security, neither of whom happened to be looking our way or, seemingly, to be concerned with anything other than their own conversation.

Why did I drive with him to Ramallah that afternoon instead of keeping my date with Apter? Because he told me so many times that I had to? Had to see with my own eyes the occupier's mockery of justice; had to observe with my own eyes the legal system behind which the occupier attempted to conceal his oppressive colonizing; had to postpone whatever I was doing to visit with him the army courtroom where the youngest brother of one of his friends was being tried on trumped-up charges and where I would witness the cynical corruption of every Jewish value cherished by every decent Diaspora Jew.

The charge against his friend's brother was of throwing Molotov cocktails at Israeli soldiers, a charge "unsupported by a single shred of evidence, unsubstantiated, another filthy lie." The boy had been picked up at a demonstration and then "interrogated." Interrogation consisted of covering his head with a hood, soaking him alternately with hot and cold showers, then making him stand outside, whatever the weather, the hood still over his head, enshrouding his eyes, ears, nose, and mouth—hooded like that for forty-five days and forty-five nights until the boy "confessed." I had to see what this boy looked like after those forty-five days and forty-five nights. I had to meet George's friend, one of the most stalwart opponents of the occupation, a lawyer, a poet, a leader whom, of course, the occupier was trying to silence by arresting and torturing his beloved kid brother. *I had to*, George charged me, the veins strung out like cables in his neck and his fingers in motion all the while, rapidly flexing open and shut as though there were something in the palm of each hand out of which he was squeezing the last bit of life.

We were standing beside George's car, which he'd left parked on a tiny side street a few blocks up from the market. The car had been ticketed and two policemen were waiting not far away and asked to see George's identity card, the car's registration, and his driver's license as soon as he stepped up and, making rather a show of his indifference, acknowledged the West Bank plates as his. Using George's key, the police methodically searched the trunk and beneath the seats and opened the glove compartment to examine its contents, and meanwhile, pretending to be oblivious to them, to be completely unintimidated by them, unharassed, unafraid, unhumiliated, George, like a man on the brink of a seizure, continued to tell me what I *had* to do.

The corruption of every Jewish value cherished by every decent Diaspora Jew . . . It was this fulsome praise of Diaspora Jews, whose excessiveness simply would not stop, that had finally convinced me that our meeting in the marketplace had been something other than sheer coincidence. His adamant insistence that I accompany him now to the occupier's travesty of a courtroom made me rather more certain that George Ziad had been following me—the me, that is, who he thought I had become—than that those two who'd been smoking and gabbing together beside the fruit vendor's stall in the market were Shin Bet agents who'd been following him. And this, the very best reason for my *not* doing what he told me I had to do, was exactly why I knew I had to do it.

Adolescent audacity? Writerly curiosity? Callow perversity? Jewish mischief? Whatever the impulse that informed my bad judgment, being mistaken for Moishe Pipik for the second time in less than an hour made yielding to his importuning as natural to me, as irresistible for me, as accepting Smiles-burger's donation had been at lunch.

George never stopped talking; he couldn't stop. An unbri-dled talker. An inexhaustible talker. A frightening talker. All the way out to Ramallah, even at the roadblocks, where not only his identification papers but now mine as well were checked over by the soldiers and where, each and every time, the trunk of the car was once again examined and the seats re-moved and the contents of the glove compartment emptied onto the road, he lectured me on the evolution of that guilt-laden relationship of American Jews to Israel which the Zion-ists had sinisterly exploited to subsidize their thievery. He had figured it out, thought it all through, even published an influ-ential essay in a British Marxist journal on "The Zionist Black-mailing of American Jewry," and, from the sound of it, all that publishing the essay had achieved was to leave him more de-graded and enraged and ground down. We drove by the high-rise apartment buildings of Jerusalem's northern Jewish suburbs ("A concrete jungle—so *hideous* what they build here! These aren't houses, they are fortresses! The mentality is every-where! Machine-sawed stone facing—the *vulgarity* of it!"); out past the large nondescript modern stone houses built before the Israeli occupation by wealthy Jordanians, which struck me as more vulgar by far, crowned as each was with an elongated TV aerial kitschily replicating the Eiffel Tower; and finally into the dry, stone-strewn valley of the countryside. And as we drove, embittered analysis streamed forth unabated, of Jewish history, Jewish mythology, Jewish psychosis and soci-ology, each sentence delivered with an alarming air of intellec-tual wantonness, the whole a pungent ideological mulch of overstatement and lucidity, of insight and stupidity, of precise historical data and willful historical ignorance, a loose array of observations as disjointed as it was coherent and as shallow as it was deep—the shrewd and vacuous diatribe of a man whose brain, once as good as anyone's, was now as much a menace to him as the anger and the loathing that, by 1988, after twenty years of the occupation and forty years of the Jewish state, had corroded everything moderate in him, everything practical, realistic, and to the point. The stupendous quarrel, the perpetual emergency, the monumental unhappiness, the battered pride, the intoxication of resistance had rendered him incapable of even nibbling at the truth, however intelligent he still happened to be. By the time his ideas wormed their way through all that emotion, they had been so distorted and intensified as only barely to resemble human thought. Despite the unremitting determination to comprehend the enemy, as though in understanding them there was still, for him, some hope, despite the thin veneer of professorial brilliance, which gave even his most dubious and bungled ideas a certain intellectual gloss, now at the core of everything was hatred and the great disabling fantasy of revenge.

And I said nothing, did not so much as challenge one excessive claim or do anything to clarify his thinking or to take exception where I knew he didn't know what he was talking about. Instead, employing the disguise of my own face and name, I listened intently to all the suppositions spawned by his unbearable grievance, to the suffering spilling out of him in every word; I studied him with the coldhearted fascination and intense excitement of a well-placed spy.

Here is a condensation of his argument, a good deal more cogent for being summarized. I won't describe the collisions and the pileups that George only narrowly avoided while he held forth. Suffice it to say that, even without an uprising under way and violence breaking out everywhere, it is extremely hazardous to sit beside a man making a long speech at the wheel of a car. On the drive that afternoon between Jerusalem and Ramallah, there was not a half-mile without its excitements. George did not always fulminate looking straight ahead.

In summary, then, George's lecture on that topic I could not really remember having chosen to shadow me like this, from birth to death; the topic whose obsessive examination I had always thought I could someday leave behind; the topic whose persistent intrusion into matters high and low it was not always easy to know what to make of; the pervasive, engulfing, wearying topic that encapsulated the largest problem and most amazing experience of my life and that, despite every honorable attempt to resist its spell, appeared by now to be the irrational power that had run away with my life—and, from the sound of things, not mine alone . . . that topic called *the Jews.*

First—according to George's historical breakdown of the cycle of Jewish corruption—were the pre-Holocaust, postimmigration years of 1900 to 1939: a period of renouncing the Old Country for the New; of dealienization and naturalization, of extinguishing the memories of families and communities abandoned, of forgetting parents left to age and die without their most adventurous children to comfort and console them—the feverish period of toiling to construct in America, and in English, a new life and identity as Jews. After this, the period of calculated amnesia, 1939 to 1945, the years of the immeasurable catastrophe, when, with lightning speed, those families and communities from which the newly, incompletely Americanized Jews had voluntarily severed their strongest ties were quite literally obliterated by Hitler. The destruction of European Jewry registered as a cataclysmic shock on American Jews not only because of its sheer horror but also because this horror, viewed irrationally through the prism of their grief, seemed to them in some indefinable way *ignited* by them— yes, instigated by the wish to put an end to Jewish life in Europe that their massive emigration had embodied, as though between the bestial destructiveness of Hitlerian anti-Semitism and their own passionate desire to be delivered from the humiliations of their European imprisonment there had existed some horrible, unthinkable interrelationship, bordering on complicity. And a misgiving very similar, an undivulgeable self-denunciation perhaps even more ominous, could be imputed to the Zionists and their Zionism. For were the Zionists without contempt for Jewish life in Europe when they embarked for Palestine? Didn't the militants who pioneered the Jewish state feel an even more drastic revulsion for the Yiddish-speaking masses of the shtetl than did those practical-minded immigrants who'd managed their escape to America without the blight of an ideology like Ben-Gurion's? Admittedly, migration, and not mass murder, was the solution proposed by Zionism; nevertheless, disgust for their own origins these Zionists made manifest in a thousand ways, most tellingly in choosing as the official tongue of the Jewish state the language of the remote biblical past rather than the shaming European vulgate that issued from the mouths of their powerless forebears.

So: Hitler's slaughter of all those millions whom these Jews had unwittingly abandoned to their fate, the destruction of the humiliating culture whose future they had wanted no part of, the annihilation of the society that had compromised their virility and restricted their development—this left the unimperiled Jews of America as well as Israel's defiantly bold founding fathers with a legacy not only of grief but of inexpungible guilt so damning as to warp the Jewish soul for decades thereafter, if not for centuries to come.

Following the catastrophe came the great period of postwar normalization, when the emergence of Israel as a haven for the surviving remnant of European Jewry coincided precisely with the advance of assimilation in America; the period of renewed energy and inspiration, when the Holocaust was itself still only dimly perceived by the public at large and before it had infested all of Jewish rhetoric; the years before the Holocaust had been commercialized by that name, when the most popular symbol for what had been endured by European Jewry was a delightful adolescent up in the attic diligently doing her homework for her daddy and when the means for contemplating everything more horrible were still generally undiscovered or suppressed, when in Israel it would be years before a holiday was officially proclaimed to commemorate the six million dead; the period when Jews everywhere wished to be known even to themselves for something more vitalizing than their victimization. In America it was the age of the nose job, the name change, the ebbing of the quota system, and the exaltations of suburban life, the dawn of the era of big corporate promotions, whopping Ivy League admissions, hedonistic holidays, and all manner of dwindling prohibitions—and of the emergence of a corps of surprisingly goylike Jewish children, dopey and confident and happy in ways that previous generations of anxious Jewish parents had never dared to imagine possible for their own. The pastoralization of the ghetto,

George Ziad called it, the pasteurization of the faith. "Green lawns, white Jews—you wrote about it. You crystallized it in your first book. That's what the hoopla was all about. 1959. The Jewish success story in its heyday, all new and thrilling and funny and fun. Liberated new Jews, normalized Jews, ridiculous and wonderful. The triumph of the untragic. Brenda Patimkin dethrones Anne Frank. Hot sex, fresh fruit, and Big Ten basketball—who could imagine a happier ending for the Jewish people?"

Then 1967: the Israeli victory in the Six Day War. And with this, the confirmation not of Jewish dealienization or of Jewish assimilation or of Jewish normalization but of Jewish *might*, the cynical institutionalization of the Holocaust begins. It is precisely here, with a Jewish military state gloating and triumphant, that it becomes official Jewish policy to remind the world, minute by minute, hour by hour, day in and day out, that the Jews were victims before they were conquerors and that they are conquerors only because they are victims. This is the public-relations campaign cunningly devised by the terrorist Begin: to establish Israeli military expansionism as historically just by joining it to the memory of Jewish victimization; to rationalize—as historical justice, as just retribution, as nothing more than self-defense—the gobbling up of the Occupied Territories and the driving of the Palestinians off their land once again. What justifies seizing every opportunity to extend Israel's boundaries? Auschwitz. What justifies bombing Beirut civilians? Auschwitz. What justifies smashing the bones of Palestinian children and blowing off the limbs of Arab mayors? Auschwitz. Dachau. Buchenwald. Belsen. Treblinka. Sobibor. Belsec. "Such falseness, Philip, such brutal, cynical insincerity! To keep the territories has for them one meaning and *only* one meaning: it is to display the physical prowess that made the conquest possible! To rule the territories is to exercise a prerogative hitherto denied—the experience of oppressing and victimizing, the experience now of ruling *others*. Power-mad Jews is what they are, is *all* that they are, no different from the power-mad everywhere, except for the mythol-
ent from the power-mad everywhere, except for the mythol-
 ictimization that they use to justify their addiction to
 d their victimizing of *us*. The famous joke has it ex-
 e's no business like *Shoah* business.' During

the period of their normalization there was the innocent symbol of little Anne Frank, that was poignant enough. But now, in the era of their greatest armed might, now at the height of their insufferable arrogance, now there are sixteen hours of *Shoah* with which to pulverize audiences all over the world, now there is 'Holocaust' on NBC once a week, starring as a Jew Meryl Streep! And the American Jewish leaders who come here, they know this *Shoah* business very well—they arrive here from New York, Los Angeles, Chicago, these officials of the Jewish establishment, and to those few Israelis who still have some truthfulness in them and some self-respect, who still know how to utter something other than the propaganda and the lies, they say, 'Don't *tell* me how the Palestinians are becoming accommodating. Don't *tell* me how the Palestinians have legitimate claims. Don't *tell* me how the Palestinians are oppressed and that an injustice has been done. Stop that immediately! I cannot raise money in America with that. Tell me about how we are threatened, tell me about terrorism, tell me about anti-Semitism and the Holocaust!' And this explains why there is the show trial of this stupid Ukrainian—to reinforce the cornerstone of Israeli power politics by bolstering the ideology of the victim. No, they will not stop describing themselves as victims and identifying themselves with the past. But it is not exactly as though the past has been ignored—the very existence of this state is evidence of that. By now surely this obsessive narrative of theirs has come to violate their sense of reality—it certainly violates ours. Don't tell *us* about their victimization! We are the last people in the *world* to understand that! *Of course* Ukrainian anti-Semitism is real. There are many causes that we all know, having to do with the role the Jews played there in the economic structure, with the cynical role assigned to them by Stalin in the farm collectivization—all this is clear. But whether this stupid Ukrainian is Ivan the Terrible is not *at all* clear, it *can't* be clear after forty years, and so, if you have any honesty as a nation, any respect left at all for the law, you let him go. If you must have your vengeance, you send him back to the Ukraine and let the Russians deal with him—that should be satisfaction enough. But to try h~~im~~ in the courtroom and over the radio and on the tel~~ev~~ in the papers, this has only one purpose—~~a~~

stunt à la the Holocaust-monger Begin and the gangster Shamir; public relations to justify Jewish might, to justify Jewish rule by perpetuating into the next one hundred millennia the image of the Jewish victim. But is public relations the purpose of a system of criminal justice? The criminal-justice system has a *legal* purpose, not a public-relations purpose. To educate the public? No, that's the purpose of an *educational* system. I repeat: Demjanjuk is here to maintain the mythology that is this country's lifeblood. Because without the Holocaust, where are they? *Who* are they? It is through the Holocaust that they sustain their connection to world Jewry, especially to privileged, secure American Jewry, with its exploitable guilt over being unimperiled and successful. Without the connection to world Jewry, where is their historical claim to the land? Nowhere! If they were to lose their custodianship of the Holocaust, if the mythology of the dispersion were to be exposed as a sham—*what then?* What *happens* when American Jews shed their guilt and come to their senses? What *happens* when American Jews realize that these people, with their incredible arrogance, have taken on a mission and a meaning that is utterly preposterous, that is *pure mythology?* What *happens* when they come to realize that they have been sold a bill of goods and that, far from being superior to Diaspora Jewry, these Zionists are inferior *by every measure of civilization?* What *happens* when American Jews discover that they have been duped, that they have constructed an allegiance to Israel on the basis of irrational guilt, of vengeful fantasies, above all, *above all,* based on the most naive delusions about the moral identity of this state? *Because this state has no moral identity.* It has *forfeited* its moral identity, if it ever had any to begin with. By relentlessly institutionalizing the Holocaust it has even forfeited its claim to the Holocaust! The state of Israel has drawn the last of its moral credit out of the bank of the dead six million—this is what they have done by breaking the hands of Arab children on the orders of their illustrious minister of defense. Even to world Jewry it will be clear: this is a state founded on force and maintained by force, a Machiavellian state that deals violently with the uprising of an oppressed people in an occupied territory, a Machiavellian state in, admittedly, a Machiavellian world, but about as saintly as the

Chicago Police Department. They have advertised this state for forty years as essential to the existence of Jewish culture, people, heritage; they have tried with all their cunning to advertise Israel as a no-choice reality when, in fact, it is an *option*, to be examined in terms of *quality* and *value*. And when you dare to examine it like this, what do you actually find? Arrogance! Arrogance! Arrogance! And beyond the arrogance? Nothing! And beyond the nothing—*more arrogance!* And now it is there for the whole world to see every night on television—a primitive capacity for sadistic violence that has finally put the lie to *all* their mythology! 'The Law of the Return'? As if any self-respecting civilized Jew would *want* to 'return' to a place like this! 'The Ingathering of the Exiles'? As if 'exile' from Jewishness begins to describe the Jewish condition anywhere but *here*! 'The Holocaust'? The Holocaust is over. Unbeknownst to them, the Zionists themselves officially declared it over three days ago at Manara Square in Ramallah. I will take you there and show you the place where the decree was written. A wall where the soldiers took innocent Palestinian civilians and clubbed and beat them to a pulp. Forget the publicity stunt of that show trial. The end of the Holocaust is written on that wall in Palestinian blood. Philip! Old friend! All your life you have devoted to saving the Jews from themselves, exposing to them their self-delusions. All your life, as a writer, ever since you began writing those stories out at Chicago, you have been opposing their flattering self-stereotypes. You have been attacked for this, you have been reviled for this, the conspiracy against you in the Jewish press began at the beginning and has barely let up to this day, a smear campaign the likes of which has befallen no Jewish writer since Spinoza. Do I exaggerate? All I know is that if a goy publicly insulted a Jew the way they have publicly insulted you, the B'nai B'rith would be screaming from every pulpit and every talk show, 'Anti-Semitism!' They have called you the filthiest names, charged you with the most treacherous acts of betrayal, and yet you continue to feel responsible to them, to fear for them, you persist, in the face of their self-righteous stupidity, to be their loving, loyal son. You are a great patriot of your people, and because of this, much of what I have been saying has angered and offended you. I see it in the set of your face, I hear it in your silence. You think, He is crazy, hysterical, reckless, wild. And what if I am—*wouldn't you be?* Jews! Jews! Jews! How can I not think continually about Jews! Jews are my jailers, I am their prisoner. And, as my wife will tell you, there is nothing I have less talent for than being a prisoner. My talent was to be a professor, not a slave to a master. My talent was to teach Dostoyevsky, not to live drowning in spite and resentment like the underground man! My talent was to explicate the interminable monologues of his seething madmen, not to turn into a seething madman whose own interminable monologues he cannot stifle even in his sleep. Why don't I restrain myself if I know what I'm doing to myself? My poor wife asks this question every day. Why can't we move back to Boston before the stroke that killed the ranting father kills the ranting son? Why? Because I, who will not capitulate, am a patriot *too*, who loves and hates his defeated, cringing Palestinians probably in the same proportion that *you*, Philip, love and hate your smug, self-satisfied Jews. You say nothing. You are shocked to see debonair Zee in a state of blind, consuming rage, and you are too ironical, too worldly, too skeptical to accept with graciousness what I am about to tell you now, but, Philip, *you are a Jewish prophet and you always have been*. You are a Jewish *seer*, and with your trip to Poland you have taken a visionary, bold, historical step. And for it you will now be more than just reviled in the press—you will be threatened, you will be menaced, you may very well be physically attacked. I wouldn't doubt that they will even try to arrest you—to implicate you in some criminal act and put you in jail to shut you up. These are ruthless people here, and Philip Roth has dared to fly directly in the face of their national lie. For forty years they have been dragging Jews from all over the world, making payoffs, cutting deals, bribing officials in a dozen different countries so as to get their hands on more and more Jews and drag them here to perpetuate their myth of a Jewish homeland. And now comes Philip Roth to do everything he can to encourage these same Jews to stop squatting on somebody else's land and to leave this make-believe country of theirs before these unregenerate, power-mad, vengeful Zionists implicate the whole of world Jewry in their brutality and bring a catastrophe down upon the Jews from which they will never recover. Old friend, we need you, we all need you, the occupiers as much as the occupied need your Diaspora boldness and your Diaspora brains. You are not in bondage to this conflict, you are not helpless in the grip of this thing. You come with a vision, a fresh and brilliant vision to resolve it—not a lunatic utopian Palestinian dream or a terrible Zionist final solution but a profoundly conceived historical arrangement that is workable, that is *just*. Old friend, dear, dear old friend—how can I serve you? How can *we* serve you? We are not without our resources. Tell me what we must do and we will do it."

5

I Am Pipik

THE Ramallah military court lay within the walls of a jail built by the British during the Mandate, a low, concrete, bunkerlike complex whose purpose it would have been hard to misconstrue—it was a punishment just to look at it. The jail was perched atop a bald, sandy hill at the edge of the city, and we turned at the roundabout at the foot of the hill and drove up to the high chain fence, topped by a double roll of barbed wire, that enclosed the outermost perimeter of the four or five acres separating the jail from the road below. George and I got out of the car and approached the gate to present our papers to one of three armed guards. Without speaking, the guard examined them and handed them back, and we were permitted to advance another hundred feet to a second gatehouse, where a submachine gun jutting out the window was aimed at whatever ascended the drive. The gun was manned by a grim, unshaven young soldier, who eyed us soberly while we handed our papers over to another guard, who tossed them onto his desk and, with a truculent gesture, indicated that we could go on.

"Sephardic boys," George told me as we continued toward a side door of the jail. "Moroccans. The Ashkenazis prefer to keep their hands clean. They get their darker brethren to do their torturing for them. The ignorant Arab haters from the Orient furnish the refined Ashkenazis with a very useful, all-purpose proletarian mob. Of course when they lived in Morocco they didn't hate Arabs. They lived harmoniously with Arabs for a thousand years. But the white Israelis have taught them that, too—how to hate the Arabs and how to hate themselves. The white Israelis have turned them into their thugs."

The side door was guarded by a pair of soldiers who, like those we'd just encountered, looked to have been recruited from the meanest city streets. They let us through without a word, and we stepped into a shabby courtroom barely large enough for a couple of dozen spectators. Occupying half the seats were more Israeli soldiers, who weren't carrying weapons that I could see but who didn't appear as though they'd have much trouble putting down a disturbance with just their bare hands. In scruffy fatigues and combat boots, their shirt collars open and their heads bare, they sat lazily sprawled about but nonetheless looking very proprietary with their arms spread to either side along the back rail of the wooden benches. My first impression was of young toughs lolling in the outer lobby of an employment agency that specialized in placing bouncers.

On the raised dais at the front of the courtroom, between two large Israeli flags pinned to the wall behind him, sat the judge, a uniformed army officer in his thirties. Slender, slightly balding, clean-shaven, carefully turned out, he listened to the proceedings with the perspicacious air of a mild, judicious person—one of "us."

In the second row down from the dais, a seated spectator gestured toward George, and we two slipped quietly in beside him. No soldiers sat in this row. They had grouped themselves together further back, near a door at the rear of the room, which I saw opened onto the detention area for the defendants. Before the door was pulled shut, I glimpsed an Arab boy. You could read the terror on his face even from thirty feet away.

We had joined the poet-lawyer whose brother was accused of throwing Molotov cocktails and whom George had described as a formidable opponent of the Israeli occupation. When George introduced us he took my hand and pressed it warmly. Kamil° was his name, a tall, mustached man, skeletally thin, with the molten, black, meaningful eyes of what they used to call a ladies' man and a manner that reminded me of the persuasively debonair disguise that George had worn back when he was Zee in Chicago.

Kamil explained to George, in English, that his brother's case had still not been heard. George lifted a finger toward the dock to greet the brother, a boy of about sixteen or seventeen whose vacant expression suggested to me that he was, at least for the moment, paralyzed more by boredom than by fear. Altogether there were five Arab defendants in the dock, four teenagers and a man of about twenty-five whose case had been argued since morning. Kamil explained to me in a whisper that the prosecution was trying to renew the detention order of the older defendant, an alleged thief said to have stolen two hundred dinars, but that the Arab policeman testifying for the prosecution had only just arrived in the court. I looked to where the policeman was being cross-examined by the defense lawyer, who, to my surprise, wasn't an Arab but an Orthodox Jew, an imposingly bearded bear of a man, probably in his fifties, wearing a skullcap along with his black legal gown. The interpreter, seated at the center of the proceedings just down from the judge, was a Druze, Kamil told me, an Israeli soldier who spoke Arabic and Hebrew. The lawyer for the prosecution was, like the judge, an army officer in uniform, a delicate-looking young fellow who had the air of someone engaged in an exceedingly tiresome task, though momentarily he seemed amused, as did the judge, by a remark of the policeman's just translated by the interpreter.

My second Jewish courtroom in two days. Jewish judges. Jewish laws. Jewish flags. And non-Jewish defendants. Courtrooms such as Jews had envisioned in their fantasies for many hundreds of years, answering longings even more unimaginable than those for an army or a state. One day *we* will determine justice!

Well, the day had arrived, amazingly enough, and here we were, determining it. The unidealized realization of another hope-filled human dream.

My two companions focused only briefly on the cross-examination; soon George had a pad in his hand and was making notes to himself while Kamil was once again whispering directly into my face, "My brother has been given an injection."

I thought at first that he'd said "injunction."

"Meaning what?" I asked.

"An *injection*." He illustrated by pressing his thumb into my upper arm.

"For what?"

"For nothing. To weaken his constitution. Now he aches all over. Look at him. He can barely hold his head up. A sixteen-year-old," he said, plaintively unfurling his hands before him, "and they have made him sick with an injection." The hands indicated that this was what they did and there was no way to stop them. "They use medical personnel. Tomorrow I'll go complain to the Israeli medical society. And they will accuse me of libel."

"Maybe he got an injection from medical personnel," I whispered back, "because he was already ill."

Kamil smiled as you smile at a child who plays with its toys while, in the hospital, one of its parents is dying. Then he put his lips to my ear to hiss, "It is *they* who are ill. This is how they suppress the revolt of the nationalist core. Torturing in ways that don't leave marks." He motioned toward the policeman on the witness stand. "Another sham. The case goes on and on only to extend our agony. This is the fourth day this has happened. They think that if they frustrate us long enough we will run away to live on the moon."

The next time Kamil turned to whisper to me, he took my hand in his as he spoke. "Everywhere I meet people from South Africa," he whispered. "I talk to them. I ask them questions. Because this gets so much like that every day."

Kamil's whispering was beginning to get on my nerves, as was the role in which I'd cast myself for whatever perverse and unexplained reason. *How can we serve you?* Either Kamil was working to recruit me as an ally against the Jews or he was testing to see if my usefulness was anything like George had surmised it to be on the basis of my visit with Lech Walesa. I thought, I've been putting myself in difficulties like this all my life but, up till now, by and large in fiction. How exactly do I get out of this?

Again there was the pressure of Kamil's shoulder against my own and his warm breath on my skin. "Is this not correct? If it weren't that Israel was Jewish—"

There was the sharp smack of a gavel striking, the judge's way of suggesting to Kamil that perhaps it was time to shut up. Kamil, imperturbable, sighed and, crossing his hands in his lap, bore his reprimand in a state of ruminative meditation for about two minutes. Then he was at my ear again. "If it weren't that Israel was Jewish, would not the same American Jewish liberals who are so identified with its well-being, would they not condemn it as harshly as South Africa for how it treats its Arab population?"

I chose again not to reply, but this discouraged him no more than the gavel had. "Of course, South Africa is irrelevant now. Now that they are breaking hands and giving their prisoners medical injections, now one thinks not of South Africa but of Nazi Germany."

Here I turned my face to his as instinctively as I would hit the brake if something darted out in front of my car. And gazing altogether unaggressively at me were those liquid eyes with that bottomless eloquence which was all opacity to me. I had only to nod sympathetically, to nod and arrange my face in my gravest expression, in order to carry on the masquerade—but what was the *purpose* of this masquerade? If it had ever had a purpose, I was too provoked by my taunter's reckless rhetoric to remember what it was and get on with the act. I'd heard enough. "Look," I said, starting quiet and low but, surprisingly, as the words came, all at once flaring out of control, "Nazis didn't break hands. They engaged in industrial annihilation of human beings. They made a manufacturing process of death. Please, no metaphors where there is recorded history!"

With that I sprang to my feet, but as I pushed past George's legs the judge swung the gavel, twice this time, and in the row at the back four soldiers promptly stood and I saw the armed guard at the door toward which I was headed move to block my way. Then the perspicacious judge, speaking in English, ringingly announced to the courtroom, "Mr. Roth is morally appalled by our neocolonialism. Make way. The man needs air." He spoke next in Hebrew and the guard blocking the door moved aside and I pushed the door open and stepped into the yard. But I had barely a moment to begin to figure out how I was going to find my way back to Jerusalem on my own before everyone I had left behind came pouring through the door after me. Everyone but George and Kamil. Had they been arrested? When I peered back through the open door I saw that the prisoners had been removed from the dock and, except at the dais, the room was empty. And there beside the chair of the army judge, who'd apparently called a recess in order to address them privately, stood my two missing companions. The judge happened at the moment to be listening and not speaking. It was George who was speaking. *Foaming.*

Kamil stood quietly beside him, a very tall man with his hands in his pockets, an attacker whose onslaught was tamed by a cunning camouflaged to look just like forbearance.

The defense lawyer, the large bearded man in the skullcap, industriously smoked a cigarette only a few feet away from me. He smiled when I turned his way, a smile with a needle in it. "So," he said, as though before we had even exchanged a word we had already reached a stalemate. He lit a second cigarette with the butt of his first and, after a little frenzy of deep inhalations, spoke again. "So you're the one they're all talking about."

Inasmuch as he'd seen me tête-à-tête in the courtroom with the locally renowned brother of an Arab defendant and had to have assumed from that, however incorrectly, that my bias, if I had one, couldn't be entirely antithetical to his, I was unprepared for the flagrant disdain. *Another* antagonist. But mine or Pipik's? As it turned out, a little of each.

"Yes, you open your mouth," he said, "and whatever comes out, the whole world takes notice. The Jews begin to beat their breasts. 'Why is he against us? Why isn't he for us?' That must be a wonderful feeling, its mattering so much what you are for or against."

"A better feeling, I assure you, than being a lawyer pleading petty-theft cases out in the sticks."

"A two-hundred-and-fifty-pound Orthodox Jewish lawyer. Don't minimize my insignificance."

"Go away," I said.

"You know, when the schmucks here get on me for defending Arabs, I don't usually bother to listen. 'It's a living,' I tell them. 'What do you expect from a shyster like me?' I tell them that the Arab respects a fat man, a fat man can screw them really good. But when George Ziad brings to this courtroom his celebrity leftists, then I seem to myself nearly as despicable as they are. At least you have the excuse of self-advancement. How will you get to Stockholm without your Third World credentials?"

"Of course. All a part of the assault on the prize."

"The glamorous one, their courtroom bard, has he told you yet about the burning building? 'If you jump out of a burning building, you may land on the back of a man who happens to be walking along the street. That is a bad enough accident. You then don't have to start beating him over the head with a stick. But that is what is happening on the West Bank. First they landed on people's backs, in order to save themselves, and now they are beating them over the head.' So folkloric. So very authentic. Hasn't he taken you by the hand yet? He will, very stirringly, when you are ready to go. This is when Kamil gets the Academy Award. 'You will leave here and forget, and she will leave here and forget, and George will leave here, and for all I know perhaps even George will forget. But the one who receives the strokes, he has an experience different from that of the one who counts the strokes.' Yes, they have a great catch in you, Mr. Roth. A Jewish Jesse Jackson—worth a thousand Chomskys. And here they are," he said, looking to where George and Kamil had stepped through the courtroom door and into the yard, "the world's pet victims. What is their dream? Palestine or Palestine and Israel too? Ask them sometime to try and tell you the truth."

What George and Kamil did first when they joined us was to shake the large lawyer's hand; in turn he offered each a cigarette, and when I refused one, he lit himself another and began to laugh, a harsh, tearing noise with cavernous undertones that did not bring good tidings from the bronchial tubes; another thousand packs and he might never again have to endure the sickly naiveté of celebrity leftists like Jesse Jackson and me. "The eminent author," he explained to George and Kamil, "doesn't know what to make of our cordiality." To me he then confided, "This is the Middle East. We all know how to lie with a smile. Sincerity is not of this world, but these native boys make a specialty of underdoing it. That's something you find out about Arabs—perfectly natural in both roles at the same time. So convincing one way—just like you when you write—and then, the next moment, someone will walk out of the room, they'll turn around and be just the opposite."

"And how do you account for this?" I asked him.

"One's interest allows anything. Very, very basic. Comes from the desert. That blade of grass is mine and my animal is going to get it or die. It's my animal or your animal. That's where interest begins and it justifies all duplicity. There is in Islam this idea of *taqiya*. Generally called in English 'dissimulation.' It's especially strong in Shi'ite Islam but it's all over Islamic culture. Doctrinally speaking, dissimulation is *part* of Islamic culture, and the permission to dissimulate is widespread. The culture doesn't expect that you'll speak in a way that endangers you and certainly not that you'll be candid and sincere. You would be considered foolish to do that. People say one thing, adopt a public position, and are then quite different on the inside and privately act in a totally different way. They have an expression for this; 'the shifting sands' —*ramál mutaharrika.* An example. For all their bravado about opposing Zionism, throughout the Mandate they sold land to the Jews. Not just their run-of-the-mill opportunists but also their big leadership. But they have a wonderful proverb to justify this as well. *Ad-daroori lih achkaam.* 'Necessity has its own rules.' Dissimulation, two-facedness, secretiveness—all highly regarded values among your friends," he told me. "They don't think that other people have to know what is really on their minds. Very different from Jews, you see, telling everything that's on their minds to everyone nonstop. I used to think that God has given the Jew the Arab to bedevil his conscience and keep it Jewish. I know better since meeting George and the bard. God sent us the Arab so we could learn from him how to refine our own deviousness."

"And why," George asked him, "did God give the Arab the Jew?"

"To punish him," the lawyer answered. "You know that better than anyone. To punish him, of course, for falling away from Allah. George is a great sinner," he said to me. "He can tell you some entertaining stories about falling away."

"And Shmuel° is a greater actor even than I am a sinner," said George. "In our communities he plays the role of a saint—a Jew who defends the Arab's civil rights. To be represented by a Jewish lawyer—this way there is at least a chance in the courtroom. Even Demjanjuk thinks this way. Demjanjuk fired his Mr. O'Brien and hired Sheftel because he too is deluded enough to think it will help. I heard the other day that Demjanjuk told Sheftel, 'If I had a Jewish lawyer to begin with, I'd never be in this trouble now.' Shmuel, admittedly, is no Sheftel. Sheftel is the antiestablishment superstar—he'll squeeze those Ukrainians for all they're worth. He'll make half

a million on this Treblinka guard. That isn't the humble way
of Saint Shmuel. Saint Shmuel doesn't care how little he is
paid by his impoverished defendants. Why should he? He receives his paycheck elsewhere. It isn't enough that Shin Bet
corrodes our life here by buying an informer in every family. It
isn't enough to play the serpent like that with people already
oppressed and, you would think, humiliated quite enough
already. No, even the civil-rights lawyer must be a spy, even
that they must corrupt."

"George is not fair to his informers," the Jewish lawyer told
me. "Yes, there are a great many of them, but why not? It is a
traditional occupation in this region, one at which its practi-
tioners are marvelously adept. Informing has a long and noble
history here. Informing goes back not just to the British, not
just to the Turks, it goes all the way back to Judas. Be a good
cultural relativist, George—informing is a way of life here, no
less deserving of your respect than the way of life indigenous
to any society. You spent so many years abroad as an intellectual playboy, you were away so long from your own people,
that you judge them, if I may say so, almost with the eyes of a
condescending Israeli imperialist dog. You speak of informing,
but informing offers a little *relief* from all that humiliation. Informing lends status, informing offers privileges. You really
should not be so quick to slit the throats of your collaborators
when collaborating is one of you society's most estimable
achievements. It is actually on the order of an anthropological
crime to burn their hands and stone them to death—and for
someone in your shoes, it is stupid as well. Since everybody in
Ramallah already suspects everyone else of informing, some
foolish hothead might someday be so misguided as to take *you*
for a collaborator and slit your throat too. What if I were to
spread the rumor myself? I might not find doing that too
unpleasant."

"Shmuel," George replied, "do what you do, spread false
rumors if you like—"

While their bantering continued, Kamil stood apart smoking in silence. He did not seem even to be listening, nor was
there any reason why he should have been, since this bitter
little vaudeville turn was clearly for the sake of my, and not his,
education.

The soldier who'd been smoking together at the other end of the yard started back toward courtroom door and, after expectorating into the dust from behind one hand, the lawyer Shmuel, too, abruptly headed off without another insult for any of us.

Kamil said to me, now that Shmuel had gone, "I mistook you for somebody else."

Who this time? I wondered. I waited to hear more but for a while there was nothing more and his thoughts appeared to be elsewhere again. "There are too many things to do," he finally explained, "in not enough time. We are all overworked and overstrained. No sleep begins to make you stupid." A grave apology—and the gravity I found as unnerving as everything else about him. Because his rage wasn't flaring up in your face every two minutes, it struck me as more fearsome than George's to be near. It was like being in the vicinity of one of those bombs they unearth during urban excavations, the big ones that have lain unexploded since World War II. I imagined—as I didn't when thinking about George—that Kamil could do a lot of damage when and if he ever went off.

"Whom did you mistake me for?" I asked.

He surprised me by smiling. "Yourself."

I did not like this smile from a man who I surmised *never* horsed around. Did he know what he was saying or was he saying that he had nothing more to say? All this performing didn't mean that a play was in progress; it meant the opposite.

"Yes," I said, feigning friendliness, "I can see how you might be misled. But I assure you that I am no more myself than anyone else around here."

Something in that response made him promptly turn even more severe-looking than before the dubious gift of that smile. I really couldn't understand what he was up to. Kamil spoke as though in a code known only to himself; or perhaps he was just trying to frighten me.

"The judge," George said, "has agreed that his brother should go to the hospital. Kamil is staying to be sure it happens."

"I hope nothing's wrong with your brother," I said, but Kamil continued to look at me as though I were the one who had given the boy the injection. Now that he had apologized for having mistaken me for somebody else, he seemed to have concluded that I was even more contemptible than the other guy.

"Yes," Kamil replied. "You are sympathetic. Very sympathetic. It is difficult not to be sympathetic when you see with your own eyes what is being perpetrated here. But let me tell you what will happen to your sympathy. You will leave here, and in a week, two weeks, a month at the most, you will forget. And Mr. Shmuel the lawyer, he will go home tonight and, even before he is in the front door, before he has even eaten his dinner and played with his children, he will forget. And George will leave here and perhaps even George will forget. If not today, tomorrow. George forgot once before." Angrily he pointed back to the jail, but his voice was exceedingly gentle when he said, "The one who receives the strokes has an experience different from that of the one who counts the strokes." And with that went back to where his brother was a prisoner of the Jews.

George wanted to telephone his wife to tell her he would shortly be home with a guest, so we walked around to a door at the front of the complex, where there was no one standing guard, and George simply pushed it open and went in, with me following closely behind. I was astonished that a Palestinian like George and a perfect stranger like me could just start down the corridor without anyone's stopping us, especially when I remembered that no one had checked at any point to see if we were armed. In an office at the end of the corridor, three female soldiers, Israeli girls of about eighteen or nineteen, were typing away, their radio tuned to the standard rock stuff—we had only to roll a grenade through the open door to take our revenge for Kamil's brother. How come no one seemed alert to this possibility? One of the typists looked up when he asked in Hebrew if he could use the phone. She nodded perfunctorily, "Shalom, George," and that's when I thought, He *is* a collaborator.

George, speaking English, was telling his wife how he'd run into me in Jerusalem, the great friend he hadn't seen since 1955, and I looked at the posters on the walls of the dirty, drab little room, tacked up probably by the soldier-typists to help them forget where they worked—there was a travel poster from Colombia, a poster of little ducklings swimming cutely in

a lily pond, a poster of wildflowers growing abundantly in a
peaceful field—and all the while I pretended to be engaged by
them and nothing more, I was thinking, He's an Israeli spy—
and who he is spying on is me. Only what kind of spy can he
be if he doesn't know that I'm not the right me? And why
should Shmuel have exposed him if Shmuel works for Shin Bet
himself? No, he's a spy for the PLO. No, he's a spy for no one.
No one's a spy. *I'm* the spy!

Where everything is words, you'd think I'd have some
mastery and know my way around, but all this churning
hatred, each man a verbal firing squad, immeasurable suspicions, a flood of mocking, angry talk, all of life a vicious debate, conversations in which there is nothing that cannot be
said . . . no, I'd be better off in the jungle, I thought, where
a roar's a roar and one is hard put to miss its meaning. Here I
had only the weakest understanding of what might underlie
the fighting and the shadow fighting; nor was my own behavior much more plausible to me than anyone else's.

As we walked together down the hill and out past the
guarded gatehouses, George berated himself for having imposed the miseries of the occupation on his wife and his son,
neither of whom had the fortitude for a frontline existence,
even though for Anna° there was compensation of a sort in living virtually next door to the widowed father whose failing
health had been such a source of anxiety to her in America. He
was a wealthy Ramallah businessman, nearly eighty, who had
seen that Anna was sent to the best schools from the time she
was ten, first, in the mid-fifties, to a Christian girls' school in
Beirut, after that to the United States, where she'd met and
married George, who was also Christian. Anna had worked for
years as a layout artist with a Boston advertising agency; here
she ran a workshop for the production of propaganda posters,
leaflets, and handouts, an operation whose clandestine nature
took its toll in a daily dose of nagging medical problems and a
weekly bout of migraines. Her abiding fear was of the Israelis
coming at night and arresting not her but their fifteen-year-old
son, Michael.°

Yet for George himself had there been a choice? In Boston
he'd held the line against Israel's defenders at the Middle East
seminars in Coolidge Hall, he obstinately opposed his Jewish

friends even when it meant ruining his own dinner parties, he wrote op-ed pieces for the *Globe* and went on WGBH whenever Chris Lydon wanted someone to battle for three minutes with the local Netanyahu on his show; but idealistically resisting the occupier from the satisfying security of his tenured American professorship turned out to be even less tolerable to his conscience than the memory of going around all those years disavowing any connection to the struggle at all. Yet here in Ramallah, true to his duty, he worried continually about what returning with him was doing to Anna and, even more, to Michael, whose rebellion George hadn't foreseen, though when he described it I wondered how he could have failed to. However heroic the cause had seemed to Michael amid the patriotic graffiti decorating his bedroom walls in suburban Newton, he felt now as only an adolescent son can toward what he sees as an obstacle to his self-realization raised by an obtuse father mandating an outmoded way of life. Most reluctantly, George was on the brink of accepting his father-in-law's financial help and, at Anna's insistence, sending Michael back to a New England boarding school for his remaining high school years. To George—who believed the boy was big enough to stay and be educated here in the hard truth of their lives, old enough now to share in the tribulation that was inescapably theirs and to embrace the consequences of being George's son—the arguments with Michael were all the more punishing for being a reenactment of the bitter conflict that had alienated him from his own father and embittered them both.

My heart went out to Michael, however callow a youth he might be. The shaming nationalism that the fathers throw on the backs of their sons, each generation, I thought, imposing its struggle on the next. Yet that was their family's big drama and the one that weighed on George Ziad like a stone. Here is Michael, whose entitlement, his teenage American instinct tells him, is to be a new ungrateful generation, ahistorical and free, and here is another father in the heartbreaking history of fathers, who expects everything blindly selfish in a young son to capitulate before his own adult need to appease the ghost of the father whom he had affronted with his own selfishness. Yes, making amends to father had taken possession of George and, as anyone knows who's tried it, making amends to father is hard work—all that hacking through the undergrowth of stale pathology with the machete of one's guilt. But George was out to settle the issue of self-division once and for all, and that meant, as it usually does, immoderation with a vengeance. Half-measures are out for these people—but hadn't they always been for George? He wanted a life that merged with that of others, first, as Zee in Chicago, with ours and now all over again here with theirs—subdue the inner quarrel with an act of ruthless simplification—and it never worked. But sensibly occupying the middle ground in Boston hadn't worked either. His life couldn't seem to merge with anyone's anywhere no matter what drastic experiment in remodeling he tried. Amazing, that something as tiny, really, as a self should contain contending subselves—and that these subselves should themselves be constructed of subselves, and on and on and on. And yet, even *more* amazing, a grown man, an educated adult, a full professor, who seeks *self-integration*!

Multiple selves had been on my mind for months now, beginning with my Halcion breakdown and fomented anew by the appearance of Moishe Pipik, and so perhaps my thinking about George was overly subjective; but what I was determined to understand, however imperfectly, was why whatever George said, even when, like a guy in a bar, he despaired about people as close to him as his wife and his child, didn't seem to me quite to make sense. I kept hearing a man as out of his depth as he was out of control, convulsed by all his contradictions and destined never to arrive where he belonged, let alone at "being himself." Maybe what it all came down to was that an academic, scholarly disposition had been overtaken by the mad rage to make history and *that*, his temperamental unfitness, rather than the urgency of a bad conscience, accounted for all this disjointedness I saw, the overexcitability, the maniacal loquacity, the intellectual duplicity, the deficiencies of judgment, the agitprop rhetoric—for the fact that amiable, subtle, endearing George Ziad had been turned completely inside out. Or maybe it just came down to injustice: isn't a colossal, enduring injustice enough to drive a decent man mad?

Our pilgrimage to the bloodstained wall where Israeli soldiers had dragged the local inhabitants to break their bones and beat them into submission was thwarted by a ring of impassable roadblocks around the central square, and we had, in fact, to detour up through the outlying hills to reach George's house at the other side of Ramallah. "My father used to weep nostalgically about these hills, too. Even in spring, he'd say, he could smell the almond blossoms. You can't," George told me, "not in spring—they bloom in February. I was always kind enough to correct his hyperbole. Why couldn't he be a man about those trees and stop crying?"

In a tone of self-castigating resignation George wearily compiled an indictment of recollections like these all the way up, around, and down the back roads into the city—so perhaps I'd been right the first time, and it *was* remorse that, if not alone in determining the scale of this harsh transformation, intensified the wretched despair that polluted everything and had made hyperbole standard fare for George, too. For having sniped at a ruined father's sentimental maunderings with a faultfinding adolescent's spiteful tongue, Dr. Ziad's little boy looked now to be paying the full middle-aged price and then some.

Unless, of course, it was all an act.

George's was one of half a dozen stone houses separated by large patches of garden and clustered loosely around a picturesque old olive grove that stretched down to a small ravine—originally, during Anna's early childhood, this had been a family compound full of brothers and cousins but most of them had emigrated by now. There was a biting chill in the air as it was getting to be dusk, and inside the house, in a tiny fireplace at the end of the narrow living room, a few sticks of wood were burning, a pretty sight but without effect against the chill pervasive dankness that went right to one's bones. The place was cheerily fixed up, however, with bright textiles splashed about on the chairs and the sofa and several rugs with modernistic geometric designs scattered across the uneven stone floor. To my surprise I didn't see books anywhere—maybe George felt his books were more secure at his university office—though there were a lot of Arabic magazines and newspapers strewn atop a table beside the sofa. Anna and Michael wore heavy sweaters as we sat close to the fire drinking our hot tea, and I warmed my hands on the cup, thinking, This

above-ground cellar, after Boston. The cold smell of a dungeon on top of everything else. There was also the smell of a
kerosene heater burning—one that might not have been in the
best state of repair—but it seemed to be off in another room.
This room opened through multipaned French doors onto the
garden, and a four-bladed fan hung by a very long stem from
an arched ceiling that must have been fifteen feet high, and
though I could see how the place might have its charm once
the weather grew warm, right now this wasn't a home to inspire a mood of snug relaxation.

Anna was a tiny, almost weightless woman whose anatomy's
whole purpose seemed to be to furnish the housing for her astonishing eyes. There wasn't much else to her. There were the
eyes, intense and globular, eyes to see with in the dark, set like
a lemur's in a triangular face not very much larger than a man's
fist, and then there was the tent of the sweater enshrouding
the anorexic rest of her and, peeping out at the bottom, two
feet in baby's running shoes. I would have figured as a mate
for the George I'd known a nocturnal creature fuller and fur-
rier than Anna, but perhaps when they'd met and married in
Boston some two decades back there'd been more in her of
the sprightly gamine than of this preyed-upon animal who
lives by night—if you can call it living—and during the day is
gone.

Michael was already a head taller than his father, an excruciatingly skinny, delicate brunette with marbleized skin, a pretty-
ish boy whose shyness (or maybe just exasperation) rendered
him mute and immobile. His father was explaining that Diasporism was the first original idea that he had heard from a Jew
in forty years, the first that promised a solution based on honest historical and moral foundations, the first that acknowledged that the only just way to partition Palestine was by
transferring not the population that was indigenous to the
region but the population to whom this region had been,
from the start, foreign and inimical . . . and all the while
Michael's eyes remained rigidly fixed on some invisible dot
that compelled his entire attention and that was situated in the
air about a foot above my knee. Nor did Anna appear to take
much hope from the fact that Jewry's leading Diasporist was

visiting her home for tea. Only George, I thought, is so far gone, only he is so crazily desperate . . . unless it's all an act.

Of course George understood that such a proposal would be received with nothing but scorn by the Zionists, whose every sacrosanct precept Diasporism exposed as fraudulent; and he went on to explain that even among Palestinians, who should be my ardent advocates, there would be those, like Kamil, lacking the imagination to grasp its political potential, who would stupidly misconstrue Diasporism as an exercise in Jewish nostalgia—

"So that was his take," I said, daring to interrupt the unbridled talker who, it occurred to me, perhaps with his voice alone had reduced his wife to little more than those eyes and battered his son into silence. "A nostalgic Jew, dreaming Broadway dreams about a musical-comedy shtetl."

"Yes. Kamil said to me, 'One Woody Allen is enough.'"

"Did he? In the courtroom? Why Woody Allen?"

"Woody Allen wrote something in *The New York Times*," George said. "An op-ed article. Ask Anna. Ask Michael. They read it and couldn't believe their eyes. It was reprinted here. It ranks as Woody Allen's best joke yet. Philip, the guy isn't a shlimazl just in the movies. Woody Allen believes that Jews aren't capable of violence. Woody Allen doesn't believe that he is reading the papers correctly—he just can't believe that Jews break bones. Tell us another one, Woody. The first bone they break in defense—to put it charitably; the second in winning; the third gives them pleasure; and the fourth is already a reflex. Kamil hasn't patience for this idiot, and he figured you for another. But it doesn't matter in Tunis what Kamil thinks in Ramallah about Philip Roth. It hardly matters any longer in Ramallah what Kamil thinks about anything."

"Tunis?"

"I assure you that Arafat can differentiate between Woody Allen and Philip Roth."

This was surely the strangest sentence I had ever heard spoken in my life. I decided to top it. If this is the way George wants to play it, then this is the way we shall go. I am not writing this thing. They are. I don't even exist.

"Any meeting with Arafat," I heard myself telling him,

"must be completely secret. For obvious reasons. But I *will* meet with him, any place and any time, Tunis or anywhere, and tomorrow is none too soon. It might be communicated to Arafat that through the good offices of Lech Walesa it's likely that I'll be meeting secretly at the Vatican with the Pope, probably next month. Walesa is already committed to my cause, as you know. He maintains that the Pope will find in Diasporism not only a means of resolving the Arab-Israeli conflict but an instrument for the moral rehabilitation and spiritual reawakening of all of Europe. I am myself not as sanguine as he is about the boldness of this pope. It's all well and good for His Holiness to be pro-Palestinian and to berate the Jews for appropriating property to which they have no legal right. It's something else again to espouse the corollary of this position and to invite a million-plus Jews to consider themselves at home in the heart of Western Christendom. Yes, it would be something if the Pope were to call upon Europe publicly and openly to invite its Jews to return from their exile in Israel, and for him to mean it; if he were to call on Europe to confess to its complicity in their uprooting and destruction; if he were to call on Europe to purge itself of a thousand years of anti-Semitism and to make room in its midst for a vital Jewish presence to multiply and flourish there and, in anticipation of the third millennium of Christianity, to declare by proclamation in all its parliaments the right of the Jewish uprooted to resettle in their European homeland and to live as Jews there, free, secure, and welcome. That would be simply wonderful. But I have my doubts. Walesa's Polish pope may even prefer Europe as Hitler passed it on to his European heirs—His Holiness may not really care to undo Hitler's little miracle. But Arafat is another matter. Arafat—" On I went, usurping the identity of the usurper who had usurped mine, heedless of truth, liberated from all doubt, assured of the indisputable rightness of my cause—seer, savior, very likely the Jews' Messiah.

So this is how it's done, I thought. This is how they do it. You just say everything.

No, I didn't stop for a very long time. On and on and on, obeying an impulse I did nothing to quash, ostentatiously free of uncertainty and without a trace of conscience to rein in my raving. I was telling them about the meeting of the World Diasporist Congress to take place in December, fittingly enough in Basel, the site of the first World Zionist Congress just ninety years ago. At that first Zionist Congress there had been only a couple of hundred delegates—*my* goal was to have twice that many, Jewish delegations from every European country where the Israeli Ashkenazis would soon resume the European Jewish life that Hitler had all but extinguished. Walesa, I told them, had already agreed to appear as keynote speaker or to send his wife in his behalf if he concluded that he could not safely leave Poland. I was talking about the Armenians, suddenly, about whom I knew nothing. "Did the Armenians suffer because they were in a Diaspora? No, because they were *at home* and the Turks moved in and massacred them *there*." I heard myself next praising the greatest Diasporist of all, the father of the new Diasporist movement, Irving Berlin. "People ask where I got the idea. Well, I got it listening to the radio. The radio was playing 'Easter Parade' and I thought, But this is Jewish genius on a par with the Ten Commandments. God gave Moses the Ten Commandments and then He gave to Irving Berlin 'Easter Parade' and 'White Christmas.' The two holidays that celebrate the divinity of Christ—the divinity that's the very heart of the Jewish rejection of Christianity—and what does Irving Berlin brilliantly do? He de-Christs them both! Easter he turns into a fashion show and Christmas into a holiday about snow. Gone is the gore and the murder of Christ —down with the crucifix and up with the bonnet! *He turns their religion into schlock.* But nicely! Nicely! So nicely the goyim don't even know what hit 'em. They love it. *Everybody* loves it. The Jews especially. Jews loathe Jesus. People always tell me Jesus is Jewish. I never believe them. It's like when people used to tell me Cary Grant was Jewish. Bull*shit*. Jews don't want to *hear* about Jesus. And can you blame them? So—Bing Crosby replaces Jesus as the beloved Son of God, and the Jews, the *Jews*, go around whistling about Easter! And is that so disgraceful a means of defusing the enmity of centuries? Is anyone really dishonored by this? If schlockified Christianity is Christianity cleansed of Jew hatred, then three cheers for schlock. If supplanting Jesus Christ with snow can enable my people to cozy up to Christmas, then let it snow, let it snow, let it snow! Do you see my point?" I took more pride,

I told them, in "Easter Parade" than in the victory of the Six
Day War, found more security in "White Christmas" than in
the Israeli nuclear reactor. I told them that if the Israelis ever
reached a point where they believed their survival depended
not merely on breaking hands but on dropping a nuclear
bomb, that would be the end of Judaism, even if the state of
Israel should survive. "Jews as Jews will simply disappear. A
generation after Jews use nuclear weapons to save themselves
from their enemies, there will no longer be people identify
themselves as Jews. The Israelis will have saved their state by
destroying their people. They will never survive morally after
that; and if they don't, why survive as Jews at all? They barely
have the wherewithal to survive morally now. To put all these
Jews in this tiny place, surrounded on all sides by tremendous
hostility—how *can* you survive morally? Better to be marginal
neurotics, anxious assimilationists, and everything else that the
Zionists despise, better to *lose* the state than to lose your moral
being by unleashing a nuclear war. Better Irving Berlin than
Ariel Sharon. Better Irving Berlin than the Wailing Wall. Better Irving Berlin than Holy Jerusalem! What does owning
Jerusalem, of all places, have to do with being Jews in 1988?
Jerusalem is by now the *worst* thing that could possibly have
happened to us. *Last* year in Jerusalem! Next year in Warsaw!
Next year in Bucharest! Next year in Vilna and Cracow! Look,
I know people call Diasporism a revolutionary idea, but it's
not a revolution that I'm proposing, it's a *retroversion*, a turning back, the very thing Zionism itself once was. You go back
to the crossing point and cross back *the other way*. Zionism
went back too far, that's what went wrong with Zionism.
Zionism went back to the crossing point of the dispersion—
Diasporism goes back to the crossing point of *Zionism*."

My sympathies were entirely with George's wife. I didn't
know which was more insufferable to her, the fervor with
which I presented my Diasporist blah-blah or the thoughtful-
ness with which George sat there taking it in. Her husband
had finally stopped talking—only to listen to this! Either to
warm herself or to contain herself she'd enwrapped herself in
her own arms and, like a woman on the brink of keening, she
began almost imperceptibly rocking and swaying to and fro.
And the message in those eyes of hers couldn't have been

plainer: I was more than even she could bear, she who had by now borne everything. *He suffers enough without you. Shut up. Go away. Disappear.*

All right, I'll address this woman's fears directly. Wouldn't Moishe Pipik? "Anna, I'd be skeptical too if I were you. I'd be thinking, just as you are, This writer is one of those writers with no grasp on reality. This is all the nonsensical fantasy of a man who understands nothing. This is not even literature, let alone politics, this is a fable and a fairy tale. You are thinking of the thousand reasons why Diasporism can only fail, and I am telling you that I know the thousand reasons, I know the *million* reasons. But I am also here to tell you, to tell George, to tell Kamil, to tell whoever here will listen that it cannot fail *because it must not fail*, because the absurdity is not Diasporism but its alternative: Destruction. What people once thought about Zionism you are now thinking about Diasporism: an impossible pipe dream. You are thinking that I am just one more victim of the madness here that is on both sides —that this mad, crazy, tragic predicament has engulfed my sanity too. I see how miserable I am making you by exciting expectations in George that you know to be utopian and beyond implementation—that George, in *his* heart of hearts, knows to be utopian. But let me show you both something I received just a few hours ago that may cause you to think otherwise. It was given to me by an elderly survivor of Auschwitz."

I removed from my jacket the envelope containing Smiles-burger's check and handed it to Anna. "Given to me by some-one as desperate as you are to bring this maddening conflict to a just and honorable and workable conclusion. His contribution to the Diasporist movement."

When Anna saw the check, she began to laugh very softly, as though this were a private joke intended especially for her amusement.

"Let me see," said George, but for the moment she would not relinquish it. Wearily he asked her, "Why do you laugh? I prefer that, mind you, to the tears, but why do you laugh like this?"

"From happiness. From joy. I'm laughing because it's all over. Tomorrow the Jews are going to line up at the airline

office to get their one-way tickets for Berlin. Michael, look."
And she drew the boy close to her to show him the check.
"Now you will be able to live in wonderful Palestine for the
rest of your life. The Jews are leaving. Mr. Roth is the anti-
Moses leading them out of Israel. Here is the money for their
airfare." But the pale, elongated, beautiful boy, without so
much as glancing at the check in his mother's hand, clenched
his teeth and pulled away violently. This did not stop Anna,
however—the check was merely the pretext she needed to deliver *her* diatribe. "Now there can be a Palestinian flag flying
from every building and everybody can stand up and salute it
twenty times a day. Now we can have our own money, with
Father Arafat's portrait on our very own bills. In our pockets
we can jingle coins bearing the profile of Abu Nidal. I'm
laughing," she said, "because Palestinian Paradise is at hand."

"Please," George said, "this is the royal road to the migraine." He motioned impatiently for her to hand him my
check. Pipik's check.

"Another victim who can't forget," said Anna, meanwhile
studying the face of the check with those globular eyes as
though there at last she might find the clue to why fate had delivered her into this misery. "All these victims and their horrible scars. But, tell me," she asked, and as simply as a child asks
why the grass is green, "how many victims can possibly stand
on this tiny bit of soil?"

"But he *agrees* with you," her husband said. "That is why he
is *here*."

In America," she told me, "I thought I had married a man
who had left all this victimization behind, a man of cultivation
who knew what made life rich and full. I didn't think I had
married another Kamil, who can't start being a human being
until the occupation is over. These perpetual little brothers,
claiming they can't live, they can't breathe, because somebody
is casting a shadow over them! The moral childishness of these
people! A man with George's brain, strangling on spurious issues of *loyalty*! Why aren't you loyal," she cried, wildly turning
on George, "to your *intellect*? Why aren't you loyal to *literature*? People like you"—meaning me as well—"run for their
lives from backwater provinces like this one. You ran, you were

right to run, both of you, as far as you could from the provincialism and the egocentricity and the xenophobia and the lamentations, you were not poisoned by the sentimentality of these childish, stupid ethnic mythologies, you plunged into a big, new, free world with all your intellect and all your energy, truly free young men, devoted to art, books, reason, scholarship, to *seriousness*—"

"Yes, to everything noble and elevated. Look," said George, "you are merely describing two snobbish graduate students—and we were not so pure even then. You paint a ridiculously naive portrait that would have struck us as laughable even then."

"Well, all I mean," she answered contemptuously, "is that you couldn't possibly have been as idiotic as you are now."

"You just prefer the high-minded idiocy of universities to the lowminded idiocy of political struggle. No one says it isn't idiotic and stupid and perhaps even futile. But that is what it's like, you see, for a human being to live on this earth."

"No amount of money," she said, ignoring the condescension to address me again about my check, "will change a single thing. Stay here, *you'll* see. There is nothing in the future for these Jews and these Arabs but more tragedy, suffering, and blood. The hatred on both sides is too enormous, it envelops everything. There is no trust and there will not be for another thousand years. 'To live on this earth.' Living in Boston was living on this earth—" she angrily reminded George. "Or isn't it 'life' any longer when people have a big, bright apartment and quiet, intelligent neighbors and the simple civilized pleasure of a good job and raising children? Isn't it 'life' when you read books and listen to music and choose your friends because of their qualities and not because they share your roots? Roots! A concept for *cavemen* to live by! Is the survival of Palestinian culture, Palestinian people, Palestinian heritage, is that really a 'must' in the evolution of humanity? Is all that mythology a greater must than the survival of my son?"

"He's going back," George quietly replied.

"When? *When?*" She shook the check in George's face. "When Philip Roth collects a thousand more checks from crazy Jews and the airlift to Poland begins? When Philip Roth and the Pope sit down together in the Vatican and solve our problems for us? I will not sacrifice my son to any more fanatics and their megalomaniacal fantasies!"

"He will go back," George repeated sternly.

"Palestine is a lie! Zionism is a lie! Diasporism is a lie! The biggest lie yet! I will not sacrifice Michael to more lies!"

George phoned to downtown Ramallah for a taxi to come to his house to drive me to Jerusalem. The driver was a weathered-looking old man who seemed awfully sleepy given that it was only seven in the evening. I wondered aloud if this was the best George could do.

First George told him in Arabic where to take me, then, in English, he said, "He's used to the checkpoints, and the soldiers there are familiar with him. You'll get back all right."

"To me he looks a little the worse for wear."

"Don't worry," George said. He had wanted, in fact, to take me back himself, but in their bedroom, where Anna had gone to lie down in the dark, she had warned George that if he dared to go off in the evening to drive to Jerusalem and back, neither she nor Michael would be there when he returned, *if* he returned and didn't wind up beaten to death by the army or shot by vigilante Jews. "It's the migraine talking," George explained. "I don't want to make it worse."

"I'm afraid," I said, "I already have."

"Philip, we'll speak tomorrow. There are many things to discuss. I'll come in the morning. I want to take you somewhere. I want you to meet someone. You will be free in the morning?"

I had arranged a meeting with Aharon, I had somehow to get to see Apter, but I said, "For you, yes, of course. Say goodbye to Michael for me. And to Anna. . . ."

"He's in there holding her hand."

"Maybe this *is* all too much for him."

"It does begin to look that way." He closed his eyes and pressed his fingers to his forehead. "My *stupidity*," he moaned. "My fucking stupidity!"

At the door he embraced me. "Do you know what you're doing? Do you know what it's going to mean for you when the Mossad finds out you've met with Arafat?"

"Arrange the meeting, Zee."

"Oh, you're the best of them!" he said emotionally. "The very best!"

Bullshit artist, I thought, actor, liar, fake, but all I did was return the embrace with no less fervent duplicitousness than was being proffered.

To circumvent the Ramallah roadblocks, which still barred the entrance to the city center and access to the telltale blood-stained wall, the taxi driver took the circuitous route through the hills that George had used earlier to get home. There were no lights to be seen anywhere once we were headed away from the complex of stone houses at the edge of the ravine, no cars appeared on the hillside roads, and for a long time I kept my eyes fixed on the path cut by our headlamps and was too apprehensive to think of anything other than making it safely back to Jerusalem. Shouldn't he be driving with his brights on? Or were those feeble beams the brights? Going back with this old Arab, I thought, had to be a mistake but so was coming out with George, so, surely, was everything I had just said and done. This little leave I had taken not merely of my senses but of my life was inexplicable to me—it was as though reality had stopped and I had gotten off to do what I did and now I was being driven along these dark roads to where reality would be waiting for me to climb back on board and resume doing what I used to do. Had I even been present? Yes, yes, I most certainly had been, hidden no more than an inch or two behind that mild exercise in malicious cynicism. And yet I could swear that my carrying-on was completely innocent. The lengths I had gone to to mislead George hadn't seemed to me any more underhanded than if we'd been two children at play in a sandpile, no more insidious and about as mindless —for one of the few times in my life I couldn't really satirize myself for thinking too much. What had I yielded to? How did I get here? The rattling car, the sleepy driver, the sinister road . . . it was all the unforeseen outcome of the convergence of my falseness with his, dissimulation to match dissimulation . . . unless George hadn't been dissimulating, *unless the only act was mine!* But could he possibly have taken that blather seriously about Irving Berlin? No, no—*here's* what they're up to: They're thinking of the infantile idealism and immeasurable egoism of all those writers who step momentarily onto the vast stage of history by shaking the hand of the revolutionary leader in charge of the local egalitarian dictatorship; they're thinking of how, aside from flattering a writer's vanity, it lends his life a sense of significance that he just can't seem to get finding the mot juste (if he even comes anywhere close to finding it one out of five hundred times); they're thinking that nothing does that egoism quite so much good as the illusion of submerging it for three or four days in a great and selfless, highly visible cause; they're thinking along the lines that Shmuel the lawyer had been thinking when he observed that it might just be that I'd come round to the courtroom in the clutches of "the world's pet victims" to beef up my credentials for the big prize. They're thinking of Jesse Jackson, of Vanessa Redgrave, smiling in those news photographs arm in arm with their leader, and of how, in the public-relations battle with the Jews, which well might decide more in the end than all of the terrorism would, a photograph in *Time* with a celebrity Jew might just be worth ten seconds of the leader's precious time. Of course! They're setting me up for a photo opportunity, and the looniness of my Diasporism is inconsequential—Jesse Jackson isn't exactly Gramsci either. Mitterrand has Styron, Castro has Márquez, Ortega has Pinter, and Arafat is about to have me.

No, a man's character isn't his fate; a man's fate is the joke that his life plays on his character.

We hadn't yet reached the houses sporting their Eiffel Tower TV antennas but we were out of the hills and on the main road south to Jerusalem when the taxi driver spoke his first words to me. In English, which he did not pronounce with much assurance, he asked, "Are you a Zionist?"

"I'm an old friend of Mr. Ziad's," I replied. "We went to university together in America. He is an old friend."

"Are you a Zionist?"

And who is *this* guy? I thought. This time I ignored him and continued looking out the window for some unmistakable sign, like those TV aerials, that we were approaching the outskirts of Jerusalem. Only what if we weren't anywhere near the road to Jerusalem but on the road to somewhere else? Where were the Israeli checkpoints? So far we hadn't passed one.

"Are you a Zionist?"

"Tell me," I replied as agreeably as I could, "what you mean by a Zionist and I'll tell you if I'm a Zionist."

"Are you a Zionist?" he repeated flatly.

"Look," I snapped back, thinking, Why don't you just say no? "what business is that of yours? Drive, please. This is the road to Jerusalem, is it not?"

"Are you a Zionist?"

The car was now perceptibly losing speed, the road was pitch-black, and beyond it I could see nothing.

"Why are you slowing down?"

"Bad car. Not work."

"It was working a few minutes ago."

"Are you a Zionist?"

We were barely rolling along now.

"Shift," I said, "shift the car down and give it some gas."

But here the car stopped.

"What's going on!"

He did not answer but got out of the car with a flashlight, which he began clicking on and off.

"Answer me! Why are you stopping out here like this? Where are we? Why are you flashing that light?"

I didn't know whether to stay in the car or to jump out of the car or whether either was going to make any difference to whatever was about to befall me. "Look," I shouted, leaping after him onto the road, "did you understand me? I am George Ziad's *friend*!"

But I couldn't find him. He was gone.

And this is what you get for fucking around in the middle of a civil insurrection! This is what you get for not listening to Claire and not turning everything over to lawyers! This is what you get for failing to comply with a sense of reality like everyone else's! *Easter Parade!* This is what you get for your bad jokes!

"Hey!" I shouted. "Hey, you! Where are you?"

When there was no reply, I opened the driver's door and felt around for the ignition: *he'd left the keys.* I got in and shut the door and, without hesitating, started the car, accelerating hard in neutral to prevent it from stalling. Then I pulled onto the road and tried to build-up speed—there must be a checkpoint *somewhere*! But I hadn't driven fifty feet before the driver appeared in the dim beam of the headlights waving one hand for me to stop and clutching his trousers around his knees with the other. I had to swerve wildly to avoid hitting him, and then, instead of stopping to let him get back in and drive me the rest of the way, I gunned the motor and pumped the gas pedal but nothing was able to get the thing to pick up speed and, only seconds later, the motor conked out.

Back behind me in the road I saw the flashlight wavering in the air, and in a few minutes the old driver was standing, breathless, beside the car. I got out and handed him the keys and he got back in and, after two or three attempts, started the motor, and we began to move off, jerkily at first, but then everything seemed to be all right and we were driving along once again in what I decided to believe was the right direction.

"You should have said you had to shit. What was I supposed to think when you just stopped the car and disappeared?"

"Sick." he answered. "Stomach."

"You should have told me that. I misunderstood."

"Are you a Zionist?"

"Why do you keep *asking* that? If you mean Meir Kahane, then I am not a Zionist. If you mean Shimon Peres . . ." But why was I favoring with an answer this harmless old man with bowel problems, answering him seriously in a language he understood only barely . . . where the hell *was* my sense of reality? "Drive, please," I said. "Jerusalem. Just get me to Jerusalem. And without talking!"

But we hadn't got more than three or four miles closer to Jerusalem when he drove the car over the shoulder, shut off the engine, took up the flashlight, and got out. This time I sat calmly in the back seat while he found himself some spot off the road to take another crap. I even began to laugh about at how I had exaggerated the menacing side of all this, when suddenly I was blinded by headlights barreling straight toward the taxi. Just inches from the front bumper, the other vehicle stopped, although I had braced for the impact and may even have begun to scream. Then there was noise everywhere, people shouting, a second vehicle, a third, there was a burst of light whitening everything, a second burst and I was being dragged out of the car and onto the road. I didn't know which language I was hearing. I could discern virtually nothing in all that incandescence, and I didn't know what to fear more, to have fallen into the violent hands of marauding Arabs or a violent band of Israeli settlers. "English!" I shouted, even as I tumbled along the surface of the highway. "I speak English!"

I was up and doubled over the car fender and then I was yanked and spun around and something knocked glancingly against the back of my skull and then I saw, hovering enormously overhead, a helicopter. I heard myself shouting, "Don't hit me, God damn it, I'm a Jew!" I'd realized that these were just the people I'd been looking for to get me safely back to my hotel.

I couldn't have counted all the soldiers pointing rifles at me even if I could have managed successfully to count—more soldiers even than there'd been in the Ramallah courtroom, helmeted and armed now, shouting instructions that I couldn't have heard, even if their language was one I understood, because of the noise of the helicopter.

"I hired this taxi in Ramallah!" I shouted back to them. "The driver stopped to shit!"

"Speak English!" someone shouted to me.

"THIS IS ENGLISH! HE STOPPED TO MOVE HIS BOWELS!"

"Yes? Him?"

"The driver! The Arab driver!" But where was he? Was I the only one they'd caught? "*There was a driver!*"

"Too late at night!"

"Is it? I didn't know."

"Shit?" a voice asked.

"Yes—we stopped for the driver to shit, he was only flashing the flashlight—"

"*To shit!*"

"*Yes!*"

Whoever had been asking the questions began to laugh. "That's all?" he shouted.

"As far as I know, *yes*. I could be wrong."

"*You are!*"

Just then one of them approached, a young, heavyset soldier, and he had a hand extended toward mine. In his other hand was a pistol. "Here." He gave me my wallet. "You dropped this."

"Thank you."

"This is quite a coincidence," he said politely in perfect English, "I just today, this afternoon, finished one of your books."

Thirty minutes later, I was safely at the door of my hotel, chauffeured there in an army jeep by Gal Metzler,° the young lieutenant who that very afternoon had read the whole of *The Ghost Writer*. Gal was the twenty-two-year-old son of a successful Haifa manufacturer who'd been in Auschwitz as a boy and with whom Gal had a relationship, he told me, exactly like the one Nathan Zuckerman had with *his* father in my book. Side by side in the jeep's front seats, we sat in the parking area in front of the hotel while Gal talked to me about his father and himself, and while I was thinking that the only son I'd seen yet in Greater Israel who was *not* in conflict with his father was John Demjanjuk, Jr. There there was only harmony.

Gal told me that in six months he would be finishing four years as an army officer. Could he continue to maintain his sanity that long? He didn't know. That's why he was devouring two and three books a day—to remove himself every minute that he possibly could from the madness of this life. At night, he said, every night, he dreamed about leaving Israel after his time was up and going to NYU to study film. Did I know the film school at NYU? He mentioned the names of some teachers there. Did I know these people?

"How long," I asked him, "will you stay in America?"

"I don't know. If Sharon comes to power . . . I don't know. Now I go home on leave, and my mother tiptoes around me as though I'm somebody just released from the hospital, as though I'm crippled or an invalid. I can stand only so much of it. Then I start shouting at her. 'Look, you want to know if I personally beat anyone? I didn't. But I had to do an awful lot of maneuvering to avoid it!' She's glad and she cries and it makes her feel better. But then my father starts shouting at the two of us. 'Breaking hands? It happens in New York City every night. The victims are black. Will you go running from America because they break hands in America?' My father says, 'Take the British, put them here, face them with what we are facing—they would act out of morality? The Canadians would act out of morality? The French? A state does not act out of moral ideology, a state acts out of self-interest. A state acts to preserve its existence.' 'Then maybe I prefer to be stateless,' I tell him. He laughs at me. 'We tried it,' he tells me. 'It didn't work out.' As if I need his stupid sarcasm—as if half of me doesn't believe exactly what *he* believes! Still I have to deal with women and children who look me in the eyes and scream. They look at me ordering my troops to take away their brothers and their sons, and what they see is an Israeli monster in sunglasses and boots. My father is disgusted with me when I say such things. He throws his dishes on the floor in the middle of the meal. My mother starts crying. *I* start crying. I cry! And I never cry. But I love my father, Mr. Roth, so I cry! Everything I've done in my life, I've done to make my father proud of me. That was why I became an officer. My father survived Auschwitz when he was ten years younger than I am now. I am humiliated that I can't survive this. I know what reality is. I'm not a fool who believes that he is pure or that life is simple. It is Israel's fate to live in an Arab sea. Jews accepted this fate rather than have nothing and no fate. Jews accepted partition and the Arabs did not. If they'd said yes, my father reminds me, they would be celebrating forty years of statehood too. But every political decision with which they have been confronted, invariably they have made the wrong choice. *I know all this.* Nine tenths of their misery they owe to the idiocy of their own political leaders. *I know that.* But still I look at my own government and I want to vomit. Would you write a recommendation for me to NYU?"

A big soldier armed with a pistol, a two-hundred-pound leader of men whose face was darkly stubbled with several days' whiskers and whose combat uniform foully reeked of sweat, and yet, the more he recounted of his unhappiness with his father and his father's with him, the younger and more defenseless he had seemed to me. And now this request, uttered almost in the voice of a child. "So—" I laughed—"*that's* why you saved my life out there. That's why you didn't let them break my hands—so I could write your recommendation."

"No, no, *no*," he quickly replied, a humorless boy distressed by my laughter and even more grave now than he'd been before, "no—no one would have hurt you. Yes, it's there, of course it's there, I'm not saying it's not there—some of the boys *are* brutal. Most because they are frightened, some because they know the others are watching and they don't want to be cowards, and some because they think, 'Better them than us, better him than me.' But no, I assure you—you were never in real danger."

"It's you who's in real danger."

"Of falling apart? You can tell that? You can see that?"

"You know what I see?" I said. "I see that you are a Diasporist and you don't even know it. You don't even know what a Diasporist is. You don't know what your choices really are."

"A Diasporist? A Jew who lives in the Diaspora."

"No, no. More than that. Much more. It is a Jew for whom *authenticity* as a Jew means living in the Diaspora, for whom the Diaspora is the normal condition and Zionism is the abnormality—a Diasporist is a Jew who believes that the only Jews who matter are the Jews of the Diaspora, that the only Jews who will survive are the Jews of the Diaspora, that the only Jews who *are* Jews are the Jews of the Diaspora—"

It would have been hard to say where I found the energy after what I'd been through in just forty-eight hours, but suddenly here in Jerusalem something was running away with me again and there seemed to be nothing I had more strength for than this playing-at-Pipik. That lubricious sensation that is fluency took over, my eloquence grew, and on I went calling for the de-Israelization of the Jews, on and on once again, obeying an intoxicating urge that did not leave me feeling quite so sure of myself as I may have sounded to poor Gal, torn in two as he was by the rebellious and delinquent feelings of a loyal, loving son.

TWO

6

His Story

W HEN I went up to the desk for the key to my room, the young clerk smiled and said, "But you have it, sir."

"If I had it I wouldn't be asking for it."

"Earlier, when you came out of the bar, I gave it to you, sir."

"I haven't been in the bar. I've been everywhere in Israel but the bar. Look, I'm thirsty. I'm hungry. I'm dirty and I need a bath. I'm out on my feet. The key."

"Yes, a key!" he chirped, pretending to laugh at his own stupidity, and turned away to find one for me while slowly I caught up with the meaning of what I had just heard.

I sat with my key in one of the wicker chairs in the corner of the lobby. The desk clerk by whom I'd first been confused tiptoed up to me after about twenty minutes and asked in a quiet voice whether I needed assistance to my room; worried that I might be ill, he had brought, on a tray, a bottle of mineral water and a glass. I took the water and drank it all down, and then, when he remained at my side, looking concerned, I assured him that I was all right and could make my way to my room alone.

It was almost eleven. If I waited another hour, might he not leave on his own—or would he just get into my pajamas and go to bed? Perhaps the solution was to take a taxi over to the King David Hotel and ask for his key as casually as he, apparently, had walked off with mine. Yes, go there and sleep there. With her. And tomorrow he meets with Aharon to complete our conversation while she and I get on with the promotion of the cause. I just pick up where I left off in the jeep.

I remained half dozing in that corner chair, groggily thinking that this was still last summer and that everything I took to be actuality—the Jewish courtroom in Ramallah, George's desperate wife and child, my impersonating Moishe Pipik for them, the farcical taxi ride with the shitting driver, my alarming run-in with the Israeli army, my impersonating Moishe Pipik for Gal—was all a Halcion hallucination. Moishe Pipik was *himself* a Halcion hallucination; as was Jinx Possesski; as was this Arab hotel; as was the city of Jerusalem. If this were Jerusalem I'd be where I always stay, the municipal guest house, Mishkenot Sha'ananim. I would have seen Apter and all my friends here. . . .

With a start, I surfaced, and there to either side of me was a large potted fern; there too was the kind clerk, offering water again and asking if I was sure I didn't need help. I saw by my watch that it was half past eleven. "Tell me please, the day, the month, and the year."

"Tuesday, January 26, 1988. In thirty minutes, sir, it will be the twenty-seventh."

"And this is Jerusalem."

He smiled. "Yes, sir."

"Thank you. That's all."

I put my hand in my inside jacket pocket. Had that been a Halcion hallucination as well, the cashier's check for a million dollars? Must have been. The envelope was gone.

Instead of telling the clerk to get the manager or the security officer and advising them that an intruder posing as me and probably crazy and maybe even armed had gained access to my room, I got up and went across the lobby and into the restaurant to find out if it was possible at this late hour to get something to eat. I stopped first in the doorway to see if Pipik and Jinx might be dining there; she could very well have been with him when he'd come out of the bar earlier to get my key from the front desk—perhaps they were not yet up fucking together in my room but down here eating together at my expense. Why not that, too?

But except for a party of four men lingering over coffee at a round table in the furthest corner of the restaurant, the place was empty even of waiters. The four seemed to be having a good time, quietly laughing over something together, and only when one of them came to his feet did I recognize that he was Demjanjuk's son and that the late diners with him were his father's legal team, Chumak the Canadian, Gill the American, and Sheftel the Israeli. Probably they'd been working out the next day's strategy over dinner and now they were bidding

good night to John junior. He was no longer in the neat dark
suit he'd been wearing in the courtroom but dressed casually
in slacks and a sports shirt, and when I saw that he was carrying a plastic bottle of water in one hand, I remembered reading in my clipping file that except for Sheftel, whose home and
office were forty-five minutes away, in Tel Aviv, the lawyers
and the Demjanjuk family members were staying at the American Colony; he must be taking the water to his room.

Leaving the dining room, young Demjanjuk passed directly
beside me and, as though it were he for whom I'd been waiting there, I turned and followed after him, thinking exactly as
I had the day before when I'd seen him headed from the
courtroom for the street: Should this boy be unprotected?
Isn't there a single survivor of the camps whose children or
sister or brother or parents or husband or wife had been murdered there, someone who had been mutilated there or mad-
dened for life, ready to take vengeance on Demjanjuk senior
through Demjanjuk junior? Isn't there anyone prepared to
hold the son hostage until the father confesses? It was difficult
to account for what was keeping him alive and safe in this
country, populated as it was by the last of the generation to
whose decimation his namesake stood accused of having made
such a wholehearted contribution. Isn't there one Jack Ruby
in all of Israel?

And then it occurred to me: How about you?

Lagging only some four or five feet behind him, I followed
young Demjanjuk through the lobby and up the stairs, suppressing the impulse to stop him and say, "Look, I for one
don't hold it against you that you believe your father is being
framed. How could you believe otherwise and be the good
American son that you are? Your belief in your father does not
make you my enemy. But some people here may see it differently. You're taking an awfully big chance walking around like
this. You, your sisters, and your mother have suffered enough
already. But so too, remember, have a lot of Jews. You'll never
recover from this no matter how you may delude yourself, but
then neither have a lot of Jews quite recuperated yet from
what they and their families have been through. You might
really be asking a little too much of them to go walking around
here in a nice sports shirt and a clean pair of slacks, with a full

bottle of mineral water in your hand. . . . Innocuous enough from your point of view, I'm sure: what's the water have to do with anything? But don't provoke memories unnecessarily, don't tempt some enraged and broken soul to lose control and do something regrettable. . . ."

When my quarry turned into the corridor off the landing I proceeded on up the stairs to the hotel's top floor, where my room was situated midway down the hall. I moved as quietly as I could to the door of my room and listened there for sounds from within, while back by the staircase someone was standing and looking my way—someone who had been following only steps behind me while I had been following Demjanjuk's son. A plainclothesman, of course! Stationed here by the police and watching out for John junior's safety. Or is this the plainclothesman shadowing me, imagining that I'm Moishe Pipik? Or is he stalking Pipik, thinking that Pipik is me? Or is he here to investigate why we are two and what we two are conspiring to do?

Though nothing could be heard from within the room and though he had perhaps come and gone, having already stolen or destroyed whatever he was after, I was convinced that even if there was only the remotest chance that he was inside, it would still be foolish to enter alone and so I turned and started back toward the staircase just as the door to my room opened a ways and there, peering out of it, was Moishe Pipik's head. I was actually hastening in double time along the corridor by then, but because I didn't want him to know how afraid of him I had become, I stopped and even took a few slow steps back toward where he was standing now, half in and half out of the room. And what I saw, as I stepped closer, so shocked me that I had all I could do not to turn and run full speed for help. His face was the face I remembered seeing in the mirror during the months when I was breaking down. His glasses were off, and I saw in his eyes my own dreadful panic of the summer before, my eyes at their most fearful, back when I could think of little other than how to kill myself. He wore on his face what had so terrified Claire: my look of perpetual grief.

"You," he said. That was all. But for him that was the accusation: I who was I.

"Come in," he said, weakly.

"No, you come out. Get your shoes"—he was in his stocking feet and his shirt was hanging out of his trousers—"get whatever is yours, hand over the key, and get out of here."

Without even bothering to answer he turned back into the room. I approached as far as the door and looked inside to see if Jinx was with him. But he was stretched diagonally across the bed, all alone and looking sorrowfully at the whitewashed, vaulted ceiling. The pillows were wadded up by the headboard, and the spread was turned back and dragged down onto the tile floor, and beside him on the bed was an opened book, my copy of Aharon Appelfeld's novel *Tzili*. In the small room nothing else appeared to have been disarranged; I am orderly with my things, even in a hotel room, and everything of mine looked to me as I'd left it. I hadn't had much with me to begin with: on the little desk by the large, arched window was the folder containing the notes of my conversations with Aharon, the three tapes Aharon and I had made so far, and Aharon's books in English translation. Because my tape recorder was in my one suitcase and the suitcase locked inside the closet, whose key was in my wallet, he couldn't have listened to the tapes; perhaps he'd rifled through the shirts and socks and underwear laid out in the middle bureau drawer, perhaps I'd find later that he'd even defiled them in some way, but so long as he hadn't sacrificed a goat in the bathtub, I knew enough to consider myself lucky.

"Look," I said to him from the doorway, "I'm going to get the house detective. He's going to call the police. You've broken into my room. You've trespassed on my property. I don't know what you may have taken—"

"What *I've* taken?" And saying this, he swung about and sat himself up on the edge of the bed, cradling his head in his hands so that for the moment I couldn't see the grief-stricken face and the resemblance to my own, by which I was still transfixed and horrified. Nor could he see me and the resemblance to which he had succumbed out of a motive that was still anything but clear in its personal particulars. I understood that people are trying to transform themselves all the time: the universal urge to be otherwise. So as not to look as they look, sound as they sound, be treated as they are treated, suffer in the ways they suffer, etc., etc., they change hairdos, tailors, spouses, accents, friends, they change their addresses, their noses, their wallpaper, even their forms of government, all to be more like themselves or less like themselves, or more like or less like that exemplary prototype whose image is theirs to emulate or to repudiate obsessively for life. It wasn't even that Pipik had gone further than most—he was, in the mirror, improbably evolved into somebody else already; there was very little more for him to imitate or fantasize. I could understand the temptation to quash oneself and become imperfect and a sham in entertainingly new ways—I had succumbed too, and not just a few hours earlier with the Ziads and then with Gal, but more sweepingly even than that in my books: looking like myself, sounding like myself, even laying claim to convenient scraps of my biography, and yet, beneath the disguise of me, someone entirely other.

But this was no book, and it wouldn't do. "Get off my bed," I told him, "get out!"

But he had picked up Aharon's *Tzili* and was showing me how far he'd got in reading it. "This stuff is real poison," he said. "Everything Diasporism fights against. Why do you think highly of this guy when he is the *last* thing we need? He will never relinquish anti-Semitism. It's the rock he builds his whole world on. Eternal and unshakable anti-Semitism. The man is irreparably damaged by the Holocaust—why do you want to encourage people to read this fear-ridden stuff?"

"You miss the point—I want only to encourage you to leave."

"It astonishes me that you, of all people, after all that you have written, should want to reinforce the stereotype of the Jewish victim. I read your dialogue with Primo Levi last year in the *Times*. I heard you had a breakdown after he killed himself."

"Who'd you hear it from? Walesa?"

"From your brother. From Sandy."

"You're in touch with my brother, too? He's never mentioned it."

"Come in. Close the door. We have a lot to talk about. We have been intertwined for decades in a thousand different ways. You don't want to know how uncanny this whole thing is, do you? All you want is to get rid of it. But it goes back, Philip, all the way back to Chancellor Avenue School."

"Yes, you went to Chancellor?"

He began quietly to sing, in a soft baritone voice—a singing voice chillingly familiar to me—a few bars of the Chancellor Avenue School song, words that had been set, early in the thirties, to the tune of "On Wisconsin." ". . . We will do our best . . . try to always be victorious . . . put us through the test, rah-rah-rah . . ." He smiled at me wanly with the grief-stricken face. "Remember the cop who crossed you at the corner of Chancellor and Summit? Nineteen thirty-eight—the year you started kindergarten. Remember his name?"

While he spoke I glanced back toward the staircase, and there, to my relief, I saw just the person I was looking for. He paused at the landing, a short, stocky man in shirtsleeves, with closely cropped black hair and a masklike, inexpressive face, or so the face appeared from that distance. He looked toward me now without any attempt to disguise the fact that he was there and that he too sensed that something suspicious was going on. It was the plainclothesman.

"Al," Pipik was saying once again, his head falling back on the pillows. "Al the Cop," he repeated wistfully.

While Pipik babbled on from the bed, the plainclothesman, without my even signaling him, started along the corridor toward where I was waiting in the open doorway.

"You used to jump up to touch his arms," Pipik was reminding me. "He'd hold his arms straight out to stop the traffic, and you little kids would jump up and touch his arms as you crossed the street. Every morning, 'Hi, Al!' and jump up and touch his arms. Nineteen thirty-eight. Remember?"

"Sure," I said, and as the plainclothesman approached, I smiled to let him know that, although he was needed, the situation was not yet out of control. He leaned close to my ear and mumbled something. He spoke in English but because of his accent the softly uttered words were unintelligible at first.

"What?" I whispered.

"Want me to blow you?" he whispered back.

"Oh, no—thanks, no. My mistake." And I stepped into the room and pulled the door firmly shut.

"Pardon the intrusion," I said.

"Remember Al?"

I sat down in the easy chair by the window, not quite knowing what else to do now that I was locked in with him. "You don't look so hot, Pipik."

"Pardon?"

"You look awful. You look physically ill. This business is not doing you a world of good—you look like somebody in very serious trouble."

"Pipik?" He was sitting up now on the bed. Contemptuously he asked, "You call me *Pipik*?"

"Don't take it so hard. What else should I call you?"

"Cut the shit—I came for the check."

"What check?"

"*My* check!"

"Yours? Please. Did anyone ever tell you about my great-aunt who lived in Danbury, Pipik? My grandfather's older sister on my father's side. Nobody tell you yet about our Meema Gitcha?"

"*I want that check.*"

"You found out about Al the Cop, somebody taught you all the words to the Chancellor song, so now perhaps it's time you learned about Meema Gitcha, the family ancient, and how we would visit her and the phone calls we made to her when we got home from her house, safe and sound. You're so interested in 1938—this is about 1940."

"You're not stealing from *me* stealing that check, you're not stealing from Smilesburger—*you're stealing from the Jewish people.*"

"Please. *Please.* Enough. Meema Gitcha was also a Jewish person, you know—*listen to me.*" I can't say that I had any idea of what I was doing but I told myself that if I just took charge and kept talking I could wear him down to nothing and then proceed from there . . . But to do what? "Meema Gitcha—a very foreign-looking Old Country woman, big and bossy and bustling, and she wore a wig and shawls and long dark dresses, and going to visit her in Danbury was a terrific outing, almost like leaving America."

"I want that check. Now."

"Pipik, pipe down."

"Cut the Pipik crap!"

"Then *listen*. This is *interesting*. Once every six months or
so we went out in two carloads to visit Meema Gitcha for the
weekend. Her husband had been a hatter in Danbury. He used
to work at Fishman's in Newark with my grandfather, who was
also a hatter for a while, but when the hat factories left for
Connecticut, Gitcha and her family moved up with them to
Danbury. About ten years later, Gitcha's husband, working in
off-hours, taking a stock of finished hats to the shipping room,
was trapped and died in an accident in the elevator. Gitcha was
on her own and so two, three times a year, we all went north
to see her. A five-hour car ride in those days. Aunts, uncles,
cousins, my grandmother, all packed in together, coming and
going. It was somehow the most Jewishy-Yiddishy event of my
childhood—we *could* have been driving all the way back to the
folkland of Galicia traveling up to Danbury on those trips.
Meema Gitcha's was a household with a lot of melancholy and
confusion—poor lighting, food always cooking, illness in the
wings, some new tragedy always imminent—relatives very different from the lively, healthy, Americanized contingent
stuffed into the new Studebakers. Meema Gitcha never got
over her husband's accident. She was always sure we were
going to be killed in a car crash on the way up, and when we
weren't, she was sure we would be killed in a crash on the way
down, and so the custom was that as soon as we got home on
Sunday night, the very moment we stepped through the door,
before anybody even went to the bathroom or got out of his
coat, Meema Gitcha had to be phoned and reassured that we
were still alive. But, of course, in those days, in our world, a
long-distance phone call was unheard of—other than in an
emergency, nobody would dream of making one. Nonetheless,
when we got home from Meema Gitcha's, no matter how late
it was, my mother got on the phone and, as though what she
was doing was entirely on the up and up, dialed the operator
and asked to place a long-distance call to Meema Gitcha's Connecticut number and to speak there person-to-person with
Moishe Pipik. Even while my mother was holding the phone,
my brother and I used to put our ears up next to hers on
the receiver because it was tremendously exciting to hear the
goyisch operator trying to get her tongue around 'Moishe

Pipik.' She always got it wrong, and my mother, who was wonderful at this and celebrated for it in the family, my mother very calmly, very precisely, would say, 'No, operator, no—person-to-person to Moí-she . . . Pí-pik. Mr. Moishe . . . *Pipik*.' And when finally the operator got it marginally right, we would hear the voice of Meema Gitcha jumping in at the other end—'Moishe Pipik? He's not here! He left half an hour ago!' and immediately, bang, she'd hang up before the phone company caught on to what we were doing and threw the whole bunch of us in jail."

Something about the story—could just have been its length—seemed to have sedated him a little, and he lay there on the bed as though for the moment he were no threat to anyone, including even himself. His eyes were closed when he said, very wearily, "What does this have to do with what you have done to me? Anything? Have you no imagination for what you did to me today?"

I thought then that he was like some errant son of mine, like the child I'd never had, some ne'er-do-well infantile grown-up who bears the family name and the facial features of a larger-than-life dad and doesn't much like feeling suffocated by him and has gone everywhere to learn to breathe and, after decades on his motorcycle, having succeeded at nothing but strumming on an electric guitar, appears at the doorstep of the old manse to vent the impotence of a lifetime and then, following twenty-four hours of frenzied indictment and frightening tears, ends up back in his boyhood bedroom, momentarily drained of recrimination, while the father sits kindly beside him, mentally ticking off all his offspring's deficiencies, thinking, "At your age I had already. . . ," and aloud, trying in vain, with funny stories, to amuse this beast of prey into a change of heart, at least until he'll accept the check he came for and go away to some place where he can repair automobiles.

The check. The check was no hallucination and the check was gone. It was all no hallucination. This is worse than Halcion—this is happening.

"You're thinking Pipik was our fall guy," I said, "the scapegoat's scapegoat—but, no, Pipik was protean, a hundred different things. Very human in that regard. Moishe Pipik was someone who didn't exist and couldn't possibly exist, and yet

we were claiming he was so real he could answer the telephone. To a seven-year-old child this was all hilarious. But
then Meema Gitcha would say, 'He left half an hour ago,' and
I was suddenly as stupid as the operator and I believed her. I
could *see* him leaving. He wanted to stay and talk more with
Meema Gitcha. Going to visit her reassured him of something.
That he wasn't entirely alone, I suppose. There weren't that
many Jews in Danbury. How had poor little Moishe Pipik got
there in the first place? Oddly, Gitcha could be a very reassuring bulk of a person for all that there was nothing that didn't
worry her. But the worries she attacked like a dragon slayer—
maybe that was it. I imagined them speaking in Yiddish,
Meema Gitcha and Moishe Pipik. He was a refugee boy who
wore an Old Country refugee cap, and she gave him food to
eat out of the cooking pots and her dead husband's old coat to
wear. Sometimes she slipped him a dollar. But whenever he
happened to come around to see her after the New Jersey relatives had been visiting for the weekend, and he sat at the table
telling her his problems, she would sit there eyeing the kitchen
clock, and then suddenly she would jump up and say, 'Go,
Moishe! Look at the time! God forbid you should be here
when they call!' And in the midst of everything, *in mitn dri-
nen*, you know, he grabbed his cap and he ran. Pipik ran and
he ran and he ran and he never stopped running until fifty
years later he finally reached Jerusalem and all that running
had made him *so* tired and *so* lonely that all he could do when
he got to Jerusalem was to find a bed, any bed, even somebody
else's bed. . . ."

I had put my sonny boy to sleep, with my story anesthetized
him. I remained in the chair by the window wishing that it had
killed him. When I was younger my Jewish betters used to accuse me of writing short stories that endangered Jewish lives—
would that I could! A narrative as deadly as a gun!

I took a look at him, a good long hungry look of the kind I
hadn't quite been able to take while he was looking back at
me. Poor bastard. The resemblance *was* striking. As his trousers
were gathered up on his legs because of the way he had fallen
to sleep, I could see that he even had my spindly ankles—or I
his. The minutes passed quietly. I'd done it. Worn him down.
Knocked him out. It was the first peaceful moment I'd known

all day. So this, I thought, is what I look like sleeping. I hadn't seen myself as quite so long in a bed though maybe it was just that this bed was short. Anyway, this is what the women see when they awaken to contemplate the wisdom of what they have done and with whom. This is what I would look like if I were to die tonight in that bed. This is my corpse. I am sitting here alive even though I am dead. I am sitting here after my death. Maybe it's before my birth. I am sitting here and, like Meema Gitcha's Moishe Pipik, I do not exist. I left half an hour ago. I am here sitting *shivah* for myself.

This is stranger even than I thought.

No, not that tack. No, just a different person similarly embodied, the physical analogue to what in poetry would be a near rhyme. Nothing more revelatory than that.

I lifted the phone on the table beside me and very, very quietly asked the switchboard operator to get me the King David Hotel.

"Philip Roth, please," I said, when the operator came on at the King David.

The phone in their room was answered by Jinx.

I whispered her name.

"Honey! Where are you? I'm going crazy!"

Weakly I replied, "Still here."

"*Where?*"

"His room."

"God! Didn't you find it?"

"Nowhere."

"Then that's it—leave!"

"I'm waiting for him."

"Don't! No!"

"My million, damn it!"

"But you sound awful—you sound *worse*. You took too much again. You can't take that much."

"I took what it takes."

"But it's *too much*. How bad is it? Is it very bad?"

"I'm resting."

"You sound ghastly! You're in pain! Come back! Philip, come back! He'll turn everything around! It'll be you who stole from *him*! He's a vicious, ruthless egomaniac who'll say *anything* to win!"

This deserved a laugh. "Him? Frighten me?"

"He frightens *me*! *Come back!*"

"Him? He's shitting his pants with fear of *me*. He thinks it's all a dream. I'll show him what a dream is. He won't know what hit him when I've finished scrambling his fucking brains."

"Hon, this is *suicide*."

"I love you, Jinx."

"Really? Am I anything at all to you anymore?"

"What are you wearing?" I whispered, keeping my eye on the bed.

"What?"

"What do you have on?"

"Just my jeans. My bra."

"The jeans."

"Not now."

"The jeans."

"This is crazy. If he comes back . . ."

"The jeans."

"They are. They are."

"Off?"

"I'm pulling them off."

"Around your ankles. Leave them around your ankles."

"They are."

"The panties."

"You too."

"Yes," I said, "oh, yes."

"Yes? Is it out?"

"I'm on his bed."

"You crazy man."

"On his bed. I've got it out. Oh, it's out, all right."

"Is it big?"

"It's big."

"Very big?"

"Very big."

"My nipples are hard as a fucking rock. My tits are spilling out. Oh, hon, they're spilling over—"

"All of it. Say all of it."

"I'm nobody's cunt but your cunt—"

"Ever?"

"Nobody's."

"All of it."

"I worship your stiff cock."

"All of it."

"My lips around your stiff stiff cock—"

On the bed Pipik had opened his eyes and I hung up the phone.

"Feel better?" I asked.

He looked at me as if a man deep in a coma and, seemingly seeing nothing, closed his eyes again.

"Too much medication," I said.

I decided not to call Jinx back and finish off the job. I'd got the idea.

When he came around next there was a mask of perspiration clinging to his forehead and his cheeks.

"Shall I get a doctor?" I asked. "Do you want me to call Miss Possesski?"

"I just want you, I just want you . . ." But tears appeared in his eyes and he couldn't go on.

"What *do* you want?"

"What you stole."

"Look, you're a sick man. You're in a lot of pain, aren't you? You're taking painkilling drugs that are bending your mind. You're taking tremendous doses of those drugs, that's the story, isn't it? I know from experience what that's like. I know how they can make you behave. Look, I don't particularly want to send a Demerol addict to jail. But if that's what it takes to get you to leave me alone, I don't care how sick you are or how much pain you're in or how loony the drugs are making you act, I will take it as my business to see that that happens. I'll be absolutely merciless with you if I find that I have to be. But *do* I have to be? How much do you need to get out of here and to go somewhere with Miss Possesski and try to get some peace and quiet? Because this other thing is a stupid farce, it means nothing, it can come to nothing, you're bound to fail. It's very likely to end for you two in a stupid catastrophe brought on by yourselves. I'm willing to pay your way to wherever you want to go. Two round-trip first-class airplane tickets to anyplace your two hearts desire. Something toward expenses too, to tide you over until you sort things out. Doesn't that seem reasonable? I press no charges. You go away. Please, let's negotiate a settlement and put an end to this."

"Easy as that." He didn't seem quite as bleary now as when he'd first come round, but there was still perspiration beading his upper lip and no color at all in his face. "'Moishe Pipik Gets Paid Off. NBA Winner Wins Again.'"

"Would the Jewish police be a more humane solution? A payoff isn't always without dignity in a mess like this. I'll give you ten thousand bucks. That's a lot of money. I have a publisher here"—and why hadn't I thought of calling *him*!—"and I'll arrange to have ten thousand dollars in cash in your hands by noon tomorrow—"

"'Providing you are out of Jerusalem by nightfall.'"

"By nightfall tomorrow, yes."

"I get ten and you get the balance."

"There is no balance. That's it."

"No balance?" He began to laugh. "No balance?" All at once he was sitting up straight and seemed entirely resuscitated. Either the drugs had suddenly worn off or they had suddenly kicked in, but Pipik was himself again (whoever that might be). "You who studied arithmetic with Miss Duchin at Chancellor Avenue School, you tell me there is *no balance* when"—and here he began gesturing as though he were a Jewish comic, his two hands to the left, his two hands to the right, distinguishing *this* from *that*, *that* from *this*—"when the subtrahend is ten thousand and the minuend is one million? You got B's in arithmetic all through Chancellor. Subtraction is one of the four fundamental operations of arithmetic. Let me refresh your recollection. It is the inverse of addition. The result of subtracting one number from another is called the difference. The symbol for this operation is our friend the minus sign. Any of this ring a bell? As in addition, only like qualities can be subtracted. Dollars from dollars, for instance, work very nicely. Dollars from dollars, Phil, is what subtraction was made for."

What *was* he? Was he fifty-one percent smart or was he fifty-one percent stupid? Was he fifty-one percent crazy or was he fifty-one percent sane? Was he fifty-one percent reckless or was he fifty-one percent cunning? In every case it was a very close call.

"Miss Duchin. I must confess," I said, "I'd forgotten Miss Duchin."

"You played Columbus for Hana Duchin in the Columbus Day play. Fourth grade. She adored you. Best Columbus she ever had. They all adored you. Your mother, your Aunt Mim, your Aunt Honey, your Grandma Finkel—when you were a tot they used to stand around the crib, and when your mother changed your diaper, they used to take turns kissing your *tuchas*. Women have been lining up to kiss your *tuchas* ever since."

Well, we were both laughing now. "What are you, Pipik? What's your game? You have this amusing side to you, don't you? You're obviously much more than just a fool, you have a stunning companion who is full of life, you don't lack for audacity or daring, you even have some brains. I hate to be the one to say it but the vehemence and intelligence of your criticism of Israel makes you into something more than just a crackpot. Is this just a malicious comedy about convictions? The argument for Diasporism isn't always as farcical as you make it sound. There's a mad plausibility about it. There's more than a grain of truth in recognizing and acknowledging the Eurocentrism of Judaism, of the Judaism that gave birth to Zionism, and so forth. Yet it also strikes me, I'm afraid, like the voice of puerile wishful thinking. Tell me, please, what *is* this really all about? Identity theft? It's the stupidest con going. You've *got* to get caught. Who are you? Tell me what you do for a living when you aren't doing this. As far as I know— though correct me if I'm wrong—you've never plugged into my American Express card. So on what do you survive? Your wits alone?"

"Guess." Oh, he was very bright and sparkly now, practically flirtatious. *Guess.* Don't tell me he's bisexual! Don't tell me this is more of the guy in the hallway! Don't tell me he wants us to have it off together, Philip Roth fucking Philip Roth! That, I'm afraid, is a form of masturbation too fancy even for me.

"I can't guess. You're a blank to me," I said. "I even get the feeling that without me around you're a blank to yourself. A little urbane, a little intelligent, a little self-confident, maybe even a little fascinating—Jinx-like creatures don't just drop from the sky—but mostly somebody who never arrived at a clear idea of what his life was for, mostly uncohesive, disappointed, a very shadowy, formless, fragmented thing. A kind of wildly delineated nothing. What enkindles you when I'm not here? Under 'me' isn't there at least a *little* you? What do you aim for in life other than getting people to think that you are somebody else?"

"What do *you* aim for other than that?"

"Yes, I take your point, but the question asked of you has a broader meaning, no? Pipik, what do you do for a real life?"

"I'm a licensed law-enforcement official," he said. "How's that grab you? I'm a private investigator. Here."

His ID. Could have been a bad picture of me. License No. 7794. Date of Expiration 06/01/90. ". . . A duly licensed private investigator . . . and is vested with all the authorities allowed him by law." And his signature. My signature.

"I run an agency in Chicago," he said. "Three guys and me. That's all. Small agency. We list what most everybody else lists —thefts, white- and blue-collar crime, missing persons, matrimonial surveillance. We do lie detection. Narcotics. We do murders. I do all the missing-persons cases. Missing persons is what Philip Roth is known for throughout the Midwest. I've been as far as Mexico and Alaska. Twenty-one years and I found everybody I was ever contracted to find. I also handle all the murders."

I gave back the ID card and watched him return it to his wallet. Were there a hundred more phony cards in there, all of them bearing that name? I didn't think it wise to ask just then—he'd caught me up short with "I handle all the murders."

"You like the dangerous assignments," I said.

"I have to be challenged twenty-four hours a day, seven days a week. I like to live on the edge, always up—it keeps my adrenaline going. Anything other than that I consider boring."

"Well, I'm stunned."

"I see that."

"I had you figured for an adrenaline freak but it wasn't exactly a law *enforcer* that I would have thought to call you."

"It's impossible for a Jew to be a private detective?"

"No."

"It's impossible for a detective to look like me? Or like you?"

"No, it's not even that."

"You just think I'm a liar. It's a cozy universe you've got going—you're the truth-telling Philip and I'm the lying Philip, you're the honest Philip and I'm the dishonest Philip, you're the reasonable Philip and I'm the manic psychopath."

"I like the missing-persons bit. I like that that's your specialty. Very witty in the circumstances. And what got you into detective work? Tell me that, while we're at it."

"I was always the type of person who wanted to help other people. Since I was a kid I couldn't stand injustice. It drove me crazy. It still does. It always will. Injustice is my obsession. I think it has to do with being a Jewish kid growing up in the war era. America wasn't always fair to Jews in those days. Beaten up in high school. Just like Jonathan Pollard. I could even have gone in the same direction as Pollard. Acting out of my love of Jews, I could have done it. I had the Pollard fantasies, volunteering for Israel, working for the Mossad. At home, FBI, CIA, they both turned me down. Never found out why. I sometimes wonder if it wasn't because of you, because they thought it was just too much bother, a guy who was a veritable duplicate of somebody in the public eye. But I'll never know. I used to draw a cartoon strip for myself when I was a kid. 'A Jew in the FBI.' Pollard is very important to me. What the Dreyfus case was to Herzl, the Pollard case is to me. Through my PI contacts I've heard that the FBI attached Pollard to a polygraph machine, gave him lists of prominent American Jews, and told him to identify the other spies. He wouldn't do it. Everything about the guy repels me except that. I live in dread of a second Pollard. I live in dread of what that will mean."

"So, is what I'm supposed to gather from all this that you became a detective to help Jews?"

"Look, you tell me you know nothing about me and you're at a disadvantage because I know so much about you. I'm explaining to you that it's my profession to know as much as I know, not just about you but about *everyone*. You ask me to level with you. That's what I'm trying to do. Except all I meet

with is a barrage of disbelief. You want *me* to take a polygraph?
I could pass it with flying colors. Okay, I haven't been calm
and collected with you. It surprises me, too. I wrote and apologized for that. Some people blitz you, no matter who you
are. I have to tell you that you are only the second person in
my life to blitz me like this. In my line of work I'm hardened
to everything and I see everything and I have to learn to handle everything. The only other time it happened before, that I
was blitzed anything like this, was in 1963, when I met the
president. He came to Chicago. I was doing some bodyguard
work then. Usually I was employed by a private contractor, but
at this time I was employed by the public sector, too. It was
the mayor's office. I couldn't speak when he shook my hand.
The words wouldn't come out. That doesn't usually happen.
Words are a large part of my business and account for ninety
percent of my success. Words and brains. It was probably
because I was having masturbatory fantasies in those days
about his wife on her water skis and I felt guilty. Do you know
what the president said to me? He said, 'I know your friend
Styron. You've got to come down to Washington and have
dinner with us and the Styrons some night.' Then he said, 'I'm
a great admirer of *Letting Go.*' That was in August 1963. Three
months later he was shot."

"Kennedy mixed you up with me. The president of the
United States thought a bodyguard in the mayor's office was a
novelist on the side."

"The guy shook a million hands a day. He took me for another dignitary. It wasn't hard—there was my name, my looks,
and besides, people are always taking a bodyguard for somebody else. That's part of the job. Somebody desires protection.
Somebody like you, say, who might be feeling threatened. You
ride around with them. You pretend you're a friend or something. Sure, some guys tell you they want to make it obvious
that you're a bodyguard, so you play that part. Nice dark
suit, the sunglasses, you carry a gun. The goon outfit. That's
what they want, you do it. They want it obvious—they like the
flash, the glitter of it. I had one client I worked with all the
time in Chicago, a big contractor and developer, lots of money,
and a lot of people who might be after him, and he loved the
show. I'd go to Vegas with him. Him and his limousine and his

friends—they wanted it always to be a big thing. I had to watch the women when they went to the bathroom. I had to go into the bathroom with them without their knowing it."

"Difficult?"

"I was twenty-seven, twenty-eight, I managed it. Things have changed now but at this time I was the only Jewish body-guard in the whole Midwest. I broke ground out there. The other Jewish boys were all in law school. That was what the families wanted. Didn't your old man want you to go to law school instead of to Chicago to become an English teacher?"

"Who told you that?"

"Clive Cummis, your brother's friend. Big New Jersey attorney now. Before you went out to graduate school to study literature, your father asked Clive to take you aside to plead with you to go to law school instead."

"I don't myself remember that happening."

"Sure. Clive took you into the bedroom on Leslie Street. He said you'd never make a living teaching English. But you told him you weren't having any of that stuff and to forget it."

"Well, that's an incident that slips my mind."

"Clive remembers it."

"You see Clive Cummis, too?"

"I get business from lawyers all over the country. I have a lot of law firms we work very closely with. We are exclusive agents for them. They'll turn over all the cases to us where they need an investigator in Chicago. We'll turn cases over to them, they'll turn cases over to us. I've got a great working relationship with about two hundred police departments, basically in Illinois, Wisconsin, and Indiana. We have a great relationship with the county police, tremendous arrest record with the counties. I brought in a lot of people for them."

I have to tell you that I was beginning to believe him.

"Look, I never *ever* wanted to do the Jewish thing," he said. "That always seemed to me to be our big mistake. Law school to me was just another ghetto. So was what you did, the writing, the books, the schools, all that scorn for the material world. Books to me were too Jewish, just another way to hide from fear of the goyim. You see, I was having Diasporist thoughts even then. It was crude, it wasn't formulated, but the instinct was there from the start. These people here call it 'assimilation' in order to disparage it—I called it living like a man. I joined the army to go to Korea. I *wanted* to fight the Communists. I never got sent. They made me an MP at Fort Benning. I built my body in the gym there. I learned to direct traffic. I became a pistol expert. I fell in love with weapons. I studied the martial arts. You quit ROTC because you were against the military establishment at Bucknell, and I became the best fucking MP they ever saw in Georgia. I *showed* the fucking rednecks. Don't be afraid, I told myself, don't run away—beat them at their fucking game. And through this technique I developed a tremendous sense of self-worth."

"What happened to it?" I asked.

"Please, don't insult me *too* much. I don't carry a gun, the cancer has knocked the shit out of my body, the drugs, you're right, they're no good for the brain, they fuck up your nature, and, on top of everything, I am in awe of you—that's true and always will be. It's as it *should* be. I know my place vis-à-vis you. I'm willing to take shit from you that I never took before in my life. I'm a little powerless where you're concerned. But I happen also to understand your predicament better than you give me credit for. You're blitzed too, Phil, this isn't the easiest situation for a classic Jewish paranoid to handle. That's what I'm trying to address right now—your paranoid response. That's why I'm explaining to you who I am and where I'm coming from. I'm not an alien from outer space. I'm not a schizoid delusion. And however much fun it is for you to think so, I'm not Meema Gitcha's Moishe Pipik, either. Far from it. I'm Philip Roth. I'm a Jewish private detective from Chicago who has got cancer and is doomed to die of it, but not before he makes his contribution. I am not ashamed of what I have done for people up until now. I am not ashamed of being a bodyguard for people who needed a bodyguard. A bodyguard is a piece of meat, but I never gave anybody less than the best. I did matrimonial surveillance for years. I know it's the comic-relief end of the business, catching people with their pants down, I know it's not being a novelist who wins prizes for excellence—but that's not the Philip Roth who I was. I was the Philip Roth who went up to the desk manager at the Palmer House and showed him my badge or gave him some other pretense so I could get to the registration book to see

that they had actually signed in and what room they were in. I
am the Philip Roth who in order to get up there would say I
was a floral-delivery person and I gotta be sure this is personally done because the guy gave me a hundred dollars to get it
up there. I am the Philip Roth who would get the maid and
make up a story for her: 'I forgot my key, this is my room, you
can check downstairs that this is my room.' I am the Philip
Roth who could always get a key, who could always get in the
room—*always*."

"Just like here," I said, but that didn't stop him.

"I am the Philip Roth who rushes into the room with his
Minolta and gets his pictures before they know what's happened. Nobody gives you awards for this, but I was never
ashamed, I put in my years, and when I finally had the money,
I opened my own agency. And the rest is history. People are
missing and Philip Roth finds them. I'm the Philip Roth who
is dealing with desperate people all the time, and not just in
some book. Crime is desperate. The person who reported them
is desperate and the person who is on the lam is desperate, and
so desperation is my life, day and night. Kids run away from
home and I find them. They run away and they get pulled into
the world of people who are scum. They need a place to stay,
and so the people take advantage of that. My last case, before I
got cancer, was a fifteen-year-old girl from Highland Park. Her
mother came to me, she was a mess, a lot of tears and screaming. Donna registered for her high school class in September,
went for the first two days, and then disappeared. She winds
up with a known felon, warrants for his arrest, a bad guy. A
Dominican. I found this apartment building in Calumet City
where his grandmother lived, and I staked it out. It was all I
had to go on. I staked it out for days. I sat upwards of twenty-
six hours once without relief. With nothing happening. You
have to have patience, *tremendous* patience. Even reading the
newspapers is chancy because something could happen in a
split second and you might miss it. There for hours and you
have to be inventive. You hide in the vehicle, you sit low in the
vehicle, you pretend you're just hanging out like anybody else
in the vehicle. Sometimes you go to the bathroom in the
vehicle—you can't help it. And meanwhile I am always putting
myself in the criminal's mind, how he's going to react and

what he's going to do. Every criminal is different and every scenario I come up with is different. When you're a criminal and you're stupid, you don't think, but if you're a detective you have to be intelligent enough to not-think in the way this guy doesn't think. Well, he turns up at the grandmother's finally. I follow him on foot when he comes out. He goes to make a drug purchase. Then he comes back to the car. I make a pass by the car and there she is—I make a positive identification that it is Donna. It turned out later that he was doing drugs in the car himself. To shorten a long story, the car chase lasted twenty-five minutes. We're driving about eighty miles an hour down side roads through four Indiana towns. The guy is charged with sixteen different counts. Eluding police, resisting arrest, kidnapping—he's in deep shit. I interrogated the girl. I said, 'How you doin', Donna?' She says, 'I don't know what you're talking about, my name is Pepper. I'm from California. I've been in town a week.' This nice Highland Park high school girl of fifteen has the intelligence of a hardened con and her story is perfect. She's been gone eleven months, and she had a fake birth certificate, a driver's license, a whole bunch of fake IDs. Her behavior indicated to me that this guy was using her for prostitution. We found condoms in her pocketbook, sexual devices in the car and things."

I thought, He's got it all down pat from TV. If only I'd watched more "L.A. Law" and read less Dostoyevsky I'd know what's going on here, I'd know in two minutes what show it is exactly. Maybe motifs from fifteen shows, with a dozen detective movies thrown in. The joke is that more than likely there's a terrifically popular network program that everyone stays home for on Friday nights, and not only is it about a private investigator who specializes in missing kids but it's a Jewish private investigator, and the episode about the high school girl (sweet cheerleader, square parents, mind of her own) and the addict-pimp abductor (dirty dancer, folkloric grandmother, pitted skin) was probably the last one seen by Pipik before he'd hopped on the plane for Tel Aviv to play me. Maybe it was the in-flight movie on El Al. Probably everybody in America over three years of age knows about how detectives shit in their cars and call the cars vehicles, probably everybody over three in America knows exactly what is meant by a sexual device and only the aging author of *Portnoy's Complaint* has to ask. What fun it must be for him putting me on like this. But is the masquerading relentless for the sake of the shakedown, or is the shakedown a pretext for the performance and all the real fun in the act? What if this isn't simply a con but his parody of my vocation, what's now known to mankind as a "roast." Yes, suppose this Pipik of mine is none other than the Satiric Spirit in the flesh, and the whole thing a send-up, a satire of authorship! How could I have missed it? Yes, yes, the Spirit of Satire is of course who he is, here to poke fun at me and other outmoded devotees of what is important and what is real, here to divert us all from the Jewish savagery that doesn't bear thinking about, come with his road show to Jerusalem to make everyone miserable laugh.

"What are the sexual devices?" I asked him.

"She had a vibrator. There was a blackjack in the car. I forget what else we had."

"What's the blackjack, a kind of dildo? I suppose dildos are a dime a dozen on prime time by now. What the Hula-Hoop used to be."

"They use blackjacks for S & M. For beating and punishing and things like that."

"What happened to Donna? Is she white? I didn't catch this show. Who plays you? Ron Liebman or George Segal? Or is it you playing them for me?"

"I don't know many writers," he replied. "Is this the way they all think? That out there everybody is *playing*? Man! You listened too religiously to that kiddie program when you were a little boy—you and Sandy may have loved it too much. Saturday mornings. Remember? Nineteen forty also. Eleven a.m. Eastern Standard Time. Da-*dum*-da-dadada, *dum*-da-dadada, *dum*-dada-da-dum."

He was humming the tune that used to introduce "Let's Pretend," a fairy-tale half hour that little unmediaized American children adored back in the thirties and forties, my brother and I but two of the millions.

"Maybe," he said, "your perception of reality got arrested at the 'Let's Pretend' level."

To this I did not even bother to reply.

"Oh, that's a cliché, is it? Am I boring you? Well," he said, "now that you're pushing sixty and 'Let's Pretend' isn't on the air anymore, someone *should* bore you long enough to explain that, one, the world is real, two, the stakes are high, and, three, nobody is pretending anymore except *you*. I have been inside your head for so long now and yet not until this moment have I understood what a writer is all about: you guys think it's *all* make-believe."

"I don't think *any* of it is make-believe, Pipik. I think—I *know*—that you are a real liar and a real fake. It's the stories that purport to be about 'it,' it's the struggle to describe 'it,' where the make-believe comes in. Five-year-old children may take the stories for real, but by the time you're pushing sixty, deciphering the pathology of story making comes to be just another middle-age specialty. By the time you're pushing sixty, the representations of 'it' *are* 'it.' They're everything. Follow me?"

"Nothing hard to follow except your relevance. Cynicism increases with age because the bullshit piles up on your head. What's that got to do with us?"

I heard myself ask aloud, "Am I conversing with this person, am I truly trying to make *sense* with him? *Why?*"

"Why *not!* Why should you converse with Aharon Appelfeld," he said, holding up and shaking Aharon's book, "and not with me!"

"A thousand reasons."

He was all at once in a jealous rage because I talked seriously to Aharon but not to him. "Name *one!*" he cried.

Because, I thought, of Aharon's and my distinctly radical *twoness*, a condition with which you appear to have no affinity at all; because we are anything *but* the duplicates that everyone is supposed to believe you and me to be; because Aharon and I each embody the *reverse* of the other's experience; because each recognizes in the other the Jewish man he is *not*; because of the all but incompatible orientations that shape our very different lives and very different books and that result from *antithetical* twentieth-century Jewish biographies; because we are the heirs jointly of a drastically *bifurcated* legacy—because of the sum of all these Jewish *antinomies*, yes, we have much to talk about and are intimate friends.

"Name *one!*" he challenged for a second time but on this

subject I simply remained silent and, sensibly for a change, kept my thinking to myself. "You recognize Appelfeld for the person he claims to be; why do you refuse that with me? All you *do* is resist me. Resist me, ignore me, insult me, defame me, rant and rave at me—*and steal from me.* Why must there be this bad blood? Why *you* should see *me* as a rival—I cannot understand it. Why is this relationship so belligerent from your end? Why must it be destructive when together we could achieve so much? We could have a creative relationship, we could be partners—copersonalities working in tandem rather than stupidly divided in two!"

"Look, I've got more personalities than I can use already. All you are is one too many. This is the end of the line. I don't want to go into business with you. I just want you to go away."

"We could at least be friends."

He sounded so forlorn I had to laugh. "Never. Profound, unbridgeable, unmistakable differences that far outweigh the superficial similarity—no, we can't be friends, either. This is it."

He looked, to my astonishment, about to burst into tears because of what I'd said. Or maybe it was just the ebb tide of those drugs. "Look, you never told me what happened to Donna," I said. "Entertain us a little more, and then, what do you say, let's bring this little error to an end. What became of Highland Park High's fifteen-year-old dominatrix? How'd that show wind up?"

But this, of course, riled him again.

"Shows! You really think I watch PI shows? There isn't one that depicts what's real, not *one.* If I had a choice between watching "Magnum, P.I." and "Sixty Minutes," I'd watch "Sixty Minutes" anytime. Shall I tell you something? Donna turned out to be Jewish. Her mother, I found out later, was the reason why she left. I won't go into that, you don't care. But I did, I got involved in those cases—they were my life before I got sick. I would try to find out what the reasons were they left and try to get them to stay. I would try to help them. That was very rewarding. Unfortunately this Dominican with Donna—his name was Hector—Donna had a problem with him—"

"He had this power over her," I said, "and to this day she's trying to contact him."

"That happens to be the case. That's true. She was charged with receiving stolen property, resisting arrest, eluding police too—she's in a detention center."

"And the day she's released from the detention center, she'll run away again," I said. "Great story. Everybody can identify, as they say. Beginning with you. She doesn't want to be Dr. and Mrs. Jew's Donna anymore, she wants to be Hector's Dominican Pepper. All this autobiographical fantasy, is it nationwide? Is it worldwide? Maybe this stuff everybody is watching has inspired half the human population with the yearning for a massive transfer of souls, maybe that's what *you* embody—the longings for metempsychosis inspired in mankind by all those TV shows."

"Idiot!" he shouted. "It's staring you right in the *face* what I embody!"

It is, I thought: exactly nothing. There is no meaning here at all. *That's* the meaning. I can stop there. I could have started there. Nothing could look more like it meant something than this, and nothing could mean less.

"So, what happened finally to Hector?" I asked him, hoping now that if I could lead him to the end of something, of anything, it might present an opportunity to get him up from my bed and out of the room without my having to call down to the desk for assistance. I never felt less inclined than at that moment to see this poor possessed scoundrel wind up in trouble. Not only was he meaningless but, having observed him for nearly an hour, I was hard-pressed to believe any longer that he was violent. In this way we *weren't* dissimilar: the violence was all verbal. I had, in fact, actively to prevent myself from despising him less than was warranted, given the maddening mix-up he'd made of my life and the repercussions of this encounter, which I was sure were going to dog me in unpleasant ways in the future.

"Hector?" he said. "Hector made bail, he's out on bail." Unexpectedly he began to laugh, but a laugh that was as hopeless and weary as any sound emitted by him yet. "You and Hector. I never saw the parallel till now. As if I don't have enough grief from you, with all the ways you want to fuck me over, I've got Hector waiting in the wings. He called me, he spoke to me, he threatened my life—Hector told me he was going to kill me. This is just before I went into the hospital. I've arrested a lot of people, you realize, put a lot of people in prison. They phone me, they track me down, and I don't hide. If somebody wants to get even with me, there's nothing I can do. But I don't look over my shoulder. I told Hector what I tell them all. 'I'm listed in the book, man. Philip Roth. Come and get me.'"

With this I raised my arms over my head, I howled, I clapped my hands together, once, then again, until I found myself applauding him. "Bravo! You're wonderful! What a finish! What a flourish! On the phone, the dedicated Jewish savior, the Jewish statesman, Theodor Herzl turned inside out. Then face-to-face outside the trial, a zany fan blushing with adoration. And now this, the masterstroke—the detective who doesn't look over his shoulder. 'I'm in the book, man. Philip Roth. Come and get me.' The *book*!" From out of my depths roared all the laughter that I should have been laughing from the day I first heard that this preposterous mouthpiece claimed to exist.

But he was suddenly screaming from the bed, "I want the check! I want my check! You've stolen a million dollars!"

"I lost it, Pipik. I lost it on the highway from Ramallah. The check is gone."

Aghast, he stared straight at me, at the person in all the world who most reminded him of himself, the person he saw as the rest of him, the completion of him, the one who'd come to be his very reason for being, his mirror image, his meal ticket, his hidden potential, his public persona, his alibi, his future, the one in whom he sought refuge from himself, the other whom he called himself, the person in whose service he had repudiated his own identity, the breakthrough to the other half of his life . . . and he saw instead, laughing at him uncontrollably from behind the mask of his very own face, his worst enemy, the one to whom the only bond is hatred. But how could Pipik have failed to know that I would have to hate him no less than he hated me? Did he honestly expect that when we met I'd fall in love and set up shop and have a creative relationship with him like Macbeth and his wife?

"I lost it. It's a great story, too, nearly rivals yours for unbelievability. The check is gone," I told him again. "A million bucks blowing away across the desert sands, probably halfway down to Mecca by now. And with that million you could have convened that first Diasporist Congress in Basel. You could have shipped the first lucky Jews back to Poland. You could have established a chapter of A-S.A. right in Vatican City. Meetings in the basement of St. Peter's Church. Full house every night. 'My name is Eugenio Pacelli. I'm a recovering anti-Semite.' Pipik, who sent you to me in my hour of need? Who made me this wonderful gift? Know what Heine liked to say? There is a God, and his name is Aristophanes. *You* prove it. It's Aristophanes they should be worshiping over at the Wailing Wall—if he were the God of Israel I'd be in shul three times a day!"

I was laughing the way people cry at funerals in the countries where they let go and really have at it. They rend their clothes. They rake their faces with their nails. They howl. They swoon. They faint. They grab at the coffin with their twisted hands and fling themselves shrieking into the hole. Well, this is how I was laughing, if you can picture it. To judge from Pipik's face—our face!—it was something to behold. Why *isn't* God Aristophanes? Would we be any further from the truth?

"Surrender yourself to what is real," were my first words to him when I could talk again. "I speak from experience—surrender to reality, Pipik. There's nothing in the world quite like it."

I suppose I should have laughed even more uproariously at what happened next; as a newly anointed convert to the Old Comedy, I should have bounded to my feet, cried aloud, "Hallelujah!" and sung the praises of He Who Created Us, He Who Formed Us from the Mud, the One and Only Comic Almighty, OUR SOVEREIGN REDEEMER, ARISTOPHANES, but for reasons all too profane (total mental paralysis) I could only dumbly gape at the sight of nothing less than the highly entertaining Aristophanic erection that Pipik had produced, as

though it were a rabbit, from his fly, an oversized pole right
out of *Lysistrata* that, to my further astonishment, he proceeded to crank in a rotary motion, to position, with one hand
cupped over the knobby doll-like head, as if he were moving
the floor shift on a prewar car. Then he was lunging with it
across the bed.

"*There's* reality. Like a rock!"

He was ridiculously light, as though the disease had eaten
through his bones, as though inside there was nothing left of
him and he was as hollow as Mortimer Snerd. I caught hold of
his arm just as he landed, and with a blow between his shoulder blades and another, nastier, at the base of the spine, I spun
him out the door (who'd opened it?) and shoved him ass-first
into the corridor. Then there was the split second in which,
across the threshold, each of us was frozen in place by the reflection of the malformed mistake that was the other. Then the
door seemed to spring to life again to assist me—the door was
closed and locked but afterward I could have sworn I'd had as
little to do with its shutting as with its opening.

"My shoes!"

He was screaming for his shoes just as my phone began to
ring. So—we were *not* alone, this Arab hotel in Arab East
Jerusalem had not been emptied of Demjanjuk's son and
Demjanjuk's lawyers, the place had not been evacuated of all
its guests and sealed off by the Jewish authorities so that this
struggle for supremacy between Roth and "Roth" could rage
on undisturbed until the cataclysmic end—no, a complaint at
long last from the outer world about the intemperate acting
out of this primordial dream.

His shoes were beside the bed, cordovans with the strap that
pulls across the instep, Brooks Brothers shoes of the kind I'd
been wearing since I'd first admired them on the feet of a dapperly Princetonian Shakespeare professor at Bucknell. I bent to
pick up Pipik's shoes and saw that, along the back lateral
curve, the heels were sharply worn away exactly as were the
heels of the pair I had on. I looked at mine, at his, and then
opened and shut the door so quickly that all I caught sight of
as I hurled his cordovans into the corridor was the part in his
hair. I saw the part as he rushed the door, and when the door
was locked again I realized that it was on the opposite side

from my own. I reached a hand up to my scalp to be certain. He'd modeled himself on my photograph! Then this, I said to myself, is most definitely someone else, and, depleted beyond depletion, I dropped with my arms outspread on the disheveled bed from which he and his erection had just arisen. That man is not me! I am here and I am whole and part what hair I still possess on the *right* side. Yet in spite of this, and of differences even more telling—our central nervous systems, for example—he's going to proceed down the stairs and out of the hotel like that, he's going to parade through the lobby like that, he's going to walk across Jerusalem like that, and when the police finally run him down and go to take him in for indecent exposure, he's going to tell them what he tells them all—"I'm in the book. Philip Roth. Come and get me."

"My glasses!"

The glasses I found right there beside me on the bed. I snapped them in two and hurled the pieces against the wall. Let him be blind!

"They're broken! *Go!*"

My phone continued ringing and I was no longer laughing like a good Aristophanian but quivering with irreligious, unenlightened rage.

I picked up the phone and said nothing.

"Philip Roth?"

"Not here."

"Philip Roth, where was God between 1939 and 1945? I'm sure He was at the Creation. I'm sure He was at Mount Sinai with Moses. My problem is where He was between 1939 and 1945. That was a dereliction of duty for which even He, *especially* He, cannot ever be forgiven."

I was being addressed in a thick, grave Old Country accent, a hoarse, rough, emphysemic voice that sounded as though it originated in something massively debilitated.

Meanwhile someone had struck up a light, rhythmic knuckle rapping on my door. Shave and a haircut . . . *two bits*. Could it be Pipik on the phone if it was also Pipik at the door? How many of him were there?

"Who is this?" I asked into the phone.

"I spit on this God who was on vacation from 1939 to 1945!"

I hung up.

Shave and a haircut . . . *two bits.*

I waited and waited but the rapping would not go away.

"Who is that?" I finally whispered, but so softly that I thought I might not even be heard. I could almost believe I was smart enough not to be asking.

The whisper back seemed to waft through the keyhole, carried on a wire-thin current of cool air. "Want me to blow you?"

"Go away!"

"I'll blow both of you."

I am looking down on an open-air hospital ward or public clinic that is set out on a vast playing field that reminds me of School Stadium on Bloomfield Avenue in Newark, where Newark's rivalrous high schools—the Italian high school, the Irish high school, the Jewish high school, the Negro high school—played football doubleheaders when I was a boy. But this arena is ten times the size of our stadium and the crowd is as huge as the crowd at a bowl game, tens upon tens of thousands of excited fans, snugly layered with clothing and warming their dark insides with steaming containers of coffee. White pennants wave everywhere, rhythmically the crowd takes up the chant, "Give me an M! Give me an E! Give me a T! Give me an E!" while down on the field white-clad doctors glide agilely about in clinical silence—I am able to see through my binoculars their serious, dedicated faces and the faces, too, of those who lie still as stone, each hooked up to an IV drip, their souls draining into the body on the next gurney. And what is horrifying is that the face of every one of them, even of the women and of the little children, is the face of Ivan of Treblinka. From the stands, the cheering fans can see nothing but the balloon of a big, stupid, friendly face swelling out of each of the bodies strapped to the gurneys, but with my binoculars I see concentrated in that emerging face everything in humanity that there is to hate. Yet the electrified crowd seethes with hope. "All will be different from now on! Everybody will be nice from now on! Everybody will belong to a church like Mr. Demjanjuk! Everybody will raise a garden like Mr. Demjanjuk! Everybody will work hard and come home at night to a wonderful family like Mr. Demjanjuk!" I alone have binoculars and am witness to the unfolding catastrophe. "That is

Ivan!" But nobody can hear me above the hurrahs and the exuberant cheering. "Give me an O! Give me an S!" I am still
shouting that it is Ivan, Ivan from Treblinka, when they pluck
me lightly out of my seat and, rolling me down atop the soft
tassels of the white woolen caps worn by all the fans, pass my
body (swathed now in a white pennant bearing a big blue
"M") over a low brick wall that has painted across it "The
Memory Barrier. Players Only," and into the arms of two waiting doctors, who strap me tightly to a gurney of my own and
wheel me out to midfield just as the band strikes up a quick-
time march. When the IV needle pierces my wrist, I hear the
mighty roar that precedes the big game. "Who's playing?" I
ask the nurse in the white uniform who attends me. She is Jinx,
Jinx Possesski. She pats my hand and whispers, "University of
Metempsychosis." I begin to scream, "I don't want to play!"
but Jinx smiles reassuringly and says, "You must—you're the
starting halfback."

"HALF BACK" was sounding the alarm in my ear when I
scrambled upright in the bed with no idea in what dimension-
less black room I had awakened. I concluded at first that it was
the previous summer and that I needed a light to find the pillbox beside the bed. I need half of a second Halcion to get me
through the rest of the night. But I'm reluctant to turn on the
light for fear of finding paw prints not just on the bedsheets
and the pillowcases but climbing the walls and crossing the
ceiling. Then my phone begins to ring again. "What is the real
life of man?" I am asked this by the emphysemic old Jew with
the tired voice and the heavy accent. "I give up. What *is* the
real life of man?" "There is none. There is only the urge to attain a real life. Everything that is not real is the real life of
man." "Okay. I've got one for you. Tell me the meaning of
today." "Error. Error upon error. Error, misprision, fakery,
fantasy, ignorance, falsification, and mischief, of course, irrepressible mischief. An ordinary day in the life of anyone."
"*Where* is the error?" *In his bed*, I think, and, dreaming on, I
am in the bed of someone who has just died of a highly conta-
gious disease, and then I am dying myself. For locking myself
into this little room with him, for ridiculing and chastising him
from only an arm's length away, for telling this ego-blank

megalomaniacal pseudo-being that he is no more to me than a mere Moishe Pipik, for my failing to understand that he is not a joke, Moishe Pipik murders me and there I expire, emptied of all my blood, until I am ejected like a pilot from the burning cockpit into the discovery that I have had a wet dream for the first time in twenty-five years.

Fully awake, I left the bed at long last and, in the dark, crossed to the arched window in front of the desk to see if I could spot him keeping a lookout on my room from the street below, and what I saw, not in the narrow street bordering this side of the hotel but two streets beyond, was a convoy of buses under the glow of the lamps and several hundred soldiers, each with a rifle slung over his shoulder, waiting to board them. I couldn't even hear the boots striking against the pavement, so easily did the soldiers amble along, one by one, once the signal to move out had been given. There was a high wall running the length of the far side of the street and on the near side was a block-long stone structure with a corrugated iron roof that must have been a garage or a warehouse, an L-shaped building that made the street a hidden cul-de-sac. There were six buses, and I stood there watching until the last soldier climbed aboard with his weapon and the buses began to roll away, heading out more than likely for the West Bank, replacement troops to put down the riots, armed Jews, what Pipik maintains makes a second Holocaust imminent, what Pipik claims he can render unnecessary through the benevolent agency of A-S.A. . . .

I decided then—it was a little after two—to leave Jerusalem. If I got to it immediately, I'd have time enough to compose another three or four questions to round out the interview. Aharon's house was in a development village some twenty minutes due west of Jerusalem, just off the road to the airport. At dawn I'd have the taxi stop there briefly so that I could give to Aharon those last questions and then proceed on to the airport and London.

Why didn't you just *pretend* to be his partner? Your error was derision. You'll pay plenty for breaking those glasses.

By two that night I was so done in by the unsurpassable confusion of the day before, so unable any longer to assess the truth of anything amid all this turmoil, that these three sentences, softly uttered aloud by me while beginning to prepare for my dawn departure, I took to be spoken by Pipik from the other side of the door. *The lunatic is back! He's armed!* And it was no less astonishing—and in its way *more* frightening— when, in the next instant, I understood that it was my own voice that I had heard and mistaken for his, that it was only me talking to myself as might any lonely traveler who'd found himself wide awake, far from home, in a strange hotel in the middle of the night.

I was suddenly in a terrible state. All that I had struggled to retrieve since the breakdown of the previous summer rapidly began to give way before an onslaught of overpowering dread. I was all at once terrified that I did not have the strength to hold myself together very much longer and that I would be carried off into some new nightmare of disintegration unless I could forcibly stop this unraveling with my few remaining ounces of self-control.

What I did was to move the bureau in front of the door, not so much anticipating that he would return and dare to use again the key to my room that was still in his pocket, but for fear that I might find myself *volunteering* to open the door to allow him to make some last proposal for a rapprochement. Watching out for my bad back, I slowly dragged the bureau away from where it was positioned opposite the bed and, turning back the oriental rug in the center of the room, edged it as noiselessly as I could along the tiles until it obstructed access to the door. Now I couldn't possibly let him have at me, however entertaining, intimidating, or heartfelt his petition to reenter. Using the bureau to block the door was the second-best precaution I could think to take against my own stupidity; the first was flight, getting myself a thousand miles away from him and my demonstrable incapacity to contend on my own with the mesmeric craziness of this provocation. But for now, I thought, sit it out, barricaded in. Until the light came up and the hotel reawakened to life and I could leave the room accompanied by a bellhop and make my departure in a taxi drawn right up in front of the entrance, I would sit it out right there.

For the next two hours I remained at the desk in front of the window, fully aware of just how visible I was to anyone lurking in the street below. I did not bother to pull the curtains, since a piece of fabric is no protection against a well-aimed rifle shot. I could have pushed the desk away from the window and along the adjacent wall, but sanity balked here and simply would not permit a further rearrangement of the furniture. I could have sat up on the bed and composed from there my remaining questions for Aharon, but instead, to safeguard what little equilibrium I still possessed, I chose to sit as I have been sitting all my life, in a chair, at a desk, under a lamp, substantiating my peculiar existence in the most consolidating way I know, taming temporarily with a string of words the unruly tyranny of my incoherence.

In *To the Land of the Cattails* [I wrote], a Jewish woman and her grown son, the offspring of a Gentile father, are journeying back to the remote Ruthenian countryside where she was born. It's the summer of 1938. The closer they get to her home the more menacing is the threat of Gentile violence. The mother says to her son, "They are many, and we are few." Then you write: "The word *goy* rose up from within her. She smiled as if hearing a distant memory. Her father would sometimes, though only occasionally, use that word to indicate hopeless obtuseness."

The Gentile with whom the Jews of your books seem to share their world is usually the embodiment of hopeless obtuseness and of menacing, primitive social behavior—the *goy* as drunkard, wife beater, as the coarse, brutal semisavage who is "not in control of himself." Though obviously there's more to be said about the non-Jewish world in those provinces where your books are set—and also about the capacity of Jews, in their own world, to be obtuse and primitive, too—even a non-Jewish European would have to recognize that the power of this image over the Jewish imagination is rooted in real experience. Alternatively the *goy* is pictured as an "earthy soul . . . overflowing with health." *Enviable* health. As the mother in *Cattails* says of her half-Gentile son, "He's not nervous like me. Other, quiet blood flows in his veins."

I'd say that it's impossible to know anything really about the Jewish imagination without investigating the place that the *goy* has occupied in the folk mythology that's been exploited in America by Jewish comedians like Lenny Bruce and Jackie Mason and, at quite another level, by Jewish novelists. American fiction's most single-minded portrait of the *goy* is in *The Assistant* by Bernard Malamud. The *goy* is Frank Alpine, the down-and-out thief who robs the failing grocery store of the Jew, Bober, later attempts to rape Bober's studious daughter, and eventually, in a conversion to Bober's brand of suffering Judaism, symbolically renounces *goyish* savagery. The New York Jewish hero of Saul Bellow's second novel, *The Victim*, is plagued by an alcoholic Gentile misfit named Allbee, who is no less of a bum and a drifter than Alpine, even if his assault on Leventhal's hard-won composure is intellectually more urbane. The most imposing Gentile in all of Bellow's work, however, is Henderson—the self-exploring rain king who, to restore his psychic health, takes his blunted instincts off to Africa. For Bellow no less than for Appelfeld, the truly "earthy soul" is not the Jew, nor is the search to retrieve primitive energies portrayed as the quest of a Jew. For Bellow no less than for Appelfeld, and, astonishingly, for Mailer no less than for Appelfeld—we all know that in Mailer when a man is a sadistic sexual aggressor his name is Sergius O'Shaugnessy, when he is a wife killer his name is Stephen Rojack, and when he is a menacing murderer he isn't Lepke Buchalter or Gurrah Shapiro, he's Gary Gilmore.

Here, succumbing finally to my anxiety, I turned off the desk lamp and sat in the dark. And soon I could see into the street below. And someone *was* there! A figure, a man, running across the dimly lit pavement not twenty-five feet from my window. He ran crouching over but I recognized him anyway.

I stood at the desk. "Pipik!" I shouted, flinging open the window. "Moishe Pipik, you son of a bitch!"

He turned to look toward the open window and I saw that in either hand he held a large rock. He raised the rocks over his head and shouted back at me. He was masked. He was shouting in Arabic. Then he ran on. Then a second figure was running by, then a third, then a fourth, each of them carrying a rock in either hand and all their faces hidden by ski masks. Their source of supply was a pyramid-shaped rock pile, a rock pile that resembled a memorial cairn and that stood just inside an alleyway across from the hotel. The four ran up and down the street with their rocks until the cairn was gone. Then the street was empty again and I shut the window and went back to work.

In *The Immortal Bartfuss*, your newly translated novel, Bartfuss asks irreverently of his dying mistress's ex-husband, "What have we Holocaust survivors done? Has our great experience changed us at all?" This is the question with which the novel somehow or other engages itself on virtually every page. We sense in Bartfuss's lonely longing and regret, in his baffled effort to overcome his own remoteness, in his avidity for human contact, in his mute wanderings along the Israeli coast and his enigmatic encounters in dirty cafés, the agony that life can become in the wake of a great disaster. Of the Jewish survivors who wind up smuggling and black-marketeering in Italy directly after the war, you write, "No one knew what to do with the lives that had been saved."

My last question, growing out of your preoccupation in *The Immortal Bartfuss*, is, perhaps, extremely comprehensive, but think about it, please, and reply as you choose. From what you observed as a homeless youngster wandering in Europe after the war, and from what you've learned during four decades in Israel, do you discern distinguishing patterns in the experience of those whose lives were saved? What *have* the Holocaust survivors done and in what ways were they ineluctably changed?

7
Her Story

H E'D taken nothing. Not even a sock was missing from the bureau drawer where I'd laid my loose clothing, and, in searching for the check that meant everything to him, he hadn't disarranged a thing. He'd borrowed *Tzili* to read while waiting on the bed for my return but that seemed to have been the only possession of mine—my identity aside—that he had dared to touch. I began to doubt, while I packed my bag to go, if he actually had searched the room and, disturbingly for a moment, even to wonder if he had ever been here. But if he hadn't come to claim the check as his, why had he risked my wrath (and perhaps worse) by breaking in?

I had my jacket on and my bag packed. I was only waiting for dawn. I had but one goal and that was to disappear. The rest I'd puzzle out or not when I'd successfully accomplished an escape. And don't write about it afterward, I told myself. Even the gullible now have contempt for the idea of objectivity; the latest thing they've swallowed whole is that it's impossible to report anything faithfully other than one's own temperature; everything is allegory—so what possible chance would I have to persuade anyone of a reality like this one? Ask Aharon, when you say goodbye to him, please to be silent and forget it. Even in London, when Claire returns and asks what happened, tell her all is well. "Nothing happened, he never turned up." Otherwise you can explain these two days for the rest of your life and no one will ever believe your version to be anything other than your version.

Folded in thirds in the inside pocket of my jacket were the fresh sheets of hotel stationery onto which I'd copied, in legible block letters, my remaining questions for Aharon. In my bag I had all our other questions and answers and all the tapes. I had managed despite everything to do the job, maybe not as I'd looked forward to doing it back in New York . . . I remembered Apter suddenly. Could I catch him at his rooming house on my way out of Jerusalem? Or would I find Pipik already waiting there, Pipik pretending to poor Apter that he's me!

The lights were off in my room. I'd been sitting in the dark for half an hour, waiting at the little desk by the large window with my fully packed bag up against my leg and watching the masked men who had resumed their rock conveying directly below, as though for my singular edification, as though daring me to pick up the phone to notify the army or the police. These are rocks, I thought, to split open the heads of Jews, but I also thought, I belong elsewhere, this struggle is over territory that is not mine . . . I counted the number of rocks they were moving. When I reached a hundred I could stand it no longer, and I called the desk and asked to be put through to the police. I was told that the line was engaged. "It's an emergency," I replied. "Is something wrong? Are you ill, sir?" "Please, I want to report something to the police." "As soon as I get a free line, sir. The police are very busy tonight. You lost something, Mr. Roth?"

A woman spoke from the other side of the door just as I was hanging up. "Let me in," she whispered, "it's Jinx Possesski. Something terrible is happening."

I pretended not to be there, but she began rapping lightly on the door—she must have overheard me on the phone.

"He's going to kidnap Demjanjuk's son."

But I had only my one objective and didn't bother to answer her. *You can't make a mistake doing nothing.*

"They're plotting right this minute to kidnap Demjanjuk's son!"

Outside the door Pipik's Possesski, below the window the Arabs in ski masks running rocks—I closed my eyes to compose in my head a last question to leave with Aharon before I flew off. *Living in this society, you are bombarded by news and political disputation. Yet, as a novelist, you have, by and large, pushed aside the Israeli daily turbulence—*

"Mr. Roth, they intend to do it!"

—in order to contemplate markedly different Jewish predicaments. What does this turbulence mean to a novelist like yourself? How does being a citizen of—

Jinx was softly sobbing now. "He wears this. Walesa gave it to him. Mr. Roth, you've got to help . . ."

—of this self-revealing, self-asserting, self-challenging, self-leg-endizing society affect your writing life? Does this news-produc-ing reality ever tempt your imagination?

"This will be the end of him."

Everything dictated silence and self-control but I couldn't restrain myself and spoke my mind. "Good!"

"It'll destroy everything he's done."

"Perfect!"

"You must take *some* responsibility."

"None!"

Meanwhile I had got down on my hands and knees and was trying to reach under the bureau to see what she had pushed beneath the door. I was able, finally, to fish it out with my shoe.

A jagged piece of fabric about the size of my hand and as weightless as a swatch of gauze—a cloth Star of David, some-thing I'd only seen before in those photographs of pedestrians on the streets of occupied Europe, Jews tagged as Jews with a bit of yellow material. This surprise shouldn't have exasperated me more than anything else issuing from Pipik's excesses but it did, it exasperated me violently. Stop. Breathe. Think. His pathology is his, not yours. Treat it with realistic humor—and *go!* But instead I gave way to my feelings. *Hold off, hold off,* but I couldn't—there seemed no way for me to treat the appear-ance of this tragic memento as just a harmless amusement. There was absolutely nothing he wouldn't turn into a farce. A blasphemer even of *this.* I cannot endure him.

"Who is this madman! Tell me who this madman is!"

"I will! Let me in!"

"Everything! The truth!"

"All I know! I will!"

"You're alone?"

"All alone. I am. I swear to you I am."

"Wait."

Stop. Breathe. Think. But I did instead what I'd decided not to do until it was time to make a safe exit. I edged the big bu-reau away from the door just enough to open it, and then I unlocked the door and let squeeze into the room the cocon-spirator he had sent to entice me, dressed for those pickup bars where the oncology nurses used to go to irrigate themselves of all that death and dying back when Jinx Possesski was still a full-fledged, unreclaimed hater of Jews. Big dark glasses covered half her face, and the black dress she was wearing couldn't have made her look any shapelier. She couldn't have looked any shapelier without it. It was a great cheap dress. Lots of lipstick, the unkempt pale pile of Polish cornsilk, and enough of her protruding for me to conclude not only that she was up to no good but that it may not have been my terrible temper alone that had enjoined me from stopping and breathing and thinking, that I had let Jinx past my barricade because I was up to no good myself and had been for some time now. It occurred to me, friends, when she wriggled through the door and then turned the key to lock us in—and him out?—that I should never have left the front stoop in Newark. I never longed so passionately, not for her, not that quite yet, but for my life before impersonation and imitation and twofoldedness set in, life before self-mockery and self-idealization (and the idealization of the mockery; and the mockery of the idealization; and the idealization of the idealization; and the mockery of the mockery), before the alternating exaltations of hyperobjectivity and hypersubjectivity (and the hyperobjectivity about the hypersubjectivity; and the hypersubjectivity about the hyperobjectivity), back when what was outside was outside and what was inside was inside, when everything still divided cleanly and nothing happened that couldn't be explained. I left the front stoop on Leslie Street, ate of the fruit of the tree of fiction, and nothing, neither reality nor myself, had been the same since.

I didn't want this temptress, I wanted to be ten; despite a lifelong determinedly antinostalgic stance, I wanted to be ten and back in the neighborhood when life was not yet a blind passage out but still like baseball, where you came home, and when the voluptuous earthliness of women other than my mamma was nothing I yet wished to gorge myself on.

"Mr. Roth, he's waiting to hear from Meir Kahane. They're going to do it. Somebody has to stop them!"

"Why did you bring this?" I said, angrily thrusting the yellow star in her face.

"I told you. Walesa gave it to him. In Gdansk. Philip wept. Now he wears it under his shirt."

"The truth! The truth! Why at three in the morning do you

come with this star and this story? How did you get this far anyway? How did you pass the desk downstairs? How do you get across Jerusalem at this hour, with all this danger and dressed like fucking Jezebel? This is a city seething with hatred, the violence will be terrible, it's dreadful already, and *look* at how he sent you here! Look at how he's fitted you out in this femme fatale Bond movie get-up! The man has got the instincts of a pimp! Forget the crazy Arabs—a crazy pack of pious Jews could have stoned you to death in this dress!"

"But they are going to kidnap Demjanjuk's son and send him back piece by piece until Demjanjuk confesses! They're writing Demjanjuk's confession right now. They say to Philip, 'You, writer—do it good!' Toe by toe, finger by finger, eyeball by eyeball, until his father speaks the truth, they are going to torture the son. Religious people in skullcaps, and you should hear what they are saying—and Philip sits there writing the confession! Kahane! Philip is *anti*-Kahane, calls him a *savage*, and he's sitting there waiting for a phone call from the savage fanatic he hates most in the world!"

"Answer me please with the truth. Why did he send you here in this dress? With this star? How does a person like him *come about*? The chicanery is *inexhaustible*."

"I ran! I told him, 'I cannot listen anymore. I cannot watch you destroy everything!' I ran away!"

"To me."

"You must give him back the check!"

"I lost the check. I don't have the check. I told him that. Something untoward happened. Certainly the girlfriend of your boyfriend can understand that. The check is gone."

"But your keeping the money is what's making him wild! Why did you accept Mr. Smilesburger's money when you *knew* it wasn't meant for you!"

I pushed the cloth star into her hand. "Take this with you and get out of here."

"But Demjanjuk's *son*!"

"Miss, I was not born to Bess and Herman Roth in Newark's Beth Israel Hospital to protect this man Demjanjuk's son."

"Then protect *Philip*!"

"That is what I'm doing."

"But it's to prove himself to you that *he's* doing what *he's* doing. He's out of his mind for your admiration. You are the hero, like it or not!"

"Please, with a dick like his he doesn't need me for a hero. He was nice enough to come here to show it to me. Did you know that? He's not particularly pestered by inhibitions, is he?"

"No," she muttered, "oh, no," and here she caved in and dropped to the edge of the bed in tears.

"Nope," I said, "uh-uh, you two aren't taking turns—*get up and get out.*"

But she was crying so pathetically that all I could do was to return to the easy chair by the window and sit there until she had exhausted herself on my pillow. That she was clutching that cloth star while she wept disgusted and infuriated me.

Down in the street the masked Arabs were gone. I didn't seem to have been born to stop them either.

When I couldn't any longer stand the sight of her with the star, I came over to the bed and pulled it out of her hands, and then I unzipped my suitcase and shoved it in with my things. I still have it. I am looking at it while I write.

"It's an implant," she said.

"What is? What are you saying?"

"It isn't 'his.' It's a plastic implant."

"Oh? Tell me more."

"Everything's been cut out of him. He couldn't stand how it left him. So he had the procedure. Plastic rods are in there. In-side the penis is a penile implant. Why do you laugh? How can you *laugh*! You're laughing at somebody's terrible suffering!"

"I'm not at all—I'm laughing at all the lies. Poland, Walesa, Kahane, even the *cancer's* a lie—Demjanjuk's *son* is a lie. And this prick he's so proud of, come clean, in what Amsterdam doodad shop did you two find *that* nutty joke? It's *Hellzapoppin'* with Possesski and Pipik, it's a gag a minute with you two madcap kids—who *wouldn't* laugh? The prick was great, I have to admit, but I think I'll always love best the Poles at the Warsaw railroad station ecstatically welcoming back their Jews. Diasporism! Diasporism is a plot for a Marx Brothers movie—Groucho selling Jews to Chancellor Kohl! I lived eleven years in London—not in bigoted, backwater, pope-ridden Poland but in civilized, secularized, worldly-wise England. When the first hundred thousand Jews come rolling into Waterloo Station with all their belongings in tow, I really want to be there to see it. Invite me, won't you? When the first hundred thousand Diasporist evacuees voluntarily surrender their criminal Zionist homeland to the suffering Palestinians and disembark on England's green and pleasant land, I want to see with my very own eyes the welcoming committee of English goyim waiting on the platform with their champagne. 'They're here! More Jews! Jolly good!' No, *fewer* Jews is my sense of how Europe prefers things, *as few of them as possible*. Diasporism, my dear, seriously misses the *point* about the *depths* of the antipathy. But then, that shouldn't come as news to a charter member of A-S.A. That poor old Smilesburger was nearly suckered by Diasporism's founding father out of a million bucks—well, I don't think this Smilesburger is all there either."

"What Mr. Smilesburger does with his money," she shot back, her face rapidly melting down into the defeated grimace of a thwarted child, "*is up to Mr. Smilesburger!*"

"Then tell Mr. Smilesburger to stop the check, why don't you? Go play the interceding woman with him. It's not going to work here, so go try it with him. Tell him he gave the check to the wrong Philip Roth."

"I'm crashing," she moaned, "damn it, I'm *crashing*," and she grabbed the phone from the tin-topped table squeezed in by the wall at the inside corner of the bed and asked the clerk at the hotel switchboard for the King David Hotel. All roads lead back to him. I decided too late to wrestle the phone away from her. Among all the other things contributing to the disorganization of my thinking was the immediacy of her sensuality on that bed.

"It's me," she said when the connection was made. ". . . With him. . . . Yes I am. . . . His room! . . . No! . . . No! Not with *them*! . . . I can't go on, Phil. I'm on the damn brink. Kahane is crazy, you said so, not me. . . . *No!* . . . I am crashing, Philip, I am going to crash!" Here she thrust the phone at me. "You stop him! You must!"

Because for some reason the phone was wired into the wall furthest from the door, the cord had to be pulled across the width of the bed and I had to lean directly across her to speak into the mouthpiece. Maybe that was *why* I spoke into the mouthpiece. There could be no other reason. To anyone watching us through that one big window, it would have been she and I who looked like coconspirators now. Propinquity and piquancy seemed as if one word derived from the single explosive root syllable *Jinx*.

"On to yet another hilarious idea, I hear," said I into the telephone.

The reply was calm, amused, his voice my own restrained mild voice! "Of yours," he said.

"Repeat that."

"Your idea," he said, and I hung up.

But no sooner was I off the phone than it was ringing again.

"Let it be," I told her.

"Okay, that's it," she said, "that's gotta be it."

"Right. Just let it ring."

The return trip to the chair beside the desk was one long temptation-ridden journey, rich with pleas to the baser yearnings for caution and common sense, a great deal of convulsive conflict compressed into a very short space, a kind of synthesis of my whole adult life. Seating myself as far as I could get in that room from this rash, precipitate complicity of ours, I said, "Leaving aside for the moment who *you* are, who is this antic fellow who goes around as me?" I signaled with a finger that she was not to touch the ringing phone. "Concentrate on my question. Answer me. Who is he?"

"My patient. I told you that."

"Another lie."

"*Everything* can't be a lie. Stop *saying* that. It doesn't help anyone. You protect yourself from the truth by calling everything you won't believe a lie. Everything that's too much for you, you say, 'That's a lie.' But that's denial, Mr. Roth, of what living *is*! These lies of yours are my damn life! *The phone is no lie!*" And she lifted the phone and cried into the mouthpiece, "I won't! It's over! I'm not coming back!" But what she heard through the receiver sucked the angry blood engorging her face all the way back down to her feet as though she'd been upended and "hourglass" were no mere metaphor with which to describe her shape. Very meekly she offered me the phone.

"The police," she said, horrified and uttering "police" as she must once have heard patients freshly apprised of their chances repeat the oncologist's "terminal." "Don't," she begged me, "he won't survive it!"

The Jerusalem police were responding to my call. Because the rock runners were gone I had now been put through to them—or maybe all phone lines *had* indeed been tied up earlier, unlikely as that still seemed to me. I described to the police what I'd seen from my window. They asked me to describe what was going on there now. I told them that the street was empty. They asked my name and I gave it to them. I gave them my U.S. passport number. I did not go on to tell them that someone bearing a duplicate passport, a counterfeit of mine, was at that very moment conspiring at the King David Hotel to kidnap and torture John Demjanjuk's son. Let him try it, I thought. If she's not lying, if he's resolved, like his antihero Jonathan Pollard, to be a Jewish savior regardless of the cost—or even if the motive is merely personal, if he's just determined to take a leading role in my life like the boy who shot Reagan to wow Jodie Foster—let the fantasies evolve grandiosely without my interference, this time let him overstep something more than just my boundaries and collide head-on with the Jerusalem police. I could not myself arrange a more satisfying conclusion to this stupid drama of no importance. Two minutes into it they'll nab him in his bid for historical significance and that will be the end of Moishe Pipik.

She had closed her eyes and crossed her arms and laid them protectively over her breasts while I hung just inches above her talking to the police. And she remained like that, absolutely mummified, while I traversed the room and sat back down in my chair once again, thinking, as I looked at the bed, that she could have been waiting to be removed by the undertaker. And that made me think of my first wife, who, some twenty years earlier, at just about Jinx's age, had been killed in a car crash in New York. We had embarked on a disastrous three-year marriage after she had falsified the results of a pregnancy test in the aftermath of our lurid love affair and then threatened suicide if I didn't marry her. Six years after my leaving the marriage against her will, I'd still been unable to win her consent to a divorce, and when she was abruptly killed in 1968, I wandered around Central Park, the site of her fatal accident, reciting to myself a ferociously apt little couplet by John

Dryden, the one that goes, "Here lies my wife: here let her lie!/Now she's at rest; and so am I."

Jinx was taller than her by half a foot and substantial physically in a rather more riveting way, but seeing her laid out in repose, as though for burial, I was struck by a racial resemblance to the square-headed northern good looks of my long-dead enemy. What if it was she risen from the dead to take her revenge . . . if she was the mastermind who'd trained and disguised him, taught him my mannerisms and how I speak . . . plotted out the intricacies of the identity theft with the same demoniacal resolve with which she'd dished up to the Second Avenue pharmacist that false urine specimen. . . . These were the thoughts lapping at the semiconscious brain of a fitfully dozing man struggling still to remain alert. The woman in the black dress stretched across the bed was no more the ghost of my first wife's corpse than Pipik was the ghost of me, yet there was now a dreamlike distortion muddling my mind against which I was only intermittently able to mobilize my rational defenses. I felt drugged by too many incomprehensible events and, after twenty-four hours of going without sleep, I was shadowboxing none too deftly with an inchoate, dimming consciousness.

"Wanda Jane 'Jinx' Possesski—open your eyes, Wanda Jane, and tell me the truth. It is time."

"You're going?"

"Open your eyes."

"Put me in your bag and take me with you," she moaned. "Get me out of here."

"Who are you?"

"Oh, you know," she said wearily, her eyes still closed, "the fucked-up shiksa. Nothing new."

I waited to hear more. She wasn't laughing when she said, once again, "Take me with you, Philip Roth."

It *is* my first wife. I must be saved and you must save me. I am drowning and you did it. I am the fucked-up shiksa. Take me with you.

We slept this time round for more than just a few minutes, she in the bed, I in the chair, arguing as of old with the resurrected wife. "Can't you even return from *death* without screaming about the morality of your position versus the immorality of mine? Is alimony all you think about even there? What is the source of the eternal claim on my income? On what possible grounds did you conclude that somebody owed you his life?"

Then I was put ashore again in the tangible world where she wasn't, back with my flesh and Wanda Jane's in the fairy tale of material existence.

"Wake up."

"Oh, yes . . . I'm here."

"Fucked-up how?"

"How else? Family." She opened her eyes. "Low-class. Beer-drinking. Fighting. Stupid people." Dreamily she said, "I didn't like them."

Neither did she. Hated them. I was the last best chance. Take me with you, I'm pregnant, you must.

"Raised Catholic," I said.

She positioned herself up on her elbows and melodramatically blinked. "My God," she asked, "which one are you?"

"The only one."

"Wanna put your million on it?"

"I want to know who you are. I want to know finally what is going on—I want the truth!"

"Father Polish," she said lightly, ticking off the facts, "mother Irish, Irish grandmother a real doozy, Catholic schools —church until I was probably twelve years old."

"Then?"

She smiled at the earnest "Then," an intimate smile that was no more, really, than a slow curling at the corner of the mouth, something that could only be measured in millimeters but that was, in my book, the very epitome of sexual magic.

I ignored it, if you can describe failing still to get up and leave as ignoring anything.

" 'Then?' Then I learned how to roll a joint," she said. "I ran away from home to California. I got involved with drugs and all that hippie stuff. Fourteen. Hitchhiked. It wasn't un-common."

"And then?"

" 'And then?' Well, out there I remember going through a Hare Krishna event in San Francisco. I liked that a lot. It was very passionate. People were dancing. People were very taken over by the emotion of it. I didn't get involved in that. I got involved with the Jesus people. Just before that I had been going back to Mass. I guess I was interested in getting involved in some sort of religion. What exactly are you trying to figure out again?"

"What do you think I'm trying to figure out? *Him.*"

"Gee, and I thought you were interested in little me."

"The Jesus people. You got involved."

"Well . . ."

"*Go ahead.*"

"Well, there was a pastor, a very passionate little guy. . . . There was always a passionate guy. . . . I looked like a waif, I guess. I was dressed like a hippie. I guess I was wearing a long skirt, I had long hair. Little peasant outfit. You've seen 'em. Well, this guy gave an altar call at the end of the service, the first one I ever went to, and he asked whoever wanted to accept Jesus into his heart to stand up. The spiel is if you want peace, if you want happiness, accept Jesus into your heart as your personal savior. I was sitting in the front row with my girlfriend. I stood up. Halfway through standing, I realized that I was the only one standing. He came down from the altar and prayed over me that I would receive the baptism of the Holy Spirit. Looking back on it, I think I just hyperventilated. But I had some sort of rush, some sort of profound feeling. And I did begin to speak in some sort of language. I'm sure it was made up. It's supposed to be communication with God. Without bothering with language. Your eyes are closed. I did feel a tingling. Sort of detached from what was going on around me. In my own world. Being able to forget who I was and what I was doing. And just do this. It went on for a couple of minutes. He put his hand on my head and I was thrilled. I think I was just vulnerable to anything."

"Why?"

"Usual reasons. Everybody's reason. Because of who my parents were. I got very little attention at home. None. So walking into a place where suddenly I'm a star, everybody loves me and wants me, how could I resist? I was a Christian for twelve years. Age of fifteen to the age of twenty-seven. One of those hippies who found the Lord. It became my life. I hadn't been going to school. I had dropped out of school, and actually I went back to grammar school, I finished grammar school at sixteen in San Francisco. I had these breasts even back then and there I was with them, sitting at a grammar school desk next to all those little kids."

"Your cross," I said, "carried before instead of aft."

"Sometimes it sure seems that way. The doctors were always rubbing up against me when we worked together. Anyway, I'd failed all my life in school and suddenly, tits and all, I started doing okay. And I read the Bible. I liked all that death-to-self stuff. I felt like shit already and it sort of confirmed my feeling of shit. I'm worthless, I'm nothing. God is Everything. It can be very passionate. Just imagine that somebody loved you enough to die for you. That's big-time love."

"You took it personally."

"Oh, absolutely. That's me all over. Yes, yes. I loved to pray. I would be very passionate and I would pray and I would love God and I would be ecstatic. I remember training myself not to look at anything when I was walking on the street. I would only look straight ahead. I didn't want to be distracted from contemplating God. But that can't last. It's too hard. That would sort of dissipate—then I'd be overcome with guilt."

Where had she disposed of all the "like"s and the "okay"s and the "you know"s? Where was the tarty, tough-talking nurse from the day before? Her tones were as soft now as those of a well-behaved ten-year-old child, the pitter-patter, innocent treble of a sweet and intelligent little ten-year-old who has just discovered the pleasures of being informative. She might have weighed seventy pounds, a freshly eloquent prepubescent, home helping her mother bake a cake, so unjaded was the voice with which she'd warmed to all this attention. She might have been chattering away while helping her father wash the car on a Sunday afternoon. I supposed I was hearing the voice of the abundantly breasted hippie at the grammar school desk who'd found Jesus.

"Why guilt?" I asked her.

"Because I wasn't being as in love with God as He deserved. My guilt was that I was interested in things of this world. Especially as I got older."

I saw the two of us drying the dishes in Youngstown, Ohio. Was she my daughter or my wife? This was now the nonsensical background to the ambiguous foreground. My mind, at this stage, was an uncontrollable thing, but then it was a marvel to me that I could continue to remain awake and that she and I—and he—could still be at it at four a.m. the next day—a marvel too that, listening to this lengthy story that couldn't make a scrap of difference, I was only plunging further under their spell.

"Which things?" I asked her. "Which things of this world?"

"My appearance. Trivial things. My friends. Entertainment. Vanity. Myself. I was not supposed to be interested in myself. That's how I decided to go into nursing. I didn't want to go into nursing, but nursing was selfless, something I could do for other people and forget about what I looked like. I could serve Christ through being a nurse. This way I would still be in good with God. I moved back to the Midwest and I joined a new church in Chicago. A New Testament church. All of us attempting to follow Christ's recommendations for living on earth. Love one another and be involved in one another's lives. Take care of your brothers and sisters. It was total bullshit. None of it actually happened, it was just a lot of talk. Some people tried. But they never succeeded."

"So what brought the Christianity to an end?"

"Well, I was working in a hospital and I started getting more involved with people I was working with. I loved people to take an interest in me because I was a waif. But twenty-five! I was getting old to be a waif. And then a guy I got involved with, a guy named Walter Sweeney, he died. He was thirty-four years old. Very young. Very passionate. Always that. And he decided that God wanted him to go on a fast. Suffering is very big, you see, a certain brand of Christian believes that God allows us to suffer to make us better servants of Him. Getting rid of the dross they call it. Well, Walter Sweeney got rid of the dross, all right. Went on a fast to purify himself. So that he could be closer to God. And he died. I found him in his apartment on his knees. And that always stayed with me, and that became the whole experience for me. Dying on his knees. Fuck that."

"You slept with Walter Sweeney."

"Yep. First one. I was chaste from about fifteen to twenty-five. I wasn't a virgin at fifteen, but from fifteen to twenty-five,

I didn't even have a date. I got involved with Sweeney, then he died, and I got involved with another guy, a married man in the church. That had a lot to do with it too. Especially because his wife was a good friend of mine. I couldn't live with that. I couldn't face God anymore, so I stopped praying. It wasn't long, maybe a couple of months, but long enough to lose fifteen pounds. I tortured myself about it. I liked the idea of sex. I never could figure out the prohibition on sex. I still can't figure it out. What's the big deal? Who cares? It was senseless to me. I went to a therapist. Because I was suicidal. But he was no good. Christian Interpersonal Therapy Workshop. Guy named Rodney."

"What's Christian Interpersonal Therapy?"

"Oh, it's just Rodney talking to people. More bullshit. But then I met a guy who wasn't a Christian and I got involved with him. And it was gradual. I don't know how to make it any more clear. I grew out of it. In every sense."

"So it's sex that got you out of the church. Men."

"It's probably what got me in and, yeah, probably it helped to get me out."

"You left the world of men and then you came back to the world of men. That's the story you tell, anyway."

"Well, that was certainly part of the world I left. I also left the world of my dismal family and the world of living chaotically. And then when I was strong enough, I was able to do things on my own. I went to nursing school. That was a big move for me away from Christianity. Part of what Christianity was about for me was about not thinking. About being able to go to the elders and ask them what I should do. And going to God. In my twenties I realized that God doesn't answer. And that the elders are no smarter than I am. That I could think for myself. Still, Christianity saved me from a lot of craziness. It got me back to school, stopped me from doing drugs, from being promiscuous. Who knows where I could have ended up?"

"Here," I said. "Here is where you could have ended up—where you ended up. With him. Living chaotically with him."

You are not here to help her understand herself. Go no further. You are not the Jewish Interpersonal Therapy Workshop. It only looks that way tonight. One patient shows up, spends his hour telling you his favorite lies, then he exits, after exposing himself, and another materializes, takes possession of the pillow, and begins telling *her* favorite lies. The storification of everyday life, the poetry you hear on the Phil Donahue show, stuff *she* probably hears on the Donahue show, and I sit here as if I hadn't heard the fucked-up-shiksa story from the Scheherazade of fucked-up shiksas; as if I hadn't got myself morbidly enfolded in its pathos over thirty years ago, I sit and I listen as though to do so is my fate. In the face of a story, any story, I sit captivated. Either I am listening to them or I am telling them. Everything originates there.

"Christianity saved me from a lot of craziness," she said, "but not from anti-Semitism. I think I really got into hating Jews when I was a Christian. Before, it was just my family's stupid thing. Know why I started hating Jews? Because they didn't have to put up with any of this Christian nonsense. Death to self, you have to kill yourself, suffering makes you a better servant of Him—and they *laughed* at all our suffering. Only allow God to live through you so that you become nothing more than a vessel. So I became nothing more than a vessel while the Jews became doctors and lawyers and rich. They laughed at our suffering, they laughed at *His* suffering. Look, don't get me wrong, I loved being nothing. I mean I loved it and I hated it. I could be what I believed I was, a piece of shit, and get *praised* for it. I wore little plaid skirts, wore my hair in a ponytail, didn't fuck, and meanwhile the Jews were all smart, they were middle class, they were fucking, they were educated, they were down in the Caribbean at Christmastime, and I hated them. That started when I was a Christian, and it just kept growing at the hospital. Now, from A-S.A., I understand why else I hated them. Their cohesiveness, I hated that. Their superiority, what the Gentiles call greed, I hated that. Their paranoia and their defensiveness, always being strategic and careful, always clever—the Jews drove me crazy just by being Jews. Anyway, that was my legacy from Jesus. Until Philip."

"From Jesus to Philip."

"Yeah, looks that way. Done it all over again, haven't I? With him." She sounded amazed. An amazing experience and it was hers.

And mine? From Jesus to Philip—to Philip. From Jesus to

Walter Sweeney to Rodney to Philip to Philip. I am the next apocalyptic solution.

"And it's only just dawning on you here," I asked, "that he might constitute a bit of a relapse?"

"I was coasting along, you see, winging along there, being a nurse, seven years—I told you about all that, I told you about killing somebody—"

"Yes, you did."

"But with him I didn't know how to get *out*. I *never* know how to get out. One guy is battier than the other and I don't know how to get out. My trouble is I get very passionate and ecstatic. It takes me a long time to get disillusioned with the whole unreality of everything. I guess I was still loving people taking an interest in me the way he took an interest in my anti-Semitism. Yeah, he *did* take over from Jesus. He was going to purify me like the church. I need it black and white, I guess. There's really very little that is black and white, and I realize that the whole world is nothing but gray areas, but these mad dogmatic people, they're kind of protection, you know?"

"Who is he? Who is this mad dogmatic person?"

"He's not a crook, he's not a fake, you're all wrong thinking that. His whole *life* is the Jews."

"Who is he, Wanda Jane?"

"Yeah, Wanda Jane. That's me. Perfect little Wanda Jane, who has to be invisible and a servant. Jinx the Battler, Jinx the Amazon, Jinx who thinks for herself, who answers for herself, who makes decisions for herself and stands up for herself, Jinx who holds the dying in her arms and watches every kind of suffering a human being can suffer, Jinx Possesski who's afraid of nothing and is like an Earth Mother to her dying people, and Wanda Jane who is nothing and is afraid of everything. Don't call me Wanda Jane. It's not funny. It reminds me of those people I once lived with in Ohio. You know who I always hated more than the Jews? Want to know my secret? I hated the fucking Christians. I ran and ran and ran until all I did was circle back. Is that what everybody does or just me? Catholicism goes very deep. And the craziness and the stupidity goes very deep. God! Jesus! Judaism makes my third great religion and I'm still not even thirty-five. I got a ways to go yet with God. I ought to sashay over tomorrow to the Muhammadans

and sign on with them. They sound like they got it all together. Great on women. The *Bible*. I didn't *read* the Bible—I
would *open* the Bible and *point*, and whatever phrase I was
pointing at would give me an answer. An answer! It was *games*.
The whole thing is lunatic games. Yet I freed myself. I did it. I
got better. I got born again as an atheist. Hallelujah. So life
isn't perfect and I was an anti-Semite. If that was the worst
that I wound up, given where I began, that was a *victory*, for
God's sake. Who doesn't have something they hate? Who was
I harming? A nurse who shot off her mouth about Jews. So
what. Live with it. But, no, still couldn't bear being their offspring, still couldn't stand anything if it came from Ohio, and
this is how I got involved with Philip and A-S.A. I've just spent
a year with a lunatic Jew. *And didn't know it.* Wanda Jane
didn't know it until he got on the phone one hour ago and put
in a call to Meir Kahane, to the absolute king of religious nuts,
to the Jewish Avenger himself. I'm sitting in Jerusalem, in a
hotel room, with three crazy bastards in skullcaps screaming all
at once for Philip to write down Demjanjuk's confession,
screaming where they are going to take Demjanjuk's son and
how they are going to cut him up into little pieces and mail
him back to his dad, and *still* I don't understand. Not until he
puts in that call to Kahane's number does it dawn on me that I
am living an anti-Semite's nightmare. Everything I learned at
A-S.A., right down the tube. A roomful of screaming Jews
plotting to murder a Gentile child—my Polish grandfather
who drove the tractor used to tell me that that's what they did
all the *time* back in Poland! Maybe you intellectuals can turn
your noses up at this stuff and think that it's all beneath you,
but all this crazy stuff you think is trashy lies is just more life to
me. Crazy stuff's what most people I've known live with every
day. It's Walter Sweeney all over again. Dying on his knees—
and I found him there. Imagine what *that* was like. You know
what my Philip said when I told him about finding Walter
Sweeney praying on his knees and dead of starvation? 'Christianity,' he said, '*goyische nachis*,' and he spat. I just go from
one to the next. Rodney. Want to know what it was, Rodney's
Christian Interpersonal Therapy? A guy who hadn't even graduated high school, and Wanda Jane goes to *him* for therapy.
Well, I got therapy, all right. Yeah, you guessed it. Don't talk

to me about that penile implant. Don't make me talk about *that.*"

When she said "implant," I thought of the way an explorer, concluding his epochal voyage, claims all the land he sees for the crown by implanting the royal flag—before they send him back in chains and he is beheaded for treason. "You might as well tell me everything," I said.

"But you think everything is *lies* when it's true, so terribly, terribly, terribly *true.*"

"Tell me about the implant."

"He got it for me."

"That I can believe."

She was crying now. Rolling down her cheeks were plump tears that had all the fullness of her own beautifully upholstered frame, an embattled child's enormous outpouring of pent-up tears, attesting to a tender nature that was simply indisputable now even to me. This raving madman had somehow got himself a wonderful woman, an out-and-out saint with a wonderful heart whose selfless life had gone monstrously wrong.

"He was afraid," she said. "He wept and wept. It was so awful. He was going to lose me to some other man, a man who could still do it. He was going to lose me, he said. I would leave him all alone to die in agony with the cancer—and how could I say no? How can Wanda Jane say no when someone is suffering like that? How can a nurse who has seen all I've seen say no to a penile implant if that is going to give him the strength to fight on? Sometimes I think that I am the only one who follows the teachings of our Lord. That's what I sometimes think when I feel him pushing that thing inside me."

"And who is he? Tell me who he is."

"Another fucked-up Jewish boy. The fucked-up shiksa's fucked-up Jewish boyfriend, a wild, hysterical animal, that's who he is. That's who I am. That's who we are. Everything's about his mother."

"Not really."

"His mother didn't love him enough."

"But that's out of my book, isn't it?"

"I wouldn't know."

"I wrote a book, a hundred years ago."

"I know *that*. But I don't read. He gave it to me but I didn't read it. I have to hear the words. That was the hardest part of school, the reading. I have a lot of trouble with my *d*'s and *b*'s."

"As in 'double'."

"I'm dyslexic."

"You've had a lot to overcome, haven't you?"

"You can say that again."

"Tell me about his mother."

"She used to lock him out of the house. On the landing out-side their apartment. He was all of five years old. 'You don't live here anymore.' That's what she would tell him. 'You are not our little boy. You belong to somebody else.'"

"Where was this? In what city? Where was the father in all this?"

"Don't know, he doesn't say anything about the father. All he ever says is that he was always locked out by the mother."

"But what had he done?"

"Who knows? Assault. Armed robbery. Murder. Crimes beyond description. I guess the mother knew. He used to set his jaw and wait on the landing for her to open up. But she was as stubborn as he was and wouldn't give in. A little five-year-old boy was not going to be in charge of *her*. A sad story, isn't it? Then it got dark. That's when he folded. He'd start to whimper like a dog and beg for his dinner. She'd say, 'Get din-ner from the people you belong to.' Then he'd beg to be for-given six or seven times more and she would figure he was broken enough and open up the door. Philip's whole child-hood is about that door."

"So this is what made the outlaw."

"Is it? I thought it's what made the detective."

"Might be what made both. The angry boy outside the door, overcome by helplessness. Unjust persecution. What a rage must have boiled up in that five-year-old child. What de-fiance must have been born in him out there on that landing. The thing excluded. Cast out. Banished. The family monster. I am alone and despicable. No, that's not my book, I don't go anywhere like that far. I believe he got that from another book. The infant put out by his parents to perish. Ever hear of *Oedi-pus Rex*?"

Can I help it if I felt tickled with adoration for this beguiling woman on my bed when she said to me, gaily, with the Mae West slyness in her voice of the woman rich with amorous surprises, "Honey, even us dyslexics know about *Oedipus Rex*."

"I don't know what to make of you," I said, truthfully.

"It's not easy to know what to make of you, either."

A pause followed, filled with fantasies of our future together. A long, long pause and a long, long look, from the chair to the bed and back.

"So. How did he settle on me?" I asked.

"How?" She laughed. "You're joking."

"Yes, how?" I was laughing now too.

"Look in the mirror someday. Who else was he going to settle on, Michael Jackson? I can't *believe* you two. I see you guys coming and going. Look, don't think this has been easy for me. It's totally weird. I think I'm dreaming."

"Well, not totally. It took *some* doing on his part."

"Well, not much." And that's when I got that particular smile again, that slow curling upward at the corner of the mouth that was to me the epitome of sexual magic, as I've said. It has to be clear even to a small child reading this confession that from the moment I'd pushed back the bureau and let her slip into my room in that dress, I had been struggling to neutralize her erotic attraction and to eradicate the carnal thoughts aroused in me by the desperate, disheveled look of her recumbent on my bed. Don't think it'd been easy for me, honey, when she'd moaned in a whisper, "Put me in your bag and take me with you." But while drinking in the roman-fleuve of her baffled quest for guardianship (among the Protestants, the Catholics, and the Jews), I had maintained as best I could the maximum skepticism. Charm there was, admittedly, but her verbal authority was really not great, and I told myself that, in any circumstance less drastic than this (if, say, I'd sidled up to her at one of those Chicago singles bars when she was a nurse hanging out), after five minutes of listening I would have been hard put not to try my luck with someone who wasn't being endlessly reborn. Yet, all this said, the effect of her smile was to make me tumescent.

I *didn't* know what to make of her. A woman forged by the commonplace at its most cruelly ridiculous smiles up from a hotel bed at a man who has every reason in the world to be nowhere near her, a man to whom she is the mate in no way whatsoever, and the man is underground with Persephone. You are in awe of eros's mythological depths when something like that happens to you. What Jung calls "the uncontrollability of real things," what a registered nurse just calls "life."

"We aren't indistinguishable, you know."

"That word. That's the word. He uses it a hundred times a day. 'We're indistinguishable.' He's looking in the mirror and that's what he says—'We're indistinguishable.'"

"Well, we're not," I informed her, "not by a long shot."

"No? What is it then, you've got a different Life line? I do palmistry. I learned it once, hitchhiking. I read palms instead of books."

And I did next the stupidest thing I'd yet done in Jerusalem and perhaps in my entire life. I got up from the chair by the window and stepped across to the bed and took hold of the hand that she was extending. I placed my hand in hers, in the nurse's hand that had been everywhere, the nurse's tabooless, transgressive hand, and she ran her thumb lightly along my palm and then palpated in turn each of its cushioned corners. For at least a full minute she said only, "Ummm . . . ummm . . . ," all the while carefully studying my hand. "It's not surprising," she finally told me very, very quietly, as though not to awaken a third person in the bed, "that the Head line is surprisingly long and deep. Your Head line is the strongest line in the hand. It's a Head line dominated by imagination rather than by money or heart or reason or intellect. There's a strong warlike component to your Fate line. Your Fate line sort of rises in the Mount of Mars. You actually have three Fate lines. Which is very unusual. Most people don't have any."

"How many does your boyfriend have?"

"Only one."

And I was thinking, If you want to get killed, if you are determined to die on your knees like Walter Sweeney, then this is the way to get the job done. This palm reader is his treasure. This recovering anti-Semite fingering your Fate line is that madman's prize!

"All of these lines from the Mount of Venus into your Life

line indicate how deeply you're ruled by your passions. The deep, deep clear lines on this part of the hand—see?—intersect with the Life line. They actually aren't crossed, which means that rather than passion bringing you misfortune, it doesn't. If they were crossed, I'd say that in you sexual appetite leads to decadence and corruption. But that's not true. Your sexual appetite is quite pure."

"What do you know," I replied, thinking, Do this and he will hunt you down to the ends of the earth and kill you. You should have fled. You didn't need her answers to all your questions. Her answers are as useless to you if they are true as they are if they are false. This is his trap, I thought, just as she looked up into my face with that smile that was *her* Fate line and said, "It's all such complete bullshit but it's sort of fun—you know?" Stop. Breathe. Think. She believes you are in possession of Smilesburger's million and is simply changing sides. Anything could be happening and you'd be the last to know.

"It's sort of the hand of a . . . I mean if I didn't know anything about you, if I were reading the hands of a stranger and didn't know who you were, I would say it's sort of the hand of a . . . of a great leader."

I should have fled. Instead I implanted myself and then I fled. I penetrated her and I ran. Both. Talk about the commonplace at its most ridiculous.

8

The Uncontrollability of Real Things

HERE is the Pipik plot so far.

A middle-aged American Jew settles into a suite at Jerusalem's King David Hotel and proposes publicly that Israeli Jews of Ashkenazi descent, who make up the more influential half of the country's population and who constituted the original cadre that settled the state, return to their countries of origin to resurrect the European Jewish life that Hitler all but annihilated between 1939 and 1945. He argues that this post-Zionist political program, which he has called "Diasporism," is the only means by which to avert a "second Holocaust," in which either the three million Jews of Israel will be massacred by their Arab enemies or the enemies will be decimated by Israeli nuclear weapons, a victory that, like a defeat, would destroy the moral foundations of Jewish life for good. He believes that, with assistance from traditional Jewish philanthropic sources, he can raise the money and marshal the political will of influential Jews everywhere to institute and realize this program by the year 2000. He justifies his hopefulness by alluding to the history of Zionism and comparing his supposedly unattainable dream to the Herzlian plan for a Jewish state, which, in its own time, struck Herzl's numerous Jewish critics as contemptibly ludicrous, if not insane. He concedes the troubling persistence of a substantial anti-Semitic European population but proposes to implement a massive recovery program that will rehabilitate those several tens of millions still powerless before the temptations of traditional anti-Semitism and enable them to learn to control their antipathy to their Jewish compatriots once the Jews have been rerooted in Europe. He calls the organization that will implement this program Anti-Semites Anonymous and is accompanied on his proselytizing fund-raising travels by a member of the charter chapter of A-S.A., an American nurse of Polish and Irish Catholic extraction, who identifies herself as a "recovering anti-Semite" and who came to be influenced by his ideology when he was her cancer patient in the Chicago hospital where she worked.

The champion of Diasporism and founder of A-S.A. turns out to have had a prior career as a private detective, running his own small agency in Chicago, which specialized in missing-persons cases. His involvement with political ideas and his concern for the survival of the Jews and of Jewish ideals seems to date from the cancer battle, when he felt himself summoned to dedicate to a higher calling whatever life remained to him. (In addition, the conviction of the American Jew Jonathan Pollard as an Israeli spy sensitively positioned within the U.S. defense establishment—and Pollard's coldhearted abandonment by his Israeli Secret Service handlers the moment his operation was compromised—seems to have had a strong effect on the formulation of his ideas, consolidating his fears for Diaspora Jewry so long as they are an expendable, exploitable resource to a Jewish state that, as he sees it, Machiavellianly exacts from them unquestioning loyalty.) Little is known of his earlier life other than that, as a young man, he conscientiously set out to disassociate himself from any social or vocational role that might mark him as a Jew. His acolyte mistress has spoken of a mother who disciplined him pitilessly as a small child, but otherwise his biography is a blank and, even in its sketchy outline, seems a story patched together by the same unhistorical imagination that dreamed up the improbabilities and exaggerations of Diasporism.

Now it so happens that this man bears a decided physical resemblance to the American writer Philip Roth, claims that Philip Roth is his name as well, and is not averse to playing upon this unaccountable, if not utterly fantastical, coincidence to foster the belief that he *is* the author and thus to advance the cause of Diasporism. Through this subterfuge he is able to convince Louis B. Smilesburger, an elderly, disabled Holocaust victim who has retired unhappily to Jerusalem after having made his fortune as a New York jeweler, to contribute to him one million dollars. But, when Smilesburger sets out to deliver the check personally to the Diasporist Philip Roth, who should he come upon but the writer Philip Roth, who had arrived in Jerusalem just two days earlier to interview the Israeli novelist Aharon Appelfeld. The writer is having lunch with Appelfeld at a Jerusalem café when Smilesburger locates him there and, mistakenly imagining that the writer and the Diasporist are one, approaches the wrong man with the check.

By this time the paths of the two look-alikes have already crossed not far from the Jerusalem courtroom where John Demjanjuk, a Ukrainian American autoworker extradited to Israel from Cleveland by the U.S. Department of Justice, is on trial, accused of being the sadistic Treblinka guard and mass murderer of Jews known to his victims as Ivan the Terrible. This trial and the uprising against the Israeli government by the Arabs in the Occupied Territories—both events the subject of worldwide media coverage—constitute the turbulent backdrop against which the pair enact their hostile encounters, the first of which results in the writer Roth warning the Diasporist Roth that unless the impostor immediately repudiates his false identity he will be brought before the authorities on criminal charges.

The writer, still smarting from the inflammatory meeting with the Diasporist when Mr. Smilesburger appears at the café, impulsively pretends to be who he has been taken to be (himself!) and accepts Mr. Smilesburger's envelope without, of course, realizing when he does so the improbable size of the donation. Later that day, following a perturbing visit, with a Palestinian friend from his graduate school days, to an Israeli court in occupied Ramallah (where the writer is again mistaken for the Diasporist and, to his own astonished dismay, not only allows the error to go unnoted for a second time but, afterward, at his friend's home, fortifies it with an implausible lecture *extolling* Diasporism), he, the writer, loses the Smilesburger check (or it is confiscated) when a platoon of Israeli soldiers conducts a frightening search of the writer and his Arab driver as they are headed erratically back in a taxicab along the road from Ramallah to Jerusalem early that evening.

The writer, who some seven months earlier had suffered a frightening nervous breakdown presumably generated by a hazardous sleeping medication prescribed in the aftermath of a botched-up minor surgical procedure, is so perplexed by all these events and by his own incongruously self-subverting behavior in response to them that he begins to fear that he is headed for a relapse. The implausibility of so much that is happening even causes him, in an extreme moment of disorientation, to ask himself if any of it *is* happening and if he is not in his rural Connecticut home living through one of those hallucinatory episodes whose unimpeachable persuasiveness had brought him close to committing suicide the summer before. His control over himself begins to seem nearly as tenuous to him as his influence over the other Philip Roth, whom, in fact, he refuses to think of as "the other Philip Roth" or the "impostor" or his "double" but instead takes to calling Moishe Pipik, a benignly deflating Yiddish nickname out of the daily comedy of his humble childhood world that translates literally to Moses Bellybutton and that he hopes will at least serve to curb his own perhaps paranoid assessment of the other one's dangerousness and power.

On the road from Ramallah, the writer is rescued from the soldiers' hair-raising ambush by a young officer in charge of the platoon, who has recognized him as the author of a book he happened to have been reading that very day. To make amends to the writer for the unwarranted assault, Gal, the lieutenant, personally drives him by jeep back to his hotel in the Arab quarter of East Jerusalem, voluntarily confessing along the way—to one he clearly holds in high esteem—his own grave qualms about his unconscionable position as an instrument of Israeli military policy. In response, the writer launches into a renewed exposition of Diasporism, which strikes him as no less ludicrous than the lecture he gave in Ramallah but which he delivers in the jeep with undiminished fervor.

At the hotel the writer discovers that Moishe Pipik, having easily misled the desk clerk into thinking that he is Philip Roth, has gained access to his room and is waiting there for him on his bed. Pipik demands that Roth hand over to him the Smilesburger check. An agitated exchange follows; there is a calm, deceptively friendly, even intimate, interlude, during which Pipik discloses his adventures as a Chicago private detective, but Pipik's anger erupts once again when the writer reiterates that the Smilesburger check is lost, and the episode concludes with Pipik, seething with rage and overcome by hysteria, exposing his erection to the writer as he is pushed and pummeled out of the room and into the hotel corridor.

So overwrought is the writer by this burgeoning chaos that

he decides to flee Israel on the morning plane to London and, after barricading his door as much against his ineptitude in the face of Pipik's provocations as against Pipik's return, he sits down at the desk by the window of his room to compose a few final questions for the Appelfeld interview, which he plans to leave with Appelfeld when he departs at dawn for the airport. From the window he is able to observe several hundred Israeli soldiers, in a nearby cul-de-sac, boarding buses that will transport them to the rioting West Bank towns. Directly below the hotel, he sees half a dozen masked Arab men stealthily racing back and forth, moving rocks from one end of the street to the other; after completing his questions for Appelfeld, he decides that he must report this rock running to the Israeli authorities.

However, no sooner does he attempt, without success, to place a call to the police than he hears Pipik's consort whispering tearfully to him from the other side of his barricaded door, explaining that Pipik, whom she gallingly persists in calling Philip, is back at the King David Hotel plotting with Orthodox Jewish militants to kidnap Demjanjuk's son and to hold him and mutilate him until Demjanjuk confesses to being Ivan the Terrible. She slides beneath the door a cloth star of the kind European Jews were forced to wear for identification during the war years, and when she tells the writer that Moishe Pipik has worn the star beneath his clothes ever since it was given to him as a present by Lech Walesa in Gdansk, the writer is so affronted that he loses emotional control and once again finds himself swallowed up in the very madness from which he had determined to disengage himself by running away.

On the condition that she disclose to him Moishe Pipik's true identity, he unbarricades the door and lets her slip into the room. It turns out that she is herself in flight from Pipik and has crossed Jerusalem to call on the writer not so much in the expectation of recovering Smilesburger's check, although she at first makes a feeble attempt at just that, or of persuading the writer to prevent the kidnapping of young Demjanjuk but in the hope of finding asylum from the "anti-Semite's nightmare" in which, paradoxically, she has been ensnared by the zealot she cannot stop nursing. Tantalizingly stretched (outstretched, stretched out, sprawled, surrendered) across the writer's hotel bed—hers now the second unlikely head to seek restitution on his pillow that night—and wearing a low-fashion dress that makes the writer as uncertain of her motives as of his own, she spins a tale of lifelong servitude and serial transformations: from the unloved Catholic child of bigoted ignoramuses into the mindless promiscuous hippie waif, from the mindless promiscuous hippie waif into the chaste fundamentalist stupefyingly subjugated to Jesus, from the chaste fundamentalist stupefyingly subjugated to Jesus into a death-poisoned Jew-hating oncology nurse, from a death-poisoned Jew-hating oncology nurse into an obedient recovering anti-Semite . . . and from this last way station on the journey out of Ohio, from this to what new self-mortification? What metamorphosis next for Wanda Jane "Jinx" Possesski and, too, for the mentally woozy, emotionally depleted, nutrient-deprived, erotically bedazzled writer who, having most rashly implanted himself inside her, discovers himself, even more perilously, half in love with her?

This is the plot up to the moment when the writer leaves the woman still dolefully enmeshed in it, and, suitcase in hand, tiptoeing so as not to disturb her postcoital rest, he himself slips silently out of the plot on the grounds of its general implausibility, a total lack of gravity, reliance at too many key points on unlikely coincidence, an absence of inner coherence, and not even the most tenuous evidence of anything resembling a serious meaning or purpose. The story so far is frivolously plotted, overplotted, for his taste altogether too freakishly plotted, with outlandish events so wildly careening around every corner that there is nowhere for intelligence to establish a foothold and develop a perspective. As if the look-alike at the story's storm center isn't farfetched enough, there is the capricious loss of the Smilesburger check (there is the fortuitous appearance of the Smilesburger check; there is Louis B. Smilesburger himself, Borscht Belt deus ex machina), which sets the action on its unconvincing course and serves to reinforce the writer's sense that the story has been intentionally conceived as a prank, and a nasty prank at that, considering the struggles of Jewish existence that are said to be at issue by his antagonist.

And what, if anything, is there of consequence about the antagonist who has conceived it? What in his self-presentation warrants his consideration as a figure of depth or dimension?

The macho livelihood. The penile implant. The ridiculously transparent impersonation. The grandiose rationale. The labile personality. The hysterical monomania. The chicanery, the anguish, the nurse, the creepy pride in being "indistinguishable" —all of it adding up to someone *trying* to be real without any idea of how to go about it, someone who knows neither how to be fictitious—and persuasively pass himself off as someone he is not—nor how to actualize himself in life as he is. He can no more portray himself as a whole, harmonious character or establish himself as a perplexing, indecipherable puzzle or even simply exist as an unpredictable satiric force than he can generate a plot of sequential integrity that an adult reader can contemplate seriously. His being as an antagonist, his being *altogether*, is wholly dependent on the writer, from whom he parasitically pirates what meager selfhood he is able to make even faintly credible.

But why, in exchange, does the writer pirate from *him?* This is the question plaguing the writer as his taxi carries him safely through Jerusalem's western hills and onto the highway for the airport. It would be comforting for him to believe that his impersonation of his impersonator springs from an aesthetic impulse to intensify the being of this hollow antagonist and apprehend him imaginatively, to make the objective subjective and the subjective objective, which is, after all, no more than what writers are paid to do. It would be comforting to understand his performances in Ramallah with George and in the jeep with Gal—as well as the passionate session locked up with the nurse, culminating in that wordless vocal obbligato with which she'd flung herself upon the floodtide of her pleasure, the streaming throaty rising and falling, at once husky and murmurous, somewhere between the trilling of a tree toad and the purring of a cat, that luxuriantly articulated the blissful climax and that still sounded sirenishly in his ears all those hours later—as the triumph of a plucky, spontaneous, audacious vitality over paranoia and fear, as a heartening manifestation of an artist's inexhaustible playfulness and of an irrepressibly comic fitness for life. It would be comforting to think that those episodes encapsulate whatever true freedom of spirit is his, that embodied in the impersonation is the distinctively personal form that his fortitude takes and that he has no reason at this stage of life to be bewildered by or ashamed of. It would be comforting to think that, far from having pathologically toyed with an explosive situation (with George, Gal, or Jinx) or having been polluted by an infusion of the very extremism by which he feels so menaced and from which he is now in flight, he has answered the challenge of Moishe Pipik with exactly the parodic defiance it warrants. It would be comforting to think that, within the confines of a plot over which he's had no authorial control, he has not demeaned or disgraced himself unduly and that his serious blunders and miscalculations have resulted largely from a sentimental excess of compassion for his enemy's ailments rather than from a mind (his own) too unhinged by the paranoid threat to be able to think out an effective counterplot in which to subsume the Pipikesque imbecility. It would be comforting, it would be only natural, to assume that in a narrative contest (in the realistic mode) with this impostor, the real writer would easily emerge as inventive champion, scoring overwhelming victories in Sophistication of Means, Subtlety of Effects, Cunningness of Structure, Ironic Complexity, Intellectual Interest, Psychological Credibility, Verbal Precision, and Overall Verisimilitude; but instead the Jerusalem Gold Medal for Vivid Realism has gone to a narrative klutz who takes the cake for wholesale indifference to the traditional criteria for judgment in every category of the competition. His artifice is phony to the core, a hysterical caricature of the art of illusion, hyperbole fueled by perversity (and perhaps even insanity), exaggeration as the principle of invention, everything progressively overdrawn, super-simplified, divorced from the concrete evidence of the mind and the senses—and yet he wins! Well, let him. See him not as a terrifying incubus insufficiently existent who manufactures his being cannibalistically, not as a demoniacal amnesiac who is hiding from himself in you and can only experience himself if he experiences himself as someone else, not as something half-born or half-dead or half-crazed or half-charlatan/half-psychopath—see this bisected thing as the achievement that he is and grant him the victory graciously. The plot that prevails is Pipik's. He wins, you lose, go home—better to relinquish the Medal for Vivid Realism, however unjustly, to fifty percent of a man than to be defeated in the struggle for

recovery of your own stability and to wind up again fifty percent of yourself. Demjanjuk's son will or will not be kidnapped
and tortured through Pipik's plotting whether you remain in
Jerusalem or are back in London. Should it happen while
you're here, the newspaper stories will bear not only your
name as the perpetrator but your picture and your bio in a
sidebar; if you are not here, however, if you are there, then
there will be a minimum of confusion all around when he is
tracked to his Dead Sea cave and caught with the captive and
with his bearded accomplices. That he is determined to actualize a thought that merely passed through your mind when you
first saw young Demjanjuk unprotected cannot possibly im-
pute culpability to you, however strenuously *he* attributes to
you the prize-winning plot and claims, once his interrogation
begins, merely to be the Chicago hired gun, the private detective engaged for a fee to enact, as stand-in, as stuntman, your
drastic self-intoxicated melodrama of justice and revenge. Of
course, there will be those who will be only too thrilled to
believe him. It won't be hard for them either: they'll blame it
(compassionately, no doubt) on your Halcion madness the
way Jekyll blame Hyde on his drugs; they'll say, "He never recovered from that breakdown and this was the result. It had to
be the breakdown—not even he was that dreadful a novelist."

But I never did escape from this plot-driven world into a more
congenial, subtly probable, innerly propelled narrative of my
own devising—didn't make it to the airport, didn't even get as
far as Aharon's house—and that was because in the taxi I remembered a political cartoon I'd seen in the British papers
when I was living in London during the Lebanon war, a de-
testable cartoon of a big-nosed Jew, his hands meekly opened
out in front of him and his shoulders raised in a shrug as
though to disavow responsibility, standing atop a pyramid
of dead Arab bodies. Purportedly a caricature of Menachem
Begin, then prime minister of Israel, the drawing was, in fact, a
perfectly realistic, unequivocal depiction of a kike as classically
represented in the Nazi press. This cartoon was what turned
me around. Barely ten minutes out of Jerusalem I told the
driver to take me back to the King David Hotel. I thought,
When he starts slicing off the boy's toes and mailing them one

at a time to Demjanjuk's cell, the *Guardian* will have a field day. Demjanjuk's lawyers had already challenged the integrity of the proceedings publicly, daring to announce to three Jewish judges in a Jewish courtroom that the prosecution of John Demjanjuk for crimes committed at Treblinka had the characteristics of nothing less than the Dreyfus trial. Wouldn't the kidnapping dramatically underscore this claim as it was even less delicately made by Demjanjuk's Ukrainian supporters in America and Canada and by his defenders, left- and right-wing, in the Western press—namely that it was impossible for anyone with a name suffixed *juk* to receive justice from Jews, that Demjanjuk was the Jews' scapegoat, that the Jewish state was a lawless state, that the "show trial" convened in Jerusalem was intended to perpetuate the self-justifying Jewish myth of victimization, that revenge alone was the Jews' objective? To drum up world sympathy for their client and to bolster their allegations of bias and prejudgment, Demjanjuk's supporters could not themselves have hit on a publicity stunt more brilliant than the one that Moishe Pipik was planning to perform in order to vent his rage with me.

If it hadn't been so infuriatingly clear that it was I who was the challenge he meant to defy, that this crazy kidnapping, potentially damaging to a cause perhaps even more poignant than his own, originated in his single-minded fixation on me, I might have told the driver to take me not to the King David Hotel but directly to the Jerusalem police. If it hadn't seemed to me that I had been humiliatingly outfoxed at every turn by an adversary who was in no way my equal and that I had compounded my ineptness by unthinkingly accepting Smilesburger's check—and subsequently elaborated on that error by failing to grasp the scale of the West Bank conflict and getting myself caught after dark on the Ramallah road by an Israeli patrol in no mood to observe the niceties of a legal search—I might not have felt that it was now incumbent on me, and on me alone, to face down this bastard once and for all. This is as far as his pathology goes. As far as *mine* goes. I'd overmagnified the menace of him from the start. You don't have to call out the Israeli marines, I told myself, to put an end to Moishe Pipik. He's got a foot in the grave already. All he needs is a little push. It's simple: crush him.

Crush him. I was indignant enough to think that I could. I certainly knew that I should. Our moment had arrived, the face-to-face showdown between just the two of us: the genuine versus the fake, the responsible versus the reckless, the serious versus the superficial, the resilient versus the ravaged, the multiform versus the monomaniacal, the accomplished versus the unfulfilled, the imaginative versus the escapist, the literate versus the unschooled, the judicious versus the fanatic, the essential versus the superfluous, the constructive versus the useless. . . .

The taxi waited for me in the circular drive outside the King David Hotel while, at this early hour, the armed security guard at the hotel door accompanied me to the front desk. I repeated to the desk clerk what I'd told the guard: Mr. Roth was expecting me.

The clerk smiled. "Your brother."

I nodded.

"Twin."

I nodded again. Why not?

"He is gone. No longer with us." He looked at the clock on the wall. "Your brother left half an hour ago."

Meema Gitcha's words exactly!

"They all left?" I asked. "Our Orthodox cousins, too?"

"He was alone, sir."

"No. Couldn't be. I was to meet him here with our cousins. Three bearded men in yarmulkes."

"Not tonight, Mr. Roth."

"They didn't show up," I said.

"I don't believe so, sir."

"And he's gone. At four-thirty. And not coming back. No message for me."

"Nothing, sir."

"Did he say where he was going?"

"I believe to Romania."

"At four-thirty in the morning. Of course. And did Meir Kahane visit my brother tonight, by any chance? You know who I mean? Rabbi Meir Kahane?"

"I know who Rabbi Kahane is, sir. Rabbi Kahane was not in the hotel."

I asked if I might use the pay phone across the lobby. I

dialed the American Colony and asked for my old room. I had told the clerk there, after paying the bill, that my wife was asleep and would be leaving in the morning. But it turned out that she had left already.

"You're sure?" I asked him.

"Mister and Missus. They're both gone."

I hung up, waited a minute, and phoned the hotel again.

"Mr. Demjanjuk's room," I said.

"Who is calling, please?"

"This is the jail calling."

A moment later I heard an anxious, sharp "Hello?"

"You all right?" I asked.

"Hello? Who is this? Who *is* this?"

He was there, I was here, they were gone. I hung up. They were gone, he was safe. They'd fled their *own* plot!

And that plot's purpose? Only larceny? Or was the whole hoax merely that, a hoax, two crazy X's off on a lark?

Standing at the phone and thinking that this entire mishap might just have come to a sudden end, I was more mystified than ever, wondering if these were two X's who were themselves escaping the world or two X's whom the world itself was escaping or two X's who'd only been falsifying everything so as to befuddle me . . . though why that should be a goal of anyone's was the most mystifying question of all. And it looked now as though I'd probably never know the answer—and as though what had enthralled me from the start was the question! Had they wanted only me to think that all their falseness was real, or had they themselves imagined it to be real, or was their excitement in creating the Pirandellian effect by derealizing everything and everyone, beginning with themselves? Some hoax *that* was!

I returned to the front desk. "I'll take my brother's room."

"Let me give you a room that has not been occupied, sir."

I pulled a fifty-dollar bill from my wallet. "His will be just fine."

"Your passport, please, Mr. Roth."

"Our parents liked the name so much," I explained, passing it across the counter with the fifty, "that they gave it to both of us."

I waited while he examined my photograph and recorded the passport number in the registration book. He handed the passport back to me without any comment. I then filled out the registration card and received the key to suite 511. The security guard had meanwhile returned to the front door of the hotel. I gave him twenty dollars to pay the taxi driver and told him to keep the change for himself.

For the next half hour, until it was dawn, I searched Pipik's room and found nothing in any of the drawers, nothing on the desk, no notes on the notepad, no magazines or newspapers left behind, nothing beneath the bed, nothing behind the cushions of the armchair, nothing hanging in the closet or lying on the closet floor. When I peeled back the bedspread and the blanket, the sheets and pillowcases were freshly ironed and smelled still of the laundry. No one had slept there since housekeeping had made up the room the previous morning. The towels in the bathroom were also fresh. Only when I lifted the toilet seat did I find a trace of his occupancy. A kinked spiral of dark pubic hair about the size of a fourteen-point ampersand adhered to the enamel rim of the bowl. I tweezed it loose between two fingernails and deposited it into a hotel envelope from the stationery drawer of the desk. I searched the bathroom floor for a strand of her hair, an eyelash, a snippet of toenail, but the tiles had been swept spotlessly clean—nothing there either. I got up off my knees to wash my hands in the sink, and it was there that I discovered along the lip of the basin, just beneath the hot-water tap, the minute filings of a man's beard. I blotted them carefully into a square of toilet tissue—a scattering of maybe ten filings in all—folded the tissue in quarters, and put it into a second envelope. The filings could, of course, have been anyone's—they could even have been my own; he could have found them when *he* was snooping around *my* hotel bathroom and, to *seal* our oneness, transferred them here to his. Having done everything else he'd done, why not that too? Perhaps even the pubic hair was mine. It certainly could have passed for mine, but then, with coils of stray pubic hair, it's difficult often, using just the naked eye, to distinguish exactly whose is whose. Still, I took it—if he could disguise himself as the writer, I could pretend to be the detective.

These two envelopes, along with the cloth star and his handwritten "Ten Tenets of A-S.A.," are beside me on the desk as I write, here to attest to the tangibility of a visitation that even I must be continually reassured was only cloaked in the appearance of a nonsensical, crude, phantasmagorical farce. These envelopes and their contents remind me that the spectral, half-demented *appearance* was, in fact, the very earmark of its indisputable lifelike realness and that, when life looks least like what it's supposed to look like, it may then be most like whatever it is.

I also have here the audiotape cassette that, to my astonishment, I found when I went to play one of Aharon Appelfeld's taped conversations with me on my return to London. It had been inserted in the very tape recorder that I'd locked away in the hotel closet at the American Colony and that I hadn't opened or used since I'd stolen with my bag out of that room, leaving Jinx asleep in the bed. There is no way for me to explain how the cassette had got placed into my machine before I'd returned to the room other than to think that Pipik had picked the closet lock using the skills he had acquired as a tracer of missing persons. The handwriting on the label that looks so like mine is, of course, his; so is the voice babbling the toxic babble of the people who destroyed almost everything, the maddening, diseased, murderous arraignment that only *sounds* unreal. The label reads: "A-S.A. Workout Tape #2. 'Did the Six Million Really Die?' Copyright Anti-Semites Anonymous, 1988. All rights reserved."

I leave it to readers of this confession to conjecture about his purpose and, in this way perhaps, to share something of the confusion of that week in Jerusalem, the extravagant confusion aroused in me by this "Philip Roth" by whom I was beset, someone about whom (as this recording confirms) it was impossible ever to say just how much of a charlatan he really was.

Here he is, the ritual impersonator, the mask modeled with my features and conveying the general idea of me—here he is, once again, exulting in being somebody else. Within that mouth, how many tongues? Within the man, how many men? How many wounds? How many unendurable wounds!

Did six million really die? Come off it. The Jews pulled a fast one on us again, keeping alive their new religion, Holocaustomania. Read the revisionists. What it really comes down to is *there were no gas chambers*. Jews love numbers. They love to manipulate numbers. Six million. They're not talking about the six million anymore, are they? Auschwitz was mainly a plant to produce synthetic rubber. And that's why it was so evil-smelling. They didn't send them to the gas chamber, they sent them there to work. Because there were no gas chambers, as we now found out. From chemistry. Which is hard science. Freud. That was soft science. Masson over at Berkeley has now proved that Freud's basic research was false because he did not believe these women when they talked about how they were abused. Sexually abused. Because he said society wouldn't accept it. So he changed it to child sexuality. That Siggy. The whole basis of psychoanalysis is false. You can forget that. Einstein, of course, he's been called the bomb father. He and Oppenheimer. Now they're ranting and raving against them—why did you create *that*? So you can forget about Einstein. Marx [*chuckle*], well, you know what happened to Marx. Elie Wiesel. Another Jewish genius. Only no one likes Elie Wiesel. Just like they don't like Saul Bellow. I'll give you five thousand dollars if you find someone around here, in the Chicago area, who likes Saul Bellow. Something wrong with that guy. They know he made a lot of money in real estate. Chicago has the biggest Polish population outside of Warsaw. The Poles are united by three things. The Roman Catholic Church. Fear of Russia. And hatred of the Jews. Why do they hate Jews? The Russian czars constantly sent their bad-ass Jews into Poland and they were money changers, ghetto dwellers. Jews are very ugly people. The nose doctors, etc. Notice the Jew, notice the Jew from the hips down, especially below the knees, they're all fucked up, big, long flat feet, and they have twisted feet and are bowlegged —that's a lot the part of inbreeding. The Jews don't have any friends at all. Even niggers hate Jews. The blacks growing up in the projects see five white people in their life. The Irish or Italian cop—that's changing—they see the Jewish landlord, the Jewish grocer, the Jewish schoolteacher, and the Jewish social worker. Well, of course, their landlord now is the federal government. But they feel the Jews have made a great deal of money from the blacks, but they've never given them anything but a lot of hot air. The niggers turn against Jews, *everyone* turns against Jews. Jews suffer from something called Paget's disease. People don't know about that. Look at Ted Koppel. Look at the other ones. Woody Allen, little dork asshole. Mike Wallace. The bone thickens and their legs get bowed. The women get what is called the Hebrew hump. Their nails get very hard. Hard as rocks. They have a slack in their lower jaw. You notice the Jewesses who are older, they have that slack look in the jaws as if they're a dimwit. That's why they hate us, because we don't have that. Because we remain firm. We might get a little fat. But we remain firm. You know what a Jew is. A Jew's an Arab who was born in Poland. They get heavy. Kissinger. He's got that heavy look. Heavy nose. Heavy features. And that's why they dislike us. Look at Philip Roth, for God's sake. A real ugly buggy. A real asshole. I stopped reading him when he talked about that thing in *My Life as a Man*, when he was just a neurotc fucked-up graduate student at the U. of C.—oh, Jesus, are they ever! Dirty, oh Christ, you see them. He was so hot for shiksas that he grabbed a waitress, a mental case, a divorcée with a couple of kids, he thought this was great. Nitwit. Now he's coming back into the Jewish fold again because he wants to win the Nobel Prize. Jews obviously know how to get it, they got it for Wiesel, Singer, and Bellow. Graham Greene, of course, never got it. Isaac Stern—Mozart, Schubert, Stern just can't cut it. Doesn't understand it. Well, anyway . . . where were we? Hitler had no plan to exterminate the Jews. The Wannsee conference. A. J. P. Taylor's done a lot of work on this, the British historian. He says that the documents don't exist. Hilberg, who is a real Jewish creep, says I can read documents and I know code words—oh, go fuck yourself. [*Chuckle.*] Of course, they're great for code words, symbolisms, numerology—Jewish girls are into numerology, stars, all this other stuff, futurology, they're all screwed up. By the way, the Germans do have the capacity to exterminate people. They didn't have to. They wanted to work the Jews. I would say the Germans do have a cruel streak, but so do we. We exterminated the Indians. But what happened was, they worked them—there were no gas chambers. Six million didn't die. There weren't six million Jews *in* Europe. That's one of the reasons people attack the six million figure. Now it's down to a hundred and fifty to three hundred thousand, and the reason they died was because of the breakdown of the German supply system at the end of the war and because scurvy, typhus just rampaged through the camps. You and I know the State Department didn't want them *here*. No one wanted them *anywhere*. They would appear at the Dutch border, at the Swiss border, they were turned away. No one wanted Jews in their country. Why? The Jew has a tendency—as I say, even niggers hate Jews—the Jew has a tendency to alienate every other group within society. Then when he gets in trouble, he asks people for help. Why should they give it? The Jew came out of the ghetto in eastern Europe during Napoleon's time, he was liberated, and, Christ, he ran rampant. Once they get a lock on things, they keep it. The Jews got a lock on music with Schoenberg. They haven't produced any fuckin' music worth a shit. Hollywood. It's a piece of shit. Why is it? They got a lock on it. We hear about how the Jews created Hollywood. Jews aren't creative. What have they created? Nothing. Painting. Pissarro. Did you ever read Richard Wagner on the Jews? Superficiality. That's why all their art fails. They will not assimilate with the culture in the nation in which they reside. They have superficial popularity, someone like Herman Wouk or that other guy who writes dirty books, that dopey-looking jerk, Mailer, but it doesn't last, because it's not tied to the cultural roots of the society. Saul Bellow is their nominee. Jesus Christ, he's a sad sack, right? [*Chuckle.*] He was wearing his hat—covering his bald head and also to show the world he was a kike [*chuckle*]—when he had the press conference when he won the Nobel Prize. Roth. Roth is just a fuckin' masturbator, a wanker, man, in the john, whackin' off. Arthur Miller. Doesn't he look like a fuckin' junk-man, like a fuckin' junkyard owner? Their fuckin' looks go, man, they really look bad. He always had that big, long look, goofy-lookin' jerk, you know, he'll *defend your right*, whatever the fuck that means. The cultural output from the Jews has been very, very low. Very low and very poor. Well, and of course Wall Street. You know, the arrest of Boesky and the rest of them is a goy plot to discredit the wonderful Jew who has given us our prosperity. It's bullshit. They haven't given us our prosperity. They only exist in a society that's on the brink of having inflation. All their deals are predicated on inflation coming about. If you don't have inflation, if you have deflation, they are fucked. Cultural? Bullshit. They might *own* the cultural institutions but they can't produce anything. Take a look at the shit. Anything vulgar on TV, a Jewish name is on it. Norman Lear, he's one. Hides behind a Gentile name, but there's another one with the bowed legs and the whole gig. Guy I know at the NIH did a study on a whole group of rabbis. About twenty, twenty-five years ago. Said they had specific Jewish diseases. Inbreeding caused these diseases, they've been inbred too much. Nine specific Jewish diseases that hit children —Down's syndrome is one of them. They always hide people like that. Because, you know, Jews are all geniuses. They're all violin players. Nuclear physicists. And of course Wall Street geniuses like Ivan Boesky. [*Snicker, chuckle.*] You know, you never hear about the idiots, which is really because of inbreeding. They're *all* nuts. They continually have children among themselves. But of course Kissinger and so many others, they get married, have two kids, then get rid of her, then they go after their ugly shiksa bookkeeper. [*Sneering chuckle.*] Poor fuckin' sad assholes. Right? Jesus Christ, all the big dough they pay hookers. Well, let's just jump on. First of all, there's a Jewish Mafia. Try to explain to people Jacob Rubinstein, you know him as Jack Ruby, the guy who offed Oswald—well, he was a member of the Jewish Mafia, on the West Side of Chicago. Arthur Miller. He made money off of Marilyn Monroe, he and Billy Wilder, and, who's that other one, Tony Curtis, dragged her into that movie, *Some Like It Hot*, I believe when she was pregnant, and she lost the baby. Watch that movie, she's frankly pregnant. But, of course, Miller had a piece of the film—a real fuckin' scumbag *defending your right.* Really a sea-dwelling slug. The Jews who marry Gentiles are always telling them they're stupid. Had a girlfriend who was married to a Jew. The most anti-Semitic people I've ever met are people who have been married to Jews. They tell you they're fuckin' neurotic, man. I know a broad who lived with a Jew for eight or nine years. She said only ten or fif-teen times did he relax and we had good sex. He was so aware of his Jewishness and he's fuckin' a shiksa. You should see the way his par-ents treated her, just like she was dogshit. Jesus, these Jews, they have all kinds of trouble. All they fuckin' do is whine. Jonathan Pollard. I knew a guy who went to high school with the fucking guy. Pollard says that when he went to high school in South Bend, Indiana—his father was a professor at Notre Dame, Notre Dame Medical School—the gangs used to lay in wait and beat him up. It's all bullshit, man. His old man had lots of dough and he got him a scholarship at Stan-ford—typical Jew shit, you know, probably said he had no money. Went down to Stanford, went to Washington, he was *crazy.* The Israelis thought he was crazy, he was a fuckin' walk-in. They treated him well, this guy's giving us some information, but the guy's a fuckin' nut case. But, anyway, where were we? The Jew always whines, he always brings up anti-Semitism. I've never seen an article about a Jew, a Hollywood star, a politician, or anyone, for Christ's sake, he could sell hot dogs, where he doesn't talk about how, in high school, when he was going for his violin lesson, the gangs laid in wait to beat him up. And how he experienced anti-Semitism when he went to the hot-dog college and he got summa cum laude in hot-dogology and he couldn't get a job at the hot-dog place, and all the bullshit, of course. And, of course, now we found out about those SAT tests, that the rabbis who run schools in Brooklyn and in other Jewish commu-nities are selling the SAT things, that's why these Jews are such fuck-ing geniuses and getting into Harvard, Yale, and Princeton and all these schools. I've worked with them, you know. Christ, you never get any fuckin' work out of them, always around the phone, they know about networking, man, they *never* do any fucking work. [*Chuckle.*] Christ, they're neurotic. They have millions and millions of dollars to fight anti-Semitism. So anti-Semitism has gone under-ground. Most of these screwball KKK, Nazis, etc., are plants. They're Jewish plants, they're set up. Friend of mine attended one of these things at the temple. They get 'em in and show them pictures of the Holocaust, you know, the bodies, then they see a picture [*laughing*]

of some guy down South, screaming, with his Nazi uniform—he's a
Jewish stooge. Yeah, it's for the temple. If I got in a Nazi uniform and
started to yell, they would come around with pictures and photographs and all the other stuff, and then they would run it in every
temple and make the old pitch for the money. Jesus Christ, you ever
talk to a Farrakhan guy? What they say about the Jews is beyond belief. That we're controlled by the Jews. We're not *that* controlled by
the Jews. We're controlled by their publicity, but when the numbers
come out, you'd rather have the money made by Kenny Rogers and
Willie Nelson than by Streisand. Streisand. *She's* got the look. Friend
of mine in California is very close to the film industry [*cackle*], he's
not so happy with the Jews. You know, there is a little Gentile remnant there. Disney used to be their home. But it's all been taken over.
They'll tell you that any business the Jew is in is filled with kickbacks,
payoffs, trading off, networking, but networking fucks you. They got
to hire the nitwit brother-in-law. Why? Because the father-in-law has
invested in the business, and, Jesus, they shake their head, but of
course you can't fire him. So he just sits at a desk or takes long
lunches, you hope. But if he gets actively involved, he fucks up everything. Jews don't put trust in the bank, they have private trusts. I
know from my business experience. Jesus Christ, I dealt with so many
Jews in my time. All of them have Jewish attorneys, all of them sharp
dealers, all of them this, all of them that, right? My boss knows how
to treat 'em, he says this is the price, fuck you. He treats them like
shit. [*Laughter.*] He treats them like shit right away, when they come
in. I wondered why he did it. He says, I used to be nice to these fucking people but you can't be nice to them. He makes them write
letters, which they don't like. They *love* that fuckin' telephone.
Because if they bid on something, well, I'll pay three hundred and
forty thousand for it, then they come in and say, well, you know I told
you three twenty on the phone, they like to fuck over your head, and
with their sharp business practices they create enemies. They know
they're disliked. Why? It's because of *what* they *do*! But still you can't
say anything against Ivan Boesky or any of these other people. If
you say anything about them you are therefore [*whispering*] *an anti-
Semite.* No wonder anti-Semitism has gone underground—it *has* to.
Man, how can you *not* be anti-Semitic? When you see them they're all
on the fucking telephone, manipulating. For better jobs. Or helping
their friends. Jesus Christ, they're born with the PR gene. Born with
this aggressive gene. It's just amazing. Of course, if you fire *them*—
especially if you make a Jew fire a Jew. Jesus Christ, I guess there's no
such thing. Very weird and strange people. See, one of the things
about Jews that I really dislike is that they don't understand the Gen-

tile mind. You can say to the Gentile, "We suffered," and we agree, the German did push you around. Then you come out with the six million, then you extract money from the Bonn government based on six million, then you talk about this and that, then people start chipping away at that six million. Bring the six million even down to eight hundred thousand, let's say. They don't understand the goy mind. Have you ever seen any publicity about a Jew who hasn't suffered because of his faith? The "survivors." Everyone survived. There are so many Auschwitz "survivors." No one, of course, asks the question if maybe you survived by turning in your friend. The "survivors" all wrote books. You ever notice they're all the same books? *Because they're all copying from another book.* They're all the same because Jewish Control Central said, Here's the line on Auschwitz, *write it!* Oh, sly fucking devils. *Sly!*

When my phone rang at almost eight a.m. I had been asleep in the chair beside it since I'd last checked on Demjanjuk's son at about five-thirty. I had dreamed that I owed $128 million on my water bill. That was what my mind came up with after all I'd just been through.

On awakening I smelled something enormous putrefying. I smelled must and feces. I smelled the walls of a damp old chimney. I smelled the fermenting smell of sperm. I smelled her asleep in my trousers—she was that heavy, clinging, muttony stench and she was also that pleasingly unpleasing brackishness on the middle fingers of the hand that picked up the receiver of the ringing phone. My unwashed face was rank with her. Dipped in her. In everyone. I smelled of them all. The shitting driver. The fat lawyer. Pipik. He was the smell of incense and old, dried blood. I smelled of every second of every minute of my last twenty-four hours, smelled like the container of something forgotten in the refrigerator whose lid you pop open after three weeks. Not until I decompose in my coffin will I ever be so immensely pungent again.

The phone was ringing in a hotel room where nobody I knew knew that I was.

A man said, "Roth?" Again a man with an accent. "*Roth?* You there?"

"Who . . . ?"

"The office of Rabbi Meir Kahane."

"Wants *Roth*?"

"This Roth? I am the press secretary. Why do you call the rabbi?"

"Pipik!" I cried.

"Hello? This is *the* Roth, the self-hating Jewish assimilationist?"

"Pipik, where are you?"

"And fuck you too."

I bathe.

Two words.

I dress in clean clothes.

Five words.

I no longer smell.

Four words.

Eleven words, and I no longer know if I ever *did* smell like my corpse.

And this, I thought, my mind already, first thing, careening around its densely overstocked little store of concerns, this is how Demjanjuk does it. Everything putrid in the past just snaps off and falls away. Only America happened. Only the children and the friends and the church and the garden and the job have happened. The accusations? Well, they might as well charge him with owing $128 million on the water bill. Even if they had his signature on the water bill, even if they had his photograph on the water bill, how could it possibly be his water bill? How could anyone use that much water? Admittedly he bathed, sprinkled the lawn, wet down the garden, washed the car, there was a washer-dryer, an automatic dishwasher, there was water for cooking, there were houseplants to water, there were floors to wash every week, they were a family of five, and five people use water—but does that add up to $128 million worth of water? You sent me the bill for the city of Cleveland. You sent me the bill for the state of Ohio. You sent me the bill for the whole fucking world! Look at me in this courtroom, under all this, and still at the end of the day all I have sipped from my glass is maybe three or four ounces of water. I'm not saying that I don't take a drink of water when I'm thirsty, of course I do, and in the summertime I drink my fill after going out and weeding the garden. But do I look to you like somebody who could be wasteful of water to the tune of $128 *million*? Do I strike you as somebody who, twenty-four hours a day, thirty days a month, twelve months a year, year in and year out, is thinking about water and nothing else? Is water running out of my nose and my mouth? Are my clothes sopping wet? Is there a puddle where I walk, is there water under the chair where I sit? Pardon me, but you've got the wrong man. Some Jew, if I may say so, stuck six zeros on my bill just because I am Ukrainian and supposed to be stupid. But I am not so stupid that I don't know my own water bill. My bill is *one hundred and twenty-eight dollars*—one—two—eight! There has been a mistake. I am just an average suburban consumer of water and I should not be on trial for this gigantic bill!

As I was leaving the room on my way to get something to eat before racing off to the trial, I suddenly remembered Apter, and the thought of him wondering if I had abandoned him, the thought of his vulnerability, of his lonely, fear-ridden, fragile existence, sent me back into the room to phone him, at least to assure him that he hadn't been forgotten and that as soon as I possibly could, I would come to see him . . . but it turned out that I *had* seen him. It turned out that I'd had lunch with him just the day before: while Aharon and I had been eating together at the Ticho House, Apter and I had been eating together only a few blocks away at a vegetarian restaurant off Ethiopia Street where we'd always gone in the past for our meal together. It turned out that while Smilesburger was presenting me with his staggering contribution, Apter had been telling me again that he was afraid to go to his stall in the Old City for fear that the Arabs there would kill him with their knives. He was afraid now even to leave his room. And even in his bed, he lay awake, watchful all night long, afraid that if he were to so much as blink his eyes, they would steal through his window and devour him. He had cried and begged me to take him back with me to America, he had lost control of himself completely, bawling and shrieking that he was powerless and that only I could save him.

And I had acceded. At lunch with him I had agreed. He was to come to live in my barn in Connecticut. I had told him that I would build a big new room for him in the unused barn, fix up a room with a skylight and a bed and whitewashed walls, where he could live securely and paint his landscapes and never again have to worry about being eaten alive while he slept.

On the phone he wept with gratitude even as he reminded me of all that I had promised the day before . . . and so how could I tell him that it hadn't been me? And was I even certain that it had been Pipik? It couldn't be! It had to be Apter dreaming aloud, under the pressure of the Arab uprising; it had to be the eruption of the hysteria of a resourceless, deformed, infolded spirit on whom the grip of a horrible past was never relaxed, someone who, even without an insurrection in progress, hourly awaited his execution. It had to be Apter pining for that restful safety he could never possibly know, longing for the lost family and the stolen life; it had to be the unreality of the hysteria of this little blank-faced man shut off and in dread of everything, whose whole existence was shrinking; it had to be withdrawal and longing and fear—because if it wasn't that and had indeed been Pipik conscientiously back at work pretending he was me, if it wasn't either Apter cut loose from his tiny anchor to life and fantastically deluded or Apter openly lying, Apter simulating Apter so as to alarm me into understanding how fantastically deluded existing as Apter required him to be, if Pipik had really made it his business to hunt him down and take him to lunch and toy like this with Apter's ruined life, then I'd been exaggerating nothing, then I was up against a purpose that was as diabolical as it was intangible, I was up against someone wearing my mask who wasn't human at all, someone who could get up to anything in order to make things into what they were not. Which does Pipik despise more, reality or me?

"I won't be a small boy—don't worry, Cousin Philip. I'll just be in the barn, that's all."

"Yes," I said, "yes," and this was the only thing I was able to say.

"I'll be no bother. I won't bother anyone. I need nothing at all," Apter assured me. "I'll paint. I'll paint the American countryside. I'll paint the stone walls you told me about. I'll paint the big maple trees. I'll paint pictures of the barns and of the banks of the river."

On he went, the whole load of his life falling away as he gave free rein, at fifty-four, to his naked need and the fairy tale it engendered of the perfect refuge. I wanted to ask, "Did this happen, Apter? Did he take you to lunch and tell you about the stone walls? Or has the violence so filled you with terror that, whether you know it or not, you are making all this up?" But even as Apter fell deeper and deeper under the spell of the dream of the unhaunted life, I heard myself asking Pipik, "Did you really do this to him? Did you really excite in this banished being who can barely maintain his equilibrium this beautiful vision of an American *Gan Eden* where he will be saved from the blight and din of his past? Answer me, Pipik!" Whereupon Pipik replied, "I couldn't resist, I couldn't do otherwise, neither as a Diasporist nor as a human being. Every word he spoke was filled with his fears. How could I deny him what he's craved all his life? Why are you so outraged? What have I done that's so awful? No more than any Jew would do for a frightened Jewish relative in trouble." "And now you are my conscience, too?" I cried. "You, *you* are going to instruct me in matters of decency, responsibility, and ethical obligation? Is there nothing that you will not pollute with your mouth? I want a serious answer! Is there nothing that you will not befoul? Is there anyone you will not mislead? What joy do you take in raising false hopes and sowing all this confusion?"

I want a serious answer. From Moishe Pipik. And after that, how about peace on earth and goodwill among men? *I want a serious answer*—as who doesn't?

"Apter," I wanted to say, "you are out of contact with reality. I did not take you to lunch yesterday. I had lunch with Aharon Appelfeld, I took *him* to lunch. If you had this conversation at lunch yesterday, it was not with me. Either it was with that man who is in Jerusalem pretending to be me or it was perhaps a conversation with yourself—is it possibly an exchange you imagined?"

But every word he spoke *was* so filled with fear that I did not have the heart to do anything other than repeat "Yes" to it all. I would leave him to awaken by himself from this delusion . . . and if it was no delusion? I imagined myself ripping the tongue out of Pipik's mouth with my own two hands. I imagined myself . . . but I could not give any more thought to the possibility that this was other than a delusion of Apter's for the simple reason that I would have exploded.

That morning's *Jerusalem Post* was outside my door when I left the room, and I picked it up and quickly scanned the front page. The first lead story was about the 1988 Israeli budget— "Worry over Exports Casts Shadow on New State Budget." The second lead story concerned three judges who were to be put on trial and three others who were facing disciplinary action on charges of corruption. Situated between these stories was a photograph of the defense minister visiting the wall that George had tried to take me to see the day before, and beneath that were three stories about the West Bank violence, one datelined Ramallah and headed, "Rabin Inspects Wall of Bloody Beatings." On the lower half of the page I spotted the words "PLO" and "Hezbollah" and "Mubarak" and "Washington" but nowhere the name "Demjanjuk." Nor did I find my name. I ran quickly over the paper's remaining nine pages while going down in the elevator. The only mention of the trial I could find was under the television listings. "Israel Channel 2. 8.30 Demjanjuk trial—live broadcast." And further on, "20.00 Demjanjuk trial roundup." That was all. Nothing calamitous was reported to have happened to any Demjanjuk in the night.

Nonetheless, I decided to skip breakfast at the hotel and to proceed immediately to the courtroom to be sure that Pipik was not there. I'd had no food at all since lunch with Aharon the previous noon, but I could pick up something at the coffee bar just off the entrance hall to the courtroom, and that would replenish me for now. I realized from the TV listings that the trial began much earlier in the day than I had thought, and I had to be there from the very first moment—I was bent on ousting him today, on supplanting him and taking charge completely; if necessary, I would sit in that courtroom through both the morning and the afternoon sessions so as to avert, before it could even get going, anything that he might still be plotting. Today Moishe Pipik was to be obliterated (if, by any chance, he hadn't already been the night before). Today was the end of it: Wednesday, January 27, 1988 • Shevat 8, 5748 • Jomada Tani 9, 1408.

Those were the dates printed in a row beneath the logo of the *Post*. 1988. 5748. 1408. Agreement on nothing but the last digit, dissension over everything, beginning with where to begin. It's no wonder "Rabin Inspects Wall of Bloody Beatings" when the discrepancy between 5748 and 1408 is a matter not of decades or even of a few little centuries but of four thousand three hundred and forty years. The father is superseded by the rivalrous, triumphant firstborn—rejected, suppressed, persecuted, expelled, shunned, terrorized by the firstborn and reviled as the enemy—and then, having barely escaped extinction for the crime of being the father, resuscitates himself, revives and rises up to struggle bloodily over property rights with the second-born, who is raging with envy and the grievances of usurpation, neglect, and ravaged pride. 1988. 5748. 1408. The tragic story's all in the numbers, the successor monotheists' implacable feud with the ancient progenitor whose crime it is, whose *sin* it is, to have endured the most unspeakable devastation and still, somehow, to be *in the way*.

The Jews are in the way.

The moment I stepped out of the elevator, two teenagers, a boy and a girl, jumped up from where they were sitting in the lobby and came toward me, calling my name. The girl was redheaded, freckled, on the dumpy side, and she smiled shyly as she approached; the boy was my height, a skinny, very serious, oldish-seeming boy, cavern-faced and scholarly-looking, who, in his awkwardness, seemed to be climbing over a series of low fences to reach me. "Mr. Roth!" He spoke out in a strong voice a little loud for the lobby. "Mr. Roth! We are two students in the eleventh grade of Liyad Ha-nahar High School in the Jordan Valley. I am Tal.° This is Deborah.°"

"Yes?"

Deborah then stepped forward to greet me, speaking as though she were beginning a public address. "We are a group of high school students that has found your stories very provocative in our English class. We read 'Eli, the Fanatic' and 'Defender of the Faith.' Both created question marks about the state of the American Jew. We wonder if it would be possible for you to visit us. Here is a letter to you from our teacher."

"I'm in a hurry right now," I said, accepting the envelope she handed me, which I saw was addressed in Hebrew. "I'll read this and answer it as soon as I can."

"Our class sent you last week, all the students, each one, a letter to the hotel," Deborah said. "When we received no answer the class voted to send Tal and me on the bus to make our offer directly. We'll be delighted if you accept our class's offer."

"I never got your class's letters." Because *he* had gotten them. Of course! I wondered what could possibly have constrained him from going out to their school and answering questions about his provocative stories. Too busy elsewhere? It horrified me to think about the invitations to speak he had received and accepted here if this was one he considered too inconsequential even to bother to decline. Schoolkids weren't his style. No headlines in schoolkids. And no money. The schoolkids he left to me. I could hear him calming me down. "I wouldn't dare to interfere in literary matters. I respect you too much as a writer for that." And I needed calming down when I thought about him getting and opening the mail people thought they were addressing to me.

"First of all," Tal was saying to me, "we would like to know how *you* live as a Jew in America, and how you have solved the conflicts you brought up in your stories. What's with the 'American dream'? From the story 'Eli, the Fanatic' it seems like the only way of being a Jew in America is being a fanatic. *Is* it the only way? What about making aliyah? In Israel, in our society, the religious fanatics are seen in a negative way. You talk about suffering—"

Deborah saw my impatience with Tal's on-the-spot inquiry and interrupted to tell me, softly now, quite charmingly in that very faintly off-ish English, "We have a beautiful school, near the Kinneret Lake, with a lot of trees, grass, and flowers. It's a very beautiful place, under the Golan mountains. It is so beautiful it is considered to be Paradise. I think you would enjoy it."

"We were impressed," Tal continued, "by the beautiful style of literature you write, but still not all of the problems were solved in our mind. The conflict between the Jewish identity and being a part of another nation, the situation in the West Bank and Gaza, and the problem of double loyalty as in the Pollard case and its influence on the American Jewish community—"

I put a hand up to stop him. "I appreciate your interest. Right now I've got to be somewhere else. I'll write your teacher."

But the boy had come from the Jordan Valley on a very early bus to Jerusalem and had waited nervously in the lobby for me to wake up and get started, and he wasn't prepared, having gotten up his head of steam, to back off yet. "What comes first," he asked me, "nationality or Jewish identity? Tell us about your identity crisis."

"Not right now."

"In Israel," he said, "many youngsters have an identity crisis and make *hozer b'tshuva* without knowing what they are getting into—"

A rather stern-looking, unsmiling man, very decorously— and, in this country, uncharacteristically—dressed in a dark double-breasted suit and tie, had been watching from a sofa only a few feet away as I tried to extricate myself and be on my way. He was seated with a briefcase in his lap, and now he came to his feet and, as he approached, addressed a few words to Deborah and Tal. I was surprised that he spoke Hebrew. From his looks as well as his dress I would have taken him for a northern European, a German, a Dutchman, a Dane. He spoke quietly but very authoritatively to the two teenagers, and when Tal responded, intemperately, in Hebrew, he listened without flinching until the boy was finished and only then did he turn his cast-iron face to me, to say, in English, and in an English accent, "Please, forgive their audacity and accept them and their questions as a token of the tremendous esteem in which you are held here. I am David Supposnik,° an antiquarian. My office is in Tel Aviv. I too have come to bother you." He handed me a card that identified him as a dealer in old and rare books, German, English, Hebrew, and Yiddish.

"The annual teaching of your story 'Eli, the Fanatic' is always an experience for the high school students," Supposnik said. "Our pupils are mesmerized by Eli's plight and identify wholly with his dilemma despite their innate contempt for all things fanatically religious."

"Yes," agreed Deborah while Tal, resentful, remained silent.

"Nothing would give the students greater pleasure than a

visit from you. But they know it is unlikely and that is why this young man has seized the opportunity to interrogate you here and now."

"It's not been the worst interrogation of my life," I replied, "but I'm in a rush this morning."

"I'm sure that, if you could see your way, in response to his questions, to sending a collective reply to all the students in the class, that would be sufficient and they would be extremely flattered and grateful."

Deborah spoke up, obviously feeling as bullied as Tal did by the outsider's unsought intervention. "But," she said to me, pleadingly, "they would still prefer if you *came*."

"He has explained to you," said Supposnik, no less brusque now with the girl than he'd been with the boy, "that he has business in Jerusalem. That is quite enough. A man cannot be in two places at one time."

"Goodbye," I said, extending my hand, and it was shaken first by Deborah, then reluctantly by Tal before, finally, they turned and left.

Who can't be in two places at one time? Me? And who is this Supposnik and why has he forced those youngsters out of my life if not to force himself in?

What I saw was a man with a long head, deep-set, smallish light-colored eyes, and a strongly molded forehead from which his light brown hair was combed straight back close to the skull—an officer type, a colonial officer who might have trained at Sandhurst and served here with the British during the Mandate. I would never have had him pegged as a dealer in rare Yiddish books.

Crisply, reading my mind, Supposnik said, "Who I am and what I want."

"Quickly, yes, if you don't mind."

"In just fifteen minutes I can make everything clear."

"I don't have fifteen minutes."

"Mr. Roth, I wish to enlist your talent in the struggle against anti-Semitism, a struggle to which I know you are not indifferent. The Demjanjuk trial is not irrelevant to my purpose. Is that not where you are hurrying off to?"

"Is it?"

"Sir, everybody in Israel knows what you are doing here."

Just then I saw George Ziad walk into the hotel and approach the front desk.

"Please," I said to Supposnik, "one moment."

At the desk, where George embraced me, I found he was at the same pitch of emotion as when I'd left him the evening before.

"You're all right," he whispered. "I thought the worst."

"I'm fine."

He would not let me free myself. "They detained you? They questioned you? Did they beat you?"

"They never detained me. Beat me? Of course not. It was all a big mistake. George, *relax*," I told him but was only able to secure my release by pressing my fists against his shoulders until we were finally an arm's length apart.

The desk clerk, a young man who hadn't been on duty when I'd checked in, said to me, "Good morning, Mr. Roth. How are things this morning?" Very jovially, he said to George, "This is no longer the lobby of the King David Hotel, it's the rabbinical court of Rabbi Roth. All his fans won't leave him alone. Every morning, they are lining up, the schoolchildren, the journalists, the politicians—we have had nothing like it," he said, with a laugh, "since Sammy Davis, Jr., came to pray at the Wailing Wall."

"The comparison is too flattering," I said. "You exaggerate my importance."

"Everyone in Israel wants to meet Mr. Roth," the clerk said.

Hooking my arm in his, I led George away from the desk and the desk clerk. "Is this the best place for you to be, this hotel?"

"I had to come. The phone is no use here. Everything is tapped and taped and will turn up either at my trial or at yours."

"George, come off it. Nobody's putting me on trial. Nobody beat me. That's all ridiculous."

"This is a military state, established by force, maintained by force, committed to force and repression."

"Please, I don't see it that way. Stop. Not now. No slogans. I'm your friend."

"Slogans? They didn't demonstrate to you last night that this is a police state? They could have shot you, Philip, then and there, and blamed the Arab driver. These are the great specialists in assassination. That is no slogan, that is the truth. They train assassins for fascist governments all over the world. They have no compunctions about whom they murder. Opposition from a Jew is intolerable to them. They can murder a Jew they don't like as easily as they murder one of us. They can and they *do*."

"Zee, Zee, you're way over the top, man. The trouble last night was the driver, stopping and starting his car, flashing his light—it was a comedy of errors. The guy had to take a shit. He aroused the suspicion of this patrol. It all meant nothing, means nothing, was nothing."

"In Prague it means something to you, in Warsaw it means something to you—only here you, even you, fail to understand what it means. They are out to frighten you, Philip. They are out to scare you to death. What you are preaching here is anathema to them—you are challenging them at the very heart of their Zionist lie. You are the opposition. And the opposition they 'neutralize.'"

"Look," I said, "talk coherently to me. This is not making sense. Let me get rid of this guy and then you and I will have to have a talk."

"Which guy? Who is he?"

"An antiquarian from Tel Aviv. A rare-book dealer."

"You know him?"

"No. He came here to see me."

All the while I explained, George looked boldly across the lobby to where Supposnik had taken a seat on the sofa, waiting for me to return.

"He's the police. He's Shin Bet."

"George, you're in a bad way. You're overwrought and you're going to explode. This is not the police."

"Philip, you are an innocent! I won't have them brutalizing you, not you too!"

"But I'm *fine*. Stop this, please. Look, this is the texture of things over here. I don't have to tell you that. There is rough stuff on the roads. I was in the wrong place at the wrong time. There is a mix-up, all right, but that's between you and me, I'm afraid. You are not responsible. If anyone is responsible, I am responsible. You and I have to have a talk. You're confused about why I'm here. Something most unusual has been happening and I haven't been at all clever dealing with it. I confused you and Anna yesterday—I acted very stupidly at your house. Unforgivably so. Let's not talk now. You'll come with me—I have to be at the Demjanjuk trial, you'll come with me and in the taxi I'll explain everything. This has all gotten out of hand and the fault is largely mine."

"Philip, while this court for Demjanjuk is carefully weighing evidence for the benefit of the world press, scrutinizing meticulously, with all kinds of experts, the handwriting and the photograph and the imprint of the paper clip and the age of the ink and the paper stock, while this charade of Israeli justice is being played out on the radio and the television and in the world press, the death penalty is being enacted all over the West Bank. Without experts. Without trials. Without justice. With live bullets. Against innocent people. Philip," he said, speaking very quietly now, "there is somebody for you to talk to in Athens. There is somebody in Athens who believes in what you believe in and what you want to do. Somebody with money who believes in Diasporism for the Jews and justice for the Palestinians. There are people who can help you in Athens. They are Jews but they are our friends. We can arrange a meeting."

I am being recruited, I thought, recruited by George Ziad for the PLO.

"Wait. Wait here," I said. "We have to talk. Is it better for you to wait here or outside?"

"No, here," he said, smiling ruefully, "here it is positively ideal for me. They wouldn't dare to beat an Arab in the lobby of the King David Hotel, not in front of all the liberal American Jews whose money props up their fascist regime. No, here I'm much safer than in my house in Ramallah."

I made the mistake then of returning to explain politely to Supposnik that he and I would not be able to continue our conversation. He did not give me a chance, however, to say even one word, but for ten minutes stood barely half a foot from my chest delivering his lecture entitled "Who I Am." Each time I retreated an inch, preparatory to ducking away, he drew an inch closer to me, and I realized that short of shouting at him or striking him or streaking out of the lobby as fast as I could, I would have to hear him out. There was a commanding incongruousness about this Teutonically handsome Tel Aviv Jew who'd taught himself to speak English in the impeccable accent of the educated English upper class, and something also touchingly absurd about the bookish erudition of his hotel-lobby lecture and the pedantic donnish air with which it was so beautifully articulated. If I hadn't felt that I was needed urgently elsewhere, I might have been more entertained than I was; in the circumstances, I was, in fact, far more entertained than I should have been, but this is a professional weakness and accounts for any number of my mistakes. I am a relentless collector of scripts. I stand around half-amazed by these audacious perspectives, I stand there excited, almost erotically, by these stories so unlike my own, I stand listening like a five-year-old to some stranger's most fantastic tale as though it were the news of the week in review, stupidly I stand there enjoying all the pleasures of gullibility while I ought instead to be either wielding my great skepticism or running for my life. Half-amazed with Pipik, half-amazed with Jinx, and now this Shylock specialist whom half-amazing George Ziad had identified for me as a member of the Israeli secret police.

"Who I am. I am one of the children, like your friend Appelfeld," Supposnik told me. "We were one hundred thousand Jewish children in Europe, wandering. Who would take us in? Nobody. America? England? No one. After the Holocaust and the wandering, I decided to become a Jew. The ones who harmed me were the non-Jews, and the ones who helped me were the Jews. After this I loved the Jew and developed a hatred for the non-Jew. Who I am. Someone who has collected books in four languages for three decades now and who has read all his life the greatest of all English writers. Particularly when I was a young student at the Hebrew University, I studied the Shakespeare play that is second only to *Hamlet* in the number of times it has been performed on the London stage in the first half of the twentieth century. And in the very first line, the opening line of the third scene of the very first act, I came with a shock upon the three words with which Shylock introduced himself onto the world stage nearly four hundred years ago. Yes, for four hundred years now, Jewish people have lived in the shadow of this Shylock. In the modern world, the Jew has been perpetually on trial; still *today* the Jew is on trial, in the person of the Israeli—and this modern trial of the Jew, this trial which never ends, begins with the trial of Shylock. To the audiences of the world Shylock is the embodiment of the Jew in the way that Uncle Sam embodies for them the spirit of the United States. Only, in Shylock's case, there is an overwhelming Shakespearean reality, a terrifying Shakespearean aliveness that your pasteboard Uncle Sam cannot begin to possess. I studied those three words by which the savage, repellent, and villainous Jew, deformed by hatred and revenge, entered as our doppelgänger into the consciousness of the enlightened West. Three words encompassing all that is hateful in the Jew, three words that have stigmatized the Jew through two Christian millennia and that determine the Jewish fate until this very day, and that only the greatest English writer of them all could have had the prescience to isolate and dramatize as he did. You remember Shylock's opening line? You remember the three words? What Jew can forget them? What Christian can forgive them? '*Three thousand ducats.*' Five blunt, unbeautiful English syllables and the stage Jew is elevated to its apogee by a genius, catapulted into eternal notoriety by 'Three thousand ducats.' The English actor who performed as Shylock for fifty years during the eighteenth century, the Shylock of his day, was a Mr. Charles Macklin. We are told that Mr. Macklin would mouth the two *th*'s and the two *s*'s in 'Three thousand ducats' with such oiliness that he instantaneously aroused, with just those three words, all of the audience's hatred of Shylock's race. 'Th-th-th-three th-th-th-thous-s-s-sand ducats-s-s.' When Mr. Macklin whetted his knife to carve from Antonio's chest his pound of flesh, people in the pit fell unconscious—and this at the zenith of the Age of Reason. Admirable Macklin! The Victorian conception of Shylock, however—Shylock as a wronged Jew rightfully vengeful —the portrayal that descends through the Keans to Irving and into our century, is a vulgar sentimental offense not only against the genuine abhorrence of the Jew that animated Shakespeare and his era but to the long illustrious chronicle of European Jew-baiting. The hateful, hateable Jew whose artistic roots extend back to the Crucifixion pageants at York, whose endurance as the villain of history no less than of drama is unparalleled, the hook-nosed moneylender, the miserly, money-maddened, egotistical degenerate, the Jew who goes to *synagogue* to plan the murder of the virtuous Christian—*this* is Europe's Jew, the Jew expelled in 1290 by the English, the Jew banished in 1492 by the Spanish, the Jew terrorized by Poles, butchered by Russians, incinerated by Germans, spurned by the British and the Americans while the furnaces roared at Treblinka. The vile Victorian varnish that sought to humanize the Jew, to dignify the Jew, has never deceived the enlightened European mind about the three thousand ducats, never has and never will. Who I am, Mr. Roth, is an antiquarian bookseller dwelling in the Mediterranean's tiniest country—still considered too large by all the world—a bookish shopkeeper, a retiring bibliophile, nobody from nowhere, really, who has dreamed nonetheless, since his student days, an impresario's dreams, at night in his bed envisioning himself impresario, producer, director, leading actor of Supposnik's Anti-Semitic Theater Company. I dream of full houses and standing ovations, and of myself, hungry, dirty little Supposnik, one of the hundred thousand wandering children, enacting, in the unsentimental manner of Macklin, in the true spirit of Shakespeare, that chilling and ferocious Jew whose villainy flows inexorably from the innate corruption of his religion. Every winter touring the capitals of the civilized world with his Anti-Semitic Drama Festival, performing in repertory the great Jew-hating dramas of Europe, night after night the Austrian plays, the German plays, Marlowe and the other Elizabethans, and concluding always as star of the masterpiece that was to prophesy, in the expulsion of the unregenerate Jew Shylock from the harmonious universe of the angelic Christian Portia, the Hitlerian dream of a *Judenrein* Europe. Today a Shylockless Venice, tomorrow a Shylockless world. As the stage direction so succinctly puts it after Shylock has been robbed of his daughter, stripped of his wealth, and compelled to convert by his Christian betters: *Exit Jew.* This is who I am. Now for what I want. Here."

I took from him what he handed me, two notebooks bound in imitation leather, each about the size of a billfold. One was red, and impressed on its cover, in white cursive script, were the words "My Trip." The other, whose brown cover was a bit scratched and mildewed, was identified as "Travels Abroad" in gold letters that were stylized to look exotically non-Occidental. Engraved in a semicircular constellation around those words were postage-stamp-sized representations of the varied forms of locomotion that the intrepid wayfarer would encounter on his journey—a ship sailing along on the wavy waves, an airliner, a rickshaw pulled by a pigtailed coolie, bearing a woman with a parasol, an elephant with a driver perched atop his head and a passenger seated in an awninged cabinet on his back, a camel ridden by a robed Arabian, and, at the bottom edge of the cover, the most elaborately detailed of the six engraved images: a full moon, a starry sky, a serene lagoon, a gondola, a gondolier. . . .

"Nothing like this," said Supposnik, "has turned up since the discovery at the end of the war of the diary of Anne Frank."

"Whose are they?" I asked.

"Open them," he said. "Read."

I opened the red book. At the top of the entry I'd turned to, where there were lines provided for "Date," "Place," and "Weather," I read "2-2-76," "Mexico," and "Good." The entry itself, in legible largish handwriting inscribed with a fountain pen in blue ink, began, "Beautiful flight. A little rough. Arrived on time. Mexico City has a population of 5,000,000 people. Our guide took us through some sections of the city. We went to a residential section that was built on lava. The homes ranged from $30,000 to $160,000. They were very modern and beautiful. The flowers were very colorful." I skipped ahead. "Wed. 2-14-76. San Huso De Puria. We had an early lunch and then went into the pool. There are 4 of them here. Each is supposed to have curative waters. Then we went to the Spa building. The girls had a mud pack on their faces and then we went into the mikva or baths. Marilyn and I shared one. It is called a family bath. It was the most delightful experience. All my friends should visit this place. Even some of my enemies. It is great."

"Well," I said to Supposnik, "they're not André Gide's."

"It's written whose they are—at the beginning."

I turned to the beginning. There was a page titled "Time Keeping at Sea," a page about "Changing the Clock," information about "Latitude and Longitude," "Miles and Knots," "The Barometer," "The Tides," "Ocean Lanes and Distances," "Port and Starboard," a full page explaining "Conversion from US-$ into Foreign Currencies," and then the page headed "Identification," where all but a few of the blanks had been filled in by the same diarist with the same fountain pen.

My Name.	Leon Klinghoffer				
My Residence.	70 E. 10th St. NY, NY 10003				
My Occupation.	Appliance manufacturer (Queens)				
Ht.	5-7½	*Wgt.*	170	*Born*	1916
Color	W.	*Hair*	Brown	*Eyes*	Brown

I AM KNOWN TO HAVE THE FOLLOWING

Diagnosis ——————————————————————————

Social Security No. ——————————————————————

Religion ———————————— Hebrew ————————————

IN CASE OF ACCIDENT NOTIFY

Name ———————— Marilyn Klinghoffer ————————

"Now you see," said Supposnik gravely.

"I do," I said, "yes," and opened the brown diary he'd given me. "9-3-79. Naples. Weather cloudy. Breakfast. Took tour to Pompeii again. Very interesting. Hot. Back to ship. Wrote cards. Had drink. Met 2 nice young people from London. Barbara and Lawrence. Safety drill. Weather turned nice. Going to Captain's cocktail party in the swank [illegible] Room."

"This is *the* Klinghoffer?" I asked. "From the *Achille Lauro* hijacking?"

"The Klinghoffer they killed, yes. The defenseless Jew crippled in a wheelchair that the brave Palestinian freedom fighters shot in the head and threw into the Mediterranean Sea. These are his travel diaries."

"From that trip?"

"No, from happier trips. The diary from that trip has disappeared. Perhaps it was in his pocket when they tossed him overboard. Perhaps the brave freedom fighters used it for paper to cleanse their heroic Palestinian behinds. No, these are from the pleasant trips he made with his wife and his friends in the years before. They've come to me through the Klinghoffer daughters. I heard about the diaries. I contacted the daughters. I flew to New York to meet with them. Two specialists here in Israel, one of them associated with the forensic investigation unit of the attorney general's office, have assured me that the handwriting is Klinghoffer's. I brought back with me documents and letters from his business office files—the handwriting there corresponds to the diary handwriting in every last particular. The pen, the ink, the manufacturing date of the diaries themselves—I have expert documentation for their authenticity. The daughters have asked me to act as their representative to help them find an Israeli publisher for their late father's diaries. They want to publish them here as a memorial to him and as a token of the devotion that he felt to Israel. They have asked for the proceeds to be donated to the Hadassah Hospital in Jerusalem, a favorite charity of their father's. I told these two young women that when Otto Frank returned to Amsterdam from the camps after the war and found the diary kept by his little daughter while the Frank family hid from the Nazis in their attic, he too wanted it only to be published privately, as a memorial to her for a small group of Dutch friends. And as you well know, having yourself made Anne Frank into the heroine of a literary work, that was the modest, unassuming way in which the Anne Frank diary first appeared. I of course will follow the wishes of the Klinghoffer daughters. But I happen also to know that, like the diary of little Anne Frank, *The Travel Diaries of Leon Klinghoffer* are destined to reach a far wider audience, a worldwide audience—if, that is, I can secure the assistance of Philip Roth. Mr. Roth, the introduction to the first American publication of *The Diary of Anne Frank* was written by Eleanor Roosevelt, the much-esteemed widow of your wartime president. A few hundred words from Mrs. Roosevelt and Anne Frank's words became a moving entry in the history of Jewish suffering and Jewish survival. Philip Roth can do the same for the martyred Klinghoffer."

"I'm sorry, I can't." However, when I made to hand back the two volumes, he wouldn't accept them.

"Read them through," Supposnik said. "I'll leave them for you to read through."

"Don't be ridiculous. I can't be responsible. Here."

But again he refused to take them. "Leon Klinghoffer," he said, "could very easily have been a man out of one of your books. He's no stranger to you. Neither is the idiom in which he expresses here, simply, awkwardly, sincerely, his delight in living, his love for his wife, his pride in his children, his devotion to his fellow Jews, his love for Israel. I know the feeling you have for the achievement that these men, burdened by all the limitations of their immigrant family backgrounds, nonetheless made of their American lives. They are the fathers of your heroes. You know them, you understand them; without sentimentalizing them, you respect them. Only you can bring to these two little travel diaries the compassionate knowledge that will reveal to the world exactly who it was and what it was that was murdered on the cruise ship *Achille Lauro* on October 8, 1985. No other writer writes about these Jewish men in the way that you do. I'll return tomorrow morning."

"It's not likely I'll be here tomorrow morning. Look," I said angrily, "you cannot leave these things with me."

"I cannot think of anyone more reliable to entrust them to." And with that he turned and left me there holding the two diaries.

The Smilesburger million-dollar check. The Lech Walesa six-pointed star. Now the Leon Klinghoffer travel diaries. What next, the false nose worn by the admirable Macklin? Whatever Jewish treasure isn't nailed down comes flying straight into my face! I went immediately to the front desk and asked for an envelope large enough to hold the two diaries and wrote Supposnik's name across it and my own in the upper left-hand corner. "When the gentleman returns," I said to the clerk, "give him this package, will you?"

He nodded to assure me that he would, but no sooner had he turned to place the envelope in my room's pigeonhole than I imagined Pipik popping up to claim the package for his own the moment after I'd departed for the courtroom. However much evidence there was that I had finally prevailed and that the two of them had abandoned the hoax and taken flight, I still couldn't convince myself that he wasn't lurking nearby, fully aware of everything that had just transpired, any more than I could be one hundred percent certain that he wasn't already at the courtroom with his Orthodox coconspirators, poised to undertake the folly of kidnapping Demjanjuk's son. If Pipik returns to steal these . . . well, that's Supposnik's hard luck, not mine!

Nonetheless I turned back to the desk from which I'd turned away and asked the clerk to hand me the package that I had only just deposited with him. While he watched with a barely discernible smirk suggesting that he, rather like me, saw in this scene great untapped comic potential, I tore it open, put the red diary ("My Trip") into one of my jacket pockets and the brown diary ("Travels Abroad") into the other, and then quickly left the hotel with George, who all this while, submerged in his malice, racked by God only knew what unendurable fantasies of restitution and revenge, had sat in a chair close by the door smoking cigarette after cigarette, observing the brisk stirrings of another busy day in the sedate, attractive lobby of a four-star Jewish hotel whose prosperous guests and resourceful staff were, of course, utterly indifferent to the misery caused him by their matter-of-factly manageable existence.

As we stepped into the bright sunlight, I surveyed the cars parked along the street to see if Pipik might be in one of them, hiding the way he'd hidden in his "vehicle" as a Chicago detective. I saw a figure standing on the roof of the YMCA building across the street from the hotel. It could be him, he could be anywhere—and for a moment I *saw* him everywhere. Now that she's told him how I seduced her, I thought, he's my terrorist for life. I'll be sighting him on rooftops for years to come, just as he'll be seeing me, sighted in the cross hairs of his rage.

9

Forgery, Paranoia, Disinformation, Lies

BEFORE stepping into the taxi I quickly checked out the driver, a tiny Turkish-looking Jew a foot and a half shorter than Pipik or me and crowned with ten times more wiry black hair than the two of us possessed together. His English was less than rudimentary, and once we were in the cab George had to repeat our destination to him in Hebrew. We were as good as alone in that cab, and so between the hotel and the courtroom, I told George Ziad everything that I should have told him the day before. He listened silently and, to my astonishment, did not seem startled or at all incredulous to learn that there had been another "me" in Jerusalem all the while he'd assumed that there was only the one with whom he had been to graduate school three decades earlier. He wasn't even ruffled (he who enjoyed so few moments without his veins and arteries visibly vibrating) when I tried to diagnose for him the perverse impulse that had led me to masquerade before his wife and his son as the Diasporist fanatic tendering manic homage to Irving Berlin.

"No apologies necessary," he replied in a calmly cutting voice. "You are still who you were. Always on the stage. How could I have failed to remember? You're an actor, an amusing actor performing endlessly for the admiration of his friends. You're a satirist, always looking for the laugh, and how can a satirist be expected to suppress himself with a raving, ranting, slobbering Arab?"

"I don't know these days what I am," I said. "What I did was stupid—stupid and inexplicable—and I'm sorry. It was the last thing Anna and Michael needed."

"But what about what *you* needed? Your comic fix. What do an oppressed people's problems matter to a great comic artist like you? The show must go on. Say no more. You're a very amusing performer—and a moral idiot!"

So no more was said by either of us during the remaining few minutes before we reached the courtroom, and whether

George was a deluded madman or a cunning liar—or a great comic artist in his own right—or whether the network of intrigue he claimed to represent existed (and whether a man so out of control and continually at the breaking point could be its representative) I had no way now of finding out. *There is somebody for you to talk to in Athens. There are people who can help you there. They are Jews but they are also our friends. . . .* Jews bankrolling the PLO? Is *that* what he'd been telling me?

At the courthouse, when George hopped out of his side of the taxi before I even had a chance to pay the driver, I believed I'd never see him again. Yet there he was, already at the back of the courtroom, when I slipped inside a minute or two later. Quickly catching hold of my hand, he whispered, "You're the Dostoyevsky of disinformation," and only then proceeded past me to look for a seat by himself.

The courtroom that morning was less than half full. According to *The Jerusalem Post*, all the witnesses had been heard and this was to be the third day of the summing up. I could see clearly down to where Demjanjuk's son was sitting in the second row, just to the left of the center of the hall and directly in line with the chair on the stage where his father was seated between his two guards and back of the defense counsel's table. When I saw that in the row behind Demjanjuk junior nearly all the chairs were unoccupied, I made my way there and quickly sat down, as the court was already in session.

I'd got a set of earphones at the desk by the entrance door and, slipping them over my head, turned the dial to the channel for the English translation of the proceedings. It was a minute or two, however, before I could take in what one of the judges—the chief judge, Israeli Supreme Court Justice Levin—was saying to the witness on the stand. He was the first witness of the day, a compactly built, sturdy-looking Jewish man in his late sixties, whose substantial head—a weighty boulder onto which a pair of thick spectacles had incongruously been set—was stacked squarely atop a torso of cement building blocks. He wore slacks and a surprisingly sporty red and black pullover sweater, something in which a clean-cut young athlete might show up for a date, and his hands, a laborer's hands, a dockworker's hands, hands that looked hard as nails, were fastened to the lip of the lectern with the impassioned, bottled-up nervous ferocity of a heavyweight bursting to catapult into battle at the sound of the bell.

His name was Eliahu Rosenberg and this was not his first round in court with Demjanjuk, as I knew from a startling photograph in the Demjanjuk clipping file that had caught my attention the day I'd arrived, one in which a friendly, grinning Demjanjuk is warmly offering Rosenberg his hand to shake. The photograph had been taken about a year before, on the seventh day of the trial, when Rosenberg was asked by the prosecution to leave the witness stand and step up to the defendant's chair, some twenty feet away, to make his identification. Rosenberg had been called to testify as one of seven prosecution witnesses who claimed to recognize John Demjanjuk of Cleveland, Ohio, as the Ivan the Terrible they had known while they were prisoners at Treblinka. According to Rosenberg, he and Ivan, both men then in their early twenties, had worked in close proximity every day for nearly a year, Ivan as the guard who operated the gas chamber and supervised the detail of Jewish prisoners, the "death commandos," whose job was to empty the gas chamber of corpses, to clean it of urine and excrement so as to make it ready for the gassing of the next shipment of Jews, and to whitewash the walls, outside as well as inside, so as to cover over the bloodstains (for Ivan and the other guards oftentimes drew blood while driving the Jews into the gas with knives and clubs and iron pipes). Twenty-one-year-old Eliahu Rosenberg, recently of Warsaw, was one of the death commandos, those thirty or so living Jews whose other job, after each gassing, was carrying on stretchers— running all the while at top speed—the naked corpses of the freshly killed Jews to the open-air "roast" where, after their gold teeth were extracted for the German state treasury by the prisoner "dentist," the bodies were skillfully piled to be incinerated, children and women at the bottom for kindling, and men at the top, where they ignited more easily.

Now, eleven months later, Rosenberg had been surprisingly recalled, this time by the defense, in the midst of its summing up. The judge was telling Rosenberg, "You will listen carefully to the questions put to you and you will reply and confine yourself to the questions put to you. You will not enter into polemics nor will you lose your self-control as, unfortunately, happened more than once in the course of your testimony—"

But, as I have said, during my first few minutes inside the courtroom, I could not focus on the English translation coming through my headphones, not with young Demjanjuk in the row before me, mine to maintain surveillance over, mine to sit by and protect—if protection was indeed warranted—from the machinating Moishe Pipik, and not with these two diaries filling my pockets. *Were* they the diaries of Leon Klinghoffer? Unobtrusively as I could, I lifted them out of either pocket and turned them over and over in my hands; I even put them up to my nose, quickly one and then the other, to sniff their papery odor, that pleasant moldering smell that faintly perfumes old library stacks. Holding the red diary open in my lap, I read for a moment from a page midway through. "Thurs. 9/23/78. On way to Yugoslavia. Du Brovnik. Went past Messina and Straits. Reminded us of 1969 trip to city of Messina. New crowd got aboard at Genoa. Show tonight was great. Everyone has coughing spells. I don't know why, weather is perfect."

That comma setting off "why" from "weather"—is it likely, I asked myself, that a man in the appliance business in Queens would have deftly dropped a comma in there? In jottings as rudimentary as these should I be finding any punctuation at all? And no spelling errors anywhere other than in the writing of an unfamiliar place name? *New crowd got aboard at Genoa.* Deliberately planted there, that item? There perhaps to presage what would happen seven years hence, when, in the new crowd that boarded the *Achille Lauro* at some Italian port or other—maybe it was even at Genoa—were hidden the three Palestinian terrorists who would kill this very same diarist? Or was that simply a report of what had happened on their cruise of September 1978—a new crowd had boarded at Genoa and, for the Klinghoffers, nothing horrible ensued.

But distracted as I was from following the judge's opening remarks by the presence, in the seat before me, of young Demjanjuk, not yet kidnapped and still unharmed; distracted as I was by the diaries that had been forced on me by Supposnik—wondering whether they were forged, wondering whether

Supposnik was a charlatan who was a party to the forgery or a passionate Jewish survivor who was its unsuspecting victim, wondering whether the diaries were exactly what he'd said they were, and, if so, wondering whether it really was somehow my Jewish duty to write the introduction that might then elicit publishing interest in them other than just in Israel—I was still further disconcerted by trying to puzzle out why everything I'd truthfully told George Ziad in the taxi could have been assumed by him to be, of all things, "disinformation."

It must be because he assumed, first off, that, like the antiquarian bookseller Supposnik, our tiny taxi driver was another of those Israeli secret police men that he'd been directing my attention to everwhere we met; it must be that he assumed not only that we two were under close surveillance but that I had surmised this upon getting into the cab and had then, ingeniously, come up with the story of the second Philip Roth in order to jam the interloper's circuits with so much cuckoo nonsense. Otherwise I didn't know what to make of this word "disinformation" or of the affectionate grip in which he'd taken my hand only minutes after angrily informing me that I was a moral idiot.

Admittedly, the story of my double was difficult to accept at face value. The story of anyone's double would be. It was my own difficulty accepting it that largely accounted for why I had so mismanaged just about everything having to do with Pipik and was probably mismanaging it still. But however hard it was to swallow the existence of a character as audaciously fraudulent as Moishe Pipik or to imagine him meeting with any success whatsoever, I'd have thought it still easier for George to accept this double's unlikely existence than to believe that (1) I could seriously be the proponent of a political scheme as antihistorically harebrained as Diasporism or that (2) Diasporism could possibly constitute a source of hope for the Palestinian national movement, especially one worthy of financial backing. No, only the insane desperation of a zealot who knew himself to be powerless and who had lived too long in behalf of a cause on the brink of total failure could lead someone as intelligent as George Ziad to seize with such reckless enthusiasm on an idea so spurious. And yet if George were that blinded, that defeated by suffering, that disfigured by impotent rage, then

surely he would have disqualified himself long ago from anything like the position of influence that he claimed enabled
him to come to see me, as he had this morning, to make
arrangements for the secret Athens meeting. On the other
hand, perhaps by now the mind of my old Chicago friend was
so savagely unhinged by despair that he had taken to living in
a dream of his own devising, "Athens" his Palestinian Xanadu
and those rich Jewish backers of the PLO no more real than
the imaginary friends of a lonely child.

It was not for me, after these last seventy-two hours, to reject as too outlandish the possibility that the situation for him
here had driven George crazy. Yet I did reject it. It was just too
insipid a conclusion. Not everybody was crazy. Resolute is not
crazy. Deluded is not crazy. To be thwarted, vengeful, terrified, treacherous—this is not to be crazy. Not even fanatically
held illusions are crazy, and deceit certainly isn't crazy—deceit,
deviousness, cunning, cynicism, all of that is far from crazy
. . . and there, that, *deceit*, there was the key to my confusion! Of course! It wasn't I who'd been deceiving George, it
was George who was deceiving me! I had been suckered by the
tragic melodrama of the pitiful victim who is driven nearly insane by injustice and exile. George's madness was Hamlet's—
an act.

Yes, here's an explanation to it all! Eminent Jewish writer
shows up in Jerusalem espousing a massive transfer of Israel's
Ashkenazi population back to their European countries of origin. The idea may appear as grossly unrealistic to a Palestinian
militant as to Menachen Begin, but that an eminent writer
should come up with such an idea might not seem unrealistic
to either; no, nothing peculiar to them about an eminent
writer who imagines there is some correlation between his
own feverish, ignorant apocalyptic fantasies and the way that
struggles between contending political forces are won and lost
in actuality. Of course, politically speaking, the eminent writer
is a joke; of course nothing the man thinks moves anyone in
Israel or anywhere else to act one way or another, but he's a
cultural celebrity, he commands column inches all over the
world, and consequently the eminent writer who thinks that
the Jews should get the hell out of Palestine is not to be ignored or ridiculed but to be encouraged and exploited.

George knows him. He's an old American buddy of George's.
Seduce him, George, with our suffering. Between books all
these eminent writers love five or six days in a good hotel, enmeshed in the turbulent tragedies of the heroically oppressed.
Track him down. Find him. Tell him how they torture us—it's
the ones who stay in the best hotels who are, understandably,
particularly sensitized to the horrors of injustice. If a dirty fork
on the breakfast tray elicits an angry protest to room service,
imagine their outrage over the cattle prod. Rant, rave, display
your wounds, give him the Celebrity Tour—the military
courtrooms, the bloodstained walls—tell him that you'll take
him to talk with Father Arafat himself. Let's see what kind of
coverage George can whip up for Mr. Roth's little publicity
stunt. Let's put this megalomaniac Jew on the cover of *Time*!

But what then of the other Jew, the megalomaniac double?
All these suppositions might explain why George Ziad had
damned me in the taxicab as a moral idiot and then, only minutes later, in a whispered aside at the rear of the courtroom,
lauded me as the Dostoyevsky of disinformation. This spy
story I'd been spinning out could indeed provide the key to
George's ostensibly haywire behavior, to his so fortuitously
stumbling on me in the marketplace, to his following me and
pursuing me and taking me dead seriously no matter how
bizarre my own performance, except for one formidable impediment to its logic: the ubiquitous Moishe Pipik. Everything
that George had appeared to discount as concocted by me to
confound the Israeli intelligence agent driving our cab, local
Palestinian intelligence—had it taken the slightest interest in
me—would already have known to be the truth through its
contacts at the two hotels where Pipik and I were each openly
registered in my name. And if the higher-ups in Palestinian intelligence were well aware that the Diasporist and the novelist
were different people, that the King David P.R. was an impostor and the American Colony P.R. the real thing, why then
would they—more precisely, why then would their agent,
George Ziad—pretend to me to think that the two were identical? Particularly when they knew that I knew as well as they
did of the existence of the other one!

No, Moishe Pipik's existence argued too powerfully against
the plausibility of the story with which I was trying to con-

vince myself that George Ziad was something other than insane and that there was a meaning more humanly interesting
than that lurking beneath all this confusion. Unless, of course,
they'd planted Pipik in the first place—unless, as I'd all but
doped out the very first time I made contact with Pipik and interviewed him from London as Pierre Roget, *unless Pipik had
been working for them from the start*. Of course! That's what intelligence agencies do all the time. They'd stumbled accidentally on my look-alike, who might actually be, for all I knew, in
the seedy end of the detective business, and, for a fee, they had
put him up to some propagandistic mischief—to spouting to
whoever would listen all this thinly camouflaged anti-Zionist
crap that called itself Diasporism. He was being run by my old
friend George Ziad, George his coach, his contact, his brains.
The last thing they'd expected was that, in the midst of it all, *I*
would turn up in Jerusalem too. Or maybe that was what
they'd *planned*. They had set Pipik out as the bait. But to lure
me into doing what?

Why, exactly what I was doing. Exactly what I had done!
Exactly what I was going to do. They're not just running him,
they're running *me* without my knowing it! They have been
since I got here!

I stopped myself right there. Everything I had been thinking
—and, what's worse, eagerly believing—shocked me and
frightened me. What I was elaborating so thoroughly as a rational explanation of reality was infused with just the sort of
rationality that the psychiatrists regularly hear from the most
far-gone paranoid on the schizophrenic ward. I stopped myself
and stepped back in alarm from the hole where I was blindly
headed, realizing that in order to make George Ziad "more
humanly interesting" than someone simply nuts and out of
control, I was making *myself* nuts. Better for real things to be
uncontrollable, better for one's life to be indecipherable and
intellectually impenetrable than to attempt to make causal
sense of what is unknown with a fantasy that is mad. Better, I
thought, that the events of these three days should remain incomprehensible to me forever than to posit, as I had just been
doing, a conspiracy of foreign intelligence agents who are determined to control my mind. We've all heard that one before.

Mr. Rosenberg had been recalled to be questioned about a sixty-eight-page document that only now, in the closing hours of the year-long trial, had been discovered by the defense at a Warsaw historical institute. It was a 1945 report about Treblinka and the fate of the Jews there, written in Eliahu Rosenberg's own hand and in Yiddish, his first language, nearly thirty months after his escape from Treblinka, while he was a soldier in the Polish army. Encouraged to recount the story of the death camp by some Poles in Cracow, where he was then billeted, Rosenberg had spent two days writing down his memories and then gave the manuscript to a Cracow landlady, a Mrs. Wasser, to pass on to the appropriate institution for whatever historical usefulness it might have. He had not seen his Treblinka memoir again until on that morning a photocopy of the original was handed to him on the witness stand and he was asked by defense counsel Chumak to examine the signature and to tell the court if it was his own.

Rosenberg said it was, and when there was no objection from the prosecution, the 1945 memoir was admitted into evidence "for the purposes," said Justice Levin, "of questioning the witness in conjunction with what it states in same on the events of the uprising at Treblinka on the second of August, 1943. And specifically," Levin continued, "on the subject of the death of Ivan as written down in said statement."

The death of Ivan? At the sound of those four words coming through the earphones in English translation, young Demjanjuk, seated directly in front of me, began to nod his head vigorously, but otherwise there wasn't a movement to be discerned in the courtroom, not a sound was to be heard until Chumak, with his confident matter-of-factness, set out in his Canadian-accented English to review with Rosenberg the relevant pages of this memoir, in which, apparently just months after the end of the European war, Rosenberg had written of the death of the very man into whose "murderous eyes" he had gazed with such horror and revulsion back on the seventh day of the trial, or so he had sworn.

"I would like to go directly to the relevant portion with Mr. Rosenberg, where you wrote, 'After a few days, the date for the uprising was set for the second day of the eighth month with no excuse'—can you find that on page sixty-six of the document?"

Chumak then took him through his description of the heat in the middle of the day of August 2, 1943, a heat so fierce that the "boys," as Rosenberg had described his fellow death commandos, who had been working since four a.m., sobbed from pain and fell down with the stretchers while transferring exhumed corpses to be incinerated. The revolt had been set for four p.m., but fifteen minutes before, there was a hand-grenade explosion and several shots rang out, signaling that the uprising had begun. Rosenberg read aloud the Yiddish text and then translated into Hebrew a description of how one of the boys, Shmuel, was the first to run out of the barracks, loudly shouting the uprising's passwords, "Revolution in Berlin! There is a revolt in Berlin!" and how Mendel and Chaim, two other boys, then jumped the Ukrainian barracks guard and took the rifle from his hands.

"Now you wrote these lines, sir, and they are correct," said Chumak. "That's what happened at the time, is that correct?"

"If it pleases the court," said Rosenberg, "I think I have to explain. Because what I say here, I had heard. I hadn't seen it. There's a big difference between the two."

"But what you just read to us, sir, that Shmuel was the first to leave the barracks. Did you see him leave the barracks?"

Rosenberg said that no, he hadn't seen it himself, and that in much of what he'd written he had been reporting what others had seen and what they had told one another once they had gotten over all the fences and safely escaped into the forest.

"So," said Chumak, who was not about to let him be on this subject, "you don't write in your document that they told us about it in the forest later, you are writing it as it is happening in the document, which you have admitted your memory was better in '45 than it is today. And I put it to you that if you wrote this, you must have seen it."

Again Rosenberg set out to clarify that what he'd written was based, of necessity, on what he had been able to observe as a participant in the uprising and on what all the others had told him afterward, in the forest, about their involvement and what they had seen and done.

Zvi Tal, the bearded judge in the skullcap, stereotypically judicious-looking with his glasses set halfway down his nose, finally interrupted the repetitious duologue between Chumak and Rosenberg and asked the witness, "Why didn't you point out later, in the forest, I saw, I heard such and such—why did you write it as though you saw it yourself?"

"Perhaps it was a mistake on my part," replied Rosenberg. "Perhaps I should have noted it, but the fact of the matter is that I did hear all of this, and I have always said that in the course of the uprising, I didn't see what was happening all around me because the bullets were shrieking all around us and I just wanted to get away as quickly as possible from that inferno."

"Naturally," said Chumak, "everyone would want to get away as quickly as possible from that inferno, but if I could proceed, did you see this guard being strangled by everybody and thrown into the well—did you see that?"

"No," said Rosenberg, "it was told to me in the forest, not just to me, everyone heard about it, and there were many versions, not only that one. . . ."

Justice Levin asked the witness, "You were inclined to believe what people told you, people who had escaped as you did, to freedom from the camp?"

"Yes, Your Honor," said Rosenberg. "It was a symbol of our great success, the very fact that we heard what had been done to those *Vachmanns*, for us it was a wish come true. Of course I believed that they had been killed and that they had been strangled—it was a success for us. Can you imagine, sir, such a success, this wish come true, where people succeeded in killing their assassins, their killers? Did I have to doubt it? I believed it with my whole heart. And would that it had been true. I hoped it was true."

All of this having been explained yet again, Chumak nonetheless resumed questioning Rosenberg along the very same lines—"Didn't you see all of these events, sir, that I have read out to you?"—until finally the chief prosecutor rose to object.

"I believe," the prosecutor said, "that the witness has already replied to this question several times."

The bench, however, allowed Chumak to continue and even

Judge Tal intervened again, more or less along the line of what *he* had asked Rosenberg only minutes before. "Do you agree," he said to the witness, "that it emerges from what you wrote down, if one just reads what you wrote down—that one simply cannot tell what you actually saw for yourself and what you heard about later? In other words, anyone reading this would be inclined to think that you saw everything. Do you agree?"

While the questioning dragged on about the method by which Rosenberg had composed his memoir, I thought, Why is his technique so hard to understand? The man is not a skilled verbalist, he was never a historian, a reporter, or a writer of any kind, nor was he, in 1945, a university student who knew from studying the critical prefaces of Henry James all there is to know about the dramatization of conflicting points of view and the ironic uses of contradictory testimony. He was a meagerly educated twenty-three-year-old Polish Jewish survivor of a Nazi death camp who had been given paper and a pen and then placed for some fifteen or twenty hours at a table in a Cracow rooming house, where he had written not the story, strictly told, of his own singular experience at Treblinka but rather what he had been asked to write: a memoir of Treblinka life, a *collective* memoir in which he simply, probably without giving the matter a moment's thought, subsumed the experiences of the others and became the choral voice for them all, moving throughout from the first-person plural to the third-person plural, sometimes from one to the other within the very same sentence. That such a person's handwritten memoir, written straight out in a couple of sittings, should lack the thoughtful discriminations of self-conscious narration did not strike me, for one, as surprising.

"Now," Chumak was saying, "now this is really the heart of the whole exercise, Mr. Rosenberg—the next line of what you wrote in December of 1945." He asked Rosenberg to read aloud what came next.

"'We then went into the engine room, to Ivan, he—who was sleeping there—'" Rosenberg slowly translated from the Yiddish in a forceful voice, "'and Gustav hit him with a shovel on the head. And he remained lying down for keeps.'"

"In other words, he was dead?" Chumak asked.

"Yes, correct."

"Sir, on December 20, 1945, in your handwriting?"

"Correct."

"And I suppose this would be one very important piece of information in your document, sir, would it not be?"

"Of course it would be a very important piece of information," Rosenberg replied, "if it were the truth."

"Well, when I asked you about the whole document, sir, the sixty-eight pages—I asked you whether you made an accurate and correct version or recital of what occurred at Treblinka. You said, at the very beinning of my cross-examination—"

"I say again yes. But there are things which I heard."

In front of me young Demjanjuk was shaking his head in disbelief at Rosenberg's contention that eyewitness testimony recorded in 1945 could be based on unreliable evidence. Rosenberg was lying and, thought the son of the accused, lying because of his own unappeasable guilt. Because of how he had managed to live while all the others died. Because of what the Nazis had ordered him to do with the bodies of his fellow Jews and what he obediently had done, loathsome as it was for him to do it. Because to survive not only was it necessary to steal, which he did, which of course they all did all the time—from the dead, from the dying, from the living, from the ill, from one another and everyone—but also it was necessary to bribe their torturers, to betray their friends, to lie to everyone, to take every humiliation in silence, like a whipped and broken animal. He was lying because he was worse than an animal, because he'd become a monster who had burned the little bodies of Jewish children, thousands upon thousands of them burned by him for kindling, and the only means he has to justify becoming a monster is to lay his sins on my father's head. My innocent father is the scapegoat not merely for those millions who died but for all the Rosenbergs who did the monstrous things they did to survive and now cannot live with their monstrous guilt. The other one is the monster, says Rosenberg, Demjanjuk is the monster. I am the one who catches the monster, who identifies the monster and sees that he is slain. There, in the flesh, is the criminal monster, John Demjanjuk of Cleveland, Ohio, and I, Eliahu Rosenberg of Treblinka, am cleansed.

Or were these not at all like young Demjanjuk's thoughts? Why is Rosenberg lying? Because he is a Jew who hates Ukrainians. Because the Jews are out to get the Ukrainians. Because this is a plot, a conspiracy by all these Jews to put all Ukrainians on trial and vilify them before the world.

Or were *these* nothing like John junior's thoughts either? Why is this Rosenberg lying about my father? Because he is a publicity hound, a crazy egomaniac who wants to see his picture in the paper and to be their great Jewish hero. Rosenberg thinks, When I finish with this stupid Ukrainian, they'll put my picture on a postage stamp.

Why does Rosenberg lie about my father? Because he is a liar. The man in the dock is my father, so he must be truthful, and the man in the witness box is somebody else's father, so he must be lying. Perhaps it was as simple for the son as that: John Demjanjuk is my father, any father of mine is innocent, therefore John Demjanjuk is innocent—maybe nothing more need be thought beyond the childish pathos of this filial logic.

And in a row somewhere behind me, what was George Ziad thinking? Two words: public relations. Rosenberg is their Holocaust PR man. The smoke from the incinerators of Treblinka . . . behind the darkness of that darkness they still contrive to hide from the world their dark and evil deeds. The cynicism of it! To exploit with shameless flamboyance the smoke from the burning bodies of their own martyred dead!

Why is he lying? Because that's what public relations is—for a weekly paycheck they lie. They call it image making: whatever works, whatever suits the need of the client, whatever serves the propaganda machine. Marlboro has the Marlboro Man, Israel has its Holocaust Man. Why does he say what he says? Ask why the ad agencies say what they say. FOR THE SMOKESCREEN THAT HIDES EVERYTHING, SMOKE HOLOCAUST.

Or was George thinking about me and my usefulness, about making me into *his* PR man? Maybe without me to intimidate with all that righteous rage, he was taking a quiet philosophical break and thinking to himself only this: Yes, it's all a battle for TV time and column inches. Who controls the Nielsen ratings controls the world. It's all publicity, a matter of which of us comes up with the more spectacular drama to popularize his claim. Treblinka is theirs, the uprising is ours—may the best propaganda machine win.

Or maybe he was thinking, wistfully, sinisterly, utterly realistically, If only *we* had the corpses. Yes, I thought, maybe it's a pathologically desperate desire for bloody mayhem that lies behind this uprising, their need for a massacre, for piles of slaughtered corpses that will dramatize conclusively for worldwide TV just who are the victims this time round. Maybe that's why the children are in the first wave, why, instead of fighting against the enemy with grown men, they are dispatching children, armed only with stones, to provoke the firepower of the Israeli army. Yes, to make the networks forget their Holocaust we will stage *our* Holocaust. On the bodies of our children the Jews will perpetrate a Holocaust, and at last the TV audience will understand our plight. Send in the children and then summon the networks—we'll beat the Holocaust-mongers at their own game!

And what was *I* thinking? I was thinking, What are they thinking? I was thinking about Moishe Pipik and what *he* was thinking. And wondering every second where he was. Even as I continued to follow the courtroom proceedings I looked around me for some sign of his presence. I remembered the balcony. What if he was up with the journalists and the TV crews, sighting down on me from there?

I turned but from my seat could see nothing beyond the balcony railing. If he's up there, I thought, he is thinking, What is Roth thinking? What is Roth doing? How do we kidnap the monster's son if Roth is in the way?

There were uniformed policemen in the four corners of the courtroom and plainclothesmen, with walkie-talkies, standing at the back of the courtroom and regularly moving up and down the aisles—shouldn't I get hold of one and take him with me up to the balcony to apprehend Moishe Pipik? But Pipik's gone, I thought, it's over. . . .

This is what I was thinking when I was not thinking the opposite and everything else.

As to what the accused was thinking while Rosenberg explained to the court why the Treblinka memoir was erroneous, the person who best knew that sat at the defense table, the

Israeli lawyer, Sheftel, to whom Demjanjuk had been passing note after note throughout Chumak's examination of Rosenberg, notes written, I supposed, in the defendant's weak English. Demjanjuk scribbled feverishly away, but after he'd passed each note to Sheftel over the lawyer's shoulder, it did not look to me as though Sheftel gave more than a cursory glance to it before setting it down atop the others on the table.* In the Ukrainian American community, I was thinking, these notes, if they were ever to be collected and published, would have an impact on Demjanjuk's *landsmen* something like that of those famous prison letters written in immigrantese by Sacco and Vanzetti. Or the impact on the conscience of the civilized world that Supposnik immoderately posits for Klinghoffer's travel diaries should they ever be graced by an introduction by me.

All this writing by nonwriters, I thought, all these diaries, memoirs, and notes written clumsily with the most minimal skill, employing one one-thousandth of the resources of a written language, and yet the testimony they bear is no less

---

*It was Sheftel, by the way, who would have benefited from a bodyguard to protect him against attack. Perhaps my most unthinking mistake of all in Jerusalem was to have allowed myself to become convinced that at the culmination of this inflammatory trial, the violent rage of a wild Jewish avenger, if and when it should erupt, would be directed at a Gentile and not, as I initially thought, and as happened—and as even the least cynical of Jewish ironists could have foreseen—at another Jew.

On December 1, 1988, during the funeral for Demjanjuk's auxiliary Israeli lawyer—one who'd joined Sheftel, after Demjanjuk's conviction, to help prepare the Supreme Court appeal and who mysteriously committed suicide only weeks later—Sheftel was approached by Yisroel Yehezkeli, a seventy-year-old Holocaust survivor and a frequent spectator at the Demjanjuk trial, who shouted at him, "Everything's because of you," and threw hydrochloric acid in the lawyer's face. The acid completely destroyed the protective cover over the cornea of his left eye and Sheftel was virtually blind in that eye until he came to Boston some eight weeks later, where he underwent a cell transplant, a four-hour operation by a Harvard surgeon, that restored his sight. During Sheftel's Boston sojourn and subsequent recovery, he was accompanied by John Demjanjuk, Jr., who acted as his nurse and chauffeur.

As for Yisroel Yehezkeli, he was convicted of aggravated assault. He was sentenced by a Jerusalem judge, who found him "unrepentant," and served three years in jail. The court psychiatrist's report described the assailant as "not psychotic, although slightly paranoid." Most of Yehezkeli's family had been killed at Treblinka.

persuasive for that, is in fact that much more searing precisely because the expressive powers are so blunt and primitive.

Chumak was now asking Rosenberg, "So how can you possibly come to this court and point your finger at this gentleman when you wrote in 1945 that Ivan was killed by Gustav?"

"Mr. Chumak," he quickly replied, "did I say that I saw him kill him?"

"Don't answer with another question," Justice Levin cautioned Rosenberg.

"He didn't come back from the dead, Mr. Rosenberg," Chumak continued.

"I did not say so. I did not say so. I personally did not say that I saw him being killed," said Rosenberg. "But, Mr. Chumak, I would like to see him—I did not—but I did not see him. It was my fondest wish. I was in Paradise when I heard—not only Gustav but also others told me—I wanted, I wanted to believe, Mr. Chumak. I wanted to believe that this creature does not exist. Is not alive any longer. But, unfortunately, to my great sorrow, I would have liked to see him torn apart as he had torn apart our people. And I believed with all my heart that he had been liquidated. Can you understand, Mr. Chumak? It was their fondest wish. It was our dream to finish him off, together with others. But he had managed to get out, get away, survive—what luck he had!"

"Sir, you wrote in your handwriting, in Yiddish—not in German, not in Polish, not in English, but in your own language—you wrote that he was hit on the head by Gustav with a spade, leaving him lying there for keeps. You wrote that. And you told us that you wrote the truth when you made these statements in 1945. Are you saying that's not true?"

"No, it is true, this is the truth what it says here—but what the boys told us was not the truth. They wanted to boast. They were lending expression to their dream. They aspired to, their fondest wish was to kill this person—but they hadn't."

"Why didn't you write then," Chumak asked him, "it was the boys' fondest wish to kill this man and I heard later in the forest that he was killed in such and such a way—or in another way. Why didn't you write it all down, all these versions?"

Rosenberg replied, "I preferred to write this particular version."

"Who was present with you when this version was given, this version about the boys wanting to kill him, and everyone wanting to be a hero, and killing this awful man?"

"In the forest, when they told this version there were a great many around, and we sat around for some hours before we went our own way. And there, sir, they were sitting down and each was telling his version and I took it in. And this is what I remember, I took this in and I really wanted to believe firmly that this is what had happened. But it had not come about."

When I looked at Demjanjuk I saw him smiling directly back, not at me, of course, but at his loyal son, seated in the chair in front of me. Demjanjuk was amused by the absurdity of the testimony, tremendously amused by it, even triumphant-looking because of it, as though Rosenberg's claim that he had reported accurately in 1945 what his sources, unbeknownst to him, had themselves reported inaccurately was all the exculpation necessary and he was as good as free. Was he dim-witted enough to believe that? Why *was* he smiling? To raise the spirits of his son and supporters? To register for the audience his contempt? The smile was eerie and mystifying and, to Rosenberg, as anyone could see, as odious as the hand of friendship and the warm "Shalom" that had been tendered him by Demjanjuk the year before. Had Rosenberg's hatred been combustible and had a match been struck anywhere near the witness stand, the entire courtroom would have gone up in flames. Rosenberg's dockworker's fingers bit into the lectern and his jaw was locked as though to suppress a roar.

"Now," Chumak continued, "based on the 'version' as you now call it, this version of Ivan being killed, he was struck in the head with a spade. Would you therefore expect, sir, the man who was struck with the spade to have a scar or a fractured skull or some serious injury to his head? If that happened to Ivan in the engine room?"

"Of course," replied Rosenberg, "if I were sure he had been hit and in accordance with the version I wrote down, he was then dead—where is the scar? But he wasn't there. And he wasn't there—because he wasn't there." Rosenberg looked beyond Chumak now and, pointing at Demjanjuk, addressed him directly. "And if he had been there, he would not be sitting across from me. This hero is grinning!" Rosenberg cried in disgust.

But Demjanjuk was no longer merely grinning, he was laughing, laughing aloud at Rosenberg's words, at Rosenberg's rage, laughing at the court, laughing at the trial, laughing at the absurdity of these monstrous charges, at the outrageousness of a family man from a Cleveland suburb, a Ford factory employee, a church member, prized by his friends, trusted by his neighbors, adored by his family, of such a man as this being mistaken for the psychotic ghoul who prowled the Polish forests forty-five years ago as Ivan the Terrible, the vicious, sadistic murderer of innocent Jews. Either he was laughing because a man wholly innocent of any such crimes had no choice but to laugh after a year of these nightmarish courtroom shenanigans and all that the judiciary of the state of Israel had put him and his poor family through or he was laughing because he was guilty of these crimes, because he *was* Ivan the Terrible, and Ivan the Terrible was not simply a psychotic ghoul but the devil himself. Because, if Demjanjuk was not innocent, who but the devil could have laughed aloud like that at Rosenberg?

Still laughing, Demjanjuk rose suddenly from his chair, and, speaking toward the open microphone on the defense lawyers' table, he shouted at Rosenberg, "*Atah shakran!*" and laughed even louder.

Demjanjuk had spoken in Hebrew—for the second time the man accused of being Ivan the Terrible had addressed this Treblinka Jew who claimed to be his victim in the language of the Jews.

Justice Levin spoke next, also in Hebrew. On my headphones I heard the translation. "The accused's words," Justice Levin noted, "which have been placed on record—which were, 'You are a liar!'—have been—have gone on record."

Only minutes later, Chumak concluded his examination of Rosenberg, and Justice Levin declared a recess until eleven. I left the courtroom as quickly as I could, feeling bereft and spent and uncomprehending, as numb as though I were walking away from the funeral of someone I dearly loved. Never before had I witnessed an encounter so charged with pain and savagery as that frightful face-off between Demjanjuk and Rosenberg, a collision of two lives as immensely inimical as any two substances could be even on this rift-ravaged planet. Perhaps because of everything abominable in all I'd just seen or simply because of the unintended fast I'd been on now for almost twenty-four hours, as I tried to hold my place amid the spectators pushing toward the coffee machine in the snack bar off the lobby, there was a ragged overlay of words and pictures disturbingly adhering together in my mind, a grating collage consisting of what Rosenberg should have said to clarify himself and of the gold teeth being pulled from the gassed Jews' mouths for the German treasury and of a Hebrew-English primer, the book from which Demjanjuk had studiously taught himself, in his cell, to say correctly, "You're a liar." Interlaced with *You're a liar* were the words *Three thousand ducats.* I could hear distinctly the admirable Macklin oleaginously enunciating "Three thousand ducats" as I handed across my shekels to the old man taking the money at the snack bar, who, to my astonishment, was the crippled old survivor, Smilesburger, the man whose million-dollar check I'd "stolen" from Pipik and then lost. The crowd was so tightly packed behind me that no sooner had I paid for coffee and a bun than I was forced aside and had all I could do to keep the coffee in the container as I pressed toward the open lobby facing outdoors.

So now I was seeing things too. Working the cash register from atop a stool in the snack bar was just another old man with a bald head and a scaling skull, who could not possibly have been the retired New York jeweler disenchanted with Israel. I'm seeing double, I thought, doubles, I thought, but because of not eating, because of barely getting any sleep, or because I'm coming apart again for the second time in a year? How could I have convinced myself that I alone am personally responsible for overseeing the safety of Demjanjuk's son if I *weren't* coming apart? In the aftermath of that testimony, in the aftermath of Demjanjuk's laughter and Rosenberg's rage, how could the asinine clowning of that nonsensical Pipik continue to make a claim on my life?

But just then I heard shouting outside the building and, through the glass doors, saw two soldiers armed with rifles running at full speed toward the parking lot. I ran out of the lobby after them, toward where some twenty or thirty people had now gathered to encircle whatever disturbance was transpiring. And when I heard from within that circle a voice loudly shouting in English, I knew for sure that he was here and the worst had happened. The all-out paranoid who I had by now become was asserting his panicked confidence in the unstoppable unraveling of the disaster; our mutual outrage with each other had been churned into a real catastrophe by that octopus of paranoia that, interlinked, the *two* of us had become.

But the man who was shouting looked to be nearly seven feet tall, taller by far than either Pipik or me, a treelike person, a gigantic redheaded creature with an amazing chin the shape of a boxing glove. His big bowl of a forehead was flushed with his fury, and the hands he waved about high in the air looked to be as large as cymbals—you wouldn't want your two little ears caught between the clanging of those two huge hands.

In either hand he clutched a white pamphlet, which he fluttered violently over the heads of the onlookers. Although a few in the crowd held copies of the pamphlet and were flipping through its pages, mostly the pamphlets were strewn on the pavement underfoot. The Jewish giant's English was limited, but his voice was a large, cascading thing, every inch of him in that swelling voice, and when he spoke the effect was of someone sounding an organ. He was the biggest and the loudest Jew that I had ever seen and he was booming down at a priest, an elderly, round-faced Catholic priest, who, though of medium height and rather stoutly built, looked, by comparison, like a little, shatterable statuette of a Catholic priest. He stood very rigidly, holding his ground, doing his best not to be intimidated by this gigantic Jew.

I stooped to pick up one of the pamphlets. In the center of the white cover was a blue trident whose middle prong was in the shape of the Cross; the pamphlet, a dozen or so pages long, bore the English title "Millennium of Christianity in Ukraine." The priest must have been distributing the pamphlets to those who'd left the courtroom and come outside for air. I read the first sentence of the pamphlet's first page. "1988 is a significant year for Ukrainian Christians throughout the world—it is the 1,000th anniversary of the introduction of Christianity to the land called Ukraine."

The crowd, mostly Israelis, seemed to understand neither the pamphlet's contents nor what the dispute was about, and because his English was so poor, it was a moment before what the Jewish giant was shouting was intelligible even to me and I understood that he was assaulting the priest with the names of Ukrainians whom he identified as the instigators of violent pogroms. The one name I recognized was Chmielnicki, who I seemed to recall was a national hero on the order of Jan Hus or Garibaldi. I had lived among working-class Ukrainians on the Lower East Side when I'd first come to New York in the mid-fifties and remembered vaguely the annual block parties where dozens of little children danced around the streets dressed in folk costumes. There were speeches from an outdoor stage denouncing Communism and the Soviet Union, and the names Chmielnicki and Saint Volodymyr showed up on the crayoned signs in the local shop windows and outside the Orthodox Ukrainian church just around the corner from my basement apartment.

"Where murderer Chmielnicki in book!" were the words that I finally understood the giant Jew to be shouting. "Where murderer Bandera in book! Where murderer Petlura son of bitch! Killer! Murderer! All Ukrainian anti-Semite!"

Defiantly cocking his head, the priest snapped back, "Petlura, if you knew anything, was himself murdered. Martyred. In Paris. By Soviet agents." He was an American, as it turned out, a Ukrainian Orthodox priest who, from the sound of his voice, was more than likely a New Yorker and who seemed to have come to Jerusalem all the way from New York, perhaps even from Second Avenue and Eighth Street, specifically to distribute his pamphlets celebrating the thousand years of Ukrainian Christianity to the Jews attending the Demjanjuk trial. Wasn't he in his right mind, either?

And then I realized that I was the one who had to be out of his mind to be taking him for a priest and that this was more of the masquerade, a performance designed to create a disturbance, to distract the police and soldiers, to draw away the crowd . . . I could no more free myself of the thought that Pipik was behind it all than Pipik could free himself of

the thought that I was perpetually behind him. This priest is
Pipik's decoy and part of Pipik's plot.

"No!" the Jewish giant was shouting. "Petlura murdered,
yes—by *Jew*! For killing *Jew*! By brave *Jew*!"

"Please," said the priest, "you have had your say, you have
spoken. Everybody can hear you from here to Canarsie—allow
me, will you, please, to address those good people here who
might like to listen to somebody else for a change." And turning away from the Jewish giant, he resumed the lecture he'd
apparently been delivering before their ruckus had begun. As
he spoke, the crowd grew larger, *just as Pipik had anticipated.*
"Around the year 860," the priest was telling them, "two
blood brothers, Cyril and Methodius, left their monastery in
Greece to preach Christianity among the Slavic people. Our
forefathers had no alphabet and no written language. These
brothers created for us an alphabet called the Cyrillic alphabet,
after the name of one of the brothers—"

But again the Jewish giant interposed himself between the
onlookers and the priest, and again he began to shout at him
in that astoundingly large voice. "Hitler and Ukrainian! Two
brother! One thing! Kill Jew! I know! Mother! Sister! Everybody! Ukrainian kill!"

"Listen, bud," said the priest, his fingers whitening around
the thick stack of pamphlets that he was still clutching to his
chest, "Hitler, for your information, was no friend of the
Ukrainian people. Hitler gave away half of my country to Na-
zified Poland, in case you haven't heard. Hilter gave Bukovina
to Fascist Romania, Hitler gave Bessarabia—"

"No! Shut up! Hitler give you big present! Hitler give you
big, big present! Hitler," he boomed, "give you Jew to kill!"

"Cyril and Methodius," the priest resumed, again bravely
turning his back on the giant to address the crowd, "translated
the Bible and the Holy Mass into Slavonic, as the language was
called. They set out to Rome, to obtain permission from Pope
Adrian II to say Mass in the language they had translated.
Pope Adrian approved it and our Slavonic Mass, or Ukrainian
liturgy, was celebrated—"

That was as much about the brothers Cyril and Methodius
as the giant Jew could bear to hear. He reached out for the
priest with his two giant's hands and I saw him suddenly as

created not by a malfunctioning pituitary gland but by a thousand years of Jewish dreaming. Our final solution to the Ukrainian Christianity problem. Not Zionism, not Diasporism, but Gigantism—Golemism! The five soldiers looking on with their rifles from the edge of the crowd surged forward to intervene and protect the priest, but what happened happened so quickly that before the soldiers could stop anything, everything was over and everyone was laughing and already walking away—laughing not because the priest from New York City had been lifted into the air and smashed to the ground and dispatched from this life into the next by the enormous muddy boots on the giant's two feet but because a couple of hundred pamphlets went sailing up over our heads and that was the end of that. The giant had yanked from the priest's hands all of his pamphlets, hurled them as high as he could, and with that the incident was over.

As the crowd dispersed to return to the courtroom, I stood there watching the priest set out to recover his pamphlets, some of which were scattered as far as fifty feet away. And I saw the giant, still shouting, moving off alone toward the street, where buses were running and traffic was flowing as though it was what indeed it was, in Jerusalem as everywhere else: just another day. A sunny, pleasant day at that. The priest, of course, had nothing at all to do with Pipik, and the plot that I had resolved to foil existed nowhere other than in my head. Whatever I thought or did was wrong and for the simple reason that there was, I now realized, no *right thing* for someone whose double in this world was Mr. Moishe Pipik—so long as he and I both lived, this mental chaos would prevail. I'll never again know what's really going on or whether my thoughts are nonsense or not; everything I can't immediately understand will have for me a bizarre significance and, even if I have no idea where he is and never hear tell of him again, so long as he goes about, as he does, giving my life its shallowest meaning, I'll never be free of exaggerated thoughts or these insufferable sieges of confusion. Even worse than never being free of him, I'll never again be free of myself; and nobody can know any better than I do that this is a punishment without limits. Pipik will follow me all the days of my life, and I will dwell in the house of Ambiguity forever.

The priest continued to gather up the pamphlets one by one, and because he was much older than I'd realized when he was defiantly standing up to the giant, the effort was not easy for him. He was a very weak, very stout old man, and although the encounter had not ended violently, it seemed to have left him as enfeebled as if he had in fact received a terrible blow. Maybe bending over picking up the pamphlets was making him dizzy, because he didn't look at all well. He was terrifyingly ashen, whereas facing down the giant, he had been a pluckier, much more vivid shade.

"Why," I said to him, "why, in all of this world, do you come here with those pamphlets on a day like this one?"

He'd fallen to his knees to gather together the pamphlets more easily, and from his knees he answered me. "To save Jews." A little of his strength seemed to return when he repeated to me, "To save you Jews."

"You might do better to worry about yourself." Although this had not been my intention, I stepped forward to offer him my hand; I didn't see how else he could get back on his feet. Two bystanders, two young men in jeans, two very tough customers indeed, young and lithe and scornful, were watching us from only a few feet away. The rest of the crowd had all moved off.

"If they convict an innocent man," the priest said as I tried to remember where I'd seen these two in jeans before, "this will have the same result as the Crucifixion of Jesus."

"Oh, for God's sake, not that old chestnut, Father. Not the Crucifixion of Christ *again!*" I said, steadying him now that he was standing erect.

His voice shook when he replied, not because he was winded but because my angry response had left him incensed. "Through two thousand years, Jewish people paid for that— rightly or wrongly, they paid for the Crucifixion. I don't want the conviction of Johnny to have similar results!"

And it was just here that I felt myself leaving the ground. I was being removed from where I was to somewhere else. I did not know what was happening but I felt as though a pipe were digging into either side of me and on these pipes I was being hoisted and carried away. My feet were cycling in the air, and then they met the ground and I saw that the two pipes were arms belonging to the two men in jeans.

"Don't shout," one of them said.

"Don't struggle," the other said.

"Do nothing," the first one said.

"But—" I began.

"Don't speak."

"You speak too much."

"You speak to everyone."

"You speak speak speak."

"Speak speak speak speak speak speak—"

They put me into a car, and someone drove us away. Roughly the two men patted me all over to see if I was carrying a weapon.

"You have the wrong man," I said.

The driver laughed loudly. "Good. We want the wrong man."

"Oh," I heard myself asking through a great fog of terror, "is this going to be a humorous experience?"

"For us," replied the driver, "or for you?"

"Who are you?" I cried. "Palestinians? Jews?"

"Why," said the driver, "that's the very question we want to ask you."

I thought it best to say no more, though "thought" does not describe in any way the process by which my mind was now operating. I began to vomit, which did not endear me to my captors.

I was driven to a stone building in a decaying neighborhood just back of the central market, not far from where I'd run into George the day before and somewhere very near where Apter lived. There were some six or seven tiny Orthodox children, their skulls crystalline, playing a game in the street, strikingly transparent little things, whose youngish mothers, most of them pregnant, stood not far away, holding bags of groceries from their shopping expeditions and animatedly gossiping together. Huddling close to the women were three pigtailed little girls wearing long white stockings and they alone blandly looked my way as I was propelled past them into a narrow alleyway and back through to where freshly washed undergarments were strung up on lines crisscrossing a small courtyard. We turned into a stone stairway, a door was unlocked, and we entered the rear foyer of what looked to me to be a very shabby dentist's or doctor's office. I saw a table littered with Hebrew magazines, there was a woman receptionist speaking on the phone, and then I was through another door and into a tiny bathroom, where a light was flipped on and I was told to wash.

I was a long time soaking my face and my clothes and repeatedly rinsing out my mouth. That they allowed me to be alone like this, that apparently they didn't want me to be left disgustingly smelly, that I had not been gagged or blindfolded, that nobody was banging on the door of the cubicle with the butt of a pistol telling me to hurry up—all this provided my first tinge of hope and suggested to me that these were not Palestinians but Pipik's Jews, the Orthodox coconspirators whom he had double-crossed by ducking out and who now had me confused with him.

Once I was clean I was led, and now without too much force from behind, out of the washroom and down the corridor to a narrow staircase whose twenty-three shallow steps took us to a second story, where four classrooms angled off of a central landing. Overhead there was a skylight, opaque with soot, and the floorboards beneath my shoes were badly scuffed and worn. The place reeked of stale cigarette smoke, a smell that carried me back some forty-five years, to the little Talmud Torah, one flight above our local synagogue, where I went unenthusiastically with my friends to study Hebrew for an hour in the late afternoons three days a week in the early 1940s. The rabbi who ran the show there had been a heavy smoker and, as best I could remember it, that second floor of the synagogue back in Newark, aside from smelling exactly the same, hadn't looked too unlike this place either—shabby, dreary, just a little disagreeably slummy.

They put me in one of the classrooms and closed the door. I was alone again. Nobody had kicked me or slapped me or tied my hands or shackled my legs. On the blackboard I saw something written in Hebrew. Nine words. I couldn't read one of them. Four decades after those three years of afternoon classes at the Hebrew school, I could no longer even identify the letters of the alphabet. There was a nondescript wooden table at the front of the classroom, and in back of it a slatted chair for the teacher. On the table was a TV set. *That* we did not have in 1943, nor did we sit on these movable molded-plastic student chairs but on long benches nailed to the floor before sloped wooden desks on which we wrote our lessons from right to left. For one hour a day, three days a week, fresh from six and a half hours of public school, we sat there and learned to write backwards, to write as though the sun rose in the west and the leaves fell in the spring, as though Canada lay to the south, Mexico to the north, and we put our shoes on before our socks; then we escaped back into our cozy American world, aligned just the other way around, where all that was plausible, recognizable, predictable, reasonable, intelligible, and useful unfolded its meaning to us from left to right, and the only place we proceeded in reverse, where it was natural, logical, in the very nature of things, the singular and unchallengeable exception, was on the sandlot diamond. In the early 1940s, reading and writing from right to left made about as much sense to me as belting the ball over the outfielder's head and expecting to be credited with a triple for running from third to second to first.

I hadn't heard a bolt turn in the door, and when I hurried over to the windows I found not only that they were unlocked but that one was open at the bottom. I had merely to push it up all the way to be able to crawl out, hang full length from the sill, and then drop from the window the ten or twelve feet to the courtyard below. I could then race the twenty yards down the alleyway and, once out into the street, start shouting for help—or make directly for Apter's. Only what if they opened fire? What if I hurt myself jumping and they caught me and dragged me back inside? Because I still didn't know who my captors were, I couldn't decide which was the bigger risk: to escape or not to try to escape. That they hadn't chained me to the wall of a windowless dungeon didn't necessarily mean that they were nice fellows or that they would take lightly any failure to cooperate. But to cooperate with *what*? Hang around, I thought, and you'll find out.

I soundlessly opened the window all the way, but when I peered out to gauge the drop, a pain went jaggedly crackling through the left hemisphere of my head and whatever can pulsate in a man began to pulsate in me. I wasn't a man, I was now an engine being revved up by something beyond my control. I pulled the window down as soundlessly as I'd pulled it open, leaving it ajar at the bottom precisely as I'd found it, and, crossing to the center of the room, like the eager student who arrives first in the class, I took a seat in front of the blackboard, two rows from the teacher's table and the TV set, convinced that I had no need to jump, because I had nothing to fear from Jews, and simultaneously stunned by my childish ingenuousness. Jews couldn't beat me, starve me, torture me? No Jew could kill me?

Again I went over to the window, although this time all I did was look out into the courtyard, hoping that someone looking in would see me and understand from whatever I was able silently to signal that I was here against my will. And I was thinking that whatever it was that was happening to me and had been happening now for three days, it had all begun back when I'd first taken my seat in that small, ill-ventilated classroom that was the Newark original of this makeshift Jerusalem replica, during those darkening hours when I could barely bring myself to pay attention after a full day in the school where my heart was somehow always light, the public school from which I understood clearly, every day in a thousand ways, my real future was to arise. But how could anything come of going to Hebrew school? The teachers were lonely foreigners, poorly paid refugees, and the students—the best among us along with the worst—were bored, restless American kids, ten, eleven, twelve years old, resentful of being cooped up like this year after year, through the fall, winter, and spring, when everything seasonal was exciting the senses and beckoning us to partake freely of all our American delights. Hebrew school wasn't school at all but a part of the deal that our parents had cut with *their* parents, the sop to pacify the old generation—who wanted the grandchildren to be Jews the way that they were Jews, bound as they were to the old millennial ways—and, at the same time, the leash to restrain the breakaway young, who had it in their heads to be Jews in a way no one had ever dared to be Jew in our three-thousand-year history: speaking and thinking American English, *only* American

English, with all the apostasy that was bound to beget. Our put-upon parents were simply middlemen in the classic American squeeze, negotiating between the shtetl-born and the Newark-born and taking blows from either side, telling the old ones, "Listen, it's a new world—the kids have to make their way here," while sternly rebuking the young ones, "You must, you have to, you cannot turn your back on everything!" What a compromise! What could possibly come of those three or four hundred hours of the worst possible teaching in the worst possible atmosphere for learning? Why, everything—what came of it was *everything!* That cryptography whose signification I could no longer decode had marked me indelibly four decades ago; out of the inscrutable words written on this blackboard had evolved every English word I had ever written. Yes, all and everything had originated there, including Moishe Pipik.

I began to make a plan. I would tell them the story of Moishe Pipik. I would differentiate for them between what he was up to and what I was up to. I would answer any questions they had about George Ziad—I had nothing to hide about our meetings and conversations or even about my own Diaspora diatribes. I would tell them about Jinx, describe every last thing that they wanted to know. "I am guilty of nothing," I would tell them, "except perhaps failing to notify the police about Pipik's threat to kidnap young Demjanjuk, and even that I can explain. I can explain everything. I came only to interview Aharon Appelfeld." But if the people holding me here are indeed Pipik's coconspirators, and if they have gotten me out of the way like this precisely now to go ahead and abduct young Demjanjuk, then that is the *last* thing I should say!

Exactly what justification should I offer—and who will swallow it anyway? Who that comes to interrogate me will believe that there is no conspiracy to which I am a party, no plot in which I have had a hand, that there is no collusion here, no secret machinations between Moishe Pipik and me or between George Ziad and me, that I have not put anyone up to anything for any personal, political, or propagandistic reason whatsoever, that I have devised no strategy to assist Palestinians or to compromise Jews or to intervene in this struggle in any way? How can I convince them that there is nothing artful here, no subtle aim or hidden plan undergirding everything, that these events are nonsensical and empty of meaning, that there is no pattern or sequence arising from some dark or sinister motive of mine or any motive of *mine* at all, that this is in no way an imaginative creation accessible to an interpretive critique but simply a muddle, a mix-up, and a silly fucking mess!

I remembered how, in the mid-sixties, a Professor Popkin had come forward with a carefully argued theory that there was not just a single Lee Harvey Oswald involved in killing Kennedy on November 22, 1963, but a second Oswald, a double of Oswald, who had been deliberately conspicuous around Dallas during the weeks before the assassination. The Warren Commission had dismissed these sightings of a second Oswald —at times when Oswald himself could be proved to have been elsewhere—as a case of mistaken identification, but Popkin argued that the instances of duplication were too frequent and the reports too well founded to be discounted, especially the reports of those episodes in which the look-alike had been seen shopping in a gun store and flamboyantly firing weapons at a local rifle range. The second Oswald was a real person, Popkin concluded, one of the assassins in a conspiracy in which the first Oswald played the role of a decoy or perhaps, unwittingly, of a patsy.

And it's this, I thought, that I'm about to go up against, some conspiracy genius for whom it's unimaginable that anyone like me or Lee Harvey Oswald could be out there plotless and on his own. My Pipik will father my Popkin, and the patsy this time will be me.

I spent nearly three hours alone in that classroom. Instead of jumping from the window into the courtyard and making a run for it, instead of opening the room's unlocked door to see if it was possible simply to walk out the way I'd come in, I finally went back to my seat in the second row and sat there doing what I've done throughout my professional life: I tried to think, first, how to make credible a somewhat extreme, if not outright ridiculous, story and, next, how, after telling it, to fortify and defend myself from the affronted who read into the story an intention having perhaps to do less with the author's perversity than with their own. Fellow writers will understand when I say that, excepting the difference in what might be at stake here and the dreadful imaginings that this fomented,

preparing myself in that room to tell my story to my inter-
rogator struck me as being not unlike waiting to see the review
of your new book by the dumbest, clumsiest, shallowest, most
thick-witted, wrongheaded, tone-deaf, tin-eared, insensate,
and cliché-recycling book-reviewing dolt in the business.
There's not much hope of getting through. Who wouldn't
consider jumping out the window instead?

About midway through my second hour, when no one had
as yet appeared to tie me up or beat me up or put a pistol to
my head and begin to ask me my opinions, I began to wonder
if I might not be the victim of a practical joke and nothing
more perilous than that. Three thugs and their car had been
hired by Pipik to scare the life out of me—it could have cost
him as little as two hundred bucks and, who knows, maybe not
even half that much. They'd swept me up, dumped me off,
and then gone on their merry way, nothing worse to show for
their half hour's work than my vomit on the tips of their shoes.
It was pure Pipik, a brainstorm bearing all the earmarks of the
putative private eye whose capacity for ostentatious provocation appeared to me inexhaustible. For all I knew, there was a
peephole somewhere in this very room from behind which he
was now watching me disgracefully being held prisoner by no
one but myself. His revenge for my stealing his million dollars.
His mockery for my stealing his Wanda Jane. The payoff for
my breaking his glasses. Maybe she's with him, pantyless on
his lap, heroically planted on his implant and conscientiously
feeding his excitement by peeping at me too. I am their peep
show. I have been all along. The inventiveness of this nemesis
is abysmal and bottomless.

But I drove this possibility out of my mind by studying the
nine words on the blackboard, focusing on each character as
though if I looked long and hard enough I might unexpectedly regain possession of my lost tongue and a secret message
would be revealed to me. But no foreign language could have
been any more foreign. The only feature of Hebrew that I
could remember was that the lower dots and dashes were vowels and the upper markings generally consonants. Otherwise
all memory of it had been extinguished.

Obeying an impulse nearly as old as I was, I took out my
pen, and, on the back of my bill from the American Colony, I

slowly copied down the words written on the blackboard. Perhaps they weren't even words. I would have been no less stupid copying Chinese. All those hundreds of hours spent drawing these letters had disappeared without a trace, those hours might just as well have been a dream, and yet a dream in which I discovered everything that was forever thereafter to obsess my consciousness however much I might wish it otherwise.

This is what I painstakingly copied down, thinking that afterward, if there was an afterward, these markings might provide the clue to exactly where I'd been held captive and by whom.

$$\text{וַיְוָתֵר יַעֲקֹב לְבַדּוֹ וַיֵּאָבֵק}$$
$$\text{אִישׁ עַד עֲלוֹת הַשָּׁחַר}$$

I startled myself then by speaking out loud. I had been trying to convince myself that not everything sensible in me had as yet been stultified by fear, that I had strength enough left in me to sit tight and wait to see who and what I was truly up against, but instead I heard myself saying to an empty classroom, "Pipik, I know you are there," the first words I'd uttered since in the car I'd asked my captors if they were Palestinians or Jews. "Abduction on top of identity theft. Pipik, the case against you gets worse by the hour. It's still possible, if you want it, to negotiate a truce. I don't press charges and you leave me alone. Speak and tell me that you are there."

But no one spoke other than me.

I approached him next more practically. "How much would it take for you to leave me alone? Name a figure."

Although an all but irrefutable argument could have been made at that moment—and was, by me—that he did not answer because he had nothing to do with my abduction, was nowhere nearby, and more than likely had left Jerusalem the night before, the long silence that once again followed my calling out to him simultaneously intensified my belief that he *was* there and that he did not respond either because I had not as yet found the formula that would provoke a response or because he was enjoying this spectacle far too much to inter-vene or interrupt and intended to hide the face that he went around Jerusalem advertising as my own until I had reached the uttermost limits of mortification and was contritely beg-ging on my knees for mercy. Of course I knew how patheti-cally ridiculous I must appear if the abduction that bore all the clownish signs of Pipik's authorship was the handiwork of someone else entirely, someone not at all clownish who consti-tuted an even more drastic threat to me than he did and who was in fact monitoring me now, someone who far from con-niving a singularly intimate, uncanny affiliation with me, one that might make him at least a little susceptible to my tender supplications, was beyond the reach of any appeal or offer or entreaty I might make. Because I feared that scrutinizing me in my molded-plastic student chair there might well be a sur-veillant even more alien than Pipik, lethally indifferent to my every need, to whom my name and my face could not have meant less, I discovered myself desperate to hear the voice of Moishe Pipik echoing mine. The plot that I had set out to flee at dawn on the grounds of its general implausibility, its total lack of gravity, its reliance on unlikely coincidence, the absence of inner coherence and of anything resembling a serious mean-ing or purpose, that outlandish plot of Pipik's that had dis-gusted me as much by its puerility as by its treachery and deceitfulness, now seemed to be my only hope. Would that I were still a ludicrous character in his lousy book!

"Pipik, are you with me, are you here? Is this or is this not your stinking idea? If it is, tell me so. Speak. I never was your enemy. Think back on what's happened, review all the details, will you, please? Have I no right to claim that I have been pro-voked? Are you blameless entirely? Whatever pain my public standing may have caused you in those years before we met—well, how can I be responsible for that? And was it that injuri-ous? Was the resemblance to me ever really much more than what most people would think of as a nuisance? It's not I who told you to come to Jerusalem and pretend that we two were one—I cannot, in all fairness, be saddled with that. Do you hear me? Yes, you hear me—you don't answer because that's not what you hold against me. My offense is that I did not treat you with respect. I was not willing to entertain your proposal that we set up shop as partners. I was rude and caustic. I was dismissive and contemptuous. I was furious and threatening from the moment I saw you and, even before that, when I laid a trap on the phone as Pierre Roget. Look, that there is room for improvement I admit. Next time I will try harder to see your side of things before I take aim and fire. 'Stop, breathe, think,' instead of 'Ready, aim, fire'—I'm trying hard to learn. Perhaps I *was* too antagonistic—perhaps. I don't really know. I am not out to bullshit you, Pipik. You would despise me even more than you do already if, because you have the upper hand, I started kowtowing and kissing your ass. I am simply trying to explain that my response on meeting you, however offensive, was well within the range of what you might have expected from anyone in my position. But your grievance is deeper even than that. The million bucks. That's a lot of money. Never mind that you extorted it by passing yourself off as me. Maybe you're right and that's not my business. Why should I care? Especially if it's money in behalf of a good cause—and if you see it that way and say that it is, who am I to say it isn't? I'm willing to believe that that was all between Smilesburger and you. Caveat emptor, Mr. Smilesburger. Though that's not my crime either, is it? My crime is that it was I posing as you rather than you posing as me who extorted the money under false pretenses—by pretending to be you, I took what was not mine. In your eyes this amounts to grand larceny. You make the deal, I reap the harvest. Well, if it makes you feel better, I haven't come away with a red cent. I haven't got the check. I'm in your custody here, the boys who picked me up are your boys—you're in charge in every way, and so I'm not about to lie to you. The check was lost. I lost it. You may or may not know this but I haven't been contending here solely with you. The story is too long to tell, and you wouldn't believe it anyway, so suffice it to say that the check disappeared in a situation where I was utterly powerless. Can't we now go together to Mr. Smilesburger and explain to him his confusion? Get him to stop the old check and issue a new one? I would bet another million that the first check isn't in anyone's pocket but either got blown away by the wind or was trampled into the ground when some soldiers roughed me up on the road from Ramallah. That's the story you won't believe, though you ought to, really—it's not a lot stranger than yours. I got caught in the crossfire of the fight being fought here, and that's when your check disappeared. We'll get you another one. I'll help you get it. I'll do everything I can in your behalf. Isn't that what you've been asking from the start? My cooperation? Well, you've got it. This does it. I'm on your side. We'll get you your million bucks back."

I waited in vain for him to speak, but either he believed that I was lying and holding out on him, that his million was already in my account, or he wanted even more, or he wasn't there.

"And I apologize," I said, "about Jinx. Wanda Jane. For a man who's gone through and survived the physical anguish that you've suffered, of course that's bitterly infuriating. This probably has incensed you even more than the money. I don't expect that you would believe me if I were to tell you that to pierce your heart was not my motive or intention. You think otherwise, of course. You think I meant to punish and humiliate you. You think I mean to steal what you prize most. You think I mean to strike a blow where you are most vulnerable. It won't do me any good to try to tell you that you're wrong. Particularly as you could be partially right. Human psychology being what it is, you could even be entirely right. But since the truth is the truth, let me add insult to insult and injury to injury—I did not do what I did without some feeling. For her, I mean. I mean that muzzling a virile response to her kind of magnetism has turned out to be no easier for me than it is for you. There's yet another resemblance between us. I realize this was never the kind of partnership you had in mind but . . . But nothing. Enough. Wrong tack. I did it. I did it and in similar circumstances I would probably try to do it again. But there will be no such circumstances, that I promise you. The incident will never be repeated. I only ask you now to accept that by having been abducted and detained like this, by tasting all the terror that goes with sitting in this room not knowing what's in store for me, I have been sufficiently disciplined for trespassing against you as I have."

I waited for an answer. *This was never the kind of partnership you had in mind.* I needn't have said *that,* but otherwise, I thought, in a predicament as ambiguously menacing as this, no one could have spoken much more adroitly. Nor had I been craven. I had said more or less what he wanted me to say while still saying what was more or less true.

But when still no answer was forthcoming, I all at once lost whatever adroitness I may have had and announced in a voice no longer calm and steady, "Pipík, if you cannot forgive me, give me a sign that you're there, that you're here, that you hear me, that I am not talking to a wall!" Or, I thought, to someone even less forgiving than you and capable of a rebuke sterner even than your silence. "What do you require, burnt offerings? I will never again go near your girl, we'll get you back your goddamn money—now say something! Speak!"

And only then did I understand what he *did* require of me, not to mention understanding finally just how very maladroit I was with him and had been from the start, how unforgivably self-damaging a miscalculation it had been to deny this impostor the thing that any impostor covets and can least do without and that only I could meaningfully anoint him with. Only when I spoke my name as though I believed it was his name as well, only then would Pipik reveal himself and negotiations commence to propitiate his rage.

"Philip," I said.

He did not answer.

· "Philip," I said again, "I am not your enemy. I don't want to be your enemy. I would like to establish cordial relations. I am nearly overcome by how this has turned out and, if it's not too late, I'd like to be your friend."

Nothing. No one.

"I was sardonic and unfeeling and I'm chastened," I said. "It was not right to exalt myself and denigrate you by addressing you as I have. I should have called you by your name as you called me by mine. And from now on I will. I will. I am Philip Roth and you are Philip Roth, I am like you and you are like me, in name and not only in name. . . ."

But he wasn't buying it or else he wasn't there.

He *wasn't* there. An hour later the door opened and into the classroom hobbled Smilesburger.

"Good of you to wait," he said. "Terribly sorry, but I was detained."

10

You Shall Not Hate
Your Brother in Your Heart

I WAS reading when he came in. To make it appear to whoever might be observing me that I was not yet incapacitated by fear or running wild with hallucination, that I was waiting as though for nothing more than my turn in the dental chair or at the barbershop, to force my attention to something other than the timorousness that kept me nailed warily to my seat— even more urgently, to focus on something other than the overbold boldness insistently charging me now to jump out the window—I had removed from my pockets the purported diaries of Leon Klinghoffer and shunted myself, with a huge mental effort, onto the verbal track.

How pleased my teachers would be, I thought—reading, even here! But then this was not the first time, or the last, when, powerless before the uncertainty at hand, I looked to print to subjugate my fears and keep the world from coming apart. In 1960, not a hundred yards from the Vatican walls, I had sat one evening in the empty waiting room of an unknown Italian doctor's office reading a novel of Edith Wharton's, while on the far side of the doctor's door, my then wife underwent an illegal abortion. Once on a plane with a badly smoking engine, I had heard the pilot's horrifyingly calm announcement as to how and where he planned to set down and had quickly told myself, "You just concentrate on Conrad," and continued my reading of *Nostromo*, mordantly keeping at the back of my mind the thought that at least I would die as I'd lived. And two years after escaping Jerusalem unharmed, when I wound up one night an emergency patient in the coronary unit of New York Hospital, an oxygen tube in my nose and an array of doctors and nurses fastidiously monitoring my vital signs, I waited for a decision to be made about operating on my obstructed arteries while reading, not without some pleasure, the jokes in Bellow's *The Bellarosa Connection*. The book you clutch while awaiting the worst is a book you may never be capable of summarizing coherently but whose clutching you never forget.

When I was a small boy in my first classroom—I remembered this, sitting obediently as a middle-aged man in what I could not help thinking might be my last classroom—I had been transfixed by the alphabet as it appeared in white on a black frieze some six inches high that extended horizontally atop the blackboard, "Aa Bb Cc Dd Ee," each letter exhibited there twice, in cursive script, parent and child, object and shadow, sound and echo, etc., etc. The twenty-six asymmetrical pairings suggested to an intelligent five-year-old every duality and correspondence a little mind could possibly conceive. Each was so variously interlocked and at odds, any two taken together so tantalizing in their faintly unharmonious apposition that, even if viewed as I, for one, first apprehended the alphabet frieze—as figures in profile, the way Nineveh's low-relief sculptors depicted the royal lion hunt in 1000 B.C.—the procession marching immobilely toward the classroom door constituted an associative grab bag of inexhaustible proportions. And when it registered on me that the couples in this configuration—whose pictorial properties alone furnished such pure Rorschachish delight—each had a name of its own, mental delirium of the sweetest sort set in, as it might in anyone of any age. It only remained for me to be instructed in the secret of how these letters could be inveigled to become words for the ecstasy to be complete. There had been no pleasure so fortifying and none that so dynamically expanded the scope of consciousness since I'd learned to walk some fifteen hundred days before; and there would be nothing as remotely inspirational again until a stimulant no less potent than the force of language—the hazardous allurements of the flesh and the pecker's irrepressible urge to squirt—overturned angelic childhood.

So this explains why I happened to be reading when Smilesburger appeared. The alphabet is all there is to protect me; it's what I was given instead of a gun.

In September 1979, six years before he was thrown in his wheelchair over the side of the *Achille Lauro* by Palestinian terrorists, Klinghoffer and his wife were on a cruise ship bound for Israel. This is what I read of what he'd written in the leather-bound diary with the rickshaw, the elephant, the camel, the gondola, the airliner, and the passenger ship engraved in gold on its cover.

9/5
Weather clear
Friday. Sunny

Took tour through Greek port of Piraeus and city of Athens. Guide was excellent. The city of Athens is a modern bustling city. Lots of traffic. Went up to the Acropolis and saw all the ancient ruins. It was a well-guided and interesting tour. Got home about 2.30. Quarter of 4 on way to Haifa, Israel. A very interesting afternoon. Tonight was the night. After dinner there was a singer from Israel. Gave a performance. I was one of the judges for queen of the ship. It was all hilarious. What a night. To bed at 12.30.

9/6 Sea calm
Weather good

Another pleasant day. Young Dr. and his wife going to Israel to look into opening a hospital with a group of French Jewish doctors in a large town in the south of Israel. In case something happens in France they will have a foot in Israel and an investment. Met many people, made a lot of friends in 7 days. They all loved Marilyn. She never looked so rested and pretty. Bed late. Up early. Ship to dock at Haifa tomorrow.

9/7
Haifa

What excitement. Young and old alike. Many away on tours for as long as 40 days. Some longer. Ziv and wife for 3 months singing in America. Others just cruising. What expressions of joy to be home in their country. How they love Israel. Hotel Dan a beautiful place. Accommodations good.

9/8
Haifa to Tel Aviv

The trip from Haifa to Tel Aviv over 1½ hours. The roads modern. Traffic some parts heavy. Building going on all over. Houses. Factories. It is astonishing for a country born of war and living a war to be so vibrant. The soldiers all over the place with their full packs and rifles. Girls and boys alike. Booked for tours all over the place. We are tired. Worth the tiredness. Listening to radio in lovely room looking over the blue Mediterranean.

9/8 W. sunny
Tel Aviv

Up at 7. Started to tour. Tel Aviv. Yaffo. Rehovoth. Ashdod. 50 kilometers around Tel Aviv. The activity. The building. The reclaiming of sand dunes and making towns and cities grow is astonishing. The old Arab city of Yaffo is being torn down and instead of slums that have existed for years a new city has been planned and is being erected.
The Agricultural College, the Chaim Weizmann Institute is a garden spot in Rehovoth. Its beautiful buildings, its hall of learning, its surroundings are something to see. A busy delightful educational day and a new respect for the land born of war and still plagued.

9/9 Sunny
Tel Aviv

Up at 5.45 to go to the Dead Sea. Sodom. Beersheba. Over the steep hills and down to the lowest spot on earth. What a day. 12 hours again. Terrific what is going on in this small country. Building. Roads. Irrigation. Planning and fighting. It was a very hard day but a rewarding one. Visited kibbutz at the end of the earth where young married families live in complete loneliness and unfriendly neighbors to build a land. Guts. Plain guts.

9/10
Jerusalem

What a city. What activity. New roads. New factories. New housing. Thousands of tourists from all over. Jew and Gentile alike. Got here at 11 and went on tour. The shrine of the Holocaust. And my Marilyn broke down. I had tears in my eyes also. The city is a series of hills. New and old. The garden where Billy Rose's art exhibit is. Also the museum is in the most beautiful setting. The museum is large, roomy, and full of art objects. Looking over the city from this site is grand. Supper. Walked the streets. To bed at 10.

9/11 Thursday

Looking at the hills of Jerusalem in the year 1979. It is a beautiful view. The geography is the same but with modern living, good roads, trucks, busses, cars, air conditioning to make life better. The climate here is cool at night, warm during the day except when the wind blows from the desert.

9/12
Sunny

Went to the Old City of Jerusalem. Wailing Wall. Jesus tomb. David's. Walked through narrow streets of the Arab quarter. Full of stores which are small stalls. Smells and dirt predominant. Our hotel was the border line between Israel and Jordan. The goings on in front of the W.W. were interesting. The constant praying. Bar Mitzvahs. Weddings. Etc. Got home at 1. Again tired after all touring. 2½ hour tour, all walking. No cars in the Old City. Next Hadassah Hospital. The women of America should be proud of what their efforts have done. On the grounds there is a building that is used as a research center and houses pictures of Jews killed in Germany. Horrifying between resentment and tears that well up in your eyes. You wonder how a civilized Christian nation could allow a little pimp to lead them to such atrocities. Then on to where Herzl the founder of Zionism and his family were buried. Also a cemetery built on the hills of men who died in all the wars. Ages ranging from 13 to 79. All soldiers. Then to the Knesset, college, and other important centers of government and learning.

This city is just beautiful. Full of history and wonders. All roads lead to Jerusalem not Rome. I am glad to have the opportunity to get here.

9/13
Shabbas and
Rosh Hoshana

It is 6 o'clock A.M. And from our room in the King David Hotel we have the most beautiful view, looking over the hills of Jerusalem. Just 500 yards away from our hotel was the Jordanian border where snipers stood in the ruins of the Old City and shot into the New City. There were 39 houses of worship there and the Arabs blew them all up in the last War. These people deserve all the help and praise of all of the Diaspora. The defenders of this country are 18 to 25. There are soldiers all over the city but inconspicuous. It is a modern city with all of the old ruins preserved. This is our final day in the city the Jews prayed to come back to for 2000 years and I can now understand why. I hope they never have to leave.

I was reading when Smilesburger came in, and I was also writing, making notes—while I went probingly through each plodding page of the diaries—for the introduction that Supposnik claimed would expedite Klinghoffer's American and

European publication. What else was I to do? What else do I know *how* to do? It was not even in my hands. The thoughts began to drift in a bit at a time and I began groping both to disentangle them and to piece them together—an inherent activity, a perpetual need, especially under the pressure of strong emotions like fear. I wrote not on the back of the American Colony bill, where I'd already recorded the mysterious Hebrew words chalked up on the blackboard, but in the dozen or so unused pages at the tail end of the red diary. I had nothing else on which to record anything of any length, and gradually, when the old habituated state of mind firmly took root and, as a protest perhaps against this inscrutable semicaptivity, I found myself working step by step into the familiar abyss, the initial shock of appending one's own profane handwriting to the handwriting of a murdered martyr—the transgressive feelings of a good citizen vandalizing, if not exactly a sacred work, certainly a not insignificant archival curio—gave way before an absurdly schoolboyish assessment of my situation: I had been brutally abducted and carted off to this classroom specifically for this purpose and would not be freed until a serious introduction, with the correct Jewish outlook, was satisfactorily composed and handed in.

Here are the impressions I had begun to elaborate when Smilesburger made his wily appearance and loquaciously announced why in fact I was there. As I would learn by the time he was done with me, two thousand words countenancing Klinghoffer's humanity was the *least* the situation demanded.

The terrific ordinariness of these entries. The very reasonable ordinariness of K. A wife he's proud of. Friends he loves to be with. A little money in his pocket to take a cruise. To do what he wants to do in his own artless way. The very embodiment, these diaries, of Jewish "normalization."

An ordinary person who purely by accident gets caught in the historical struggle. A life annotated by history in the last place you expect history to intervene. On a cruise, which is out of history in every way.

The cruise. Nothing could be safer. The floating lockup. You go nowhere. It's a circle. A lot of movement but no progress. Life suspended. A ritual of in-betweenness. All the time in the world. Insulated, like a moon shot. Travel within their own environment. With old friends. Don't have to learn any languages. Don't have to worry about new foods. In neutral territory, the protected trip. *But there is no neutral territory.* "You, Klinghoffer, of the Diaspora," crows the militant Zionist, "even at the point where you thought you were most safe, you weren't. You were a Jew: not even on a cruise is a Jew on a cruise." The Zionist preys on the Jewish urge for normalcy anywhere but in Fortress Israel.

The shrewdness of the PLO: they will always figure out the way to worm their way into the tranquilizing fantasy of the Jew. The PLO too denies the plausibility of Jewish safety other than armed to the teeth.

You read K.'s diaries with the whole design in mind, as you read the diary of A.F. You know he's going to die and how, and so you read it through the ending back. You know he's going to be pushed over the side, so all these boring thoughts he has—which are the sum total of everybody's existence—take on a brutal eloquence and K. is suddenly a living soul whose subject is the bliss of life.

Would Jews without enemies be just as boring as everybody else? These diaries suggest as much. What makes extraordinary all the harmless banality is the bullet in the head.

Without the Gestapo and the PLO, these two Jewish writers (A.F. and L.K.) would be unpublished and unknown; without the Gestapo and the PLO any number of Jewish writers would be, if not necessarily unknown, completely unlike the writers they are.

In idiom, interests, mental rhythms, diaries like K.'s and A.F.'s confirm the same glaring pathos: one, that Jews are ordinary; two, that they are denied ordinary lives. Ordinariness, blessed, humdrum, dazzling ordinariness, it's there in every observation, every sentiment, every thought. The center of the Jewish dream, what feeds the fervor both of Zionism and Diasporism: the way Jews would be people if they could forget they were Jews. Ordinariness. Blandness. Uneventful monotony. Unembattled existence. The repetitious security of one's own little cruise. But this is not to be. The incredible drama of being a Jew.

Although I'd only met Smilesburger the day before at lunch, my shock at the sight of him advancing on his crutches through the classroom door was akin to the astonishment of catching sight on the street, after thirty or forty years, of a school friend or a roommate or a lover, a famously unimpaired ingenue whom time has obviously reveled in recasting in the most unbefitting of character roles. Smilesburger might even have been some intimate whom I had thought long dead, so agitatingly eerie was the impact of discovering that it was he and not Pipik into whose custody I had been forcibly taken.

Unless, because of the "stolen" million, he had joined forces with Pipik . . . unless it was he who had engaged Pipik to entrap me in the first place . . . unless *I* had somehow ensnared *them*, unless there was something I was doing that I was not aware of doing, that I could not stop doing, that was the very opposite of what I wanted to be doing, and that was making everything that was happening to me seem to be happening to me without my doing anything. But assigning myself a leading role when I couldn't have felt more like everyone's puppet was the most debilitating mental development yet, and I fought off the idea with what little rationality I retained after almost three hours of waiting alone in that room. Blaming myself was only another way of not thinking, the most primitive adaptation imaginable to a chain of unlikely events, a platitudinous, catchall fantasy that told me nothing about what my relations were to whatever was going on here. I had not summoned forth, by some subterranean magic, this cripple who called himself Smilesburger just because I'd imagined that I'd seen him in the refreshment area adjacent to the courtroom when, in fact, taking the cash was an elderly man who, I now realized, bore little resemblance to him at all. I had blundered idiotically and even been half-demented, but I had not myself summoned up *any* of this: it wasn't my imagination calling the shots but my imagination that was being shattered by theirs, whoever "they" might be.

He was dressed just as he'd been at lunchtime the day before, in the neat blue businessman's suit, the bow tie, and the cardigan sweater over his starched white shirt, the attire of the fastidious jewelry-store owner; and his strangely grooved skull and scaling skin still suggested that, in handing him problems, life had not settled for half-measures and restricted his experience of loss merely to the use of his legs. His torso swung like a partially filled sandbag between the crutches whose horseshoe-shaped supports cupped his forearms, the burden of ambula-tion as torturous for him today as it had been yesterday and, more than likely, ever since he'd been impeded by the handicap that gave his face the wasted, worn-down look of someone sen-tenced to perpetually struggle uphill even when he feels the need of nothing more than a glass of water. And his English was still spoken with the immigrant accent of the tradesmen who sold cotton goods from a pushcart and herring from a barrel in the slum where my grandparents had settled and my father had grown up. What was new since yesterday, when there had ap-peared to be penned into this body nothing but the most un-speakable experience of life, was the mood of gracious warmth, the keen peal of exhilaration in the raw, rumbling voice, as though he were not ponderously poling himself forward on two sticks but slaloming the slopes at Gstaad. The demon-stration of dynamism by this wreck struck me as either self-satire at its most savage or a sign that encaged in this overabundantly beleaguered human frame was nothing but resistance.

"Good of you to wait," he said, swinging to within inches of my chair. "Terribly sorry, but I was detained. At least you brought something to read. Why didn't you turn on the tele-vision? Mr. Shaked is summing up." Spinning himself about with three little hops, virtually pirouetting on his crutches, he advanced to the teacher's table at the front of the classroom and pressed the button that brought the trial to life on the screen. There, indeed, was Michael Shaked, addressing the three judges in Hebrew. "This has made him a sex symbol—all the women in Israel are now in love with the prosecutor. They didn't open a window? So stuffy here! Have you eaten? Noth-ing to eat? No lunch? Soup? Some salads? Broiled chicken? To drink—a beer? A soda? Tell me what you like. Uri!'" he called. Into the open doorway stepped one of that pair of bejeaned abductors who had looked vaguely familiar to me out in the parking lot where my last act as a free man was to lend a help-ing hand to an anti-Semitic priest. "Why no lunch, Uri? Why are the windows shut? No one turns on television for him? No-body does anything! Smell it! They play cards and they smoke cigarettes. Occasionally they kill someone—and they think this is the whole job. Lunch for Mr. Roth!"

Uri laughed and left the room, pulling the classroom door shut behind him.

Lunch for Mr. Roth? Meaning what? The improbable fluency of that heavily accented English, the gracious amiability, the edge of paternal tenderness in that deeply masculine voice . . . all of it meaning what?

"He would have torn to pieces anyone who came within an inch of you," Smilesburger said. "A more ferocious watchdog than Uri I could not have found for you. What is the book?"

But it was not for me to explain anything, even what I was reading. I didn't know what to say, didn't even know what to ask—all I could think to do was to start shouting, and I was too frightened for that.

Maneuvering his carcass into the chair, Smilesburger said, "No one told you? They told you nothing? Inexcusable. No one told you I was coming? No one told you you could go? No one came to explain that I would be late?"

No reply necessary to sadistic baiting. Don't tell them again that they've got the wrong man. Nothing you say can make anything better; all you've said so far in Jerusalem has only made things worse.

"Why are Jews so thoughtless with one another? To keep you sitting here in the dark like this," said Smilesburger ruefully, "without even offering a cup of coffee. It persists and persists and I do not understand. Why are the Jews so lacking in the fundamental courtesies of social intercourse even between themselves? Why must every affront be magnified? Why must every provocation initiate a feud?"

I had affronted no one. I had provoked no one. I could explain that million dollars. But to his satisfaction? Without Uri reappearing *to feed me my lunch*? I didn't answer.

"The Jew's lack of love for his fellow Jew," Smilesburger said, "is the cause of much suffering among our people. The animosity, the ridicule, the sheer hatred of one Jew for another—why? Where is our forbearance and forgiveness of our neighbor? Why is there such divisiveness among Jews? It isn't only in Jerusalem in 1988 that there is suddenly this discord—it was in the ghetto, God knows, a hundred years ago; it was at the destruction of the Second Temple two thousand years ago. Why was the Second Temple destroyed? Because of this hatred of one Jew for another. Why has the Messiah not come? Because of the angry hatred of one Jew for another. We not only need Anti-Semites Anonymous for the goy—we need it for the Jew himself. Angry disputes, verbal abuse, malicious backbiting, mocking gossip, scoffing, faultfinding, complaining, condemning, insulting—the blackest mark against our people is not the eating of pork, it is not even marrying with the non-Jew: worse than both is the sin of Jewish speech. We talk too much, we say too much, and we do not know when to stop. Part of the Jewish problem is that they never know what voice to speak in. Refined? Rabbinical? Hysterical? Ironical? Part of the Jewish problem is that the voice is too loud. Too insistent. Too aggressive. No matter what he says or how he says it, it's inappropriate. *Inappropriateness* is the Jewish style. Awful. 'For each and every moment that a person remains silent, he earns a reward too great to be conceived of by any created being.' This is the Vilna Gaon quoting from the Midrash. 'What should a person's job be in this world? To make himself like a mute.' This is from the Sages. As one of our most revered rabbinical scholars has beautifully expressed it in an admirably simple sentence not ten syllables long, 'Words generally only spoil things.' You do not wish to speak? Good. When a Jew is as angry as you are, there is almost nothing harder for him than to control his speech. You are a heroic Jew. On the day of reckoning, the account of Philip Roth will be credited with merits for the restraint he has displayed here by remaining silent. Where did the Jew get it in his head that he has always to be talking, to be shouting, to be telling jokes at somebody's expense, to be analyzing over the telephone for a whole evening the terrible faults of his dearest friend? 'You shall not go about as a tale bearer among your people.' This is what is written. You shall not! It is forbidden! This is law! 'Grant me that I should say nothing that is unnecessary. . . .' This is from the prayer of the Chofetz Chaim. I am a disciple of the Chofetz Chaim. No Jew had more love for his fellow Jews than the Chofetz Chaim. You don't know the teachings of the Chofetz Chaim? A great man, a humble scholar, a revered rabbi from Radin, in Poland, he devoted his long life to trying to get Jews to shut up. He died at ninety-three in Poland the year that you were born in America. It is he who formulated the detailed laws of speech for our people and tried to cure them of the bad habits of centuries. The Chofetz Chaim formulated the laws of evil speech, or *loshon hora*, the laws that forbid Jews' making derogatory or damaging remarks about their fellow Jews, even if they are true. If they are false, of course it's worse. It is forbidden to speak *loshon hora* and it is forbidden to listen to *loshon hora*, even if you don't believe it. In his old age, the Chofetz Chaim extolled his deafness because it prevented him from hearing *loshon hora*. You can imagine how bad it had to have been for a great conversationalist like the Chofetz Chaim to say a thing like that. There is nothing about *loshon hora* that the Chofetz Chaim did not clarify and regulate: *loshon hora* said in jest, *loshon hora* without mentioning names, *loshon hora* that is common knowledge, *loshon hora* about relatives, about in-laws, about children, about the dead, about heretics and ignoramuses and known transgressors, even about merchandise—all forbidden. Even if someone has spoken *loshon hora* about you, you cannot speak *loshon hora* about him. Even if you are falsely accused of having committed a *crime*, you are forbidden to say who did do the crime. You cannot say 'He did it,' because that is *loshon hora*. You can only say 'I didn't do it.' Does it give you an idea of what the Chofetz Chaim was up against if he had to go that far to stop Jewish people's blaming and accusing their neighbors of everything and anything? Can you imagine the animosity he witnessed? Everyone feeling wronged, being hurt, bristling at insults and slights; everything everybody says taken as a personal affront and a deliberate attack; everyone saying something derogatory about everyone else. Anti-Semitism on the one side, *loshon hora* on the other, and in between, being squeezed to death, the beautiful soul of the Jewish people! The poor Chofetz Chaim was an Anti-Defamation League unto himself—only to get Jews to stop defaming *one another*. Someone else with his sensitivity to *loshon hora* would have become a murderer. But he loved his people and could not bear to see them brought low by their chattering mouths. He could not stand their quarreling, and so he set himself the impossible task of promoting Jewish harmony and Jewish unity instead of bitter Jewish divisiveness. Why couldn't the Jews be one people? Why must Jews be in conflict with one

another? Why must they be in conflict with themselves?
Because the divisiveness is not just between Jew and Jew—it is
within the individual Jew. Is there a more manifold personality
in all the world? I don't say divided. Divided is nothing. Even
the goyim are divided. But inside every Jew there is a *mob* of
Jews. The good Jew, the bad Jew. The new Jew, the old Jew.
The lover of Jews, the hater of Jews. The friend of the goy, the
enemy of the goy. The arrogant Jew, the wounded Jew.
The pious Jew, the rascal Jew. The coarse Jew, the gentle Jew.
The defiant Jew, the appeasing Jew. The Jewish Jew, the de-
Jewed Jew. Shall I go on? Do I have to expound upon the Jew
as a three-thousand-year amassment of mirrored fragments to
one who has made his fortune as a leading Jewologist of international literature? Is it any wonder that the Jew is always dis-
puting? He *is* a dispute, incarnate! Is it any wonder that he is
always talking, that he talks imprudently and impulsively and
thoughtlessly and embarrassingly and clownishly and that he
cannot purify his speech of ridicule and insult and accusation
and anger? Our poor Chofetz Chaim! He prayed to God,
'Grant me that I should say nothing that is unnecessary and
that all my speech should be for the sake of Heaven,' and
meanwhile his Jews were speaking everywhere simply for the
sake of *speaking*. All the time! Couldn't stop! Why? Because
inside each Jew were *so many speakers*. Shut up one and the
other talks. Shut him up, and there is a third, a fourth, a fifth
Jew with something more to say. The Chofetz Chaim prayed,
'I will be careful not to speak about individuals,' and meanwhile individuals were all his beloved Jews could talk about
day and night. For Freud in Vienna life was simpler, believe
me, than it was for the Chofetz Chaim in Radin. They came to
Freud, the talking Jews, and what did Freud tell them? Keep
talking. Say everything. No word is forbidden. The more *loshon
hora* the better. To Freud a silent Jew was the worst thing
imaginable—to him a silent Jew was bad for the Jew and bad
for business. A Jew who will not speak evil? A Jew who will not
get enraged? A Jew with no ill word for anyone? A Jew who
will not feud with his neighbor, his boss, his wife, his child, his
parents? A Jew who refuses to make any remark that could
possibly hurt someone else? A Jew who says only what is
strictly permissible? A world of such Jews as the Chofetz Chaim

dreamed of, and Sigmund Freud will starve to death and take all the other psychoanalysts with him. But Freud was no fool and he knew his Jews, knew them better, I am sad to say, than his Jewish contemporary, the Jewish heads to his Jewish tails, our beloved Chofetz Chaim. To Freud they flocked, the Jews who couldn't stop talking, and to Freud they spoke such *loshon hora* as was never heard from the mouths of Jews since the destruction of the Second Temple. The result? Freud became Freud because he let them say everything, and the Chofetz Chaim, who told them to refrain from saying practically everything they wanted to say, who told them they must spit the *loshon hora* out of their mouths the way they would spit out of their mouths a piece of pork that they had inadvertently begun to eat, with the same disgust and nausea and contempt, who told them that unless they were one hundred percent certain that a remark was NOT *loshon hora*, they must suppose that it was and shut up—the Chofetz Chaim did not become popular among the Jewish people like Dr. Sigmund Freud. Now, it can be argued, cynically, that speaking *loshon hora* is what makes Jews Jews and that there was nothing more Jewishly Jewish to be conceived of than what Freud prescribed in his office for his Jewish patients. Take away from the Jews their *loshon hora*, and what do you have left? You have nice goyim. But this statement is itself *loshon hora*, the worst *loshon hora* there is, because to speak *loshon hora* about the Jewish people *as a whole* is the gravest sin of all. To berate the Jewish people for speaking *loshon hora*, as I do, is itself to commit *loshon hora*. Yet I not only speak the worst *loshon hora* but compound my sin by forcing you to sit here and listen to it. I am the very Jew I am berating. I am *worse* than that Jew. That Jew is too stupid to know what he is doing, while I am a disciple of the Chofetz Chaim, who knows that, so long as there is all this *loshon hora*, the Messiah will never come to save us— and still I speak *loshon hora* as I just this moment did when I called this other Jew stupid. What hope is there then for the dream of the Chofetz Chaim? Perhaps if all the pious Jews who do not eat on Yom Kippur were instead to give up for one day speaking *loshon hora* . . . if, for one moment in time, there were not a single word of *loshon hora* spoken by a single Jew . . . if together all the Jews on the face of the earth would simply shut up for *one second.* . . . But as even a *second* of Jewish silence is an impossibility, what hope can there be for our people? I personally believe that why the Jews left those villages in Galicia like Radin and ran to America and came to Palestine was, as much as anything, to escape their own *loshon hora.* If it drove crazy a saint of forbearance and great conversationalist like the Chofetz Chaim, who was even glad to go *deaf* so as to hear no more of it, one can only imagine what it did to the mind of the average nervous Jew. The early Zionists never said so, but privately more than one of them had to have been thinking, I will even go to Palestine, where there is typhoid, yellow fever, malaria, where there are temperatures of over a hundred degrees, so as never again to have to hear this terrible *loshon hora*! Yes, in the Land of Israel, away from the goyim, who hate us and thwart us and mock us, away from their persecution and all the chaos this causes within us, away from their loathing and all the anxiety and uncertainty and frustration and anger this engenders in every last Jewish soul, away from the indignity of being locked up by them and shut out by them, we will make a country of our own, where we are free and where we belong, where we will not insult one another and maliciously speak behind one another's backs, where the Jew, no longer awash with all his inner turmoil, will not defame and derogate his fellow Jews. Well, I can testify to it—I am, unfortunately, an example of it—the *loshon hora* in Eretz Yisroel is a hundred times worse, a thousand times worse, than it ever was in Poland in the lifetime of the Chofetz Chaim. Here there is *nothing* we will not say. Here there is such divisiveness that there is no restraint whatsoever. In Poland there was the anti-Semitism, which at least made you silent about the faults of your fellow Jews in the presence of the goyim. But here, with no goyim to worry about, the sky is the limit; here no one has the least idea that, even without goyim to be ashamed in front of, there are still things you cannot and you must not say and that maybe a Jewish person should think twice before he opens wide a Jewish mouth and announces proudly, as Sigmund Freud urged him to, the worst thoughts about people he has in his head. A statement that will cause hatred—they say it. A statement that will cause resentment—they make it. A malicious joke at somebody's expense—they tell it, they print it, they broadcast it over the nightly news. Read the Israeli press and you will read worse things said about us there than a hundred George Ziads are able to say. When it comes to defaming Jews, the Palestinians are *pisherkehs* next to *Ha'aretz*. Even at *that* we are better than they are! Now, once again it can be cynically argued that in this phenomenon lies the very triumph and glory of Zionism, that what we have achieved in the Land of Israel that we could never hope to attain with the goyim listening is the full flowering of the Jewish *genius* for *loshon hora*. Delivered at last from our long subjugation to the Gentiles' ears, we have been able to evolve and bring to perfection *in less than half a century* what the Chofetz Chaim most dreaded to behold: a shameless Jew who will say anything."

And what, I was frantically asking myself, is this overelaborated outpouring leading us on to? I could not fathom the subject here. Was this some shadowy bill of attainder condemning me for *my* language sins? What's any of it got to do with the missing money? His extravagant lamentation for this Chofetz Chaim was merely self-entertainment, brutishly spun out to pass the time until Uri arrived with *my lunch* and the real sadistic fun began—this was my best and most horrifying guess. Assaulted and battered by yet another tyrannical talker whose weapon of revenge is his unloosened mouth, somebody whose purposes lurk hidden, ready to spring, behind the foliage of tens of thousands of words—another unbridled performer, another coldly calculating actor, who, for all I knew, wasn't even crippled but only crashed about on a couple of crutches the better to enact his bitterness. This is the hater who *invented loshon hora*, the unshockable one, the unillusioned one, pretending to be shocked by the human disgrace, the misanthrope whose misanthropic delight is to claim loudly and tearfully that it's hatred he most hates. I am in the custody of a mocker who despises everything.

"It's said," Smilesburger resumed, "that only one law of *loshon hora* remained unclear to the Chofetz Chaim. Yes, a Jew could not, under any circumstances, defame and denigrate a fellow Jew, but was it also forbidden to say something damaging about, to denigrate and to belittle, oneself? About this the Chofetz Chaim remained uncertain for years. Only in his very old age did something happen that made up his mind for him on this troublesome point. Traveling away from Radin in a coach one day, he found himself seated beside another Jew, whom he soon engaged in a friendly conversation. He asked the Jew who he was and where he was going. With excitement the Jew told the old man that he was going to hear the Chofetz Chaim. The Jew did not know that the old man he was addressing happened to be the Chofetz Chaim himself and began to heap praise on the sage he was on his way to hear give a speech. The Chofetz Chaim listened quietly to this glorification of himself. Then he said to the Jew, 'He's really not such hot stuff, you know.' The Jew was stunned at what the old man had dared to say to him. 'Do you know who you are talking about? Do you realize what you are saying?' 'Yes,' replied the Chofetz Chaim, 'I realize very well what I am saying. I happen to know the Chofetz Chaim, and he really isn't all he's cracked up to be.' Back and forth went the conversation, the Chofetz Chaim repeating and elaborating his reservations about himself and the Jew growing angrier by the moment. At last the Jew couldn't stand this scandalous talk any longer and he slapped the old man's face. The coach by then had rolled up to its stop in the next town. The streets all around were jammed with followers of the Chofetz Chaim excitedly awaiting his arrival. He disembarked, a roar went up, and only then did the Jew in the coach understand whom he had slapped. Imagine the poor man's mortification. And imagine the impression that his mortification made on as loving and gentle a soul as the Chofetz Chaim. From that moment onward, the Chofetz Chaim decreed that a person must not utter *loshon hora* even about himself."

He had charmingly recounted the story, expertly, wittily, so very graceful in his speech despite his heavy accent, his tone mellifluous and quite spellbinding, as though with a treasured folktale he were coaxing a little grandchild to sleep. I wanted to say, "Why do you entertain me, in preparation for what? Why am I here? Who exactly are you? Who are these others? What is Pipik's place in all of this?" I suddenly wanted *so much* to speak—to shout for help, to cry out in distress, to demand from him some explanation—that I felt ready to jump not from the window but from my own skin. Yet by this time the wordlessness that had begun as something closely resembling hysterical aphonia had become the bedrock on which I was building my self-defense. Silence had settled in now like a tactic, albeit a tactic that even I recognized he—Uri—they—whoever—wouldn't have much trouble negating.

"Where is Uri now?" Smilesburger asked, looking down at his watch. "The man is half a man and half a panther. If on the way to the restaurant there is a pretty soldier girl . . . But this is the price you pay for a specimen like Uri. Again I apologize. It's days since you've eaten a nutritious meal. Someone else might not be so gracious about this terrible situation. Another man of your eminence reeling with hunger might not be so civil and restrained. Henry Kissinger would be screaming at the top of his lungs had he been made to wait alone in a stuffy room like this for the likes of a crippled old nobody like me. A Henry Kissinger would have got up and stormed out of here hours ago, would have hit the ceiling, and I wouldn't blame him. But you, your even temper, your self-possession, your cool head . . ." Hoisting himself up on his feet, he hobbled to the blackboard, where, with a stump of chalk he wrote in English, "YOU SHALL NOT HATE YOUR BROTHER IN YOUR HEART." Beneath that he wrote, "YOU SHALL NOT TAKE VENGEANCE OR BEAR ANY GRUDGE AGAINST THE CHILDREN OF YOUR PEOPLE." "But then maybe secretly," he said while he wrote, "you are amused and this explains your patient composure. You have one of those Jewish intellects that seize naturally on the comical side of things. Maybe everything is a joke to you. Is it? Is *he* a joke?" Having finished at the blackboard, he was gesturing to the TV screen, where the camera had momentarily focused on Demjanjuk as he scribbled a note for his defense attorney. "In the beginning he used to nudge Sheftel all the time. Sheftel must have told him, 'John, don't nudge me, write me notes,' so now he writes notes that Sheftel doesn't read. And why is his alibi so hopeless? Doesn't that surprise you? Why such a contradictory jumble of places and dates that any first-year law student could discredit? Demjanjuk's not intelligent but I thought at least he was cunning. You would think he would have got someone long ago at least to help him with the alibi. But then this would entail telling someone the truth, and that he *has* been too cunning for. I doubt if even the wife knows. The friends don't. The poor son doesn't. Your friend Mr. Ziad calls it a 'show trial.' Ten years of hearings in America by American immigration and the American courts. A trial in Jerusalem before three distinguished judges and under the scrutiny of the entire world press already going on for over a year. A trial where nearly two days are taken up with arguing over the paper clip on the identity card to establish if the paper clip is authentic or not. Mr. Ziad must be making a joke. So many jokes. Too many jokes. Do you know what it amuses some people to say? That it's a Jew who runs the PLO. That surrounded by a circle of henchmen as inept as he is, Arafat could not himself, without at least *some* Jewish assistance, administer a multinational racket with ten billion dollars in assets. People say that, if there is not a Jew to whom Arafat reports, there must be a Jew in charge of the money. Who but a Jew could rescue this organization from all the mismanagement and corruption? When the bottom fell out of the Lebanese pound, who but a Jew prevented the PLO from taking a bath at the Beirut banks? Who now manages the capital outlay for this rebellion that is their latest futile public-relations stunt? Look, *look* at Sheftel," he said, drawing my attention once again to the TV set. Demjanjuk's Israeli lawyer had just risen to raise an objection to some remark of the prosecutors. "When he was in law school here and the government had canceled Meyer Lansky's entry visa, Sheftel became chairman of Students for Meyer Lansky. Later he became Lansky's lawyer and *got* Lansky a visa to come. Sheftel calls this American Jewish gangster the most brilliant man he ever met. 'If Lansky had been in Treblinka,' Sheftel says, 'the Ukrainians and the Nazis wouldn't have lasted three months.' Does Sheftel believe Demjanjuk? That isn't the point. It's more that Sheftel can never believe the state. He would rather defend the accused war criminal and the renowned gangster than side with the Israeli establishment. But even this is still a very long way from a Jew who manages the PLO portfolio, let alone a Jew who makes them charitable contributions. Do you know what Demjanjuk said to Sheftel after the Jews had fired the Irishman O'Connor and put Sheftel in charge of the case? Demjanjuk told Sheftel, 'If I'd had a Jewish lawyer to begin with, I'd never be in this trouble now.' A joke? Apparently not. The man who sits accused of being Ivan the Terrible is reported to have said it: 'If only I'd had a Jewish lawyer. . . .' So I ask once again, is it necessarily a joke, and only a joke, that the sound investments in stocks, in bonds, in real estate, in motels and currency and radio stations that have given the PLO some financial independence from their Arab brothers are said to have been made for them by Jewish advisers? But just who *are* these Jews, if they really exist? What is their motive, if they really exist? Is this only stupid Arab propaganda, designed to try to embarrass the Jews, or is it true and truly embarrassing? I can more readily sympathize with the motives of a traitorous Jew like Mr. Vanunu, who gives to the British press our nuclear secrets, than the motives of a rich Jew who gives his money to the PLO. I wonder if even the Chofetz Chaim could find it in his heart to forgive a Jew so defiant of the Torah prohibition that tells us we must not take vengeance against the children of our people. What is the worst *loshon hora* compared to putting Jewish money in the pockets of Arab terrorists who machine-gun our youngsters while they play on the beaches? True, it is told to us by the Chofetz Chaim that the only money you can take with you when you die is what you spent here in charity—but charity to the PLO? That is surely not the way to amass treasures in Heaven. You shall not hate your brother in your heart, you shall not follow a multitude to do evil, and you shall not write checks to terrorists who kill Jews. I would like to know the names that are signed on those checks. I would like to have a chance to talk to these people and to ask what they think they are doing. But first I must find out if they truly exist other than in the hate-filled imagination of this mischievous friend of yours, so bursting with troublemaking tricks and lies. I never know whether George Ziad is completely crazy, completely devious, or completely both. But then this is the problem we have with the people in this region. Are there really in Athens rich Jews waiting to meet you who support our worst enemy, Jews ready to put their wealth at the disposal of those who have wished to destroy us from the moment that this country first drew breath? Suppose for the sake of argument that there are five of them. Suppose there are *ten* of them. How much can they contribute—a million apiece? Inconsequential beside what's given to Arafat every year by a single corrupt little Arabian sheikh. Is it worth tracking them down for a measly ten million? Can you just go around killing rich Jews because you don't like the people they give their money to? On the other hand, can you reason with them instead, people so poisoned with perversity to begin with? Probably it is best to forget about them and leave them to their everlasting shame. And yet I can't. I am obsessed by them, these seemingly responsible members of the community, these two-faced fifth-column Jews. All I want to do is to converse with one of them, if such a one exists, the way I am conversing with you. Am I misguided in my Jewish zeal? Am I being made a fool of by an Arab liar? The Chofetz Chaim reminds us, and I believe it, that 'the world rests on those who silence themselves during an argument.' But perhaps the world will not cave in immediately if you should dare now to say a few words. *Should* such Jews prey on my mind like this? What is your opinion? With all the work still to be done for the Jews of the Soviet Union, with all the problems of security that beset our tiny state, why devote one's precious energy to hunting down a few self-hating Jews in order to discover what makes them tick? About these Jews who defame the Jewish people, the Chofetz Chaim has told us everything anyway. They are driven by *loshon hora*, and like all who are driven by *loshon hora*, they will be punished in the world to come. And so why, in our world, should I pursue them? That is the first question I have for you. The second is this: If I do, can I count on Philip Roth to assist me?"

As though at last the cue had been uttered for which he'd been waiting, Uri entered the classroom.

"Lunch," said Smilesburger, smiling warmly.

The dishes were crammed onto a cafeteria tray. Uri set the tray beside the TV set, and Smilesburger invited me to pull up my chair and begin to eat.

The soup wasn't plastic, the bread was not cardboard, the potato was a potato and not a rock. Everything was what it was supposed to be. Nothing as clear as this lunch had happened to me in days.

It was only with the food passing into my gullet that I remembered I'd first seen Uri the day before. Two young men in jeans and sweatshirts who had looked to me to be produce

workers had been identified by George Ziad as Israeli secret
police. Uri was one of them. The other, I now realized, was
the guy at the hotel who'd offered to blow me and Pipik. As
for this classroom, I thought, they'd just borrowed it, maybe
because they figured, not so stupidly, that it would be a particularly effective place to lock me in. They'd gone to the princi-
pal and said, "You were in the army, we know about you,
we've read your file, you're a patriotic guy. Get everybody the
fuck out of your school after one this afternoon. This afternoon the kids are off." And probably he never complained. In
this country, the secret police get everything they want.

At the conclusion of my lunch, Smilesburger handed me, for
the second time, the envelope with the million-dollar check.
"You dropped this last night," he said, "on your way back
from Ramallah."

Of the questions I asked Smilesburger that afternoon, the ones
to which I could least believe I was being given a straight answer had to do with Moishe Pipik. Smilesburger claimed that
they had no better idea than I did of where this double of mine
had emerged from, of who he was or whom he might be working for—he certainly wasn't working for them. "The God of
Chance delivered him," Smilesburger explained to me. "It is
with intelligence agencies as it is with novelists—the God of
Chance creates in us. First the fake one came along. Then the
real one came along. Last the enterprising Ziad came along.
From this we improvise."

"You're telling me that he's nothing but a crackpot con man."

"To you there must be more, to you this must be a singular
occurrence rich with paranoidal meaning. But charlatans like
him? The airlines offer them special rates. They spend their
lives crisscrossing the globe. Yours took the morning flight to
New York. He is back in America."

"You made no effort to stop him."

"To the contrary. Every effort was made to help him on his
way."

"And the woman?"

"I know nothing about the woman. After last night, I would
think that you know more than anyone does. The woman, I
suppose, is one of those women for whom adventure with a

crook is irresistible. Phallika, the Goddess of Male Desire. Am
I mistaken?"

"They are both gone."

"Yes. We are down to just one of you, the one not a crackpot, not a charlatan, not a fool or a weakling either, the one
who knows how to be silent, to be patient, to be cautious, how
to remain unprovoked in the most unsettling circumstances.
You have received high grades. All instincts excellent. Never
mind how you quaked inside or even that you vomited—you
did not shit yourself or take a wrong step. The God of Chance
could not have presented a better Jew for the job."

But I was not taking the job. I had not been extricated from
one implausible plot of someone else's devising to be intimidated into being an actor in yet another. The more Smilesburger explained about the intelligence operation for which he
bore the code name "Smilesburger" and for which he proposed I volunteer, the more infuriated I became, not merely
because his overbearing playfulness was no longer a bewilder-
ing puzzle that kept me stunned and on my guard, but
because, once I had finally eaten something and begun to calm
down, it registered on me just how cruelly misused I had been
by these phenomenally high-handed Israelis playing an espionage game that seemed to me to have at the heart of it a fantasy forged in the misguided brain of no less a talent than
Oliver North. My initial gratitude toward the putative captors
who had been kind enough to feed me a piece of cold chicken
after having forcibly abducted me and then held me prisoner
here against my will so as to see how well I might hold up on a
mission for *them*—the gratitude gave way, now that I felt liberated, to outrage. The magnitude of my indignation alarmed
even me, yet I could do nothing to control the eruption once
it had begun. And Uri's brutish, contemptuous stare—he'd
returned with a Silex to pour me a fresh cup of coffee—enraged me still more, especially after Smilesburger told me that
this subordinate of his who'd fetched my lunch had been following me everywhere. "The ambush out on the Ramallah
road?" Uri, I learned, had been there for that, too. They had
been running me like a rat through a maze without my knowledge or consent and, from everything I could gather, with no
precise idea of what, if any, the payoff for them might be.

Smilesburger had been operating on no more than a hunch, inspired by the presence in Jerusalem of Pipik—whom an informant had identified as an impostor only hours after he'd been ushered through immigration with the phony passport identifying him as me—and then by my arrival a week later. How could Smilesburger call himself professional if a coincidence so fraught with the potential for creative subterfuge had failed to ignite his curiosity? Surely a novelist could understand what it meant to be confronted with a situation so evocative. Yes, he was like a writer, a very lucky writer, he explained, warming sardonically to the comparison, who had fallen upon his own true subject in all its complex purity. That his art was aesthetically impure, a decidedly lesser form of contrivance owing to its gross utilitarian function, Smilesburger was willing to grant—but still the puzzle presented to him was exactly the writer's: there is the dense kernel, the compacted core, and how to set loose the chain reaction is the question that tantalizes, how to produce the illuminating explosion without, in the process, mutilating oneself. You do as the writer does, Smilesburger told me: you begin to speculate, and to speculate with any scope requires a principled disregard for the confining conventions, a gambler's taste for running a risk, a daring to tamper with the taboo, which, he added flatteringly, had always marked my own best work. His work too was guesswork, morally speaking. You try your luck, he told me. You make mistakes. You overdo and underdo and doggedly follow an imaginative line that yields nothing. Then something creeps in, an arguably stupid detail, a ridiculous gag, an embarrassingly bald ploy, and this opens out into the significant action that makes the mess an *operation*, rounded, pointed, structured, yet projecting the illusion of having been as spontaneously generated, as coincidental, untidy, and improbably probable, as life. "Who knows where Athens might lead? Go, for George Ziad, to Athens, and if you convincingly play your role there, then this meeting he dangled before you, the introduction, in Tunis, to Arafat, could well come to pass. Such things do happen. For you this would be a great adventure, and for us, of course, having you in Tunis would be no small achievement. I myself once spent a week with Arafat. Yasir is good for a laugh. He has a wonderful twinkle. He's a show-man. Very, very demonstrative. In his outward behavior, he's a terrific charmer. You'd enjoy him."

In response I shook in his face the embarrassingly bald ploy itself, the ridiculous gag, the stupid detail that was his million-dollar check. "I am an American citizen," I said. "I am here on a journalistic assignment for an American newspaper. I am not a Jewish soldier of fortune. I am not a Jewish undercover agent. I am not a Jonathan Pollard, nor do I wish to assassi-nate Yasir Arafat. I am here to interview another writer. I am here to talk to him about his books. You have followed me and bugged me and baited me, you have physically manhandled me, psychologically abused me, maneuvered me about like your toy for whatever reason suited you, and now you have the audacity—"

Uri had taken a seat on the windowsill and was grinning at me while I unleashed all my contempt for these unforgivable excesses and the wanton indecency with which I had been so misused.

"You are free to leave," said Smilesburger.

"I am also free to bring an action. This is actionable," I told him, remembering all the good it had done me to make the same claim to Pipik at our first face-to-face encounter. "You have held me here for hours on end without giving me any idea of where I was or who you were or what might be going to happen to me. And all in behalf of some trivial scheme so ridiculous that I can hardly believe my ears when you associate it with the word 'intelligence.' These absurdities you concoct without the slightest regard for my rights or my privacy or my safety—this is intelligence?"

"Perhaps we were also protecting you."

"Who asked you to? On the Ramallah road you were pro-tecting me? I could have been beaten to death out there. I could have been shot."

"Yet you were not even bruised."

"The experience was nonetheless most unpleasant."

"Uri will chauffeur you to the American Embassy, where you can lodge a complaint with your ambassador."

"Just call a taxi. I've had enough Uri."

"Do as he says," Smilesburger told Uri.

"And where am I? Where exactly?" I asked, after Uri had left the room. "What is this place?"

"It's not a prison, clearly. You haven't been chained to a pipe in a windowless room with a blindfold around your eyes and a gag in your mouth."

"Don't tell me how lucky I am that this isn't Beirut. Tell me something useful—tell me who this impostor is."

"You might do better to ask George Ziad. Perhaps you have been even more misused by your Palestinian friends than by me."

"Is this so? This is something you *know*?"

"Would you believe me if I said yes? I think you will have to gather your information from someone more trustworthy as I will have to gather mine with the assistance of someone a little less easily affronted. Ambassador Pickering will contact whom he sees fit to about my conduct, and, whatever the consequences, I will live with them as best I can. I cannot believe, however, that this has been an ordeal that will scar you forever. You may even be grateful someday for whatever my contribution may have been to the book that emerges. It may not be all that such a book might be if you chose to proceed a bit further with us, but then you know just how little adventure a talent like yours requires. And in the end no intelligence agency, however reckless, can rival a novelist's fantastical creations. You can get on now, without interference from all this crude reality, creating for yourself characters more meaningful than a simple thug like Uri or a tryingly facetious thug like me. Who is the impostor? Your novelist's imagination will come up with something far more seductive than whatever may be the ridiculous and trivial truth. Who is George Ziad, what is *his* game? He too will become a problem more complexly resonant than whatever the puerile truth may be. Reality. So banal, so foolish, so *incoherent*—such a baffling and disappointing nuisance. Not like being in that study in Connecticut, where the only thing that's real is you."

Uri poked his head into the room. "Taxi!"

"Good," said Smilesburger, flipping off the TV set. "Here begins your journey back to everything that is self-willed."

But could I be sure this taxi was going to turn out to be a

taxi, when I was increasingly uncertain that these people had any affiliation whatsoever with Israeli intelligence? What proof *was* there? The profound illogic of it all—was *that* the proof? At the thought of that "taxi," I suddenly felt endangered more by leaving than by staying and listening for as long as it took to figure out the safest possible means of extricating myself.

"Who are you?" I asked. "Who assigned you to me?"

"Don't worry about that. Represent me in your book however you like. Do you prefer to romanticize me or to demonize me? Do you wish to heroize me or do you want instead to make jokes? Suit yourself."

"Suppose there *are* ten rich Jews who give their money to the Palestinians. Tell me why that is your business."

"Do you want to take the taxi to the American Embassy to lodge your complaint or do you want to continue to listen to someone you cannot believe? The taxi will not wait. For waiting you need a limousine."

"A limousine then."

"Do as he says," Smilesburger said to Uri.

"Cash or credit card?" Uri replied in perfect English, laughing loudly as he went off.

"Why does he stupidly laugh all the time?"

"This is how he pretends not to have a sense of humor. It's meant to frighten you. But you have held up admirably. You are doing wonderfully. Continue."

"These Jews who may or may not be contributing money to the PLO, why haven't they a perfect right to do with their money whatever they wish without interference from the likes of you?"

"Not only do they have a right as Jews, they have an inescapable moral duty as Jews, to make reparations to the Palestinians in whatever form they choose. What we have done to the Palestinians is wicked. We have displaced them and we have oppressed them. We have expelled them, beaten them, tortured them, and murdered them. The Jewish state, from the day of its inception, has been dedicated to eliminating a Palestinian presence in historical Palestine and expropriating the land of an indigenous people. The Palestinians have been driven out, dispersed, and conquered by the Jews. To make a Jewish state we have betrayed our history—we have done unto

the Palestinians what the Christians have done unto us: sys-
tematically transformed them into the despised and subjugated
Other, thereby depriving them of their human status. Irrespec-
tive of terrorism or terrorists or the political stupidity of Yasir
Arafat, the fact is this: as a people the Palestinians are totally
innocent and as a people the Jews are totally guilty. To me the
horror is not that a handful of rich Jews make large financial
contributions to the PLO but that every last Jew in the world
does not have it in his heart to contribute as well."

"The line two minutes ago was somewhat at variance with
this one."

"You think I say these things cynically."

"You say everything cynically."

"I speak sincerely. They are innocent, we are guilty; they are
right, we are wrong; they are the violated, we the violators. I
am a ruthless man working in a ruthless job for a ruthless
country and I am ruthless knowingly and voluntarily. If someday there is a Palestinian victory and if there is then a war-
crimes trial here in Jerusalem, held, say, in the very hall where
they now try Mr. Demjanjuk, and if at this trial there are not
just big shots in the dock but minor functionaries like me as
well, I will have no defense to make for myself in the face of
the Palestinian accusation. Indeed, those Jews who contributed freely to the PLO will be held up to me as people of conscience, as people of *Jewish* conscience, who, despite every
Jewish pressure to collaborate in the oppression of the Palestinians, chose instead to remain at one with the spiritual and
moral heritage of their own long-suffering people. My brutality will be measured against their righteousness and I shall hang
by my neck until I am dead. And what will I say to the court,
after I have been judged and found guilty by my enemy? Will I
invoke as my justification the millennial history of degrading,
humiliating, terrifying, savage, murderous anti-Semitism? Will
I repeat the story of our claim on this land, the millennial history of Jewish settlement here? Will I invoke the horrors of the
Holocaust? Absolutely not. I don't justify myself in this way
now and I will not stoop to doing it then. I will not plead the
simple truth: 'I am a tribesman who stood with his tribe,' nor
will I plead the complex truth: 'Born as a Jew where and when
I was, I am, I always have been, whichever way I turn, con-

demned.' I will offer no stirring rhetoric when I am asked by the court to speak my last words but will tell my judges only this: 'I did what I did to you because I did what I did to you.' And if that is not the truth, it's as close as I know how to come to it. 'I do what I do because I do what I do.' And your last words to the judges? You will hide behind Aharon Appelfeld. You do it now and you will do it then. You will say, 'I did not approve of Sharon, I did not approve of Shamir, and my conscience was confused and troubled when I saw the suffering of my friend George Ziad and how this injustice had made him crazy with hatred.' You will say, 'I did not approve of Gush Emunim and I did not approve of the West Bank settlements, and the bombing of Beirut filled me with horror.' You will demonstrate in a thousand ways what a humane, compassionate fellow you are, and then they will ask you, 'But did you approve of Israel and the existence of Israel, did you approve of the imperialist, colonialist theft that *was* the state of Israel?' And that's when you will hide behind Appelfeld. And the Palestinians will hang you, too, as indeed they should. For what justification is Mr. Appelfeld from Csernowitz, Bukovina, for the theft from them of Haifa and Jaffa? They will hang you right alongside me, unless, of course, they mistake you for the other Philip Roth. If they take you for him, you will at least have a chance. For that Philip Roth, who campaigned for Europe's Jews to vacate the property they had stolen, to return to Europe and to the European Diaspora where they belonged, *that* Philip Roth was their friend, their ally, their Jewish hero. And that Philip Roth is your only hope. This man, your monster, is, in fact, your salvation—*the impostor is your innocence.* Pretend at your trial to be him and not yourself, trick them with all your wiles into believing you two are one and the same. Otherwise you will be judged a Jew just as hateful as Smilesburger. *More* hateful, for hiding from the truth the way you do."

"Limousine!" It was Uri back at the door of the classroom, the smiling muscleman, mockingly unantagonistic, a creature who clearly didn't share my rationalized conception of life. His was a presence I couldn't seem to adapt to, one of those powerfully packaged little five-footers who have organized just a bit too skillfully everything that's disparate and fluctuating in the rest of us. The eloquence of all that sinewy tissue unimpaired by intellect made me feel, despite the considerable advantage of my height, like a very small and helpless boy. Back when the battlers settled everything and anything that was in dispute, the whole male half of the human species must have looked more or less like Uri, beasts of prey camouflaged as men, men who didn't need to be drafted into armies and put through specialized training in order to learn how to kill.

"Go," said Smilesburger. "Go to Appelfeld. Go to New York. Go to Ramallah. Go to the American Embassy. You are free to indulge your virtue freely. Go to wherever you feel most blissfully unblamable. That is the delightful luxury of the utterly transformed American Jew. Enjoy it. You are that marvelous, unlikely, most magnificent phenomenon, the truly liberated Jew. The Jew who is not accountable. The Jew who finds the world perfectly to his liking. The *comfortable* Jew. The *happy* Jew. Go. Choose. Take. Have. You are the blessed Jew condemned to nothing, least of all to our historical struggle."

"No," I said, "not a hundred percent true. I am a happy Jew condemned to nothing who is condemned, however, from time to time to listen to superior Jewish windbags reveling in how they are condemned to everything. Is this show finally over? All rhetorical strategies exhausted? No means of persuasion left? What about turning loose your panther now that nothing else has shattered my nerves? He can tear open my throat, for a start!"

I was shouting.

Here the old cripple swung up onto his crutches and poled himself to the blackboard, where he half effaced with his open palm the scriptural admonitions he'd written there in English, while the Hebrew words that someone else had written he let stand untouched. "Class dismissed," he informed Uri and then, turning back to me, said, disappointedly, "Outraged *still* at having been 'abducted'?"—and at that moment he resembled almost exactly the sickly and vanquished old man, speaking a rather more meager and circumscribed English, whom he had impersonated at lunch the day before, blasted-looking suddenly, like someone bested by life long ago. But *I* hadn't bested him, that was for sure. Perhaps it had just been a very long day of thinking up ways of trapping rich Jews who

weren't giving money to the UJA. "Mr. Roth Number One—use your good Jewish brain. How better to mislead your Palestinian admirers than to let them observe us forcibly abducting their treasured anti-Zionist celebrity Jew?"

With that, even I had heard enough, and after close to five hours as Smilesburger's captive I finally worked up the courage to leave through the door. I might be risking my life but I simply could not listen any longer to how nicely it fit in with their phantasmagoria to do with me whatever they liked.

And nobody did anything to stop me. Uri, happy-go-lucky Uri, pushed the door open all the way and then, clownishly standing at rigid attention like the lackey he was not, pressed himself against the wall to allow maximum passageway for my exit.

I was out in the foyer at the top of the landing when I heard Smilesburger call out, "You forgot something."

"Oh no I didn't," I called back, but Uri was already beside me, holding the little red book that I had been reading earlier to try to concentrate my forces.

"Beside your chair," Smilesburger answered, "you left one of Klinghoffer's diaries."

I took the diary from Uri just as Smilesburger appeared in the classroom door. "We are lucky, for an embattled little country. There are many talented Jews like yourself out in our far-flung Diaspora. I myself happened to have had the privilege of recruiting the distinguished colleague of yours who created these diaries for us. It was a task that he came to enjoy. At first he declined—he said, 'Why not Roth? It's right up his alley.' But I told him, 'We have something else in mind for Mr. Roth.'"

Epilogue:
Words Generally Only Spoil Things

I HAVE elected to delete my final chapter, twelve thousand words describing the people I convened with in Athens, the circumstances at brought us together, and the subsequent expedition, to a second European capital, that developed out of that educational Athens weekend. Of this entire book, whose completed manuscript Smilesburger had asked to inspect, only the contents of chapter 11, "Operation Shylock," were deemed by him to contain information too seriously detrimental to his agency's interests and to the Israeli government to be published in English, let alone in some fifteen other languages. I was, of course, no more obliged to him, his agency, or the state of Israel to suppress those forty-odd pages than I was to submit the entire manuscript or any part of it for a prepublication reading. I had signed no statement beforehand promising to refrain from publishing anything about my mission or to seek clearance for publication from them, nor had this subject been discussed during the briefings that took place in Tel Aviv on the two days after my abduction. This was a potentially disruptive issue which neither party had wished to raise, at least for the time being, my handlers because they must have believed that it was not so much the good Jew in me as the ambitious writer in me consenting, finally, to gather intelligence for them about "Jewish anti-Zionist elements threatening the security of Israel" and I because I had concluded that the best way to serve my professional interest was to act as though it were nothing *but* the good Jew, rising to the call of duty, who was signing on as an Israeli operative.

But why *did* I do it—given all the risks and uncertainties that exceeded by far the dangers of the unknown that adhere to writing—and enter into that reality where the brutal forces were in combat and something serious was at stake? Under the enchantment of these alluringly effervescent characters with their deluge of dangerous talk, spinning inside the whirlpool of their contradictory views—and without the least control over this narrative Ping-Pong in which I appear as the little white ball—was I simply susceptible as never before to a new intensification of the excitement? Had my arresting walk through the wilderness of this world—the one that began with Halcion, that Slough of Despond, and after the battle with Pipik, King of the Bottomless Pit, concluded in the dungeon of the Giant Mossad—germinated a new logic for my Jewish pilgrimage? Or, rather than betraying my old nature, was I succumbing at long last to a basic law of my existence, to the instinct for impersonation by which I had so far enacted and energized my contradictions solely within the realm of fiction? I really couldn't see what was behind what I was doing, and that too may have accounted for why I was doing it: I was enlivened by its imbecilic side—maybe *nothing* was behind it. To do something *without* clarity, an inexplicable act, something unknowable even to oneself, to step outside responsibility and give way fully to a very great curiosity, to be appropriated unresistingly by the strangeness, by the dislocation of the unforeseen . . . No, I could not name for myself what it was that drew me in or understand whether what was impinging on this decision was absolutely everything or absolutely nothing, and yet, lacking the professional's ideology to fire my fanaticism—or fueled perhaps by the ideology of the professionally unideological like myself—I undertook to give the most extreme performance of my life and seriously to mislead others in something more drastic than a mere book.

Smilesburger's private request that he have the opportunity, before publication, to read about whatever aspect of the operation I might "see fit to exploit someday for a best-selling book" was made some two and a half years before I even decided to embark on this nonfictional treatment rather than to plumb the idea in the context, say, of a Zuckerman sequel to *The Counterlife*. Since, once the job for him was completed, I never heard from Smilesburger again, it shouldn't have been difficult by the time I got around to finishing the eleventh chapter of *Operation Shylock* nearly five years later to pretend to have forgotten his request—irritatingly tendered, at our parting, with that trademark taunting facetiousness—or to simply disregard it and proceed, for good or bad, to publish the whole of this book as I had its predecessors: as an unconstrained writer independent of any interference from apprehensive outside parties eager to encroach on the text.

But when I'd come to the end of the manuscript, I found I had reasons of my own for wanting Smilesburger to take a look at it. For one thing, now that all those years had passed since I'd been of service to him, he might possibly be more forthcoming about the several key factors still mystifying me, particularly the question of Pipik's identity and his role in all of this, which I remained convinced was more fully documented in Smilesburger's files than in mine. He could also, if he was willing, correct whatever errors had crept into my depiction of the operation, and, if I could persuade him, he might even tell me a little something about his own history before he'd become Smilesburger for me. But mostly, I wanted him to confirm that what I was reporting as having happened had, in fact, taken place. I had extensive journal notes made at the time to authenticate my story; I had memories that had remained all but indelible; yet, odd as it may strike those who haven't spent a lifetime writing fiction, when I finished chapter 11 and sat down to reread the entire manuscript, I discovered myself strangely uncertain about the book's verisimilitude. It wasn't that, after the fact, I could no longer believe that the unlikely had befallen me as easily as it does anyone else; it was that three decades as a novelist had so accustomed me to *imagining* whatever obstructed my impeded protagonists—even where raw reality had provided the stimulus—that I began to half believe that even if I had not invented *Operation Shylock* outright, a novelist's instincts had grossly overdramatized it. I wanted Smilesburger to dispel my own vague dubiousness by corroborating that I was neither imperfectly remembering what had happened nor taking liberties that falsified the reality.

There was no one other than Smilesburger I could look to for this certification. Aharon had been there at lunch when a semidisguised Smilesburger dropped off his check, but he had otherwise witnessed nothing at first hand. A bit exuberantly, I had recounted to Aharon the details of my first meetings in Jerusalem with Pipik and Jinx, but I'd never told him anything more, and afterward I asked him as a friend to treat confidentially what I'd said and to repeat the stories to no one. I even wondered if, when Aharon came to read *Operation Shylock*, he might not be tempted to think that what he'd actually seen was all there was and that the rest was only a tale, an elaborately rounded out and coherent scenario I had invented as the setting for a tantalizingly suggestive experience that had amounted, in reality, to absolutely nothing, certainly to nothing coherent. I could easily imagine him believing this, because, as I've said, on first reading through the finished manuscript even I had begun to wonder if Pipik in Jerusalem could have been any more slippery than I was being in this book about him—a queer, destabilizing thought for anyone other than a novelist to have, a thought of the kind that, when carried far enough, gives rise to a very tenuous and even tortured moral existence.

Soon enough I found myself wondering if it might be *best* to present the book not as an autobiographical confession that any number of readers, both hostile *and* sympathetic, might feel impelled to challenge on the grounds of credibility, not as a story whose very *point* was its improbable reality, but—claiming myself to have imagined what had been munificently provided, free of charge, by superinventive actuality—as fiction, as a conscious dream contrivance, one whose latent content the author had devised as deliberately as he had the baldly manifest. I could even envision *Operation Shylock*, misleadingly presented as a novel, being understood by an ingenious few as a chronicle of the Halcion hallucination that, momentarily, even I, during one of the more astounding episodes in Jerusalem, almost supposed it might be.

Why not *forget* Smilesburger? Inasmuch, I told myself, as his existence is now, by my sovereign decree, no more real than is anything else earnestly attested to here, corroboration by him of the book's factual basis is no longer possible anyway. Publish the manuscript uncut, uncensored, as it stands, only inserting at the front of the book the standard disclaimer, and you will more than likely have neutralized whatever objections Smilesburger might have wished to raise had he been given access to the manuscript. You will also be sidestepping a confrontation with the Mossad that might not have been to your liking. And, best, you will have spontaneously performed on the body of your book the sacrosanct prank of artistic transubstantiation, the changed elements retaining the appearance of autobiography while acquiring the potentialities of the novel. Less than fifty familiar words is all it takes for all your problems to be solved.

This book is a work of fiction. Names, characters, places, and incidents either are products of the author's imagination or are used fictitiously. Any resemblance to actual events or locales or persons, living or dead, is entirely coincidental.

Yes, those three formulaic sentences placed at the front of the book and I'd not only satisfy Smilesburger but give it to Pipik once and for all. Just wait till that thief opens this book to find that I've stolen his act! No revenge could possibly be more sadistically apt! Providing, of course, that Pipik was alive and able to savor sufficiently—and to suffer painfully—how I had swallowed him whole. . . .

I had no idea what had become of Pipik, and my never having heard from or about him again after those few days in Jerusalem made me wonder if perhaps he had even died. Intermittently I tried to convince myself, on the basis of no evidence other than his absence, that he had indeed been felled by the cancer. I even developed a scenario of the circumstances in which his life had ended that was intended to parallel the flagrantly pathological course of what I surmised about how it had been lived. I pointedly set myself to working up the kind of veiled homicidal daydream that occurs often enough in angry people but that's generally too blatantly suffused by wishful thinking to afford the assurance that I was groping for. I needed a demise for him neither more nor less incredible than everything else about the lie that he was, needed it so as to proceed *as if* I had been delivered from his interference for good and it was safe to write truthfully of what had happened, without my having to fear that publishing my book would provoke a visitation a lot more terrible for me than his aborted Jerusalem debut.

I came up with this. I imagined a letter from Jinx turning up in my mailbox, written in a hand so minuscule that I could only decipher it with the aid of the magnifying lens from my two-volume set of the *OED*. The letter, some seven pages long, had the look of a document smuggled out of a prison, while the calligraphy itself suggested the art of the lacemaker or the microsurgeon. At first glance I found it impossible to attribute this letter to a woman as robustly formed and sensuously supple as Pipik's buxom Wanda Jane, who had claimed, moreover, to be on such bad terms with the alphabet. How could this exquisite stitching be her handiwork? It wasn't until I remembered the hippie waif who'd found Jesus, the servile believer whose comfort had come from telling herself, "I'm worthless, I'm nothing, God is everything," that I could even begin to move beyond my initial incredulity to query the likelihood of the narrative so peepingly revealed there.

As it happened, there was nothing I read in that letter, extreme though it was, that I couldn't bring myself to believe about *him*. However, what made me more suspicious than even the handwriting was the alarming confession, halfway through, that Wanda Jane made about herself. It was simply too shocking to believe that the woman whom Smilesburger labeled "Phallika" in deference to her natural juiciness had performed the act of necrophilia that she reported almost as blithely as if she were remembering her first French kiss at the age of thirteen. His maniacal power over her couldn't possibly have been so grotesque as that. Surely what I was reading was a description not of something she had done but of something that he wanted me to think she had done, a fantasy specifically devised to inform his eternal rival of just how dazzlingly unbreakable a hammerlock he had on her life—intended, moreover, to so contaminate her memory for me as to render her eternally taboo. It was malicious pornography and could not have happened. What she had inscribed here, as though with the point of a pin, attesting to his hold on her and to her worshipful, ghoulish adoration of him, was what her dictator had dictated in the hope of keeping her and me from ever coupling again, not merely after his death but during his life, which—as I was forced to deduce from this quintessentially Pipikish ploy —had by no means come to its sorry end.

So he lived—he was back. Far from assuring me that he was gone, never again to return to plague me, this letter— admittedly, as perhaps only I would interpret it—proclaimed with his usual sadistic ingenuity the resurgence of Pipik's powers and the resumption of his role as my succubus. He and no one else had written this letter to plunge me back into that paranoiac no-man's-land where there is no demarcation between improbability and certainty and where the reality of what menaces you is all the more portentous for being inestimable and obscure. He had imagined her here as he would have her be: a ministering instrument serving him in extremis and, after his death, worshiping his virility in a most unimaginable way. I could even explain the unvarnished self-portrait he presented of a dying man perpetually on the verge of all-out insanity as the most conclusive evidence he could think to offer of the miraculous devotion he could inspire in her regardless of how fiendishly he might behave. No, it didn't surprise me that he would make not the slightest effort to conceal the depths of his untruthfulness or to disguise or soften in any way the vulgar, terrifying charlatan to whom she was enslaved. To the contrary, why should he not *exaggerate* his awfulness, misrepresent himself as even more monstrous than he was, if his intention was to frighten me off her forever?

And I *was* frightened. I had almost forgotten how readily I could be undone by the bold audacity of his lies until that letter arrived, ostensibly from Wanda Jane, asking me to believe that my all too indestructible nemesis was no more. What better measure of my dread of his reappearing than the masochistic perversity with which I quickly transformed the welcome news of his death into the confirmation of his continued existence? Why not take a cue instead from what had happened in Jerusalem and recognize in everything hyperbolical the most telling proof of the letter's authenticity? Of course she's telling the truth—there is nothing here at all inconsistent with what you already know of them, *least* of all what is most repugnant. And why go to the trouble even to imagine a letter like this if, instead of taking heart from the news of having outlasted him, instead of being fortified by your victory over him, you self-destructively build into the letter egregious ambiguities that you then exploit to undermine the very equanimity you are out to achieve?

Answer: Because what I have learned from what I've gone through with them—and with George, with Smilesburger, with Supposnik, with *all* of them—is that any letter less dismayingly ambiguous (or any more easily decipherable) that failed to belie itself in even the minutest way, any letter whose message inspired my wholehearted belief and purged, if only temporarily, the uncertainties most bedeviling to me, wouldn't convince me of anything other than the power over my imagination of that altogether human desire to be convinced by lies.

So here then is the substance of the letter I came up with to spur me on to tell the whole of this story, as I have, without the fear of being impeded by his reprisal. Someone else might have found a more effective way to quiet his own anxiety. But, Moishe Pipik's dissent notwithstanding, I am not someone else.

When it became apparent that Philip had probably less than a year to live, they had moved up from Mexico—where, in desperation, he had imprudently put his faith in a last-ditch course of drug therapy outlawed in the United States—and sublet a furnished little house in Hackensack, New Jersey, half an hour north of my hometown of Newark. That was another catastrophe, and six months later they had moved on to the Berkshires, only some forty miles north of where I have been living for the last twenty years. In a small farmhouse they rented on a remote dirt road halfway up a wooded mountainside, he set about, with his waning strength, to dictate into a tape recorder was to have been his grand treatise on Diasporism, while Wanda Jane got work as an emergency-room nurse in a nearby hospital. And it was here that they found some respite at last from the melodrama that had forged their indissoluble union. Life became calm. Harmony was restored. Love was rekindled. A miracle.

Death came suddenly four months later, on Thursday, January 17, 1991, just hours after the first Iraqi Scud missiles exploded in residential Tel Aviv. Ever since he'd been working with the tapes, his physical degeneration had become all but imperceptible, and to Wanda it had seemed as though the cancer might once again have gone into remission, perhaps even as a consequence of the progress that he made each day on the book and that he talked about so hopefully each evening when she came home from the hospital to bathe him and make dinner. But when the pictures flashed over CNN of the wounded on stretchers being hurriedly carried from the badly damaged apartment buildings, he was beyond consoling. The shock of the bombardment made him cry like a child. It was too late now, he told her, for Diasporism to save the Jews. He could bear neither to witness the slaughter of Tel Aviv's Jews nor to contemplate the consequences of the nuclear counterattack that he was certain the Israelis would launch before dawn, and, brokenhearted, Philip died that night.

For two days, wearing her nightgown and watching CNN, Wanda remained beside the body in the bed. She comforted him with the news that no Israeli strike of any sort was going to be launched in retaliation; she told him about the Patriot missile installations, manned by American servicemen, protecting the Israelis against renewed attacks; she described to him the precautions that the Israelis were taking against the threat of Iraqi germ warfare—"They are not slaughtering Jews," she assured him, "they're going to be all right!" But no encouragement she was able to offer could bring him back to life. In the hope that it might resuscitate the rest of him, she made love to his penile implant. Oddly enough, it was the one bodily part, she wrote to me, "that looked alive and felt like him." She confessed without so much as a trace of shame that the erection that had outlived him had given her solace for two days and two nights. "We fucked and we talked and we watched TV. It was like the good old days." And then she added, "Anybody who thinks that was wrong doesn't know what real love is. I was far nuttier as a little Catholic taking Communion than having sex with my dead Jew."

Her sole regret was having failed to relinquish him to the Jews to bury like a Jew within twenty-four hours of his death. *That* was wrong, sinfully wrong, particularly for him. But caring for Philip as if for her own sick little boy in the isolation of that quiet little mountainside house, she had fallen more deeply in love with him than ever before and as a result had been unable to let him go without reenacting, in that posthumous honeymoon, the passion and the intimacy of their "good old days." In her defense she could only say that once she understood—and she was herself so far gone that the realization had been awfully slow in coming—that no amount of sexual excitement could ever resurrect his corpse, she had acted with dispatch and had had him promptly buried, with traditional Jewish rites, in a local cemetery dating back to

pre-Revolutionary Massachusetts. He had chosen the plot
there himself. To be surrounded in death by all these old Yankee families, with their prototypical Yankee names, had seemed
to him exactly as it should be for the man whose gravestone
was to bear beneath *his* name the just, if forlorn, epithet "The
Father of Diasporism."

His aversion to me—or was it to my shadow?—had apparently reached its maniacal crescendo some months earlier,
when they were living in New Jersey. After Mexico, she wrote,
he had decided they would make their home there while he set
to work on *His Way*, the scandalous exposé of me whose writing had taken possession of him and whose publication as a
full-length book was to reveal me to the public as a sham and a
charlatan. They took pointless drives around blighted Newark,
where he was determined to unearth "documentation" that
would disclose how I was not at all the person I pretended to
be. Sitting with him in their car across the street from the hospital where I was born, and where drug-dealers now congre-
gated not two minutes away, she wept and begged him to
come to his senses while he fulminated for hours about my
lies. One morning, as they ate breakfast in the kitchen of their
Hackensack house, he explained that he had restrained himself
long enough and that, against the opponent I had revealed
myself to be in Jerusalem, he could be bridled no longer by the
rules of fair play. He had made up his mind to confront my
aged father that very day with "the truth about his fraudulent
son." "*What* truth?" she had cried. "*The* truth! That everything about him is a lie! That his success in life is based on a
lie! That the role he plays in life is a lie! That misleading people
about who he is is the only talent the little shit has! *He's* the
fake, *that's* the irony—*he's the fucking double*, a dishonest impostor and fucking hypocritical fake, and I intend to tell the
world, starting today with his stupid old man!" And when she
then refused to drive him to my father's Elizabeth address
(which he'd written on a piece of paper he'd kept in his wallet
since their return from Mexico), he lunged at her with his
fork, sharply stabbing the back of the hand that, just in the
nick of time, she had thrown out to protect her eyes.

Now, not a day had passed since they'd moved to New Jersey
—some days, not even an hour—when she had not plotted

running away from him. But even when she looked down at the holes punched into her skin by the tines of his fork and at her blood seeping out of them, even then she could find neither the strength nor the weakness to abandon him to his illness and run for her life. Instead she began to scream at him that what was enraging him was the failure of the Mexican cure—the charlatan was the phony doctor in Mexico, all of whose claims had been filthy lies. At the root of his rage was the *cancer*. And that was when he told her that it was the writer who had *given* him the cancer—contending for three decades with the treachery of that writer was what had brought him, at only fifty-eight, face-to-face with death. And that was when even the self-sacrificing devotion of Nurse Possesski gave way and she announced that she could no longer live with someone who was out of his mind—she was leaving!

"For him!" he exclaimed in a triumphant voice, as though it were the cure for his cancer that she had finally revealed. "Leaving the one who loves you for that lying son of a bitch who fucks you every which way and then disappears!"

She said no, but of course it was true—the dream of being rescued was of being rescued by me; it was the very dream she'd enacted on the night she'd pushed Walesa's six-pointed star beneath the door of my hotel room in Arab Jerusalem and pleaded to be given refuge by the original whose existence so inflamed the duplicate.

"I'm going! I'm getting out of here, Philip, before something worse happens! I cannot live with a savage child!"

But when she rose from the breakfast table, at long last primed to break the bonds of this inexplicable martyrdom, he sobbed hysterically, "Oh, Mommy, I'm sorry," and tumbled to his knees on the kitchen floor. Pressing her bleeding hand against his mouth, he told her, "Forgive me—I promise I'll never stab you again!" And then this man who was all malaise, this unshameable, intemperate, conniving madman driven as recklessly by ungovernable compulsion as by meticulous, minute-by-minute miscalculation, this mutilated victim who was all incompleteness and deficiency, whose every scheme was a fiasco and against whose hyperbole she was, as always, undefended, began to lick the wound he had inflicted. Grunting with contrition, growling showily with remorse, he lapped

thirstily away at her with his tongue as though the blood oozing out of this woman's veins were the very elixir for which
he'd been searching to prolong the calamity that was his life.

Because by this time he didn't weigh much over a hundred
pounds, it wasn't that difficult for someone with her strength
to lift him off the floor and virtually carry him in her arms up
the stairs to the bed. And while she sat beside him there, holding his trembling hands in hers, he revealed where he really
came from and who he really was, a story irreconcilable with
everything he had told her before. She refused to believe him
and, in her letter to me, would not repeat even one detail of
the things to which he pleaded guilty. He had to have been
delirious, she wrote, because, if he wasn't, then she would
have had to have him either arrested or institutionalized.
When, at last, there was nothing disgraceful that a man could
do that was left for him to confess to, darkness had enveloped
their street and it was time to feed him dinner with her throb-
bing bandaged hand. But first, using a sponge and a basin of
warm water, she gently bathed him right there in the bed and,
as she did every night, massaged his legs until he purred. What
did it matter in the end who he was and what he had done, or
who he thought he was and what he thought he had done or
was capable of doing or was emboldened enough to have done
or was ill enough to have imagined he had done or imagined
he must have done to have made himself fatally ill? Pure or depraved, harmless or ruthless, would-be Jewish savior or thrill-
seeking, duplicitous, perverted betrayer, he was suffering, and
she was there to assuage that suffering as she had been from
the start. This woman whom he had stabbed in the hand at
breakfast (while aiming for her face) put him to sleep—without
his even having to ask—with a sweetly milking, all-consuming
blow job that blotted out all his words, or so she said, or so
said whoever had told her what to say in that letter in order to
warn me off ever writing a single sentence for publication
about these coarse, barbaric irrationalists of mine, these two
catastrophists sustained by their demonic conflict and the theatrical, maddening trivia of psychosis. Her letter's message to
me was this: *Find your comedy elsewhere. You bow out, and we'll
bow out. He'll be as good as dead. But dare to ridicule either one
of us in a book, and we'll never leave you alone again. You have*

met your match in Pipik and Jinx, both of whom are alive and well. And this message, of course, was the very antithesis of the assurance that the letter had been conceived to provide.

The morning after the reconciliation, everything that worked to drain away her courage started up once again, even though it seemed at first that the shock even to him of the savagery with that fork might have at last reined in his desperation. He addressed her, on that morning after, "in a soothing voice like yours," she wrote, a voice contained, modulated, expressive of all that she longed for and sometimes secretly dreamed of finding by taking the unthinkable revenge of fleeing to the sanctuary of me.

He informed her that they were leaving New Jersey. She was to go out to the backyard and burn in the barbecue pit the four first-draft chapters of *His Way.* That abhorrent obsession was over. They were going.

She was ecstatic—now she could stay on at her task of keeping him alive (as if, she admitted, she could ever have left him to die in agony by himself). Making a life with his namesake was a fairy tale anyway. I, as he'd reminded her, had wanted her "only for sex" while what he wanted from her, with all the scorching intensity that only the dying can feel, alone and resourceless on their island of fear, was "*everything,*" she wrote, "everything" that she had in her to give to a patient.

They were leaving New Jersey to move to the Berkshires, where he would write the book on Diasporism that would be his legacy to the Jews.

Since dyslexic Wanda had never read a page I or any other novelist had written, it wasn't until they'd settled down in western Massachusetts that she learned it was where I'd located the home of the wearily heroic E. I. Lonoff, whose example of Flaubertian anchoritism confirms the highest literary ideals of writer-worshiping Nathan Zuckerman, the young novice of *The Ghost Writer.* However, if she could not understand how, having begun by stealing my identity, Pipik was now bent on further compounding the theft by turning into parody (*his* way) the self-obliterating dedication of the selfless Lonoff, she did know that I made my home less than an hour south, in Connecticut's northwestern hills. And the provocation my proximity was bound to be was enough to reawaken her dread, and with that, of course, the inextinguishable fantasies of breaking free that the edifying encounter with me had inspired. (I should never have found her irresistible, I thought. It didn't take a genius to foresee this.)

"Oh, darling," she cried, "forget him, I beg you. We'll burn *His Way* and forget he ever existed! You can't leave where he was born to go to live where he's living now! You can't keep following him like this! Our time together is too precious for that! Being anywhere near this man drives you nuts! You'll only fill up with poison again! Being there will just make you crazy again!"

"Being near him now can only make me sane," he told her, as senseless on the subject as ever. "Being near him can only make me strong. Being near him is the antidote—it's how I am going to beat this thing. Being near him is *the cure*."

"As far from him as we can!" she pleaded.

"As close to him as we can," he replied.

"Tempting fate!" she cried.

"Not at all," he answered. "See him if you want to."

"I didn't mean *me* and fate—I meant *you*. First you tell me he gave you the cancer, now you tell me he's the cure! But he has nothing to do with it *either way*. Forget him! Forgive him!"

"But I do forgive him. I forgive him for who he is, I forgive myself for who I am, I even forgive you for who you are. I repeat to you—see him if you wish. See him again, seduce him again—"

"I don't want to! You're my man, Philip, my only man! I wouldn't be here otherwise!"

"Did you say—did I hear you right? Did you actually say 'You're my Manson, Philip'?"

"My man! Man! You're my M-A-N!"

"No. You said 'Manson.' Why did you say Manson?"

"I did *not* say Manson."

"You said I was your Charles Manson, and I would like to know why."

"But I *didn't*!"

"Didn't what? Say Charles or say Manson? If you didn't say Charles but only Manson, did you mean merely to say manson, did you only mean I was your infantile, helpless creep,

your 'savage child,' as you told me yesterday, did you mean
only to insult me like that again first thing today, or did you
mean *what you meant*—that you live with me like those zom-
bie girls who worshiped Manson's tattooed dick? *Do* I terror-
ize you like Charles Manson? Do I Svengali you and enslave
you and scare you into submission—is that the reason you remain loyal to a man who is already half a corpse?"

"But *that's* what's doing this to you—death!"

"It's *you* who's doing this to me. *You said I was your Charles
Manson!*"

And here she screamed, "You are! Yesterday! All those horrible, horrible stories! You are! *You're worse!*"

"I see," he replied in my soothing voice, the voice that only
minutes earlier had awakened so much hope in her. "So this is
what comes of the fork. You haven't forgiven me at all. You ask
me forgive him for his diabolical hatred of me, *and I do*, but
you cannot find it in your heart to forgive four little pinpricks
on the back of your hand. I tell horrible stories, horrible, *horrible* stories, and *you* believe me."

"I didn't believe you! I definitely did *not* believe you."

"So, you *don't* believe me. But you never believe me. I can't
win, even with you. I tell you the truth and you *don't* believe
me, I tell you lies and you *do* believe me—"

"Oh, death is doing this, *death*—this isn't you!"

"Oops—not me? Who then? Shall I guess? Can't you think
for one single moment about anybody but him? Is looking at
me and thinking of him what gets you through our awful life?
Is that what you imagine in the bed, is that how you are able,
without vomiting, to satisfy my repellent desires—by pretending you're in Jerusalem satisfying his? What's the stumbling
block? That his is real and mine is fake? That he is healthy and
I am sick? That I will die and disappear and he will live on forever through all those wonderful books?"

Later in the morning, while he was sleeping off that tirade in
their bed, she did as he had instructed and, in the barbecue pit
on the back lawn, destroyed the unfinished manuscript of *His
Way*. She knew that even if he awakened he was far too depleted to haul himself over to the window to watch her, and
so, before dumping the contents of his briefcase straight into

the flames, she quickly looked to read what she could of his exposé of me. Only there was nothing there. All the pages were blank.

And so too were the tapes on which he'd claimed to have been recording his Diasporism book while she was off working her hospital shift during those last months of his life in the Berkshires. Six weeks after his death, though she still feared that hearing his disembodied voice might unleash those paroxysms of grief that had nearly killed her in the days after she'd relinquished his body to be buried by the Jews, she found herself one night yearning so for his presence that she had sat down with the tape recorder at the kitchen table and discovered that the tapes were blank as well. Alone in that remote little mountainside house, vainly listening for his voice on one tape after another, sitting all night and into the morning playing side after side and hearing absolutely nothing—and remembering too those mystifyingly empty pages that she had burned to cinders that awful morning in New Jersey—she understood, as people will often fully perceive the suffering of their loved ones only after they are gone, that I was the barrier to everything. He had not been lying about that. I was the obstacle to the fulfillment of his most altruistic dreams, choking off the torrent of all the potential originally his. At the end of his life, despite everything that he had been ordained to tell the Jews to prevent their destruction, the thought of my implacable hostility had impeded him from telling them anything, just as the menace of his Mansonish hatred (if I understood this letter correctly) was now supposed to stifle me.

Dear Jinx [I wrote],

You have my sympathy. I don't know how you survived intact such a harrowing experience. Your stamina, patience, endurance, tolerance, loyalty, courage, forbearance, strength, compassion, your unwavering devotion while watching him struggle helplessly in the death grip of all those deep-buried devils that were tearing to pieces the last of his life—it's all no less astonishing than the ordeal itself. You must feel that you've awakened from a colossal nightmare even as you continue to grieve over your loss.

I'll never understand the excesses he was driven to by me—or by his mystique of me—all the while pleading the highest motives. Was it enchantment, that I cast a spell? It felt the other way round to me. Was it all about death and his struggle to elude it—to elude it as me, to be born again in me, to consign dying to me? I'd like to be able someday to understand what he was saving himself from. Though maybe to understand that is not my duty.

Recently I listened again to the so-called A-S.A. workout tape that found its way into my tape recorder back in my Jerusalem hotel. What was *that* chilling thought-stream about? This time round I wondered if maybe he wasn't Jewish at all but a pathological Gentile, stuck with the Jewish look and out to exact unbridled revenge on the whole vile subspecies as represented by me. Could that possibly be true? Of his entire arsenal of stupid stunts, that sham—if such it was—remains the most sinister, demented, and, alas, compelling . . . yes, aesthetically alluring to me in its repugnant, sickish, Céline-like way. (Céline was also unhinged, a genius French novelist and clamorous anti-Semite circa World War II whom I try hard to despise—and whose reckless books I teach to my students.) But what then to conclude? All I know for sure is that the dreadful wound that never healed preceded my appearance as a writer, I'm certain of that—I'm not, I can't be, the terrible original blow. All the dizzying energy, all the chaos and the frenzy behind the pointlessness of contending with me, points to something else.

That he was immobilized as an author is not my fault, either. The deathbed tapes were blank and all those pages empty for very good reasons other than fear of my blockading publication. It's writing that closes people off from writing. The power of the paranoid to project doesn't necessarily extend to the page, bursting though he may be with ideologies to save the imperiled and with exposés to unfrock the fakes. The inexhaustible access to falsification that fortifies paranoidal rage has nothing in common with the illusion that lifts a book free of the ground.

His Way was never his to write. *His Way* was what lay in his way, the crowning impossibility to the unrealizable task of burying the shame of what shamed him most. Can you tell me what was so unbearably humiliating about whoever he originally was? Could what he began as have been any more scandalous or any less legitimate than what he became in the effort to escape it by becoming somebody else? The seeming paradox is that he could go so shamelessly overboard in the guise of me while, if my guess is right, he was all but annihilated by shame as himself. In this, actually, he came closer to the experience of authorship than he ever did thinking about writing those books and enacted, albeit back to front, a strategy for clinging to sanity that wouldn't be unfamiliar to many novelists.

But is anything I'm saying of interest to you? Maybe all you want to know is if I want to get together again now that he's finally out of the way. I could take a drive up some afternoon. You could show me his grave. I wouldn't mind seeing it, despite the oddness of reading the name on his stone. I wouldn't mind seeing you, either. Your abundant forthcomingness left a strong impression. The temptation is enormous to mine you for every last bit of information you can supply about him, though that, admittedly, isn't the enticement that comes most pictorially to mind.

Well, I'd love to get together with you—yet I can't think of a worse idea for either one of us. He may have been resonant with fragments of my inner life but, as best I can figure it out, that wasn't the charge he carried for you. Rather, there was a macabre, nothing-to-lose, staring-death-in-the-face kind of manhood there, some macabre sense of freedom he had because he was dying—willing to take all kinds of risks and do anything because there's so little time left—that appeals to a certain type of woman, a macabre manliness that makes the woman romantically selfless. I understand the seduction, I think: something about the way he takes that leads you to give the way you give. But it's something about the frighteningly enticing way you give that leads me to wonder about what *you* take in exchange for the crazy burden. In short, you'll have to complete the recovery from anti-Semitism without me. I'm sure you'll find that for a woman so willing to sacrifice herself so much, for a nurse with a body and soul like yours, with your hands, your health, your illness, there will be plenty of Jewish men around who will volunteer to help you on your way to loving our people as you should. But I'm too old for heavy work like that. It's already taken up enough of my life.

The most I can offer is this: what he couldn't write I'll ghost-write for him and publish under his name. I'll do my best to be no less paranoid than he would have been and to do everything I can to make people believe that it was written by him, his way, a treatise on Diasporism that he would have been proud of. "We could be part-ners," he told me, "copersonalities who work in tandem rather than stupidly divided in two." Well, so we shall be. "All you do," he protested, "is resist me." That's true. While he lived and raged I couldn't do otherwise. I had to surmount him. But in death I em-brace him and see him for the achievement that he was—I'd be a very foolish writer, now that he's gone, not to be my impostor's creature and, in my workshop, partake of his treasure (by which I no longer mean you). Your other P.R. assures you that the impostor's voice will not be stifled by him (meaning me).

This letter remained unanswered.

It was only a week after I'd sent a copy of my final manuscript to his office that Smilesburger phoned from Kennedy Airport. He had received the book and read it. Should he come to Connecticut for us to talk it over, or would I prefer to meet in Manhattan? He was staying with his son and his daughter-in-law on the Upper West Side.

The moment I heard the resonating deep rumble of that Old Country voice—or rather, heard in response the note of respectful compliance in my own, disquieted though I was by his abrupt and irritating materialization—I realized how specious were my reasons for getting myself to do as he'd asked. What with the journals I'd kept and the imprint of the experience on my memory, it was transparently ridiculous to have convinced myself that I needed Smilesburger to corroborate my facts or to confirm the accuracy of what I'd written, as ridiculous as it was to believe that I had undertaken that operation for him solely to serve my own professional interests. I had done what I'd done because he had wanted me to do it; I'd obeyed him just as any other of his subordinates would have—I might as well have been Uri, and I couldn't explain to myself why.

Never in my life had I submitted a manuscript to any inspector anywhere for this sort of scrutiny. To do so ran counter to all the inclinations of one whose independence as a writer, whose *counter-suggestiveness* a writer, was simply second nature and had contributed as much to his limitations and his miscalculations as to his durability. To be degenerating into an acquiescent Jewish boy pleasing his law-giving elders when, whether I liked it or not, I had myself acquired all the markings of a Jewish elder was more than a little regressive. Jews who found me guilty of the crime of "informing" had been calling for me to be "responsible" from the time I began publishing in my middle twenties, but my youthful scorn had been plentiful and so were my untested artistic convictions, and, though not as untrammeled by the assault as I pretended, I had been able to hold my ground. I hadn't chosen to be a writer, I announced, only to be told by others what was permissible to write. The writer redefined the permissible. *That*

was the responsibility. Nothing need hide itself in fiction. And
so on.

And yet there I was, more than twice the age of the redefin-
ing young writer who'd spontaneously taken "Stand Alone!"
as his defiant credo, driving the hundred miles down to New
York early the next morning to learn from Smilesburger what
he wanted removed from my book. Nothing need hide itself in
fiction but are there no limits where there's no disguise? The
Mossad was going to tell me.

Why *am* I a sucker for him? Is it just what happens between
two men, one being susceptible to the manipulations of the
other who feels to him more powerful? Is his that brand of authoritative manhood that is able to persuade me to do its bidding? Or is there something in my sense of his worldliness that
I just don't feel I measure up to, because he's swimming in the
abrasive tragedies of life and I'm only swimming in art? Is
there something in that big, tough—almost romantically
tough—mind at work that I am intellectually vulnerable to and
that makes me trust in his judgment more than in my own,
something perhaps about his moving the pieces on the chess-
board the way Jews always wished their fathers could so no
one would pull those emblematic beards? There's something
in Smilesburger that evokes not my real father but my *fantastic* one—that takes over, *that takes charge of me.* I vanquish
the bogus Philip Roth and Smilesburger vanquishes the real
one! I push against him, I argue against him, and always in the
end I do what he wants—in the end I give in and do everything he says!

Well, not this time. This time the terms are mine.

Smilesburger had chosen as the site for our editorial meeting a Jewish food store on Amsterdam Avenue, specializing in
smoked fish, that served breakfast and lunch on a dozen
Formica-topped tables in a room adjacent to the bagel and
bialy counter and that looked as though, years back, when
someone got the bright idea to "modernize," the attempt at
redecoration had been sensibly curtailed halfway through. The
place reminded me of the humble street-level living quarters of
some of my boyhood friends, whose parents would hurriedly
eat their meals in a closet-sized storeroom just behind the shop
to keep an eye on the register and the help. In Newark, back in

the forties, we used to buy, for our household's special Sunday breakfasts, silky slices of precious lox, shining fat little chubs, chunks of pale, meaty carp and paprikaed sable, all double-wrapped in heavy wax paper, at a family-run store around the corner that looked and smelled pretty much as this one did—the tiled floor sprinkled with sawdust, the shelves stacked with fish canned in sauces and oils, up by the cash register a prodigious loaf of halvah soon to be sawed into crumbly slabs, and, wafting up from behind the showcase running the length of the serving counter, the bitter fragrance of vinegar, of onions, of whitefish and red herring, of everything pickled, peppered, salted, smoked, soaked, stewed, marinated, and dried, smells with a lineage that, like these stores themselves, more than likely led straight back through the shtetl to the medieval ghetto and the nutrients of those who lived frugally and could not afford to dine à la mode, the diet of sailors and common folk, for whom the flavor of the ancient preservatives was life. And the neighborhood delicatessen restaurants where we extravagantly ate "out" as a treat once a month bore the same stamp of provisional homeliness, that hallmark look of something that hadn't quite been transformed out of the eyesore it used to be into the eyesore it aspired to become. Nothing distracted the eye, the mind, or the ear from what was sitting on the plate. Satisfying folk cuisine eaten in simple surroundings, on tables, to be sure, and without people spitting in their plates, but otherwise earthly sustenance partaken in an environment just about as unsumptuous as a feasting place can get, gourmandizing at its most commonplace, the other end of the spectrum of Jewish culinary establishments from the commodiously chandeliered dining salon at Miami Beach's Fontainebleau. Barley, eggs, onions, soups of cabbage, of beets, inexpensive everyday dishes prepared in the old style and devoured happily, without much fuss, off of bargain-basement crockery.

By now, of course, what was once the ordinary fare of the Jewish masses had become an exotic stimulant for Upper West Siders two and three generations removed from the great immigration and just getting by as professionals in Manhattan on annual salaries that, a century earlier, would have provided daily banquets all year long for every last Jew in Galicia. I'd see these people—among them, sometimes, lawyers, journalists, or editors I knew—taking pleasure, mouthful by mouthful, in their kasha varnishkas and their gefilte fish (and riveted, all the while they unstintingly ate, to the pages of one, two, or even three daily papers) on those occasions when I came down to Manhattan from Connecticut and took an hour off from whatever else I was doing to satisfy my own inextinguishable appetite for the chopped-herring salad as it was unceremoniously served up (*that* was the ceremony) at one of those very same tables, facing onto the trucks, taxis, and fire engines streaming north, where Smilesburger had suggested that we meet for breakfast at ten a.m. to discuss my book.

After shaking Smilesburger's hand and sitting down directly across from him and the coatrack against which his forearm crutches were leaning, I told him how I rarely came to New York without stopping off here for either a breakfast or a lunch, and he answered that he knew all about that. "My daughter-in-law spotted you a couple of times. She lives just around the corner."

"What does she do?"

"Art historian. Tenured professor."

"And your son?"

"International entrepreneur."

"And his name?"

"Definitely not 'Smilesburger,'" he said, smiling kindly. And then, with an open, appealing, spirited warmth that I was unprepared for from this master of derisive artifice and that, despite its disarming depth of realness, couldn't possibly have been purged of all his callous shrewdness, he carried me almost to the edge of gullibility by saying, "And so how are you, Philip? You had heart surgery. Your father died. I read *Patrimony*. Warmhearted but tough. You've been through the wringer. Yet you look wonderful. Younger even than when I saw you last."

"You too," I said.

He clapped his hands together with relish. "Retired," he replied. "Eighteen months ago, freed of it all, of everything vile and sinister. Deceptions. Disinformation. Fakery. 'Our revels now are ended, . . . melted into air, into thin air.'"

This was strange news in the light of why we were meeting, and I wondered if he wasn't simply attempting to gain his customary inquisitorial upper hand, here at the very outset, by misleading me once again, this time, for a change, by encouraging me to believe that my situation was in *no* way threatening and that I couldn't possibly be shanghaied into anything but a game of checkers by a happy-go-lucky senior citizen like him, a pensioner wittily quoting Prospero, wandless old Prospero, bereft of magical power and casting a gentle sunset glow over a career of godlike treachery. Of course, I told myself, there's no apartment just around the corner where he's staying with a daughter-in-law who'd spotted me eating here before; and the chocolaty tan that had led to a dramatic improvement of his skin condition and that gave an embalmed-looking glow of life to that heavily lined, cadaverous face stemmed, more than likely, from a round of ultraviolet therapy administered by a dermatologist rather than from retirement to the Negev. But the story I got was that, in a desert development community, he and his wife were now happily gardening together only a mile down the road from where his daughter, her husband, and their three adolescent children had been living since the son-in-law had moved his textile business to Beersheba. The decision to fly to America to see me, and, while here, to spend a few days with his two American grandchildren, had been made wholly on his own. My manuscript had been forwarded to him from his old office, where he hadn't set foot since his retirement; as far as he could tell, no one had opened the sealed envelope and read the manuscript, although it wouldn't be difficult for either of us, he said, to imagine the response there if anyone had.

"Same as yours," I offered.

"No. Not so considered as mine."

"There's nothing I can do about that. And nothing they can do about it."

"And, on your part, no responsibility."

"Look, I've been around this track as a writer before. My failed 'responsibility' has been the leitmotif of my career with the Jews. We signed no contract. I made no promises. I performed a service for you—I believe I performed it adequately."

"More than adequately. Your modesty is glaring. You performed it expertly. It's one thing to be an extremist with your mouth. And even that is risky for writers. To then go and do what you did—there was nothing in your life to prepare you for this, nothing. I knew you could think. I knew you could write. I knew you could do things in your head. I didn't know you could do something as large in reality. I don't imagine that you knew it either. Of course you feel proud of your accomplishment. Of course you want to broadcast your daring to the whole world. I would too if I were you."

When I looked up at the young waiter who was pouring coffee into our cups, I saw, as did Smilesburger, that he was either Indian or Pakistani.

After he moved off, having left behind our menus, Smilesburger asked, "Who will fall captive to whom in this city? The Indian to the Jew, the Jew to the Indian, or both to the Latino? Yesterday I made my way to Seventy-second Street. All along Broadway blacks eating bagels baked by Puerto Ricans, sold by Koreans. . . . You know the old joke about a Jewish restaurant like this one?"

"Do I? Probably."

"About the Chinese waiter in the Jewish restaurant. Who speaks perfect Yiddish."

"I was sufficiently entertained in Jerusalem with the Chofetz Chaim—you don't have to tell me Jewish jokes in New York. We're talking about my book. Nothing was said beforehand, not one word, about what I might or might not write afterward. You yourself drew my attention to the professional possibilities the operation offered. As an enticement, if you recall. 'I see quite a book coming out of this,' you told me. An even better book if I went on to Athens for you than if I didn't. And that was before the book had even entered my mind."

"Hard to believe," he responded mildly, "but if you say so."

"It was what you said that put it *into* my mind. And now that I've written that book you've changed your mind and decided that what would truly make it a better book, for your purposes if not mine, would be if I were to leave Athens out entirely."

"I haven't said that or anything like it."

"Mr. Smilesburger, there's no advantage to be gained by the old-geezer act."

"Well"—shrugging his shoulders, grinning, offering it for whatever an old geezer's opinion was worth—"if you fictionalized a little, well, no, I suppose it might not hurt."

"But it's not a book of fiction. And 'a little' fictionalization isn't what you're talking about. You want me to invent another operation entirely."

"I want?" he said. "I want only what is best for you."

The Indian waiter was back and waiting to take the order.

"What do you eat here?" Smilesburger asked me. "What do you like?" So insipid a man in retirement that he wouldn't dare order without my help.

"The chopped-herring salad on a lightly toasted onion bagel," I said to the waiter. "Tomato on the side. And bring me a glass of orange juice."

"Me too," said Smilesburger. "The same exactly."

"You are here," I said to Smilesburger, "to give me a hundred other ideas, just as good and just as true to life. You can find me a story even more wonderful than this one. Together we can come up with something even more exciting and interesting for my readers than what happened to have happened that weekend in Athens. Only I don't want something else. Is that clear?"

"Of course you don't. This is the richest material you have ever gotten firsthand. You couldn't be clearer or more disagreeable."

"Good," I said. "I went where I went, did what I did, met whom I met, saw what I saw, learned what I learned—and nothing that occurred in Athens, absolutely nothing, is interchangeable with something else. The implications of these events are intrinsic to these events and to none other."

"Makes sense."

"I didn't go looking for this job. This job came looking for me, and with a vengeance. I have adhered to every condition agreed on between us, including sending a copy of the manuscript to you well before publication. In fact, you're the first person to have read it. Nothing was forcing me to do this. I am back in America. I'm no longer recovering from that Halcion madness. This is the fourth book I've written since then. I'm myself again, solidly back on my own ground. Yet I did do it: you asked to see it, and you've seen it."

"And it was a good idea to show it. Better me now than someone less well disposed to you later."

"Yes? What are you trying to tell me? Will the Mossad put a contract out on me the way the Ayatollah did with Rushdie?"

"I can only tell you that this last chapter will not go unnoticed."

"Well, if anyone should come complaining to me, I'll direct them to your garden in the Negev."

"It won't help. They'll assume that, no matter what 'enticement' I offered back then, no matter how irresistible an adventure it may be for you to write about and to crow about, you should know by now how detrimental your publishing this could be to the interests of the state. They'll maintain that confidence was placed in your loyalty and that with this chapter you have betrayed that confidence."

"I am not now, nor was I ever, an employee of yours."

"Theirs."

"I was offered no compensation, and I asked for none."

"No more or less than Jews all around the world who volunteer their services where their expertise can make a difference. Diaspora Jews constitute a pool of foreign nationals such as no other intelligence agency in the world can call on for loyal service. This is an immeasurable asset. The security demands of this tiny state are so great that, without these Jews to help, it would be in a very bad way. People who do work of the kind you did find compensation not in financial payment and not in exploiting their knowledge elsewhere for personal gain but in fostering the security and welfare of the Jewish state. They find their compensation, *all of it*, in having fulfilled a Jewish duty."

"Well, I didn't see it that way then and I don't now."

Here our food arrived, and for the next few minutes, as we began to eat, Smilesburger pedantically discussed the ingredients of his late beloved mother's chopped herring with the young Indian waiter: her proportion of herring to vinegar, vinegar to sugar, chopped egg to chopped onion, etc. "This meets the highest specifications for chopped herring," he told him. To me he said, "You didn't give me a bum steer."

"Why would I?"

"Because I don't think you've come to like me as much as I've come to like you."

"I probably have," I replied. "As much exactly."

"At what point in the life of a negative cynic does this yearning for the flavors of innocent childhood reassert itself? And may I tell the joke, now that the sugared herring is running in your blood? A man comes into a Jewish restaurant like this one. He sits at a table and picks up the menu and he looks it over and decides what he's going to eat and when he looks up again there is the waiter and he's Chinese. The waiter says, '*Vos vilt ihr essen?*' In perfect Yiddish, the Chinese waiter asks him, 'What do you want to eat?' The customer is astonished but he goes ahead and orders and, with each course that arrives, the Chinese waiter says here is your this and I hope you enjoyed that, and all of it in perfect Yiddish. When the meal's over, the customer picks up the check and goes to the cash register, where the owner is sitting, exactly as that heavyset fellow in the apron is sitting at the register over there. In a funny accent much like my own, the owner says to the customer, 'Everything was all right? Everything was okay?' And the customer is ecstatic. 'It was perfect,' he tells him, 'everything was great. And the waiter—this is the most amazing thing—the waiter is Chinese and yet he speaks *absolutely perfect Yiddish*.' '*Shah,* shhh,' says the owner, 'not so loud—he thinks he's learning English.'"

I began to laugh, and he said, smiling, "Never heard that before?"

"You would think by now I'd have heard all the jokes there are about Jews and Chinese waiters, but no, not that one."

"And it's an old one."

"I never heard it."

I wondered while we ate in silence if there could be any truth in this man at all, if anything could exist more passionately in him than did the instinct for maneuver, contrivance, and manipulation. Pipik should have studied under him. Maybe he had.

"Tell me," I suddenly said. "Who hired Moishe Pipik? It's time I was told."

"That's paranoia asking, if I may say so, and not you—the organizing preconception of the shallow mind faced with chaotic phenomena, the unthinking man's intellectual life, and the everyday occupational hazard of our work. It's a paranoid universe but don't overdo it. Who hired Pipik? Life hired Pipik. If all the intelligence agencies in the world were abolished overnight, there would still be Pipiks aplenty to complicate and wreck people's orderly lives. Self-employed, nonessential nudniks whose purpose is simply *balagan*, meaningless mayhem, a mess, are probably rooted more deeply in reality than are those who are only dedicated, as you and I are, to coherent, essential, and lofty goals. Let's not waste any more frenzied dreaming on the mystery of irrationality. It needs no explanation. There is something frighteningly absent from life. One gets from someone like your Moishe Pipik a faint idea of all that's missing. This revelation one must learn to endure without venerating it with fantasy. Let us move on. Let us be serious. Listen to me. I am here at my own expense. I am here, on my own, as a friend. I am here because of you. You may not feel responsible to me, but I happen to feel responsible to you. I *am* responsible to you. Jonathan Pollard will never forgive his handlers for abandoning him in his hour of need. When the FBI closed in on Pollard, Mr. Yagur and Mr. Eitan left him utterly on his own to fend for himself. So did Mr. Peres and Mr. Shamir. They did not, in Pollard's words, 'take the minimum precaution with my personal security,' and now Pollard is incarcerated for life in the worst maximum-security prison in America."

"The cases are somewhat dissimilar."

"And that's what I'm pointing out. I recruited you, perhaps even with a false enticement, and now I will do *everything* to prevent your exposing yourself to the difficulties that the publication of this last chapter could cause for a very long time to come."

"Be explicit."

"I can't be explicit, because I am no longer a member of the club. I only can tell you, from past experience, that when someone causes the kind of consternation that is going to be caused by publishing this chapter as it now stands, indifference is never the result. If anyone should think that you have jeopardized the security of a single agent, a single contact—"

"In short, I am being threatened by you."

"A retired functionary like me is in no position to threaten anyone. Don't mistake a warning for a threat. I came to New York because I couldn't possibly have communicated to you on the phone or through the mail the seriousness of your indiscretion. *Please* listen to me. In the Negev now, I have begun to catch up on my reading after many years. I started out by reading all of your books. Even the book about baseball, which, you have to understand, for someone of my background was a bit like reading *Finnegans Wake*."

"You wanted to see if I was worth saving."

"No, I wanted to have a good time. And I did. I like you, Philip, whether you believe me or not. First through our work together and then through your books, I have come to have considerable respect for you. Even, quite unprofessionally, something like familial affection. You are a fine man, and I don't wish to see you being harmed by those who will want to discredit you and to smear your name or perhaps to do even worse."

"Well, you still give a beguiling performance, retired or not. You are a highly entertaining deceiver altogether. But I don't think that it's a sense of responsibility to me that's operating here. You have come on behalf of your people to intimidate me into shutting my mouth."

"I come quite on my own, at substantial personal expense actually, to ask you, for your own good, here at the end of this book, to do nothing more than you have been doing as a writer all your life. A little imagination, please—it won't kill you. To the contrary."

"If I were to do as you ask, the whole book would be specious. Calling fiction fact would undermine everything."

"Then call it fiction instead. Append a note: 'I made this up.' Then you will be guilty of betraying no one—not yourself, your readers, or those whom, so far, you have served faultlessly."

"Not possible. Not possible in any way."

"Here's a better suggestion, then. Instead of replacing it

with something imaginary, do yourself the biggest favor of your life and just lop off the chapter entirely."

"Publish the book without its ending."

"Yes, incomplete, like me. Deformed can be effectual too, in its own unsightly way."

"Don't include what I went specifically to Athens to get."

"Why do you persist in maintaining that you undertook this operation as a writer only, when in your heart you know as well as I now do, having only recently enjoyed all your books, that you undertook and carried it out as a loyal Jew? Why are you so determined to deny the Jewish patriotism, you in whom I realize, from your writings, the Jew is lodged like nothing else except, perhaps, for the male libido? Why camouflage your Jewish motives like this, when you are in fact no less ideologically committed than your fellow patriot Jonathan Pollard was? I, like you, prefer never to do the obvious thing if I can help it, but continuing to pretend that you went to Athens only for the sake of your calling—is this really less compromising to your independence than admitting that you did it because you happen to be Jewish to the core? Being as Jewish as you are is your most secret vice. Any reader of your work knows that. As a Jew you went to Athens and as a Jew you will suppress this chapter. The Jews have suppressed plenty for you. Even you'll admit that."

"Yes? Have they? Suppressed what?"

"The very strong desire to pick up a stick and knock your teeth down your throat. Yet in forty years nobody's done it. Because they are Jews and you are a writer, they give you prizes and honorary degrees instead. Not exactly how his kind have rewarded Rushdie. Just who would you be without the Jews? *What* would you be without the Jews? All your writing you owe to them, including even that book about baseball and the wandering team without a home. Jewishness is the problem they have set for you—without the Jews driving you crazy with that problem there would be no writer at all. Show some gratitude. You're almost sixty—best to give while your hand is still warm. I remind you that tithing was once a widespread custom among the Jews as well as the Christians. One tenth of their earnings to support their religion. Can you not cede to the Jews, who have given you *everything*, one eleventh of this book? A mere one fiftieth, probably, of one percent of all the pages you have ever published, *thanks to them?* Cede to them chapter 11 and then go overboard and, whether it is true or not, call what remains a work of art. When the newspapers ask, tell them, 'Smilesburger? That blabbering cripple with the comical accent an Israeli intelligence officer? Figment of my fecund imagination. Moishe Pipik? Wanda Jane? Fooled you again. Could such walking dreams as those two have possibly crossed *anyone's* path? Hallucinatory projections, pure delirium—that's the book's whole point.' Say something to them along these lines and you will save yourself a lot of *tsuras*. I leave the exact wording to you."

"Yes. Pipik too? Are you finally answering me about who hired Pipik? Are you telling me that Pipik is a product of *your* fecund imagination? Why? Why? I cannot understand why. To get me to Israel? But I was already coming to Israel to see Aharon Appelfeld. To lure me into conversation with George? But I already knew George. To get me to the Demjanjuk trial? You had to know that I'm interested in those things and would have found it on my own. Why did you need him to get me involved? Because of Jinx? You could have gotten another Jinx. What is the reason from your side for constructing this creature? From the point of view of the Mossad, which is an intelligence operation, goal-oriented, *why did you produce this Pipik?*"

"And if I had a ready answer, could I in good conscience tell it to a writer with a mouth like yours? Accept my explanation and be done with Pipik, please. Pipik is not the product of Zionism. Pipik is not even the product of Diasporism. Pipik is the product of perhaps the most powerful of all the senseless influences on human affairs and that is *Pipikism*, the antitragic force that inconsequentializes everything—farcicalizes everything, trivializes everything, superficializes everything—our suffering as Jews not excluded. *Enough* about Pipik. I'm suggesting to you only how to give coherence to what you tell the newspapers. Keep it simple, they're only journalists. 'No exceptions, fellas: hypothetical book from beginning to end.'"

"George Ziad included."

"George you don't have to worry about. Didn't his wife write to you? I would have thought, since you were such friends. . . . *Don't* you know? Then I have to shock you. Your PLO handler is dead."

"Is this so? Is *this* fact?"

"A horrible fact. Murdered in Ramallah. He was with his son. Five times he was stabbed by masked men. They didn't touch the boy. About a year ago. Michael and his mother are living again in Boston."

Free at last in Boston—and now never to be free—of fealty to the father's quest. One more accursed son. All the wasted passion that will now be Michael's dilemma for life! "But *why?*" I asked. "Murdered for what reason?"

"The Israelis say murdered as a collaborator by Palestinians. They murder one another like this every day. The Palestinians say murdered by Israelis—because Israelis are murderers."

"And what do you say?"

"I say everything. I say maybe he was a collaborator who was murdered for the Israelis by Palestinians who are also collaborators—and then maybe not. To you who have written this book, I say I don't know. I say the permutations are infinite in a situation like ours, where the object is to create an atmosphere in which no Arab can feel secure as to who is his enemy and who is his friend. *Nothing is secure.* This is the message to the Arab population in the territories. Of what is going on all around them, they should know very little and get everything wrong. And they do know very little and they do get everything wrong. And if this is the case with those who live there, then it follows that for someone like you, who lives *here*, you know even less and get even more wrong. That's why to describe your book, laid in Jerusalem, as a figment of your imagination might not be as misleading as you fear. It might be altogether accurate to call the *entire* five hundred and forty-seven pages hypothetical formulation. You think I'm such a deceiver, so let me now be cruelly blunt about his book to a writer whose work I otherwise admire. I am not qualified to judge writing in English, though the writing strikes me as excellent. But as for the content—well, in all candor, I read it and I laughed, and not only when I was supposed to. This is not a report of what happened, because, very simply, you haven't the slightest idea of what happened. You grasp almost nothing of the objective reality. Its meaning evades you completely. I cannot imagine a more innocent version of what was going on and what it signified. I won't go so far as to say that this is the reality as a ten-year-old might understand it. I prefer to think of it as subjectivism at its most extreme, a vision of things so specific to the mind of the observer that to publish it as anything *other* than fiction would be the biggest lie of all. Call it an artistic creation and you will only be calling it what it more or less is anyway."

We had finished eating a good twenty minutes earlier and the waiter had removed all the dishes except our coffee cups, which he'd already been back to refill several times. I had till then been oblivious to everything but the conversation and only now saw that customers were beginning to drift in for lunch and that among them were my friend Ted Solotaroff and his son Ivan, who were at a table up by the window and hadn't yet noticed me. Of course I'd known that I wasn't meeting Smilesburger in the subterranean parking garage where Woodward and Bernstein used to go to commune with Deep Throat, but still, at the sudden sight of someone here I knew, my heart thumped and I felt like a married man who, spotted at a restaurant in ardent conversation with an illicit lover, quickly begins to calculate how best to introduce her.

"Your contradictions," I said softly to Smilesburger, "don't add up to a convincing argument, but then, with me, you don't believe you need any argument. You're counting on my secret vice to prevail. The rest is an entertainment, amusing rhetoric, words as bamboozlement, your technique here as it was there. Do you even bother to keep track of your barrage? On the one hand, with this book—the whole of it now, not merely the final chapter—I am, in your certifiably *un*paranoid view, serving up to the enemy information that could jeopardize the security of your agents and their contacts, information that, from the sound of it, could lay the state of Israel open to God only knows what kind of disaster and compromise the welfare and security of the Jewish people for centuries to come. On the other hand, the book presents such a warped and ignorant misrepresentation of objective reality that to save my literary reputation and protect myself against the ridicule of all the clear-eyed empiricists, or from punishments that you intimate might be far, far worse, I ought to recognize this thing for what it is and publish *Operation Shylock* as—as what? Subtitled 'A Fable'?"

"Excellent idea. A subjectivist fable. That solves everything."

"Except the problem of accuracy."

"But how could you know that?"

"You mean chained to the wall of my subjectivity and seeing only my shadow? Look, this is all nonsense." I raised my arm to signal to the waiter for our check and unintentionally caught Ivan Solotaroff's eye as well. I'd known Ivan since he was an infant back in Chicago in the mid-fifties, when the late George Ziad was there studying Dostoyevsky and Kierkegaard and Ivan's father and I were bristling graduate students teaching freshman composition together at the university. Ivan waved back, pointed out to Ted where I was sitting, and Ted turned and gave a shrug that indicated there could be no place on earth more appropriate than here for us to have run into each other after all our months of trying in vain to arrange to get together for a meal. I realized then the unequivocal way in which to introduce Smilesburger, and this made my heart thump again, only now in triumph.

"Let's cut it short," I said to Smilesburger when the check was placed on the table. "I cannot know things-in-themselves, but you can. I cannot transcend myself, but you can. I cannot exist apart from myself, but you can. I know nothing beyond my own existence and my own ideas, my mind determines entirely how reality appears to me, but for you the mind works differently. You know the world as it really is, and I know it only as it appears. Your argument is kiddie philosophy and dime-store psychology and is too absurd even to oppose."

"You refuse absolutely."

"Of course I do."

"You'll neither describe your book as what it is not nor censor out what they're sure not to like."

"How could I?"

"And if I were to rise above kiddie philosophy and dime-store psychology and invoke the wisdom of the Chofetz Chaim? 'Grant me that I should say nothing unnecessary. . . .' Would I be wasting my breath if, as a final plea, I reminded you of the laws of *loshon hora*?"

"It would not even help to quote Scripture."

"Everything must be undertaken alone, out of personal conviction. You're that sure of yourself. You're that convinced that only you are right."

"On this matter? Why not?"

"And the consequences of proceeding uncompromisingly, independent of every judgment but your own—to these consequences you are indifferent?"

"Don't I have to be?"

"Well," he said, while I snapped up the check before he could take it and compromisingly charge breakfast to the Mossad, "then that's that. Too bad."

Here he turned to the crutches that were balanced behind him on the coatrack. I came around to assist him to his feet, but he was already standing. The disappointment in his face, when his eyes engaged mine, looked as though it couldn't possibly have been manufactured to deceive. And must there not be a point even in him, where manipulation stops? It caused a soundless but not inconsiderable emotional upheaval in me to think that he might actually have shed his disguises and come here out of a genuine concern for my welfare, determined to spare me any further misfortune. But even if that was so, was it any reason to cave in and voluntarily give them a pound of my flesh?

"You've come a long way from that broken man whom you describe as yourself in the first chapter of this book." He had somehow gathered up his attaché case along with the crutches and clutched the handle round with what I noticed, for the very first time, were the powerful, tiny, tufted fingers of a primate somewhat down the scale from man, something that could swing through a jungle by its prehensile tail in the time that it would take Smilesburger to get from our table to the street. I assumed that in the attaché case was my manuscript. "All that uncertainty, all that fear and discomposure—it all seems safely behind you now. You are impermeable," he said. "Mazel tov."

"For now," I replied, "for now. Nothing is secure. Man the pillar of instability. Isn't that the message? The unsureness of everything."

"The message of your book? I wouldn't say so. It's a happy book, as I read it. Happiness radiates from it. There are all

kinds of ordeals and trials but it's about someone who is recovering. There's so much élan and energy in his encounters
with the people he meets along the way that anytime he feels
his recovery is slipping and that thing is coming over him
again, why, he rights himself and comes through unscathed.
It's a comedy in the classic sense. He comes through it *all*
unscathed."

"Only up to this point, however."

"That too is true," said Smilesburger, nodding sadly.

"But what I meant by 'the unsureness of everything' was the
message of *your* work. I meant the inculcation of pervasive uncertainty."

"That? But that's a permanent, irrevocable crisis that comes
with living, wouldn't you say?"

This is the Jewish handler who handles me. I could have
done worse, I thought. Pollard did. Yes, Smilesburger is my
kind of Jew, he is what "Jew" *is* to me, the best of it to me.
Worldly negativity. Seductive verbosity. Intellectual venery.
The hatred. The lying. The distrust. The this-worldliness. The
truthfulness. The intelligence. The malice. The comedy. The
endurance. The acting. The injury. The impairment.

I followed behind him until I saw Ted rise to say hello. "Mr.
Smilesburger," I said, "one minute. I want you to meet Mr.
Solotaroff, the editor and writer. And this is Ivan Solotaroff.
Ivan's a journalist. Mr. Smilesburger pretends to be a gardener
in the desert these days, fulfilling the commandments of our
Lord. In fact, he's an Israeli spymaster, the very handler who
handles me. If there is an inmost room in Israel where somebody is able to say, 'Here lies our advantage,' then it's the joy
of the Smilesburgers to obtain it. Israel's enemies would tell
you that he is, institutionally, simply the sharp end of national
and patriotic and ethnic psychosis. I would say, from my experience, that if there is such a thing in that frenetic state as central will, it appears to me to be invested in him. He is, to be
sure, as befits his occupation, also an enigma. Is he, for instance, assing around on these crutches? Is he actually a great
athlete? This too could be. At any rate, he has treated me to
some wonderfully confusing adventures, which you will soon
be reading about in my book."

Smiling almost sheepishly, Smilesburger shook hands first with the father and then with the son.

"Spying for Jews?" Ivan asked me, amused. "I thought you made a living spying *on* them."

"A distinction, in this case, without a difference—and a source of contention between Mr. Smilesburger and me."

"Your friend," said Smilesburger to Ted, "is impatient to construct his own disaster. Has he always been in this hurry to overdo things?"

"Ted, I'll call you," I said, even while Ted stood towering above Smilesburger, puzzling over what sort of connection we might have other than the one I had so deliberately and loquaciously delineated. "Ivan, good to see you. So long!"

Softly Ted said to Smilesburger, "Take care now," and together my handler and I made our way to the register, where I paid the bill, and then we were out of the store and into the street.

On the corner of West Eighty-sixth Street, only a few feet from the steps of a church where a destitute black couple slept beneath a filthy blanket as the midday traffic rolled noisily by, Smilesburger offered me his attaché case and asked me to open it for him. I found inside the photocopied pages of the original eleven chapters of this book, still in the large manila envelope in which I'd initially mailed them to him, and beneath that, a second, smaller envelope, thick and oblong, just about the size and shape of a brick, my name written boldly across the face of it.

"What's this?" I asked. But I had only to heft the envelope in my hand to realize what it contained. "Whose idea is this?"

"Not mine."

"How much is in here?"

"I don't know. I would think quite a lot."

I had a violent urge to heave the envelope as far as I could out into the street, but then I saw the shopping cart crammed with all the worldly goods belonging to the black couple on the steps of the church and thought to just go over and drop it in there. "Three thousand ducats," I said to Smilesburger, repeating aloud for the first time since Athens the identifying code words that I'd been given to use by him before leaving on the mission purportedly for George.

"However much it is," he said, "it's yours."

"For what? For services already rendered or for what I'm now being advised to do?"

"I found it in my briefcase when I got off the plane. Nobody has told me anything. I opened the briefcase on the way in from Kennedy. There it was."

"Oh, for Christ's sake!" I shouted at him. "This is what they did to Pollard—shtupped the poor schnuk with money until he was compromised up to his ears!"

"Philip, I don't want what doesn't belong to me. I don't wish to be accused of stealing what isn't mine. I ask you please to take this off my hands before I am the one who is compromised in the middle of an affair where I no longer play any role. Look, you never put in for your Athens expenses. You charged the hotel to American Express and even got stuck with a big restaurant bill. Here. To cover the costs you incurred spying at the fountainhead of Western civilization."

"I was thinking, just before, that I could have done much worse than you," I said. "Now it's hard to imagine how." I held the envelope containing my manuscript under my arm while placing the envelope full of money back in the attaché case. "Here," I said, snapping the case shut and offering it to Smilesburger, but he held tightly to his crutches, refusing to accept it back. "All right," I said and, seeing that the woman who'd been sleeping beside her companion on the church steps was awake now and cautiously watching the two of us, I set the case down on the pavement before Smilesburger's feet. "The Mossad Fund for Homeless Non-Jews."

"No jokes, please—pick up the case," he said, "and take it. You don't know what could be in store for you otherwise. Take the money and do what they want. Ruining reputations is no less serious an intelligence operation than destroying nuclear reactors. When they are out to silence a voice they don't like, they know how to accomplish it without the blundering of our Islamic brothers. They don't issue a stupid, barbaric *fatwa* that makes a martyred hero out of the author of a book that nobody can read—they quietly go to work on the reputation instead. And I don't mean halfheartedly, as they did in the past with you, turning loose the intellectual stooges at their magazine. I mean hardball—*loshon hora*: the whispering campaign that cannot be stopped, rumors that it's impossible to quash, besmirchment from which you will never be cleansed, slanderous stories to belittle your professional qualifications, derisive reports of your business deceptions and your perverse aberrations, outraged polemics denouncing your moral failings, misdeeds, and faulty character traits—you shallowness, your vulgarity, your cowardice, your avarice, your indecency, your falseness, your selfishness, your treachery. Derogatory information. Defamatory statements. Insulting witticisms. Disparaging anecdotes. Idle mockery. Bitchy chatter. Malicious absurdities. Galling wisecracks. Fantastic lies. *Loshon hora* of such spectacular dimensions that it is guaranteed not only to bring on fear, distress, disease, spiritual isolation, and financial loss but to significantly shorten a life. They will make a shambles of the position that you have worked nearly sixty years to achieve. No area of your life will go uncontaminated. And if you think this is an exaggeration you really *are* deficient in a sense of reality. Nobody can ever say of a secret service, 'That's something they don't do.' Knowledge is too dispersed for that conclusion to be drawn. They can only say, 'Within my experience, it wasn't done. And beyond that again, there's always a first time.' Philip, remember what happened to your friend Kosinski! The Chofetz Chaim wasn't just whistling Dixie: there is no verbal excess, no angry word, no evil speech that is unutterable to a Jew with an unguarded tongue. You are *not* Jonathan Pollard—you are being neither abandoned nor disowned. Instead you are being given the benefit of a lifetime's experience by someone who has developed the highest regard for you and cannot sit by and watch you destroyed. The consequences of what you've written are simply beyond calculation. I fear for you. Name a raw nerve and you recruit it. It is not a quiet book you've written—it is a *suicidal* book, even within the extremely Jewish stance you assume. Take the money, please. I beg you. I beg you. Otherwise the misery you suffered from Moishe Pipik will seem like a drop in the bucket of humiliation and shame. They will turn you into a walking joke beside which Moishe Pipik will look like Elie Wiesel, speaking words that are only holy and pure. You'll *yearn* for the indignities of a double like Pipik; when they get done desecrating you and your name, Pipik will seem the personification of modesty, dignity, and the passion for truth. Lead them not into temptation, because their creativity knows no bounds when the job is to assassinate the character even of a *tzaddik* like you. A righteous person, a man of moral rectitude, that is what I have come to understand you to be—and against the disgrace of such a person it is my human obligation to cry out! Philip, pick up the attaché case, take it home, and put the money in your mattress. Nobody will ever know."

"And in return?"

"Let your Jewish conscience be your guide."

Note to the Reader

THIS book is a work of fiction. The formal conversational exchange with Aharon Appelfeld quoted in chapters 3 and 4 first appeared in *The New York Times* on March 11, 1988; the verbatim minutes of the January 27, 1988, morning session of the trial of John Demjanjuk in Jerusalem District Court provided the courtroom exchanges quoted in chapter 9. Otherwise the names, characters, places, and incidents either are products of the author's imagination or are used fictitiously. Any resemblance to actual events or locales or persons, living or dead, is entirely coincidental. This confession is false.

SABBATH'S THEATER

For Two Friends

Janet Hobhouse
1948–1991

Melvin Tumin
1919–1994

PROSPERO:
Every third thought shall be my grave.
—*The Tempest*, act V, scene I

1

There's Nothing That Keeps Its Promise

Eいたた forswear fucking others or the affair is over.

This was the ultimatum, the maddeningly improbable, wholly unforeseen ultimatum, that the mistress of fifty-two delivered in tears to her lover of sixty-four on the anniversary of an attachment that had persisted with an amazing licentiousness—and that, no less amazingly, had stayed their secret—for thirteen years. But now with hormonal infusions ebbing, with the prostate enlarging, with probably no more than another few years of semi-dependable potency still his—with perhaps not that much more life remaining—here at the approach of the end of everything, he was being charged, on pain of losing her, to turn himself inside out.

She was Drenka Balich, the innkeeper's popular partner in business and marriage, esteemed for the attention she showered on all her guests, for her warmhearted, mothering tenderness not only with visiting children and the old folks but with the local girls who cleaned the rooms and served the meals, and he was the forgotten puppeteer Mickey Sabbath, a short, heavyset, white-bearded man with unnerving green eyes and painfully arthritic fingers who, had he said yes to Jim Henson some thirty-odd years earlier, before *Sesame Street* started up, when Henson had taken him to lunch on the Upper East Side and asked him to join his clique of four or five people, could have been inside Big Bird all these years. Instead of Caroll Spinney, it would have been Sabbath who was the fellow inside Big Bird, Sabbath who had got himself a star on the Hollywood Walk of Fame, Sabbath who had been to China with Bob Hope—or so his wife, Roseanna, delighted in reminding him back when she was still drinking herself to death for her two unchallengeable reasons: because of all that had not happened and because of all that had. But as Sabbath wouldn't have been any happier inside Big Bird than he was inside Roseanna, he was not much bruised by the heckling. In 1989, when Sabbath had been publicly disgraced for the gross sexual harassment of a girl forty years his junior, Roseanna had had to be interned for a month in a psychiatric institution because of the alcoholic breakdown brought on by the humiliation of the scandal.

"One monogamous mate isn't enough for you?" he asked Drenka. "You like monogamy so much with him you want it with me too? Is there no connection you can see between your husband's enviable fidelity and the fact that he physically repels you?" Pompously he continued, "We who have never stopped exciting each other impose on each other no vows, no oaths, no restrictions, whereas with him the fucking is sickening even for the two minutes a month he bends you over the dinner table and does it from behind. And why is that? Matija is big, powerful, virile, a head of black hair like a porcupine. His hairs are *quills*. Every old dame in the county is in love with him, and not just for his Slavic charm. His looks turn them on. Your little waitresses are all nuts about the cleft in his chin. I've watched him back in the kitchen when it's a hundred degrees in August and they're waiting ten deep on the terrace for tables. I've seen him churning out the dinners, grilling those kebabs in his sopping T-shirt. All agleam with grease, he turns *me* on. Only his wife he repels. Why? The ostentatiously monogamous nature, that is why."

Drenka dragged herself mournfully beside him, up the steep wooded hillside to the heights where their bathing brook bubbled forth, clear water rippling down a staircase of granite boulders brokenly spiraling between the storm-slanted, silvery-green birches that overhung the banks. During the early months of the affair, on a solitary hiking expedition in search of just such a love nest, she had discovered, within a clump of ancient fir trees not far from the brook, three boulders, each the size and the shade of a small elephant, that enclosed the triangular clearing they would have instead of a home. Because of mud, snow, or drunken hunters out shooting up the woods, the crest of the hill was not accessible in all seasons, but from May through early October, except when it rained, it was here they retreated to renovate their lives. Years back a helicopter had once appeared out of nowhere to hover momentarily a hundred feet overhead while they were naked on the tarpaulin below, but otherwise, though the Grotto, as they'd come to call the hideaway, was fifteen minutes by foot from the only paved road connecting Madamaska Falls to the valley, no human presence had ever threatened their secret encampment.

Drenka was a dark, Italian-looking Croat from the Dalmatian coast, on the short side like Sabbath, a full, firmly made woman at the provocative edge of being just overweight, her shape, at her heaviest, reminiscent of those clay figurines molded circa 2000 B.C., fat little dolls with big breasts and big thighs unearthed all the way from Europe down to Asia Minor and worshiped under a dozen different names as the great mother of the gods. She was pretty in a rather efficient, businesslike way, except for her nose, a surprisingly bridgeless prizefighter's nose that created a sort of blur at the heart of her face, a nose slightly out of plumb with the full mouth and the large dark eyes, and the telltale sign, as Sabbath came to view it, of everything malleable and indeterminate in her seemingly well-deployed nature. She looked as though she had once been mauled, in earliest childhood damaged by a crushing blow, when in fact she was the daughter of kindly parents, both of them high school teachers religiously devoted to the tyrannical platitudes of Tito's Communist party. Their only child, she had been abundantly loved by these nice, dreary people.

The blow in the family had been delivered by Drenka. At twenty-two, an assistant bookkeeper with the national railway, she married Matija Balić, a handsome young waiter with aspirations whom she had met when she went for her vacation to the hotel that belonged to the railroad syndicate workers on the island of Brač, just off Split. The two went to Trieste for their honeymoon and never returned home. They ran away not merely to become rich in the West but because Matija's grandfather had been imprisoned in 1948, when Tito broke with the Soviet Union and the grandfather, a local party bureaucrat, a Communist since 1923 and an idealist about big Mother Russia, had dared to discuss the matter openly. "My both parents," Drenka had explained to Sabbath, "were convinced Communists and they loved Comrade Tito, who is there with his smile like a smiling monster, and so I figured out early how to love Tito more than any other child in Yugoslavia. We were all Pioneers, little boys and girls who would go out and sing wearing a red scarf. We would sing songs about Tito and how he is this flower, this violet flower, and how all the youth loves him. But with Matija it was different. He was a little boy who loved his grandfather. And somebody told on his grandfather—is that the word? Reported. He was reported. As an enemy of the regime. And the enemies of the regime were all sent to this horrible prison. It was the most horrible time when they were like cattle thrown into the ships. Taken by ships from the mainland to the island. And who survives survives and who doesn't doesn't. It was a place where the stone was the only element. All they had to do, they had to work those stones, cut them, without a reason. Many families had someone who went to this Goli Otok that means Naked Island. People report on others for whatever reason—to advance, for hatred, for whatever. There was a big threat always hanging in the air about being proper, and proper is to support the regime. On this island they didn't feed them, they didn't give them water even. An island just off the coast, a little bit north of Split—from the coast you can see the island in the distance. His grandfather got hepatitis there and he died just before Matija graduated from high school. Died of cirrhosis. He suffered all those years. The prisoners would send cards home, and they had to claim in the cards that they were reformed. His mother told Matija that her father was not good and that he did not listen to Comrade Tito and that's why he has to go to prison. Matija was nine. She knew what she was telling him when she was telling that. So at school he would not be provoked to say something else. His grandfather said he would be good and love *Drug* Tito, so he was only in jail for ten months. But he got hepatitis there. When he came back, Matija's mother makes a big party. He came back, he was forty kilos. That's ninety pounds or so. And he was, like Maté, a big man. Totally destroyed physically. There was a guy that told on him and that was that. And this is why Matija wished to run away after we married."

"And why did *you* wish to run away?"

"Me? I didn't care about politics. I was like my parents. During the old Yugoslavia, the king and all that stuff, before Communism, they loved the king. Then Communism came and they loved Communism. I didn't care, so I said yes, yes to the smiling monster. What I loved was the adventure. America seemed so grand and so glamorous and so enormously different. America! Hollywood! Money! Why did I go? I was a girl. Wherever would be the most fun."

Drenka shamed her parents by fleeing to this imperialist country, broke their hearts, and they too died, both of cancer, not long after her defection. However, she so loved money and so loved "fun" that she probably had the tender attentions of these convinced Communists to thank for whatever impeded the full, youthful body with the tantalizingly thuggish face from doing with itself something even more capricious than becoming enslaved to capitalism.

The only man she would ever admit to having charged for the night was the puppeteer Sabbath, and over the thirteen years this had occurred only once, when he had presented the offering of Christa, the runaway German au pair working at the gourmet food shop, whom he had scouted and patiently recruited for their joint delectation. "Cash," Drenka had informed him, though for months now, ever since Sabbath had first come upon Christa hitchhiking into town, Drenka had anticipated the adventure with no less excitement than Sabbath and needed no urging to conspire. "Crisp bills," she said, prankishly narrowing her eyes but meaning it all the same. "Stiff and new." Adapting without hesitation to the role she'd so swiftly devised for him, he asked, "How many?" Tartly she answered, "Ten." "Can't afford ten." "Forget it then. Leave me out." "You're a hard woman." "Yes. Hard," she replied with relish. "I have a sense of my worth." "It's taken some doing to arrange this, you know. It's not been a snap setting this up. Christa may be a wayward child but she still requires a lot of attention. It's I who ought to be paid by you." "I don't want to be treated like a fake whore. I want to be treated like a real whore. A thousand dollars or I stay home." "You're asking the impossible." "Never mind then." "Five hundred." "Seven fifty." "Five hundred. The best I can do." "Then I must be paid before we get there. I want to walk in with the money in my purse knowing that I've got a job to do. I want to feel like a real whore." "I doubt," suggested Sabbath, "that, to feel

like a real whore, money alone will suffice." "It will for me."
"Lucky you." "Lucky *you*," said Drenka defiantly—"okay, five
hundred. But before. I have to have all of it the night before."

The terms of the deal were negotiated while they manipulated each other manually on the tarpaulin up at the Grotto.

Now, Sabbath had no interest in money. But since arthritis
had finished him off as a performing puppeteer at the international festivals, and his Puppet Workshop was no longer welcome in the curriculum of the four-college program because of
his unmasking there as a degenerate, he was dependent for
support on his wife, with the result that it was not painless for
him to peel off five of the two hundred and twenty hundred-
dollar bills earned annually by Roseanna at the regional high
school and hand them over to a woman whose family-run inn
netted $150,000 a year.

He could have told her to fuck off, of course, especially as
Drenka would have participated as ardently in the threesome
without the money as with, but to agree for a night to act as
her john seemed to do as much for him as it did for her to pretend to be his prostitute. Sabbath, moreover, had no right *not*
to yield—her licentious abandon owed its full flowering to
him. Her systematic efficiency as hostess-manager of the inn—
just the sheer pleasure, year after year, of banking all that
dough—might long ago have mummified her lower life had
not Sabbath suspected from the flatness of the nose, from the
roundness of the limbs—from nothing more than that to
begin with—that Drenka Balich's perfectionism on the job
was not her only immoderate inclination. It was Sabbath who,
a step at a time, the most patient of instructors, had assisted
her in becoming estranged from her orderly life and in discovering the indecency to supplement the deficiencies of her regular diet.

Indecency? Who knows? Do as you like, Sabbath said, and
she did and liked it and liked telling him about how much she
had liked it no less than he liked hearing about it. Husbands,
after weekending at the inn with their wives and children,
phoned Drenka secretly from their offices to tell her they had
to see her. The excavator, the carpenter, the electrician, the
painter, all the laborers assisting around the inn invariably maneuvered to eat their lunches close to the office where she did

the bookkeeping. Men wherever she went sensed the intangible aura of invitation. Once Sabbath had sanctioned for her the force that wants more and more—a force to whose urging she was never wholly averse even before Sabbath had come along—men began to understand that this shortish, less than startling-looking middle-aged woman corseted by all her smiling courtesy was powered by a carnality much like their own. Inside this woman was someone who thought like a man. And the man she thought like was Sabbath. She was, as she put it, his sidekicker.

How could he, in good conscience, say no to the five hundred bucks? No was not a part of the deal. To be what she had learned to want to be (to be what he needed her to be), what she needed from Sabbath was yes. Never mind that she used the money to buy power tools for her son's basement workshop. Matthew was married and a state trooper with the barracks down in the valley; Drenka adored him and, once he became a cop, worried about him all the time. He was not big and handsome with porcupinish black hair and a deep cleft in his chin like the father whose anglicized name he bore but much more patently Drenka's offspring, short in stature—only five feet eight and 135 pounds, he'd been the smallest guy in his class at the police academy as well as the youngest—and at the center of his face a bit of a blur, the noseless nose a replica of hers. He had been groomed to one day be proprietor of the inn and had left his father desolated by quitting hotel management school after just a year to become a muscular, crew-cutted trooper with the big hat, the badge, and lots of power, the kid cop whose first assignment running radar with the traffic squad, driving the chase car up and down the main highways, was the greatest job in the world. You meet so many people, every car you stop is different, a different person, different circumstances, a different speed. . . . Drenka repeated to Sabbath everything Matthew Junior told her about life as a trooper, from the day he had entered the academy seven years earlier and the instructors there began to yell at them and he swore to his mother, "I'm not going to let this beat me," until the day he graduated and, little as he was, they awarded him an excellence pin in physical fitness and told him and the classmates who had survived the twenty-four-week course, "You're

not God but you're the next closest thing to him." She described to Sabbath the virtues of Matthew's fifteen-shot nine-
millimeter pistol and how he carried it in his boot or at the
back in his belt when he was off duty and how that terrified
her. She was constantly afraid that he was going to be killed,
especially when he was transferred from the traffic squad to the
barracks and had to work the midnight shift every few weeks.
Matthew himself came to love cruising in his car as much as
he'd loved running radar. "Once you're gone on your shift,
you're your own boss out there. Once you get into that car,
you can do what you want out there. Freedom, Ma. Lots of
freedom. Unless something happens, all you do is ride. Alone
in the car, cruising, just driving the roads until they call you for
something." He'd grown up in what the state police called the
North Patrol. Knew the area, all the roads, the woods, knew
the businesses in the towns and found an enormous manly satisfaction in driving by at night and checking them out, checking out the banks, checking out the bars, watching the people
leaving the bars to see how bad off they were. Matthew had a
front seat, he told his mother, at the greatest show on earth—
accidents, burglaries, domestic disputes, suicides. Most people
never see a suicide victim, but a girl whom Matthew had gone
to school with had blown her head off in the woods, sat under
an oak tree and blew out her brains, and Matthew, in his first
year out of the academy, was the cop on the scene to call the
medical examiner and wait for him to come. In that first year,
Matthew told his mother, he was so pumped up, felt so invin-
cible, he believed he could stop bullets with his teeth. Matthew walks in on a domestic dispute where both of the people
are drunk and screaming at each other and hating each other
and throwing punches and he, her son, talks to them and
calms them down so that by the time he leaves everything is
okay and neither of them has to be pinched for breach of
peace. And sometimes they're so bad he does pinch 'em, handcuffs the woman and handcuffs the man, and then waits for
another trooper to come, and they take the couple in before
they kill each other. When a kid was showing a gun in a pizza
place on 63, flashing it around before leaving, it was Matthew
who found the car the kid was driving and, without any
backup, knowing the kid had a gun, told him over the loud-

speaker to come out with his hands in the air and had his own gun drawn right on the guy . . . and these stories, establishing for his mother that Matthew was a good cop who wanted to do a good job, to do it as he'd been taught to do it, frightened her so that she bought a scanner, a little box with an antenna and a crystal that monitored the police signals on Matthew's frequency, and sometimes when he was on the midnight shift and she couldn't sleep, she would turn on the scanner and listen to it all night long. The scanner would pick up the signal every time Matthew was called, so that Drenka knew more or less where he was and where he was going and that he was still alive. When she heard his number—415B—boom, she was awake. But so was Matthew's father—and enraged to be reminded yet again that the son he had been training every summer in the kitchen, the heir to the business he had built from nothing as a penniless immigrant, was now an expert in karate and judo instead, out at three in the morning stupidly trailing an old pickup truck that was going suspiciously slowly crossing Battle Mountain. The bitterness between father and son had grown so bad that it was only with Sabbath that Drenka could share her fears about Matthew's safety and recount her pride in the amount of motor vehicle activity he was able to produce in a week: "It's out there," he told her. "There's always something—speeding, stop signs, taillights out, all kind of violations. . . ." To Sabbath, then, it came as no surprise when Drenka admitted that with the five hundred dollars he had paid her to complete the trio with Christa and himself she had bought, for Matthew's birthday, a portable Makita table saw and a nice set of dado blades.

All in all, things couldn't have worked out better for everyone. Drenka had found the means by which to be her husband's dearest friend. The one-time puppet master of the Indecent Theater of Manhattan made more than merely tolerable for her the routines of marriage that previously had almost killed her—now she cherished those deadly routines for the counterweight they provided her recklessness. Far from seething with disgust for her unimaginative husband, she had never been more appreciative of Matija's stolidity.

Five hundred was *cheap* for all that everyone was getting in the way of solace and satisfaction, and so, however much it disturbed him to fork over those stiff, new banknotes, Sabbath displayed toward Drenka the same sangfroid that she affected as, lightly enjoying the movie cliché, she folded the bills in half and deposited them into her bra, down between the breasts whose soft fullness had never ceased to captivate him. It was supposed to be otherwise, with the musculature everywhere losing its firmness, but even where her skin had gone papery at the low point of her neckline, even that palm-size diamond of minutely crosshatched flesh intensified not merely her enduring allure but his tender feeling for her as well. He was now six short years from seventy: what had him grasping at the broadening buttocks as though the tattooist Time had ornamented neither of them with its comical festoonery was his knowing inescapably that the game was just about over.

Lately, when Sabbath suckled at Drenka's uberous breasts— uberous, the root word of *exuberant*, which is itself *ex* plus *uberare*, to be fruitful, to overflow like Juno lying prone in Tintoretto's painting where the Milky Way is coming out of her tit—suckled with an unrelenting frenzy that caused Drenka to roll her head ecstatically back and to groan (as Juno herself may have once groaned), "I feel it deep down in my cunt," he was pierced by the sharpest of longings for his late little mother. Her primacy was nearly as absolute as it had been in their first incomparable decade together. Sabbath felt something close to veneration for that natural sense of a destiny she'd enjoyed and, too—in a woman with as physical a life as a horse's—for the soul embedded in all that vibrating energy, a soul as unmistakably present as the odorous cakes baking in the oven after school. Emotions were stirred up in him that he had not felt since he was eight and nine years old and she had found the delight of delights in mothering her two boys. Yes, it had been the apex of her life, raising Morty and Mickey. How her memory, her *meaning*, expanded in Sabbath when he recalled the alacrity with which she had prepared each spring for Passover, all the work of packing away the year-round dishes, two sets of them, and then lugging in their cartons, from the garage, the glass Passover dishes, washing them, shelving them—in less than a day, between the time he and Morty left for school in the morning and they returned in midafternoon, she'd emptied the pantry of *chumitz* and cleansed and scoured the kitchen in accordance with every last holiday prescription. Hard to determine from the way she tackled her tasks whether it was she who was serving necessity or necessity that was serving her. A slight woman with a large nose and curly dark hair, she hopped and darted to and fro like a bird in a berry bush, trilling and twittering a series of notes as liquidly bright as a cardinal's song, a tune she exuded no less naturally than she dusted, ironed, mended, polished, and sewed. Folding things, straightening things, arranging things, stacking things, packing things, sorting things, opening things, separating things, bundling things—her agile fingers never stopped nor did the whistling ever cease, all throughout his childhood. That was how content she was, immersed in everything that had to be done to keep her husband's accounts in order, to live peaceably alongside her elderly mother-in-law, to manage the daily needs of the two boys, to see to it, during even the worst of the Depression, that however little money the butter-and-egg business yielded, the budget she devised did not impinge on their happy development and that, for instance, everything handed down from Morty to Mickey, which was nearly everything Mickey wore, was impeccably patched, freshly aired, spotlessly clean. Her husband proudly proclaimed to his customers that his wife had eyes in the back of her head and two pairs of hands.

Then Morty went off to the war and it all changed. Always they had done everything as a family. They had never been separated. They were never so poor that they would rent out the house in the summer and, like half the neighbors living as close to the beach as the Sabbaths did, move in back to a shitty little apartment over the garage, but they were still a poor family by American standards and none of them had ever gone anywhere. But then Morty was gone and for the first time in his life Mickey slept alone in their room. Once they went up to see Morty when he was training in Oswego, New York. For six months he trained in Atlantic City and they drove to see him there on Sundays. And when he was in pilot school in North Carolina, they took the drive all the way down south, even though his father had to turn the truck over to a neighbor he paid to run deliveries the days they were gone. Morty had bad skin and wasn't particularly handsome, he wasn't great in school—a B-C student in everything but shop and gym—he had never had much success with girls, and yet everybody knew that with his physical strength and his strong character he would be able to take care of himself, whatever difficulties life presented. He played clarinet in a dance band in high school. He was a track star. A terrific swimmer. He helped his father with the business. He helped his mother in the house. He was great with his hands, but then, they all were: the delicacy of his powerful father candling the eggs, the fastidious dexterity of his mother ordering the house—the Sabbath digital artfulness that Mickey, too, would one day exhibit to the world. All their freedom was in their hands. Morty could repair plumbing, electrical appliances, anything. Give it to Morty, his mother used to say, Morty'll fix it. And she did not exaggerate when she said that he was the kindest older brother in the world. He enlisted in the Army Air Corps at eighteen, a kid just out of Asbury High, rather than wait to be drafted. He went in at eighteen and he was dead at twenty. Shot down over the Philippines December 12, 1944.

For nearly a year Sabbath's mother wouldn't get out of bed. Couldn't. Never again was she spoken of as a woman with eyes in the back of her head. She acted at times as though she didn't even have eyes in the front of her head, and, as far as the surviving son could still recall while panting and gulping as though to drain Drenka dry, she was never again heard to whistle her signature song. Now the seaside cottage was silent when he walked up the sandy alleyway after school, and he could not tell till he got inside if she was even in the house. No honey cake, no date and nut bread, no cupcakes, nothing ever again baking in the oven after school. When the weather turned nice, she sat on the boardwalk bench overlooking the beach to which she used to rush out with the boys at dawn to buy flounder off the fishing boats at half what it cost in the store. After the war, when everybody came home, she went there to talk to Mort. As the decades passed, she talked to him more rather than less, until in the nursing home in Long Branch where Sabbath had to put her at ninety she talked to Morty alone. She had no idea who Sabbath was when he drove the four and a half hours to visit her during the last two years of her life. The living son she ceased to recognize. But that had begun as long ago as 1944.

And now Sabbath talked to *her*. And this he had not expected. To his father, who had never deserted Mickey however much Morty's death had broken him too, who primitively stood by Mickey no matter how incomprehensible to him his boy's life became when he went to sea after high school or began to perform with puppets on the streets of New York, to his late father, a simple, uneducated man, who, unlike his wife had been born on the other side and had come to America all on his own at thirteen and who, within seven years, had earned enough money to send for his parents and his two younger brothers, Sabbath had never uttered a word since the retired butter-and-egg man died in his sleep, at the age of eighty-one, fourteen years earlier. Never had he felt the shadow of his father's presence hovering nearby. This was not only because his father had always been the least talkative one in the family but because no evidence had ever been offered Sabbath to persuade him that the dead were anything other than dead. To talk to them, admittedly, was to indulge in the most defensible of irrational human activities, but to Sabbath it was alien just the same. Sabbath was a realist, ferociously a realist, so that by sixty-four he had all but given up on making contact with the living, let alone discussing his problems with the dead.

Yet precisely this he now did daily. His mother was there every day and he was talking to her and she was communing with him. Exactly how present *are* you, Ma? Are you only here or are you everywhere? Would you look like yourself if I had the means to see you? The picture I have keeps shifting. Do you know only what you knew when you were living, or do you now know everything, or is "knowing" no longer an issue? What's the story? Are you still so miserably sad? That would be the best news of all—that you are your whistling old self again because Morty's with you. Is he? Is Dad? And if there's you three, why not God too? Or is an incorporeal existence just like everything else, in the nature of things, and God no more necessary there than he is here? Or don't you inquire any further about being dead than you did about being alive? Is being dead just something you do the way you ran the house?

Eerie, incomprehensible, ridiculous, the visitation was nonetheless real: no matter how he explained it to himself he could
not make his mother go away. He knew she was there in the
same way he knew when he was in the sun or in the shade.
There was something too natural about his perceiving her for
the perception to evaporate before his mocking resistance. She
didn't just show up when he was in despair, it didn't happen
only in the middle of the night when he awoke in dire need of
a substitute for everything disappearing—his mother was up in
the woods, up at the Grotto with him and Drenka, hovering
above their half-clad bodies like that helicopter. Maybe the
helicopter had *been* his mother. His dead mother was with
him, watching him, everywhere encircling him. His mother
had been loosed on him. She had returned to take him to his
death.

Fuck others and the affair is over.
    He asked her why.
    "Because I want you to."
    "That won't do."
    "Won't it?" said Drenka tearfully. "It would if you loved me."
    "Yes, love is slavery?"
    "You are the man of my life! Not Matija—you! Either I am
your woman, your *only* woman, or this all *has* to be over!"
It was the week before Memorial Day, a luminous May
afternoon, and up in the woods a high wind was blowing
sprigs of new leaves off the great trees and the sweet scent of
everything flowering and sprouting and shooting up reminded
him of Sciarappa's Barber Shop in Bradley, where Morty took
him for his haircuts when he was a small kid and where they
brought their clothes to be fixed by Sciarappa's wife. Nothing
was merely itself any longer; it all reminded him of something
long gone or of everything that was going. Mentally he addressed his mother. "Smell the smells, can you? Does the out-
of-doors register in any way? Is being dead even worse than
heading there? Or is it Mrs. Balich that's the awfulness? Or
don't the trivialities bother you now one way or the other?"
    Either he was sitting in his dead mother's lap or she was sit-
ting in his. Perhaps she was snaking in through his nose along

with the scent of the mountain in bloom, wafting through him as oxygen. Encircling him and embodied within him.

"And just when did you decide this? What has happened to bring this on? You are not yourself, Drenka."

"I am. *This is myself*. Tell me you will be faithful to me. Please tell me that that's what you will do!"

"First tell me why."

"I'm *suffering*."

She was. He'd seen her suffer and this was what it looked like. The blurriness broadened out from the middle of her face rather like an eraser crossing a blackboard and leaving in its wake a wide streak of negated meaning. You didn't see a face any longer but a bowl of stupefaction. Whenever the rift between her husband and their son erupted in a screaming fight she invariably wound up looking just this awful when she ran to Sabbath, numb and incoherent with fear, her sprightly cunning having evaporated before their improbable capacity for rage and its vile rhetoric. Sabbath assured her—largely without conviction—that they would not kill each other. But more than once he had himself contemplated with a shudder what might be roiling away beneath the lid of the relentlessly genial good manners that made the Balich men so impenetrably dull. Why *had* the boy become a cop? Why did he want to be out risking his life looking for criminals with a revolver and handcuffs and a lethal little club when there was a small fortune to be made pleasing the happy guests at the inn? And, after seven years, why couldn't the amiable father forgive him? Why did he wind up charging his son with wrecking his life every single time they met? Granted that each had his own hidden reality, that like everyone else they were not without duality, granted that they were not entirely rational people and that they lacked wit or irony of any kind—nonetheless, where *was* the bottom in these Matthews? Sabbath privately conceded that Drenka had good reason to be as agitated as she was by the tremendous force of their antagonism (especially as one of them was armed), but since she was never remotely their target, he advised her neither to take a side nor to intercede —in time the heat would have to die down, et cetera, et cetera. And eventually, when her terror had begun to lift and the liveliness that was Drenka repossessed her features, she told him that she loved him, that she couldn't possibly live without him, that, as she so spartanly put it, "I couldn't carry out my responsibilities without you." Without what they got up to together, she could never be so good! Licking those sizable breasts, whose breastish reality seemed no less tantalizingly outlandish than it would have when he was fourteen, Sabbath told her that he felt the same about her, allowed it while looking up at her with that smile of his that did not make entirely clear who or what precisely he had it in mind to deride— confessed it certainly with nothing like her declamatory ardor, said it almost as though deliberately to make it appear perfunctory, and yet, stripped of all its derisive trappings, his "Feel the same way about you" happened to be true. Life was as unthinkable for Sabbath without the successful innkeeper's promiscuous wife as it was for her without the remorseless puppeteer. No one to conspire with, no one on earth with whom to give free rein to his most vital need!

"And you?" he asked. "Will you be faithful to me? Is that what you are suggesting?"

"I don't *want* anyone else."

"Since when? Drenka, I see you suffering, I don't want you to suffer, but I cannot take seriously what you are asking of me. How do you justify wishing to impose on me restrictions that you have never imposed on yourself? You are asking for fidelity of a kind that you've never bothered to bestow on your own husband and that, were I to do what you request, you would still be denying him because of *me*. You want monogamy outside marriage and adultery inside marriage. Maybe you're right and that's the only way to do it. But for that you will have to find a more rectitudinous old man." Elaborate. Formal. Perfectly overprecise.

"Your answer is no."

"Could it possibly be yes?"

"And so now you will get rid of me? Overnight? Like that? After thirteen years?"

"I am confused by you. I can't follow you. What exactly is happening here today? It's not I but you who proposed this ultimatum out of the fucking blue. It's you who presented *me* with the either/or. It's you who is getting rid of *me*

overnight . . . unless, of course, I consent to become
overnight a sexual creature of the kind I am not and never
have been. Follow me, please. I must become a sexual creature
of the kind that you have yourself never dreamed of being. In
order to preserve what we have remarkably sustained by forthrightly pursuing together our sexual desires—are you with me?
—*my* sexual desires must be deformed, since it is unarguable
that, like you—you until today, that is—I am not by nature, inclination, practice, or belief a monogamous being. Period. You
wish to impose a condition that either deforms me or turns me
into a dishonest man with you. But like all other living creatures I suffer when I am deformed. And it shocks me, I might
add, to think that the forthrightness that has sustained and excited us both, that provides such a healthy contrast to the routine deceitfulness that is the hallmark of a hundred million
marriages, including yours and mine, is now less to your taste
than the solace of conventional lies and repressive puritanism.
As a self-imposed challenge, repressive puritanism is fine with
me, but it is Titoism, Drenka, *inhuman Titoism*, when it seeks
to impose its norms on others by self-righteously suppressing
the satanic side of sex."

"You *sound* like stupid Tito when you lecture me like this!
Please stop it!"

They hadn't spread their tarpaulin or removed a single item
of their clothing but had remained in their sweatshirts and
jeans, and Sabbath in his knitted seaman's cap, sitting backed
against a rock. Drenka meanwhile paced in rapid circles the
high ring of elephantine boulders, her hands fluttering anx-
iously through her hair or reaching out to feel against her fingertips the cool familiar surface of their hideaway's rough
walls—and could not but remind him of Nikki in the last act of
The Cherry Orchard. Nikki, his first wife, the fragile, volatile
Greek American girl whose pervasive sense of crisis he'd mistaken for a deep spirit and whom he had Chekhovianly nick-
named "A-Crisis-a-Day" until a day came when the crisis of
being herself simply swept Nikki away.

The Cherry Orchard was one of the first plays he'd directed
in New York after the two years of puppet school on the GI
Bill in Rome. Nikki had played Madame Ranyevskaya as a
ruined flapper, for someone so absurdly young in that role,

counterbalancing delicately the satire and the pathos. In the last act, when everything has been packed and the distraught family is preparing to abandon forever the ancestral home, Sabbath had asked Nikki to go silently around the empty room brushing all the walls with the tips of her fingers. No tears, please. Just circle the room touching the bare walls and then leave—that'll do it. And everything she was asked to do, Nikki did exquisitely . . . and it was for him rendered not quite satisfactory by the fact that whatever she played, however well, she was still also Nikki. This "also" in actors drove him eventually back to puppets, who had never to pretend, who never acted. That he generated their movement and gave each a voice never compromised their reality for Sabbath in the way that Nikki, fresh and eager and with all that talent, seemed always less than convincing to him because of being a real person. With puppets you never had to banish the actor from the role. There was nothing false or artificial about puppets, nor were they "metaphors" for human beings. They were what they were, and no one had to worry that a puppet would disappear, as Nikki had, right off the face of the earth.

"Why," Drenka cried, "are you making fun of me? Of *course* you outsmart me, you outsmart everyone, *outtalk* every—"

"Yes, yes," he replied. "Luxurious unseriousness was what the outsmarter often felt the greater the seriousness with which he conversed. Detailed, scrupulous, loquacious rationality was generally to be suspected when Morris Sabbath was the speaker. Though not even he could always be certain whether the nonsense so articulated was wholly nonsensical. No, there was nothing simple about being as misleading—"

"Stop it! Stop it, please, being a maniac!"

"Only if *you* stop it being an idiot! Why on this issue are you suddenly so stupid? Exactly what am I to do, Drenka? Take an oath? Are you going to administer an oath? What are the words to the oath? Please list all the things that I am not allowed to do. Penetration. Is that it, is that all? What about a kiss? What about a phone call? And will you take the oath too? And how will I know if you've upheld it? You never have before."

And just when Silvija is coming back, Sabbath was thinking. Is that what's provoked all this, her fear of what she might be impelled to do for Sabbath in the excitement of the excitement? The summer before, Silvija, Matija's niece, had lived with the Baliches up at the house while working as a waitress in the inn's dining room. Silvija was an eighteen-year-old college student in Split and had taken her vacation in America to improve her English. Having shed any and all qualms in twenty-four hours, Drenka had brought to Sabbath, sometimes stuffed in her pocket, sometimes hidden in her purse, Silvija's soiled underthings. She wore them for him and pretended to be Silvija. She passed them up and down the length of his long white beard and pressed them to his parted lips. She bandaged his erection in the straps and cups, stroked him enwrapped in the silky fabric of Silvija's tiny bra. She drew his feet through the legs of Silvija's bikini underpants and worked them up as far as she could along his heavy thighs. "Say the things," he told her, "say everything," and she did. "Yes, you have my permission, you dirty man, yes," she said, "you can have her, I give her to you, you can have her tight young pussy, you dirty, filthy man. . . ." Silvija was a slight, seraphic thing with very white skin and reddish ringlets who wore small round glasses with metal frames that made her look like a studious child. "Photographs," Sabbath instructed Drenka, "find photographs. There must be photographs, they all take photographs." No, no way. Not meek little Silvija. Impossible, said Drenka, but the next day, going through Silvija's dresser, Drenka uncovered from beneath her cotton nighties a stack of Polaroids that Silvija had brought from Split to keep from becoming homesick. They were mainly pictures of her mother and father, her older sister, her boyfriend, her dog, but one photograph was of Silvija and another girl her age wearing only pantyhose and posing sideways in the doorway between two rooms of an apartment. The other girl was much larger than Silvija, a robust, bulky, big-breasted girl with a pumpkin-ish face who was hugging Silvija from behind while Silvija bent forward, her minute buttocks thrust into the other one's groin. Silvija had her head thrown back and her mouth wide open, feigning ecstasy or perhaps just laughing heartily at the silliness of what they were up to. On the reverse side of the photograph, in the half inch at the top where she carefully identified the people in each of the pictures, Silvija had written, in Serbo-Croatian, "Nera odpozadi"—Nera from the rear. The "odpozadi" was no less inflammatory than the picture, and he looked from one side of the photograph to the other all the while that Drenka improvised for him with Silvija's toylike brassiere. One Monday, when the kitchen at the inn was closed and Matija had taken Silvija off for the day to see historic Boston, Drenka squeezed into the folk dirndl with the full black skirt and the tight, embroidered bodice in which Silvija, like the other waitresses, served the Baliches' customers and, in the guest room where Silvija was spending the summer, laid herself fully clothed across the bed. There was she "seduced," "Silvija" protesting all the while that "Mr. Sabbath" must promise never to tell her aunt and her uncle what she had agreed to do for money. "I never had a man before. I only had my boyfriend, and he comes so soon. I never had a man like you." "Can I come inside you, Silvija?" "Yes, yes, I always wanted a man to come inside me. Just don't tell my aunt and my uncle!" "I fuck your aunt. I fuck Drenka." "Oh, do you? My aunt? Do you? Is she a better fuck than me?" "No, never, no." "Is her pussy tight like me?" "Oh, Silvija—your aunt is standing at the door. She's watching us!" "Oh, my God—!" "She wants to fuck with us, too." "Oh, my God, I never tried that before—"

Little was left undone that first afternoon, and Sabbath was still safely out of Silvija's room hours before the girl returned with her uncle. They couldn't have enjoyed themselves more —so said Silvija, Matija, Drenka, Sabbath. Everybody was happy that summer, including even Sabbath's wife, to whom he was more kindly disposed than he had been for years—there were times now over breakfast when he not only pretended to inquire about her AA meeting but pretended to listen to her answer. And Matija, who on his Mondays off drove Silvija into Vermont and New Hampshire and, on one occasion, to the very end of Cape Cod, seemed to have rediscovered in the role of uncle to his brother's daughter something akin to the satisfaction he had once derived from, all too successfully, making a real American out of his son. The summer had been an idyll for everyone, and when she left for home after Labor Day Silvija was speaking endearingly unidiomatic English and carried a letter from Drenka to her parents—*not* the one devilishly composed in English by Sabbath—reiterating the invitation for the youngster to return to work in the restaurant and live with them again the next summer.

To Sabbath's question—whether, if she herself were to swear to an oath of fidelity, she would have the strength to uphold it—Drenka replied of course she would, yes, she *loved* him.

"You love your husband, too. You love Matija."

"That is not the same."

"But what about six months from now? For years you were angry at him and hated him. Felt so imprisoned by him you even thought of poisoning him. That's how crazy one man was making you. Then you began to love another man and discovered in time that you could now love Matija as well. If you didn't have to pretend to desire him, you could be a good and happy wife to him. Because of you I'm not entirely horrible to Roseanna. I admire Roseanna, she's a real soldier, trooping off to AA every night—those meetings are for her what this is for us, a whole other life to make home endurable. But now you want to change all that, not just for us, but for Roseanna and Matija. Yet why you want to do this you won't tell me."

"Because I want you to say, after thirteen years, 'Drenka, I love you, and you are the only woman I want.' The time has come to *tell* me that!"

"Why has it come? Have I missed something?"

She was crying again when she said, "I sometimes think you miss everything."

"I don't. No. I disagree. I actually don't think I miss anything. I haven't missed the fact that you were frightened to leave Matija even when things were at their worst, because if you left you'd be high and dry, without your share of the inn. You were afraid to leave Matija because he speaks your language and ties you to your past. You were afraid to leave Matija because he is, without doubt, a kind, strong, responsible man. But mostly Matija means money. Despite all this love you have for me, you never once suggested that we leave our mates and run off together, for the simple reason that I am penniless and he is rich. You don't want to be a pauper's wife, though it is all right to be a pauper's girlfriend, especially when

you are able, with the pauper's encouragement, to fuck everybody else on the side."

This made Drenka smile—even in her misery the cunning
smile that few aside from Sabbath had ever got to admire.
"Yes? And if I had announced I was leaving Matija, you would
have run away with me? As stupid as I am? Yes? As bad an accent as I have? Without all the life that I am bound by? Of
course it's you that makes marriage to Matija possible—but it's
Matija that makes it work for *you*."

"So you stay with Matija to make me happy."

"As much as anything—yes!"

"And that explains the other men as well."

"But it does!"

"And Christa?"

"Of course it was for you. You know it was for you. To
please you, to excite you, to give you what you wanted, to give
you the woman you never had! I love you, Mickey. I love
being dirty for you, doing everything for you. I would give
you anything, but I can no longer endure you to have other
women. It hurts too much. The pain is just too great!"

As it happened, since picking up Christa several years back
Sabbath had not really been the adventurous libertine Drenka
claimed she could no longer endure, and consequently she
already had the monogamous man she wanted, even if she
didn't know it. To women other than her, Sabbath was by now
quite unalluring, not just because he was absurdly bearded and
obstinately peculiar and overweight and aging in every obvious way but because, in the aftermath of the scandal four years
earlier with Kathy Goolsbee, he'd become more dedicated
than ever to marshaling the antipathy of just about everyone as
though he were, in fact, battling for his rights. What he continued to tell Drenka, and what Drenka continued to believe,
were lies, and yet deluding her about his seductive powers was
so simple that it amazed him, and if he failed to stop himself it
was not to delude himself as well, or to preen himself in her
eyes, but because the situation was irresistible: gullible Drenka
hotly pleading, "What happened? Tell me everything. Don't
leave anything out," even while he eased into her the way Nera
pretended in the Polaroid to be penetrating Silvija. Drenka remembered the smallest detail of his exciting stories long after

he had forgotten even the broad outline, but then he was as naively transfixed by her stories, the difference being that hers were about people who were real. He knew they were real because, after each new liaison had got under way, he would listen on the extension while, beside him on the bed, holding the portable phone in one hand and his erection in the other, she drove the latest lover crazy with the words that never failed to do the trick. And afterward, each of these sated fellows said to her exactly the same thing: the ponytailed electrician with whom she took baths in his apartment, the uptight psychiatrist whom she saw alternate Thursdays in a motel across the state line, the young musician who played jazz piano one summer at the inn, the nameless middle-aged stranger with the JFK smile whom she met in the elevator of the Ritz-Carlton . . . each one of them said, once he had recovered his breath—and Sabbath heard them saying it, craved their saying it, exulted in their saying it, knew it himself to be one of the few wonderfully indisputable, unequivocal truths a man could live by— each one conceded to Drenka, "There's no one like you."

And now she was telling him that she no longer wished to be this woman unanimously acknowledged as unlike all others. At fifty-two, stimulating enough still to make even conventional men reckless, she wanted to change and become somebody else—but did she know why? The secret realm of thrills and concealment, this was the poetry of her existence. Her crudeness was the most distinguishing force in her life, lent her life its distinction. What was she otherwise? What was *he* otherwise? She was his last link with another world, she and her great taste for the impermissible. As a teacher of estrangement from the ordinary, he had never trained a more gifted pupil; instead of being joined by the contractual they were interconnected by the instinctual and together could eroticize anything (except their spouses). Each of their marriages cried out for a countermarriage in which the adulterers attack their feelings of captivity. Didn't she know a marvel when she saw one?

He was badgering her so relentlessly because he was fighting for his life.

She not merely sounded as though she were fighting for hers but she looked it, looked as though she and not his mother were the ghost. During the last six months or so Drenka had been suffering with abdominal pains and nausea, and he wondered now if they were not symptoms of the anxiety that had been mounting in her as she approached the day in May that she had chosen to present this crazy ultimatum. Until today he had tended to account for her cramps and the occasional bouts of vomiting as the result of the pressures at the inn. Having been at the job for over twenty-three years, she was herself not surprised by the toll the work was now taking on her health. "You have to know food," she lamented wearily, "you have to know the law, you have to know every aspect of life there is. This happens in this business, Mickey, when you have to serve the public all the time—you become a burnt-out case. And Matija still cannot be flexible. This rule, that rule—but the smarter thing is to accommodate the people where you can instead of to say always no. If I could just get a break from the bookkeeping part of it. If I could get away from the staff part of it. Our older staff, they are people full of problems all their lives. The people who are married, the housekeepers, the dishwashers, you can know from the way they behave something is going on that has nothing to do with us. They bring in what's going on outside. And they never go to Matija to tell him what's wrong. They go to me, because I'm the easier one. Every summer he is going, going, going, and I'll say, 'So-and-so did this, did that,' and Matija says to me, 'Why do you always bring me these problems? Why don't you tell me something pleasant!' Well, because I'm upset by what's going on. To have these kids on the staff. I can't take any more kids. They don't know shit from Adams. So I wind up doing their job on the floor, like I'm the kid. Trays all over the place. I clean up. Carrying trays. A busgirl. It builds up, Mickey. If we had our son with us. But Matthew thinks the business is stupid. And sometimes I don't blame him. We have a million dollars' worth of liability insurance. Now I have to get *another* million dollars. We are advised to do this. The dock in the water at the inn's beach that everybody enjoys? The insurance company says, 'Don't do that anymore. Somebody's going to hurt themselves.' So the good things you would like to provide to the American public, they will just get you in trouble. And now—computers!"

The big thing was to get computers in before the summer, an expensive system that had to be wired all over the place. Everybody had to learn to use the new system, and Drenka had to teach them after she had learned herself at a two-month course at Mount Kendall Community College (a course taken also by Sabbath so that once a week they could meet afterward, just down from Mount Kendall, at the Bo-Peep Motel). For Drenka, with her bookkeeping skills, the computer course had been a snap, though teaching the staff was not. "You have to think like that computer thinks," she told Sabbath, "and most of my staff don't even think like a human being yet." "Then why do you keep working so hard? You keep getting sick—you don't enjoy anything any longer." "I do. The money. I still enjoy that. And mine is not the hard job anyway. In the kitchen is the harder job. I don't care how hard for me my job is, how big an emotional strain it is. The physical stamina that you need in the kitchen—you have to be a horse to do that. Matija is a gentleman, thank God, and he doesn't resent that he has the horse's job. Yes, I enjoy the profit. I enjoy that the business is running. Only this year for the first time in twenty-three years we will not go forward financially. That's something else to get sick about. We will go backward. I keep the books, I see week by week how much our restaurant has been declining since Reagan. In the eighties the people from Boston were coming. They didn't mind eating dinner at nine-thirty on a Saturday night, so we'd get the turnover. But the people from around here don't want to do that. There was all the money around then, there was not the competition then. . . ."

No wonder she had cramps . . . the hard work, the worry, profits down, new computers in, and all her men besides. And me—the work with me! Talk about the horse's job. "I can't do everything," she complained to Sabbath when the pain was at its worst. "I can only be who I *am*." Which, Sabbath still believed, was someone who *could* do everything.

When, while he was fucking Drenka up at the Grotto, his mother hovering just above his shoulder, over him like the home plate umpire peering in from behind the catcher's back, he would wonder if she had somehow popped out of Drenka's cunt the moment before he entered it, if that was where his mother's spirit lay curled up, patiently awaiting his appearance. Where else should ghosts come from? Unlike Drenka, who seemed for no reason to have been seized by the taboos, his tiny dynamo of a mother was now beyond all taboos—she could be on the lookout for him anywhere, and wherever she was he could detect her as though there were something supernatural about him as well, as though he transmitted a beam of filial waves that bounced off his invisible mother's presence and gave him her exact location. Either that, or he was going crazy. One way or another, he knew she was about a foot to the right of Drenka's blood-drained face. Perhaps she was not only listening to his every word from there, perhaps every provocative word he spoke she had a puppeteer's power to *make* him speak. It might even be she who was leading him to the disaster of losing the only solace he had. Suddenly his mother's focus had changed and, for the first time since 1944, the living son was more real to her than the dead one.

The final kink, thought Sabbath, searching the dilemma for a solution—the final kink is for the libertines to be faithful. Why not tell Drenka, "Yes, dear, I'll do it"?

Drenka had dropped in exhaustion onto the large granite outcropping near the center of the enclosure where they sometimes sat on beautiful days like this one eating the sandwiches she'd brought in her knapsack. There was a wilted bouquet at her feet, the first wildflowers of the spring, there from when she'd plucked them the week before while tramping up through the woods to meet him. Each year she taught him the names of the flowers, in her language and in his, and from one year to the next he could not remember even the English. For nearly thirty years Sabbath had been exiled in these mountains, and still he could name hardly anything. They didn't have this stuff where he came from. All these things growing were beside the point there. He was from the shore. There was sand and ocean, horizon and sky, daytime and nighttime—the light, the dark, the tide, the stars, the boats, the sun, the mists, the gulls. There were the jetties, the piers, the boardwalk, the booming, silent, limitless sea. Where he grew up they had the Atlantic. You could touch with your toes where America began. They lived in a stucco bungalow two short streets from the edge of America. The house. The porch. The screens. The icebox. The tub. The linoleum. The broom. The pantry. The ants. The sofa. The radio. The garage. The outside shower with the slatted wooden floor Morty had built and the drain that always clogged. In summer, the salty sea breeze and the dazzling light; in September, the hurricanes; in January, the storms. They had January, February, March, April, May, June, July, August, September, October, November, December. And then January. And then again January, no end to the stockpile of Januaries, of Mays, of Marches. August, December, April— name a month, and they had it in spades. They'd had endless-ness. He'd grown up on endlessness and his mother—in the beginning they were the same thing. His mother, his mother, his mother, his mother, his mother . . . and then there was his mother, his father, Grandma, Morty, and the Atlantic at the end of the street. The ocean, the beach, the first two streets in America, then the house, and in the house a mother who never stopped whistling until December 1944.

If Morty had come home alive, if the endlessness had ended naturally instead of with the telegram, if after the war Morty had started doing electrical work and plumbing for people, had become a builder at the shore, gone into the construction business just as the boom in Monmouth County was begin-ning . . . Didn't matter. Take your pick. Get betrayed by the fantasy of endlessness or by the fact of finitude. No, Sabbath could only have wound up Sabbath, begging for what he was begging, bound to what he was bound, saying what he did not wish to stop himself from saying.

"I'll tell you what"—his milk-of-human-kindness intonation —"I'll make a deal. I'll make the sacrifice you want. I will give up every woman but you. I'll say, 'Drenka, I love only you and want only you and will take whatever oath you wish to admin-ister itemizing everything that I am forbidden to do.' But in return you must make a sacrifice."

"I will!" Excitedly she rose to her feet. "I want to! Never an-other man! Only you! To the end!"

"No," he said, approaching with his arms extended to her, "no, no, I don't mean that. That, you tell me, constitutes *no* sacrifice. No, I'm asking for something to test your stoicism and to test your truthfulness as you will be testing mine, a task just as repugnant to you as breaking the sacrament of infidelity is to me."

His arms were around her now, grasping her plump buttocks through her jeans. *You like when I turn around on you and you can see my ass. All men like that. But only you stick it in there, only you, Mickey, can fuck me there!* Not true, but a nice sentiment.

"I will give up all other women. In return," he told her, "you must suck off your husband twice a week."

"Aacch!"

"Aacch, yes. Aacch, exactly. You're gagging already. 'Aacch, I could never do that!' Can't I find something kinder? No."

Sobbing, she pulled herself free of him and pleaded, "Be *serious—this is serious!*"

"I am being serious. How odious can it be? It's merely monogamy at its most inhumane. Pretend it's someone else. That's what all good women do. Pretend it's the electrician. Pretend it's the credit-card magnate. Matija comes in two seconds anyway. You'll be getting everything you want and surprising a husband in the bargain, and it'll take only four seconds a week. And think of how it will excite *me.* The most promiscuous thing you have ever done. Sucking off your husband to please your lover. You want to feel like a real whore? That ought to do it."

"Stop!" she cried out, throwing her hands over his mouth. "I have cancer, Mickey! Stop! The pain has been because of cancer! I can't believe it! I *don't*! I can *die*!"

Just then the oddest thing happened. For the second time in a year a helicopter flew over the woods and then circled back and hovered directly above them. This time it had to be his mother.

"Oh, my God," said Drenka and, with her arms around him, squeezed so tightly that the full weight of her clinging caused his knees to buckle—or perhaps they were about to buckle anyway.

Mother, he thought, this can't be so. First Morty, then you, then Nikki, now Drenka. There's nothing on earth that keeps its promise.

"Oh, I wanted, oh," cried Drenka as the helicopter's energy roared above them, a dynamic force to magnify the monstrous loneliness, a wall of noise tumbling down on them, their whole carnal edifice caving in. "I wanted you to say it without *knowing*, I wanted you to do it on your *own*," and here she wailed the wail that authenticates the final act of a classical tragedy. "I can die! If they can't stop it, darling, I will be dead in a year!"

Mercifully she was dead in six months, killed by a pulmonary embolus before there was time for the cancer, which had spread omnivorously from her ovaries throughout her system, to torture Drenka beyond even the tough capacity of her own ruthless strength.

UNABLE to sleep, Sabbath lay beside Roseanna overcome by a stupendous, deforming emotion of which he had never before had firsthand knowledge. He was jealous now of the very men about whom, when Drenka was living, he could never hear enough. He thought about the men she had met in elevators, airports, parking lots, department stores, at hotel association conferences and food conventions, men she had to have because their looks appealed to her, men she slept with just once or had prolonged flings with, men who five and six years after she'd last been to bed with them would unexpectedly phone the inn to extol her, to praise her, often without sparing the graphic obscenities to tell her how she was the least inhibited woman they had ever known. He remembered her explaining to him—because he had asked her to—what exactly made her choose one man in a room over another, and now he felt like the most foolishly innocent of husbands who uncovers the true history of an unfaithful wife—he felt as stupid as the holy simpleton Dr. Charles Bovary. The diabolical pleasure this had once afforded him! The happiness! When she was alive, nothing excited or entertained him more than hearing, detail by detail, the stories of her second life. Her *third* life—*he* was the second. "It's a very physical feeling that I get. It's the appearance, it's something chemical, I almost would like to say. There's an energy that I sense. It makes me very aroused and I feel it then, I become sexualized, and I feel it in my nipples. I feel it inside, in my body. If he is physical, if he is strong, the way he walks, the way he sits, the way he's himself, if he's juicy. Guys with small dry lips, they turn me off, or if they smell bookish—you know, this dry pencil smell of men. I often look at their hands to see if they have strong, expressive hands. Then I imagine that they have a big dick. If there is any truth to this I don't know, but I do it anyway as a little research. Some kind of confidence in the way they move. It isn't that they have to look elegant—it is rather an animalistic appearance under the elegance. So it's a very intuitive thing. And I

know it right away and I have always known it. And so I say,
'Okay, I go and fuck him.' Well, I have to open the channels
for him. So I look at him and I flirt with him. I just start laughing or show my legs and sort of show him that it's all right.
Sometimes I make a real bold gesture. 'I wouldn't mind
having an affair with you.' Yeah," she said, laughing at the extent of her own impulsiveness, "I could say something like
that. That guy I had in Aspen, I felt his interest. But he was in
his fifties and there I always question how hard can they get.
With a younger guy you know it's an easier thing. With an
older one you don't know. But I felt this kind of vibration and
I was really turned on. And, you know, you move your arm
closer or he moves his arm closer and you know you're in this
aura of sexual feeling together and everybody else in the room
is excluded. I think with that man I actually openly stated that
it was okay, that I was interested."

The boldness with which she went after them! The ardor
and skill with which she aroused them! The delight she found
in watching them jerk off! And the pleasure she then took in
telling all she'd learned about lust and what it is for men
. . . and the torment all this was to him now. He'd not had
the faintest idea that he could feel such distress. "What I enjoyed was to see how they were by themselves. That I could be
the observer there, and to see how they played with their dick
and how it was formed, the shape of it, and when it became
hard, and also the way they held their hand—it turned me on.
Everybody jerks their dick differently. And when they abandon
themselves into it, when they allow themselves to abandon
themselves, this is very exciting. And to see them come that
way. This Lewis guy, he was in his sixties and he'd never jerked
off, he said, in front of a woman. And he was sort of holding
his hand this way"—she turned her wrist so that the little finger was at the top of her fist and the second knuckle of her
thumb at the bottom—"well, to see that particularity of it and,
as I say, to see when they get so hot they can't stop themselves
in spite of being shy, that's very exciting. That's what I like
best—watching them lose control." The shy ones she would
softly suck for a few minutes and then place their hands for
them on themselves and help them along until they were safely
into it and on their own. Then, beginning lightly to finger

herself, she would lean back and look on. When she next saw
Sabbath she would demonstrate on him the peculiar "particularity" of each man's technique. He was tremendously stirred
by this . . . and now it made him jealous, maddeningly jealous—now that she was dead he wanted to shake her and shout
at her and tell her to stop. "Only me! Fuck your husband
when you have to, but otherwise, no one but me!"

In fact, he didn't want her to fuck Matija either. Him least
of all. On the rare occasions when she used to report those details to Sabbath, too, they had hardly engrossed him, provoked
not the slightest erotic interest. Yet now there was barely a
night when he was free of the mortifying memory of Drenka
allowing her husband to take her like a wife. "Checking Matija
in bed, I saw his erection. I was certain he would not act on it
without my taking first initiative, so quickly I undressed. I
could not get aroused even if I had strong, tender feelings for
my husband. Seeing his hard cock, smaller than yours, Mickey,
and with a foreskin, which when the skin is pulled down is
much redder than yours . . . thinking about the way we had
just fucked . . . well, longing for your big, hard dick, it was
almost painful. How could I abandon myself to this man who
loves me? When he penetrated me, lying on top of me, Matija
was moaning louder than I ever recollect. It was almost as if he
was crying. Since it never takes him long to come, the whole
thing was over soon. After sleeping one or two hours I woke
up sick to my stomach. I had to throw up and take some My-
lanta."

How dare he! What *chutzpah*! Sabbath wanted to murder
Matija. And why didn't I? Why didn't *we*? Uncircumcised dog!
Smite him *thus*!

. . . One brilliantly sunny day back in February, Sabbath
had come upon Drenka's widowered husband up at the Stop
& Shop in Cumberland. For the first time that winter it hadn't
snowed in four consecutive days and so, after donning an old
knit seaman's cap in which to swab down the bathroom and
kitchen floors and give the house a vacuuming, Sabbath had
driven up to Cumberland—blinded much of the way by the
light off the gargantuan drifts banked at the side of the road—
to do the grocery shopping, one of his weekly household
chores. And there was Matija, almost unrecognizable since

he'd seen him silent and stone-faced at the funeral. His black hair had gone white, completely white in just the three months. He looked so weak, so slight, his face emaciated—and all of this in just three months! He could have passed for a senior citizen, older even than Sabbath, and he was only in his mid-fifties. The inn was closed every year from New Year's Day to April 1, and so Matija was out shopping for the few things he needed living alone in the Baliches' big new house up from the lake and the inn.

Balich was directly behind him in the checkout line and, though he nodded when Sabbath looked his way, registered no recognition.

"Mr. Balich, my name is Mickey Sabbath."

"Yes? How do you do?"

"Does 'Mickey Sabbath' mean anything to you?"

"Yes," said Balich kindly after feigning a moment's thought, "I believe you have been a patron of mine. I recognize you from the inn."

"No," said Sabbath, "I live in Madamaska Falls but we don't eat out much."

"I see," replied Balich and, after smiling for a few seconds more, somberly returned to his thoughts.

"I'll tell you how we know each other," said Sabbath.

"Yes?"

"My wife was your son's art teacher at the high school. Roseanna Sabbath. She and your Matthew became great friends."

"Ahhh." Again he smiled courteously.

Sabbath had never realized before how much there was in Drenka's husband of the subdued and courtly European gentleman. Maybe it was the white hair, the grief, the accent, but he had about him the magisterial air of a senior diplomat from a small country. No, Sabbath hadn't known this about him, the dignified composure came as a surprise, but then the other guy is often just a blur. Even if he's your best friend or the fellow across the street who more than once has jump-started your car, he *becomes* a blur. He becomes *the husband*, and sympathetic imagination dwindles away, right along with conscience.

The only time Sabbath ever before had occasion to observe

Matija in public was the April preceding the Kathy Goolsbee scandal, when he went over to the inn on the third Tuesday of the month—with the thirty or so Rotarians who gathered there for their luncheon meeting the third Tuesday of every month—as a guest of Gus Kroll, the service station owner, who never failed to pass on to Sabbath the jokes he heard from the truckers who stopped to gas up and use the facilities. Gus had a great audience in Sabbath, because even when the jokes were not uniformly of the first rank, the fact that Gus rarely bothered to wear his dentures while he was telling them furnished Sabbath with sufficient delight. Gus's impassioned commitment to repeating the jokes had long ago led the puppeteer to understand that they were what gave unity to Gus's vision of life, that they alone answered the need of his spiritual being for a clarifying narrative with which to face day after day at the pump. With every joke that poured forth from Gus's toothless mouth, Sabbath was reassured that not even a simple guy like Gus was free of the human need to find a strand of significance that will hold together everything that isn't on TV.

Sabbath had asked Gus if he would be kind enough to invite him to the meeting to hear Matija Balich address the Rotary Club on the topic "Innkeeping Today." By then Sabbath already knew that Matija had been agonizingly preparing the speech for weeks—Sabbath had even read the speech, or the first short version of it, when Drenka had brought it to him to look at. She had typed the six pages for her husband, done her best to catch the errors, but she wanted Sabbath to double-check the English and amiably he agreed to help. "It's fascinating," he said after twice reading it through. "It is?" "It moves along the track like a goddamn train. Really, it's wonderful. Two problems, however. It's too short. He's not thorough enough. It's got to be three times as long. And this expression, this idiom here, is wrong. It isn't 'nuts and bolts.' You don't say in English, 'If you watch the nuts and bolts. . . .'" "No?" "Who told him it was 'nuts and bolts,' Drenka?" "Stupid Drenka did," she replied. "Nuts and *bulbs*," said Sabbath. "Nuts and bulbs," she repeated and wrote on the back of the last page. "And write down there that he stops too soon," said

Sabbath. "Three times as long, at least. They'll listen," he told her. "This is stuff nobody knows."

Gus came by Brick Furnace Road to pick up Sabbath in the tow truck, and no sooner were they off than Gus started in entertaining him with what he knew to be taboo for what Gus called the "churchy guys" in town.

"Can you take a joke that's not too appreciative of women?" Gus asked him.

"The only kind I *can* take."

"Well, this truck driver, whenever he goes away, his wife, she gets cold and lonely. So when he comes back from a trip he brings her a skunk, a big, furry live skunk, and he tells her that next time he goes away she should take it to bed with her and when she goes to sleep she should put it between her legs. So she says to him, 'What about the smell?' And he says, 'He'll get used to it. I did.'"

"Well, if you like that one," said Gus when he heard Sabbath's laughter, "I got another one along the same lines," and so in no time they arrived for the meeting.

The Rotarians were already milling around in the rustic barroom with the exposed beams across the low ceiling and the cheerful white tile hearth, all of them packed closely together in the one smallish room, perhaps because of the cozy fire burning there on a cold, gusty spring day or perhaps because of the platters, on the bar, of *ćevapčići*, a Yugoslav national specialty that was also a specialty of the inn. "I have to feed you with *ćevapčići*," Drenka had told Sabbath when they were still newly lovers, playing post-coital pranks in bed. "Feed me anything you want." "Three types of meat," she told him, "one is beef, one is pork, then is lamb. All is ground. Then some onions are added to it and some pepper. It is like a meatball but a different shape. Very small. It is obligatory to eat *ćevapčići* with onion. An onion cut into small pieces. You can have little peppers, too. Red. Very hot." "It doesn't sound bad at all," said Sabbath, full of pleasure with her, smiling away. "Yes, I am going to feed you *ćevapčići*," she said adoringly. "And I, in turn, will fuck your brains out." "Oh, my American boyfriend—that means you will fuck me seriously?" "Quite seriously." "It means hard?" "Very hard." "And it means what else? I have learned to do it in Croatian, to say all the words and not be shy, but never anyone has taught me to do it in American. Tell me! Teach me! Teach me what all the things mean in American!" "It means every which way." And then, as conscientiously as she had explained to him how to make *ćevapčići*, he went ahead to teach her what every which way meant.

. . . Or perhaps they were in the barroom because, tending bar, Drenka was wearing a black crepe blouse that buttoned up to a V-neck and that did her plumpness full justice whenever she ducked down to fill a glass with ice. Sabbath stood back by the door for close to half an hour watching her flirting with the chiropractor, a strong young fellow with a loud bark of a laugh who didn't do at all well hiding his sexual orientation, and then with the former state representative who was owner of the three branches of Cumberland BanCorp, and finally even with Gus, who, fully fitted out now in his uppers and lowers and for the occasion wearing a string tie at the neck of his coveralls, was just the man he'd like to see her fuck to be assured that she was as wonderful as he thought she was. Oh, she was jolly, all right—the only woman amid all these men, the blissful stimulus serving their blissful stimulant, plainly ecstatic just to be living on earth.

When Sabbath pushed through the hubbub up to the bar and asked for a beer, she registered her surprise at his presence by instantly turning white. "What kind do you like, Mr. Sabbath?" "Do you have Pussy from Yugoslavia?" "From the tap or a bottle?" "Which do you recommend?" "More foam from the tap," she said, smiling at him, now that she had recovered her wits, with a smile that he would have taken for a startlingly open proclamation of their secret had he not seen the same smile bestowed earlier on Gus. "Draw me one, will ya?" he said with a wink. "I like the foam."

When the meal ended—big pork chops with apple rings in a Calvados sauce, chocolate ice cream sundaes, cigars, and for those who wanted an after-luncheon drink, Prošek, a sweetish white Dalmatian wine that Drenka, as their charming Old World hostess, ordinarily served to paying guests compliments of the house—Matija was introduced by the Rotary president as "Matt Balik." The innkeeper was wearing a red cashmere turtleneck, a blazer with gold buttons, new cavalry-twill trousers, and unworn, unmarked Bally boots polished to a high gloss. Snappily decked out like that, he looked more impressively brawny even than when he was working in a T-shirt and worn jeans. The allure of a heavily muscled male figure conventionally clothed for social intercourse. *An animalistic appearance under the elegance.* Sabbath had had it himself once, or so Nikki used to tell him when she urged him to buy a dark blue suit with a vest so the world could appreciate how gorgeous he was. Gorgeous Sabbath. Those were the fifties.

Matija's passion was to rebuild the stone walls falling to pieces in the fifty acres of fields adjacent to the house and the inn. On the island of Brač, where he had relatives and where he had been working as a waiter when he met Drenka, there was a tradition of masonry, and while he was on the island he would spend his days off helping a cousin who was building himself a house of stone. And, of course, Matija had never forgotten the grandfather cutting stone in the quarries, an aging man imprisoned on Goli Otok as an enemy of the regime . . . which made lugging the big stones and setting them in place something almost of a commemorative rite for Matija. That was how he spent his breaks from the kitchen: outside half an hour moving rocks and he was ready for another three, four, five hours on his feet in a temperature of a hundred degrees. He spent much of each winter moving those rocks. "His only friends," reported Drenka, sadly, "are the walls and me."

"Some people," Matija began, "think this business is fun. It is not fun. It is a business. Read the industry magazines. People say, 'I want to get away from corporate life. An inn, this is my dream.' But I am dedicated to this inn as though I am *going* every day to a corporate structure."

The pace at which Matija read made it possible for his audience to follow without trouble, despite his heavy accent. At the end of every sentence he allowed them a long moment to consider all the implications of what he had just said. Sabbath enjoyed the pauses no less than the monotony of the uninflected sentences they separated, sentences that caused him to remember for the first time in many years a lonely archipelago of uninhabitable islands that the merchant ships passed leaving Veracruz for the south. Sabbath enjoyed the pauses because he was responsible for them. He had told Drenka to instruct Matija to be sure to take his time. Amateur speakers always rush. Don't rush, he told her to tell him. There's a lot for an audience to digest. The slower the better.

"For instance, we have been audited twice," Matija told them.

From the large bay windows at the head of the rectangular dining room, Sabbath and the guests on his side of the table could see clear down to where the wind was whipping up Lake Madamaska. Their eyes could have traveled from one end to the other of that long washboard of a lake before Matija appeared to conclude that the impact of the two audits had been fully absorbed.

"There is nothing wrong," he then continued. "My wife keeps our books straight and we go to an accountant for advices. So we run it as a business and it is our livelihood. If you watch the nuts and bulbs, the business works for you. If you don't watch, and go out and talk with the guests all the time, you are losing money.

"Years ago we did not serve all the time through the afternoon on Saturday. We still don't. But we make food available to the people. The smart thing is to give people what they want rather than say no, I have this rule, I have that rule. I am pretty strict about the way I think about things. But the public teaches me to be not so strict.

"We have fifty in staff, including part-time. Serving staff is thirty-five—waitresses, bus staff, dining room supervisors. We have twelve rooms plus the annex. We can take twenty-eight people and are full most weekends, though not during the week.

"In the restaurant we can seat one hundred and thirty inside and one hundred on the terrace. But we never seat two hundred and thirty people altogether. The cooking line can't handle it. What we look for is turnover.

"The other serious problem comes with the staff. . . ."

This went on for an hour. There was a fire blazing in the main dining room, as well as the smaller one burning in the bar, and because of the cold winds blowing outside, the windows were all shut tight. The fireplace was only some six feet behind Matija, but the heat of it did not seem to affect him the way it did the Scotch drinkers at the table. They were the first to pass out. The beer drinkers were able to hold on longer.

"We are not absentee owners. I am the main fellow. If everybody else leaves, I am still standing here. My wife can do everything except two cooking-line jobs. She can't work on the broiler, because she has no idea how to cook. And she can't do the sauté, where you are basically frying in pans. But all other jobs she can do: the bartender, the dishwasher, serving, bookkeeping, working the floor. . . ."

Gus, on the wagon these days, drank Tab, but Sabbath saw that Gus was out. Just from Tab. And now the beer drinkers were losing their grip and beginning to look enfeebled—the owner of the bank, the chiropractor, the big mustached guy who ran the gardening center. . . .

Drenka was listening from the bar. When the puppeteer turned in his seat to smile at her, he saw that, leaning over the bar on her elbows, her face balanced on her fists, she was crying, and this was with half the Rotarians still clinging to consciousness.

"It is not always nice for us that our staff doesn't like us. I think some of our staff likes us a lot. A lot of them don't care for us at all. In some places the bar is open to the staff after hours. We don't have that kind of thing here. Those are the places that go bankrupt and where the staff is in terrible auto accidents on the way home. Not here. Here it is not party time with the owners. Here it is not fun. My wife and I are not fun at all. We are work. We are a business. All Yugoslavs when they go abroad, they are very hardworking. Something in our history pushes them for survival. Thank you."

There were no questions, but then there were barely a handful at the long table still capable of asking one. The Rotary president said, "Well, thanks, Matt, thanks a million. That took us through the process pretty thoroughly." Soon people began to wake up to go back to work.

On Friday of that same week, Drenka went to Boston and fucked her dermatologist, the credit-card magnate, the university dean, and then, back at home, just before midnight—making a total of four for the day—she was fucked, holding her breath for the few minutes it lasted, by the orator she was married to.

Now, down in the abandoned center of Cumberland, where the movie theater was long gone and the stores mostly vacant, there was an impoverished wreck of a grocery where Sabbath liked to get a container of coffee and drink it standing up right there after he'd done the weekly shopping. The place, Flo 'n Bert's, was dark, with dirty, worn wooden floors, undusted shelves largely empty of goods, and the most wretched potatoes and bananas Sabbath had ever seen for sale anywhere. But Flo 'n Bert's, grisly mortuary though it was, smelled exactly like the old grocery in the basement of the LaReine Arms, a block away from their house, where Sabbath used to go first thing every morning to get two fresh rolls for his mother so she could make Morty sandwiches to take to his high school for lunch—cream cheese and olive, peanut butter and jelly, but mainly canned tuna, the sandwiches double-wrapped with wax paper and stuffed in the paper bag from the LaReine Arms. Each week, after Stop & Shop, Sabbath walked around Flo 'n Bert's with his coffee container in his hand, trying to figure out what the ingredients were that went into that smell, which was also like something he smelled up at the Grotto in late autumn, after the fallen leaves and the dying underbrush had been dampened down by the rains and begun to rot. Maybe it was that: damp rot. He loved it. The coffee that he had to drink there was undrinkable but he could never resist the pleasure of that smell.

Sabbath stationed himself outside the door to Stop & Shop and, when Balich emerged carrying a plastic bag in either hand, he said, "Mr. Balich, how about a hot cup of coffee?"

"Thank you, sir, no."

"Come on," said Sabbath good-naturedly, "why not? It's ten degrees out here." Should he convert that into Celsius for him, as he would for Drenka when she telephoned, before going up to the Grotto, to ask what it *really* was outside? "There's a place down the hill. Follow me. The Chevy. A cup of coffee to warm you up."

Leading Balich's car between the one-story-high snowbanks and across the railroad tracks agleam from the frost, Sabbath had to admit that he had no idea what he was planning to do. All he could think of was this guy daring to lie across his Drenka, moaning with pleasure as though he were crying, penetrating her with a dog-red cock that afterward made her throw up.

Yes, it was time that he and Balich met—to go through life without meeting him face-to-face would be making life too easy for himself. He would long ago have died of boredom without his extensive difficulties.

The putrid coffee was poured from the Silex by a sullen, stupid girl in her late teens who had been a sullen, stupid girl in her late teens ever since Sabbath had begun dropping in to smell Flo 'n Bert's some fifteen years back. Maybe they were all from the same family, daughters of Flo and Bert who successively grew into the job, or maybe, more likely, there was an inexhaustible supply of these girls turned out by the Cumberland school system. On-the-prowl, insinuating, unselective Sabbath had never been able to get anything more than a grunt out of any of them.

Involuntarily Balich made a face when he tasted the coffee— which turned out to be about as cold as the day—but politely said, "Oh no, very good, but one is enough," when Sabbath asked if he'd like a second cup.

"It has not been easy for you without your wife," Sabbath said. "You look very thin."

"These have been dark days," Balich replied.

"Still?"

He nodded sadly. "It's awful still. I'm right at the bottom. After thirty-one years, I'm in my third month of a new regime. Somehow in some ways every day it gets worse."

That it does. "And your son?"

"He's in a bit of a state of shock too. He misses her terribly. But he's young, he's strong. Sometimes, his wife tells me, in the dark hours of the night . . . but he seems to be coping."

"That's good," Sabbath said. "That is about the strongest bond in the world, the mother and the little boy. There couldn't be anything stronger."

"Yes, yes," said Balich, his soft gray eyes growing teary from talking to somebody so understanding. "Yes, and when I looked at her dead, with my son at the hospital in the middle of the night . . . she was lying there with all the tubes and when I looked at her and I saw that it was broken, that bond with our son, I could not believe that this strongest thing in the world that you say was no longer in existence. There she was, all her beauty lying there, and that strongest thing wasn't anymore. She was gone. So I kissed her good-bye, my son did and I did, and they took all the tubes out. And this piece of human sunlight was there, but dead."

"How old was she?"

"Fifty-two. It's the most cruel thing that could have happened."

"Of all the people in the world who would have died in their fifties like that," said Sabbath, "I would never have imagined your wife on the list. The few times I ever saw her in town, as you say, she lit up everything. And your son works with you at the inn?"

"Innkeeping is not on my mind at all. Whether that comes back ever, I don't know. I do have a staff of good workers, but innkeeping is not on my mind. Our whole marriage was tied up with the inn. I am thinking of leasing the business. If some Japanese corporation wanted to come along and buy it . . . Every time I go into her office to try to deal with her things, it's awful, it makes me sick. I don't want to be there and I go."

Sabbath had not been mistaken, he thought, to have never written Drenka a single letter or to have insisted that it should be he, and not she, who filed away for safekeeping the Polaroids he'd taken of her at the Bo-Peep.

"The letters," Balich said, looking imploringly toward Sabbath, as though to make an appeal. "Two hundred and fifty-six letters."

"Of consolation?" asked Sabbath, who, of course, had not himself received a single one. When Nikki disappeared, however, he'd got mail about her, care of the theater. Though by now he'd forgotten how much—maybe fifty letters in all—at the time he'd been stupefied enough to keep a careful count, too.

"Of sympathy, yes. Two hundred and fifty-six. I shouldn't have been amazed at how she lit up everyone's life. I'm getting letters still. And from people I can't even remember. Some came to the inn when we first opened at the other end of the lake. Letters from all kinds of people about her and about how she affected their life. And I believe them. They are true. I got a long two-page letter, a handwritten letter, from the ex-mayor of Worcester."

"Really?"

"He remembers our barbecues for the guests and how she made everyone happy. How she came into the dining room at breakfast and talked to everybody. She just touched everybody. I am strict, I have a rule for everything. But she knew how to treat the guests. Everything was always possible for the guests. For her to be pleasant it was never an effort. One owner is strict, the other is flexible and pleasant. We were a perfect pair to make a successful inn. It's amazing what she did. A thousand different things. She did it all gracefully and always with great pleasure. I can't stop dwelling on it. There is nothing that can take away even a little of this misery. It's impossible to believe. One minute here, the next minute not."

The ex-mayor of Worcester? Well, she had secrets from both of us, Matija.

"And what is your son's occupation?"

"A state trooper."

"Married?"

"His wife is pregnant. The baby will be Drenka if it is a girl."

"Drenka?"

"My wife's name," said Balich. "Drenka, Drenka," he muttered. "There will never be another Drenka."

"Do you see him much, your son?"

"Yes," he lied, unless since Drenka's death there had been a rapprochement.

Balich suddenly had no more to say. Sabbath used the break to smell the moribund market's smell. Either Balich did not want to talk about his grief over Drenka with a stranger any longer or he did not want to talk about his grief over his state trooper son who thought innkeeping was a stupid business.

"How come your son isn't a partner in the inn? Why doesn't he take over with you, now that your wife is gone?"

"I see," said Balich after carefully setting his half-full cup on the counter beside the register, "that you have arthritic fingers. This is a painful disorder. My brother has arthritic fingers."

"Really? Silvija's father?" asked Sabbath.

Openly surprised, Balich said, "You know my little niece?"

"My wife met her. My wife told me about her. She said she was a very, very pretty and charming child."

"Silvija loved her aunt very much. She worshiped her aunt. Silvija became our daughter, too." In his quiet voice there was little intonation now other than the unmistakable intonation of sorrow.

"Is Silvija at the inn in the summertime? My wife said she was working there to learn English."

"Silvija comes every summer while she is in university."

"What are you doing—training *her* to take over your wife's job?"

"No, no," said Balich, and Sabbath was surprised by how disappointed he was to hear this. "She will be a computer programmer."

"That's too bad," said Sabbath.

"That's what she wants to be," said Balich flatly.

"But if she could help you run the inn, if she could light up the place the way your wife did . . ."

Balich reached into his pocket for money. Sabbath said, "Please—" but Balich was not listening any longer. Doesn't like me, Sabbath thought. Didn't take to me. Must have said the wrong thing.

"My coffee?" Balich asked the sullen girl at the register.

She answered with as few sounded consonants as possible. Other things on her mind.

"What?" Balich asked her.

Sabbath translated. "Half a dollar."

Balich paid and, nodding formally at Sabbath, concluded his initial encounter with someone he clearly did not wish to meet ever again. It was Silvija that had done it, Sabbath's modifying "very" with "very." But that was as close as the puppeteer had come to telling Balich in their first five minutes together that the woman who had vomited after having had to fuck him had had every reason to vomit, because all the while she had been as good as someone else's wife. Of course he understood Balich's feelings—for him, too, the shock of her death was only getting worse by the day—but that didn't mean that Sabbath could forgive him.

Five months after her death, a damp, warm April night with a full moon canonizing itself above the tree line, effortlessly floating—luminously blessed—toward the throne of God, Sabbath stretched out on the ground that covered her coffin and said, "You filthy, wonderful Drenka cunt! Marry me! Marry me!" And with his white beard down in the dirt—the plot was still grassless and without a stone—he envisioned his Drenka: it was bright inside the box and she looked just like herself before the cancer stripped her of all that appealing roundness—ripe, full, ready for contact. Tonight she was wearing Silvija's dirndl. And she was laughing at him.

"So now you want me all to yourself. Now," she said, "when you don't have to have only me and live only with me and be bored only by me, now I am good enough to be your wife."

"Marry me!"

Smiling invitingly, she replied, "First you'll have to die," and raised Silvija's dress to reveal that she was without underpants —dark stockings and a garter belt but no underpants. Even dead, Drenka gave him a hard-on; alive *or* dead, Drenka made him twenty again. Even with temperatures below zero, he would grow hard whenever, from her coffin, she enticed him like this. He had learned to stand with his back to the north so that the icy wind did not blow directly on his dick but still he had to remove one of his gloves to jerk off successfully, and sometimes the gloveless hand would get so cold that he would have to put that glove back on and switch to the other hand. He came on her grave many nights.

The old cemetery was six miles out of town on a little-used road that curved up into the woods and then zigzagged down the western side of the mountain, where it emptied into a superannuated truck route to Albany. The cemetery was set into an open hillside that rolled gently up to an ancient stand of hemlock and white pine. It was beautiful, still, aesthetically charming, melancholy perhaps, but not a cemetery that made you downhearted when you entered it—it was so charming that it sometimes looked as though it had nothing to do with death. It was old, very old, though there were some even older in the nearby hills, their eroded tombstones, fallen aslant, dating back to the earliest years of colonial America. The first burial here—of a certain John Driscoll—had been in 1745; the last burial had been of Drenka, on the last day of November 1993.

Because of the seventeen snowstorms that winter it was often impossible for him to make his way up to the cemetery, even on nights when Roseanna had hurried off to an AA meeting in her four-wheel drive and he was all alone. But when the roads were plowed, the weather was good, the sun down, and Roseanna gone, he drove his Chevy up to the top of Battle Mountain and parked at the cleared entrance to a hiking path about a quarter mile east of the cemetery and made his way along the highway to the graveyard and then, using a flashlight as sparingly as he could, across the treacherous glaze of the drifted snow to her grave. He never drove out during the day, however much he needed to, for fear of running into one of her Matthews or, for that matter, anyone who could take to wondering why, at the coldest spot in the state's "icebox" county, in the midst of the worst winter in local history, the disgraced puppeteer was paying his respects to the remains of the innkeeper's peppy wife. At night he could do what he wished to do, unseen by anyone but his mother's ghost.

"What do you want? If you want to say something . . ." But his mother never did communicate with him, and just because she didn't he came dangerously close to believing that she was not a hallucination—if he was hallucinating, then easily enough he could hallucinate speech for her, enlarge her reality with a voice of the kind with which he used to enliven his puppets. These visitations had been going on too regularly to be a mental aberration . . . unless he was mentally aberrant and the unreality was going to worsen as life became even more unendurable. Without Drenka it *was* unendurable—he didn't have a life, except at the cemetery.

The first April after her death, on this early spring night, Sabbath lay spread-eagled atop her grave, reminiscing with her about Christa. "Never forget you coming," he whispered into the dirt, "never forget you begging her, 'More, more. . . .'" Invoking Christa did not exacerbate his jealousy, remembering Drenka lying back in his arms while Christa maintained the steady pressure of the point of her tongue on Drenka's clitoris (for close to an hour—he'd timed them) only intensified the loss, even though, shortly after the three had first got together, Christa began taking Drenka to a bar in Spottsfield to dance. She went so far as to make Drenka the gift of a gold chain that she'd lifted from her former employer's jewelry drawer on the morning she'd decided she'd had enough of looking after a kid so hyperactive that he was about to be enrolled in a special school for the "gifted." She told Drenka that the value of *everything* she'd walked off with (including a pair of diamond stud earrings and a slithery little bracelet of diamonds) didn't come to half of what she was entitled to for having been stuck, sight unseen, with that kid.

Christa lived in an attic room on Town Street, overlooking the green, just above the gourmet food shop where she worked. Her rent was free, lunches were free, and in addition she was paid twenty-five dollars a week. For two months, on Wednesday nights, Drenka and Sabbath would go, in separate cars, to lie with Christa in the attic. Nothing was open on Town Street after dark, and they could get up unobserved to Christa's by an outside back staircase. Three times Drenka had been by herself to see Christa there but, fearful that Sabbath would be angry with her if he knew, she did not tell him until a year after Christa had turned against the two of them and moved out to the countryside, into the rented farmhouse of a history instructor on the Athena faculty, a woman of thirty with whom Christa had begun a love affair even before she had undertaken her little caprice with the elderly. Abruptly she stopped answering Sabbath's phone calls, and when he ran into her one day—while he pretended to be studying the window display of the gourmet shop, a display which hadn't changed since Tip-Top Grocery Company had evolved in the late sixties into Tip-Top Gourmet Company to accommodate the ardor of the times—she said to him angrily, her mouth so minute it looked like something omitted from her face, "I don't want to talk to you anymore." "Why? What happened?" "You two exploited me." "I don't think that's true, Christa. To exploit someone means to use someone selfishly for one's own ends or to utilize them for profit. I don't think either of us exploited you any more than you exploited either of us." "You're an old man! I am twenty years old! I do not want to talk to you!" "Won't you at least talk to Drenka?" "Leave me

alone! You're nothing but a fat old man!" "So was Falstaff,
kiddo. So was that huge hill of flesh Sir John Paunch, sweet
creator of bombast! 'That villainous abominable misleader of
youth, Falstaff, that old white-bearded Satan'!—" but she was
by this time already into the shop, leaving Sabbath to sadly
contemplate—along with a Christaless future—two jars of Mi-
Kee Chinese Duck Sauce, two jars of Krinos Grape Leaves in
Brine, two cans of La Victoria Refried Beans, and two cans of
Baxter's Cream of Smoked Trout Soup, all of them encircling
a bottle fancily wrapped in a sun-faded whitish paper shroud
and positioned on a pedestal at the center of the window as if
it were the answer to all our cravings, a bottle of Lea & Perrins
Worcestershire Sauce. Yes, a relic much like Sabbath himself of
what was considered oh-so-spicy in a bygone era less . . . in a
bygone era more . . . in a bygone era when . . . in a bygone era whose . . . Idiot! The mistake was never to have
given her money. The mistake was to have given Drenka the
money instead. All he'd slipped Christa—and this only to get a
foot in the door the first time—was thirty-five dollars for a
quilt she'd made. He should have been slipping her that much
per week. To have imagined that Christa was in it for the fun
of making Drenka crazy, that Drenka's coming was for her re-
muneration enough—idiot! idiot!

Sabbath and Christa had met one night in 1989 when he'd
given her a lift home. He saw her out on the shoulder of 144,
wearing a tuxedo, and he circled back. If she had a knife, she
had a knife—did it matter living a few years more or less? It
was impossible to leave standing all alone on the side of the
road with her thumb lifted a young blond girl in a tuxedo who
looked like a young blond boy in a tuxedo.

She explained her outfit by saying she had been to a dance
down in Athena, at the college, where you were to come wearing "something crazy." She was petite but hardly childlike—
more a miniaturized woman, with a very crisp, self-confident
air about her and a tightly held little mouth. The German accent was gentle but inflammatory (for Sabbath, any attractive
woman's accent was inflammatory), the haircut was short as a
Marine recruit's, and the tuxedo suggested that she was not
without the inclination to play a provocative role in life. Otherwise the kid was all business: no sentiment, no longings, no il-

lusions, no follies, and, he'd bet his life on it—he had—no taboos to speak of. Sabbath liked the cruel toughness, the shrewdness of the calculating, mistrustful little German mouth and saw the possibilities right off. Remote, but there. Admiringly he thought, Unbesmirched by selflessness, a budding beast of prey.

As he drove along he had been listening to a tape of Benny Goodman's *Live at Carnegie Hall*. He and Drenka had just parted for the night at the Bo-Peep, some twenty miles south on 144.

"Are they black?" the German girl asked.

"No. A few are black but mainly, Miss, they are white. White jazz musicians. Carnegie Hall in New York. The night of January 16, 1938."

"You were there?" she asked.

"Yes. I took my children, my little children. So they would be present at a musical milestone. Wanted them beside me the night that America changed forever."

Together they listened to "Honeysuckle Rose," Goodman's boys jamming with half a dozen members of the Basie band. "This is jumpin'," Sabbath told her. "This is what's called a foot mover. Keeps your feet movin'. . . . Hear that guitar back there? Notice how that rhythm section is driving them on? . . . Basie. Very lean piano playing. . . . Hear that guitar there? Carryin' this thing. . . . *That's* black music. You're hearin' black music now. . . . Now you're going to hear a riff. That's James. . . . Underneath all this is that steady rhythm section carrying this whole thing. . . . Freddie Green on guitar. . . . James. Always have the feeling he's tearing that instrument apart—you can hear it tear. . . . This figure they're just dreaming up—watch them build it now. . . . They're workin' their way into the ride-out. Here it comes. They're all tuned into each other. . . . They're off. They're *off*. . . . Well, what do you make of that?" Sabbath asked her.

"It's like the music in cartoons. You know, the cartoons for kids on TV?"

"Yes?" said Sabbath. "And it was thought to be hot stuff at the time. The innocent old ways of life—everywhere you look, except in our sleepy village here," he said, stroking his beard, "the world's at war against them. And you, what brings you to

Madamaska Falls?" asked Father Time jovially. There is no
other way to play it.

She told him about the tedium of her au pair job in New
York, how by the second year she couldn't stand the child anymore, and so she had just picked up one day and run off. She
had found Madamaska Falls by closing her eyes and putting
her finger down on a map of the Northeast. Madamaska Falls
wasn't even on the map, but she had got a ride as far as the
traffic light by the green, stopped for a coffee at the gourmet
shop, and, when she asked if there was any work around, a job
materialized right there. For five months now the gentleman's
sleepy village had been her home.

"You were escaping your job in New York with the kid."

"I was going crazy."

"What else are you escaping?" he asked, but lightly, lightly,
probing not at all.

"Me? I'm not escaping anything. Just to get a taste of life.
In Germany there is no adventure for me. I know everything
and how it works. Here a lot of things happen to me that
would never have happened to me back home."

"You don't get lonely?" asked the nice, concerned man.

"Sure. I get lonely. It's hard to make friendships with Americans."

"Is it?"

"In New York it is. Sure. They want to use you. In any possible way. That's the first idea that comes to their mind."

"I'm surprised to hear this. People in New York are worse
than people in Germany? History would seem to some to tell a
different story."

"Oh no, definitely. And cynical. In New York they keep
their true motives to themselves and announce to you other
motives."

"Young people?"

"No, mostly older than me. In their twenties."

"Did you get hurt?"

"Yeah. Yeah. But then they're very friendly—'Hi, how are
you doing? It's very lovely to see you.'" She enjoyed her imitation of an American dope and he laughed appreciatively, too.
"And you don't even *know* this person. Germany is very different," she told him. "Here there's all this friendliness—and it's

fake. 'Hey, hi, how are you?' You have to. The American way. I was very naive when I came here. I was eighteen. I run into lots of people, strangers I don't know. I go out for coffee. You have to be naive when you come as a stranger. Of course you learn. You learn all right."

The trio—Benny, Krupa, Teddy Wilson's piano. "Body and Soul." Very dreamy, very danceable, just lovely, right down to the Krupa three-thump finale. Though Morty thought that Krupa's pyrotechnics were always ruining the damn thing. "Just let it *swing*," Morty would say. "Krupa is the worst thing that ever happened to Goodman. Too obtrusive," and Mickey would repeat this as his own opinion at school. Morty would say, "Benny's never shy about taking up half the piece," and Mickey would repeat that. "A beautiful clarinet player, nobody near him," and that, too, he repeated. . . . He wondered if it might not soften up this German girl, the late-night languor-inducing beat and that tactful, torchy something in Goodman's playing, and so for three minutes he said nothing to her and, to the seductive coherence of "Body and Soul," the two drove on through the dark of the wooded hills. Nobody else abroad. Also seductive. He could take her anywhere. He could turn at Shear Shop Corner and take her up to Battle Mountain and strangle her to death in her tuxedo. Painting by Otto Dix. Maybe not in congenial Germany but in cynical, exploitative America she was running a risk out on the road in that tuxedo. Or would have been, had she been picked up by one of those Americans rather more American than I.

"The Man I Love." Wilson playing Gershwin like Gershwin was Shostakovich. Uncanny eeriness of Hamp on the vibes. January 1938. I am almost nine, Morty is soon to be fourteen. Winter. McCabe Avenue beach. He is teaching me to throw the discus on the empty beach after school. Endless.

"May I ask how you got hurt?" said Sabbath.

"They're there for you if you're pretty and outgoing and smiling, but if you have any trouble, 'Come back when you're better.' I had very few true friends in New York. Most of them were just crap."

"Where did you meet these people?"

"Clubs. At night I go to clubs. To get away from the job. To get my mind on something else. Being with a kid all day . . . brrrr. I couldn't stand it, but it got me to New York. I would just go to clubs where people I know come."

"Clubs? I'm out of my element. What are clubs?"

"Well, I have one club I go to. I get in free. I get drinks, tickets. I don't have to worry about that, I just show up. I was going there for over a year. The same people come all the time. People you don't even know their names. They have club names. You never know what they're doing in the daytime."

"And they come to the club to do what?"

"To have a good time."

"Do they?"

"Sure. Where I go there are five different floors. The basement is reggae, and black people come there. The next floor is dance music, disco. Yuppies stay on the floor with the disco, people like that. And then there is techno, and then there is more techno—music made by a machine. It's a sound that just makes you dance. The lights can make you crazy. But that's because you get to feel the music very good. You dance. You dance for three, four hours."

"Whom do you dance with?"

"People just stand and dance by themselves. It's a meditation kind of thing. The big main scene is a mix of everybody, standing and dancing by themselves."

"Well, you can't dance by yourself to 'Sugarfoot Stomp.' Hear that?' said Sabbath, good-natured and grinning. "To 'Sugarfoot Stomp' you've got to dance the lindy and you've got to dance the lindy with somebody else. To this you must jitterbug, my dear."

"Yes," she said politely, "it's very beautiful." Respect for the aged. This callous girl has a sweet side after all.

"What about drugs—at the clubs?"

"Drugs? Yeah, it exists."

He'd fucked up with "Sugarfoot Stomp." Alienated her completely, managed even to arouse her repugnance by overplaying how unmenacing, unfrightening an old fuddy-duddy he was. And deprived her of the spotlight. But then this was a situation in which there was never really a right thing to do, except to remember to be tirelessly patient. If it takes a year, it takes a year. You've just got to bank on living one more year.

This is the contact. Delight in that. Get her back to drugs, get her onto herself and the significance of her life in the clubs.

He turned off the tape. All she had to hear was Elman's klezmer trumpet oleaginizing "Bei Mir Bist Du Sheyn" and she'd leap from the moving car, even out in the middle of nowhere.

"What drugs? Which drugs?"

"Marijuana," she said. "Cocaine. They have this drug, heroin and cocaine mixed together, and they call it Special K. It's what the drag queens take to go really nuts. It's a lot of fun. They dance. They're fascinating. It's a gay scene, definitely. A lot of Hispanic. Puerto Rican guys. Lots of black men. A lot of them are young boys, nineteen, twenty. They lip-synch to some old song and they're all dressed up like Marilyn Monroe. You laugh a lot."

"How did *you* dress up?"

"I wore a black dress. Tight long dress. Low neck. A ring in my nose. Long jumbo eyelashes. Big platform shoes. Everybody's hugging each other and kissing each other and all you do is party and dance all night long. Go there at midnight. Stay till three. That's the New York I knew. The America. That's all. I thought I should see more. So here I come."

"Because you were exploited. People exploited you."

"I don't want to talk about that. There was a whole thing that just broke down. Comes down to money. I thought I had a friend but I had a friend who was using me."

"Really? How terrible. Using you how?"

"Oh, I was working with her and she gave me half of the money I was supposed to have. And I'd been working for her a lot. I thought this was a girlfriend of mine. I said, 'You cheated me out of my money. How could you do this to me?' 'Oh, you found out?' she says. 'I'm not able to pay you back.' So I'll never talk to her again. But what can you expect? The American way. Next time I have to be ready."

"I'll say. How did you meet this person?"

"Through the club scene."

"Was it painful?"

"I felt so stupid."

"What were you doing? What was the work?"

"I was dancing in a club. My past."

"You're young to have a past."

"Oh yeah," she said, laughing loudly at her unmaidenly precocity, "I do have a past."

"A girl of twenty with a past. What's your name?"

"Christa."

"Mine is Mickey, but up here the boys call me Country."

"Hi, Country."

"Most girls of twenty," he said, "haven't begun to live."

"That's the American girls. I never made an American girlfriend. Guys, yeah."

"Is meeting women what the adventure is about?"

"Yes, I would like to meet girlfriends. But mostly it's older women. You know, mother kind of types. Which is okay with me. But girls my own age? Just doesn't work out. They're kids."

"So it's mother types for Christa."

"I guess," she said, laughing again.

At Shear Shop Corner he took the turn up to Battle Mountain. The voice counseling patience was having trouble being heard. *Mother kind of types.* He could not let her get away. He could never in his life let a new discovery get away. The core of seduction is persistence. Persistence, the Jesuit ideal. Eighty percent of women will yield under tremendous pressure if the pressure is *persistent.* You must devote yourself to fucking the way a monk devotes himself to God. Most men have to fit fucking in around the edges of what they define as more pressing concerns: the pursuit of money, power, politics, fashion, Christ knows what it might be—skiing. But Sabbath had simplified his life and fit the other concerns in around fucking. Nikki had run away from him, Roseanna was fed up with him, but all in all, for a man of his stature, he had been improbably successful. Ascetic Mickey Sabbath, at it still into his sixties. The Monk of Fucking. The Evangelist of Fornication. *Ad majorem Dei gloriam.*

"What was dancing in the club like?"

"It's like—what can you say? I liked it. It was something I had to do for my own curiosity. I don't know. I just have to do everything in life."

"How long did you do that?"

"Oh, I don't want to talk about it. I listen to advice from everybody, then I go out and do my own thing."

He stopped talking and on they drove. In that silence, in that darkness, every breath assumed its importance as that which kept you alive. His aims were clear. His dick was hard. He was on automatic pilot, excited, exultant, following behind his own headlights as though in a torch-led procession to the nocturnal moisture of the starry mountaintop, where celebrants were convening already for the wild worship of the stiff prick. Dress optional.

"Hey, are we lost?" she asked.

"No."

By the time they had ascended halfway up the mountain she could take her own silence no longer. Yep, played it perfectly. "I entertained more at private parties, if you want to know. Bachelor parties. For about a year. With my girlfriend. But then you go shopping together and spend all the money anyway. These girls who do this are very lonesome. They have a bitchy mouth because they've been through a lot. And I just look at them, and I say, 'Oh, my God, I'm too young, I gotta get out of this.' Because it was because of money that I did it. And I got cheated. But that's New York. Anyway, I needed a change. I want to spend my time doing something else, a job dealing with people. And I missed the nature. In Germany I was a child in a village till my parents got divorced. I miss the nature and all that's peaceful. There are more things in life than money. So I came to live here."

"And how is it here?"

"It's great. People turn out to be very friendly. Very nice. I don't feel a stranger here. Which is nice. In New York everywhere I go people try to pick me up. It happens all the time. That's what New Yorkers love to do. I tell them go away and they go away. I'm pretty good at handling the situation. The thing is, don't show fear. I'm not afraid of you. People in New York can get a little strange. But not here. I feel at home here. I like America now. I even do patchwork," she said, with a giggle. "*Me*. I'm a real American. I make quilts."

"How did you learn?"

"I read about it in books."

"Well, I love quilts. I collect quilts," said Sabbath. "I'd like to see yours someday. Would you sell me one?"

"Sell?" she said, laughing heartily now, laughing huskily, like a boozer twice her age. "Why not? Sure, I'll sell it, Country. It's your money."

And he erupted in laughter, too. "By God, we *are* lost!"— and he made a sharp U-turn and got her back to her place over the gourmet shop in fifteen minutes. All the way there they talked animatedly about their common interest. Unimaginable as it seemed, the gap was bridged—antipathy evaporates, affinity is established, a date is made. Quilts. The American way.

"Thank you," Drenka had said to Christa when it was time for the old couple to get up and get dressed and go home, "thank you," she said, her voice faintly tremulous, "thank you thank you thank you. . . ." She took Christa back into her arms and rocked her there like a baby. "Thank you thank you." Christa gently kissed each of Drenka's breasts. Her little mouth broke out in a warm, youthful smile when she cuddled closer to Drenka and, making big eyes, girlishly said, "A lot of straight women like it."

Though Sabbath had masterminded the evening and given Drenka the money she had demanded to participate, he'd found himself more or less superfluous from the moment Drenka knocked on the door and he let her into the attic room where he'd arrived early himself, thinking that it might be necessary, even after a month of delicate diplomacy, to continue negotiations right down to the wire. There was nothing small about this endeavor, and he was still not sure how reliable a person Christa was—she had not entirely cleansed herself in Madamaska Falls of her European suspicions, nor had Sabbath observed in her, as he hoped to, a single encouraging sign of the development of a more selfless point of view. "Drenka," he said when he opened the door to let her in, "this is my friend Christa," and though previously Drenka had seen Christa only through the window of the gourmet shop—strolled by a few times at Sabbath's suggestion—she walked directly across to where Christa was sitting on the secondhand couch in tight torn jeans and a sequined velvet jacket a shade of violet matching her eyes. Sinking to her knees on the bare floorboards, Drenka grabbed Christa's close-cropped head between her two hands and kissed her strongly on the mouth. The speed with which Drenka unbuttoned Christa's jacket and with which Christa undid Drenka's silk blouse and cleared aside her push-up bra astonished Sabbath. But Drenka's boldness always astonished him. He had imagined a warm-up would be required —talking and joking overseen by him, a heart-to-heart talk, maybe even a sympathetic look through Christa's boring quilts to put the two of them at their ease—when, in fact, the five hundred dollars in Drenka's purse had emboldened her, in her words, "to just go in like a whore and do it."

Afterward Drenka couldn't say enough wonderful things about Christa. While Sabbath drove Drenka to where she'd parked behind Town Street, she snuggled adoringly into his side, kissing his beard, licking his neck—she, the woman of forty-eight, as excited as a child just home from the circus. "With a lesbian, there is a sense of *love* that I received from her. Such great experience she had in how to touch a woman's body. And the kissing! Her knowledge of the female body, how to caress it, how to kiss it, how to touch my skin and to make my nipples hard and to suck my nipples, and that loving, giving, very sexual way, very like a man, that kind of erotic vibration that she would deliver to me made me so very hot. To know exactly how to touch my body in a way almost *more* superior than sometimes men can know how to do it. To find on my cunt the little button, and to hold it there exactly the amount of time that was needed to make me come. And when she started kissing me—you know, going down and sucking me—the skill of the tongue pressure right on the right place . . . oh, that was very exciting."

Up on the bed, only inches away, following every movement like a medical student observing his first surgical procedure, he'd had a good time too and once even been able to be of assistance when Christa, her muscular tongue anchored between Drenka's thighs, went groping around the sheets searching blindly for a vibrator. Earlier on, she had removed three of them from the bedside table—ivory-colored vibrators ranging in length from three to six inches—and Sabbath was able to locate one for her, the longest of them, and to place it, correctly oriented, into her outstretched hand. "So, you didn't need me at all," he said. "Oh, no. I find it very wonderful and exciting to have another woman, but," said Drenka, lying, as it would later turn out, "I wouldn't want to have to do it alone with her. It couldn't turn me on. I have to have the male penis there, the male excitement to urge me on. But I do find very erotic a young woman's body, the beauty of it, the round curves, the small breasts, the way she is shaped, and the smell of it, and the softness of it, and then as I come down myself to the cunt, I find the cunt actually quite beautiful. I never would have thought that looking in the mirror. You come with your shame to look at yourself and you look at your sexual organs and they are not acceptable from the aesthetic perspective. But in this setting, I can see the whole thing, and although it is a mystique that I am a part of, it's a mystery to me, a total mystery."

Drenka's grave was near the base of the hill about forty feet from a pre-Revolutionary stone wall and a row of enormous maples fencing off the cemetery from the blacktop that meandered over the mountaintop. In all these months, the headlights of maybe half a dozen rattling vehicles—pickup trucks from the sound of them—had flickered by while Sabbath grieved there over his loss. He had only to drop to his knees to be as invisible from the road as any of those buried around him, and often he was on his knees already. There had not yet been a single nighttime visitor to the cemetery other than himself—a remote rural graveyard eighteen hundred feet above sea level did not strike people, even in springtime, as a place to come to roam around in after dark. Noises from beyond the cemetery—deer abounded on Battle Mountain— had seriously agitated Sabbath during his first months visiting the grave, and he was often quite sure that at the edge of his vision there was something darting among the tombstones, something he believed was his mother.

In the beginning he hadn't known that he was to become a regular visitor. But then he hadn't imagined that, looking down at the plot, he would see through to Drenka, see her inside the coffin raising her dress to the stimulating latitude at which the tops of her stockings were joined to the suspenders of her garter belt, once again see that flesh of hers that reminded him always of the layer of cream at the top of the milk bottle when he was a child and Borden delivered. It was stupid not to have figured on carnal thoughts. "Go down on me," she said to Sabbath. "Eat me, Country, the way Christa did," and Sabbath threw himself onto the grave, sobbing as he could not sob at the funeral.

Now that she was gone for good, it was incredible to Sabbath that not even when he was very much the crazy, cuntstruck lover, before Drenka became just an absorbing diversion there to have fun with, to fuck with, to plot and to scheme with, that not even back then had he thought to exchange the excruciating boredom of a drunk, de-eroticized Roseanna for marriage to someone whose affinity to him was unlike any woman's he had known outside a whorehouse. A conventional woman who would do anything. A respectable woman who was enough of a warrior to challenge his audacity with hers. There couldn't be a hundred such women in the entire country. Couldn't be fifty in all of America. And he'd had no idea. Never in thirteen years had he tired of looking down her blouse or looking up her skirt, and still he'd had no idea!

But now the thought undid him—no one would believe the scandalous town polluter, swinish Sabbath, to be susceptible to such a flood of straightforward feeling. He let go with a convulsive ardor that exceeded even her husband's on the icy November morning of the funeral. Young Matthew, wearing his trooper's uniform, betrayed no emotion other than hard-bitten rage mutely contained, the most violent of urges masterfully organized by a cop with a conscience. It was as though his mother had died not of a terrible disease but from an act of violence perpetrated by a psychopath he would go out and find and quietly take in, once the ceremony was over. Drenka had always wished that he could show the same admirable restraint as a son with his father that he did out on the road, where, to hear her tell it, he never got upset or lost control, whatever the provocation. Drenka ingenuously repeated to Sabbath, in Matthew's words, whatever Matthew boasted to her about himself. Her reveling in the boy's achievements was, to Sabbath, perhaps not the most beguiling thing about her, but it was far and away the most innocent. You wouldn't have thought—if you were yourself a guileless ingenue—that such extreme polarity in any one person was possible, but Sabbath,

a great fan of human inconsistency, was often transfixed by
how worshipful his taboo-free, thrill-seeking Drenka could be
of the son who saw the impeccable enforcement of the law as
the most serious thing in life, who no longer had any friends
but cops—who, he explained to her, had become totally mistrustful of people who *weren't* cops. When he was still fresh
out of the academy, Matthew used to tell his mother, "You
know something, I have more power than the president. You
know why? I can take people's rights away. Their rights of
freedom. 'You're under arrest. You're pinched. Your freedom
is gone.'" And it was a sense of responsibility to all this power
that caused Matthew so assiduously to toe the line. "He never
gets upset," his mother told Sabbath. "If there's another cop
who is mouthing off, calling the suspect a this or a that,
Matthew tells him, 'It's not worth it. You're going to get
yourself in trouble. We're doing what we're supposed to do.'
Last week they brought a guy in, he was kicking the cruiser
and everything, and Matthew said, 'Let him do what he's
going to do, he's pinched. What are we going to prove by
screaming at him and swearing at him? This is all stuff he can
bring up in court. It's just another reason for this guy to get
out of what he's done wrong.' Matthew says they can swear,
they can do whatever they want—they've got handcuffs on,
he's in control of the situation, not them. Matthew says, 'He's
trying to get me to lose control. There are cops who do lose
control. They start screaming at them—and why, Ma? For
what?' Matthew is just quiet and takes them in."

For Madamaska Falls, the crowd at the funeral had been
huge. Aside from friends from town and the many past and
present employees of the inn, there were, up from New York,
in from Providence and Portsmouth and Boston, dozens of
guests to whom Drenka had been the gracious, energetic hostess over the years—and among the guests were a number of
men she had fucked. In the face of each the haggard look of
loss and sorrow was clearly visible to Sabbath, who chose to
observe them from the rear of the crowd. Which was Edward?
Which was Thomas? Which was Patrick? That very tall guy
must be Scott. And not far from where Sabbath was standing,
also back as far from the coffin as he could get, was Barrett, the
new young electrician from Blackwall, the shabby town just to

the north that was home to five tough taverns and a state mental hospital. Sabbath had happened to pull in behind Barrett's pickup down in the crowded cemetery lot—across the truck's tailgate were painted the words "Barrett Electric Co. 'We'll fix your shorts.'"

Barrett, who wore his hair in a ponytail and sported a Mexican mustache, stood beside his pregnant wife. She was holding a bundle that was their tiny baby and weeping openly. Two mornings a week, when Mrs. Barrett drove down to the valley to her secretarial job with the insurance company, Drenka would drive up past the reservoir to Blackwall and take baths with Mrs. Barrett's husband. He didn't look at all well that day, maybe because his suit was tight or maybe because without a coat to wear he was freezing to death. He shifted from one long leg to the other constantly as though at the conclusion of the service he was in danger of being lynched. Barrett was Drenka's latest catch from among the workers making repairs around the inn. Last catch. A year younger than her son. He rarely spoke except when the bath was over, and then, with his hick enthusiasm, he would delight Drenka by telling her, "You are somethin', you are really somethin' else." Aside from the youth and the youthful body, what excited Drenka was that he was "a physical man." "He is not unhandsome," she told Sabbath. "He has this animal thing that I like. He is like I have a twenty-four-hour fucking service if I want it. His muscles are strong and his stomach is completely flat, and then he has this big dick, and he sweats a lot, there is all this sweat coming out of him, he is all red in his face, and he is like you, he is also, 'I don't want to come yet, Drenka, I don't want to come yet.' And then he says, 'Oh my God, I'm coming, I'm coming,' and then 'Ohhh. Ohhh,' those big sounds he makes. And the relief, it's like they collapse almost. And that he lives in a working-class environment and that I go there—all that adds to the excitement. A little apartment building with horrible horses on the walls. They have two rooms, and the taste is horrible. The other people there are attendants from the insane asylum. The bathroom has one of those old bathtubs that stand on the floor. And I say to him, 'Turn the bathtub on so I can take a bath.' I remember one time I came there at noon and I was very hungry and we were going to have a pizza. I undressed right away and I run to the bathtub. Yes, I think we get very hot in the bathtub, jerking him a little, you know. You can fuck in the bathtub, and we did, but then the water runs over. What I like is the *way* we are fucking, which is specific to him. He will sort of sit up and, because his prick is big, we sort of sit and fuck that way. We work very hard and there is a lot of sweating, a lot of physical movement, much more than I can think of with anyone else. I love to take baths *and* showers. Part of the excitement is the lathering. The soap. You start at the face and then the chest and the stomach and then you come down to the dick, and that gets big, or it is big already. And then you start to fuck. If you're standing in the shower, you stand up and fuck. Sometimes he will lift my legs up and he carries me like that in the shower. If it's in the bathtub, then I will tend to sit on top of him and fuck that way. Or I can bend over and he will fuck me. I love the bathtub, to fuck my stupid electrician there. I love it."

Her mistake was to take to Barrett the bad news. "You told me," he said, "you promised me—you weren't going to complicate everything, and here you go. I've got a baby to support, I've got a pregnant wife to look after. I got a new business to worry about, and one thing I don't need right now, from you, me, or anybody, is cancer."

Drenka phoned Sabbath and drove immediately to meet him at the Grotto. "You should never have told him," Sabbath said, seated on the granite outcropping and rocking her in his lap. "But," she said, crying pitifully, "we're lovers—I wanted him to know. I didn't know he was this *shit*." "Well, if you'd looked at it from the point of view of the pregnant wife, that might have occurred to you. You knew he was stupid. You liked that he was stupid. 'My stupid electrician.' It turned you on that he had this animal thing, lived in a horrible place, was stupid." "But I was talking to him about *cancer*. Even a *stupid* person—" "Shhh. Shhh. Not one, apparently, as stupid as Barrett."

Sabbath was completing his mourning—by scattering his seed across Drenka's oblong patch of Mother Earth—when the headlights of a car turned off the blacktop and into the wide gravel drive where the hearses ordinarily entered the cemetery. The headlights advanced waveringly and then they

were out and the quiet engine went dead. Zipping up his
trousers, Sabbath scurried, bent over, toward the nearest maple
tree. There, on his knees, he hid his white beard between the
massive tree trunk and the old stone wall. He could discern
from the silhouette of the car—more or less the shape and the
size of a hearse—that it was a limousine. And a figure was
marching steadily up in the direction of Drenka's grave, tall, in
a large overcoat, and wearing what looked to be high boots.
He was guiding himself by the beam of a flashlight that he
kept switching on and off. In the hazy half-dark of the moon-
lit cemetery he looked gigantic bounding forward on those
boots. He must have been expecting cold weather up here. He
must be from—it was the credit-card magnate! It was Scott!

Six feet five inches tall. Scott Lewis. Five-foot two-inch
Drenka had smiled up at him in an elevator in Boston and
asked if he knew the correct time. It took only that. She used
to sit on his dick in the backseat of the limo while the driver
took a slow tour of the suburbs, driving sometimes past
Lewis's own house. Scott Lewis was one of those men who
told Drenka that there was no other woman like her in the
world. Sabbath had heard him say it from the telephone of the
limousine.

"He is very interested in my body," she reported promptly
to Sabbath. "He wants to take photographs and he wants to
look at me and he wants to kiss me all the time. He is a big
cunt licker—and very tender." Yet, tender fellow that he was,
the second evening she rendezvoused with him at a Boston
hotel, a call girl Lewis had ordered came knocking at their
door only ten minutes after Drenka's arrival. "What I didn't
like about it," Drenka told Sabbath on the phone the next
morning, "was that I didn't have a *say* in it, that it was just put
upon me." "So what did you do about it?" "I just had to make
the best of it, Mickey. She comes to the hotel room dressed
like an upper-class whore. She pulls open her bag and she has
all these things in there. Do you want a little maid's uniform?
Do you want it Indian style? And then she takes out her dildos
and she says, 'Do you like this or that?' And then, okay, now
you start. But how do you get aroused by that? That was kind
of hard even for me. Anyway, I guess we sort of got started.
The idea was that the guy was more the voyeur. Interested in

seeing how two women do it. He asked her mostly to go down on me. It all seemed to me so technical and cold, but I decided, okay, I'm going to be game for it. So eventually I did some work and I was able to get excited by it. But finally I fucked more Lewis—we two were fucking while she was just sort of in the picture somewhere. After he came, I started kissing her pussy, but it was very dry, though after a while she started moving a little bit and that then became sort of my mission. Could I make a whore hot? I think maybe I did to some extent, but it was hard to know if she wasn't just playing it. You know what she said to me? To *me*? She says, when we're all getting dressed, 'You're very hard to make come!' She was *angry*. 'The husbands want me to do this all the time'—she thought we were husband and wife—'but you took unusually hard work.' Husbands and wives are very common, Mickey. The whore said that's what she does all the time." "That's difficult for you to believe?" he asked. "You mean," she replied, laughing happily, "everybody is crazy like us?" "Crazier," Sabbath assured her, "much, much crazier."

Drenka called Lewis's erection "the rainbow" because, as she liked to explain, "His dick is rather long and sort of curved. And there is a little bend to it, to one side." On Sabbath's instruction she had traced its outline on a piece of paper —Sabbath still had the drawing somewhere, probably in among those dirty pictures of her that he had not been able to look at since her death. Lewis was the only one of her men other than Sabbath whom she had allowed to fuck her in the ass. He was that special. When Lewis had wanted to do it to the whore as well, the whore said sorry, that was where she drew the line.

Oh yes, the jolly time Drenka had with this guy's crooked dick! Infuriating! And yet, back when it was happening, Sabbath frequently had to slow her down while she was telling him her stories, had to remind her that nothing was too trivial to recount, no detail too minute to bring to his attention. He used to solicit this kind of talk from her, and she obeyed. Exciting to them both. His genital mate. His greatest pupil.

It had, however, taken him years to make Drenka a decent narrator of her adventures, since her inclination, in English at least, was to pile truncated sentences one on the other until he couldn't understand what she was talking about. But gradually, as she listened to him and talked to him, there was an ever-increasing correlation between all she was thinking and what she said. She certainly became syntactically more urbane than nine-tenths of the locals up on their mountain, even though her accent remained to the end remarkably juicy: *chave* for *have*, *cheart* for *heart*; at the conclusion of *stranger* and *danger*, a strong rolling *r*; and her *l*'s almost like a Russian's, emerging from a long way back in the mouth. The effect was of a delightful shadow cast on her words, making just a little mysterious the least mysterious utterance—phonetic seduction enthralling Sabbath all the more.

She was weakest at retaining idiomatic English but managed, right up to her death, to display a knack for turning the clichéd phrase, proverb, or platitude into an object trouvé so entirely her own that Sabbath wouldn't have dreamed of intervening—indeed, some (such as "it takes two to tangle") he wound up adopting. Remembering the confidence with which she believed herself to be smoothly idiomatic, lovingly recalling from over all the years as many as he could of Drenka's malapropisms stripped him now of every defense, and once again he descended to the very pit of his sorrow: bear and grin it . . . his days are counted . . . a roof under my head . . . when the shithouse hit the fan . . . you can't compare apples and apples . . . the boy who cried "Woof!" . . . easy as a log . . . alive and cooking . . . you're pulling my leg out . . . I've got to get quacking . . . talk for yourself, Johnny . . . a closed and shut case . . . don't keep me in suspension . . . beating a dead whore . . . a little salt goes a long way . . . he thinks I'm a bottomless piss . . . let him eat his own medicine . . . the early bird is never late . . . his bark is worse than your cry . . . it took me for a loop . . . it's like bringing coals to the fireplace . . . I feel as though I've been run over by a ringer . . . I have a bone to grind with you . . . crime doesn't pay off . . . you can't teach an old dog to sit. . . . When she wanted Matija's dog to stop and wait at her side, instead of saying "Heel!" Drenka called out, "Foot!" And once when Drenka came up to Brick Furnace Road to spend an afternoon in the Sabbaths' bedroom—Roseanna was visiting her sister in Cambridge—though it was raining only lightly when she arrived, by the time they had eaten the sandwiches Sabbath had prepared and had smoked a joint and gotten into bed, the day had all but turned into a moonless night. An eerie black hour of silence passed and then the storm broke over their mountain—on the radio Sabbath later learned that a tornado had torn apart a trailer park only fifteen miles west of Madamaska Falls. When the turbulence overhead was most noisily dramatic, hammering down like artillery that had found its target in Sabbath's property, Drenka, clinging to him beneath the sheet, said to Sabbath in a woozy voice, "I hope there is a thunder catcher on this house." "I am the thunder catcher on this house," he assured her.

When Sabbath saw Lewis bending over the grave to place a bouquet on the plot, he thought, But she's mine! She belongs to me!

What Lewis did next was such an abomination that Sabbath reached crazily about in the dark for a rock or a stick with which to rush forth and beat the son of a bitch over the head. Lewis unzipped his fly and from his shorts extracted the erection whose outlined drawing Sabbath had retained in his files, he now remembered, under "Misc." He was a long time rocking back and forth, rocking and moaning, until at last he turned his face upward to the starry sky and a full, fervent basso profundo echoed across the hills. "Suck it, Drenka, suck me dry!"

Though it was not phosphorescent, enabling Sabbath visually to chart its course, though it was not sufficiently clotted or dense for him to hear it splatter to the ground even in that mountaintop silence, simply from the stillness of Lewis's silhouette and from the fact that his breathing was audible thirty feet away, Sabbath knew that the tall lover had just commingled his wad with the short one's. In the next moment Lewis had fallen to his knees and, before her grave, in a low tearful voice he was lovingly reciting, ". . . tits . . . tits . . . tits . . . tits. . . ."

Sabbath could endure only so much. A rock he'd kicked out from between the large, protuberant roots of the maple, a rock as big around as a bar of soap, he picked up and hurled in the direction of Drenka's grave. It clanged against a tombstone nearby, causing Lewis to leap to his feet and look frantically about. Then he ran down the hill to the waiting limo, whose engine immediately started up. The car backed out of the drive and into the road, and only then did the headlights come on and the limousine whiz away.

When he rushed across to Drenka's grave, Sabbath saw that Lewis's bouquet was huge, containing perhaps as many as four dozen flowers. The only ones he could recognize, with the aid of his flashlight, were the roses and the carnations. He didn't know any of the others by name, despite all those summers of Drenka's tutoring. Kneeling down, he gathered up the bouquet by its bulky bundle of stems and clutched it to his chest as he started along the dirt path toward the highway and his car. At first he imagined that the bouquet was wet from the shop, where the flowers would have been kept fresh in vases of water, but then the texture made him understand what, of course, the wet substance was. The flowers were drenched with it. His hands were covered with it. So was the chest of the dirty old hunting jacket with the enormous pockets in which he used to carry puppets down to the college before the scandal with Kathy Goolsbee.

Drenka had once told Sabbath that after her marriage, when, within their first year as émigrés, Matija grew depressed and lost all interest in fucking her, she was so desolated that she went to a doctor in Toronto, where they lived briefly after fleeing Yugoslavia, and asked him how many times a husband was supposed to do it with a wife. The doctor asked her what she thought a reasonable expectation might be. Without even stopping to think, the young bride replied, "Oh, about four times a day." The doctor asked where a working couple was to find the time that would take, other perhaps than on the weekend. She explained, her fingers doing the calculating, "You do it once about three in the morning when sometimes you hardly know you do it. You do it at seven when you wake up. You do it when you come home from work and before you sleep. You can even do it two times before you go to sleep."

Why this story had come to him as he cautiously descended the dark cemetery hill—the bespattered flowers still clutched in his hands—was because of that triumphant Friday, only seventy-two hours after Matija's Rotary speech, when she had ended the day—not the week, the day—awash with the sperm of four men. "Nobody can accuse you, Drenka, of being timid in the face of your fantasies. Four," he said. "Well, I'd be honored to be numbered among them should there ever be a next time." He found, on hearing this story, not merely his desire inflamed but his veneration, too—there *was* something great about it: something heroic. This shortish woman a little on the plump side, darkly pretty but with an oddly damaged-looking nose, this refugee who knew hardly anything of the world beyond her schoolgirl Split (pop. 99,462) and the picturesque New England village of Madamaska Falls (pop. 1,109), seemed to Sabbath *a woman of serious importance.*

"It was the time I went to Boston," she told him, "to see my dermatologist. That was very exciting. You sit in the doctor's office and you know you're his mistress and he's turned on and he shows you he has a big hard-on right in the examination room, and he takes it out and he fucked me right there. During the appointment. I used to go years ago to fuck him in his office on Saturdays. And he was a good fuck. And anyway from there I went to the credit-card magnate, the Lewis guy. And it was exciting that another man was waiting, that I could turn another guy on. Maybe I felt strong about that, to be able to seduce more than one man. Lewis fucked me and came inside me. That made me feel good. Nobody knows it but I. I am a woman walking around who has this sperm from two guys. The third guy was the dean, that college guy who stayed at the inn with his wife. His wife was in Europe so I was having dinner with him. I didn't know him—that was the first time. You want me to be really blunt about the whole thing? I discovered that I had got my period. I'd met him when we have our cocktail party for the guests. He stood next to me and he had pushed his arms onto my nipples. And he told me that he had a big hard-on, and I could almost see it. A dean at a college—this is the way we were talking at the cocktail party. Those kind of settings are what turn me on, when you do it in public, but secretly in public. So he had prepared this elaborate dinner. We were both very passionate but very shy at the same time or nervous about it. We ate in their dining room and I was answering his questions about my childhood under Communism and eventually we went upstairs, and he was sort of a strong guy and he held me and he really almost crushed my ribs. He had unbelievable manners. Maybe he was shy and frightened. He said, 'Well, we don't have to do anything if you don't want to.' I was a little hesitant because by now I had my period but I wanted to fuck him, so I went into the bathroom and took out my tampon. We started undressing and it was all very hot and very exciting. A tall guy, very strong, and he said many beautiful words. I was very excited and wanted to know the size his dick was. So when we finally undressed I was disappointed that he seemed to have a very small dick. I don't know if he was frightened of me so he couldn't really get it up. Then I said, 'Well, I have my period,' and he said, 'That doesn't matter.' I said, 'Let me go and get a towel.' So we put a towel down on the bed and we really went into it. He was doing everything with me. He couldn't really get a very good hard-on. I worked hard on getting him to have a hard-on but I think he was scared. He was frightened about me, that I was so free. That's what I sensed—that he was a bit overwhelmed. Though he did actually come three times." "Without a hard-on. *And* overwhelmed. Quite a feat," noted Sabbath. "It was a small hard-on," she explained. "How did he come? You sucked him?" "No, no, he came inside me, actually. And he sucked me even though I was bleeding all over the place. So that was a big mess, a lot of fucking and a lot of blood coming out. The fact that there was the blood—there was an added drama to it. A lot of juice and grease—it's not grease; how do I describe it? It's thick liquid, body fluids that were mixed in together. And after it's all finished and we get up—you get up, and what do you do, you don't know this person, and you're a little embarrassed, and we're stuck with this towel." "Describe the towel." "It was a white towel. And it was not completely red. The size of a bath towel. There were enormous spots. If I would wring it, it would come out, blood from it. It was like juice, a juicy liquid. But it wasn't that the whole thing was completely red, by any means. There were big, big spots on it, and it was very heavy. It's a definite—not an alibi; how do you say it in English? The opposite of that?" "Evidence?" "Yes, it's evidence of the crime. So we were discussing it and he said, 'Well, what can I do with this?' And he stood there, this tall man, this strong man, holding this towel like a child. A little embarrassed, but not wanting to show that to me. And I didn't want to be crimelike, I didn't want to pretend, 'Oh, this is a bad thing.' This was natural to me to do it, so I wanted to be cool about it. He said, 'I can't let the maid wash it and I can't throw it in the hamper. I guess I have to throw it out. But where can I throw it?' and I said, 'I'll take it.' And the relief on his face was enormous. And I put it in a plastic bag and I took it with me, this wet bundle, in a shopping bag. So he was very happy and then I drove home, and I put it into the washing. And it came out clean. And then of course he called me the next day and he said, 'Dear Drenka, this was certainly very dramatic,' and I said, 'Well, I have the towel and it's clean. Do you want it back?' and he said, 'No, thank you.' He didn't want the towel back and I guess his wife never found out about it." "And so who is the fourth you fucked that day?" "Well, I came home and I went down to the basement and threw the towel into the machine and then I came upstairs and Matija wants me to perform my marital duty at midnight. He sees me going naked into the shower and it excites him. This is something I have to do, so I do it. Thank God it's not often." "And so how does it feel after four men?" "Well, Matija fell asleep. I guess I felt very chaotic, if you really want to know. I think it is very taxing to do that. I had done three before, a number of times, but never four. Sexually it was very—very defiant and somehow exciting, even if the fourth was Maté. And maybe slightly perverse in a way. Part of me enormously enjoyed that. But in terms of what I really felt—I couldn't sleep, Mickey; it made me feel unsettled, restless, and it made me feel I did not know to whom I belong. I kept thinking of you, and that helped, but that was a high price to pay for it, all that confusion. If I could take the confusion away, how do you say—extrapolate it?—and make it just a sexual thing, I think that it's an exciting thing to do." "The most exciting ever, Donna Giovanna?" "Oh, my God," she said, laughing heartily, "I don't know about that. Let me think." "Yes, think. Il catalogo." "Oh, in the past, maybe thirty years ago, maybe more, I would go on a train, for example, through Europe, and do it with the train conductor. You know, it was pre-AIDS time. Yes, the Italian train conductor." "Where do you do it with a train conductor?" She shrugged. "You find a compartment that isn't busy." "Is that true?" Laughing again, she said, "Yes. True."

"Were you married?" "No, no, this is when I worked a year in Zagreb. I guess he would come in the train car, a little good-looking Italian guy who speaks Italian, and you know, they're sexy, and maybe my friends, we're having a party or something like that—I can't remember who initiates what. No, I did it. I sold him cigarettes. It was expensive to travel in Italy and so you take with you something to sell. You buy it cheaply in Yugoslavia. Cigarettes were inexpensive. And Italians would buy out these cigarettes. They had the names of rivers, the Yugoslav cigarettes. Drina. Morava. Ibar. Yes, they were then all words of rivers. You make twice as much, maybe three times as much as you paid, so I sold him cigarettes. That's how it started. When I was working in Zagreb that year after high school, I loved to be fucked. It made me feel very, very good to have my cunt full of sperm, of come, it was a wonderful, maybe a powerful feeling. Whoever was the boyfriend, you would go to work that next day knowing you had been well fucked and you're all wet and the pants were wet and you walked around wet—I enjoyed that. And I remember I knew this older guy. He was a retired gynecologist and somehow we were talking about this and he thought it was very healthy to keep the come in the cunt after you had fucked, and I agreed with him. This turned him on. But it was no use. He was too old. I was curious to do it with a very old man, but he was already seventy and it was a closed and shut case."

When Sabbath reached his car, he walked beyond it some twenty feet along the hiking trail into the woods and there he hurled the bouquet into the dark mass of the trees. Then he did something strange, strange even for a strange man like him, who believed himself inured to the limitless contradictions that enshroud us in life. Because of his strangeness most people couldn't stand him. Imagine then if someone had happened upon him that night, in the woods a quarter mile down from the cemetery, licking from his fingers Lewis's sperm and, beneath the full moon, chanting aloud, "I am Drenka! I am Drenka!"

Something horrible is happening to Sabbath.

B UT horrible things are happening to people all the time. The next morning Sabbath learned about Lincoln Gelman's suicide. Linc had been the producer of Sabbath's Indecent Theater (and the Bowery Basement Players) during those few years in the fifties and early sixties when Sabbath had amassed his little audience on the Lower East Side. After Nikki's disappearance, he had stayed a week with the Gelmans in their big Bronxville house.

Norman Cowan, Linc's partner, called with the news. Norman was the subdued member of the duo, if not the office's imaginative spearhead then its levelheaded guardian against Linc's overreaching. He was Linc's equilibrium. In any discussion, even of the location of the men's room down the hall, he could come to the point in about one-twentieth of the time that Linc liked to take to explain things to people. The educated son of a venal Jersey City jukebox distributor, Norman had shaped himself into a precise and canny businessman exuding the aura of quiet strength that lean, tall, prematurely balding men often appear to possess, particularly when they come, as Norman did, scrupulously attired in gray pinstripes.

"His death," Norman confided, "was a relief to many. Most of the people we're lining up to speak at the funeral haven't seen him in five years."

Sabbath hadn't seen him in thirty.

"These are all current business associates, close Manhattan friends. But they couldn't see him. Linc was impossible to be with—depressed, obsessive, trembling, frightened."

"How long was he like that?"

"Seven years ago he fell into a depression. He never again had a painless day. A painless *hour*. We carried him in the office for five years. He'd just float around with a contract in his hand, saying, 'Are we sure this is all right? Are we sure this isn't illegal?' The last two years he's been at home. A year and a half ago, Enid couldn't take it any longer and they found an apartment for Linc around the corner and Enid furnished it and he

444

lived there. A housekeeper came every day to feed him and to clean up. I would try to get over once a week, but I had to force myself. It was awful. He would sit and listen to you and then sigh and shake his head and say, 'You don't know, you don't know. . . .' For years now that's all I heard him say."

"You don't know what?"

"The dread. The anguish. Unceasing. No medication helped. His bedroom looked like a pharmacy, but not a single drug worked. They all made him sick. He hallucinated on the Prozac. He hallucinated on the Wellbutrin. Then they started giving him amphetamines—Dexedrine. For two days it looked as though something was happening. Then the vomiting began. All he ever got were the side effects. Hospitalization didn't work, either. He was hospitalized three months, and when they sent him home they said he was no longer suicidal."

His drive, his gusto, his pep, his speediness, his effectiveness, his diligence, his loquacious joking, someone—Sabbath remembered—wholly at one with his time and place, a highly adapted New Yorker tailor-made for that frenetic reality and oozing with the passion to live, to succeed, to have fun. His sentiments transported tears to his eyes too easily for Sabbath's taste, he talked rapidly in a flood of words that revealed how strong the compulsions were that fueled his hyperdynamism, but his life *was* a solid achievement, full of aim and purpose and the delight of being the energizer of others. *And then life took a turn and never righted itself. Everything vanished. The irrational overturned everything.* "Something specific set it off?" Sabbath asked.

"People come apart. And aging doesn't help. I know a number of men our age, right here in Manhattan, clients, friends, who've been going through crises like this. Some shock just undoes them around sixty—the plates shift and the earth starts shaking and all the pictures fall off the wall. I had my bout last summer."

"You? Hard to believe about you."

"I'm still on Prozac. I had the whole thing—fortunately the abridged version. Ask why and I couldn't tell you. I just stopped sleeping at some point and then, a couple of weeks later, the depression descended—the fear, the trembling, the suicide thoughts. I was going to buy a gun and blow the top of

my head off. Six weeks until the Prozac kicked in. On top of
that, it happens not to be a dick-friendly drug, at least for me.
I'm on it eight months. I don't remember what a hard-on feels
like. But at this age it's an up-and-down affair anyway. I got
out alive. Linc didn't. He got worse and worse."

"Could it have been something other than just depression?"

"Just depression's enough."

But Sabbath knew as much. His mother had never gone
ahead to take her life, but then, for fifty years after losing
Morty, she had no life to take. In 1946, at seventeen, when, instead of waiting a year to be drafted, Sabbath went to sea only
weeks after graduating high school, he was motivated as much
by his need to escape his mother's tyrannical gloom—and his
father's pathetic brokenness—as by an unsatisfied longing that
had been gathering force in him since masturbation had all but
taken charge of his life, a dream that overflowed in scenarios of
perversity and excess but that he now, in a seaman's suit, was
to encounter thigh-to-thigh, mouth-to-mouth, face-to-face:
the worldwide world of whoredom, the tens of thousands of
whores who worked the docks and the portside saloons wherever ships made anchor, flesh of every pigmentation to furnish
every conceivable pleasure, whores who in their substandard
Portuguese, French, and Spanish spoke the scatological vernacular of the gutter.

"They wanted to give Linc electric shock treatment but he
was too frightened and he refused. It might have helped, but
whenever it was suggested, he curled up in a corner and cried.
Whenever he saw Enid he broke down. Called her, 'Mommy,
Mommy, Mommy.' Sure, Linc was one of the great Jewish
criers—they play the national anthem out at Shea and he cries,
he sees the Lincoln Memorial and he cries, we take our boys
up to Cooperstown and there's Babe Ruth's mitt and Linc
starts crying. But this was something else. This was not crying,
this was bursting. This was bursting under the pressure of unspeakable pain. And in that bursting there wasn't anything of
the man I knew or you knew. By the time he died, the Linc
we'd known had been dead for seven years."

"The funeral?"

"Riverside Chapel, tomorrow. Two P.M. Amsterdam and
76th. You'll see some old faces."

"Won't see Linc's."

"Can, actually, if you want to. Somebody has to identify the body before the cremation. The law in New York. I'm doing it. Come along when they open the coffin. You'll see what happened to our friend. He looked a hundred years old. His hair completely white and his face just a terrified, tiny thing. One of those skulls the savages shrink."

"I don't know," Sabbath replied, "that I can make it tomorrow."

"If you can't, you can't. I thought you should know before you read about it in the papers. In the papers the cause of death will be a heart attack—that's the cause the family prefers. Enid wouldn't have an autopsy. Linc was dead some thirteen or fourteen hours before he was found. Dead in his bed, the story goes. But the housekeeper tells a different story. I think by now Enid has come to believe her own. All along she honestly expected him to get better. She was sure of it down to the end, even though he had already slashed his wrists ten months ago."

"Look, thanks for remembering me—thanks for calling."

"People remember you, Mickey. A lot of people remember you with great admiration. One of the people Linc got teary about was you. I mean back when he was still himself. He never thought it was a great idea to take a talent like yours out to the boondocks. He loved your theater—he thought you were a magician. 'Why did Mickey do it?' He thought you never should have left to live up there. He talked about that often."

"Well, that's all long ago."

"You should know that Linc never for a moment considered you responsible in any way for Nikki's disappearance. I certainly didn't—and don't. The fucking well poisoners—"

"Well, the well poisoners were right and you boys were wrong."

"Standard Sabbath perversity. You can't believe that. Nikki was doomed. Tremendously gifted, extremely pretty, but so frail, so needy, so neurotic and fucked-up. No *way* that girl would ever hold together, none."

"Sorry, can't make it tomorrow," and Sabbath hung up.

Roseanna's uniform these days was a Levi's jacket and washed-out jeans as narrow as her cranelike legs, and recently Hal in Athena had cut her hair so short that at breakfast that morning Sabbath intermittently kept imagining his be-denimed wife as one of Hal's pretty young homosexual friends from the college. But then, even with shoulder-length hair she'd emanated the tomboyish aura; ever since adolescence she'd had it—flat-chested and tall, with a striding gait and a way of cocking her chin when she spoke that had its appeal for Sabbath well before the disappearance of his fragile Ophelia. Roseanna looked to belong to another group of Shakespearean heroines entirely—to the saucy, robust, realistic circle of girls like Miranda and Rosalind. And she wore no more makeup than Rosalind did attired like a boy in the Forest of Arden. Her hair was still its engaging golden brown and, even clipped short, had a soft, feathery sheen that invited touching. The face was an oval, a wide oval, and there was a carved configuration to her small upturned nose and her wide, full, unboyishly seductive mouth, a hammered-and-chiseled look that, when she was younger, gave the fairy-tale illusion of a puppet infused with life. Now that she was no longer drinking, Sabbath saw traces in the modeling of Roseanna's face of the lovely child she must have been before her mother left and the father all but destroyed her. She was not only thinner by far than her husband but a head taller, and what with daily jogging and the hormone re-placement therapy, she looked—on those rare occasions when the two of them were out together—less a fifty-six-year-old wife than an anorexic daughter.

What did Roseanna hate most about Sabbath? What did Sabbath hate most about her? Well, the provocations changed with the years. For a long time she hated him for refusing even to consider having a child, and he hated her for incessantly yammering on the phone to her sister, Ella, about her "biolog-ical clock." Finally he had grabbed the phone away from her to communicate directly to Ella the degree to which he found their conversation offensive. "Surely," he told her, "Yahweh did not go to the trouble of giving me this big dick to assuage a concern as petty as your sister's!" Once her childbearing years were behind her, Roseanna was able better to pinpoint her hatred and to despise him for the simple fact that he existed, more or less in the same way that he despised *her* for existing. In addition was the predictable bread-and-butter stuff: she hated the unthinking way he brushed the crumbs onto the floor after cleaning the kitchen table, and he hated her unamusing goy humor. She hated the conglomeration of army-navy surplus he had been wearing for clothing ever since high school, and he hated that, for as long as he'd known her, she would never, even during the adulterous phase of glorious abandon, graciously swallow his come. She hated that he hadn't touched her in bed for ten years and he hated the unruffled monotone in which she spoke to her local friends on the phone—and he hated the friends, do-gooders gaga over the environment or ex-drunks in AA. Each winter the town road crew went around cutting down 150-year-old maple trees that lined the dirt roads, and each year the maple-tree lovers of Madamaska Falls lodged a petition of protest with the first selectman, and then the next year the road crew, claiming the maples were dead or diseased, would clear another sylvan lane of ancient trees and thereby pick up enough dough—by selling the logs for firewood—to keep themselves in cigarettes, porn videos, and booze. She despised his inexhaustible bitterness about his career the way he had despised her drinking—how she would be drunk and argumentative in public places and, whether at home or out, speak in an aggressively loud and insulting voice. And now that she was sober he hated her AA slogans and the way of talking she had picked up from AA meetings or from her abused women's group, where poor Roseanna was the only one who'd never been battered by a husband. Sometimes when they argued and she felt swamped Roseanna claimed Sabbath was "verbally" abusing her, but that didn't count for much with her group of predominantly uneducated rural women, who'd had their teeth knocked out or chairs broken over their heads or cigarettes held to their buttocks and breasts. And those words she used! "And afterward there was a discussion and we shared about that particular step. . . ." "I haven't shared that many times yet. . . ." "Many people shared last night. . . ." What he loathed the way good people loathe *fuck* was *sharing*. He didn't own a gun, even out on the lonely hill where they lived, because he didn't want a gun in a house with a wife who spoke daily of "sharing." She hated that he was always bolting out the door without explanation, always leaving at all hours of the day and night, and he hated that artificial laugh of hers that hid both so much and so little, that laugh that was sometimes a bray, sometimes a howl, sometimes a cackle but that never rang with genuine pleasure. She hated his self-absorption and the outbursts about the arthritic joints that had ruined his career, and she hated him, of course, for the Kathy Goolsbee scandal, though had it not been for the breakdown brought on by the disgrace of it she would never have been hospitalized and begun her recovery. And she hated that, because of the arthritis, because of the scandal, because of his being the superior, impossible failure that he was, he earned not a penny and she alone was the breadwinner, but then Sabbath hated that too—that was one of their few points of agreement. They each found it repellent to catch even a glimpse of the other unclothed: she hated his increasing girth, his drooping scrotum, his apish hairy shoulders, his white, stupid biblical beard, and he hated the jogger's skinny titlessness—ribs, pelvis, sternum, everything that in Drenka was so softly upholstered, skeletonized as on a famine victim. They had remained in the house together all these years because she was so busy drinking that she didn't know what was going on and because he had found Drenka. That had made for a very solid union.

Driving home from her job at the high school, Roseanna used to think about nothing but the first glass of chardonnay when she hit the kitchen, a second and third glass while she prepared dinner, a fourth with him when he came in from the studio, a fifth with dinner, a sixth when he went back to his studio with his dessert, and then, the rest of the evening, another bottle all for herself. As often as not, she woke up in the morning as her father used to—still dressed—and in the living room, where the night before she had stretched out on the sofa, glass in hand, the bottle beside her on the floor, to watch the flames in the fireplace. In the mornings, dreadfully hung over, feeling bloated, sweating, full of shame and self-loathing, she never exchanged a word with him, and rarely did they have their coffee together. He took his to the studio and they did not see each other again until dinnertime, when the ritual began anew. At night, though, everybody was happy, Roseanna with her chardonnay and Sabbath off in the car somewhere, going down on Drenka.

Since her "coming into recovery," all had changed. Now seven nights a week, directly after dinner, she drove off to an AA meeting from which she returned around ten with her clothes stinking of cigarette smoke and her mood decisively serene. Monday evenings there was an open discussion meeting in Athena. Tuesday evenings there was a step meeting in Cumberland, her home group, where she had recently celebrated the fourth anniversary of her sobriety. Wednesday evenings there was a step meeting in Blackwall. She didn't like that meeting much—tough-guy workers and mental hospital attendants from Blackwall who were so aggressive, angry, and obscene that it made Roseanna, who'd lived until she was thirteen in academic Cambridge, very nervous; but, despite all the angry guys screaming at one another, she went because it was the only Wednesday meeting within fifty miles of Madamaska Falls. Thursdays she went to a closed speaker meeting in Cumberland. Fridays to another step meeting, this one in Mount Kendall. And Saturdays and Sundays there were meetings in both the afternoon—in Athena—and the evening—in Cumberland—and she went to all four. Generally an alcoholic would tell his or her story and then they would choose a discussion topic such as "Honesty" or "Humility" or "Sobriety." "Part of the recovery principle," she told him, whether he wished to listen or not, "is that you try to become honest with yourself. We talked a lot about that tonight. To find out what feels comfortable within yourself." He also didn't own a gun because of the word *comfortable*. "Isn't it tedious feeling so 'comfortable'? Don't you miss all the discomforts of home?" "I haven't found it so yet. Sure, there are drunkalogs where you fall asleep when you listen to them. But what happens with the story format," she went on, oblivious not merely to his sarcasm but to the look in his eyes of someone who had taken too many sedative pills, "is that you can identify. 'I can identify with that.' I can identify with the woman who didn't drink in bars but sat secretly drinking at home at night and had similar sorts of suffering, and that's a very comfortable sort of feeling for me. I'm not unique, and somebody else can understand where I'm coming from. People that have long sobriety, that have this aura of inner peace and spirituality—that makes them appealing. Just to sit with them is something. They seem to be at peace with life. That's inspiring. You can get hope from that." "Sorry," mumbled Sabbath, hoping himself to deal her soberalog a deathblow, "can't identify." "That we know," said Roseanna, undaunted, and continued speaking her mind now that she was no longer his drunk. "You hear people at meetings say over and over that their family is what exacerbates everything. At AA you have a more neutral family that is, paradoxically, more loving, more understanding, less judgmental than your own family. And we don't interrupt each other, which is also different from at home. We call that cross-talk. We don't use cross-talk. *And* we don't tune out. One person talks and everybody listens until he or she is finished. We have to learn not just about our problems but how to listen and to be attentive." "And is the only way to get off the booze to learn to talk like a second grader?" "As an active alcoholic I compromised myself so horribly hiding alcohol, hiding the disease, hiding the behavior. You *have* to start all over, yes. If I sound like a second grader, that's fine with me. You're as sick as your secrets." It was not for the first time that he was hearing this pointless, shallow, idiotic maxim. "Wrong," he told her—as if it really mattered to him what she said or he said or anyone said, as if with their mouthings any of them approached even the borderline of truth—"you're as adventurous as your secrets, as abhorrent as your secrets, as lonely as your secrets, as alluring as your secrets, as courageous as your secrets, as vacuous as your secrets, as lost as your secrets; you are as human as—" "No. You're as unhuman, inhuman, and sick. It's the secrets that prevent you from sitting right with your internal being. You can't have secrets," she told Sabbath firmly, "and achieve internal peace." "Well, since manufacturing secrets is mankind's leading industry, that takes care of internal peace." No longer so serene as she would have liked to be, glaring at her beast with the old engulfing hatred, she went off to immerse herself in one of her AA pamphlets while he returned to his studio to read yet another book about death. That's all he did there now, read book after book about death, graves, burial, cremation, funerals, funerary architecture, funeral inscriptions, about attitudes toward death over the centuries, and how-to books dating back to Marcus Aurelius about the art of dying. That very evening he read about *la mort de toi*, something with which he had already a share of familiarity and with which he was destined to have more. "Thus far," he read, "we have illustrated two attitudes toward death. The first, the oldest, the longest held, and the most common one, is the familiar resignation to the collective destiny of the species and can be summarized by the phrase, *Et moriemur*, and we shall all die. The second, which appeared in the twelfth century, reveals the importance given throughout the entire modern period to the self, to one's own existence, and can be expressed by another phrase, *la mort de soi*, one's own death. Beginning with the eighteenth century, man in western societies tended to give death a new meaning. He exalted it, dramatized it, and thought of it as disquieting and greedy. But he already was less concerned with his own death than with *la mort de toi*, the death of the other person. . . ."

If they ever happened to be together on a weekend, walking along the half mile of Town Street, Roseanna had a hello for just about everybody passing or driving by—old ladies, delivery boys, farmers, *everyone*. One day she even waved to Christa, of all people, who was standing in the window of the gourmet shop sipping a cup of coffee. Drenka and his Christa! The same happened when they went to see a doctor or the dentist down in the valley—she knew everybody there, too, from the meetings. "Was the whole county drunk?" Sabbath asked. "Whole country's more like it," Roseanna replied. One day in Cumberland she confided that the elderly man who'd just nodded at her when he passed by had been a deputy secretary of state under Reagan—he always came early to meetings so as to make the coffee and put out the cookies for the snack. And whenever she went up to Cambridge to visit Ella overnight—great days, those, for Sabbath and Drenka—she'd return ecstatic about the meeting there, a women's meeting. "They fascinate me. I'm amazed how competent they seem to be, how accomplished, how self-assured, how well they look. Adjusted. They're really an inspiration. I go in there and I don't know anybody and they ask, 'Anybody from outside?' and I raise my hand and I say, 'I'm Roseanna from Madamaska Falls.' Everybody claps and then if I have a chance to talk, I talk about whatever is on my mind. I tell them about my child-hood in Cambridge. About my mother and father and what happened. And they listen. These terrific women listen. The sense of love that I experience, the sense of understanding of my suffering, the sense of great sympathy and empathy. And *accepting*." "*I* understand your suffering. *I* have sympathy. *I* have empathy. *I'm* accepting." "Oh, yeah, sometimes you ask how did your meeting go, that's true. I can't talk to *you*, Mickey. You wouldn't understand—you *couldn't* understand. You can't begin to understand it innately, and so it becomes boring and silly to you. Something more to satirize." "My satire is my sickness." "I think you liked it better when I was an active drunk," she said. "You enjoyed the superiority. As if you're not superior enough, you could look down on me for that, too. I could be responsible for all your disappointments. Your life had been ruined by this fucking disgusting falling-down drunk. One guy the other night was talking about how degraded he became as an alcoholic. He was living then in Troy, New York. On the streets. They, the other drunks, just stuck him in a garbage pail and he couldn't get out of the garbage pail. He sat there for hours and people would walk by on the streets and wouldn't care about this human being who was sitting there with his legs scrunched up, in a garbage pail, and who couldn't get out. And that's what I was for you when I was drinking. In a garbage pail." "I can identify with that," Sabbath said.

Now that she was four years out of the garbage pail, why did she go on with him? Sabbath was surprised by how long it was taking Barbara, the therapist in the valley, to get Roseanna to find the strength to strike out on her own like the competent, accomplished, self-assured women in Cambridge who show-ered her with so much sympathy for her suffering. But then her problem with Sabbath, the "enslavement," stemmed, ac-cording to Barbara, from her disastrous history with an emo-tionally irresponsible mother and a violent alcoholic father for *both* of whom Sabbath was the sadistic doppelgänger. Her father, Cavanaugh, a geology professor at Harvard, had raised Roseanna and Ella after their mother could stand his drinking and his bullying no longer and, in terror of him, abandoned the family to run off to Paris with a visiting professor of

Romance languages to whom she remained quite miserably bandaged for five long years before returning alone to Boston, her own birthplace, when Roseanna was thirteen and Ella eleven. She wanted the girls to come live on Bay State Road with her, and shortly after they decided that they would and left their father—of whom they, too, were terrified—and his new second wife, who couldn't stand Roseanna, he hanged himself in the attic of their Cambridge house. And this explained to Roseanna what she was doing all these years with Sabbath, to whose "domineering narcissism" she had been no less addicted than to alcohol.

These connections—between the mother, the father, and him—were far clearer to Barbara than they were to Sabbath; if there was, as she liked to put it, a "pattern" in it all, the pattern eluded him.

"And the pattern in *your* life," Roseanna asked, angrily, "that eludes you, too? Deny till you're red in the face, but it's there, it's *there*."

"Deny *it*. The verb is transitive, or used to be before the eloquence of the blockheads was loosed upon the land. As for the 'pattern' governing a life, tell Barbara it's commonly called chaos."

"Nikki was a helpless child you could dominate and I was a drunk looking for a savior, who thrived on degradation. Is that not a pattern?"

"A pattern is what is printed on a piece of cloth. We are not cloth."

"But I *was* looking for a savior, and I *did* thrive on degradation. I thought I had it coming to me. Everything in my life was frenzy and noise and mess. Three girls from Bennington living together in New York, with black underwear hanging up and drying everywhere. Boyfriends calling everybody all the time. Men calling. Older men. Some married poet naked in somebody's room. The place a mess. Never any meals. A perpetual soap opera of angry lovers and outraged parents. And then one day in the street I saw your screwy finger show and we met and you invited me to your workshop for a drink. Avenue B and 9th Street, just by the park. Five flights up and this perfectly still, tiny white room with everything in place and dormer windows. I thought I was in Europe. All the puppets in a row. Your workbench—every tool hanging in place, every-thing tidy, clean, orderly, in place. Your file cabinet. I couldn't believe it. How calm and rational and steady-seeming, and yet on the street, performing, it could have been a madman behind that screen. Your sobriety. You didn't even offer me a drink."

"Jews never do."

"I didn't know. All I knew was that you had your crazy art and that all that mattered to you in the world was your crazy art, that why I had come to New York was for *my* art, to try to paint and to sculpt, and instead all I had was a crazy *life*. You were so *focused*. So *intense*. The green eyes. You were very handsome."

"In his thirties, everyone is handsome. What are you doing with me now, Roseanna?"

"Why did you stay with me when I was a drunk?"

Had the moment come to tell her about Drenka? *Some* moment had come. Some moment had been coming for months now, since the morning he learned that Drenka was dead. For years he had been drifting without any sense of anything being imminent and now not only was the moment galloping toward him but he was rushing into the moment and away from all he'd lived through.

"Why?" Roseanna repeated.

They'd just had dinner and she was off to a meeting, and he was off, after she'd gone, to the cemetery. She was already in her denim jacket, but because she no longer feared the "con-frontations" she formerly evaded via the chardonnay, she was not leaving the house until she had forced him, this once, to take *seriously* their miserable history.

"I am sick of the humorous superiority. I am sick of the sar-casm and the perpetual joke. Answer me. Why did you stay with me?"

"Your paycheck. I stayed," he said, "to be supported."

She seemed about to cry, and bit her lip rather than try to speak.

"Come off it, Rosie. Barbara didn't break the news today."

"It's just hard to believe."

"Doubt Barbara? Next thing you know you'll be doubting God. How many people are there left in the world, let alone here in Madamaska Falls, with a full understanding of what is going on? It has always been a premise of my life that there are no such people left, and that I am their leader. But to find someone, like Barbara, with a full grasp of what is happening, to discover, out in the sticks, someone with a fairly complete idea of everything, a human being in the largest sense of the word, whose judgment is grounded in the knowledge of life she acquired at college studying psychology . . . what other dark mystery has Barbara helped you to penetrate?"

"Oh, not such a mystery."

"Tell me anyway."

"That there may have been real pleasure for you in watching me destroy myself. As you watched Nikki destroy *her*self. That could have been another inducement to stay."

"*Two* wives whose destruction I have had the pleasure of watching. The pattern! But doesn't the pattern now call for me to enjoy your disappearance as much as I enjoyed Nikki's? Doesn't the pattern now call for you to disappear, too?"

"It does; it did. It's precisely where I was headed four years ago. I was as close to death as I could come. I couldn't wait for winter. I wanted only to be under the ice of the pond. You were hoping Kathy Goolsbee would put me there. Instead she saved me. Your masochistic student-slut saved my life."

"And why do I so much enjoy the misery of my wives? I'll bet it's because I hate them."

"You hate all women."

"Can't hide a thing from Barbara."

"Your *mother*, Mickey, *your mother*."

"To blame? My little mother, who went to her death half out of her mind?"

"She's not 'to blame.' She was what she was. She was the *first* to disappear. When your brother was killed, she disappeared from your life. She deserted you."

"And that, if I follow Barbara's logic, that is why I find you so fucking boring?"

"Sooner or later you'd find any woman boring."

Not Drenka. Never Drenka.

"So when is Barbara planning to have you throw me out?"

This was further along in the confrontation than Roseanna had planned to go just yet. He knew this because she looked suddenly as she had the previous April on Patriots' Day, when she'd taken her first crack at the Boston Marathon and fainted just beyond the finish line. Yes, the subject of getting rid of Sabbath wasn't to have come up until she was just a little better prepared to be on her own.

"So for when," he repeated, "is the date set to throw me out?"

Sabbath watched her come to the decision to abandon the old schedule and tell him "Now." This necessitated her sitting down and putting her face in her hands, the keys to the car still dangling from one finger. When she looked up again there were tears running down her face—and only that morning he had overheard her telling someone on the phone, maybe even Barbara herself, "I want to live. I'll do anything it takes to get well, anything. I'm feeling strong and able to give everything to my work. I go off to work and I love every *minute* of it." And now she was in tears. "This isn't the way I wanted it to happen," she said.

"When is Barbara planning for you to throw me out?"

"Please. *Please.* You're talking about thirty-two years of my life! This is not easy at all."

"Suppose I make it easy. Throw me out tonight," Sabbath said. "Let's see if you have the sobriety for it. Throw me out, Roseanna. Tell me to go and never come back."

"This is not fair of you," she said, weeping more hysterically than he had seen her weep in years. "After my father, after all that, *please* don't say 'throw me out.' I cannot *hear* that."

"Tell me that if I don't go you're calling the cops. They're probably all pals from AA. Call the state trooper, the inn-keeper's kid, the Balich boy; tell him that you have a family at AA that is more loving, more understanding, less judgmental than your husband and you want him to be thrown *out.* Who wrote the Twelve Steps? Thomas Jefferson? Well, call *him,* share with *him,* tell him that your husband hates women and must be thrown *outtt!* Call Barbara, my Barbara. *I'll* call her. I want to ask her how long you two blameless women have been planning my eviction. You're as sick as your secrets? Well, for just how long has off-loading Morris been your little secret, dear?"

"I cannot take this! I don't deserve this! You have no anxiety about relapse—you live in a *permanent* relapse!—but I do! With great effort and enormous suffering I have reclaimed myself, Mickey. Reclaimed myself from a horrendously devastating and potentially deadly disease. And don't make a face! If I didn't tell you my difficulties, you would never know. I say this without self-pity or sentimentality. To get well has taken all my energy and commitment. But I am *still* in a great state of change. It is still often painful and frightening. And this shouting I cannot stand. I will not stand! Stop it! You are shouting at me like my *father*."

"The fuck that's who I'm shouting at you like! I'm shouting at you like *myself*!"

"Shouting is *irrational*," she cried despairingly. "You cannot think straight if you're shouting! Nor can I!"

"Wrong! It's only when I'm shouting that I *begin* to think straight! It's my rationality that *makes* me shout! Shouting is how a Jew *thinks things through*!"

"What does 'Jew' have to do with it? You're saying 'Jew' deliberately to intimidate me!"

"I do *everything* deliberately to intimidate you, Rosie!"

"But where will you *go*, if you go. You are *not* thinking. How can you *live*? You're sixty-four years old. You don't have a penny. You cannot go away," she wailed, "to kill yourself!"

It did not pain him to say "No, you couldn't endure that, could you?"

And that's how it happened. Five months after Drenka's death, that was all it took for *him* to disappear, to leave Roseanna, to pick up finally and leave their home, such as it was—to get into his car and drive to New York to see what Linc Gelman looked like.

Sabbath took the long way to Amsterdam and 76th. He had eighteen hours for a three-and-a-half-hour trip, so instead of driving east for twelve miles to hook up with the turnpike, he decided to cross over Battle Mountain to 92 and then take the back roads and catch the turnpike some forty miles south. That way he could pay a last visit to Drenka. He had no idea where he was going or what he was doing and he did not know if he would visit that cemetery ever again.

And what the hell *was* he doing? Get off her ass about AA.

Ask her about the kids at school. Give her a hug. Take her on
a trip. Eat her pussy. It's no big deal and might turn things
around. When she was a rangy aspiring artist fresh out of college living in that flat full of sex-crazed girls, you did it all the
time, couldn't get enough of those long bones of hers encircling your ears. Spirited, open, independent—someone he'd
thought not in need of round-the-clock protection, the wonderful new antithesis of Nikki. . . .

   She'd been his puppet partner for years. When they met she
had sculpted nude figures for six months and painted abstrac-
tions for six months and then started doing ceramics and making necklaces, and then, even though people liked them and
began buying them, after a year she'd lost interest in the necklaces and begun doing photography. Then through Sabbath
she discovered puppets and a use for all her skills, for drawing,
sculpting, painting, tinkering, even for collecting bits and
pieces of things, squirreling all sorts of things away, which she
had always done before but to no purpose. Her first puppet
was a bird, a hand puppet with feathers and sequins, nothing
like Sabbath's idea of a puppet. He explained that puppets
were not for children; puppets did not say, "I am innocent and
good." They said the opposite. "I will play with you," they
said, "however I like." She stood corrected, but that didn't
mean that, as a puppetmaker, she ever really stopped looking
for the happiness that she'd known at seven, when she still had
a Mom and a Dad and a childhood. Soon she was sculpting
puppets' heads for Sabbath, sculpting them out of wood like
the old European puppets. Sculpted them, sanded them,
painted them beautifully in oil paint, taught herself how to
make the eyes blink and the mouths move, sculpted the hands.
In her excitement at the beginning she naively told people, "I
start with one thing and something else happens. A good puppet makes itself. I just go with it." Then she went out and
bought a machine, the cheapest Singer, read the instructions,
and started to design and sew the costumes. Her mother had
sewed and Roseanna hadn't had the slightest interest. Now
she was at the machine half the day. All the things people discarded, Roseanna collected. "Whatever you don't want," she
began telling her friends, "give to me." Old clothes, stuff off

the street, the stuff people cleaned out of closets, it was amazing how she could use everything—Roseanna, recycler of the world. She designed the sets on a big pad, made them, painted them—sets that rolled up, sets that turned like pages—and always fastidiously, for ten and twelve hours a day the most fastidious worker. For her a puppet was a little work of art, but even more, it was a charm, magical in the way it could get people to give themselves to it, even at Sabbath's theater, where the atmosphere was insinuatingly anti-moral, vaguely menacing, and at the same time, rascally fun. Sabbath's hands, she said, gave her puppets life. "Your hand is right where the puppet's heart is. I am the carpenter and you are the soul." Though she was softly romantic about "art," high-flown and a bit superficial where he was remorselessly mischievous, they were a team nonetheless, and if never quite aglow with happiness and unity, a team that worked for a long time. A fatherless daughter, she encountered her man so soon, at a time when she was not yet fully exposed to the spikes of the world, that she was never fully exposed to her own mind, and for years and years she did not know what to think without Sabbath to tell her. There was something exotic to her about the amount of life to which he had opened himself while still so young, and that included the loss of Nikki. If she was sometimes the victim of his withering presence, she was too enamored of the withering presence to dare to be a young woman without it. He had been an avid pupil early of the hard lessons, and she innocently saw, no less in his seafaring than in his cleverness and cynicism, a crash course in survival. True, she was always in danger around him, on edge, afraid of the satire, but it was even worse if she wasn't around him. It wasn't until she went down in a vomiting stupor in her early fifties and got to AA that she located there, in that language they spoke, in those words she embraced without a shadow of irony, criticism, or even, perhaps, full understanding, a wisdom for herself that wasn't Sabbath's skepticism and sardonic wit.

Drenka. One of them is driven to drink and one of them is driven to Drenka. But then, ever since he'd been seventeen he couldn't resist an enticing whore. He should have married that one in the Yucatán when he was eighteen years old. Instead of becoming a puppet artist he should have become a pimp. At least pimps have a public and make a living and don't have to go crazy every time they turn on TV and catch sight of the Muppets' fucking mouths. Nobody thinks of whores as entertainment for kiddies—like puppetry that means anything, whores are meant to delight adults.

Delightful whores. When Sabbath and his best friend, Ron Metzner, hitchhiked up to New York a month after high school graduation and someone in New York told them they could get out of the country without a passport by going down to the Norwegian Seamen's Center in Brooklyn, young Sabbath had no idea that at the other end there was all that pussy. His sexual experience till then had been feeling up the Italian girls from Asbury and, at every opportunity, masturbating. The way he remembered it now, as a ship approached harbor in Latin America, you got this unbelievable smell of cheap perfume, coffee, and pussy. Whether it was Rio, or Santos, or Bahia, or any of the other South American ports, there was that delicious smell.

The motive, to begin with, was simply to run away to sea. He'd been looking at the Atlantic every morning of his life and thinking, "One day, one day. . . ." It was very insistent, that feeling, and he did not then wholly attach it to a desire to escape his mother's gloom. He had been looking at the sea and fishing in the sea and swimming in the sea all his life. It seemed to him—if not to his bereft parents a mere nineteen months after Morty's death—only natural that he should go to sea to get a real education now that obligatory schooling had taught him to read and write. He learned about the pussy the moment he got aboard the Norwegian tramp steamer to Havana and he saw that everybody was talking about it. To the old hands on board the fact that when you got off the ship you would head for the whores was in no way extraordinary, but to Sabbath, at seventeen—well, you can imagine.

As if it weren't sufficiently exciting to slip by moonlight past the Morro Castle in Havana harbor, as memorable an entrance to a port as any in the world, once they'd tied up he was off the ship and heading straight for the one thing he had never done before. This was in Batista's Cuba, which was one big

American whorehouse and gambling casino. In thirteen years, Castro was going to come down out of the hills and put an end to all the fun, but ordinary seaman Sabbath was lucky enough to get his licks in just in the nick of time.

When he got his merchant mariner documents and joined the union, he could choose his ships. He hung around the union hall and—since he had tasted paradise—waited for the "Romance Run": Santos, Monte, Rio, and B.A. There were guys who spent their whole lives doing the Romance Run. And the reason, for them as for Sabbath, was whores. Whores, brothels, every kind of sex known to man.

Driving slowly up toward the cemetery, he calculated that he had seventeen dollars in his pocket and three hundred in the joint checking account. At a New York bank he'd have to write a check first thing in the morning. Get the dough out before Rosie did. Had to. She was pulling down a salary check twice a month and it would be a year before he qualified for Social Security and Medicare. His only talent was this idiotic talent with his hands, and his hands were no damn good anymore. Where could he live, how would he eat, suppose he got sick? . . . If she divorced him for desertion, what would he do for medical insurance, where would he get money for his anti-inflammatory pills and for the pills he took to keep the anti-inflammatory pills from burning out his stomach, and if he couldn't afford the pills, if his hands were in pain all the time, if there was never again to be any relief . . .

He had caused his heart to begin palpitating. The car was nosed into the usual hideaway, a quarter of a mile from Drenka's grave. All he had to do was to calm down and back out and head home. He wouldn't have to explain himself. He never did. He could sleep on the sofa and tomorrow resume reveling in his old nonexistence. Roseanna could never throw him out—her father's suicide wouldn't permit it, no matter what rewards Barbara promised in the way of inner peace and comfort. As for himself, however hateful life was, it was hateful in a home and not in the gutter. Many Americans hated their homes. The number of homeless in America couldn't touch the number of Americans who had homes and families and hated the whole thing. Eat her pussy. At night, when she gets in from the meeting. It'll astonish her. *You* become the whore. Not as good as having married one, but you're six years from seventy so do it—eat her for money.

By this time, Sabbath was out of the car and prowling with his flashlight along the road to the cemetery. He had to find out if there was somebody there.

No limousine. Tonight a pickup truck. He was afraid to cross over to look at the plates, in case somebody was at the wheel. Could be just the local boys holding a moonlight circle-jerk up on the hill or sitting around on the tombstones smoking grass. Mostly he'd run into them over in Cumberland, on the checkout line at the supermarket, each with two or three little kids and a little underage wife—who already looks as though life has passed her by—with poor coloring and a pregnant belly pushing a cart piled with popcorn, cheese bugles, sausage rolls, dog food, potato chips, baby wipes, and twelve-inch-round pepperoni pizzas stacked up like money in a dream. Could tell them by the bumper stickers. Some had bumper stickers that read, "Our God Reigns," some had bumper stickers that read, "If You Don't Like The Way I Drive Dial 1-800-EAT-SHIT," some had both. A psychiatrist from the state hospital in Blackwall who ran a private practice a couple of days a week once told Sabbath, who'd asked what it was he treated people for up here in the mountains, "Incest, wife beating, drunkenness—in that order." And this was where Sabbath had lived for thirty years. Linc had it right: he should never have left after Nikki's disappearance. Norman Cowan had it right: nobody could blame him for her disappearance. Who remembered it, other than him? Maybe he was headed for New York to confirm, after all this time, that he had no more destroyed Nikki than he had killed Morty.

Nikki—all talent, enchanting talent, and absolutely nothing else. She couldn't tell her left from her right, let alone add, subtract, multiply, or divide. She could not tell north from south or east from west, even in New York, where she had lived much of her life. She couldn't bear the sight of ugly people or old people or disabled people. She was afraid of insects. She was afraid to be alone in the dark. If something made her nervous—a yellowjacket, a Parkinson's victim, a drooling child in a wheelchair—she'd pop a Miltown, and the

Miltown made her a madwoman with a wide, vacant stare and trembling hands. She jumped and cried out whenever a car backfired or someone nearby slammed a door. She knew best how to yield. When she tried to be defiant it was only minutes before she was in tears and saying, "I'll do anything you want—just don't *go* at me like this!" She did not know what reason was; either she was childishly obstinate or childishly submissive. She would startle him by wrapping herself in a towel when she came out of the shower and, if he was in her path, rushing past him for the bedroom. "Why do you do that?" "Do what?" "What you did—hide your body from me." "I didn't do any such thing." "You did, under the towel." "I was keeping warm." "Why did you run, as though you didn't want me to see?" "You're mad, Mickey, you're making this up. Why do you have to go at me all the time?" "Why do you act as though your body is ugly?" "I don't *like* my body. I hate my body! I hate my breasts! Women shouldn't have to have breasts!" Yet she could not walk by any kind of reflecting surface without taking a quick look to see if she was as fresh and lovely as in the photos displayed outside the theater. And once she was on the stage the million phobias vanished, all the peculiarities simply ceased to exist. The things that frightened her most about life she could pretend to face in a play with no difficulty at all. She did not know which was stronger, her love of Sabbath or her hatred of him—all she knew for sure was that she could not have survived without his protection. He was her armature, her coat of mail.

In her early twenties, Nikki was already as malleable an actress as a willful director like Sabbath could want. On stage, even just in rehearsal, even standing around and waiting to be given notes, there was not a sign of her jitteriness, all that fidgeting with her ring, the tracing of the fingers around the collar, the tapping on a table with whatever was at hand. She was calm, attentive, tireless, uncomplaining, clear-minded, intelligent. Whatever Sabbath asked of her, minutely pedantic or over the top, she could reproduce on the spot, exactly as he'd imagined it for himself. She was patient with the bad actors and inspired with the good ones. At work she was never discourteous toward anyone, whereas at a department store Sabbath had seen her display a snobbish superiority toward the salesgirl that made him want to slap her face. "Who do you think you are?" he asked her once they were back out on the street. "Why are you going for me *now*?" "Why treat that girl like shit?" "Oh, she was just a little tramp." "And who the fuck are you? Your father owned a lumberyard in Cleveland. Mine sold butter and eggs from a truck." "Why do you dwell on my father? I hated my father. How can you dare bring up my father!" Another of the women in Sabbath's life who reckoned her father a flop. Drenka's was a stupid party member whom she scorned for his gullible fidelity. "I can understand if you're an opportunist—but to be a *believer*." Rosie's was an alcoholic suicide who terrified her, and Nikki's was a bullying, vulgar businessman to whom cards, taverns, and girls meant rather more than his responsibility to a wife and child. Her father had met her mother when he was in Greece with his parents for the funeral of his grandmother and afterward went traveling around the country by himself, primarily to see what the pussy was like. There he courted his wife-to-be, a bourgeois girl from Salonika, and a few months later he brought her back to Cleveland, where his own father, an even more bullying and vulgar businessman, owned the lumberyard. The old man's people had been country people, and when he spoke in Greek it was with a terrible village dialect. And the cursing over the phone! "Gamóto! Gamó ti mána sou! Gamó ti panaghía sou!" Fuck it! Fuck your mother! Fuck your Holy Mother! . . . And pinching her behind, his own daughter-in-law! Nikki's mother fancied herself a poetic young woman, and her philandering husband, the coarse in-laws, provincial Cleveland, the bouzouki music these people loved—all of it drove her mad. She couldn't have made a bigger mistake than marrying Kantarakis and his horrible family, but at nineteen she was of course in flight from a domineering, old-fashioned father *she* loathed, and the high-spirited American who made her blush so easily—and, for the first time in her life, come so easily— seemed to her at the time a man called to great things.

Her salvation was the beautiful little Nikoleta. She doted on her. She took her everywhere. They were inseparable. She began to teach Nikki, who was musical, to sing in Greek and English. She read to her aloud and taught her to recite. But still the mother wept every night, and finally she moved with Nikki to New York. To support them, she worked in a laundry, then as a mailroom sorter, and eventually for Saks, first selling hats and, a few years later, as head of the millinery department. Nikki went to the High School of Performing Arts—it was she and her mother against the world until, in 1959, an obscure blood disease abruptly ended her mother's struggle. . . .

Sabbath made his way parallel to the cemetery's long stone wall, low to the ground and moving as quietly as he could over the soft earth at the margin of the road. There was somebody in the cemetery. At Drenka's grave! In jeans—lanky, pigeon-toed, his hair in a ponytail. . . . It was the *electrician's* pickup. It was Barrett, whom she'd loved to fuck in the bath-tub and lather in the shower. *You start at the face and then the chest and the stomach and then you come down to the dick, and that gets big, or it is big already.* Yes, it was Barrett's night to pay his respects to the dead, and he was indeed big already. *Sometimes he will lift my legs up and he carries me like that in the shower.* Once again Sabbath was searching for a rock. Since he was a good fifteen feet farther from Barrett than he'd been from Lewis, he looked for a light rock that he might have a chance of pitching somewhere near the strike zone. It took time in the dark to locate something the right weight and size, and all the while Barrett stood at the foot of her grave silently beating off. To bean him one right on the cock just as he started to come. Sabbath was trying to gauge the advent of the orgasm by the speed of Barrett's stroke when he saw a second figure in the cemetery, slowly ascending the hill. In a uniform. The sexton? The uniformed figure moved stealthily, unnoticed and unseen, until he was just about three feet behind Barrett, who was oblivious by now to everything except the impending surge.

Deliberately, almost languidly, the uniformed figure raised his right arm, degree by degree. In the hand he was holding a long object that culminated in a bulge. A flashlight. A drone arose from Barrett, a steady monotonous drone that suddenly terminated in a fanfare of incoherent babble. Sabbath held his fire, but the ecstatic climax turned out to be the cue as well for the man with the flashlight, who brought it down like an ax on Barrett's skull. There was a muted thud when Barrett hit the

ground, then two swift thumps—the young electrician . . .
you are somethin', you are really somethin' else . . . getting it
twice in the balls.

Only when the assailant hopped into his own car—he had
slipped it in just behind the pickup—and turned on the engine
did Sabbath realize who it was. Out of arrogant, open defiance
or plain unquenchable rage, the state trooper's cruiser pulled
away, all lights flashing.

THAT night, on the drive to New York for Linc's funeral, he thought only of Nikki. All he could talk about with his mother, who was gliding about inside the car, drifting and plunging like debris in the tide, was what had led to Nikki's disappearance. During his four years of marriage, his mother had seen Nikki only five or six times and said little or nothing to her when she did, could hardly comprehend who Nikki was or why she was there, however earnestly, with the broken-hearted naiveté of a bright, kindly child, Nikki tried to make conversation with her. What with her terror of the aged and the deformed and the ill, Nikki was scarcely up to the ordeal of Sabbath's suffering mother and she invariably got stomach cramps driving to Bradley. Once, when Mrs. Sabbath was looking particularly gaunt and unkempt as they came upon her dozing in a kitchen chair with her teeth beside her on the table's oilcloth covering, Nikki couldn't help herself and ran out the back door. From then on, Sabbath would go alone to see his mother. He took her for lunch to a Belmar seafood restaurant that served Parker House rolls, once a favorite of hers, and back in Bradley, at his insistence, he held her by the arm and they strolled on the boards for ten minutes. Much to her relief, he then took her home. He did not press her to say anything, and over the years there were visits when he said only, "How are you, Ma?" and "So long, Ma." That and two kisses, one coming, one going. Whenever he brought a box of chocolate-covered cherries he would find it the next time un-opened and exactly where she'd put it down after taking it from his hand. He never considered staying the night in Morty and his old room.

But now that she was fluttering invisibly about in his dark car, shed of affliction, drained of grief, now that his little mother was purely spirit, purely mind, an imperishable being, he reck-oned she could endure to hear the full story of the catastrophe in which the first marriage had perished. No doubt she had been present earlier to observe the ending of the second

marriage. And wasn't she there whenever he awoke at four
A.M. and couldn't fall back asleep? Hadn't he asked her in the
bathroom that very morning, while he trimmed the fringe of
his beard, if his was not a replica of the flowing beard worn
by her own father, the rabbi for whom he was named and
whom he had apparently resembled from the moment of
birth? Wasn't she regularly at his side, in his mouth, ringing his
skull, reminding him to extinguish his nonsensical life?

Nothing but death, death and the dead, for three and a half
hours, nothing but Nikki, her unaccountability, her strangeness, her appearance, the hair and the eyes primordial in their
blackness, the skin ethereal, maidenly, an angelic, powdery
white . . . Nikki and her talent to embody everything in the
soul that is contradictory and unfathomable, even the mon-
strousness that paralyzed her with fear.

When Nikki was awarded a full scholarship to the Royal
Academy of Dramatic Art in London, she moved there with
her mother. At first they relied on the generosity of a first
cousin of Nikki's mother who was married to an English
physician and lived comfortably in Kensington. Her mother
found work in an expensive hat shop on South Audley Street,
and the gracious owners, Bill and Ned, having fallen for timorous Nikki's eloquent delicacy, allowed them to rent the two
small rooms above the store for virtually nothing. They even
supplied furniture from the attic of their country house, including a small bed on which Nikki slept in the minute "extra"
room and the couch in the "parlor" where her insomniac
mother, with the help of a novel, chain-smoked herself through
each night. The toilet was downstairs, at the back of the shop.
The place was so small that Nikki could as well have been a
kangaroo in her mother's pouch. She wouldn't really have
minded if it had been smaller still, with but one bed for the
two of them.

After graduating from the drama school, Nikki returned to
New York, but her mother, who could never get over her
memories of Cleveland and who found Americans, altogether,
loud and barbarous—certainly by comparison with her customers at the up-market hat shop, who were as kind and
thoughtful as they could be to the widowed (that was the
story) milliner (of aristocratic Cretan lineage, according to Bill

and Ned)—her mother stayed in London. The time had come for Nikki to strike out on her own while her mother remained safely among the many good friends she had made through the "boys," as everyone referred to her bosses—she and Nikki were frequently invited away to somebody's country house for a holiday weekend, and not a few wealthy customers looked on Mrs. Kantarakis as a confidante. And then there was the security furnished by cousin Rena and the doctor, who had been extraordinarily generous, especially to Nikki. Everyone was generous to Nikki. She was an enchantress, though one who, upon her departure for America, had as yet no sexual experience with men. For that matter, since fleeing her father's house in her mother's arms at the age of seven, she'd had hardly any familiarity with men who were not homosexual. It remained to be seen just how much she would enchant them.

"Her mother," Sabbath told his own mother, "died early one morning. Nikki had flown there to be with her during the last stages of the illness. Her ticket was paid for by Bill and Ned. There was nothing more to be done for her in the hospital, so the mother came back to the rooms over the hat shop to die. As the end approached, Nikki sat beside her mother, holding her hand and making her comfortable for nearly four days. Then the fourth morning she went down behind the shop to use the toilet and when she came back upstairs her mother had stopped breathing. 'My mother died just now,' she told me on the phone, 'and I wasn't there. I wasn't there for her. I wasn't there for her, Mickey! She died alone!' Compliments of Bill and Ned, I flew to London on the evening plane. I arrived around breakfast time the next day and made straight for South Audley Street. What I found was Nikki looking calm and unruffled in a chair beside her mother. It was the next day and the corpse was still in her nightgown—and there. And remained there for seventy-two hours more. When I could no longer stand the spectacle of it, I shouted at Nikki, 'You are not a Sicilian peasant! Enough is enough! It is time for your mother to go!' 'No. No. *No!*' and when she started flailing at me with her fists, I backed away, retreated down the stairs, and wandered around London for hours. What I was trying to tell her was that the vigil she had initiated over the body had exceeded my sense not of what was seemly but of what was sane.

I was trying to tell her that her unconstrained intimacy with her mother's corpse, the chatty monologue with which she was entertaining the dead woman as she sat beside her through each day, knitting at her mother's unfinished knitting and welcoming the friends of the boys, the fondling of the dead woman's hands, the kissing of her face, the stroking of her hair—all this obliviousness to the raw physical fact—was rendering her taboo to me."

Was Sabbath's mother following this story? He somehow sensed that her interest lay elsewhere. He was down into Connecticut now, driving along a beautiful, creepy stretch of river, and he thought his mother might be thinking, "It wouldn't be hard out in that river." But not before I see Linc, Ma. . . . He had to see what it looked like before he did it himself.

And this was the first time that he realized or admitted what he had to do. The problem that was his life was never to be solved. His wasn't the kind of life where there are aims that are clear and means that are clear and where it is possible to say, "This is essential and that is not essential, this I will not do because I cannot endure it, and that I will do because I can endure it." There was no unsnarling an existence whose waywardness constituted its only authority and provided its primary amusement. He wanted his mother to understand that he wasn't blaming the futility on Morty's death, or on her collapse, or on Nikki's disappearance, or on his stupid profession, or on his arthritic hands—he was merely recounting to her what had happened before this had happened. That's all you could know, though if what you think happened happens to not ever match up with what somebody else thinks happened, how could you say you know even that? Everybody got everything wrong. What he was telling his mother was wrong. If it were Nikki listening instead of his mother, she would be shouting, "It wasn't like that! *I* wasn't like that! You misunderstand! You always misunderstood! You're always going at me for no reason at all!"

Homeless, wifeless, mistressless, penniless . . . jump in the cold river and drown. Climb up into the woods and go to sleep, and tomorrow morning, should you even awaken, keep climbing until you are lost. Check into a motel, borrow the night clerk's razor to shave, and slit your throat from ear to ear. It could be done. Lincoln Gelman did it. Roseanna's father did it. Probably Nikki herself had done it, and with a razor, a straight razor very like the one with which she had exited each night to kill herself in *Miss Julie*. About a week after her disappearance, it had occurred to Sabbath to go to the prop room and look for the razor that the valet, Jean, hands to Julie after she sleeps with him, feels herself polluted by him, and finally asks of him, "If you were in my place, what would you do?" "Go, now while it's light—out to the barn, . . ." replies Jean, and hands her his razor. "There's no other way to end. . . . Go!" he says. The play's last word: go! So Julie takes the razor and goes—and embattled Nikki ineluctably follows. The razor had turned up in the drawer in the prop shop just where it was supposed to be, but there were times, nonetheless, when Sabbath could still believe that the horror was autohypnosis, that their catastrophe stemmed from the selfless, ruthless sympathy with which Nikki almost criminally embraced the sufferings of the unreal. Eagerly she surrendered her large imagination not to the overbearing beastliness of Sabbath's imagination but to the overbearing beastliness of Strindberg's. Strindberg had done it for him. Who better?

"I remember thinking by the third day, 'If this goes on any longer, I'll never fuck this woman again—I won't be able to lie with her in the same bed.' It wasn't because these rites she was concocting were strange to me and at cross-purposes with rituals I was accustomed to witnessing among Jews. Had she been a Catholic, a Hindu, a Muslim, guided by the mourning practices of this religion or that; had she been an Egyptian under the reign of the great Amenhotep, observing every last detail of the ceremonial rigmarole decreed by the death god Osiris, I believe I would have done nothing more than watch in respectful silence. My chagrin was over Nikki out there *all on her own*—she and her mother against the world, apart from the world, alone together and cut off from the world, with no church, no clan to help her through, not even a simple folk formality around which her response to a dear one's death could mercifully cohere. Two days into her vigil we happened to see a priest walking by, down on South Audley Street. 'Those are the real ghouls,' Nikki said. 'I hate them all. Priests, rabbis, clergymen with their stupid fairy tale!' I had wanted to say to her, 'Then get a shovel and do it yourself. I'm no fan of the clergy myself. Get a shovel and bury her in Ned's garden.'

"Her mother was laid out on the couch, under an eider-down. She looked—before the embalmer showed up and, in Nikki's words, 'pickled her'—she looked as though she were merely sleeping out the day in our presence, her chin, just as she carried it in life, angled slightly to one side. Beyond the windows it was a fresh spring morning. The sparrows she fed every day were flitting about on the flowering trees and bathing in the gravel on top of the garden shed in the yard, and through the open rear windows you could see down to the sheen on the tulips. A bowl of half-eaten dog food lay beside the door but her mother's lapdog was gone by then, taken in by Rena. It was from Rena that I later learned what had happened on the morning of the death. Nikki had told me that an ambulance had been sent for by the doctor who had come to view the body and to write up the death certificate but that she had decided to keep her mother at home until the funeral and sent the ambulance away. Rena, who had rushed over to be with Nikki at the time, told me that the ambulance the doctor called had not been 'sent away.' When the driver had come through the door and started up the narrow stair-case, Nikki had told him, 'No, no!'; when he insisted he was only doing his job, Nikki struck him across the face so hard that he ran off and her wrist was sore for days. I had seen her rubbing the wrist on and off during the vigil but didn't know what it meant until Rena told me."

And just who did he think he was talking to? A self-induced hallucination, a betrayal of reason, something with which to magnify the inconsequentiality of a meaningless mess—*that's* what his mother was, another of his puppets, his last puppet, an invisible marionette flying around on strings, cast in the role not of guardian angel but of the departed spirit making ready to ferry him to his next abode. To a life that had come to nothing, a crude theatrical instinct was lending a garish, pa-thetic touch of last-minute drama.

The drive was interminable. Had he missed a turn or was this itself the next abode: a coffin that you endlessly steer through the placeless darkness, recounting and recounting the uncon-trollable events that induced you to become someone unforeseen. And so fast! So quickly! Everything runs away, beginning with who you are, and at some indefinable point you come to half understand that the ruthless antagonist is yourself.

His mother had by now draped her spirit around him, she had enwrapped him within herself, her way of assuring him that she did indeed exist unmastered and independent of his imagination.

"I asked Nikki, 'When will the funeral be?' But she didn't answer. 'It's quite unacceptable,' she said, 'it's quite unacceptably sad.' She was seated on the edge of the couch where her mother was laid out. I was holding one of Nikki's hands and with the other she reached over and touched her mother's face. 'Manoúlamou, manoulítsamou.' Greek diminutives for 'my dear little mother.' 'It's unbearable. It's dreadful,' Nikki said. 'I'm going to stay with her. I'll sleep here. I don't want her to be alone.' And as I didn't want Nikki to be alone, I sat with her and her mother until, late in the afternoon, a funeral director from a large London firm contacted by Rena's doctor husband came to discuss the funeral arrangements. I was a Jew accustomed to the dead's being buried when possible within twenty-four hours, but Nikki was nothing, nothing but her mother's child, and when I reminded her, while we were waiting for the funeral director, of what Jewish custom was, she said, 'To put them in the ground the next *day*? How cruel of the Jews!' 'Well, that's one way of looking at it.' 'It *is*,' she said, 'it's cruel! It's horrible!' I said no more. She had confirmed that she didn't want a funeral ever.

"The funeral director arrived in striped trousers and a black cutaway at around four. He was extremely polite and deferential and explained that he had rushed over from his third funeral of the day and hadn't had a chance to change. Nikki announced that her mother was not to be moved but was to stay right where she was. He responded at a very high level of euphemism, one to which he adhered, but for a single lapse, throughout the consultation. He affected an upper-class accent. 'As you wish, Miss Kantarakis. We won't want to give offense, however. If mother remains with you, then one of our people will have to come and give her an injection.' I took him to mean that she would have to be cleaned out and embalmed. 'Don't worry,' he assured us crisply, 'our man is the best in

England.' He smiled proudly. 'He does the royal family. A very witty fellow, in fact. You have to be in this business. We couldn't be a morbid lot.'

"A fly meanwhile had alighted on the corpse's face and I was hoping that Nikki wouldn't see it and it would go away. But she did see and jumped up, and for the first time since I arrived, there was a hysterical outburst. 'Let her,' the funeral director said to me. I, too, had jumped up to shoo the fly away. 'Let it come out,' he said sagely.

"After she had been calmed down, Nikki laid a tissue across her mother's face to keep the fly from returning. Later in the day, at her request, I went out to buy some bug repellant and came back to spray the room—careful not to spray in the corpse's direction—and Nikki took the tissue and put it in her sweater pocket. Unknowingly—or not unknowingly—around dusk she used the tissue to blow her nose . . . and that seemed to me altogether crazy. 'At the risk of being indelicate,' the funeral director asked, 'how tall was Mother? My associates will be asking when I ring.'

"He called his office some minutes later and asked what was available at the crematorium on Tuesday. It was still only Friday, and given Nikki's condition, Tuesday seemed a long way off. But as she would as soon have had no funeral and kept her mother there for good, I'd decided on Tuesday as better than never.

"The funeral director waited while they checked the crematorium schedule. Then he looked up from the phone and said to me, 'My associates say there's a one o'clock slot.' 'Oh, no,' Nikki whimpered, but I nodded okay. 'Grab it,' he snapped into the phone, and revealed at last that he was able to speak as though the world were a real place and we were real people. 'And the service?' he asked Nikki after he'd hung up. 'I don't care who does it,' she said vaguely, 'as long as they don't go on about God.' 'Nondenominational,' he said, and wrote that down in his book, along with her mother's height and the grade of coffin that Nikki had chosen to have incinerated with her. He then set about to describe, delicately, the cremation procedure and to lay out the options available. 'You can leave before the coffin disappears or you can wait until it disappears.' Nikki was too stunned by the thought to answer and so I said,

'We'll wait.' 'And the ashes?' he asked. 'In her will,' I said, 'she just asked that they be scattered.' Nikki, looking at the motionless tissue over her mother's nostrils and lips, said to no one in particular, 'I suppose we'll take them back to New York. She hated America. But I suppose they should come with us.' 'You can take them,' the funeral director replied, 'you certainly can, Miss Kantarakis. According to the law of 1902, you can do anything you wish with them.'

"The embalmer didn't arrive until seven-thirty. The funeral director had described him to me—with a trace of Dickensian enjoyment such as you might not be likely to hear from a funeral director anywhere other than in the British Isles—as 'tall, with thick spectacles, and quite witty.' But he wasn't merely tall when he appeared in the dusk at the downstairs door; he was huge, a giant strongman out of the circus, wearing the thick spectacles and completely bald but for two sprigs of black hair that stuck up at either side of his enormous head. He stood in the doorway in a black suit, bearing two large black boxes, each sizable enough to hold a child. 'You're Mr. Cummins?' I asked him. 'I'm from Ridgely's, sir.' He might as well have said he was from Satan's. I would have believed him, Cockney accent and all. He didn't look witty to me.

"I led him up to where the corpse was tucked in under her eiderdown. He removed his hat and bowed slightly to Nikki, as respectful as he might have been were we the royals themselves. 'We'll leave you alone,' I said. 'We'll take a walk and be back in about an hour.' 'Give me an hour and a half, sir,' he said. 'Fine.' 'May I ask a few questions, sir?'

"As Nikki was sufficiently astonished by his hugeness—by his hugeness on top of everything else—I didn't think she'd need to hear his questions, which could not be anything but macabre. As it was, she couldn't lift her gaze from the large black boxes, which he'd now set down. 'You go outside a moment,' I told her. 'Go downstairs and get some air while I finish up with this guy.' Silently she obeyed. She was leaving her mother for the first time since she'd gone to the toilet the day before and returned to find her dead. But anything rather than to be with that man and those boxes.

"Back inside, the embalmer asked me how the corpse should be dressed. I didn't know, but instead of rushing out to question Nikki, I told him to leave her in her nightgown. Then I realized that if he was preparing her for the funeral and the cremation, her jewelry should be removed. I asked if he would do that for us. 'Let's see what she has on, sir,' he said and beckoned for me to examine the body with him.

"I hadn't been expecting that, but as it seemed to be a matter of professional ethics for him not to remove valuables without a witness present, I stood beside him while he pulled back the eiderdown to reveal the corpse's bluish stiffened fingers and, where the nightgown had hiked up, the pipe-thin legs. He removed her ring and gave it to me and then he lifted her head to unscrew her earrings. But he couldn't manage by himself, and so I held her head while he worked the earrings. 'The pearls, too,' I said, and he slid them around on her neck so that the catch was turned to the front. Only the catch wouldn't come undone. He struggled in vain with his inordinately large circus-strongman fingers while I continued to hold the weight of her head in one hand. She and I were never physically cozy together and this was by far the most intimate we had been. The head seemed to weigh so much dead. She is so dead, I thought—and this is becoming insufferable. Eventually I took a crack at opening the catch myself and after a few minutes of fiddling, when I couldn't do it either, we gave up and drew the pearl necklace, which was a very tight fit, over her head and her hair as best we could.

"I was careful not to trip as I stepped back between his black boxes. 'All right, then,' I told him, 'I'll return in an hour and a half.' 'You'd better phone before, sir.' 'And you'll leave her exactly as she is now?' 'Yes, sir.' But then he looked at the windows that faced onto Ned's garden and the rear windows of the houses on the street opposite and he asked, 'Can they see in from over there, sir?' I was suddenly alarmed about leaving this attractive forty-five-year-old woman alone with him, dead though she was. But what I was thinking was unthinkable —I thought—and I said, 'You better pull the curtains to be safe.' The curtains were new, a birthday gift from Nikki bought the year before and hung only during the last week of her mother's illness. Her mother had insisted that she didn't need new curtains, refused even to unwrap them, and had only accepted them when, at her bedside, Nikki, lying, said to the dying woman that they had cost her less than ten pounds.

"At Rena's, where we were staying, Rena and I tried to get Nikki to bathe and to eat. She would do neither. She would not even wash her hands when I asked her to after a day of fondling her dead mother. She waited silently in a chair until it was time to go back. After an hour passed, I phoned to see how far the embalmer had got.

"'I'm finished, sir,' he said. 'Is everything as it was?' 'Yes, sir. Flowers beside her on the pillow.' They hadn't been when we left; he must have taken the flowers that Ned had picked earlier in the day and moved them. 'Had to straighten her head,' he told me. 'Best for the coffin.' 'All right. When you go, just pull the downstairs door shut behind you. We'll be right over. Can you leave a lamp on?' 'I have, sir. The little lamp by her head.' He had arranged a tableau.

"The first thing I saw—"

It was *Sabbath* he had meant to smash on the head. Of course! It was Sabbath he had set out to catch desecrating his mother's grave! For weeks, maybe even for months now, Matthew, on night patrol, must have been observing him from the cruiser. Ever since Sabbath's monstrous exploitation of Kathy Goolsbee, Matthew, like so many others in the affronted community, had come to lose his respect for Sabbath, and this he made clear, whenever his car happened to pass Sabbath's on the road, by failing to acknowledge that he recognized the driver. As he drove around, Matthew ordinarily loved to throw a salute to the folks he'd known as a kid in Madamaska Falls, and he was still well known in town for being lenient with townsfolk about their infractions. He had been ingratiatingly lenient once with Sabbath himself, when he was just a few months out of the academy, not very wily yet, and driving a chase car with the traffic squad. He'd gone after Sabbath— who was moving along well over the speed limit after a joyous afternoon up at the Grotto—and forced him, with his siren, to the side of the road. But when Matthew strode up to the driver's window and looked inside and saw who it was, he blushed and said, "Ooops." He and Roseanna had become pals during his last year at the high school, and more than once (drunk she said everything more than once) she'd remarked that Matthew Balich was among the most sensitive boys she'd ever had in a class at Cumberland. "What did I do wrong, Officer Balich?" inquired Sabbath, seriously, as every citizen is entitled to do. "Jesus, you know you were *flying*, sir." "Uh-oh," replied Sabbath. "Look, don't worry," Matthew told him, "when it comes to folks I know, I'm not your typical gung-ho trooper. You don't have to go telling people, but it just isn't in me to be that way toward somebody I know. I drove fast before I was a trooper. I'm not going to be a hypocrite." "Well, that's more than kind. What should I do?" "Well," said Matthew, grinning broadly with that noseless face—exactly as his mother had earlier in the afternoon, coming for the third or fourth time—"you could slow down, for one thing. And then you could just get out of here. Go away! See ya, Mr. Sabbath! Say hi to Roseanna!"

So that was the end of that. He could not dare visit Drenka's grave ever again. He could never return to Madamaska Falls. In flight not just from home and marriage but now from the law at its most lawless.

"The first thing I saw when we got back was that the vacuum cleaner was out of the closet and in a corner of the larger room. Had he used it to clean up? Clean what up? Then I smelled the awful chemicals.

"The woman under the eiderdown was no longer the woman we had been with all day. 'It's not her,' Nikki said and broke into tears. 'It looks like me! It's me!'

"I understood what she meant, insane as her words first sounded. Nikki possessed a severe, spectacular variant of her mother's refined good looks, and so whatever resemblance there had been before the embalming was now even chillingly stronger. She walked back to the body and stared at it. 'Her head is straight.' 'He straightened it,' I told her. 'But she always carried her head on the side.' 'She doesn't anymore.' 'Oh, you're looking awfully stern, manoulítsa,' Nikki said to the corpse.

"Stern. Sculpted. Statuelike. Very officially very dead. But Nikki nonetheless sat back down in her chair and set about resuming the vigil. The curtains were closed and only the little light was glowing and the flowers were on the pillow beside the embalmed head. I had to suppress an impulse to grab them and throw them into the wastebasket and put a stop to the whole thing. All her fluid self is gone, I thought, suctioned into those black cases and then—what? Down the toilet bowl at the back of the shop? I could just see that giant in his black suit tossing about the naked body once it was the two of them alone in the room with the curtains drawn and there was no longer any need to be as dainty as he'd been with the jewelry. Evacuating the bowels, emptying the bladder, draining the blood, injecting the formaldehyde, if formaldehyde was what I smelled.

"I should never have allowed this, I thought. We should have buried her in the garden ourselves. I was right to begin with. 'What are you going to do?' I asked. 'I'll stay here tonight,' she said. 'You can't,' I said. 'I don't want her to be alone.' 'I don't want *you* to be alone. You can't be alone. And I'm not going to sleep here. You're coming back to Rena's. You can return in the morning.' 'I can't leave her.' 'You have to come with me, Nikki.' 'When?' 'Now. Say good-bye to her now and come.' She got out of the chair and knelt beside the couch. Touching her mother's cheeks, her hair, her lips, she said, 'I did love you, manoulítsa. Oh, manoulítsamou.'

"I opened a window to air the place out. I began to clean the refrigerator at the kitchen end of the parlor. I poured the milk that was in an open carton down the drain. I found a paper bag and put the contents of the refrigerator into the bag. But when I came back to Nikki, she was still talking to her. 'It's time to go for tonight,' I said.

"Without resisting me, Nikki got up from the floor when I offered to help her. But standing in the doorway to the stairwell, she turned back to look at her mother. 'Why can't she just stay like that?' she asked.

"I led her down the stairs to the side door, carrying the garbage out with us. But again Nikki turned around and I followed her back up into the parlor with my bag of garbage. Again she went up to the body to touch it. I waited. Ma, I waited and I waited and I thought, Help her, help her out of this, but I didn't know what to do to help her, whether to tell her to stay or to force her to go. She pointed to the corpse. 'That's my mother,' she said. 'You have to come with me,' I said. Eventually, I don't know how much later, she did.

"But the next day it was worse—Nikki was better. In the morning she couldn't wait to get to her mother's and when, after dropping her off there, I phoned an hour later and asked, 'How is it?' she said, 'Oh, very peaceful. Sitting here knitting. And we had a little chat.' And so I found her at the end of the afternoon when I came to take her back to Rena's. 'We had such a nice little chat,' she said. 'I was just telling Momma . . .'

"On Sunday morning—finally, finally, finally—in a heavy rainstorm, I went around to open the door for the hearse that had come to take her away. 'It's another twenty-five pounds,' the funeral director warned me, 'to get the staff out on Sunday, sir—funerals are expensive enough already.' But I said to him, 'Just get 'em.' If Rena wouldn't pay, I would—and I had then, as now, not a dollar to spare. I didn't want Nikki to come with me, and only when she insisted that she had to did I raise my voice and say, 'Look, start thinking. It's pissing rain. It's miserable. You're not going to like it at all when they carry your mother out of that room and into this storm in a box.' 'But I must go to see her this afternoon.' 'You can, you can. I'm sure you can.' 'You must ask them if I can come this afternoon!' 'Whenever they have her ready, I'm sure you can go there. But the scene this morning you can skip. Do you want to watch her leave South Audley Street?' 'Maybe you're right,' she said, and, of course, I was wondering if I was and if watching her mother leave South Audley Street might be just what she needed for reality to begin to seep in. But what if keeping reality at bay was all that was keeping her from coming completely apart? I didn't know. No one knows. That's why the religions have the rituals that Nikki hated.

"But at three she was back with her mother at the funeral home, which happened to be not far from the flat of an English friend I had arranged to visit. I had given her the address and the phone number and told her to come to his house when she was finished. Instead she called me to say that she would stay until my visit was over and that I should then come to pick her up at the funeral home. It wasn't what I'd had in mind. She's stuck, I thought, I cannot unstick her.

"I had lingering hopes that she would show up at my friend's anyway, but when it got to be five o'clock, I walked over and, at the front door, asked the on-duty officer, who appeared to be alone on a Sunday, to call her. He said that Nikki had left a message for me to be brought to where she was 'visiting' her mother. He led me along the corridors and down a long stairway and into another corridor, lined with doors, which I imagined issued onto cubicles where bodies were laid out to be seen by relatives. Nikki was in one of those tiny rooms with her mother. She was seated in a chair drawn up beside the open coffin, working at her mother's knitting again. When she saw me she laughed lightly and said, 'We had a wonderful chat. We laughed about the room. It's just about the size of the one in Cleveland the time we ran away. Look,' she said to me, 'look at her sweet little hands.' She turned back the lace coverlet to show me her mother's intertwined fingers. 'Manoulítsamou,' she said, kissing and kissing them.

"I think even the on-duty officer, who had remained in the open doorway to accompany us upstairs, was shaken by what he'd just seen. 'We have to go,' I said flatly. She began to cry. 'A few more minutes.' 'You've been here for over two hours.' 'I love I love I love I love—' 'I know, but we have to go now.' She got up and began kissing and stroking her mother's forehead, repeating, 'I love I love I love I love—' Only gradually was I able to pull her out of the room.

"At the door she thanked the officer. 'You've all been so kind,' she said, looking a bit dazed, and then, as we came outside, she asked if the next morning I would mind if she just stopped by first thing with some fresh flowers for her mother's room. I thought, We are dealing here with *death*, fuck the flowers! but I did not really cut loose until we were back in the room at Rena's. We walked silently through Holland Park on a beautiful May Sunday, past the peacocks and the formal gardens, then down through Kensington Gardens, where the chestnut trees were blossoming, and finally we got to Rena's. 'Look,' I said to her, closing the door to our room, 'I can't stand by and watch it anymore. You are not living with the dead, you are living with the living. It's as simple as that. You are alive and your mother is dead, very sadly dead at forty-five, but this has all become too much for me. Your mother is not a doll to play with. She is not laughing with you about anything. She is dead. Nobody is laughing. This must stop.'

"But she did not seem yet to understand. She replied, 'I've seen her pass through each stage.' 'There are no stages. She is dead. That is the only stage. Do you hear me? That is the only stage, and you are not *on* the stage. This is no act. This is all becoming very offensive.' There followed a befuddled moment and then she opened her purse and took out a prescription bottle. 'I should never have taken these.' 'What are they?' 'Pills. I asked the doctor. When he came for Momma, I asked him to give me something to get through the funeral.' 'How many of these have you been taking?' 'I had to' was all she answered. And then she wept all evening and I threw the pills down the toilet.

"The next morning, after coming out of the bathroom, where she'd been brushing her teeth, she looked at me—looked at me exactly like herself—and said, 'That's over. My mother's not there anymore,' and she never went back to the funeral home, or kissed her mother's face again, or laughed with her, or bought her curtains, or anything else. And she missed her every single day thereafter—missed her, cried over her, talked to her—until she herself disappeared. And that's when I took on the job and began a life with the dead that has, by now, put those antics of Nikki's to shame. To think how repelled I was by her—as though it were Nikki and not Death who had overstepped the limits."

In 1953—nearly ten years before the notoriously histrionic decade when jugglers, magicians, musicians, folksingers, violinists, trapeze artists, agitprop acting troupes, and youngsters in odd costumes with little to go on other than what they were high on began to exhibit themselves all over Manhattan—Sabbath, twenty-four and recently returned from studying in Rome, set up his screen on the east side of Broadway and 116th, just outside the gates to Columbia University, and became a street performer. Back then his street specialty, his trademark, was to perform with his fingers. Fingers, after all, are made to move, and though their range is not enormous, when each is moving purposefully and has a distinctive voice, their power to produce their own reality can astonish people.

Sometimes, just drawing the length of a woman's sheer stocking over one hand, Sabbath was able to create all sorts of lascivious illusions. Sometimes, by piercing a hole in a tennis ball and inserting a fingertip, Sabbath gave one or more of the fingers a head, a head with a brain, and the brain provided with schemes, manias, phobias, the works; sometimes a finger would invite a spectator close to the screen to punch the little hole and then to assist further by affixing the brainy ball over the fingernail. In one of his earliest programs Sabbath liked to conclude the show by putting the middle finger of his left hand on trial. When the court had tried the finger and found it guilty—of obscenity—a small meat grinder was rolled out and the middle finger was tugged and pulled by the police (the right hand) until its tip was forced into the oval mouth at the top of the meat grinder. As the police turned the crank, the middle finger—passionately crying out that it was innocent of all charges, having done only what comes naturally to a middle finger—disappeared into the meat grinder and spaghetti strands of raw hamburger meat began to emerge from the grinder's nether spout.

In the fingers uncovered, or even suggestively clad, there is always a reference to the penis, and there were skits Sabbath developed in his first years on the street where the reference wasn't that veiled.

In one skit his hands appeared in a close-fitting pair of black kid gloves, each with a fastener at the wrist. It took ten minutes for him to slip the gloves off, finger by finger—a long time, ten minutes, and when finally the fingers had all been exposed, each by the others—and some not at all willingly—more than a few young men in the audience could have been found to be tumescent. The effect on the young women was more difficult to discern, but they stayed, they watched, they were not embarrassed, even in 1953, to drop some coins into Sabbath's Italian peaked cap when he emerged from behind the screen at the conclusion of the twenty-five-minute show, smiling most wickedly above his close-clipped black chin beard, a small, ferocious, green-eyed buccaneer, from his years at sea as massive through the chest as a bison. He had one of those chests you don't want to get in the way of, a squat man, a sturdy physical plant, obviously very sexed-up and lawless, who didn't give a damn what anybody thought. He appeared rapidly babbling bubbly Italian and broadly gesturing his gratitude, giving no indication that holding your hands up uninterruptedly for twenty-five minutes is hard work requiring endurance and frequently painful, even for someone as strong as he was in his twenties. Of course, all the voices in the show had spoken English—Sabbath spoke Italian only afterward, and simply for the fun of it. The very reason he had established the Indecent Theater of Manhattan. The very reason he'd signed on six times for the Romance Run. The very reason he'd done just about everything since leaving home seven years earlier. He wanted to do what he wanted to do. This was his cause and it led to his arrest and trial and conviction, and for precisely the crime he'd foreseen in the meat-grinder skit.

Even from behind the screen, it was possible from certain angles for Sabbath to catch a glimpse of the audience, and whenever he spotted an attractive girl among the twenty or so students who had stopped to watch, he would break off the drama in progress or wind it down, and the fingers would start in whispering together. Then the boldest finger—a middle finger—would edge nonchalantly forward, lean graciously out over the screen, and beckon her to approach. And girls did come forward, some laughing or grinning like good sports, others serious, poker-faced, as though already mildly hypnotized. After an exchange of polite chitchat, the finger would begin a serious interrogation, asking if the girl had ever dated a finger, if her family approved of fingers, if she herself could find a finger desirable, if she could imagine living happily with only a finger . . . and the other hand, meanwhile, stealthily began to unbutton or unzip her outer garment. Usually the hand went no further than that; Sabbath knew enough not to press on and the interlude ended as a harmless farce. But sometimes, when Sabbath gauged from her answers that his consort was more playful than most or uncommonly spellbound, the interrogation would abruptly turn wanton and the fingers proceed to undo her blouse. Only twice did the fingers undo a brassiere catch and only once did they endeavor to caress the nipples exposed. And it was then that Sabbath was arrested.

How could they resist each other? Nikki was just back from

RADA and answering audition calls. She lived in a room near the Columbia campus and, several days running, was among the pretty young women beckoned toward the screen by that sly, salacious middle finger. For the first time in her life she was without mother and therefore petrified on the subway, frightened on the street, fiercely lonely in her room but scared stiff about going out. She was also beginning to despair as audition after audition led nowhere, and was probably less than a week from returning across the Atlantic to the kangaroo pouch when that middle finger fingered her to join the fun. It could not have done otherwise. He was five feet five and she was nearly six feet tall, black as black can be where she was black and white as white can be where she was white. She smiled that smile that was never insignificant, the actress's smile that aroused the irrational desire to worship her even in sensible people, the smile whose message, oddly enough, was never melancholy but that said, "There are absolutely no difficulties in life"—however, she would not move an inch from where she was rooted at the far edge of the crowd. But after the show, when Sabbath burst forth with that beard and those eyes, spinning Italian sentences, Nikki had not left and did not look as though she intended to. When he approached her, begging, "Bella signorina, per favore, io non sono niente, non sono nessuno, un modest'uomo che vive solo d'aria—i soldi servono ai miei sei piccini affamati e alla mia moglie tisica—" she placed the dollar bill that was in her hand—and that represented one one-hundredth of what she had to live on per month—into his cap. This was how the couple met, how Nikki became the leading lady of the Bowery Basement Players, and how Sabbath got his chance not only to play with his fingers and his puppets but to manipulate living creatures as well.

He'd never before been a director but he was afraid of nothing, even when—especially when—he emerged guilty, with a suspended sentence and a fine, from the obscenity trial. Norman Cowan and Lincoln Gelman put up production money for the ninety-nine-seat theater on Avenue C, as poor a street as there was then in lower Manhattan. Indecent Theater finger and puppet shows were presented from six to seven three nights a week and then at eight the Bowery Basement productions, in repertory, with a company all about Sabbath's age or younger and working virtually for nothing. No one over twenty-eight or -nine was ever on stage, even in his disastrous *King Lear*, with Nikki as Cordelia and none other than the rookie director as Lear. Disastrous, but so what? The main thing is to do what you want. His cockiness, his self-exalted egoism, the menacing charm of a potentially villainous artist were insufferable to a lot of people and he made enemies easily, including a number of theater professionals who believed that his was an unseemly, brilliantly disgusting talent that had yet to discover a suitably seemly means of "disciplined" expression. Sabbath Antagonistes, busted for obscenity as far back as 1956. Sabbath Absconditus, whatever happened to him? His life was one long flight from what?

At just past 12:30 A.M. Sabbath arrived in New York and found a spot for the car a few blocks from Norman Cowan's Central Park West apartment. He hadn't been back to the city in nearly thirty years, yet upper Broadway in the dark of night looked much as he remembered it when he used to set up his screen outside the 72nd Street subway station and put on a rush-hour finger show. The side streets seemed to him unchanged, except for the bodies bundled up in rags, in blankets, under cardboard cartons, bodies encased in torn and shapeless clothing, lying up against the masonry of the apartment buildings and along the railings of the brownstones. April, yet they were sleeping out-of-doors. Sabbath knew about them only what he'd overheard Roseanna saying on the phone to the do-gooding friends. For years he had not read a paper or listened to the news if he could avoid it. The news told him nothing. The news was for people to talk about, and Sabbath, indifferent to the untransgressive run of normalized pursuits, did not wish to talk to people. He didn't care who was at war with whom or where a plane had crashed or what had befallen Bangladesh. He did not even want to know who the president was of the United States. He'd rather fuck Drenka, he'd rather fuck *anyone*, than watch Tom Brokaw. His range of pleasures was narrow and never did extend to the evening news. Sabbath was reduced the way a sauce is reduced, boiled down by his burners, the better to concentrate his essence and be defiantly himself.

But mostly he did not follow the news because of Nikki. He couldn't leaf through a paper, any paper anywhere, without searching still for some clue about Nikki. It was years before he was able to answer the ringing phone without thinking that it would be either Nikki or someone who knew about her. Crank phone calls were the worst. When Roseanna picked up the phone and it was an obscene caller or a breather, he would think, Was it somebody who knew my wife, somebody who is trying to tell me something? Could the breather have been Nikki herself? But did Nikki know where he'd moved to; had she ever even heard of Madamaska Falls? Did she know he had married Roseanna? Had she run away that night, leaving no hint of why she was going or where, because earlier in the evening she had seen him with Roseanna, the two of them crossing Tompkins Square Park and headed for his workshop?

In New York her disappearance was all he could think about—out on the streets it was obsessional, it had no end— and this was why he'd never returned. Back when he was still in their apartment on St. Marks Place, he never went out that he did not think he would pass her in the street, and so he looked at everybody and started following people. If a woman was tall and had the right hair—not that Nikki couldn't have dyed hers or taken to wearing a wig—he would follow her until he caught up and then he would measure himself against the person and, if she was about right, would step around to look directly at her face—Let me see if this is Nikki! It never was, though he made the acquaintance of some of these women anyway, took them for coffee, took them for a walk, tried to fuck them; half the time did. But he did not find Nikki, nor did the police or the FBI or the famous detective whom he went to hire with the help of Norman and Linc.

Back in those days—the forties, the fifties, the early sixties— people didn't disappear the way they do today. Today if some-body disappears you're pretty sure, you immediately know, what happened: they were murdered, they're dead. But in 1964 nobody thought first thing of foul play. If there was no certification of their death, you had to believe they were alive. People didn't just drop off the edge of the earth with anything like the frequency they do now. And so Sabbath had to think she was alive somewhere. If there wasn't a body to bury physically, he could not bury her mentally. Although since moving to Madamaska Falls he'd never told anybody, even Drenka, about the wife who disappeared, the fact was that Nikki wouldn't die until he did. He had moved to Madamaska Falls when he felt himself beginning to go crazy looking for her on the New York streets. A person could still walk everywhere in the city in those days, and that's what he did—walked everywhere, looked everywhere, found nothing.

The police had distributed circulars to police departments all around the country and in Canada. Sabbath had himself sent out hundreds of circulars, to colleges, to convents, to hospitals, to newspaper reporters, to columnists, to Greek restaurants in Greektowns all over America. The "missing" circular had been assembled and printed by the police: Nikki's photo, age, height, weight, and hair color, even what she was wearing. They knew what clothes she'd had on because Sabbath had spent a weekend going through her dresser and her closet until he was able to recall the items no longer there. She appeared to have left with only the clothes on her back. And how much money could she have had? Ten dollars? Twenty? Nothing had been drawn from their small bank account and not even the pile of change on the kitchen table had been disturbed. She had not taken even that.

A description of what she'd been wearing and her photo were all he could offer the detective. She had left no note, and, according to the detective, most people did. "Voluntary disappearances," he called these. The detective took down from the shelf behind his desk whole loose-leaf notebooks, as many as ten of them, with pictures and descriptions of people who had disappeared and still not been located. "Usually," he said, "they leave *something*—a note, a ring. . . ." Sabbath told him that Nikki was obsessed with the dead mother she had loved and the living father she hated. Maybe she had been seized by an impulse—God knew she was a creature of impulse—and had flown out to Cleveland to forgive the crass vulgarian she had not seen since she was seven—or to murder him. Or perhaps, despite the fact that her passport was still in a drawer in their apartment, she had somehow made her way back to London and to the spot alongside the Serpentine in Kensington Gardens where on a Sunday morning, with all the children floating their boats and flying kites, he had watched her scatter the ashes over the water.

But she could be anywhere, everywhere—where was the detective to begin? No, he wouldn't take the case, and so Sabbath went back to sending out more circulars, always with a handwritten letter from him that read, "This is my wife. She disappeared. Do you know or have you seen this person?" He sent the circulars to wherever his imagination could take him. He even thought of whorehouses. Nikki was beautiful, submissive, and certainly eye-catching in America, with her long, long body and her long-nosed black and white Greek looks— maybe she'd wound up in a whorehouse like the college girl in *Sanctuary*. He could remember once, though only once, coming upon a young woman of great refinement in a whorehouse, in Buenos Aires.

Two things, the American girl next door (that was Roseanna) and the exotic (Nikki, the romance of port life, brothel life), came together for him in New York when he started to go to whorehouses looking for his wife. There were places on upper Third Avenue where you *met* the girl next door. You walked up the stairs into a kind of salon and sometimes they tried to make it look like an old-fashioned salon out of Lautrec or some fake version of that. And there were young women lounging around, and there one found the girl next door but never, never Nikki. He became a customer at three or four of these places and showed Nikki's picture to the madams. He asked if they'd ever seen her around. The madams all gave the same answer: "I wish I had."

Then there were the fifty or so letters addressed to him at the theater, from people who had seen Nikki perform and who wanted to communicate their sympathy. He had stored the letters for her return in her dresser drawer, with the jewelry she had inherited from her mother, among them the pieces he and the embalmer had removed from the corpse—she had not taken any of that either. If he could forward her these letters— no, better if he could send the writers, transport them to wherever she was hiding out and seat her in a chair in the middle of the room, ask her to be still and to let them pass before her one at a time and take as long as they liked to tell her what she had meant to them in Strindberg, Chekhov, Shakespeare.

Long before they'd all stepped up to deliver to her their emotional tributes, she would be weeping uncontrollably, not for her mother but for herself now and for the gift she had abandoned. And only after her last admirer had spoken would Sabbath enter the room. And here she would stand and put on her coat—the black form-fitting coat that was missing from the closet, the one they'd bought together at Altman's—and, without any resistance, allow him to lead her back to where she could feel coherent, of a piece, and strong, where she could think of herself as controlling events, if only for two hours—back to the stage, the only place on earth where she wasn't acting and her demons ceased to be. Being on stage was what held her together—what held *them* together. The intensification she gave everything by stepping out under the lights!

The unending mourning for her mother had made her unendurable to him; it was the actress he had to save.

As with millions upon millions of young couples, in the beginning was the sexual excitement. However baffling a mixture, Nikki's narcissism, pure as a gushing geyser, and her stupendous talent for self-abnegation seemed faultlessly wedded in her when she lay nude on the bed imploringly looking up to see what he would do with her first. And the soulfulness was there, that was always there, the romantic, ethereal side of her, her ineffectual protest against everything ugly. The taut concavity that was her belly, the alabaster apple that was her cleft behind, the pale, maidenly nipples of a fifteen-year-old, the breasts so small that you could cup them in your hand the way you hold a ladybug to prevent its flying away, the impenetrability of the eyes that drew you in and in and told you nothing, yet told you nothing so eloquently—the excitement of the yielding of all that fragility! Merely looking down at her he felt that his prick was about to burst.

"You're a vulture standing there," she said. "Does that horrify you?" "Yes," she replied. They were both surprised by what they were doing together when he first struck her backside with his belt. Nikki, who was tyrannized by nearly everyone, displayed no true fear of being whipped a little. "Not too hard," but the leather grazing her, at first lightly, then not so lightly, as she lay obligingly on her stomach, put her into an exalted state. "It's, it's . . ." "Tell me!" "It's tenderness—going wild!" It was impossible to tell who was imposing whose will on whom—was it merely Nikki once again submitting or was this the meat of her desire?

There was a nonsensical side too, of course, and more than once, disengaged from the drama by its comic dimension, Sabbath would leap up on the bed to portray that. "Oh, don't take it to heart," said Nikki, laughing; "other things hurt more than that." "For example?" "Getting up in the morning." "I like your base qualities so much, Nikoleta." "I only wish I had more for you." "You will." Smiling and frowning at once, she said sadly, "I don't think so." "You'll see," said the triumphant puppeteer, standing statuelike above her, erection in one hand and the silky sash to tie her to the bedstead in the other.

It was Nikki who turned out to be right. In time, item after item disappeared from the night table—the belt, the sash, the gag, the blindfold, the baby oil heated a little in a saucepan on the stove; after a while he could enjoy fucking her only when they'd smoked a joint, and then it needn't have been Nikki who was there, or any human thing at all.

Even the orgasms that so enthralled him began to bore him after a while. Climaxes overtook her seemingly from without, breaking upon her like a caprice, a hailstorm freakishly exploding in the middle of an August day. All that had been going on before the orgasm was for her some sort of attack that she did nothing to repel but that, however arduous, she could endlessly absorb and easily survive; yet the frenzy of her climax, the thrashing, the whimpering, the loud groaning, the opaque eyes staring fixedly upward, the fingernails digging into his scalp—that seemed a barely tolerable experience from which she might never recover. Nikki's orgasm was like a convulsion, the body bolting its skin.

Roseanna's, on the other hand, had to be galloped after like the fox in the hunt, with herself in the role of bloodthirsty foxhuntress. Roseanna's orgasm required a great deal of her, an urging onward that was breathtaking to watch (until he grew bored watching *that*). Roseanna had to fight against something resisting her and committed to another cause entirely—orgasm was not a natural development but an oddity so rare that it had to be laboriously hauled into existence. There was a suspenseful, heroic dimension to her achieving a climax. You never knew until the final moment whether or not she was going to make it or whether you yourself could stand fast without an infarction. He began to wonder if there wasn't an exaggerated and false side to her struggle, as there is when an adult plays checkers with a child and pretends to be stymied by the child's every move. *Something* was wrong, seriously wrong. But then, when you'd about given up hope, she made it, she did it, in at the kill, riding atop him, her entire being compressed in her cunt. He eventually came to feel that he needn't have been there. He could have been one of those antique marionettes with a long wooden dick. He needn't have been there—so he wasn't.

With Drenka, it was like tossing a pebble into a pond. You entered and the rippling uncoiled sinuously from the center point outward until the entire pond was undulating and aquiver with light. Whenever they had to call it quits for the day or the night, it was because Sabbath was not just at the end of his endurance but dangerously beyond it for a fatso over fifty. "Coming is an industry with you," he told her; "you're a factory." "Old-timer," she said—a word he'd taught her—while he struggled to recover his breath, "you know what I want next time you get a hard-on?" "I don't know what month that will be. Tell me now and I'll never remember." "Well, I want you to stick it all the way up." "And then what?" "Then turn me inside out over your cock. Like somebody peels off a glove."

After the first year he began to fear that he might go mad looking for Nikki. And it didn't help any to leave town. Out of New York, he searched for her name in the local telephone directory. She could have changed it, of course, or shortened it, as Greek Americans frequently shortened their names for convenience' sake. The short version of Kantarakis was generally Katris—at one point Nikki had been thinking of taking Katris for a stage name, or that was the reason she gave, perhaps not even herself understanding that a new name was not going to lessen in any way her loathing for the father who had made a decent life impossible for her mother.

One winter day Sabbath was flying back from a performance at a puppet festival in Atlanta when the weather in New York became stormy and his plane was diverted to Baltimore. In the waiting room he went to a phone booth and looked up Kantarakis *and* Katris. There it was: N. Katris. He dialed the number but got no answer, and so he ran out of the airport and had a taxi take him to the address. The house was a brown wooden bungalow, not much more than a large shack, on a street of little wooden bungalows. A BEWARE DOG sign was stuck into the ground in the middle of the untended front yard. He climbed the broken steps and knocked on the door. He wandered all around the house trying to look in the windows, even going so far as to climb almost to the top of the six-foot-high wire-mesh fence surrounding the front yard. One of the neighbors must have called the police, because two officers drove up and arrested Sabbath. Only at the station house, when he was able to phone Linc and tell him what had happened and get him to explain to the police that Mr. Sabbath had indeed had a wife who had disappeared a year ago, were the charges dropped. Outside the station, despite the police's warning him against going back and prowling, he hailed another taxi to return him to the shack belonging to N. Katris. It was evening now but there were no lights on. This time in response to his knock he got the barking of what sounded like a very large dog. Sabbath shouted, "Nikki, it's me. It's Mickey. Nikki, you are in there! I know you are in there! Nikki, Nikki, please open the door!" The only answer came from the dog. Nikki would not open the door, because she never wanted to see the son of a bitch again or because she was not there, because she was dead, because she had killed herself or been raped and murdered and cut into pieces and thrown overboard in a weighted sack a couple of miles out to sea from Sheepshead Bay.

To escape the increasing wrath of the dog he ran to the next bungalow and knocked on that door. A black woman's voice called from within, "Who is that?" "I'm looking for your neighbor—Nikki!" "For what?" "I'm looking for my wife, Nikki Katris." "Nope" was all he got back from her. "Next door. Number 583, your neighbor, N. Katris. Please, I have to find my wife. She disappeared!" The door was opened by an alarmingly thin and wrinkled elderly black woman, holding herself upright with a cane and wearing dark glasses. She spoke with tender amusement. "You beat her, now you want her back to beat again." "I did not beat her." "How come she disappear? You beat a woman, she got half a brain, she run away." "Please, who lives next door? Answer me!" "Your wife, she got herself a new boyfriend by now. And know what? *He* gonna beat her. Some women is like that." With this observation she shut the door.

He got a flight to New York later that evening. It had taken that blind old black woman to get him to understand that he had been jilted, discarded, abandoned! She had spurned him, left a year ago with somebody else and he was still out looking for her and grieving for her and wondering where she was! It wasn't him fucking Roseanna that had caused her to flee! It was Nikki fucking somebody new!

At home he began to fall apart for the first time since she had disappeared, and, up with the Gelmans in Bronxville, he had cried in his room every night for two weeks. Roseanna was living with him in the apartment now, making her ceramic necklaces again and selling them to a shop in the Village so they had some money to survive on. Sabbath's drama company had very nearly dissolved and the audience had deserted him, largely because there was no one in the company—maybe no one her age in New York—with anything like Nikki's magic. Over the months the acting had become worse and worse because of Sabbath's inattention—he would watch a rehearsal and see not a thing. And he rarely went out in the streets with his finger act, because all he did out on the street was begin to look for Nikki. Look at women and follow women. Sometimes he screwed them. Might as well.

Roseanna had been hysterical when he reached home that night. "Why didn't you phone me! Where were you? Your plane landed without you! What was I to think? What do you *think* I thought?"

In the bathroom, Sabbath got down on his knees on the tile floor and said to himself, "You can't do this anymore or you *will* go crazy. Roseanna will go crazy. You will be insane for the rest of your life. I cannot cry about it ever again. Oh, God, just don't let me do this ever again!"

Not for the first time he thought of his mother sitting on

the boardwalk waiting for Morty to come back from the war. She never believed he was dead, either. The one thing you can't think is that they're dead. They have another life. You give yourself all sorts of reasons why they haven't come home. You get into the rumor business. Somebody would swear he had seen Nikki performing under another name in a summer theater in Virginia. The police would report that somebody had spotted a crazy woman who resembled her description on the Canadian border. Only Linc, when they were alone, had the courage to say to him, "Mick, don't you really know she's dead?" And the answer was always the same: "Where is the body?" No, the wound never closes, the wound remains fresh, as it had till the very end for his mother. She had been stopped when Morty was killed, stopped from going forward, and all the logic went out of her life. She wanted life, as all people do, to be logical and linear, as orderly as she made the house and her kitchen and the boys' bureau drawers. She had worked so hard to be in control of a household's destiny. All her life she waited not only for Morty but for the explanation from Morty: why? The question haunted Sabbath. Why? Why? If only someone will explain to us *why*, maybe we could accept it. Why did you die? Where did you go? However much you may have hated me, why don't you come back so we can continue with our linear, logical life like all the other couples who hate each other?

Nikki had had a performance of *Miss Julie* that night, Nikki, who never once failed to show up to work, even reeling with a fever. Sabbath, as usual, was spending the evening with Roseanna and so had not found out what happened until he got home half an hour before Nikki was due back from the theater. That was what was wonderful about having an actress for a wife—at night you always knew her whereabouts and how long she would be gone. At first he thought that maybe she had gone out looking for him; maybe because she had her suspicions, she had taken a circuitous route to the theater and come upon Sabbath crossing the park with his hand on Roseanna's ass. She might well have seen them going through the front door of the brownstone where he had his tiny work-shop room at the rear of the top floor. Nikki was explosive, crazily emotional, and could do and say bizarre things and not even remember them afterward, or remember but fail to see why they were bizarre.

Sabbath had been complaining to Roseanna that night about his wife's incapacity to separate fantasy from reality or to understand the connection between cause and effect. Early on in life either she or her mother, or both conspiring together, had cast little Nikki as the blameless victim, and consequently she could never see where she was responsible for anything. Only on the stage did she shed this pathological innocence and take over, herself determining how things were going to come out, and, with exquisite tact, turn something imagined into something real. He told Roseanna the story of her slapping the face of the ambulance driver in London and then talking to her mother's corpse for three days, about how, even down to a few days before her disappearance, Nikki was repeating how glad she was she'd "said good-bye to Momma" as she had, how satisfying that remained. She even made a crack, as she did each time she recalled the three days of fondling the corpse, about how cruel it was of the Jews to "dump" their dead as soon as they could, a remark that Sabbath decided once more not to call her on. Why correct that idiocy rather than all the other idiocies? In *Miss Julie* she was everything she couldn't be outside *Miss Julie*: cunning, knowing, radiant, imperious—everything *but* shrinking from the reality. The reality of the play. It was only the reality of reality by which she was benumbed. Nikki's aversions, her fears, her hysteria—he was full of grievance, yet another spouse absolutely steeped in it, didn't know, he told Roseanna, how much more he could take.

And he and Roseanna fucked and she left and he went to St. Marks Place, and there were Norman and Linc sitting on the steps of his building. Sabbath had hurried home to shower away Rosie's smell before Nikki got in. One night when Nikki believed Sabbath was asleep, she had begun to sniff under the blankets and he realized only then that he had forgotten Rosie's visit at lunchtime and had gone to bed having washed his face and nothing more. And that was just a week earlier.

Norman told him what had happened, while Linc sat there with his head in his hands. Nikki had no understudy and so, even though the house was sold out, as it had been since the opening, the performance had to be canceled, the money refunded, and everybody sent home. And nobody could find Sabbath to tell him. His producers had been waiting on the steps for over an hour. Linc, woefully wracked by all this, pleadingly asked Sabbath if he knew where she was. Sabbath assured him that as soon as she had calmed down and had begun to get over whatever it was that had upset her, she'd call and come back. He wasn't worried. Nikki could behave oddly, very oddly; they didn't *know* how oddly. "This," said Sabbath, "is just one of her strange things."

But upstairs in the apartment his two young producers made Sabbath call the police.

He was in New York less than five minutes when he began to be haunted all over again by "Why?" He had to restrain himself from using the tip of his muddied old boots (muddied from the treks out to the graveyard) to awaken, one by one, those bodies buried under their rags, to see if perhaps a white woman was among them who had once been his wife. Withdrawn, mannerly, intense, tremulous, unearthly, moody, mesmeric Nikki, a difficult personality impossible ever to grasp, whose mark on him was indelible, who could more confidently imitate someone than be someone, who'd clung to her emotional virginity until the day she'd disappeared, whose fears, even without danger or misfortune at hand, were streaming through her all the time, whom he had married out of sheer fascination with her gift, at only twenty-two, for unartificial self-transformation, for duplicating realities she knew virtually nothing about, who unfailingly imparted to everything anyone ever said an inward, idiosyncratic, insulting significance, who was never really at home outside the fairy tale, a juvenile whose theatrical specialty was the most mature roles . . . into whom had she been changed by an existence free of him? What had become of her? And why?

As of April 12, 1994, there was still no certification of her death, and though our need to bury our dead is strong, we have first to be sure the person *is* dead. *Had* she returned to Cleveland? To London? To Salonika to pretend there to be her mother? But she'd had neither a passport nor money. Had she run away from him or from everything, or had she run away from being an actress just when it had become overwhelmingly apparent that she could not avoid an extraordinary career? That had already begun to terrify her, the demands of that kind of success. She would be fifty-seven in May. He never failed to remember her birthday or the date she'd disappeared. What did Nikki look like now? Her mother before the formaldehyde or after? She had already outlived her mother by twelve years—if she had lived beyond November 7, 1964.

What would Morty look like now if he had walked away from his downed plane in 1944? What did Drenka look like now? If they dug her up, could you still tell she'd been a woman, the most womanly of women? Could he have fucked her after she was dead? Why not?

Yes, fleeing for New York that evening he'd believed he was running off to see Linc's corpse, but it was the body of his first wife he could never stop thinking about, *her* body, alive, that he might at last be shepherded to. It did not matter that the idea made no sense. Sabbath's sixty-four years of life had long ago released him from the falsity of sense. You would think this would make him deal better with loss than he did. Which only goes to show what everyone learns sooner or later about loss: the absence of a presence can crush the strongest people.

"But why bring it up?" he snarled at his mother. "Why Nikki, Nikki, Nikki when I'm close to death myself!" And she finally spoke out, his little mother, gave it to him on the corner of Central Park West and West 74th Street as she never dared to in life once he was twelve and already muscular and belligerently grown-up. "That's the thing you know best," she told him, "have thought about most, *and you don't know anything.*"

"STRANGE," Norman said, reflecting on Sabbath's tribulations. Sabbath waited to let sympathy work the man over just a little more before he quietly corrected him. "Extremely," said Sabbath.

"Yes," Norman shot back, "I think it's fair to say extremely."

They were at the kitchen table, a beautiful table, large glazed ivory-colored Italian tiles bordered by bright hand-painted tiles of vegetables and fruit. Michelle, Norman's wife, was asleep in their bedroom, and the two old friends, seated across from each other, were speaking softly of the night when Nikki failed to turn up at the theater and nobody knew where she was. Norman wasn't at all as at ease with Sabbath as he'd been on the phone the night before; the scope of Sabbath's transfiguration seemed to astonish him, in part perhaps because of his own mammoth treasure of satisfied dreams, apparent everywhere Sabbath looked, including into Norman's bright, brown, benevolent eyes. Tanned from a tennis vacation in the sun and as thin and athletically flexible as he'd been as a young man, he showed no sign that Sabbath could see of his recent depression. Since he was already bald by the time he left college, *nothing* about him seemed changed.

Norman was no fool, had read books and traveled widely, but to comprehend, in the flesh, a failure like Sabbath's appeared to be as difficult as coming to terms with Linc's suicide, and maybe more so. Linc's condition he had observed worsening each year, while the Sabbath who had forsaken New York in 1965 had virtually no affinity to the man sighing over a sandwich at the kitchen table in 1994. Sabbath had washed his hands, face, and beard in the bathroom, and still, he realized, he unnerved Norman no less than if he had been a tramp whom Norman had foolishly invited home to spend the night. Perhaps over the years Norman had come to inflate Sabbath's departure to a high artistic drama—a search for independence in the sticks, for spiritual purity and tranquil meditation; if

Norman thought of him at all, he would, as a spontaneously good-hearted person, have tried to remember what he admired about him. And why did that annoy Sabbath? He was irritated not nearly so much by the perfect kitchen and the perfect living room and the perfect everything in all the rooms that opened off the book-lined corridor as by the charity. That he, Sabbath, could inspire such feelings of course entertained him. Of course it was fun to see himself through Norman's eyes. But it was hideous as well.

Norman was asking if Sabbath had ever come close to picking up Nikki's trail after she had disappeared. "I left New York in order to stop trying," Sabbath replied. "It bothered me sometimes to realize that she didn't know where I lived. What if she wanted to find me? But if she did, she'd find Roseanna, too. Once I was up in the mountains I never allowed myself the pleasure of keeping Nikki in my life. I didn't imagine her with a husband and children. I was going to find her, she was going to turn up—I stopped all that. The only way for me to understand it was not to think about it. You have to take this bizarre thing and put it away in order to proceed with your life. What was the point of thinking about it?"

"And is that what the mountain represents? A place not to think about Nikki?"

Norman was trying to ask only intelligent questions, and they *were* intelligent, and they missed entirely the point of Sabbath's descent.

Sabbath went on exchanging sentences with Norman that could as well have been true as not. It was a matter of indifference to him. "My life was changed. I just couldn't go forward with that amount of speed anymore. I couldn't go forward at all. The idea of controlling anything went completely out of my head. The thing with Nikki left me," he said, smiling with what he hoped would be a wan expression, "in a somewhat awkward position."

"I would think."

If I had appeared at the door without having called from the road, if I had got by the doorman unnoticed and taken the elevator to the eighteenth floor and knocked on the Cowans' door, Norman would never have recognized the man in the foyer as me. With the oversize hunting jacket atop the rube's flannel shirt and these big muddy boots on my feet, I look like a visitor from Dogpatch, either like a bearded character in a comic strip or somebody at your doorstep in 1900, a wastrel uncle from the Russian pale who is to sleep in the cellar next to the coal bin for the rest of his American life. Through the lens of unforewarned Norman, Sabbath saw what he looked like, had come to look like, didn't care that he looked like, deliberately looked like—and it pleased him. He'd never lost the simple pleasure, which went way back, of making people uncomfortable, comfortable people especially.

Yet there was something thrilling in seeing Norman. Sabbath felt much as poor parents do when they visit their kids in the suburbs who've made it big—humbled, mystified, out of their element, but proud. He was proud of Norman. Norman had lived in the theatrical shit-world for a lifetime and had not himself become a stupid shit. Could he be so considerate on the job, so goodnatured and decent and thoughtful? They would tear him to pieces. And still to Sabbath it seemed that Norman's humane disposition had only enlarged with age and success. There wasn't enough he could do to make Sabbath feel at home. Maybe it wasn't repulsion at all that he felt but something like awe at the sight of white-bearded Sabbath, come down from his mountaintop like some holy man who has renounced ambition and worldly possessions. Can it be that there *is* something religious about me? Has what I've done—i.e., failed to do—been saintly? I'll have to phone Rosie and tell her.

Whatever lay behind it, Norman couldn't have been more solicitous. But then, he and Linc, sons of prosperous fathers and Jersey City friends since childhood, could not have been kinder from the moment they set up their partnership fresh out of Columbia and paid the expenses arising from Sabbath's obscenity trial. They had extended to Sabbath that respect edged with reverence which was associated in Sabbath's mind less with the way you deal with an entertainer (the most he'd ever been—Nikki was the artist) than with the manner in which you approach an elderly clergyman. There was something exciting for these two privileged Jewish boys in having, as they liked to say then, "discovered Mick Sabbath." It kindled their youthful idealism to learn that Sabbath was the son of a poor butter-and-egg man from a tiny working-class Jersey shore town, that instead of attending college he had shipped out as a merchant seaman at seventeen, that he'd lived two years in Rome on the GI Bill after coming out of the Army, that married only a year he was already on the prowl, that the spookily beautiful young wife whom he bossed around off the stage as well as on—an oddball herself but obviously much better born than he and probably, as an actress, a genius, too—couldn't seem to survive half an hour without him. There was an excitement about the way he affronted people without caring. He was not just a newcomer with a potentially huge theatrical talent but a young adventurer robustly colliding with life, already in his twenties a real-lifer, urged on to excess by a temperament more elemental than either of their own. Back in the fifties there was something thrillingly alien about "Mick."

Sitting safely in the Manhattan kitchen sipping the last of the beer Norman had poured him, Sabbath was by now certain whose head Officer Balich had meant to split open. Either something incriminating had turned up in Drenka's belongings or Sabbath had been observed at the cemetery at night. Wifeless, mistressless, penniless, vocationless, homeless . . . and now, to top things off, on the run. If he weren't too old to go back to sea, if his fingers weren't crippled, if Morty had lived and Nikki hadn't been insane, or he hadn't been—if there weren't war, lunacy, perversity, sickness, imbecility, suicide, and death, chances were he'd be in a lot better shape. He'd paid the full price for art, only he hadn't made any. He'd suffered all the old-fashioned artistic sufferings—isolation, poverty, despair, mental and physical obstruction—and nobody knew or cared. And though nobody knowing or caring was another form of artistic suffering, in his case it had no artistic meaning. He was just someone who had grown ugly, old, and embittered, one of billions.

Obeying the laws of disappointment, disobedient Sabbath began to cry, and not even he could tell whether the crying was an act or the measure of his misery. And then his mother spoke up for the second time that evening—in the kitchen now, and trying to comfort her only living son. "This is human life. There is a great hurt that everyone has to endure."

Sabbath (who liked to think that distrusting the sincerity of

everyone armed him a little against betrayal by everything):
I've even fooled a ghost. But while he thought this—his head
a lumpish, sobbing sandbag on the table—he also thought,
And yet how I crave to cry!

Crave? Please. No, Sabbath didn't believe a word he said
and hadn't for years; the closer he tried to get to describing
how he arrived at becoming this failure rather than another,
the further he seemed from the truth. True lives belonged to
others, or so others believed.

Norman had reached across the table to take one of Sabbath's hands in his.

Good. They'd let him stay for at least a week.

"You," he said to Norman, "you understand what matters."

"Yeah, I'm a master of the art of living. That's why I'm
eight months on Prozac."

"All I know how to do is antagonize."

"Well, that and a few other things."

"A really trivial, really shitty life."

"The beers went to your head. When someone is exhausted
and down like you, everything gets exaggerated. Linc's suicide
has a lot to do with it. We've *all* been through it."

"Repugnant to everyone."

"Come *on*," Norman replied, increasing the firmness of his
hold on Sabbath's hand . . . but when was he going to tell
him, "I think you had better move in with us"? Because Sabbath could not go back. Roseanna wouldn't have him in the
house, and Matthew Balich had found him out and was furious enough to kill him. He had nowhere to go and nothing to
do. Unless Norman said, "Move in," he was finished.

Suddenly Sabbath raised his head from the table and said,
"My mother was in a catatonic depression from the time I was
fifteen."

"You never told me that."

"My brother was killed in the war."

"I didn't know that either."

"We were one of those families with a gold star in the
window. It meant that not only was my brother dead, my
mother was dead. All day at school I thought, 'If only when I
get home, he's there; if only when the war is over, he's there.'
What a frightening thing that gold star was to see when I came

home from school. Some days I'd actually manage to forget about him, but then I'd walk home and see the gold star. Maybe that's why I went to sea, to get the fuck away from the gold star. The gold star said, 'People have suffered something terrible in this house.' The house with the gold star was a blighted house."

"Then you get married and your wife disappears."

"Yes, but that left me all the wiser. I could never again think about the future. What did the future hold for me? I never think in terms of expectations. My expectation is how to deal with bad news."

Trying to talk sensibly and reasonably about his life seemed even more false to him than the tears—every word, every *syllable*, another moth nibbling a hole in the truth.

"And it still throws you to think about Nikki?"

"No," said Sabbath, "not at all. Thirty years later all I think is, 'What the fuck was that?' It becomes more unreal the older I get. Because the things I told myself when I was young— maybe she went here, maybe she went there—those things don't apply any longer. She was struggling always for something only her mother seemed able to give—maybe she's out there looking for it still. That's what I thought then. At this distance, it's just, 'Did all that really happen?'"

"And the ramifications?" Norman asked. He was relieved to see Sabbath back under control but continued nonetheless to hold on to him. And Sabbath allowed him to, however annoying that had become. "Its effect on you. How did it injure you?"

Sabbath took time to think—and this is more or less what he was thinking: These questions are futile to answer. Behind the answer there is another answer, and an answer behind that answer, and on and on. And all Sabbath is doing, to satisfy Norman, is to pretend to be someone who does not understand this.

"I seem injured?"

They laughed together, and Norman only then let go of his hand. Another sentimental Jew. You could fry the sentimental Jews in their own grease. Something was always *moving* them. Sabbath could never really stand either of these morally earnest, supercoddled successes, Cowan *or* Gelman.

"That's like asking how much did it injure me to be born.

How can I know? What can I know about it? I can only tell you that the idea of controlling anything is out of my mind. And that's how I choose to move along in life."

"Pain, pain, so much pain," said Norman. "How can you possibly get over minding it?"

"What difference would it make if I minded? It wouldn't change anything. Do I mind? It never occurs to me to mind. Okay, I got overemotional. But *minding*? What's the point of minding? What was the point of trying to find reason or meaning in any of these things? By the time I was twenty-five I already knew there wasn't any."

"And isn't there any?"

"Ask Linc tomorrow, when they open the coffin. He'll tell you. He was antic and funny and full of energy. I remember Lincoln very well. He didn't want to know anything ugly. He wanted it to be nice. He loved his parents. I remember when his old man came backstage. A carbonated-drink manufacturer. A tycoon in seltzer if I remember correctly."

"No. Quench."

"Quench. That was the stuff."

"Quench Wild Cherry sent Linc to Taft. Linc called it Kvetch."

"A suntanned little endurer with steel-gray hair, the old man. Started out with just the crap he bottled and a truck he drove himself. In his undershirt. Crude. Ungrammatical. Built like something that had been baled. Linc was sitting on a chair in Nikki's dressing room and just took his father and pulled him onto his lap and held him there while we were all talking after the show, and neither of them thought anything of it. He adored his old man. He adored his wife. He adored his kids. At least when I knew him he did."

"He always did."

"So where's the meaning?"

"I have some ideas."

"You don't know anything, Norman—you don't know anything about anyone. Did I know Nikki? Nikki had another life. Everybody has another life. I knew she was eccentric. But so was I. I understood I wasn't living with Doris Day. A little irrational, out of touch, prone to crazy outbursts, but irrational enough and crazy enough for what happened to happen? Did

I know my mother? Sure. She went around whistling all day long. Nothing was too much for her. Look what became of her. Did I know my brother? The discus, the swimming team, the clarinet. Killed at twenty."

"Disappear. Even the word is strange."

"Stranger is the word *reappear*."

"How is Roseanna?"

Sabbath looked at his watch, a round stainless steel watch half a century old this year. Black face, white luminous dial and hands. Morty's Army Benrus, with twelve- and twenty-four-hour numbers and a second hand you could stop by pulling on the crown. For synchronization when you flew a mission. A lot of good the synchronization did Morty. Once a year Sabbath sent the watch to a place in Boston where they cleaned and oiled it and replaced worn-out parts. He had been winding the watch every morning since it became his in 1945. His grandfathers had laid tefillin every morning and thought of God; he wound Morty's watch every morning and thought of Morty. The watch had been returned by the government with Morty's things in 1945. The body came back two years later.

"Well," said Sabbath, "Roseanna . . . Just about seven hours ago, Roseanna and I split up. Now *she's* disappeared. That's what it comes down to, Mort: folks disappearin' left and right."

"Where is she? Do you know?"

"Oh, at home."

"Then it's you who have disappeared."

"Trying," said Sabbath, and again, suddenly, a great onslaught of tears, anguish so engulfing that in the first moment he could no longer even ask himself whether or not this second collapse of the evening was any more or less honestly manufactured than the first. He was drained of skepticism, cynicism, sarcasm, bitterness, mockery, self-mockery, and such lucidity, coherence, and objectivity as he possessed—had run out of everything that marked him as Sabbath except desperation; of that he had a superabundance. He had called Norman Mort. He was crying now the way anyone cries who has had it. There was passion in his crying—terror, great sadness, and defeat.

Or was there? Despite the arthritis that disfigured his fingers, in his heart he was the puppeteer still, a lover and master of guile, artifice, and the unreal—this he hadn't yet torn out of himself. When that went, he *would* be dead.

"Are you all right, Mick?" Norman had come around the table to place his hands on Sabbath's shoulders. "*Did* you leave your wife?"

Sabbath reached up to cover Norman's hands with his own. "I have amnesia suddenly about the circumstances, but . . . yes, it appears that way. She's no longer enslaved by alcohol or me. Both demons driven out by AA. What it probably comes down to is she wants to keep the paycheck for herself."

"She was supporting you."

"I had to live."

"Where will you go after the funeral?"

He looked at Norman, smiling broadly. "Why not with Linc?"

"What are you telling me? You're going to kill yourself? I want to know if that's what you're thinking. Are you thinking about suicide?"

"No, no, I'll go on to the end."

"Is that the truth?"

"I'm inclined to think so. I'm a suicide like I'm everything: a pseudosuicide."

"Look, this is serious business," Norman told him. "We're now in this together."

"Norman, I haven't seen you in a hundred years. We're not in anything together."

"We are in *this* together! If you're going to kill yourself, you're going to do it in front of me. When you're ready you have to wait for me to get there and then do it in front of me."

Sabbath did not reply.

"You have to see a doctor," Norman told him. "You have to see a doctor tomorrow. Do you need money?"

From his wallet, full of illegible notes and telephone numbers scribbled on paper scraps and matchbook covers—fat with everything but credit cards and cash—Sabbath fished out a blank check for his and Roseanna's account. He made it out for three hundred dollars. When he realized that Norman, watching him write, saw printed on the check the names of husband and wife both, Sabbath explained, "I'm cleaning it out. If she's beaten me to it and it bounces, I'll send you back the cash."

"Forget that. Where's three hundred dollars going to get you? You're in a bad way, boy."

"I have no expectations."

"You tried that on me. Why don't you sleep here tomorrow night too? Stay as long as you need us. All the children are gone. The baby, Deborah, is away at Brown. The house is empty. You can't rush off after the funeral not knowing where you're going, and feeling the way you do. You have got to see a doctor."

"No," said Sabbath, "no. I can't stay here."

"Then you have to be hospitalized."

And this brought forth Sabbath's third round of tears. He had cried like this only once before in his life, over Nikki's disappearance. And when Morty died he had watched his mother cry worse than this.

Hospitalized. Until that word was spoken he had believed that all this crying could easily be spurious, and so it was a considerable disappointment to discover that it did not seem within his power to switch it off.

While Norman coaxed him up out of the kitchen chair and walked him across the dining room, through the living room, and down the corridor to Deborah's bedroom, then steered him onto the bed, untied the caked laces of his Dogpatch boots and pulled them off his feet, Sabbath shook. If he was not coming apart but only simulating, then this was the greatest performance of his life. Even as his teeth chattered, even as he could feel his jowls tremble beneath his ridiculous beard Sabbath thought, So, something new. And more to come. And perhaps less of it to be chalked up to guile than to the fact that the inner reason for his being—whatever the hell that might be, perhaps guile itself—had ceased to exist.

He managed only three words Norman could fully understand. "Where is everybody?"

"They're here," Norman said, to soothe him. "They're all here."

"No," replied Sabbath once he was alone. "They all escaped."

While Sabbath ran a bath in the girlishly pretty pink and white bathroom just off Deborah's room, he interested himself in the contents, all jumbled together, of the two drawers beneath the sink—the lotions, the ointments, the pills, the powders, the Body Shop jars, the contact lens cleaner, the tampons, the nail polish, the polish remover. . . . Working through the clutter to the bottom of each drawer, he found not a single photograph —let alone a stash—of the kind Drenka had unearthed from among Silvija's things during the next-to-last summer of her life. The one item at all beguiling, aside from the tampons, was a tube of vaginal lubricating cream twisted back on itself and nearly empty. He removed the cap to squeeze a speck of the amber grease into the palm of his hand and rubbed it between his thumb and his middle finger, remembering things as he smeared the stuff over his fingertips, all sorts of things about Drenka. He screwed the cap back on and set the tube out on the tiled counter for experimentation later.

After undressing in Deborah's room, he had looked at all the photographs in their transparent plastic frames on her bureau and desk. He would get to the drawers and closets in time. She was a dark-haired girl with a demure, pleasing smile, an intelligent smile. He couldn't tell much else because her figure was hidden from view by the other young people in the pictures; yet of all the faces hers alone had about it at least a touch of the enigmatic. Despite the juvenile innocence she so abundantly offered the camera, she looked to have something of a mind, even some wit, and lips whose protuberance was her greatest treasure, a hungry, seductive mouth set in the most undepraved face you could imagine. Or that's how Sabbath read it at close to two A.M. He had been hoping for a girl more tantalizing, but the mouth and the youth would have to do. Before getting into the bath, he trundled in the nude back to her bedroom and took from the desk the largest picture of her he could find, a photograph in which Deborah was nestled up against the muscular shoulder of a burly redhead of about her age. He was beside her in virtually every photograph. The deadly boyfriend.

All Sabbath did for the moment was lie in the wonderful warm bath in the pink-and-white-tiled bathroom and scrutinize the picture, as though in his gaze lay the power to transport

Deborah home to her tub. Reaching out with one arm, Sabbath was able to raise the lid to expose the seat of Deborah's
pink toilet. He rubbed his hand round and round the satiny
seat and was just beginning to harden when there was a light
rap on the bathroom door. "You all right in there?" Norman
asked and pushed the door open a ways to be sure Sabbath
wasn't drowning himself.

"Fine," said Sabbath. It had taken no time to retract his
hand from the toilet seat, but the photograph was in the other
hand and the twisted tube of vaginal cream was up on the
counter. He held out the picture so that Norman could see
which one it was. "Deborah," Sabbath said.

"Yes. That is Deborah."

"Sweet," said Sabbath.

"Why do you have the photograph in the bathtub?"

"To look at it."

The silence was indecipherable—what it meant or foretold
Sabbath could not imagine. All he knew for sure was that Norman was more frightened of him than he was of Norman.
Being nude also seemed to bestow an advantage with a conscience as developed as Norman's, the advantage of seeming
defenselessness. Sabbath's talent for this sort of scene Norman
could not hope to equal: the talent of a ruined man for recklessness, of a saboteur for subversion, even the talent of a lunatic
—or a simulated lunatic—to overawe and horrify ordinary
people. Sabbath had the power, and he knew it, of being no
one with anything much to lose.

Norman hadn't seemed to notice the vaginal cream tube.

Which of us is lonelier at this moment, Sabbath wondered.
And what is he thinking? "Enter our terrorist. *I* should drown
him." But Norman needed admiration in the ways that Sabbath never had, and more than likely he wouldn't do it.

"It would be a shame," Norman finally said, "if it got wet."

Sabbath didn't believe he had an erection, but an ambiguity
in Norman's words caused him to wonder. He didn't look to
see but instead asked a perfectly innocent question. "Who's
the lucky boy?"

"Freshman-year sweetheart. Robert." Norman spoke with
his hand extended toward the photograph. "Only recently replaced by Will." Sabbath leaned forward in the tub and

handed the photograph over, noting, alas, as he moved, his dick angled upward in the water.

"You're feeling like yourself again," Norman said, staring Sabbath in the eyes.

"I am, thank you. Much better."

"It's never been easy to say what you really are, Mickey."

"Oh, failure will do."

"But at what?"

"Failure at failing, for one."

"You always fought being a human being, right from the beginning."

"To the contrary," said Sabbath. "To being a human being I've always said, 'Let it come.'"

Here Norman picked up the vaginal cream from the tile counter, opened the bottom drawer beneath the sink, and tossed in the tube. He seemed to have surprised himself more than Sabbath by the force with which he slammed the drawer shut.

"I've left a glass of milk on the nightstand," Norman said. "You may need it. Warm milk sometimes helps sedate me."

"Great," Sabbath said. "Good night. Sleep tight."

As Norman was about to leave, he took a look over at the toilet. He would never guess why the cover was up. And yet the final glance he turned on Sabbath suggested otherwise.

After Norman's departure, Sabbath lifted himself out of the tub and, dripping water as he moved, went to get the photograph from where Norman had returned it to Deborah's desk.

In the bathroom again, Sabbath opened the drawer, withdrew the vaginal cream, and held the tube to his lips. He squirted a pea-size gob on his tongue and rolled it across his palate and up against his teeth. A vaguely Vaseline-like aftertaste. That was all. But then, what was he hoping for? The tang of Deborah herself?

Back in the tub with the photograph, he resumed at the point where he had been interrupted.

Up not once to use the john. First time in years. The father's milk pacifying the prostate, or was it the daughter's bed? First he'd removed the fresh pillowcase and, scavenging with his nose, hunted down the odor of her hair clinging to the pillow itself. Then, by a process of trial and error, he'd detected a barely perceptible furrow just to the right of the mattress's vertical midpoint, a minuscule groove cast by the mold of her body, and between her sheets, on her caseless pillow, in that groove, he had *slept*. In this Laura Ashley'd room of pink and yellow, a computer comatose on the desk, a Dalton School decal decorating the mirror, teddy bears tumbled together in a wicker basket, Metropolitan Museum posters up on the walls, K. Chopin, T. Morrison, A. Tan, V. Woolf in the bookcase, along with childhood favorites—*The Yearling*, Andersen's *Fairy Tales*—and on the desk and the dresser framed photos in abundance of the gang, wearing swimsuits, skiing gear, formal attire . . . in this candy-striped room with the flowery border, where she'd first fallen upon her clitoral entitlements, Sabbath was himself seventeen again, aboard a tramp steamer full of drunken Norwegians docking at one of the great Brazilian ports—Bahia, at the entrance of Todos os Santos Bay, the Amazon, the great Amazon, unwinding not far away. There was that smell. Unbelievable. Cheap perfume, coffee, and pussy. His head wrapped round with Deborah's pillow, a full body press on her groove, he was remembering Bahia, where there was a church and a whorehouse for every day of the year. So said the Norwegian seamen, and at seventeen he had no reason not to believe them. Be nice to go back and check it out. If she were mine, I'd send Deborah there for her junior year. Free play for the imagination in Bahia. With the American sailors alone she'd have the time of her life—Hispanic, black, even Finns, Finnish Americans, every type of redneck, old men, young boys. . . . Learn more about creative writing in one month in Bahia than in four years at Brown. Let her do something unreasonable, Norman. Look what it did for me.

Whores. Played a leading role in my life. Always felt at home with whores. Particularly fond of whores. The stewlike stink of those oniony parts. What has ever meant more to me? Real reasons for existence then. But now, preposterously, the morning hard-on was gone. The things one has to put up with in life. The morning hard-on—like a crowbar in your hand, like something growing out of an ogre. Does any other species wake up with a hard-on? Do whales? Do bats? Evolution's daily reminder to male *Homo sapiens* in case, overnight, they forget why they're here. If a woman didn't know what it was, it might well scare her to death. Couldn't piss in the bowl because of that thing. Had to force it downward with your hand—had to train it as you would a dog to the leash—so that the stream struck the water and not the upturned seat. When you sat to shit, there it was, loyally looking up at its master. There eagerly waiting while you brush your teeth—"What are we going to do today?" Nothing more faithful in all of life than the lurid cravings of the morning hard-on. No deceit in it. No simulation. No insincerity. All hail to that driving force! Human living with a capital *L*! It takes a lifetime to determine what matters, and by then it's not there anymore. Well, one must learn to adapt. How is the only problem.

He tried to think of a reason to get up, let alone to go on living. Deborah's toilet seat? A glimpse of Linc's corpse? Her *things*—and remembering delving into *the things*, he was out of the bed and across to the dresser beside the Bang & Olufsen music system.

Brimming! A treasure trove! Brilliant hues of silk and satin. Childish cotton underpants with red circus stripes. String bikinis with satin behinds. Stretch satin thong bikinis. Floss your teeth with those thongs. Garter belts in purple, black, and white. Renoir's palette! Rose. Pale pink. Navy. White. Purple. Gold. Red. Peach. Underwired black embroidered bras. Lace push-up bras with little bows. Scalloped lace half-bras. Satin half-bras. C cup. A vipers' nest of multicolored pantyhose. In white, black, and a chocolatey brown, sheer silk-lace *panty* pantyhose of the kind that Drenka wore to drive him nuts. A delicious butterscotch-color silk camisole. Leopard-print panties with matching bra. Lace body stockings, *three*, and all black. A strapless black satin bodysuit with padded push-up cups, edged with lace and hooks and straps. Straps. Bra straps, garter straps, Victorian corset straps. Who in his right mind doesn't adore straps, all the abracadabra of holding and lifting? And what about strap*less*? A strapless bra. Christ, everything works. That thing they call a teddy (Roosevelt? Kennedy? Herzl?), all in one a chemise up top and, down below, loose-fitting panties with leg holes that you slip right into without removing a thing. Silk floral bikini underpants. Half-slips. Loved the outmoded half-slip. A woman in a half-slip and a

bra standing and ironing a shirt while seriously smoking a cigarette. Sentimental old Sabbath.

He sniffed the pantyhose to find a pair that hadn't been
washed, then headed with it for the bathroom. Sat to piss the
way D. did. D.'s seat. D.'s pantyhose. But the morning hard-
on was of the past. . . . Drenka! It *was* a crowbar with you!
Fifty-two years old, a source of life to a hundred men, and
dead! It isn't fair! The urge, the urge! You've seen it over and
over again, done it over and over again, and five minutes later
it fascinates you *again*. What every man knows: the urge to indulge *again*. I should never have given it up, thought Sabbath
—the life of the sensual port like Bahia, even of the shitty little
ports around the Amazon, literally jungle ports, where one
could mix with the crews of all kinds of ships, sailors of as
many colors as Debby's underthings, from all kinds of countries, and they were all going to the same place, all ended up in
the whorehouse. Everywhere, as in a lurid dream, sailors and
women, women and sailors, and I was learning my trade. The
eight-to-twelve watch and then working all day as a seaman on
deck, chipping and painting, chipping and painting, and then
the watch, the sea watch in the bow of the ship. And sometimes it was gorgeous. I had been reading O'Neill. I was reading Conrad. A guy on board had given me books. I was
reading all that stuff and jerking myself off over it. Dostoyevsky
—everybody going around with grudges and immense fury,
rage like it was all put to music, rage like it was two hundred
pounds to lose. Rascal Knockoff. I thought: Dostoyevsky fell
in love with him. Yes, I would stand in the bow on those starry
nights in the tropical sea and promise myself that I would stick
at it and go through all the shit and become a ship's officer. I
would urge myself to do all those exams and become a ship's
officer and live like that for the rest of my life. Seventeen, a
strong young kid . . . and like a kid I didn't do it.

Drawing open the curtains, he discovered that Deborah's
was a corner room whose windows looked out across Central
Park to the apartment buildings on the East Side. The daf-
fodils and the leafing of the trees still had three weeks to work
their way to Madamaska Falls, but Central Park could have
been Savannah. The panorama Debby had teethed on, but
he'd still take the shore any day. What had he been doing in a

forest on a mountaintop? When he'd fled Nikki's disappearance, he and Roseanna should have gone to Jersey to live by the sea. Should have become a commercial fisherman. Should have dumped Roseanna and gone *back* to sea. Puppets. Of all the fucking callings. Between puppets and whores, he chooses puppets. For that alone he deserves to die.

Only now did he see the assorted pieces of Deborah's underwear strewn about at the foot of the bureau, as though she had just hurriedly undressed—or been undressed—and run from the room. Pleasant to imagine. He could only guess that he had already been into the underwear during the night —he had no recollection. He must have got up in his sleep to look at her things and spilled some onto the floor. Deep into self-caricature now. I am more of a menace than I realize. This is serious. Premature senility. Senilitia, dementia, hell-bent-for-disaster erotomania.

And what of it? A natural human occurrence. The word's *rejuvenation*. Drenka is dead but Deborah lives and, round the clock at the sex factory, the furnaces are burning away.

As he dressed in what he wore wherever he went, day in and day out—frayed flannel shirt over an old khaki T-shirt, baggy bottom-heavy corduroys—he listened to hear if anyone was home. Only eight-fifteen but already emptied out. He could not at first choose, from what lay on the floor, between a black underwire bra and a pair of silk floral bikini underpants, but thinking that the bra, because of the wiring, might prove bulky and draw attention, he took the panties, shoved them into his trouser pocket, and dropped the rest into the piled-up drawer. He could play there again tonight. And in the other drawers. And in the closet.

He noticed now two sachets in that top drawer, one of mauve velvet that was lavender-scented and one of red gingham giving off the crisp odor of pine needles. Neither was the smell he was looking for. Funny—modern kid, Dalton graduate, already a connoisseur of the Metropolitan's Manets and Cézannes, yet didn't appear to have the slightest understanding that what men pay good money to sniff is not the needles of the pine. Well, Miss Cowan will find out, one way or another, once she starts wearing this underwear to something other than class.

Old salt that he was, he made up her bed square and tight.
Her bed.

Two simple words, each a syllable as old as English, and
their power over Sabbath was nothing short of tyrannical.
How tenaciously he clings to life! To youth! To pleasure! To
hard-ons! To Deborah's underthings! And yet all the while he
had been looking down from the eighteenth floor across the
green tinge of the park and thinking that the time had come to
jump. Mishima. Rothko. Hemingway. Berryman. Koestler.
Pavese. Kosinski. Arshile Gorky. Primo Levi. Hart Crane. Walter
Benjamin. Peerless bunch. Nothing dishonorable signing on
there. Faulkner as good as killed himself with booze. As did
(said Roseanna, authority now on the distinguished dead who
might be alive had they "shared" at AA) Ava Gardner. Blessed
Ava. Wasn't much about men could astonish Ava. Elegance
and filth, immaculately intertwined. Dead at sixty-two, two
years younger than me. Ava, Yvonne De Carlo—*those* are role
models! Fuck the laudable ideologies. Shallow, shallow, shallow! Enough reading and rereading of *A Room of One's Own*—
get yourself *The Collected Works of Ava Gardner*. A tweaking
and fingering lesbian virgin, V. Woolf, erotic life one part
prurience, nine parts fear—an overbred English parody of a
borzoi, effortlessly superior, as only the English can be, to all
her inferiors, who never took her clothes off in her life. But a
suicide, remember. The list grows more inspiring by the year.
I'd be the first puppeteer.

The law of living: fluctuation. For every thought a counter-
thought, for every urge a counterurge. No wonder you either
go crazy and die or decide to disappear. Too many urges, and
that's not even a tenth of the story. Mistressless, wifeless, vocationless, homeless, penniless, he steals the bikini panties of a
nineteen-year-old nothing and, riding a swell of adrenaline,
stuffs them for safekeeping in his pocket—these panties are
just what he needs. Does no one else's brain work in quite this
way? I don't believe that. This is aging, pure and simple, the
self-destroying hilarity of the last roller coaster. Sabbath meets
his match: life. The puppet is *you*. The grotesque buffoon is
you. *You're* Punch, schmuck, the puppet who toys with taboos!

In the large kitchen with the terra-cotta floor, a kitchen
ablaze with sunshine on polished copperware, robust as a

greenhouse with gleaming potted plants, Sabbath found a place set for him at the table, facing the view. Surrounding his dishes and cutlery were boxes of four brands of cereals, three differently shaped, differently shaded loaves of hearty-looking bread, a tub of margarine, a dish of butter, and eight jars of preserves, more or less the band of colors you get by passing sunlight through a prism: Black Cherry, Strawberry, Little Scarlet . . . all the way to Greengage Plum and Lemon Marmalade, a spectral yellow. There was half a honeydew as well as half a grapefruit (segmented) under a taut sheet of Saran Wrap, a small basket of nippled oranges of a suggestive variety he'd not come across before, and an assortment of tea bags in a dish beside his place setting. The breakfast crockery was that heavy yellow French stuff decorated with childlike renderings of peasants and windmills. Quimper. Beyond quimper.

Now why do I alone in America think this is shit? Why didn't *I* want to live like this? To be sure, producers character-istically provide for themselves more like pashas than trans-gressive puppeteers do, but this *is* awfully nice to wake up to. Pocket full of panties and jar upon jar of Tiptree Preserves. Af-fixed to its lid, the Little Scarlet sported a price tag reading "$8.95." What have I achieved that could possibly quimper? It's hard not to be disgusted with yourself when you see a spread like this. There is so much and I have so little of it.

There was the park again, out the kitchen window, and, to the south, the spectacle of metropolitan spectacles, midtown Manhattan. In his absence, while up on a northern mountain Sabbath futzed away the years with puppets and his prick, Norman had grown rich and remained an exemplary person, Linc had gone nuts, and Nikki had, for all he knew, become a bag lady shitting on the floor of a 42nd Street subway station, fifty-seven years old, gaga, obese—"*Why?*" he would cry, "*Why?*" and she wouldn't even know who he was. But then, she could as easily be living in a Manhattan apartment as large and luxurious as Norman's, with a Norman of her own. She could have disappeared for as ordinary a reason as that. . . . It's the shock of seeing New York still here that's reminded me of Nikki. I will not think about it. I cannot. That is the peren-nial time bomb.

Strange. The one thing you never think is that she's dead. That even goes *for* the dead. Me up here in the light and the warmth and, fucked-over as I am, with five senses, a mind, and eight kinds of preserves—and the dead dead. Immediate reality is outside that window; so big it is, so much of it, everything entangled in everything else. . . . What large thought was Sabbath struggling to express? Is he asking, "Whatever did happen to my own true life?" Was it taking place elsewhere? But how then can looking out of this window be so gigantically real? Well, that is the difference between the true and the real. We don't get to live in the truth. That's why Nikki ran away. She was an idealist, an innocent, touching, talented illusionist who wanted to live *in the truth*. Well, if you found it, kid, you're the first. In my experience the direction of life is toward incoherence—precisely what you would never confront. Maybe that was the only coherent thing you could think to do: die to deny incoherence.

"Right, Ma? You had incoherence in spades. The death of Morty still defies belief. You were right to shut up after that."

"You think like a failure," Sabbath's mother replied.

"I am a failure. I was saying that to Norm only last night. I am at the very pinnacle of failure. How else should I think?"

"All you ever wanted were whorehouses and whores. You have the ideology of a pimp. You should have been one."

Ideology, no less. How knowing she had become in the afterlife. They must give courses.

"It's too late, Ma. The black guys have got the market cornered. Try again."

"You should have led a normal and productive life. You should have had a family. You should have had a profession. You shouldn't have run away from life. Puppets!"

"It seemed a good idea at the time, Mother. I even studied in Italy."

"You studied whores in Italy. You deliberately set out to live on the wrong side of existence. You should have had *my* worries."

"But I do. I do . . ." Crying again. "I do. I have your worries exactly."

"Then why do you go around with an *alte kocker*'s beard and wearing your playground clothes—and with whores!"

"Quarrel, if you like, with the clothes and the whores, but the beard is essential if I don't want to look at my face."

"You look like a beast."

"And what should I look like? A Norman?"

"Norman was always a lovely boy."

"And I?"

"You always got your excitement in other ways. Always. Even as a tiny child you were a little stranger in the house."

"Is that true? I didn't know that. I was so happy."

"But always a little stranger, making everything into a farce."

"Everything?"

"You? Of course. Look now. Making death itself into a farce. Is there anything more serious than dying? No. But you want to make it into a farce. Even killing yourself you won't do with dignity."

"That's asking a lot. I don't think anyone who kills himself kills himself 'with dignity.' I don't believe that's possible."

"Then you be the first. Make us proud."

"But *how*, Mother?"

Beside his place setting was a longish note beginning GOOD MORNING. In caps. The note was from Norman, computer-generated.

GOOD MORNING

We're off to work. Linc's service begins at two. Riverside at 76th. See you there—will save seat with us. Cleaning woman (Rosa) comes at nine. If you want her to wash or iron anything, just ask her to. Need anything, ask Rosa. I'm at office all morning (994-6932). I hope sleep restored you some. You're under tremendous stress. I wish you would talk to a psychiatrist while you're here. Mine's no genius but smart enough. Dr. Eugene Graves (surname unfortunate but gets the job done). I phoned him and he said you should call if you want to (562-1186). He has cancellation late this afternoon. Please consider it seriously. He got me out of my summer mess. You could be helped with medication—and by talking to him. You're in bad shape and you need help. ACCEPT IT. Please call Gene. Michelle sends her regards. She'll be at the service. We expect you to have dinner at home with us tonight. Quiet, the three of us. Until you're back on your feet, we expect you to stay. The bed is yours. The place is yours. You and I are old friends. There aren't that many left.

Norman

Paper-clipped to the note there was a plain white envelope. Fifty-dollar bills. Not just the six that would have covered the check from the joint account that Sabbath had made payable to Norman the evening before but four more in addition. Mickey Sabbath had five hundred bucks. Enough to pay Drenka to fuck in a threesome if Drenka . . . Well, she wasn't, and since chances were Norman had no intention of cashing Sabbath's check—probably already had torn it up to ensure Roseanna wouldn't get screwed out of her share of the dough—Sabbath had only to hurry, find one of those check-cashing places that take ten percent for commission, and write out a new check for three hundred on the joint account. That would give him seven seventy altogether. Suddenly he had thirty to fifty percent less reason to die.

"First you make a farce of suicide, now again you make a farce of life."

"I don't know any other way to do it, Mother. Leave me be. Shut up. You don't exist. There are no ghosts."

"Wrong. There are only ghosts."

Sabbath proceeded then to enjoy an enormous breakfast. He hadn't eaten with such pleasure since before Drenka had taken ill. It made him feel magnanimous. Let Roseanna *have* the three hundred. Deborah's furrow was now his furrow. Michelle, Norman, and Dr. Coffin were going to put him back on his feet.

Graves.

After packing himself full as a suitcase so stuffed with clothing you can't zipper it shut, he rollingly strolled around the apartment with his old sailor's gait, inspecting all the rooms, the baths, the library, the sauna; opened all the closets and examined the hats, the coats, the boots, the shoes, the stacks of sheets, the differently colored piles of soft towels; wandered down the hallway lined with mahogany bookcases holding only the world's best books; admired the rugs on the floors, the watercolors on the walls; scrutinized the Cowans' quietly elegant everything—lamps, fixtures, doorknobs, even the toilet bowl cleaners appeared to have been designed by Brancusi—all the while devouring the hard heel of the seeded pumpernickel plastered thick with Little Scarlet at $8.95 a jar and pretending that the place was his.

If only things had been different, everything would be otherwise.

His fingers still sticky with the sweet jam, Sabbath ended up back in Deborah's room sifting through the drawers of her desk. Even Silvija had them. They all had them. Just a matter of finding where they stash them away. Not even Yahweh, Jesus, and Allah have been able to stamp out the fun you can have with a Polaroid. Gloria Steinem herself can't do it. In the contest between Yahweh, Jesus, Allah, and Gloria on the one side and on the other the innermost itch that gives life its tingle, I'll give you the three boys and Gloria and eighteen points.

Now where have you hidden them, Deborah? Am I hot or am I cold? The desk was a big oak antique with polished brass handles, originating probably in the office of some nineteenth-century lawyer. Unusual. Most kids like the plastic crap. Or is this what's called camp? He began removing the contents of the long top drawer. Two large leatherbound scrapbooks with dried leaves and flowers pressed between each pair of pages. Botanically beguiling, delicately done . . . but you ain't foolin' anyone. Scissors. Paper clips. Glue. Ruler. Smallish address books with floral-design covers and no addresses as yet entered in. Two gray boxes about five by six inches. Eureka! But within, only her personalized stationery, mauve like the lavender sachet. In one box, some handwritten sheets folded in two that looked promising momentarily but were only the drafts of a poem on love unrequited. "I opened my arms but no one saw . . . I opened my mouth and no one heard. . . ." You have not been reading your Ava Gardner, dear. Next drawer, please. Dalton yearbooks from 1989 to 1992. More teddy bears. Six here plus eight in the wicker basket. Camouflage. Clever. Next. Diaries! The jackpot! A stack of them, bound in cardboard with colorful flowery designs very like those on the underpants in his pocket. He took them out to quimper. Yep, matching underpants, diaries, and address books. The kid's got everything. Except. Except! Where are the pictures hidden, Debby? "Dear Di, I find myself becoming more and more drawn to him, trying to work out my feelings. Why, why are relationships so *hard*?" Why not write about fucking him? Hasn't anybody at Brown taught you what writing is for? Page after page of crap quite unworthy of her until he came upon an entry beginning as the others did—"Dear Di"—but divided by a ruled pen stroke into two columns, one labeled MY STRENGTHS and the other MY WEAKNESSES. Something here? He'd take anything by now.

MY STRENGTHS	MY WEAKNESSES
Self-discipline	Low self-esteem
My backhand	My serve
Hopefulness	Infatuations
Amy	Mother
Sarah L.	~~Low self-esteem~~
Robert (?)	Robert!!!!
Nonsmoker	Too emotional
Nondrinker	Impatience with Mom
	Thoughtlessness with Mom
	My legs
	Butting in
	Not always listening
	Eating

Whew, this is work. A thin three-ring notebook with a college decal on the front and beneath it a white label on which was typed "Yeats, Eliot, Pound. Tues. Thurs. 10:30. Solomon 002. Prof. Kransdorf." In the notebook were her class notes, along with photocopies of poems that Kransdorf must have distributed to the class. The very first was by Yeats. Called "Meru." Sabbath slowly read it . . . the first poem he'd read by Yeats—and one of the last he'd read by anyone—since leading the life of a seaman.

> Civilisation is hooped together, brought
> Under a rule, under the semblance of peace
> By manifold illusion; but man's life is thought,
> And he, despite his terror, cannot cease
> Ravening through century after century,
> Ravening, raging, and uprooting that he may come
> Into the desolation of reality:
> Egypt and Greece good-bye, and good-bye, Rome!
> Hermits upon Mount Meru or Everest,
> Caverned in night under the drifted snow,

Or where that snow and winter's dreadful blast
Beat down upon their naked bodies, know
That day brings round the night, that before dawn
His glory and his monuments are gone.
1934

Debby's notes were written on the sheet, directly below the
poem's date of composition.

Meru. Mountain in Tibet. In 1934, WBY (Irish poet) wrote introduction to Hindu friend's translation of a holy man's ascent into renouncing the world.

K: "Yeats was at the verge beyond which all art is vain."

The theme of the poem is that man is never satisfied unless he destroys all that he has created, e.g. the civilizations of Egypt and Rome.

K: "The poem's emphasis is on man's obligation to strip away all illusion in spite of the terror of nothingness with which he will be left."

Yeats comments in a letter to a friend: "We free ourselves from obsession that we may be nothing. The last kiss is given to the void."

man=human

Class criticized poem for its lack of a woman's perspective. Note unconscious gender privileging—*his* terror, *his* glory, *his* (phallic) monuments.

He ransacked the remaining drawers. Letters to Deborah
Cowan dating back to grade school. Perfect place to hide Polaroids. Patiently he went through the envelopes. Nothing. A
handful of acorns. Postcards, blank on one side, reproductions
on the other. The Prado, the National Gallery, the Uffizi . . .
Box of staples, which he opened, curious to see if this nineteen-year-old girl who pretended to love flowers and teddy
bears best of all might be using the staple box to secrete half a
dozen joints. But only staples were secreted in the staple box.
What's wrong with this kid?

Bottom drawer. Two ornamentally carved wooden boxes.
Nope. Nothing. Doodads. Tiny beaded bracelets and necklaces.

Braided hairpieces. Headbands. A hair clip with a black velvet bow. Smelling of nobody's hair. Smelling of lavender. This child is perverted, but the wrong way.

The closets packed. Pleated skirts with floral prints. Loose silk pants. Black velvet jackets. Jogging suits. Tons of paisley kerchiefs on the overhead shelf. Big baggy things that looked like maternity dresses. Short linen dresses. (With her legs?) Size 10. What size was Drenka? He could no longer remember! Loads of pants. Corduroy. Blue jeans galore. Now why does she leave at home all her underwear and all her clothes, jeans included, when she goes to school? Does she have even more stuff there—are they that ostentatiously rich?—or is this what privileged girls do, leave it all behind rather the way certain animals, to mark their terrain, leave behind them a trail of pee?

He went through the pockets of all the jackets and all the pants. He searched among the heaps of kerchiefs. By now he was getting good and angry. Where the fuck are they, Deborah?

The drawers. Calm down. There are still three drawers to go. Since he'd been in the top, the underwear drawer, more than once already, and since he was beginning to feel the pressure of time—his plan was to get downtown before the funeral to visit the site of his first and only theater—he skipped to the second drawer. It was hard to pull the drawer open, so stuffed was it with T-shirts, sweatshirts, baseball caps, and socks of every variety, some with slots of different colors for each of the toes. How cute. He plunged right through to the bottom. Nothing. He worked his hands in among the T-shirts. Nothing. He pulled open the drawer below. Bathing suits, all kinds, a delight to touch, but he'd have to examine them more exhaustively later. Also cotton flannel pajamas with nice things like hearts printed all over them, and nightgowns with ruffled hems and lace trim. Pink and white. Back to them, too. Time, time, *time* . . . and there were not only T-shirts on the carpet by the dresser but skirts and pants on the floor in the closet, kerchiefs all the way over on the bed, the desk a mess, drawers all open and her diaries scattered across the top. Everything to be put back with fingers that were now killing him.

The bottom drawer. Last chance. Camping equipment.

Vuarnet sunglasses, three pairs without cases. She had three, six, ten of everything. Except! Except! And there it was.

There it was. The gold. His gold. At the bottom of the bottom drawer, where he should have begun in the first place, in among a jumble of old schoolbooks and more teddy bears, a simple Scotties box, design of white, lilac, and pale green flowers on a lemony-white background. "Each box of Scotties offers the softness and strength you want for your family. . . ." You're no fool, D. Handwritten label on the box read, "Recipes." You cunning girl. I love you. Recipes. I'll give you teddy bears up the gazoo!

Inside the Scotties box were her recipes—"Deborah's Sponge Cake," "Deborah's Brownies," "Deborah's Chocolate Chip Cookies," "Deborah's Divine Lemon Cake"—neatly written in blue ink in her hand. A fountain pen. The last kid in America to write with a fountain pen. You won't last five minutes in Bahia.

A short, very stout woman was standing in the doorway of Deborah's bedroom screaming. Only her mouth was she able to move; the rest of her appeared to be paralyzed with the terror. She was wearing tan stretch pants stretched to their limit and a gray sweatshirt bearing the name and logo of Deborah's university. In a large, broad face excavated by irregular patches of pockmarks, only her lips were prominent, elongated and sharply etched, the lips of the indigenous, as Sabbath knew, south of the border down Mexico way. The eyes were the eyes of Yvonne De Carlo. Nearly everybody has at least one good feature, and in mammals it's usually the eyes. His own were thought by Nikki to be his arresting feature. She made much of them back when he weighed seventy pounds less. Green like Merlin's, Nikki said back when it was all still play, when she was Nikita and he was *agápe mou, Mihalákimou, Mihalió*.

"Don't shoot. No shoot me. Four childs. One here." She pointed to her belly, a belly as pierceable as a small balloon. "No shoot. Money. I find money. No money here. I show money. No shoot me, Mister. Cleaning woman."

"I don't want to shoot you," said he, from where he was seated on the carpet, the recipes in his lap. "Don't scream. Don't cry. It's okay."

Gesturing jerkily, hysterically—toward him, toward herself
—she told him, "I show money. You take. I stay. You go. No
police. All money you." She motioned now for him to follow
her out of Deborah's defiled room and down the book-lined
corridor. In the master bedroom, the big bed was as yet un-
made, books and nightclothes flung to either side of it, books
strewn about the bed like alphabet blocks in a baby's play-
room. He stopped to examine the book jackets. How does the
educated rich Jew put himself to sleep these days? Still Eldridge Cleaver? *John Kennedy: Profile of Power. Having Our
Say: The Delany Sisters' First One Hundred Years. The Warburgs* . . .

Why *don't* I live like this? The bedsheets weren't worn and
antiseptic white like those that he and Roseanna slept at either
edge of but glowed warmly, a pale golden pattern that reminded him of the radiant glory of the October day up at the
Grotto when Drenka had run roughshod over her own record
and come thirteen times. "More," she begged, "more," but in
the end he fell back with a terrible headache and told her he
couldn't continue risking his life. He seated himself heavily on
his haunches, pale, perspiring, breathless, while on her own
Drenka took over the quest. This was like nothing he had ever
seen before. He thought, It's as though she is wrestling with
Destiny, or God, or Death; it's as though, if only she can break
through to yet one more, nothing and no one will stop her
again. She looked to be in some transitional state between
woman and goddess—he had the queer feeling of watching
someone leaving this world. She was about to ascend, to ascend and ascend, trembling eternally in the ultimate, delirious
thrill, but instead something stopped her and a year later she
died.

Why does one woman love you madly when she swallows it
and another hate your guts if you suggest she even try it? Why
is the woman who swallows it with rapacity the dead mistress,
while the one who holds you to the side, so you squirt your
heart out into the air, is the living wife? Is this luck only mine,
or is it everyone's? Was it Kennedy's? The Warburgs'? The Delany sisters'? In my forty-seven-year experiment with women,
which I hereby declare officially concluded . . . And yet the
colossal balloon that was Rosa's behind piqued his curiosity no

less than the pregnant belly did. When she bent to open one of the master bedroom's bureau drawers he remembered back to his initiation in Havana, the classic old brothel where you go into a salon and the girls are marched in for the clients. The young women came in from wherever they were lounging around, wearing nothing resembling those baggy garments in Deborah's closet but all in skintight dresses. What was amazing was that while he chose Yvonne De Carlo, his friend Ron—he'd never forgotten this—chose a pregnant one. Sabbath couldn't figure out why. Then when he grew more knowledgeable, the opportunity, strangely enough, had never come his way.

Till now.

She thinks I've got a gun. Let's see where this leads us. Last time he had anything like as much fun was watching Matthew split Barrett's skull open instead of his own.

"Here," she pleaded. "Take. Go. No shoot me. Husband. Four childs."

She had opened a drawer stacked about a foot high with lingerie, not the hot stuff that the kid had ordered from some mail-order catalog but smooth, lustrous, and perfectly piled. Collector's items. And Sabbath was a collector, had been all his life. I can't tell a pansy from a marigold, but underwear? If I can't identify it, nobody can.

Rosa gingerly lifted from the drawer a generous helping of nightgowns and laid them lightly at the foot of the bed. The nightgowns had been hiding two nine-by-twelve manila envelopes. She handed him one and he opened it. One hundred hundred-dollar bills, paper-clipped together in wads of ten each.

"Whose is this? This money belongs to—?" He was pointing to the bed, to one side, then the other.

"La señora. Secret money." Rosa was looking down at her belly, her hands—chubby and astonishingly tiny—crossed there like the hands of a child being rebuked.

"Always this much? Siempre diez mil?" Virtually all his whorehouse Spanish was gone, yet he could still remember the numbers, the prices, the levy imposed, the fact that you could go out and buy it like a papaya or pomegranate or a watch or a book, like anything that you wanted enough to part with your hard-earned dough to get it. "Cuánto? Cuántos pesos?" "Para qué cosa?" Et cetera.

Rosa made the gesture to indicate sometimes more, sometimes less. If he could just calm her down long enough to break through to the base instincts . . .

"Where does she get the money?" he asked.

"No comprendo."

"Is this money she earns at work? In italiano, lavoro."

"No comprendo."

Trabajo! God, it was coming back. *Trabajo.* How he'd loved his *trabajo.* Painting, chipping, painting, chipping, and then fucking himself silly on shore. It was just as natural as getting off the ship and going into a bar and having a drink. In no way was it extraordinary. But to me and Ron it was the most extraordinary thing in the world. You got off the ship and you headed straight for the one thing you had never done before. And never would want to stop doing again.

"How does Missus make her living? Qué trabajo?"

"Odontología. Ella es una dentista."

"A dentist? La señora?" He tapped a front tooth with his fingernail.

"Sí."

Men in and out of the office all day long. Gives 'em gas. That nitrous oxide. "The other envelope," he said. "El otro, el otro, por favor."

"No money," she replied flatly. There was opposition in her now. Suddenly she looked a little like General Noriega. "No money. En el otro sobre no hay nada."

"Nothing at all? An empty envelope hidden under fifteen nightgowns at the bottom of her bottom drawer? Gimme a break, Rosa."

The woman was astonished when he concluded with "Rosa," but she appeared not to know whether to be more frightened of him or less. Spoken inadvertently enough, her name turned out to be just the thing to resuscitate her uncertainty as to what kind of madman she was dealing with.

"Absolutamente nada," she said bravely. "Está vacío, señor! Umpty!" Here she gave way and began to cry.

"I'm not going to shoot you. I told you that. You know

that. What are you afraid of? No peligro." What the whores used to tell him when he inquired about their health.

"Is umpty!" declared Rosa, sobbing like a child into the crook of her arm. "Es verdad!"

He didn't know whether to follow his inclination and put a hand out to comfort her or to appear more ruthless by reaching for the pocket where she thought the pistol was. The main thing was to keep her from screaming again and running for help. His remaining so calm while in a state of tremendous excitement he could not account for—he might not look it, he might never have looked it, but he was really a high-strung fellow. Delicate feelings. To be callous quite like this was not in his nature (except with a perpetual drunk). Sabbath did not care to make people suffer beyond the point that he wanted them to suffer; he certainly didn't want to make them suffer any more than made him happy. Nor was he ever dishonest more than was pleasant. In this regard, at least, he was much like others.

Or was Rosa having him on? He'd bet Rosa was a lot less high-strung than he was. Four childs. Cleaning woman. No English. Never enough money. On her knees, crossing herself, praying—all an act to prove what? Why drag in Jesus, who has his own troubles? A nail through either palm you sympathize with when you suffer osteoarthritis in both hands. He had roared with laughter recently (first time since Drenka's death) when Gus told him over the gas pump that his brother-in-law and sister had been in Japan at Christmas, and when they went to shop at the biggest department store in some big city there, first thing they saw up above the entrance was a gigantic Santa Claus hanging from a cross. "Japs don't get it," Gus said. Why should they? Who does? But in Madamaska Falls Sabbath kept his retort to himself. He had got into difficulty enough explaining to one of Roseanna's fellow teachers that he could take no interest in her specialty, Native American literature, because Native Americans ate *treyf*. She had to consult a Jewish American friend to find out what that meant, but when she did she let him have it. He hated them all, except Gus.

He watched Rosa *dovening*. *That's* what was bringing out the Jew in him: a Catholic down on the floor. Always did. *You*

finished? Get off! Whores can fool you. Cleaning women can
fool you. *Anybody* can fool you. Your *mother* can fool you. Oh,
Sabbath so wanted to live! He thrived on this stuff. Why die?
Had his father gone off at dawn to peddle butter and eggs so
that *both* boys should die before their time? Had his impoverished grandparents crossed from Europe in steerage so that a
grandson of theirs who had escaped the Jewish miseries should
throw away a single fun-filled moment of American life? Why
die when these envelopes are hidden away by women beneath
their Bergdorf lingerie? There alone was a reason to live to a
hundred.

He still had the ten thousand bucks in his hands. Why is
Michelle Cowan hiding this money? Whose is it? How did she
earn it? With the money he'd had to pay Drenka that first time
with Christa, she bought the power tools for Matthew; with
the hundreds that Lewis, the credit-card magnate, slipped into
her purse, she bought *tchotchkes* for the house—ornamental
plates, carved napkin rings, antique silver candelabra. To Barrett, the electrician, she *gave* money, liked to stuff a twenty
down into his jeans as he was pinching her nipples in their last
embrace. He hoped Barrett had saved that money. He might
not be fixing shorts for a while.

Norman's first wife had been Betty, the high school sweetheart, whom Sabbath no longer remembered. What Michelle
looked like he now discovered from the contents of the second
envelope. He had once again directed Rosa to take it from the
drawer, and hurriedly she obliged when he began to edge his
hand toward the pocket in which there was no gun.

He'd been looking for pictures in the wrong room. Virtual
replicas of his pictures of Drenka someone had taken of
Michelle. Norman? After thirty years and three kids, unlikely.
Besides, if Norman had taken them, why hide them? From
Deborah? Best thing for Deborah would be to give her a good
look at them.

Michelle was an extremely slender woman—narrow shoulders, fleshless arms, and straight, polelike legs. Rather longish
legs, like Nikki's, like Roseanna's, like the legs that, before
Drenka, he used to like best to climb. The breasts were a pleasant surprise in one so thin—weighty, sizable, crowned with
nipples that came out indigo on the Polaroid film. Maybe

she'd painted them. Maybe the photographer painted them.
She wore her black hair tautly pulled back. A flamenco dancer.
She's read her Ava Gardner. She in fact did resemble the white
Cuban women about whom Sabbath used to say to Ron,
"They look Jewish but without the *ish*." Nose job? Hard to
tell. The nose was not the focus of the inquiring photographer's curiosity. The picture Sabbath liked best was the least
anatomically detailed. In it Michelle was wearing nothing but
soft brown kid boots widely cuffed at her upper thigh. Elegance and filth, his bread and butter. The other pictures were
more or less standard issue, nothing mankind hadn't known
since Vesuvius had preserved Pompeii.

The edge of a chair on which she was seated in one picture,
the stretch of carpet across which she lay in another, the
window curtains to which she made love in a third . . . he
could smell the Lysol even from here. But as he knew from
watching Drenka at the Bo-Peep, the sleazy motel was a kick,
too, a kick similar to taking the lover's money as though he
were just a john.

After inserting the photographs back into the envelope, he
helped Rosa up off the floor and handed her the envelope to
return to the drawer. He did the same with the money, counting off the ten paper-clipped piles of bills to show her that he
hadn't slipped one up his sleeve. He then lifted the nightgowns off the bed and, after holding them in his hands a
minute—and shockingly, to his surprise, failing to discover in
the feel of them sufficient reason to continue living—indicated
that she should put them back atop the envelopes and shut the
drawer.

So that's it. That's all. "Terminado," as the whores who
pushed you off them would succinctly put it the split second
after you'd come.

He surveyed the whole room now. All so innocent, this luxe
I disparaged. Yes, a failure in every department. A handful of
fairy-tale years, and the rest a total loss. He'd hang himself. At
sea, with his dexterous fingers, he'd been an ace with knots. In
this room or Deborah's? He looked for what best to hang
himself from.

Thick grayish-blue wool carpet. Muted, pale plaid wallpaper.
Sixteen-foot ceilings. Ornamented plaster. Pretty pine desk.

Austere antique armoire. Comfortable easy chair in a darker plaid, one tone down from the gray plaid on the upholstered headboard of the king-size bed. Ottoman. Embroidered throw pillows. Cut flowers in crystal vases. Huge mirror in mottled pine frame on the wall back of the bed. A five-bladed ceiling fan hanging from a long stem above the foot of the bed. There it is. Stand up on the bed, tie the rope to the motor. . . . They'd catch sight of him first in the mirror, Manhattan south of 71st Street to frame his swinging corpse. An El Greco. Tormented figure in foreground, Toledo and its churches in the background, and my soul seen ascending to Christ in the upper right corner. Rosa will get me in.

He held his hands up before her eyes. There were bulging nodes behind each of his cuticles, the ring and little fingers of both hands he could hardly move at all on a morning like this one, and long ago both his thumbs had taken on the shape of spoons. He could imagine how, to a simple mind like Rosa's, his hands looked like the hands of someone bearing a curse. She might even be right—nobody really understands arthritis.

"Dolorido?" she asked sympathetically, attentively appraising the deformity of each finger.

"Sí. Muy dolorido. Repugnante."

"No, señor, no, no," even as she continued to examine him as she would a creature in a circus sideshow.

"Usted es muy simpática," he told her.

It now occurred to him that he and Ron had fucked Yvonne and the pregnant girl in the second whorehouse they'd visited that first night in Havana. What happened when they got off the ship was what happened back then in most of the places. Pimps or runners of some kind were there to urge you to the houses where they wanted to take you. They may have targeted us because we were young kids. The other sailors told them to piss off. So he and Ron were taken to a cruddy old decaying place with filthy tiled walls and tiled floors, into a salon practically barren of furniture, and out came a bunch of fat old women. That's who Rosa reminded him of—the whores in that shithole. Imagine my having the presence of mind, two months out of Asbury High, to say, "No, no, thanks," but I did. I said in English, "Young chickens. Young chickens." So the guy took them to the other place, where they found

Yvonne De Carlo and the pregnant girl, young women who passed for good-looking in the Cuban marketplace. *You finished? Get off!*

"Vámonos," he said, and obediently Rosa followed him down the corridor to Deborah's bedroom, which did indeed look as though a thief had had at it. He wouldn't have been surprised to find a mound of warm feces on the top of the desk. The savage license taken here astonished even the perpetrator.

On Deborah's bed.

He seated himself at the edge of the bed while Rosa hung back by the disheveled closet.

"I will not tell what you did, Rosa. I will not tell."

"No?"

"Absolutamente no. Prometo." He indicated, with a gesture so painful it nearly made him retch, that it was between the two of them. "Nostro segreto."

"Secreto," she said.

"Sí. Secreto."

"Me promete?"

"Sí."

He pulled one of Norman's fifties out of his wallet and motioned for her to come and take it.

"No," said Rosa.

"I don't tell. You don't tell. I don't tell you showed the señora's money, the doctor's money, you don't tell you showed me her photographs. Her pictures. Comprende? Everything we forget. How do you say 'to forget' en español? 'To forget.'" He tried to indicate with a hand something flying out of his head. Oh, oh! Voltaren! *Volare!* The Via Veneto! The whores of the Via Veneto, as flavorful as the perfumed peaches he'd buy in Trastevere, half a dozen for a dime's worth of lira.

"Olvidar?"

"Olvidar! Olvidar todos!"

She came over and, to his delight, took the money. He clutched her hand with his deformed fingers while, with the other hand, he produced a second fifty.

"No, no, señor."

"Donación," he said humbly, holding on to her.

He remembered *donación*, all right. In the days of the Romance Run, each time you went back to the same whorehouses and you brought nylons to your favorite girls. The guys said, "You like her? Give her a little *donación*. Pick her up something, and when you come back you'll give it to her. Whether she remembers you or not is another matter. She'll be glad to take the nylons anyhow." The names of those girls? In the dozens and dozens of brothels in the dozens and dozens of places, there must have been a Rosa somewhere.

"Rosa," he murmured softly, trying to pull her so that she would slide between his legs, "para usted de parte mía."

"No, gracias."

"Por favor."

"No."

"De mí para tí."

A glare that was all blackness but that looked to be the go-ahead signal anyway—you win, I lose, do it and get it over with. On Deborah's bed.

"Here," he said and managed to wedge the mass of her lower torso between his widespread legs. He grasps the sword. He eyes the bull. *El momento de verdad*. "Take it."

Without speaking, Rosa did as she was told.

Secure it with a third fifty, or was agreement reached? *Cuánto dinero? Para qué cosa?* To be back there, to be seventeen in Havana and ramming it in! *Vente y no te pavonees.* That crone, that one old bitch, always sticking her head in my room and trying to hurry me up. A madam's hard eye, heavy makeup, a butcher's thick shoulders, and, after only fifteen minutes, the scornful harangue of the slavedriver. "Vente y no te pavonees!" 1946. Come and don't show off!

"Look," he said to her sadly. "The room. Chaos."

She turned her head. "Sí. Caos." She breathed deeply—resignation? disgust? If he slipped her the third fifty, would she just slide to her knees as easily as when she prayed? Interesting if she prayed and blew him both at once. Happens a lot in Latin countries.

"*I* made this caos," Sabbath told her, and when he rubbed the tip of a spoon-shaped thumb across the pockmarked cheeks, she offered no objection. "Me. Por qué? Because I lost something. I could not find something I lost. Comprende?"

"Comprendo."

"I lost my glass eye. Ojo artificial. This one." He drew her a little closer and pointed to his right eye. He began to smell her, armpits first, then the rest. Something familiar. It is not lavender. Bahia! "This isn't a real eye. This is a glass eye."

"Vidrio?"

"Sí! Sí! Este ojo, ojo de vidrio. Glass eye."

"Glasseye," she repeated.

"Glasseye. That's it. I lost it. I took it out last night to go to sleep, just as I usually do. But because I wasn't at home, a mi casa, I didn't put it in the usual place. You follow all this? I am a guest here. Amigo de Norman Cowan. Aquí para el funeral de señor Gelman."

"No!"

"Sí."

"El señor Gelman está muerto?"

"I'm afraid so."

"Ohhhhh."

"I know. But that's how I come to be here. If he hadn't died, we two would never have met. Anyhow, I took out my glasseye to sleep, and when I woke up I couldn't remember where I'd put it. I had to get to the funeral. But could I go to a funeral without an eye? Understand me? I was trying to find my eye and so I opened all the drawers, the desk, the closet"—feverishly he pointed around the room as she nodded and nodded, her mouth no longer grimly set but rather innocently ajar—"to find the fucking eye! Where had it gone? Looking everywhere, going crazy. Loco! Demente!"

Now she was beginning to laugh at the scene he was so slapshtikishly playing out for her. "No," she said, tapping him disapprovingly on the thigh, "no loco."

"Sí! And guess where it was, Rosa? Guess. Dónde was the ojo?"

Sure a joke was on the way, she began shaking her head from side to side. "No sé."

Here he hopped energetically off the bed and, while *she* now sat on the bed to watch him, he began to mime for her how before going to sleep he popped the eye out of his head and, after looking and finding nowhere to put it—and fearful that someone who came in and saw it on Deborah's desk, say, would be horrified (this too he mimed for her, making her laugh a beguiling ripple of a girlish laugh)—he just dropped it into his trouser pocket. Then he brushed his teeth (showed her this), washed his face (showed her that), and came back into the bedroom to undress and stupidly—"Estúpido! Estúpido!" he cried, knocking his poor fists against the sides of his head and not even stopping to acknowledge the pain—hung his trousers on a pants hanger in Deborah's closet. He showed her a pants hanger on which were hanging a pair of Deborah's wide blue silk pants. Then he showed her how he had turned *his* pants upside down to hang them in the closet and how, of course, the *ojo* had fallen out of the pocket and into one of her running shoes on the floor. "Can you beat that? Into the kid's zapato! My eye!"

She was laughing so hard she had to squeeze herself with her arms as though to prevent her belly from splitting open. If you're going to fuck her, just step up to the bed and fuck her now, man. On Deborah's bed, the fattest woman you will have ever fucked. One last enormous woman, and then with a clear conscience you can hang yourself. Life won't have been for nothing.

"Here," he said and, taking one of her hands in his own, drew it toward his right eye. "Did you ever feel a glasseye before? Go ahead," he said. "Be gentle, Rosa, but go ahead, feel it. You may not have this chance again. Most men are ashamed of their infirmities. Not me; I love 'em. Make me feel alive. Touch it."

She shrugged uncertainly. "Sí?"

"Don't be afraid. It's all part of the deal. Touch it. Touch it gently."

She gasped, drawing in her breath as she laid the padded tip of her tiny pointing finger lightly on the surface of his right eye.

"Glass," he said. "Hundred percent glass."

"Feel real," she said and, indicating that it wasn't so spooky as she first had feared, looked eager to take another poke at the thing. Contrary to appearances, she was not a slow learner. And she was game. They're all game, if you take your time and use your brains—and aren't sixty-four years old. The girls! All the girls! It was killing to think about.

"Of course it feels real," he replied. "That's because it's a good one. The best. Mucho dinero."

Life's last fuck. Working since she was nine. No school. No

plumbing. No money. A pregnant, illiterate Mexican out of some slum somewhere or up from peasant poverty, and weighing about the same as yourself. It couldn't have ended otherwise. Final proof that life is perfect. Knows where it's going every inch of the way. No, human life must not be extinguished. No one could come up with anything like it again.

"Rosa, will you be a good soul and clean the room? You *are* a good soul. You weren't trying to fool me down there praying to Jesus. You were just asking his forgiveness for your leading me into temptation. You just swung right into it the way you were taught. I admire that. I wouldn't mind somebody like Jesus to turn to. Maybe he could get me some Voltaren without a prescription. Isn't that one of his specialties?" He didn't know precisely what he was saying, because his blood began draining into his boots.

"No comprendo." But she wasn't frightened, for while smiling at her, he was barely speaking above a whisper and had weakly settled back down onto the bed.

"Make order, Rosa. Make regularidad."

"Okay," she said and began zealously to pick Deborah's things up off the floor instead of having to do what this madman with the white beard and the crazy fingers and the glass eye—and more than likely a loaded pistol—expected for two lousy fifties.

"Thank you, dear," said Sabbath woozily. "You've saved my life."

And then, while he was fortunately anchored to the edge of the bed, the vertigo took him by the ears, a shot of bile surged into his throat, and he felt as he had felt riding the waves as a kid after catching a big one too late and it broke over him like the chandelier at Asbury's palatial Mayfair, the great chandelier that, in dreams he'd been having for half a century, ever since Morty was killed in the war, was tearing loose from its moorings and falling on top of his brother and him as they sat there innocently, side by side, watching *The Wizard of Oz.*

He was dying, had given himself a heart attack by going all out for Rosa's amusement. Final performance. Will not be held over. Puppet master and prick conclude career.

Rosa was kneeling next to the bed now, stroking his scalp with one of her warm little hands. "Sick?" she asked.

"Low self-esteem."

"Want doctor here?"

"No, ma'am. Hands hurt, that's all." Did they! He assumed at first the pain-riddled fingers were causing him to shake. Then the teeth began to chatter as they had the evening before and he had suddenly to fight with all his fortitude to prevent himself from throwing up. "Mother?" No answer. Her silent act again. Or was she not there? "Mama!"

"Su madre? Dónde, señor?"

"Muerto."

"Hoy?"

"Sí. This morning. Questo auroro. Aurora?" Italian again. Italy again, the Via Veneto, the peaches, the girls!

"Ah, señor, no, no."

She kindly supported his hairy cheeks with her hands, and when she pulled him to her mountainous bosom, he let her; he'd let her take the pistol out of his pocket, if he had one, and shoot him right between the eyes. She could plead self-defense. Rape. He had a harassment record a mile long already. They'd string him up by his feet outside NOW. Roseanna would see they did it to him the way they'd done it to Mussolini. And cut off his prick, for good measure, like that woman who'd used a kitchen knife twelve inches long to slice the cock off her sleeping husband, an ex-Marine and a violent bastard, for fucking her up the ass down in Virginia. "You wouldn't do that to me, darling, would you?" "I would," said R. obligingly, "if you had one." She and all her progressive friends in the valley couldn't stop talking about this case. Roseanna didn't seem anything like so upset by it as she was by circumcision. "Jewish barbarism," she told him after attending the *bris* of a friend's grandson in Boston. "Indefensible. Disgusting. I wanted to walk out." Yet the woman who'd cut off her husband's cock seemed, from the excitement with which Roseanna spoke of her, to have become a heroine. "Surely," Sabbath suggested, "she could have registered her protest another way." "How? Dial 911? Try it and see where it gets you." "No, no, not 911. That's not justice. No, stick something unpleasant up *his* ass. One of his pipes, say, if he happens to be a smoker. Maybe even one that was lit. If he is not a smoker, then she could shove a frying pan up his ass. A rectum for a rectum. Exodus 21:24.

But cutting his dick off—really, Rosie, life isn't just a series of pranks. We are no longer schoolgirls. Life is not just giggling and passing notes. We are women now. It's a serious business. Remember how Nora does it in *A Doll's House*? She doesn't cut off Torvald's dick—she walks out the fucking door. I don't believe you necessarily have to be a nineteenth-century Norwegian to walk out a door. Doors continue to exist. Even in America they are still more plentiful than knives. Only doors take guts to walk out of. Tell me, have you ever wanted to cut my dick off in the middle of the night as an amusing way of settling scores?" "Yes. Often." "But why? What did I ever do, or fail to do, to give you an idea like that? I don't believe I ever once entered your anus without a prescription from the doctor and written permission from you." "Forget it," she said. "I don't know that it's a good idea for me to forget it now that I know it. You have really had thoughts about taking a knife—" "A scissors." "A scissors and cutting off my cock." "I was drunk. I was angry." "Oh, that was just chardonnay talking tough back in the bad old days. So what about today? What would you like to cut off now that you're 'in sobriety'? What does Bill W. suggest? I offer my hands. They're no fucking good anyway. I offer my throat. What is the overpowering symbolism of the penis for you people? Keep this up and you'll make Freud look good. I don't understand you and your friends. You stage a sit-down strike in the middle of Town Street every time the road crew goes near the limb of a sacred maple tree, you throw your bodies in front of every twig, but when it comes to this unfortunate incident, you're all gung ho. If the woman had gone outside and sawed down his favorite elm for revenge, this guy might have had a chance with you all. Too bad he wasn't a tree. One of those irreplaceable redwoods. The Sierra Club would have been out in force. She would have had her head handed to her by Joan Baez. A redwood? You mutilated a redwood? You're as bad as Spiro Agnew! You're all so merciful and tender, against the death penalty even for serial killers, judging poetry contests for degenerate cannibals in maximum-security prisons. How could you be so horrified about napalming the Communist enemy in Southeast Asia and so happy about this ex-Marine having his dick cut off right here in the USA? Cut mine off, Roseanna

Cavanaugh, and I bet you ten to one, a hundred to one, you're back on the booze tomorrow. Cutting off a dick isn't as easy as you think. It isn't just snip, snip, snip, like you're darning a sock. It isn't just chop, chop, chop, like you're mincing an onion. It isn't an onion. It's a human dick. It's full of blood. Remember Lady Macbeth? They didn't have AA in Scotland, and so the poor woman went off her rocker. 'Who would have thought the old man to have had so much blood in him?' 'Here's the smell of the blood still. All the perfumes of Arabia will not sweeten this little hand.' She flips out—Lady Powerhouse Macbeth! So what's going to happen to you? That woman in Virginia *is* a heroine—as well as a despicable human being. But you don't have the guts, darling. You're just a schoolteacher in the sticks. We're talking about evil, Rosie. The worst you could do in life was become a wino. What the fuck's a wino? A dime a dozen. Any drunk can become a drunk. But not everybody can cut off a dick. I don't doubt that this splendid woman has given encouragement to dozens of other splendid women all around the country, but personally I don't think you've got anything like what it takes to get down there and do it. You'd vomit if you had to swallow my come. You told me that long ago. Well, how do you think you'd like to perform surgery on your loving husband without an anesthetic?" "Why not wait and see?" said Roseanna with a smile. "No. No. Let's not wait. I'm not going to live forever. I'll be seventy the day after tomorrow. And then you'll have missed your big chance to prove how courageous you are. Cut it off, Roseanna. Pick a night, any night. Cut it off. I dare you."

And wasn't that what he had run from and why he was here? There was a mammoth scissors in the utility closet. There was a much smaller scissors, shaped like a heron, in her sewing kit and an ordinary-size one with orange plastic handles in her middle desk drawer. There was a hedge clipper out in her potting shed. For weeks, ever since this case had begun to obsess her, he had been thinking of throwing them all in the woods up at Battle Mountain when he went at night to visit Drenka's grave. Then he remembered that her art classes were full of scissors; every kid had a pair, for cutting and pasting. And then the jury in Virginia declares this woman innocent on grounds of temporary insanity. She went crazy for two minutes. Just about how long it took Louis to knock out Schmeling in that second fight. Barely enough time to cut it off and throw it away, but she managed, she did it—shortest insanity in world history. A record. The old one-two, and that's it. Roseanna and the peaceniks were on the phone all morning. They thought it was a great decision. That was enough warning for him. Great day for women's liberation but a black day for the Marine Corps and Sabbath. He would never sleep in that house of scissors again.

And who was his comforter now? She was cradling his head as though she intended to give him suck.

"Pobre hombre," she muttered. "Pobre niño, pobre madre. . . ."

He was weeping, to Rosa's surprise out of both eyes. She continued nonetheless to soothe his sorrows, talking softly in Spanish and stroking the scalp where the pitch-black hair that strikingly offset the hot green needles that were his eyes used to grow in profusion back when he was a seventeen-year-old in a sailor's cap and everything in life led to pussy.

"How do you have one eyes?" asked Rosa, gently rocking him to and fro. "Por qué?"

"La guerra," he moaned.

"It cry, glasseye?"

"I told you, it wasn't cheap."

And under the spell of her fleshiness, pressing against her pungency, his nose sinking deeper and deeper into the deep, Sabbath felt as though he were porous, as though the last that was left of the whole concoction that had been a self was running out now drop by drop. He wouldn't need to knot a rope. He would just drip his way into death until he was dry and gone.

So then, this had been his existence. What conclusion was to be drawn? Any? Who had come to the surface in him was inexorably himself. Nobody else. Take it or leave it.

"Rosa," he wept. "Rosa. Mama. Drenka. Nikki. Roseanna. Yvonne."

"Shhhh, pobrecito, shhhhh."

"Ladies, if I have put my life to an improper use . . ."

"No comprendo, pobrecito," she said, and so he shut up, because neither really did he. He was fairly sure that he was half faking the whole collapse. Sabbath's Indecent Theater.

2

To Be or Not To Be

SABBATH hit the street with the intention of spending the hours before Linc's funeral playing Rip Van Winkle. The idea revived him. He looked the part and had been out of it longer even than Rip. RVW merely missed the Revolution— from what Sabbath had been hearing over the years, he had missed the transformation of New York into a place utterly antagonistic to sanity and civil life, a city that by the 1990s had brought to perfection the art of killing the soul. If you had a living soul (and Sabbath no longer made such a claim for himself), it could die here in a thousand different ways at any hour of the day or night. And that was not to speak of unmetaphorical death, of citizens as prey, of everyone from the helpless elderly to the littlest of schoolchildren infected with fear, nothing in the whole city, not even the turbines of Con Ed, as mighty and galvanic as fear. New York was a city completely gone wrong, where nothing but the subway was subterranean anymore. It was the city where you could obtain, sometimes with no trouble at all, sometimes at considerable expense, the worst of everything. In New York the good old days, the old way of life, was thought to have existed no further than three years back, the intensification of corruption and violence and the turnover in crazy behavior being that rapid. A showcase for degradation, overflowing with the overflow of the slums, prisons, and mental hospitals of at least two hemispheres, tyrannized by criminals, maniacs, and bands of kids who'd overturn the world for a pair of sneakers. A city where the few who bothered to consider life seriously knew themselves to be surviving in the teeth of everything inhuman—or all too human: one shuddered to think that all that was abhorrent in the city disclosed the lineaments of mass mankind as it truly longed to be.

Now, Sabbath did not swallow these stories he continually heard characterizing New York as Hell, first, because every great city is Hell; second, because if you weren't interested in the gaudier abominations of mankind, what were you doing there in the first place?; and third, because the people he heard telling these stories—the wealthy of Madamaska Falls, the tiny professional elite and the elderly who'd retired to their summer homes there—were the last people on earth you'd believe about anything.

Unlike his neighbors (if Sabbath could be said to consider anyone anywhere a neighbor), he did not naturally shrink from the worst in people, beginning with himself. Despite his having been preserved in a northern icebox for the bulk of his life, during recent years he had been thinking that he, for one, could perhaps be something other than repelled by the city's daily terrors. He might even have left Madamaska Falls (and Rosie) to return to New York long ago if it had not been for his sidekicker . . . and for the feelings still springing from Nikki's disappearance . . . and for the silly destiny that had been chosen for him instead by his tiresome superiority and threadbare paranoia.

Though his paranoia, he observed, shouldn't be exaggerated. It was never the poisoned spearhead of his thinking, never on the truly grand scale, needing absolutely nothing to unleash it. Certainly by now it was no more than a sort of everyman's paranoia, quarrelsome enough to rise to the bait but by and large frazzled and sick of itself.

Meanwhile he was trembling again, and without the comfort of Rosa's pungency and its nostalgic meaning. It seemed that once the thing had taken hold, as it had again earlier in Deborah's ransacked room, he was hard put to extinguish, by an act of will, the desire not to be alive any longer. It was walking along with him, his companion, as he headed toward the subway station. Though he hadn't walked them for decades, he saw nothing at all of those streets, so busy was he in staying abreast of his wish to die. He marched in unison with it step-by-step, keeping time to an infantry chant he'd had drummed into his head by the black cadre at Fort Dix when he was there training to be a killer of Communists after coming back from sea.

> You had a good home but you left—
> You're right!
> You had a good home but you left—

> You're right!
> Sound off, one-two,
> Sound off, three-four,
> Sound off, one-two-three-four—
> Three-four!

The-desire-not-to-be-alive-any-longer accompanied Sabbath right on down the station stairway and, after Sabbath purchased a token, continued through the turnstile clinging to his back; and when he boarded the train, it sat in his lap, facing him, and began to tick off on Sabbath's crooked fingers the many ways it could be sated. This little piggy slit his wrists, this little piggy used a dry-cleaning bag, this little piggy took sleeping pills, and this little piggy, born by the ocean, ran all the way out in the waves and drowned.

It took Sabbath and the-desire-not-to-be-alive-any-longer just the length of the ride downtown to together compose an obituary.

MORRIS SABBATH, PUPPETEER, 64, DIES

Morris "Mickey" Sabbath, a puppeteer and sometime theatrical director who made his little mark and then vanished from the Off Off Broadway scene to hide like a hunted criminal in New England, died Tuesday on the sidewalk outside 115 Central Park West. He fell from a window on the eighteenth floor.

The cause of death was suicide, said Rosa Complicata, whom Mr. Sabbath sodomized moments before taking his life. Ms. Complicata is the spokesperson for the family.

According to Ms. Complicata, he had given her two fifty-dollar bills to perform perverse acts before his jumping out the window. "But he no have hard prick," said the heavyset spokesperson, in tears.

Suspended Sentence

Mr. Sabbath began his career as a street performer in 1953. Observers of the entertainment world identify Sabbath as the "missing link" between the respectable fifties and the rambunctious sixties. A small cult developed around his Indecent Theater, where Mr. Sabbath used fingers in place of puppets to represent his ribald characters. He was prosecuted on charges of obscenity in 1956, and though he was found guilty and fined, his sentence of thirty days was suspended. Had he served the time it might have straightened him out.

Under the auspices of Norman Cowan and Lincoln Gelman (for

Gelman obituary see B7, column 3), Mr. Sabbath directed a notably insipid *King Lear* in 1959. Nikki Kantarakis was praised by our critic for her Cordelia, but Mr. Sabbath's performance as Lear was labeled "megalomaniacal suicide." Ripe tomatoes had been handed to all ticket holders as they entered the theater, and by the end of the evening Mr. Sabbath seemed to relish his besmirchment.

Pig or Perfectionist?

The RADA-trained Miss Kantarakis, star of the Bowery Basement Players and the director's wife, mysteriously disappeared from their home in November 1964. Her fate remains unknown, though murder has never been ruled out.

"The pig Flaubert murdered Louise Colet," said Countess du Plissitas, the aristocrat's feminist, in a telephone interview today. Countess du Plissitas is best known for fictionalizing biography. She is currently fictionalizing the biography of Miss Kantarakis. "The pig Fitzgerald murdered Zelda," the countess continued, "the pig Hughes murdered Sylvia Plath, and the pig Sabbath murdered Nikki. It's all there, all the different ways he murdered her, in *Nikki: The Destruction of an Actress by a Pig*."

Members of the original Bowery Basement Players contacted today agreed that Mr. Sabbath was merciless in his direction of his wife. They were all hoping that she would kill him and were disappointed when she disappeared without even having tried.

Mr. Sabbath's friend and coproducer, Norman Cowan—whose daughter, Deborah, a student in underclothing at Brown, played a starring role in the extravaganza *Farewell to a Half Century of Masturbation*, elaborately staged by Mr. Sabbath in the hours just before he leaped to his death—tells another story. "Mickey was a genuinely nice person," Mr. Cowan commented. "Never gave anybody any trouble. A bit of a loner, but always with a kind word for everyone."

First Whore Mean

Mr. Sabbath trained in the whorehouses of Central and South America, as well as the Caribbean, before establishing himself as a puppeteer in Manhattan. He never used a rubber and miraculously never contracted VD. Mr. Sabbath often recounted the story of his first whore.

"The one I chose was very interesting," he once told a person sitting next to him on the subway. "I'll never forget her as long as I live. You wouldn't forget your first one anyway. I chose her because she looked like Yvonne De Carlo, the actress, the movie actress. Anyway, here I am shaking like a leaf. This is in Old Havana. I remember how

marvelous and romantic that was, decaying streets with balconies.
Very first time. Never been laid in my life. So there I was with
Yvonne. We both started getting undressed. I remember sitting in a
chair by the door. The first thing and the most lasting thing of all is
that she had red underwear, a red brassiere and underpants. And that
was fantastic. The next thing I remember is being on top of her. And
the next thing I remember is that it was all over and she said, 'Get off
of me!' Slightly mean. 'Get off!' Now this doesn't happen every time,
but since it was my first time, I thought it did and got off. 'You finished? Get off!' There are some nasty types even among whores. I'll
never forget it. I thought, 'Okay, what do I care?' but it did strike me
as unfriendly and even mean. How did I know, a kid from the boondocks, that one out of ten would be mean and tough like that, however pretty?"

Did Nothing for Israel

Not long after the alleged murder of his first wife, Mr. Sabbath made
his way to the remote mountain village where he was supported until
his death by a second wife, who dreamed for years of cutting off his
cock and then taking sanctuary in her abused-women's group. During his three decades in hiding, aside from virtually making a prostitute of Mrs. Drenka Balich, a Croatian American neighbor, he seems
to have worked on little else but a five-minute puppet adaptation of
the hopelessly insane Nietzsche's *Beyond Good and Evil*. In his fifties
he developed erosive osteoarthritis in both hands, involving the distal
interphalangeal joints and the proximal interphalangeal joints, with
relative sparing of the metacarpophalangeal joints. The result was radical instability and function loss from persistent pain and stiffness, and
progressive deformity. Owing to his prolonged consideration of the
advantages of arthrodesis against the advantages of implant arthro-
plasty, his wife became an expert in chardonnay. The osteoarthritis
provided a wonderful pretext for being even more bitter about everything and devoting his entire day to thinking up ways to degrade Mrs.
Balich.

He is survived by the ghost of his mother, Yetta, of Beth Some-
thing-or-other Cemetery, Neptune, New Jersey, who haunted him
unceasingly during the last year of his life. His brother, Lieutenant
Morton Sabbath, was shot down over the Philippines during the Second World War. Yetta Sabbath never got over it. It is from his mother
that Mr. Sabbath inherited his own ability never to get over anything.

Also surviving is his wife, Roseanna, of Madamaska Falls, with
whom he was shacked up on the night that Miss Kantarakis disappeared or was murdered by him and her body disposed of. Mr. Sab-

bath is believed by Countess du Plissitas to have coerced Mrs. Sabbath, the former Roseanna Cavanaugh, into being an accomplice to the crime, thus initiating her plunge into alcoholism.

Mr. Sabbath did nothing for Israel.

a blur whizzing blur why now most unpleasant invention nobody think ticker tape like this I don't head coming down here stupid find what I lost idiocy Greek Village gyro sandwich souvlaki sandwich baklava you know Nikki gypsy clothes spangles beads angelically on Victorian boots never a fuck without a rape tossed in no no not there but only way she came was there god forgive those dont fuck in the ass hey gyro you know Nikki souvlaki you know Nikki St. Marks hotel $25.60 and up room rent you know Nikki tattooed tubby you know Nikki garbage still from when we left leather shops tie wrists ankles blindfold proceed want to know a secret I want to know only secrets when you use me like a boy Im your boy you are my girl my boy your puppet hand puppet make me a hand puppet Ethnic Jewelry more leather old people Im one Religious Sex Clothing Shop incense Nikki always Nikki burning gift shops T-shirts incense never out of incense fire escapes still need paint long hairs last outpost movers movers movers redfaced brick broad women Polish-American home cooking and what will I say other than why so why bother theres less chance of her being here than my being her cant stand this there is god can those be ours in the window Nikki stained them hung them disappeared I left 120 bucks of Salvation Army shit the wooden blinds she loved there they are the red tapes faded slats missing thirty years later Nikkis blinds

"Smoke? Wanna smoke?"

"Not today, honey."

"Man, I'm starvin'. I got great smokes. The real McCoy. I ain't had no breakfast, ain't had no lunch. Been out here two hours. Ain't sold shit."

"Patience, patience. 'Nothing illegal is achieved without patience.' Benjamin Franklin."

"Ain't had fuck to *eat*, man."

"How much?"

"Five."

"Two."

"Shit. This is the real McCoy."

"But as you are the one starving, the leverage is mine."

"Fuck you, old man, old Jew man."

"Tut tut. That's beneath you. 'Neither a philo- nor an anti-Semite be; / And it must follow, as the night the day, / Thou canst not then be false to any man.'"

"Someday ain't gonna be out here beggin' and sellin' shit. Gonna be Jews out here beggin'. Wait'll all the beggars is Jews. You gonna like that."

"All the Jews will be begging when there is a black Mount Rushmore, my dear, and not a day sooner—when there is a black Mount Rushmore with Michael Jackson, Jesse Jackson, Bo Jackson, and Ray Charles carved upon its face."

"Two for five. I'm starvin', man."

"The price is right—a deal. But you must learn to think more kindly of Jews. You people were here long before we were. We did not have your advantages."

Nina Cordelia Desdemona Estroff Pharmacy still here my god Freie Bibliothek u. Lesehalle Deutsches Dispensary all basements Indian boutiques Indian restaurants Tibetan trinkets Japanese restaurants Ray's Pizza Kiev 24 hours 7 days a week introduction to Hinduism always she was reading dharma artha kama and moksha release from rebirth supreme goal death certainly a worthy subject maybe the greatest certainly a solution for low self-esteem The Racing Form the Warsaw-papers the bums the bums the Bowery bums still in the stairwells head in hands piss gushing out from their pockets

"I'm on a real guilt trip, man."

"Say that again, please?"

"Guilt trip. I need somethin' to eat. I ain't had breakfast or lunch yet."

"Wouldn't worry. Nobody has."

"I'm innocent, man. I was framed. Somebody help me."

"I'll take your case, son. I believe in your innocence no less than my own."

"Thanks, man. You a lawyer?"

"No, a Hindu. And you?"

"I'm Jewish. But I studied Buddhism."

"Yes, overachiever is written all over your jeans."

"What's it all like to a wise old Hindu?"

"Oh, not for everyone, but I happen to love hardship. Live on plant foods from the forest. Seek constantly to achieve purity and self-control. Practice restraint of the senses. Perform austerities."

"I gotta eat somethin', man."

"Animal food is to be avoided."

"Shit, I don't eat animal food."

"Avoid actresses."

"How about shiksas?"

"For a Jew who studies Buddhism the shiksa is not forbidden to eat. Ben Franklin: 'God forgive those who don't fuck in the ass.'"

"You're nuts, baby. You're a great Hindu man."

"I have passed through life in the world and performed my duties to society. Now I am reinitiated into the celibate state and become like a child. I concentrate on internal sacrifices to the sacred fires in my own self."

"Far out."

"I am seeking final release from rebirth."

lamppost sex sale naked girl silhouette phone number whats that say I speak Hindi Urdu and Bangla well that leaves me out shiksa Mount Rushmore Ava Gardner Sonja Henie Ann-Margret Yvonne De Carlo strike Ann-Margret Grace Kelly she is the Abraham Lincoln of shiksas

So Sabbath passeth the time, pretending to think without punctuation, the way J. Joyce pretended people thought, pretending to be both more and less unfixed than he felt, pretending that he did and did not expect to find Nikki down in a basement with a dot on her head selling saris or in her gypsy clothes roaming these streets of theirs in search of him. So passeth Sabbath, seeing all the antipathies in collision, the villainous and the innocent, the genuine and the fraudulent, the loathsome and the laughable, a caricature of himself and entirely himself, embracing the truth and blind to the truth, self-haunted while barely what you would call a self, ex-son, ex-brother, ex-husband, ex-puppet artist without any idea what he now was or what he was seeking, whether it was to slide headlong into the stairwells with the substrata of bums or to succumb like a man to the-desire-not-to-be-alive-any-longer or to affront and affront and affront till there was no one on earth unaffronted.

At least he hadn't been witless enough to go find on Avenue C where he personally had handed tomatoes to all the first-nighters. It'd be another grim hole in the ground with Indian cuisine. Nor did he cut across Tompkins Park to where his workshop once had been, where they'd fucked so hard and so long that the couch would slide on its casters halfway to the door by the time he'd had to dress and race back to beat Nikki home from the theater. That bewitching bondage now seemed like the fantasy of a twelve-year-old boy. Yet it had happened, to him and to Roseanna Cavanaugh, fresh from Bennington College. When Nikki disappeared, aside from the grief and the tears and the torments of confusion, he was also as delighted as a young man could be. A trapdoor had opened and Nikki was gone. A dream, a sinister dream common to all. *Let her disappear. Let him disappear.* Only for Sabbath the dream came true.

Dragging him down, spewing him forth, knocking him flat, beating him like the batter in his mother's Mixmaster. Then, for the finale, a breech delivery onto the shore, leaving him abraded and stinging from where he had been dragged across the pebbled shingle by the churning of the wave he'd mis-timed. When he got up he didn't know where he was—he could be in Belmar. But out to the depths he savagely swam, back to where Morty had a gleaming arm stuck straight up and was shouting over the sound of the sea, "Hercules! Come on!" Morty caught every wave right; zinc-striped nose plowing the way, he'd ride a wave, when the tide was full, from way beyond the last rope to damn near up to the boards. They used to laugh at the Weequahic guys down from Newark. Those guys can't ride waves, they'd say. Those Newark Jewish kids were all escaping polio. If they were home they'd beg to go swimming at the amusement park pool up there in Irvington and as soon as they paid and got their ticket they immediately got polio. So their parents took them down the shore. If you were a Jew from Jersey City you went to Belmar, if you were a Jew from Newark you went to Bradley. We used to play blackjack with them under the boards. I was introduced to blackjack by those Weequahic guys, then developed my skills further at sea. Those blackjack games were legendary in our little backwater. Down for double! Up the shoot! Bai-*ja!* And the Jewish Weequahic broads at the Brinley Avenue beach in their two-piece suits, their Weequahic bellies bare. Loved it when they came in for the summer. Up till then all you did was listen to the radio and do your homework. A cloistered, quiet time. And suddenly everything was happening, the streets in Asbury were jammed with people, the boards in Bradley were jammed at night—from the moment the Memorial Day weekend began, our small-town life was over. Waitresses all over Asbury, college girls from all over the country lining up there to get a job. Asbury was the hub, next came Ocean Grove, the Methodist shtetl where you couldn't drive on Sundays, and then Bradley, and down on the beach Jewish girls from every part of Jersey. Eddie Schneer, the parking-lot thief Morty and I worked for, used to warn us, "Don't mess with Jewish girls. Save it for the shiksas. Never get nasty with Jewish girls." And the Jewish city guys from Weequahic who we said couldn't ride the waves, we used to have wave-riding contests with them, bet them and ride waves for money. Morty always won. Our great summertimes before he joined the Air Corps.

And when the tide was out and the ailing and the arthritic old drifted down to dunk themselves at the water's rippling edge, where the sunburned kids with their leaky toy buckets were shoveling for sand crabs, Morty, his pals, and "Little Sabbath" carved a large rectangular court up on the beach, drew a line dividing it, and, three or four to a side, clad in their sopping suits, they played Buzz, a deceptively ferocious beach game devised by the daredevil shore kids. When you're "it" you have to go over and touch someone on the other side and get back before they pull your arms out of the sockets. If they catch you on the line, your team pulls you one way and the other team pulls you the other way. Much like the rack. "And what happens," Drenka asked him, "if they do catch you?" "They pull you down. If they catch you, they pull you down, they tackle you, and they sodomize you. Nobody gets hurt." Drenka laughed! How he could make Drenka laugh when she asked him to tell her about being an American boy at the shore. Buzz. Sand scratching your eyes, stuffing your ears, burning your belly, packing the crotch of your suit, sand between your buttocks, up your nose, a clump of sand, stained with blood, spat from between your lips, and then, together— "Geronimo!"—everyone out again to where the surf was calm now and you could sun yourself on your back, swaying sleepily, laughing at nothing, singing "opera" at the top of your lungs— "Toreador / Don't spit on the floor / Use the cuspidor / That's what it's for!"—and then, spurred by a sudden heroic impulse, spinning about onto your belly for the dive to the ocean floor. Sixteen, eighteen, twenty feet down. *Where's the bottom?* Then the lung-bursting battle up to the oxygen with a fistful of sand to show Morty.

On Morty's days off from being a lifeguard at the West End Casino, Mickey didn't leave his side, either on land or sea. What a pounding he could take! And how great that felt when he was a happy-go-lucky kid before the war letting himself go riding the waves.

Not so now. He clutched the edge of a street vendor's stand, waiting for the coffee to save him. Thought went on independently of him, scenes summoning themselves up while he seemed to wobble perilously on a slight rise between where he was and where he wasn't. He was trapped in a process of self-division that was not at all merciful. A pale, pale analog to what must have happened to Morty when his plane was torn apart by flak: living your life backward while spinning out of control. He had the definite impression that they were re-hearsing *The Cherry Orchard* even as he carefully took the cof-fee cup in one disfigured hand and paid with the other. There was Nikki. This mark she had left on his mind could open out like the mouth of a volcano, and it was already thirty years now. There is Nikki, listening the way she listened when she was given even the minutest note—the look of voluptuous at-tention, the dark, full eyes without panic, tranquil as only they were when she was having to be someone other than herself, murmuring his words inwardly, brushing her hair off her ears so nothing was between his words and herself, breathing little sighs of defeat to acknowledge just how right he was, his state of mind her state of mind, his sense of things her sense of things, Nikki his instrument, his implement, the self-immolating register of his ready-made world. And rat-a-tat-tat Sabbath, the insuperable creator of her hiding place, born to deliver her from all losses and from all the fears they'd bred, missing not so much as the movement of an eye, punctilious to the point of madness, dangerously prodding the air with a finger so that nobody dared even to blink while he laid it out, every detail, in that overbearing way of his—how frightening he looked to her, a little bull with a big mind, a little keg filled to the spout with the intoxicating brandy of himself, his eyes *insisting* like that, warning, reminding, scolding, mimicking; it was all to Nikki like a ferocious caress, and she felt in her, overriding everything timorous, this stony obligation to be great. "*O my childhood.* That's a *question.* Don't lose that soft, questioning tone. Fill the speech with sweetness. To Trofimov: *You were only a boy then*, et cetera. Some sweet charm has gone there too. More playful, broken—charm him! Your entrance: viva-cious, excited, generous—Parisian! The dance. *I can't sit still*, et cetera. Be sure to get rid of the cup long before this. Get up. The Parisian dance with Lopakhin takes you *down*stage, *down*-stage. *Compliment* Lopakhin on this unexpected excellence in Parisian dancing. *You, Varya.* Wagging a finger at her. It's *mock* chastisement. Then teasing, quick, kissing both her cheeks, *You're just the same as ever.* The line *I don't quite follow you*—much dizzier. Laugh audibly after *mentioned in the ency-clopedia.* Don't lose the laughing and the noises—make all the delicious noises you want; they're wonderful, they're Ranyev-skaya! *Much* more teasingly provocative with Lopakhin when he goes on and on about the sale of the orchard—that's where you get your bigness. For you this business talk is just a mar-velous occasion to bewitch a new man. Bewitch him! He's as much as invited you to by saying he loves you the very mo-ment he lays eyes on you. Where are those teasing sounds? The seductive moan. The musical *Hmmmmm.* Chekhov: 'The im-portant thing is to find the right smile.' Tender, Nikki, inno-cent, lingering, false, real, lazy, vain, habitual, charming—find *the smile*, Nikki, or you'll completely fuck up. Her vanity: pow-der your face, dab a little scent, straighten up your back to make yourself look beautiful. You are vain and you are aging. Imagine that: a corrupt and weary woman and yet as vulnera-ble and innocent as Nikki. *They're from Paris.* Let us see how lightly you take that—must see that *smile*. Three steps—*only three*—up from the torn telegram before you turn back and break down. Then let's *see* the breakdown as you retreat to the table. *If only this weight could be lifted from my heart.* Look at the floor. Musingly, gently, *If only I could forget my past. Keep* looking down, reflectively, through his line—then look up and you see your mother. IT IS MOTHER. Introduces the past, which magically then appears as Petya. She sees mother in a tree—but can't recognize Petya. Why does she give Petya the money? This is not convincing as you are doing it. Does he flirt with her? Charm her? Is he a great friend of old? Something has to have been there *before* to make it credible *now*. Yasha. Who is Yasha? What is Yasha? He is living proof of her bad judgment. *There's no one there.* This whole speech, from beginning to end, is as to a child. Including *It looks like a woman.* Lopakhin's past is to be beaten with a stick—your childhood Eden was his childhood hell. Consequently he does *not* make a sentimental *tsimmes* out of purity and innocence. Unshrinkingly, Nikki, *without shrinking*, you cry, *Look! It's mother walking in the orchard!* But the last thing Lopakhin would want to see is his drunken father resurrected. Think of the play as her dream, as Lyuba's Paris dream. She is exiled in Paris, miserable with her lover, and she dreams. I dreamed that I returned home and everything was as it used to be. Mother was alive, she was there—appeared right outside the nursery window in the form of a cherry tree. I was a child again, a child of my own called Anya. And I was being courted by an idealistic student who was going to change the world. And yet at the same time I was myself, a woman with all my history, and the serf's son, Lopakhin, himself grown now too, kept warning me that if I didn't chop down the cherry orchard the estate was going to be sold. Of course I couldn't chop down the cherry orchard, so I gave a party instead. But in the middle of the dancing, Lopakhin burst in, and though we tried to beat him back with a stick, he announced that the estate had indeed been sold, and to him, to the serf's son! He drove us all out of the house and began to chop down the orchard. And then I awoke . . . Nikki, what are your first words? Tell me. *The nursery.* Yes! It's to the *nursery* that she's returned. At the one pole the nursery; at the other, Paris—the one a place impossible to retrieve, the other impossible to manage. She fled Russia to elude the consequences of her disastrous marriage; she flees Paris to leave behind the disastrous affair. A woman in flight from disorder. In *flight* from disorder, Nikoleta. Yet she carries the disorder within her—she is the disorder!"

But I was the disorder. I am disorder.

According to Morty's Benrus, eternity was officially beginning for Linc Gelman at the Riverside Memorial Chapel on Amsterdam Avenue in just about half an hour. Yet dedicated as Sabbath was to seeing what a man could make of a wreck of a life if only he had the wherewithal, when he reached the Astor Place station, instead of hurrying down for the train, he became engrossed by a small company of gifted players enacting, with effectively minimalist choreography, the last degrading stages of the struggle for survival. Their amphitheater was this acre or two of lower Manhattan where everything running north, south, east, and west comes unstuck and together again in an intricate angling of intersections and odd-shaped oases of open space.

"Don't have to be a Rockefella to help a fella, don't have to be a Rockefella to help a fella—" A black tiny being with a bashed-in face hopped up with his cup to recite for Sabbath in a gentle singsong voice rather belying the chain of events three centuries long that had culminated in this pinprick of tormented existence. This guy was barely living and yet—thought Sabbath, counting how many others were working the adjoining territory with cups of their own—clearly he was Man of the Year.

Sipping at the dregs in his own cup, Sabbath at last looked up from the submerged blunder that was his past. The present happened also to be in progress, manufactured day and night like the troop ships at Perth Amboy during the war, the venerable present that goes back to antiquity and runs right from the Renaissance to today—this always-beginning, never-ending present was what Sabbath was renouncing. Its inexhaustibility he finds repugnant. For this alone he should die. So what if he has led a stupid life? Anyone with any brains knows that he is leading a stupid life even while he is leading it. Anyone with any brains understands that he is destined to lead a stupid life *because there is no other kind.* There is nothing personal in it. Nonetheless, childish tears well up in his eyes as Mickey Sabbath—yes, *the* Mickey Sabbath, of that select band of 77 billion prize saps who constitute human history—bids good-bye to his one-and-onlyness with a half-mumbled, heartbro-ken "Who gives a shit?"

A grizzled black face, wild and wasted, eyes bereft of any de-sire to see—blurred, muzzy eyes that Sabbath took to be at the twilight edge of sanity—appeared only inches from his own grizzled face. For such wretched affliction Sabbath had the stomach and so he did not turn away. His own anguish he knew to be but the faintest imitation of a sublife as abhorrent as this one. The black man's eyes were terrifying. If deep in that pocket his fingers are twisted around the handle of a knife, I may not be doing what I should be doing by holding my ground like this.

The beggar shook his cup like a tambourine, causing the change to rattle dramatically. A heavy odor of rot polluted his breath as into Sabbath's beard he whispered conspiratorially, "It's just a job, man—somebody's got to do it."

It *was* a knife. Jabbing into Sabbath's jacket, a knife. "What's the job?" Sabbath asked him.

"Bein' a borderline case."

Try to remain calm and to look unperturbed. "You do ap-pear to have had your share of disappointment."

"America love me."

"If you say so." But when the beggar lurched heavily against him, Sabbath cried out, "Let's not have violence—you hear me? No violence!"

This provoked from his assailant a gruesome grin. "Vi-o-lence? *Vi-o-lence?* I *told* you—America *love* me!"

Now, if what Sabbath felt pushing into him was indeed the tip of a knife milliseconds from impaling his liver, if Sabbath truly had the-desire-not-to-be-alive-any-longer, why did he bring the heel of his big boot so forcefully down on that beloved American's foot? If he no longer gave a shit, why did he give a shit? On the other hand, if this limitless despair was only so much simulation, if he was not so steeped in hopeless-ness as he pretended to be, whom was he deceiving other than himself? His mother? Was a suicide required for his mother to understand that Mickey had amounted to nothing? Why else was she haunting him?

The black man howled and stumbled backward, whereupon Sabbath, fiery still with whatever impulse had saved his life, looked quickly down to discover that what he had taken for the tip of a knife was something in the shape of a grub or a slug or a maggot, a soft worm of a thing that looked as though it had been dipped in coal dust. It made you wonder what all the fuss was for.

In the meantime, nobody on those streets seemed to have noticed either the pecker that was nothing to write home about or the crazy bastard to whom it belonged and who, in what was admittedly a clumsy effort not entirely thought through, had wanted merely to become Sabbath's friend. Nor had anyone noticed Sabbath stomp him. The encounter that had left Sabbath in a sweat appeared to have been as good as invisible to two beggars who were no farther from the puppeteer than one corner of the boxing ring is from the other. They were intimately talking together across a supermarket cart and a load of transparent plastic bags stuffed to bursting with empty soda bottles and cans. The lanky one, who appeared, from the proprietary way he sprawled across it, to be the owner of the cart and its loot, was wearing a decent-enough sweat suit and sneakers that were practically brand-new. The other, shorter man was wrapped in rags that could well have been appropriated off the floor of an auto garage.

The more prosperous of the two spoke in a large, declamatory voice. "Man, there ain't enough hours in the *day* for me to do all the things I got scheduled."

"You fuckin' thief," replied the other weakly. Sabbath saw that he was weeping. "You stole it, you shitface."

"Sorry, man. I'd pencil you in, but my computers are down. The automatic car wash don't work. You don't do a drive-through at McDonald's in under seven minutes, and they get it all wrong anyway. Things we supposed to be really good at we ain't good at anymore. I call IBM. I ask them where I can buy one of them laptop computers. Call their 800 number. He says, 'I'm sorry, the computers are down.' IBM," he repeated, looking gleefully at Sabbath, "and *they* ain't got it together."

"I know, I know," said Sabbath. "The TV fucked it up."

"The TV fucked it up good, man."

"The challah machine," said Sabbath, "is the last thing that
works. Look at a window full of challah. No two exactly alike,
and yet all within the genre. And they still look like they're
plastic. And that's what a challah wants to do. Wanted to look
like plastic even before plastic. There's where they got the idea
for plastic. From challahs."

"No shit. How you know that?"

"National Public Radio. They help you understand things.
There's always National Public Radio to help me understand,
no matter how confused I may be."

The only other white man anywhere nearby was standing in
the middle of Lafayette Street, one of those bantamweight
redfaced bums of indeterminate age and Irish descent who'd
been making a home of the Bowery for decades now and so
was familiar to Sabbath from back when he had lived in the
neighborhood. He was clutching a bottle in a brown paper
bag and talking quietly to a pigeon, a wounded pigeon that
couldn't get itself up on its legs and take more than a wobbly
step or two before keeling over on its side. In the midst of the
early afternoon traffic it vainly fluttered its wings, trying to get
moving. The bum stood straddling the pigeon, using his free
hand to direct the cars to drive around and on through the intersection. Some drivers, angrily honking their horns, came
perilously close to deliberately running him down, but the
bum only cursed them and continued to stand guard over the
bird. With the flapping sole of one of the sandals he was wearing, trying gently to help the pigeon find its equilibrium, he
repeatedly nudged the bird up to its feet only to see it tumble
to its side once the assistance was removed.

It looked to Sabbath as though the pigeon had been struck
by a car or was ill and dying. He came over to the curb to
watch as the bum with the bottle, wearing a red and white
baseball cap with the logo "Handy Home Repair," leaned
down toward the helpless creature. "Here," he said, "have a
little . . . have some . . ." and he spilled a few drops from
the mouth of the bottle onto the street. Though the pigeon
obstinately worked to recover the power of self-locomotion, it
was clear how with each succeeding effort its strength was
ebbing away. So, too, was the magnanimity of the bum.

"Here—*here*, it's vodka, *take some*." But the pigeon remained oblivious to the offering. It lay on its side barely stirring, its wings unable to do much more than intermittently twitch and collapse. The bum warned, "You're gonna get killed out here —*drink*, you fucker!"

Finally, when he could no longer endure the bird's indifference, he reared back and kicked the pigeon as hard as he could out of the path of the oncoming traffic.

It landed in the gutter only feet from where Sabbath was standing to watch. The bum marched over and kicked it again, and that took care of the problem.

Spontaneously Sabbath applauded. As far as he could tell, there were no longer street performers like himself—streets far too dangerous for that—the street performers now were homeless beggars and bums. Beggar's cabaret, beggar's cabaret that was to his own long-extinct Indecent Theater what the Grand Guignol was to the darling Muppets and their mouths, all the decent Muppets, making people happy with their untainted view of life: everything is innocent, childlike, and pure, everything is going to be okay—the secret is to tame your prick, draw attention away from the prick. Oh, the timidity! *His* timidity! Not Henson's, *his*! The cowardice! The *meekness*! Finally afraid to be utterly unspeakable, choosing to hide out in the hills instead! To everyone he had ever horrified, to the appalled who'd considered him a dangerous man, loathsome, degenerate, and gross, he cried, "Not at all! My failure is failing to have gone far *enough*! My failure is not having gone *further*!"

In response, a passerby dropped something into his coffee cup. "Cocksucker, I haven't finished!" But when he plucked the object out of the cup, it wasn't chewed chewing gum or a cigar butt—for the first time in four years, Sabbath had earned a quarter.

"God bless you, sir," he called after his benefactor. "God bless you and your loved ones and your cherished home with the electrical security system and the computer-accessed long-distance services."

At it again. How he'd begun was how he'd end, he who had gone gloomily around for years believing his life of adulteries and arthritis and professional embitterment to have been senselessly lived outside the conventions, without purpose or unity.

But far from being disappointed at the malicious symmetry of his finding himself thirty years later once again on the street with his hat in his hand, he had the humorous sensation of having meandered blindly back into his own grand design. And you had to call that a triumph: he had perpetrated on himself the perfect joke.

By the time he went off to panhandle in the subway, his cup contained over two dollars in change. Clearly Sabbath had the touch, the look, the patter, the battered, capsized, repellent whatever-it-was that got under people's skins sufficiently fast for them to want to shut him down just long enough to scoot on by and never see him or hear him again.

Between Astor Place and Grand Central, where he had to change for the Suicide Express, he lumbered dutifully from car to car, shaking his cup and reciting from *King Lear* the role he hadn't had occasion to perform since he'd been assailed by his own tomatoes. A new career at sixty-four! Shakespeare in the subway, *Lear* for the masses—rich foundations love that stuff. Grants! Grants! Grants! At least let Roseanna see that he was out hustling, on his feet again, after the scandal that had cost them his twenty-five hundred a year. He was meeting her halfway. Financial equity between them was restored. Yet, even as he was regaining a working man's dignity, a residual sense of self-preservation cautioned him that he wasn't clowning on Town Street. In Madamaska Falls human corruption was considered to reside pretty much in him, Sabbath alone the menace, no one as dangerous anywhere around . . . no one but that midget Jap dean. He hated her fucking midget guts, not for her leading the coven that cost him his job—he hated the job. Not for losing the dough—he hated the dough, hated being an employee on a payroll who got a paycheck that he took to a bank where behind the counter there was a person they called a teller because she had it in her to tell even Sabbath to have a good day. He could not think of anything he hated more than endorsing that check, except perhaps looking at the stub where all the deductions were tallied up. It always got him, trying to figure out that stub, always pissed him off. Here I am at the bank endorsing my check—just what I always wanted. No, it wasn't the job, it wasn't the money, it was los-

ing those girls that killed him, a dozen of them a year, none
over twenty-one, and always at least one. . . .

That year—the fall of '89—it had been Kathy Goolsbee, a
freckled redhead with the shiksa overbite, a hefty, big-limbed
scholarship kid from Hazleton, PA, another of his treasured
six-footers, a baker's daughter who'd worked in the shop after
school from the time she was twelve and who pronounced *can*
"kin" and *going to* the way Fats Waller did when he sang, "I'm
gunna sit right down and write myself a lettuh." Kathy displayed an unlikely flair for meticulous puppet design that reminded him of Roseanna when she started out as his partner,
and so more than likely it *would* have been Kathy that year had
she not "accidentally" left on the sink of the second-floor
women's room of the college library the tape that, unknown
to her teacher, she had made of a phone conversation they'd
had only days earlier, their fourth. She swore to him that all
she intended to do was to take the tape into a toilet stall so she
could listen there in privacy; she swore to him that she'd
brought it with her to the library only because, since they'd
got going together on the telephone, her head, even without
her headset, was ablaze with little else. She swore to him that
vengefully robbing him of his only source of income had never
entered her mind.

It had all begun when Kathy phoned his home one evening
to tell Professor Sabbath she had the flu and couldn't turn in
her project the next day, and Sabbath, seizing on the surprising
call to quiz her paternally about her "goals," learned that she
was living with a boyfriend who tended bar at night in the student hangout and was at the library during the day writing a
"poli sci" dissertation. They talked for half an hour, exclusively
about Kathy, before Sabbath said, "Well, at least don't worry
about the workshop—you stay in bed with that flu," and she
replied, "I am." "And your boyfriend?" "Oh, Brian's at Bucky's,
working." "So you're not only in bed, you're not only sick,
you're all alone." "Yeah." "Well, so am I," he said. "Where is
your wife?" she asked, and Sabbath understood that Kathy was
his nominee for the school year 1989–90. When you feel a
strike like that at the end of the line, you don't have to be

much of a fisherman to know you've hooked a beaut. You get a move on when a girl who speaks only in the stunted argot of her age-group asks in an uncharacteristically languid, slitheringly restless voice, with words that waft out of her more like an odor than a sound, "Where is your wife?"

"Out," he replied. "Hmmmm." "Are you warm enough, Kathy? Is it the chills making you make that noise?" "Uh-uh." "You must be sure you're warm enough. What are you wearing in bed?" "My pj's." "With the flu? That's all?" "Oh, I'm boiling in just these. I keep having flashes. Flushes." "Well," laughing, "I do, too—" and yet, even as he began to reel her in cautiously, gently, without haste, taking all the time in the world to haul her on board, big and speckled and thumpingly alive, inwardly Sabbath was so excited he did not begin to realize that it was he being guided up through leagues of lust by the hook with which she'd pierced *him*; had no idea, he who'd passed into his sixties only the month before, that it was he being craftily landed and that someday very soon now he would discover himself eviscerated, stuffed, and hung as a trophy on the wall above the desk of Dean Kimiko Kakizaki. All the way back in Havana, when Yvonne De Carlo had said to the young merchant seaman, "You finished? Get off!" he had come to understand that in dealing with the wayward you must never allow your cunning to be set aside along with your skivvies simply because of the mad craving to come . . . and yet it never occurred to Sabbath, no, not even to wily old Sabbath, cynical now for a good fifty years, that a big strapping Pennsylvanian with all those freckles could be quite so deficient in ideals as to be setting him up for bringing him down.

It was not three weeks after her first call that Kathy was explaining to Sabbath that she had begun her evening's work listening to their tape in the stacks, at a carrel piled high with books for "Western Civ," but that after only ten minutes, the tape had made her so wet she had left everything and taken off with the headset for the ladies' bathroom. "But how did the tape wind up on the sink," Sabbath asked, "if you were listening to it in a toilet stall?" "I was taking it out to put something else in." "Why didn't you do that in the stall?" "Because I would only have started listening again. I mean, I just didn't know what to do, basically. I thought, 'This is really crazy.' I was, like, so wet and swollen, how could I concentrate? I was in the library to research my paper, only I couldn't stop masturbating." "Everybody masturbates in libraries. That's what they're for. This does not explain to me why you walk away leaving a tape—" "Somebody came *in*." "Who? Who came in?" "It doesn't *matter*. Some *girl*. I got *confused*. By then I didn't even know what I was doing anymore. This whole thing has made me crazy. I was, like, afraid from getting so crazy from the tape, and so I just walked out. I felt really awful. I was gunna call. But I was, like, afraid of *you*." "Who put you up to this, Kathy? Who put you up to taping me?"

Now, however justified Sabbath's anger may have been by what was either an unforgivable oversight or an out-and-out betrayal, as Kathy sat sobbing in the front seat of his car, unburdening herself of the news, even he knew himself to be being less than ingenuous. (He had parked, fatefully enough, across from the Battle Mountain cemetery where Drenka's body would be laid to rest just a few years later.) The truth was that he, too, had taped their conversation, not only the conversation on the tape she'd left at the library but the three that preceded it. But then, Sabbath had been taping his workshop girls for years now and planned to leave the collection to the Library of Congress. Seeing to the collection's preservation was one of the best reasons he had—the only reason he had— to one day get a lawyer to draw up a will.

Including his four with Big Kathy, there were a total of thirty-three tapes, perpetuating the words of six different students who'd taken the puppetry workshop. All were locked away in the bottom drawer of an old file cabinet, stored in two shoeboxes marked "Corres." (A third shoebox, marked "Taxes 1984," contained Polaroids of five of the girls.) Each tape was dated and all were organized alphabetically—and responsibly —by Christian names only and filed chronologically within that classification. He kept the tapes in excellent order not only so that each was easy to locate when he needed it to hand but so that they could be quickly accounted for if he ever worried, as irrationally he sometimes did, that one or another had gotten misplaced. From time to time Drenka would like to listen to the tapes while sucking him off. Otherwise they never left the locked file cabinet, and whenever he took one of his favorites to play a patch for himself, he would double-lock the studio door. Sabbath knew the danger of what he had in those shoeboxes yet he could never bring himself either to erase the tapes or to bury them in garbage at the town dump. That would have been like burning the flag. No, more like defiling a Picasso. Because there was in these tapes a kind of *art* in the way that he was able to unshackle his girls from their habit of innocence. There was a kind of art in his providing an illicit adventure not with a boy of their own age but with someone three times their age—the very repugnance that his aging body inspired in them had to make their adventure with him feel a little like a crime and thereby give free play to their budding perversity and to the confused exhilaration that comes of flirting with disgrace. Yes, despite everything, he had the artistry still to open up to them the lurid interstices of life, often for the first time since they'd given their debut "b.j." in junior high. As Kathy told him in that language which they all used and which made him want to cut their heads off, through coming to know him she felt "empowered." "I still have moments when I'm uncertain and scared. But for the most part," she said, "I just want . . . I want to spend time with you. . . . I want—to take care of you." He laughed. "You think I need taking care of?" "I *mean* it," she said earnestly. "*What* do you mean?" "I mean I can care for you . . . I mean I can take care of your body. *And* your heart." "Yes? You've seen my EKG? You're afraid when I come I'll have a coronary?" "I don't *know*. . . . I mean . . . I don't know *what* I mean but I mean it. That's what I mean—what I just said." "And can I take care of you?" "Yeah. Yeah. You kin." "Which part of you?" "My body," she dared to reply. Yes, they experienced not merely their capacity for deviancy—that they'd known of since seventh grade—but the larger risks that deviancy entailed. His gifts as a theater director and a puppet master he poured without stinting into these tapes. Once he'd passed into his fifties, the art in these tapes—the insidious art of giving license to what was already there—was the only art he had left.

And then he got nailed.

The tape Kathy "forgot" had not only landed by morning in Kakizaki's office but was somehow hijacked and rerecorded, before it even reached the dean, by an ad hoc committee call-

ing itself Women Against Sexual Abuse, Belittlement, Battering, and Telephone Harassment, whose acronym was formed
from the last seven words. By dinnertime of the following
day, SABBATH had opened up a phone line on which the tape
was continuously played. The local phone number to call—
722-2284, fortuitously enough S-A-B-B-A-T-H again—was announced by the committee's cochairpersons, two women, an
art history professor and a local pediatrician, during an hour-
long call-in show on the college radio station. The introduction prepared by SABBATH for the telephonic transmission
described the tape as "the most blatantly vile example of the
exploitation, humiliation, and sexual defilement of a college
student by her professor in the history of this academic community." "You are about to hear," the introduction began,
spoken by the pediatrician, and sounding to Sabbath appropri-
ately clinical though lawyerly as well—lawyerly with palpable
hatred—"two people talking on the telephone: one a man of
sixty and the other a young woman, a college student, who has
just turned twenty. The man is her teacher, acting in loco par-
entis. He is Morris Sabbath, adjunct professor of puppet theater in the four-college program. In order to protect her
privacy—and her innocence—the name of the young woman
has been bleeped wherever it appeared on the tape. That is the
only alteration that has been made in the original conversation, which was secretly transcribed by the young woman in
order to document what she had been subjected to by Professor Sabbath from the day she enrolled in his course. In a candid, confidential statement given voluntarily to the steering
committee of SABBATH, the young woman revealed that this
was not the first such conversation into which she had been
lured by Professor Sabbath. Moreover, she turns out to have
been only the latest of a series of students whom Professor
Sabbath has intimidated and victimized during the years he has
been associated with the program. This tape records the fourth
such telephone conversation to which the student was subjected.* The listener will quickly recognize how by this point

---

*What follows is an uncensored transcription of the entire conversation as
it was secretly taped by Kathy Goolsbee (and by Sabbath) and played by SAB-
BATH for whoever dialed 722-2284 and took the thirty minutes to listen. In just
the first twenty-four hours, over a hundred callers stayed on the line to hear

in his psychological assault on an inexperienced young woman, Professor Sabbath has been able to manipulate her into thinking that she is a willing participant. Of course, to get the woman to think that it is her fault, to get her to think that she is a 'bad girl' who has brought her humiliation on herself by her own cooperation and complicity . . ."

The car descended the slope of Battle Mountain to the lonely spot where he'd arranged to pick her up, the crossroad separating the woods from the fields that led to West Town Street. All the way down the eighteen hundred feet she wept with her whole body shaking, immersed in pain, as though he were lowering her alive into her grave. "Oh, it's unbearable. Oh, it hurts. I'm so unhappy. I don't understand why this is happening to me." She was a big girl whose production of secretions was considerable, and her tears were no exception. He'd never seen tears so large. Someone less of a connoisseur might have taken them for real.

"Extremely immature behavior," he said. "The Sobbing Scene."

---

the harassment from beginning to end. It wasn't long before tapes reproduced from the original began to turn up for sale around the state and, according to the *Cumberland Sentinel*, "as far afield as Prince Edward Island, where the tape is being used as an audio teaching aid by the Charlottetown Project on the State of Canadian Women."

What are you doing right now?
I'm on my stomach. I'm masturbating.
Where are you?
I'm home, I'm on my bed.
You all alone?
Ummmm.
How long are you alone for?
A long time. Brian's at a basketball game.
I see. How nice. You are all alone and on your own bed masturbating. Well, I'm glad you called. What are you wearing?
(*Babyish laugh*) I'm wearing my clothes.
What are you wearing?
I'm wearing jeans. And a turtleneck. Standard wear.
Yes, that's your standard wear, isn't it? I was very excited after I spoke to you last time. You're very exciting.
Ummmm.

"I want to suck you," she managed to moan through her tears.

"The emotionality of young women. Why don't they ever come up with something new?"

Across the road a couple of pickup trucks were parked in the dirt lot of the roadside nursery whose greenhouses constituted the first reassuring signs of the white man's intrusion into these wooded hills (once the heartland of the Madamaskas, to whose tribes the local falls were said—by those opposed to the profane installation of a parking lot and picnic tables—to have been sacred. It was in the numbingly cold pool of one of the remotest tributaries of those sacred falls, the brook that spilled down the rocky streambed beside the Grotto, that he and Drenka would gambol naked in the summer. See plate 4. Detail from the Madamaska vase of dancing nymph and bearded figure brandishing phallus. On bank of brook, note the wine jar, a he-goat, and a basket of figs. From the collection of the Metropolitan Museum. XX century A.D.).

"Get out. Disappear."

"I want to suck you hard."

You are. Don't you know that?

But I felt bad. I felt like I disturbed you when I called at your house.

You didn't disturb me in terms of my not wanting to hear from you. I just felt it was a good idea to stop that before it went any further.

Sorry. And I won't do it again.

Fine. You just misjudged. And why not? You're new to this. Okay. You're alone and you're on your bed.

Yeah, and also, I wanted . . . Last time we talked you said . . . about I told you I felt disgusted, you know, when I get really disgusted . . . and you said about what, and I said whatever I said, like I said, my lack of ability in workshop . . . and then I think I was just very evasive, like, I didn't really, like, I felt that I couldn't really tell you (*embarrassed laugh*). . . . It's much more specific. . . . I'm just, like . . . well, maybe it's just now . . . it's like I think about sex all the time (*confessional laugh*).

Do you?

Yes, I do. I just feel I can't do anything about it. It's very . . . I mean, it's very . . . It's very good, sometimes. (*Laugh*)

You masturbate a lot?

Well, no.

No?

Well, I don't really have the opportunity. I'm in class. And it's all so boring and my mind is just elsewhere completely. And ummmm . . .

A worker in coveralls was loading mulch sacks onto one of the trucks—otherwise there wasn't anyone in sight. Mist was rising beyond the woods to the west, the seasonal mist that to the Madamaskas undoubtedly meant something about reigning divinities or departed souls—their mothers, their fathers, their Morties, their Nikkis—but to Sabbath recalled nothing more than the opening of "Ode to Autumn." He was not an Indian, and the mist was the ghost of no one he knew. This local scandal, remember, was taking place in the fall of 1989, two years before the death of his senile mother and four before her reappearance jolted him into understanding that not everything alive is a living substance. This was back when the Great Disgrace was still to come, and for obvious reasons he could not locate its origins in the sensuous stimulus that was the innocuously experimental daughter of the Pennsylvania baker with the foreboding surname. You besmirch yourself in increments of excrement—everyone knows that much about the inevitabilities (or used to)—but not even Sabbath understood how he could lose his job at a liberal arts college for teaching a twenty-year-old to talk dirty twenty-five years after Pauline

---

You have sex thoughts.

Yeah. Constantly. And I just . . . I think it's normal but sort of extreme. And I feel—guilty, I guess.

Really? What do you feel guilty about? Having sex thoughts all the time? Everybody does.

You think so? I don't think most people think like that.

You'd be surprised at what most people think like. I wouldn't worry about it. You're young and you're healthy and you're lovely and so why shouldn't you? Right?

I guess. I don't know. Sometimes I read in psych about people, you know, diagnosed, like, "hypersexual," and I'm, like, "Hey." Now I feel I'm just gunna, like, you're gunna think I'm a nymphomaniac and I'm not. I don't . . . whatever . . . like, I'm not out having sex. I don't know. I think I just sexualize every interaction I have with people, and I feel guilty. I feel like this is . . . you know . . . no good.

You feel that with me?

Well, ummmm . . .

You sexualized our phone calls, I sexualized our phone calls—nothing wrong with that. You don't feel guilty about that, or do you?

Well, I mean . . . I don't know. I guess I don't feel guilty. I feel very empowered. But, nevertheless, I'm just, like, saying, like, in general I don't sit

Réage, fifty-five years after Henry Miller, sixty years after
D. H. Lawrence, eighty years after James Joyce, two hundred
years after John Cleland, three hundred years after John
Wilmot, second earl of Rochester—not to mention four hundred after Rabelais, two thousand after Ovid, and twenty-two
hundred after Aristophanes. By 1989 you had to be a loaf of
Papa Goolsbee's pumpernickel not to be able to talk dirty. If
only you could run a '29 penis on ruthless mistrust, cunning
negativity, and world-denouncing energy, if only you could
run a '29 penis on relentless mischief, oppositional exuberance,
and eight hundred different kinds of disgust, then he wouldn't
have needed those tapes. But the advantage a young girl has
over an old man is that she is wet at the drop of a hat, while to
engorge him it is necessary at times to drop a ton of bricks.
Aging sets problems that are no joke. The prick does not come
with a lifetime guarantee.

  The mist was rising preternaturally from the river, and the
pumpkins, ripe for carving, dotted like the freckles on Kathy's
face a big open field back of the greenhouse, and affixed to the
trees, wouldn't you know it, all the right leaves, every last one

---

around thinking I lack ability. I sit around thinking, *What* is going on in my
head? I can't stand it.

  So you're going through the time when you're obsessed with sex. It happens to everybody. Especially as nothing in school is interesting you.

  I think that's the problem. It's like I react to it. I have to rebel or something.

  It doesn't engage your mind. And so your mind is empty and something
moves in and what moves in—because you're frustrated, the thing that can answer the frustration is sex. It's very common. There's nothing on your mind,
and it's filled by this thing. Don't worry about it. Okay?

  (*Laugh*) Yeah. I'm glad. . . . You see, I feel like I could tell you this but I
couldn't tell anyone else.

  You can tell me and you have told me and it's fine with me. You're in Levi's
and you've got on your turtleneck shirt.

  Yeah.

  Yeah?

  Yeah.

  You know what I want you to do?

  What?

  Unzip your Levi's.

  Okay.

tinted to polychromatic perfection. The trees were resplendent precisely as they'd been resplendent the year before—and the year before that—a perennial profusion of pigmentation to remind him that by the waters of the Madamaskas he had every reason to weep, because that was about as far as he could have got himself from the tropical sea and the Romance Run and those grand cities like Buenos Aires, where a common seaman of seventeen could eat for peanuts in 1946 at the greatest steak houses along the Florida—they called the main street in B.A. Florida—and then cross the river, the famous Plata, to where they had *the best places*, which meant the places where there were the most beautiful girls. And in South America that meant the most beautiful girls in the world. So many hot, beautiful women. And he had sequestered himself in New England! Colorful leaves? Try Rio. They got the colors too, only instead of on trees they're on flesh.

Seventeen. Three years Kathy's junior and no ad hoc committee of mollycoddling professors to keep me from getting clap, getting rolled, or getting stabbed to death, let alone get-

———————

Undo the button.

Okay.

And unzip it.

Okay. . . . I'm in front of the mirror.

You're in front of the mirror?

Yeah.

Lying down?

Yeah.

Now pull your Levi's down. . . . Pull 'em down around your ankles.

(*Whispered*) Okay.

And take them off. . . . I'll give you time. . . . Did you get them off?

Yeah.

What do you see?

I see my legs. And I see my crotch.

Do you have bikini underpants on?

Yes.

Take your hand and put your finger right on the crotch of your underpants. Just on the outside of the underpants, rub it up and down. Just rub it gently up and down. How does that feel?

Good. Yeah. It feels real good. It feels so nice. It's wet.

Is it wet?

It's really wet.

ting my little ears molested. I went there deliberately to get myself molly-bloomed! That's what sevenfuckinteen is *for*!

Frost, he mused—thought Sabbath—passing the time until Kathy got the idea that not even with his *low* standards would he dare to risk his dick again with an out-and-out adder and that she should just slither back to the Japanese viperina. The dim meatballs who were the proud descendants of the settlers who'd usurped these hills from the Original Goyim—an epithet historically more accurate than "Indians" and more respectful, too, as Sabbath had explained to that pal of Roseanna's who taught "Hunting and Gathering" as a literature course. . . . Where was I? thought he, when once again the blandishments tumbling forth from perfidious Kathy caused him to lose his . . . the dim meatballs, long now the Reigning Goyim, all crowing gaily—as in "When Hearts Were Young and Gay"—about another frost, lower temperatures than even the night before, when Roseanna, wearing only a nightie, had been found by the state police at three A.M. stretched on her back across Town Street, waiting to be run over.

You're still outside the underpants. Just on the outside rub it. Rub it up and down. . . . Now move the underpants aside. Can you do that?

Yeah.

And now put your finger on your clitoris. And just rub it up and down. And tell me how that feels.

It feels good.

Make yourself excited that way. Tell me how that feels.

I'm putting my finger in my cunt. I'm on top of my finger.

You on your belly or on your back?

I'm sitting up.

You're sitting up. And looking in the mirror?

Yeah.

And you're going in and out?

Yeah.

Go ahead. Fuck it with your finger.

I want it to be you, though.

Tell me what you want.

I want your cock. I'll get it really, really hard.

Want me to stick it in you?

I want you to stick it into me hard.

A nice stiff cock inside you?

Ummmm. Oh, I'm touching my breasts.

An hour or so earlier she had left their house by car but had failed even to negotiate the first fifty feet of the hundred yards of curving dirt incline that lay between the carport and Brick Furnace Road. She had been speeding off not for town but for Athena, fourteen miles away, where Kathy shared an apartment with Brian a few blocks from the college, at 137 Spring. And despite having driven her Jeep into a boulder in the hay field that was their front yard, despite having to stumble without shoes or slippers two and a half miles down the twist of pitch-black lanes to the bridge that crossed the brook to Town Street, despite having lain on the asphalt insufficiently clad anywhere from fifteen minutes to half an hour before being spotted by the cop cruising by, she was clutching in one of her freezing hands a yellow Post-it note bearing—in a drunken scrawl legible by then not even to herself—the address of the girl who'd asked at the close of the tape, "When is your wife coming back?" Roseanna's intention was to tell this little whore in person just how fucking back she was, but having stumbled to the ground so many times without getting anywhere near Athena, Roseanna decided on Town that she'd be

---

You want to take your turtleneck off?

I'm just lifting it up.

You want to put the nipple between your fingers?

Yeah.

How about wetting it? Wet it with your fingers. Wet your fingers with your tongue and then wet the end of your nipple. Is that good?

Oh, God.

Now fuck your cunt again. Fuck your cunt.

Ummmm.

And tell me what you want. Tell me what you most want.

I want you on top of my back. Your cock inside me. Oh, God. Oh, God, I want *you*.

What do you want, (*bleep*)? Tell me what you want.

I want your cock. I want it everywhere. I want your hands everywhere. I want your hands on my legs. On my stomach. My back. On my breasts, squeezing my breasts.

Where do you want my cock?

Oh, I want it in my mouth.

What are you going to do when it's in your mouth?

Suck it. Suck it really hard. I want to suck your balls. I want to lick your balls. Oh, God.

And what else?

better off dead. That way the girl would never have to ask that question again. None of them would.

"I want to suck you right here."

Sabbath had not only driven some six hours that day—getting Roseanna to the private psychiatric hospital in Usher and then himself back in time to meet Kathy—but had been up confronting this newest upheaval since just after three in the morning, when he had been awakened by a loud knock at the side door and the astonishing news that it was the police returning the wife whom he had assumed was sleeping all the while in their king-size bed, not cuddled close to him, needless to say, but safely over at the far edge, where, admittedly, he had not journeyed for many a year. When they had moved up from queen-size he had remarked to a visitor that the new bed was so big he couldn't find Roseanna in it. Overhearing him from where she happened to be gardening just outside the kitchen window, she had shouted into the house, "Why don't you look?" But this was easily over a decade back, when he still spoke to people and she was drinking only a bottle a day and there was still a remnant of hope.

Oh, I just want you to squeeze me. Then I want you to start pumping me.

Pump you? I'm pumping you right now. Tell me what you want.

I want you to pump me. Oh, I want you inside me.

What are you doing now?

I'm on my stomach. I'm masturbating. I want you to suck my breasts.

I'm sucking on them right now. I'm sucking your tits now.

Oh, God.

What else do you want me to do to you?

Oh, God. I'm going to come.

You're going to come?

I want to. I want you here. I want you on top of me. I want you on top of me right now.

I'm on top of you.

Oh. God. Oh, God. I have to stop.

Why do you have to stop?

Because—I'm afraid. I'm afraid to not be able to hear.

I thought no one was coming back. I thought he was playing basketball.

Well, you never know. Oh, God. Oh, God. Oh, God, this is awful. I have to stop. I want your cock. Pumping me hard. Digging into me. Oh, God. What are you doing right now?

I have my cock in my hand.

You squeezing it and rubbing it? I want you to rub it. Tell me. I want my

Yes, there at the door, earnestly polite now, stood Matthew Balich, whom his former art teacher had failed to recognize either because of the state trooper uniform or because of the booze. She had apparently whispered to Matthew, before he authoritatively made known his mission, that they must be very quiet to avoid awakening her hardworking husband. She had even tried to tip him. Heading for Kathy's in only a nightgown, she'd still had the percipience to take her purse in case she needed to buy a drink.

It had been a long night, morning, and afternoon for Sabbath. First the Jeep had to be towed off the boulder where she'd run aground, then arrangements had to be made through the family doctor to get her a bed at Usher, then the effort had to be undertaken to force her, hung over and hysterical though she was, to agree to twenty-eight days in Usher's rehab program, and then at last there was the six-hour round-trip to the hospital, Roseanna ranting at him from the backseat the whole way there, pausing only to instruct him angrily to pull over at each service station they passed so she could try to relieve herself of her cramps.

---

mouth on it. I want to suck it. Oh, God, I want to kiss it. I want to put your cock in my ass.

What do you want to do with my cock right now?

I want to suck it right now. I want to be between your legs. You pull my head.

Hard?

No. Just gently. And then I'll move around. Let me suck you.

I'll let you. If you say please, I'll let you.

Oh, God. This is torture.

Is it? You got your finger in your cunt?

No.

It's not torture. Put your finger in your cunt, (*bleep*). Put your finger in your cunt.

Okay.

Put your finger right up inside your cunt.

Oh, God, it's so hot.

Put it up there. Now move it up and down.

Oh, God.

Move it up and down, (*bleep*). Move it up and down, (bleep). Move it up and down, (*bleep*). Fuck it, (*bleep*). Come on, fuck it. Come on, fuck it.

Oh, God! Oh, God!

Go ahead, fuck it.

Why she had to get plastered by stages in those putrid rest-
rooms instead of openly guzzling from the bottle in her purse
Sabbath did not bother to inquire. Her pride? After last night,
her pride? Nor did Sabbath do anything to stop her when she
listed the ways in which a wife whose intentions had merely
been to assist him at his work and to comfort him when there
were setbacks and to look after him when the arthritis was
most acute had herself been ruthlessly ignored, insulted, exploited, and betrayed.

Up front in the car Sabbath played the Goodman tapes to
which he and Drenka used to dance together in the motel
rooms he rented up and down the valley when first they'd
become enraptured lovers. During the 130-mile drive west to
Usher, the tapes more or less drowned out Roseanna's tirade
and allowed Sabbath some respite from all that he'd been
through since Matthew had kindly returned her. First they
fucked, then they danced, Sabbath and Matthew's mom, and
while Sabbath faultlessly sang the lyrics into her grinning, incredulous face, his come would leak out of her, making even
more lubricious the inner roundness of her thighs. The come

Oh! Oh! Oh! Mickey! Oh, my God! Ahh! Ahh! Ahh! Jesus Christ! Oh, my
God! Jesus Christ! I want you so bad! Uhhh! Uhhh! Oh, God. . . . I just
came.

Did you come?

Yeah.

Was that good?

Yeah.

Want to come again?

Uh-uh.

No?

No. I want you to come.

You want to make me come?

Yeah. I'm gunna suck your cock.

You tell me how you're going to make me come.

I'm gunna suck you. Slowly. Up and down. Slowly move my lips up and
down your cock. Move my tongue. I'm gunna suck off the top of your cock.
Really slowly. Ummm. Oh, God. . . . What do you want me to do?

Suck my balls.

Okay. Okay.

I want you to put your tongue on my ass. Want to do that?

Okay.

Make my asshole very excited with your tongue.

would stream all the way down to her heels, and after they'd danced he would massage her feet with it. Nestled down at the end of the motel bed, he would suck on her big toe, pretending it was her cock, and she pretended that his come was her own.

(And where did all those 78s disappear to? After I went to sea, what happened to the 1935 Victor recording of "Sometimes I'm Happy" that was Morty's treasure of treasures, the one with the Bunny Berigan solo that Morty called "the greatest trumpet solo ever, by anyone"? Who got Morty's records? What happened to his things after Mother died? Where are they?) Stroking with one spoon-shaped thumb the breadth of Croatian cheekbone while with the other jiggling her on-off switch, Sabbath sang "Stardust" to Drenka, not like Hoagy Carmichael, in English, but in French no less—"Suivant le silence de la nuit / Répète ton nom . . ."—exactly the way it was sung for the prom crowds by Gene Hochberg, who led the swing band in which Morty played clarinet (and who, amazingly, would wind up just like Morty flying B-25s in the Pacific and who Sabbath had always secretly wished had been

---

Yeah. I can do that.

Put your finger up my ass.

Okay.

Did you ever do that?

Nooo. Uh-uh.

Take your finger, while we're fucking. Gently put it on my asshole. And then fuck my ass with your finger. Do you think you'd like that?

Yeah. I want to make you come.

Play with it with your hand. And when a little drop comes out, you can smear the head of it with the drop. You like that?

Yeah.

Did you ever fuck a woman?

No.

Didn't you?

No.

No? Just have to ask, you know.

(*Laughter*)

Nobody at school ever tried to fuck you? No woman ever tried to fuck you in the four-college program?

Ummm, no.

Really?

Ummm, no. Not that I haven't thought about it.

You have thought about it?

the one to be shot down). A bearded barrel he indisputably was, yet Drenka cooed ecstatically, "My American boyfriend. I have an American boyfriend," while the great Goodman performances of the thirties transformed into the pavilion over the LaReine Avenue beach the room reeking of disinfectant that he had rented for six bucks in the name of Goodman's maniac trumpeter on "We Three and the Angels Sing," Ziggy Elman. At the LaReine Avenue pavilion Morty taught Mickey to jitterbug one August night in 1938, when the little boy who was his shadow was just nine. The kid's birthday present. Sabbath taught the girl from Split how to jitterbug on a snowy afternoon in 1981 in a motel in New England called the Bo-Peep. By the time they left at six to drive, in two cars, the plowed roads home, she could tell Harry James's solos from Elman's on "St. Louis Blues," she could imitate very funnily Hamp going "Ee-ee" in that screechy way he did it in the final solo of "Ding Dong Daddy," she could knowingly say about "Roll 'Em" what Morty used to knowingly say to Mickey about "Roll 'Em" after the boogie-woogie beginning starts petering out in the Stacy solo: "It's really just a fast blues in F."

Yeah.

What do you think?

I think about being on top of a woman and sucking her breasts. And putting our cunts together—and rubbing. Kissing.

Never did it?

Uh-uh.

Did you ever fuck two men?

Uh-uh.

No?

Uh-uh. (*Laughing*) Did you?

Not that I recall. You ever think about that?

Yeah.

About fucking two men.

Yeah.

You have fantasies about it?

Yeah. I guess so. I think about just sort of anonymous men. Fucking.

Did you ever fuck a man and a woman?

No.

Did you ever think about that?

I don't know.

No?

Maybe. Yeah. I guess so. Why are *you* asking all the questions?

She could even bang out on Sabbath's hairy hindquarters the Krupa tom-tom beat in her own accompaniment to "Sweet Leilani." Martha Tilton taking over from Helen Ward. Dave Tough taking over from Krupa. Bud Freeman coming over in '38 from the Dorsey band. Jimmy Mundy, from the Hines band, coming over as staff arranger. In one long winter afternoon at the Bo-Peep her American boyfriend taught Drenka things she could never learn from the devoted husband whose pleasure that day was to be out all alone in the snow, building stone walls until it got too dark even to see his own breath.

At Usher a kindly, handsome doctor twenty years Sabbath's junior assured him that if Roseanna cooperated with "the program" she would be home and on the path to sobriety in twenty-eight days. "Wanna bet?" Sabbath said, and drove back to Madamska Falls to kill Kathy. Ever since three A.M., when he learned how Roseanna, because of that tape, had stretched out on Town Street in her nightgown, waiting to be run over, he had been planning to take Kathy to the top of Battle Mountain and strangle her.

As a ripe, enormous pumpkin floated free from the darken-

Well, you can ask me questions if you want.
Did you ever fuck a man?
No.
Never?
No.
Really?
Yes.
Did you ever fuck two women?
Uh-huh.
Did you ever fuck a prostitute?
Uh-huh.
You did? Oh, my God (*laughing*).
Yeah, I fucked two women.
Did you like it?
I loved it. I love it.
Really?
Yeah. They loved it, too. It's fun. I fucked the two of them. They fucked each other. And they both sucked me. And then I would suck one of them. While the other sucked me. That was good. I had my face in her cunt. And the other one would be sucking on my cock. And then the first one would be sucking on the other one's cunt. So everybody would be sucking everybody

ing field across from the car and the high drama of a full harvest moon began, Sabbath could not have said where he found
the strength to refrain—as, for the fifth time in as many minutes, she extended yet again the offer to entrap him—from
either commencing the strangulation with his once-powerful
fingers or going ahead and taking it out in a car for the mil-
lionth time in this life.

"Kathy," he said, exhaustion giving him the sensation that he
was glimmering and fading like a dying light bulb, "Kathy," he
said, thinking as he watched the moon ascend that if only
he'd had the moon on his side things would have turned out
differently, "do us all a favor—do Brian instead. That may even
be what he's angling for by turning into a deaf-mute. Didn't
you say that the shock of hearing the tape has turned him into
a deaf-mute? Well, go home and sign him that you're going to
blow him and see if his face doesn't light up."

Not too hard on Sabbath, Reader. Neither the turbulent inner talkathon, nor the superabundance of self-subversion, nor
the years of reading about death, nor the bitter experience of
tribulation, loss, hardship, and grief make it any easier for a

---

else. And sometimes one of them sucks you and makes you hard and then she
puts it in the other one's cunt. How does that strike you?

It's good.

I like to watch them suck each other. That's always exciting. They make
each other come. There are lots of things to do, aren't there?

Yeah.

Frighten you?

Yeah.

Does it really?

A little bit. But I want to fuck you. I want to fuck you. I don't want to fuck
you with someone else.

I'm not asking you to. I'm just answering your questions. I just want to fuck
you. I want to suck your cunt. Suck your cunt for an hour. Oh, (*bleep*), I want
to come all over you.

Come on my breasts.

You like that?

Yes.

You're a very hot girl, aren't you? Tell me what your cunt looks like now.

Uh-uh.

No? You're not going to tell me what it looks like?

Uh-uh.

man of his type (perhaps for a man of any type) to get good use out of his brain when confronted by such an offer once, let alone when it is made repeatedly by a girl a third his age with an occlusion like Gene Tierney's in *Laura*. Don't be too hard on Sabbath for beginning to begin to think that maybe she was *telling the truth*: that she *had* left the tape in the library accidentally, that it *had* fallen into he Kakumoto's hands accidentally, that she *had* been helpless to resist the pressures brought on her and had capitulated only to save her skin, as who among her "peers"—that was what she called her friends —would have done otherwise? She was really a sweet and decent kid, good-natured, involved, she had presumed, in some half-crazy but harmless extracurricular amusement, Professor Sabbath's Audio-Visual Club; a large, graceless girl, ill-educated, coarse, and incoherent in the preferred style of the late-twentieth-century undergraduate, but utterly without the shifty ruthlessness necessary for the vicious stunt he was charging her with. Maybe merely because he was so enraged and exhausted, a great misapprehension had taken hold of him and he was falling victim to another of his stupid mistakes. Why

---

I can imagine it.

(*Laughter*)

It's beautiful cunt.

You know what happened?

What?

I had a gynecologist appointment. And I thought the gynecologist was coming on to me.

Was he?

She.

She was?

It was very different from anything that had ever happened to me before.

Tell me.

I don't know. She was just, like . . . She was very pretty. She was beautiful. She put the speculum in and she said, "Oh, my God, you have so much stuff in here." And she kept saying it. And she sort of lifted out this huge glob. I don't know. It was weird.

She touch you?

Yeah. She put her hand in me. I mean her fingers to do the exam.

Make you excited?

Yeah. She touched this . . . I have a little burn on my thigh, and she touched it, and she asked me what happened. I don't know. It was different. And that's when . . .

would she be crying so pitifully for so long if she was conspiring against him? Why would she cling to his side like this, if her true ties and affinities were with his supervirtuous antagonists and their angry, sinister fixed ideas about what should and should not constitute an education for twenty-year-old girls? She didn't begin to have Sabbath's skill at feigning what looked like genuine feeling . . . or did she? Why else would she be begging to blow someone wholly alien to her, inessential to her, someone who was already a month into his seventh decade on earth, if not to assert without equivocation that she was farcically, illogically, and incomprehensibly his? So little in life is knowable, Reader—don't be hard on Sabbath if he gets things wrong. Or on Kathy if *she* gets things wrong. Many farcical, illogical, incomprehensible transactions are subsumed by the manias of lust.

Twenty. Could I even survive saying no to twenty? How many twenties are left? How many thirties or forties are left? Under the sad end-of-days spell of the smoky dusk and the waning year, of the moon and its ostentatious superiority to all the trashy, petty claptrap of his sublunar existence, why does

---

That's when what?

Nothing.

Tell me.

I just felt really good. I thought I was crazy.

You thought you were crazy?

Yeah.

You're not crazy. You're a hot kid from Hazleton and you're excited. Maybe you should fuck a girl.

Uh-uh (*laughing*).

You can do whatever you want, you see? You want to make me come now?

Yeah. I'm all sweaty. It's cold here, too. Yeah, I want you to come. I want to suck your cock. I want it so bad.

Keep going.

You have your hand on it?

You bet.

Good. Are you rubbing it?

I'm jerking it.

You're jerking it?

I'm pumping it up and down. I'm pumping it up and down. I'm going to take my balls out. Oh, it feels good, (*bleep*), it feels good.

Where do you want me?

he even hesitate? The Kamizakis are your enemies whether you do anything or not, so you might as well do it. Yes, yes, if you can still do something, you *must* do it—that is the golden rule of sublunar existence, whether you are a worm cut in two or a man with a prostate like a billiard ball. If you can still do something, then you must do it! Anything living can figure that out.

In Rome . . . in Rome, he was now remembering while Kathy continued her sobbing beside him, an elderly Italian puppeteer said to have once been quite famous had come to the school to judge a competition that Sabbath proceeded to win, and afterward the puppeteer, having given a demonstration of stale wizardry with a puppet looking exactly like himself, had asked young Sabbath to accompany him to a café in the Piazza del Popolo. The puppeteer was in his seventies, small, pudgy, and bald with a poor yellowish complexion, but so haughtily autocratic was his bearing that Sabbath spontaneously followed the example of his awestruck professor and, even enjoying for a change being deferential—albeit impudently so—he addressed the old man, whose name meant

---

I want your cunt to sit right down on my cock. To slide on top of it. And to just start pumping up and down. To sit on it and go up on it.

Squeeze my breasts?

I'll squeeze 'em.

Squeeze my nipples?

Oh, I'll bite on your nipples. Your beautiful pink nipples. Oh, (*bleep*). Oh, it's filling up with come now. It's filling up with hot, thick come. It's filling up with hot white come. It's going to shoot out. Want me to come in your mouth?

Yeah. I want to suck you right now. Very fast. I want to put you in my mouth. Oh, God. I'm sucking it hard.

Suck it, (*bleep*). Suck me.

Faster and faster?

Suck me, (*bleep*).

Oh, God.

Suck me, (*bleep*). Want to suck my dick?

Yes, I want to suck you. I want to suck your cock.

Suck my stiff cock. Hard, stiff cock. Suck my hard, stiff cock.

Oh, God.

Oh, it's full of come, (*bleep*). Oh, (*bleep*), suck it now. Ahha! Ahh! Ahh! Ahh! . . . Oh, my goodness. . . . Are you still there?

Yeah.

That's good. I'm glad it's you who's still there.

nothing to him, as Maestro. In addition to his insufferable posturing there was an ascot that half hid a substantial wattle, a beret that, out-of-doors, concealed the baldness, a stick with which he tapped the table to draw the attention of the waiter—and all of this readied Sabbath for a flood of boring old bohemian self-adoration that he would just have to endure for having won the prize. But instead, no sooner had the puppeteer ordered cognac for both of them than he said, "Dimmi di tutte le ragazze che ti sei scopato a Roma"—Tell me about all the girls you fucked in Rome. And then while Sabbath answered, speaking plainly and freely of the arsenal of allurement Italy was to him, describing how more than once he had been provoked to emulate the locals and follow someone clear across the city to nail down a pickup, the master's eyes were eloquent with a sardonic superiority that caused even the ex-merchant seaman, a veteran six times over of the Romance Run, to feel a little like a model child. The old man's attention did not waver, however, nor did he interrupt other than to press for more elaboration than the American could always furnish in his limited Italian—and, repeatedly, to demand from Sabbath the precise age of each girl whose seduction he described. Eighteen, replied Sabbath obediently. Twenty, Maestro. Twenty-four. Twenty-one. Twenty-two . . .

(*Laughter*)

Oh, sweetheart.

You're an animal.

An animal? You think so?

Yeah.

A human animal?

Yeah.

And you? What are you?

A bad girl.

That's a good thing to be. It's better than the opposite. You think you have to be a good girl?

Well, it's what people expect.

Well, you be realistic and let them be unrealistic. Jesus. There's a mess here.

(*Laughter*)

Oh, lovely (*bleep*).

Are you still alone?

Yes. I'm still alone.

When's your wife coming back?

Only when Sabbath had finished did the maestro announce to him that his own current mistress was fifteen. Abruptly he rose to leave—to leave the café and to leave Sabbath with the check—but not before adding, with a derisive flick of his cane, "Naturalmente la conosco da quando aveva dodici anni"—Of course I've known her since she's twelve.

And only now, practically forty years later, with Kathy still crying for him and the oblivious blank of a moon still rising for him, with folks here in the hills and down in the valley settling in by the fire for a pleasant fall evening of listening on the phone to Kathy and him coming, did Sabbath believe that the old puppeteer had been telling him the truth. Twelve. Capisco, Maestro. You might as well go for broke.

"Katherine," he said sadly, "you were once my most trusted accomplice in the fight for the lost human cause. Listen to me. Stop crying long enough to listen to what I have to say. Your people have on tape my voice giving reality to all the worst things they want the world to know about men. They have got a hundred times more proof of my criminality than could be required by even the most lenient of deans to drive me out of every decent antiphallic educational institution in America. Must I now ejaculate on CNN? Where is the camera? Is there a telephoto lens in that pickup truck over by the nursery? I've got my breaking point, too, Kathy. If they send me up for sodomy, the result could be death. And that might not be as much fun for you as you may have been led to believe. You may have forgotten, but not even at Nuremberg was everyone sentenced to die." On he continued—in the circumstances, a lovely speech; *it* should be taped, thought he. Yes, on Sabbath went, developing with increasing cogency the argument in support of a constitutional amendment to make coming illegal for American men, regardless of race, creed, color, or ethnic origin, until Kathy cried out, "I'm of age!" and wiped her face dry of tears with the shoulder of her running jacket.

"I do what I want," she angrily asserted.

Maestro, what would *you* do? To peer down at her head cradled in your lap, your cock encircled by her foaming lips, and to watch her blowing you in tears, to patiently lather that undissipated face with that sticky confection of spit, semen, and tears, a delicate meringue icing her freckles—could life be-

stow any more wonderful last thing? She had never looked
more soulful to Sabbath, and he pointed this out to the maestro. She had never before looked soulful to Sabbath at all. But
tears made her radiant, and even to the jaded maestro she
seemed to be digging into a spiritual existence that was news
to her, as well. She *was* of age! Kathy Goolsbee had just grown
up! Yes, not only something spiritual but something primordial was going on, as there had been on that hot summer day
up in the picturesque brook beside the Grotto when he and
Drenka had pissed on each other.

"Oh, if only I could believe that you weren't in cahoots with
these filthy, lowlife, rectitudinous cunts who tell you children
these terrible lies about men, about the sinister villainy of what
is simply the ordinary grubbing about in reality of ordinary
people like your dad and me. Because that is who they are
against, honey—me and your dad. That's what it comes down
to: caricaturing us, insulting us, abhorring in us what is
nothing more than the delightful Dionysian underlayer of life.
Tell me, how can you be against what has been inherently
human going back to *antiquity*—going back to the virginal
peak of Western civ—and yourself a civilized person? Maybe
it's because she's Japanese that she doesn't dig the unparalleled mythologies of ancient Attica. I don't get it otherwise.
How would they like you to be sexually initiated? Intermittently by Brian, while he takes poli sci notes at the library? Are
they going to leave it to a dry-as-dust scholar to initiate a girl
like you? Or are you supposed to pick it up on your own? But
if you're not expected to pick up chemistry on your own, if
you're not expected to pick up physics on your own, then why
are you supposed to pick up the erotic *mysteries* on your own?
Some need seduction and don't need initiation. Some don't
need initiation but still need seduction. Kathy, *you needed both.*
Harassment? I remember the good old days when *patriotism*
was the last refuge of a scoundrel. Harassment? I have been
Virgil to your Dante in the sexual underworld! But then, how
would those professors know who Virgil is?"

"I want," she said yearningly, "to suck you so hard."

That "so"! And yet hearing the so intensifying "so," feeling
the familiar, lifelong urge to crude, natural bodily satisfaction
creep uncontrollably across every square inch of his two square

yards of yearning old hide, Sabbath thought not, as he would have hoped, of his estimable mentor, the unplatitudinous maestro, obedient to the end to the edict of excitement, but of his sick wife suffering in the hospital. Of all people! It isn't fair! The '29 as stiff as a horse's and who should he start thinking about but Roseanna! He saw before him the little cell of a room to which they'd assigned her after admission, a room beside the nurse's station, where she could be conveniently observed during the twenty-four-hour detox watch. They would take her blood pressure every half hour and do what they could for the shakes she was going to have because she had been drinking steadily for the previous three days—drinking hard right up to the hospital door. He saw her standing beside that narrow bed with the sad chenille spread, so stoop-shouldered that she looked no taller than he was. On the bed lay her suitcases. Two pleasant un-uniformed nurses, who had asked her politely to open them for inspection, meticulously went through her things, removing her eyebrow tweezers, her nail scissors, her hair dryer, her dental floss (so she wouldn't stab, electrocute, or hang herself), impounding a bottle of Listerine (so she would not drink it all down in desperation or smash the bottle to use the shards to slit her wrists or cut her throat), examining everything in her wallet and extracting from it her credit cards, driver's license, and all her cash (so she could not buy contraband whiskey smuggled into the hospital or wander off grounds to a bar in Usher village or jump-start a staff member's car and head home), rummaging through all the jeans, sweaters, underwear, and jogging stuff; and all the while Roseanna, lost, lifeless, immensely alone, hollowly looked on, her aging folksingerish good looks demolished—a woman decarnalized: simultaneously a pre-erotic juvenile and a post-erotic wreck. She might have been living all these years, not in a simple box of a house where every fall the deer fed off the apple trees in the hillside orchard beyond the screen porch, but locked away inside an automatic car wash, where there was no hiding from the battering rain and the big turning brushes and the gaping blowers pouring forth their hot air. Roseanna restored to its roots in stripped-to-its-skin, nickel-and-dime, down-to-earth reality the exalted phrase "the bludgeonings of fate."

"The cause," sobbed Roseanna, "goes free, the effect goes to jail." "Isn't that life exactly," he agreed. "Only it's not jail. It's a hospital, Rosie, and a hospital that doesn't even look like one. As soon as you stop suffering, you'll see that it's very pretty, like a big country inn. There are a lot of trees and nice walks to walk on with your friends. I noticed driving in that there is even a tennis court. I'll send your racket Federal Express." "Why are they taking my Visa card!" "Because you don't pay nightmare by nightmare and tremor by tremor; as your Catholic upbringing should have taught you, you pay through the nose at the end." "It's *your* things they should be searching! They'd come up with enough to put *you* away for good!" "Do you want the nurses to do that, to search me? For what?" "The handcuffs you use on your teenage whore!" Twenty, Sabbath thought to inform the two nurses, no longer a teenager, unfortunately; but neither nurse appeared the least bit amused or appalled by the Sabbaths' farewell banter and so he didn't bother. Foul language and loud shouting the nurses had heard before. The drunk frenetic, terrified, extremely angry at the mate, the mate even angrier with the drunk. Husbands and wives yelling and screaming and accusing were nothing new to them, nothing new to anyone—you don't have to work in a mental hospital to know about husbands and wives. He watched the nurses dutifully checking each and every pocket of all of Roseanna's jeans for a stray joint or a razor blade. They impounded her keys. Good. That was in her own best interest. Now there was no chance of her bursting unannounced into the house. He wouldn't have wanted Roseanna, in her condition, to have to deal with Drenka, too. Let's deal first with the addiction. "*You* should be locked up, Mickey—and everyone who knows you knows it!" "I'm sure one day they *will* lock me up, if that is truly the consensus. But let the others see to that. You just get sober real quick now, ya hear?" "You don't *want* me s-s-sober! You *prefer* a drunk. S-so you can s-s-s—" "Seem," he whispered, to help her over the hump. Her *s*'s always bested her when she mixed her rage with more than a quart of vodka. "S-seem to be the long s-s-s—" "Long-suffering husband?" "Yes!" "No. No. Sympathy isn't my bag. You know that. I don't ask to be s-s-seen as anything other than what I am. Though tell me again what that is—I wouldn't want to forget during the days we're apart." "A fail-ure! A fucking nons-s-s-stop failure! A s-s-s-scheming, lying, s-s-s-sick, deceiving total failure who lives off his wife and fucks *children*! He's the one," she weepingly told the nurses, "who *put* me here. I was *fine* till I met him. I wasn't this at *all*!" "And," he rushed to reassure her, "in only twenty-eight days it'll all be over and you'll be just the way you were before I made you into 'this.'" He raised his hand beside his face to shyly wave good-bye. "*You cannot leave me here!*" she cried. "The doctor said I get to see you after the first two weeks." "But what if they give me shock treatment!" "For drinking? I don't think they do that—do they, nurse? No, no. All they give you is a new outlook on life. I'm sure all they want you to do is to drop your illusions and adapt to reality like me. Bye-bye. Two little weeks." "I'll be counting the days," said Rosie's old self, but then, when she saw that he was really going to leave her there, something from within contorted her spiteful smile into a knotted lump and she began to wail.

This sound accompanied Sabbath along the corridor and down the flight of stairs and out the main hospital door, where a group of patients were having a smoke and looking upstairs to see in which of the rooms the new wailer was suffering. It accompanied him to the parking lot and into the car and then out onto the highway, and it was with him all the way back to Madamaska Falls. Louder and louder Sabbath played the tapes, but even Goodman couldn't cancel it out—even Goodman, Krupa, Wilson, and Hampton in their heyday, breaking loose with "Running Wild," even Krupa opening dramatically out with the bass drum on that last great chorus couldn't obliter-ate Roseanna's eight-bar solo flourish. A wife going off like a siren. The second crazy wife. Was there any other kind? Not for him. A second crazy wife who'd begun life hating her father and then discovered Sabbath to hate instead. But then Kathy *loved* her protective, self-sacrificing dad, who'd worked day and night in the bakery to put three Goolsbee kids into college, and a lot of good it did her. *Or* Sabbath. I can't win. No one can, when they follow Father with me.

If it was Roseanna's wail earlier in the day that gave Sabbath the determination to decline what he had never before de-clined in his life, then that was a truly record-breaking wail.

"Time to go home to blow Brian."

"But this isn't *fair*. I didn't *do* anything."

"Go home or I'll kill you."

"Don't say that—my God!"

"You would not be the first woman I killed."

"Uh-huh. Sure. Who was?"

"Nikki Kantarakis. My first wife."

"That's not funny."

"True enough. Murdering Nikki constitutes my sole claim to real gravitas. Or *was* it pure fun? I'm never entirely convinced by my assessment of anything. That ever happen to you?"

"Jesus! Like, what are you even *talking* about?"

"I'm only talking about what everybody talks about. You know what they say at the college. They say I had a wife who disappeared but that she didn't *just* disappear. Can you deny you've heard 'em say it—can you, Kathy?"

"Well . . . people say everything—don't they? I don't even remember. Who even *listens*?"

"Sparing my feelings, isn't that nice. But you needn't. You learn by sixty to accept in a sporting spirit the derision of virtuous bystanders. Besides, they happen to have it right. Thus proving that if, when speaking of a fellow creature, you give continual expression to your antipathy, a strange kind of truth may unfold."

"Why don't you say anything *seriously* to me!"

"I have never said anything more seriously to anyone: I killed a wife."

"*Please* stop this."

"You telephoned to play doctor on the phone with somebody who killed his wife."

"I did *not*."

"What drives you, anyway? At the highest levels of higher education, my identity as a murderer has been laid bare, and you phone to tell me that you are in your pj's, all alone in bed. What's inside of *you* scorching *you*? Your bondage is bondage to *what*? I am a notorious killer-diller *who strangled his wife*. Why else would I have to live in a place like this if I hadn't strangled somebody? I did it with these very hands while we were rehearsing in our bedroom, on our bed, the final act of *Othello*. My wife was a young actress. *Othello*? It's a play. It's a play in which an African Venetian strangles his white wife to death. You never heard of it because it perpetuates the stereotype of the violent black male. But back in the fifties, humanity hadn't figured out yet what was important, and students fell prey in college to a lot of wicked shit. Nikki was terrified of every new role. She suffered insufferable fears. One was of men. Unlike you, she was not wily in the ways of men. This made her perfect for the part. We rehearsed beforehand alone in our apartment to try to reduce Nikki's fears. 'I can't do it!' This I heard from her many times. I played the stereotypical violent black male. In the scene in which he murders her I did it—I went ahead and murdered her. Got carried away by the spell of her acting. It just opened something up in me to see it. Someone to whom the tangible and the immediate are repugnant, to whom only the illusion is fully real. This was the order Nikki made of her chaos. And you, what is the order you make of yours? Talking about your tits to an old man on the phone? You elude description, at least by me. Such a shameless creature and yet so bland. Perverse and treacherous, the French kiss of death, already deep into the disreputable thrills of a double life—and *bland*. As chaos goes, yours seems decidedly unchaotic. The chaos theorists ought to study you. How deep does what Katherine does or says reach down into Katherine? Whatever you want, however dangerous or deceitful, you pursue, like, impersonally, you know?"

"Okay. How *did* you kill her?"

Lifting his hands, he said, "I used these. I told you. 'Put out the light, and then put out the light.'"

"Whatja do with the body?"

"I rented a boat at Sheepshead Bay. A harbor in Brooklyn. I was a sailor boy once. I loaded the body down with bricks and dumped Nikki overboard out at sea."

"And how did you get a dead body to Brooklyn?"

"I was always carrying things around. I had an old Dodge in those days and I was always shoving into the trunk my portable stage and my props and my puppets. The neighbors saw me coming and going all the time like that. Nikki was a stringbean. She didn't weigh much. I stuffed her doubled-over into my seaman's bag. No big deal."

"I don't believe you."

"Too bad. Because I've never told anyone before. Not even Roseanna. And now I've told you. And as our little scandal teaches us, telling you isn't exactly observing the dictates of prudence. Who do you tell first? Dean Kuziduzi, or will you go straight to the Japanese high command?"

"Why must you be so racially prejudiced against Japanese!"

"Because of what they did to Alec Guinness in *The Bridge on the River Kwai*. Putting him in that fucking little box. I hate the bastards. Who will you tell first?"

"No one! I'm not telling anyone, because it's not *true*!"

"And if it were? Would you tell anyone then?"

"What? If you really were a murderer?"

"Yes. And if you knew I was. Would you turn me in the way you turned in the tape?"

"I *forgot* the tape! I left the tape *accidentally*!"

"Would you turn me in, Kathy? Yes or no?"

"Why must I answer these questions!"

"Because it's indispensable to my finding out just who the fuck you are working for."

"No one!"

"Would you turn me in? Yes or no? If it were true that I was a murderer."

"Well . . . you want a serious answer?"

"I'll take what I get."

"Well . . . it would depend."

"On?"

"On? Well, on our relationship."

"You might not turn me in if we had the right relationship? And what would that be? Describe it."

"I don't know. . . . I guess love."

"You would protect a murderer if you loved him."

"I don't *know*. You never murdered anyone. These questions are *stupid*."

"*Do* you love me? Don't worry about my feelings. Do you love me?"

"In a way."

"Yes?"

"Yes."

"Old and loathsome as I am?"

"I love . . . I love your mind. I love how you expose your mind when you talk."

"My mind? My mind is a murderer's mind."

"Stop *saying* that. You're *scaring* me."

"My mind? Well, this is quite a revelation. *I* thought you loved my ancient penis. My *mind*? This is quite a shock for a man of my years. Were you really only in it for my mind? Oh, no. All the time I was talking about fucking, you were watching me expose my mind! Paying unwanted attention to my *mind*! You dared to introduce a mental element into a setting where it has no place. Help! I've been mentally harassed! Help! I am the victim of mental harassment! God, I am getting a gastrointestinal disorder! You have extracted mental favors from me without my even knowing and against my will! I have been belittled by you! My *dick* has been belittled by you! Call the dean! My dick has been disempowered!"

With this, Kathy finally found the initiative to push open the door, but so frantically, with such force, that she tumbled from the car to the shoulder of the road. But she was up on her Reeboks almost immediately and, through the windshield, could be seen speeding north toward Athena. Puppets can fly, levitate, twirl, but only people and marionettes are confined to running and walking. That's why marionettes always bored him: all that walking they were always doing up and down the tiny stage, as though, in addition to being the subject of every marionette show, walking were the major theme of life. And those strings—too visible, too many, too blatantly metaphorical. And always slavishly imitating human theater. Whereas puppets . . . shoving your hand up a puppet and hiding your face behind a screen! Nothing like it in the animal kingdom! All the way back to Petrushka, anything goes, the crazier and uglier the better. Sabbath's cannibal puppet that won first prize from the maestro in Rome. Eating his enemies on the stage. Tearing them apart and talking about them all the while they were chewed and swallowed. The mistake is ever to think that to act and to speak is the natural domain of anyone other than a puppet. Contentment is being hands and a voice—looking to be more, students, is madness. If Nikki had been a puppet, she might still be alive.

And down the road, Kathy fleeing by the oversize light of the preposterous moon. And the smokers now gathered in moonlight, too, beneath the cell of the detoxing Roseanna, whose wailing could still be heard 130 miles away. . . . Oh, she was in for it tonight, up against an even more horrifying trial than being married to him. The doctor had warned Sabbath that she might telephone to beg him to come get her out. He counseled Sabbath to ignore the bidding of compassion and tell her no. Sabbath promised to do his best. Rather than head home to hear her ringing, he sat a while longer in the car, where, for reasons he couldn't figure out right off, he was remembering the guy who'd given him those books to read on the Standard Oil tanker, remembering how they unloaded through that great piping system at Curacao and how that guy —one of those gentlemanly, quiet types who mysteriously spend their lives at sea when you would expect them to wind up as teachers or even maybe ministers—had given him a book of poems by William Butler Yeats. A loner. A self-educated loner. The guy's silences gave you the creeps. Another American type. One met all our American types at sea. Even by that time, a good many of them Hispanic—tough, really tough Latino types. I remember one who looked like Akim Tamiroff. All kinds of our colored brothers, every type you can think of—sweet men, not so sweet men, everybody. There was a big, fat black cook on that ship where the guy who gave me that book started me off reading. I'd be lying in my top bunk with a book, and this cook would always come in and grab my balls. And start laughing. I'd have to wrestle him away. Guess that makes me "homophobic." He didn't make any more aggressive moves but would have been very pleased if I'd responded, no doubt about that. Interesting thing was that I used to see him in the whorehouses. Now, the guy who gave me the poetry was out-and-out queer yet never laid a glove on me, pretty green-eyed lad though I was. Told me which poems to read. Gave me a lot of books. Awfully nice of him, really. Guy from Nebraska. I'd memorize the poems on my watch.

Of course! Yeats to Lady Goolsbee:

> I heard all old religious man
> But yesternight declare

That he had found a text to prove
That only God, my dear,
Could love you for yourself alone
And not your yellow hair.

In only a few hours Kathy would be crossing the finish line. He could see her taping her breasts and falling into the embrace of the Immaculate Kamizoko. Breasting the tape. Kaki-zomi. Kazikomi. Who could remember their fucking names. Who wanted to. Tojo and Hirohito sufficed for him. Sobbing hysterically, she would tell the dean of his terrifying confession. And the dean might not resist believing it as Kathy had pretended to do.

Driving home he played "The Sheik of Araby." Few things in this world as right as those four zippy solos. Clarinet. Piano. Drums. Vibes.

How come nobody hates Tojo anymore? Nobody remembers that killer except me. They think Tojo's a car. But ask the Koreans about the Japanese sitting on their faces for thirty-five years. Ask the Manchurians about the civility of their conquerors. Ask the Chinese about the wonderful understanding shown them by those little flat-faced imperialist bastards. Ask about the brothels the Japs stocked for their soldiers with girls just like you. Younger. The dean thinks *I'm* the enemy. Ho, ho! Ask her about the boys back home and how they bravely fucked their way through Asia, the foreign women they enslaved and made into whores. Ask 'em in Manila about the bombs, tons of bombs dropped by Japs *after* Manila was an open city. Where is Manila? How would you know? Maybe one day Teacher will take an hour off from harassment lessons to mention to all her spotless lambs a little horror called World War II. The Japan*eez*. As racially arrogant as anyone anywhere—beside them the Ku Klux Klan is . . . But how would you know about the Ku Klux Klan? How would you know anything, given whose clutches you're in? You want the lowdown on the Japan*eez*? Ask my mother, also a woman harassed in life. Ask her.

Expansively he sang along with the quartet, pretending to be Gene Hochberg, who could really get a crowd of kids up and swingin'; delighting himself, Sabbath was, not just in the multidemeaning lyric of the old twenties anthem celebrating date rape and denigrating Arabs but in the unending, undecorous, needling performance, the joy of the job of being their savage. How could the missionaries puff themselves up without their savage? Their naive fucking impertinence about carnal lusting! Seducer of the young. Socrates, Strindberg, and me. Yet feeling great all the same. The glassy chiming of Hampton's hammering—that could fix about anything. Or maybe it was having Rosie out of the way. Or maybe it was knowing that he'd never had to please and wasn't starting now. Yes, yes, yes, he felt uncontrollable tenderness for his own shit-filled life. And a laughable hunger for more. More defeat! More disappointment! More deceit! More loneliness! More arthritis! More missionaries! God willing, more cunt! More disastrous entanglement in everything. For a pure sense of being tumultuously alive, you can't beat the nasty side of existence. I may not have been a matinee idol, but say what you will about me, it's been a real human life!

> I'm the Sheik of Araby,
> Your love belongs to me.
> At night when you're asleep,
> Into your tent I'll creep.
> The stars that shine above,
> Will light our way to love.
> You'll rule the land with me,
> I'm the Sheik of Araby.

Life *is* impenetrable. For all Sabbath knew, he had just thrown over a girl who had neither betrayed nor bebitched him and never could—a simple, adventurous girl who loved her father and would never deceive any grown man (except Father, with Sabbath); for all he knew he had just frightened off the last twenty-year-old into whose tent he would ever again creep. He had mistaken innocent, loving, loyal Cordelia for her villainous sisters Goneril and Regan. He'd got it as backward as old Lear. Lucky for his sanity there was some consolation to be had in the big bed up on Brick Furnace Road by fucking Drenka there that night and the twenty-seven nights to follow.

The only communication Sabbath received during the two weeks before he was allowed to visit Roseanna was a resoundingly factual postcard sent to him from Usher at the end of her first week there: no salutation and mailed simply to their street address in Madamaska Falls—she would not even write his name. "Meet me at Roderick House, 23rd, 4:30 p.m. Dinner at 5:15. I have AA meeting 7–8 p.m. Stay Ragged Hill Lodge in Usher if you don't want to drive home same night. R.C.S."

Just as he was getting into the car at 1:30 on the 23rd, the phone rang in the house and he raced back through the kitchen door, thinking that it must be Drenka. When he heard Roseanna, reversing the charges, he figured she was calling to ask him not to come. He'd phone Drenka with the news as soon as she hung up.

"How are you, Roseanna?"

Her voice, never highly inflected, was ironed flat, stern and angry and flat. "Are you coming?"

"I was just getting into the car. I had to run back to the house to get the phone."

"I want you to bring something. Please," she added, as though someone were there instructing her on what to say and how to say it.

"Bring something? Of course," he said. "Anything."

Her reply to this was a harsh, unscripted laugh. Followed icily by "In my file. Top drawer at the back. A blue three-ring binder. I have to have it."

"I'll bring it. But I'll have to get into the file."

"You'll need the key." More icily still, if that could be possible.

"Yes? Where would I find it?"

"In my riding boots. . . . The left boot."

But over the years he'd searched through all her boots, shoes, and sneakers. She must have moved it there recently from wherever it had been hidden from him before.

"Go get it now," she said. "Find it now. It's important. . . . Please."

"Sure. Okay. The right boot."

"The *left*!"

No, it wasn't hard to make her lose hold. And that was with two weeks already under her belt and only two to go.

He found the key and, from the file, got the blue three-ring binder and came back to the phone to assure her he had it.

"Did you lock the file?"

He lied and said yes.

"Bring the key with you. The file key. Please."

"Of course."

"And the binder. It's blue. There are two elastic bands around it."

"Got it right here."

"Please don't lose it!" she exploded. "It is a matter of life or death!"

"Are you sure you really want it?"

"Don't *argue* with me! Do as I ask you! It's not easy for me even to *talk* to you!"

"Would you rather I didn't come?" He wondered if it would be safe at this hour to drive by the inn and blow the horn twice, their signal for Drenka to meet him at the Grotto.

"If you don't want to come," she said, "don't. You're not doing anyone a favor. If you're not interested in seeing me, *that is fine with me.*"

"I am interested in seeing you. That's why I was in the car when you called. How do you feel? Are you any better?"

She answered in a wavering voice, "It isn't easy."

"I'm sure it isn't."

"It's damn hard." She began to cry. "It's *impossibly* hard."

"Are you making headway at all?"

"Oh, you don't understand! You'll never understand!" she shouted, and hung up.

In the binder were the letters that her father had sent her after she had left him to go to live with her mother, following her mother's return from France. He'd written a letter to Roseanna every single day right up to the evening that he killed himself. The suicide letter was addressed both to Roseanna and to the younger sister, Ella. Roseanna's mother had gathered the letters to her daughters together and had kept them for them until she herself had died after a long ordeal with emphysema the year before. The binder had been bequeathed to

Roseanna along with her mother's antiques, but she had never been able even to remove the elastic bands holding it shut. For a while she was determined to throw it out, but she could not do that either.

Halfway to Usher, Sabbath stopped at a highway diner. He held the binder in his lap until the waitress brought him coffee. Then he removed the elastic bands, placed them carefully in his jacket pocket, and opened to the letters.

The letter written only hours before he hanged himself was headed "My beloved children, Roseanna and Ella," and dated "Cambridge, Sept. 15, 1950." Rosie was thirteen. Professor Cavanaugh's last letter Sabbath read first:

Cambridge, Sept. 15, 1950

My beloved children, Roseanna and Ella,

I say *beloved* in spite of everything. I have always tried to do my best, but I have failed completely. I have failed in my marriages and I have failed in my work. When your mother left us, I became a broken man. And when even you, my beloved children, abandoned me, everything ended. Since then I have had total insomnia. I have no strength any longer. I am exhausted and I am ill from all the sleeping pills. I cannot go on any longer. God help me. Please do not judge me too harshly.

Live happily!
Dad

Cambridge, Feb. 6, 1950

Dear little Roseanna!

You cannot imagine how I miss my beloved little darling. I feel completely empty inside and I don't know how I'll get over it. But at the same time I feel that it was important and necessary that it happen. I have seen the change in you since May of last year. I was terribly worried since *I could not help you* and you did not wish to confide in me. You bottled yourself up and pushed me away. I did not know that you had such a hard time in school but I suspected as much since your classmates never visited you. Only pretty little Helen Kylie came sometimes and picked you up in the morning. But my little dear one, the fault was yours. You felt superior and you showed it maybe more than you knew yourself. This is exactly the same thing that happened to your mother with her friends here. Dear little Roseanna, I do not say this to accuse you but so that you can think through all of this and eventually discuss it with your mother. And then you'll learn that in life one must not be selfish. . . .

Cambridge, Feb. 8, 1950

. . . you had lost contact with your father and I could no longer penetrate the armor by which you surrounded yourself. It worried me so deeply. I understood that you needed a mother, I even tried to get you one but that failed totally. Now you have your real mother back, whom you so long have missed. Now you have all the possibilities again to become well. This will give you new courage to live. And you'll be happy again with school. In intelligence you are way, way above the average. . . .

Your father's home remains open for you, whenever you want to return, for a shorter or longer period of time. You are my most beloved child and the emptiness is enormous without you. I shall try to gain solace thinking that what happened was best for you.

Please write me something as soon as you are settled. Good-bye, my little darling! A thousand loving kisses from your lonely

Dad

Cambridge, Feb. 9, 1950

Dear little Roseanna!

I ran into Miss Lerman on the street. She was sad that you left the school. She said that all the teachers liked you so much. But she understood that you had a difficult time lately, infections, et cetera, which forced you to be absent for long periods. She also noted that lately you hadn't been together with Helen Kylie or your other nice friends, Myra, Phyllis, and Aggie. But she said these girls were committed to their studies while Roseanna has lost the desire to succeed. She hoped that you would get over your difficulties in a few years. She had seen many similar cases, she said. She also felt strongly, as I do, that a girls' school is better for girls in puberty. Unfortunately your mother does not seem to share Miss Lerman's opinion. . . .

. . . yes, dear little Roseanna, I hope you'll soon be as happy as when you were my sunshine, truthful and straightforward. But then our problems began. I wanted to help you but I couldn't since you didn't want my help. You couldn't confide your worries to me any longer. Then you needed a mother but then you did not have a mother, unfortunately. . . .

A huge hug from
Dad

Cambridge, Feb. 10, 1950

Dear Roseanna!

You promised to call and write often to me when you left. You were so sweet and open and I believed you. But love is blind. Now five days have passed since you left and I have not had one line from you. Neither did you want to speak to me last night, even though I was home. I am beginning to understand, my eyes are opening. Do you have a bad conscience? Can you no longer look your father in the eye? Is that the thank-you for all I have done for you during these five years when I alone had to take care of my children? It is cruel. It is horrible. Can you ever again come home to your father and look him in the eye? I can hardly grasp this. But I do not judge you. I understand that lately you have been under hypnosis. Your mother seems to have made it her mission to harass me to the utmost. Her only interest is my defeat. She does not seem to have changed as much as you children seem to think.

Maybe you will write a few lines and tell me what I should do. Shall I clean out your room and try to forget that you ever existed?

Why did you lie to me at the stationery store about the ten dollars? It was unnecessary. Not a beautiful last memory.

Dad

Cambridge, Feb. 11, 1950

Dearest little Roseanna!

A thousand thank-yous for your longed-for letter today! It made me so happy that I now feel like another person. The sun is shining again over my broken life. Please forgive my last letter. I was so depressed when I wrote it that I barely believed I could stand up again. But today everything feels different. Irene has now become so kind that I would even say she is *sweet*. She has probably helped me over the worst crisis—your departure. . . .

Of course you are welcome so long as you do not completely cut off contact with your father. And now, since things here at home are calm and peaceful again, your letters will be heartily welcome to us *all*. Please write as often as you can to us. It doesn't have to be a long epistle but just a short greeting that you are fine. Though sometimes you must write some lines to your father telling him how you feel in the depths of your soul, especially when sorrows drag you down.

Dearest dearest dearest regards from us all, but especially from your loving

Dad

This was the way the letters went from the February day in 1950 when Roseanna moved from Cambridge with Ella to live with her mother through the end of April, which was as far as Sabbath was able to read if he intended to be on time for dinner at the hospital. And he was sure to hear the same despondent message being beeped right on down to the end anyway—the world against him, obstructing him, insulting and crushing him. *Shall I clean out your room and try to forget that you ever existed?* From bleeding Professor Cavanaugh to his thirteen-year-old beloved after not having heard from her for five days. The suffering, crazy drunk—couldn't have been battle-free one day of his life, until the day the stone was lifted. *Please do not judge me harshly. Live happily! Dad.* And then, no longer out or tune with a thing. Everything at last under control.

Sabbath pulled into the hospital parking lot just before five. On foot he made his way up a circular drive that separated a wide bowl of green lawn from a long three-storied white clapboard house with black-shuttered windows at the top of the hill, the hospital main building, designed, coincidentally enough, very much in the style of the Baliches' colonial-style inn overlooking Lake Madamaska. In the last century there'd been a lake here, too, where now there was the lakelike lawn, and looming above it a massive Gothic mansion that had fallen into ruin after the death of the childless owners. First the roof gave way, then the stone walls, until, in 1909, the lake was drained and the spookily picturesque pile was pushed into the hole with a steam shovel and covered over to make way for a TB sanatorium. Today the old sanatorium was the main building of Usher Psychiatric Hospital but continued to be referred to as the Mansion.

Doubtless because the dinner hour was approaching, the crowd of smokers gathered outside the front door of the Mansion numbered twenty or twenty-five, a handful of them surprisingly young, boys and girls in their teens who were dressed like the students in the valley, the boys with their baseball caps on backward and the girls in college T-shirts, running shoes, and jeans. He asked the prettiest of the girls—who would also have been the tallest if only she had stood up straight—to direct him to Roderick House and observed, when she raised her arm to point the way, a horizontal slash mark across her wrist that looked to be only recently healed.

An ordinary autumn late afternoon—which is to say, radiant and extraordinary. How horrible, how *dangerous* this beauty must be to someone suicidally depressed, yet the kind of day, thought Sabbath, that perhaps makes it possible for a garden-variety depressive to believe that the cavern through which he is crawling may be leading in the direction of life. Childhood at its very best is recalled, and the abatement, if not of adulthood, at least of dread seems for the moment possible. Autumn at the psychiatric hospital, autumn and its famous meanings! How can it be autumn if I am here? How can I be here if it is autumn? *Is* it autumn? The year again in magical transition and it does not even register.

Roderick House lay just off the bottom of a turning of the road that ringed the lawn and led back out to the county highway. The house was a smaller, two-story version of the Mansion, one of seven or eight such houses set irregularly back among the trees, each with an open veranda and a grassy front yard. Coming upon Roderick from the rise of the drive, Sabbath saw four women sitting on outdoor furniture pulled close together on the lawn. The one reclining in the white plastic chaise was his wife. She was wearing sunglasses and lying perfectly still, while around her the others were in lively conversation. But then something so funny was said by someone —perhaps even by Roseanna—that she sprang to a sitting position and clapped her hands together with joy. Her laugh was more spontaneous than he'd heard it for years. They were all still laughing when Sabbath appeared, walking across the lawn. One of the women leaned toward Roseanna. "Your visitor," she whispered.

"Good day," said Sabbath and formally bowed to them. "I am the beneficiary of Rosearma's nest-building instinct and the embodiment of all the resistance she encounters in life. I am sure that each of you has an unworthy mate—I am hers. I am Mickey Sabbath. Everything you have heard about me is true. Everything is destroyed and I destroyed it. Hello, Rosie."

It did not astonish him when she failed to pop up out of the chair to embrace him. But when she took off the sunglasses and shyly said, "Hi," . . . well, the voice on the phone had not led him to expect such loveliness. Only fourteen days off the sauce and away from him, and she looked thirty-five. Her skin was clear and tawny, her shoulder-length hair shone more golden than brown, and she seemed even to have recovered the width of her mouth and that appealing width between her eyes. She had a notably broad face but her features had been vanishing within it for years. Here lay the simple origin of their suffering: her knockout girl-next-door looks. In just fourteen days she had cast off two decades of bungled life.

"These," she said awkwardly, "are some residents of the house." *Helen Kylie, Myra, Phyllis, Aggie* . . . "Would you like to see my room? We've got a little time." She was now an utterly disconcerted child, too embarrassed by a parent's presence to be anything but miserable so long as he remained among her friends.

He followed Roseanna up the stairs to the veranda—three smokers out there, youngish women like the ones on the lawn —and into the house. They passed a small kitchen and turned down a corridor lined with notices and newspaper clippings. To one side the corridor opened onto a small, dark living room where another group of women were watching TV and to the other onto the nurse's station, partitioned in glass and cheerily hung with "Peanuts" posters above the two desks. Roseanna pulled him halfway through the door. "My husband's here," she said to the young nurse on duty. "Fine," replied the nurse and nodded politely to Sabbath, whom Roseanna immediately dragged away before he told the nurse, too, that everything was destroyed and he had destroyed it, right on the money though that indictment might be.

"Roseanna!" a friendly voice called from the living room. "Roseanna Banana!"

"Hi."

"Back to Bennington," said Sabbath.

Bitterly she jumped on him. "Not *quite*!"

Her room was small, freshly painted a sparkling white, with two curtained windows looking onto the front yard, a single bed, an old wooden desk, and a dresser. All anyone needed, really. You could live in a place like this forever. He stuck his head into the bathroom, turned on a tap—"Hot water," he said approvingly—and then, when he came out, saw on the desk three framed photographs: the one of her mother wrapped in a fur coat in Paris just after the war, the old one of Ella and Paul with their two plump, blond children (Eric and Paula) and a third (Glenn) plainly on the way, and a photograph that he had never seen before, a studio portrait of a man in a suit, tie, and starched collar, a stern, broad-faced middle-aged man who did not look at all "broken" but could be no one but Cavanaugh. There was a composition notebook open on the desk, and Roseanna closed it with one quivering hand while she nervously circled the room. "Where's the binder?" she said. "You forgot the binder!" She was no longer the sylph in sunglasses he'd seen on the lawn, merrily laughing with Helen, Myra, Phyllis, and Aggie.

"I left it locked in the car. It's under the seat. It's safe."

"And what," she cried in all seriousness, "if somebody steals the car?"

"Is that likely, Roseanna? That car? I was hurrying to be on time. I thought we'd get it after dinner. But I'll leave whenever you want me to. I'll get the binder and leave now if you want me to. You looked great until two minutes ago. I'm no good for your complexion."

"I planned to show you the place. I wanted to take you around. I *did*. I wanted to show you where I swim. Now I'm confused. Terribly. I feel hollow. I feel awful." Sitting on the edge of her bed, she began to sob. "It's, it's a thousand dollars a day here" were the words she managed finally to utter.

"Is that what you're crying about?"

"No. The insurance covers it."

"Then what is making you cry?"

"Tomorrow . . . tomorrow night, at the meeting, I have to tell 'My Story.' It's my turn. I've been making notes. I'm terrified. For days I've been making notes. I'm nauseated, my stomach hurts. . . ."

"Why be terrified? Pretend you're talking to your class. Pretend they're just your kids."

"I'm not terrified of *speaking*," she replied angrily. "It's what I'm *saying*. It's my saying the *truth*."

"About?"

She couldn't believe his stupidity. "About? *About?* Him!" she cried, pointing to her father's picture. "That man!"

So. It's *that* man. It's *him*.

Innocently enough, Sabbath asked, "What did he do?"

"Everything. *Everything*."

The dining room, on the first floor of the Mansion, was pleasant and quiet and bright with light from the bay windows that looked out across to the lawn. The patients sat where they liked, mostly at oak tables large enough for eight, but a few stayed apart at tables along the wall that seated two. Again he was reminded of the inn at the lake and the pleasant mood of the dining room there when Drenka officiated as high priestess. Unlike the customers at the inn, the patients served themselves from a buffet table where tonight there were french fried potatoes, green beans, cheeseburgers, salad, and ice cream —thousand-buck-a-day cheeseburgers. Whenever Roseanna got up to refill her glass of cranberry juice, one or another of those drying out and crowded together at the juice machine smiled at her or spoke to her, and as she passed with yet another full glass, someone at a table took hold of her free hand. Because tomorrow night she had to tell "My Story" or because tonight "he" was here? He wondered if anybody at Usher—patient, doctor, or nurse—had as yet dialed across the state line to get an earful of what had put her here.

Only it was the father who had done everything who had put her here.

But how come she'd never told him of this "everything" before? Hadn't she dared to speak of it? Hadn't she dared to remember it? Or did the charge so clarify for her the history of her misery that whether it was truly rooted in fact was a cruelly irrelevant question? At last she possessed the explanation that was at once exalted and hideous and, by zeitgeist standards, more than reasonable. But where—if anywhere any longer— was a true picture of the past?

You cannot imagine how I miss my beloved little darling. I feel completely empty inside and I don't know how I'll ever get over it. You are my most beloved child and the emptiness is enormous without you. Only pretty little Helen Kylie came sometimes. When you were my sunshine, truthful and straightforward. You were so sweet and open and I believed you. But love is blind. Do you have a bad conscience? Can you no longer look your father in the eye? Your longed-for letter. The sun is shining again over my broken life.

Who had hanged himself in that Cambridge attic, a bereft father or a spurned lover?

At dinner, by talking continuously, she seemed able to pretend that Sabbath wasn't there or that whoever was sitting opposite was somebody else. "See the woman," she whispered, "two tables behind me, petite, thin, glasses, early fifties?" and she synopsized the story of *her* marital disaster—a second family, a twenty-five-year-old girlfriend and two little children three and four, the husband had secretly stashed away in the next town. "See the girl with the braids? Red-haired . . . lovely, smart kid . . . twenty-five . . . Wellesley . . . construction worker boyfriend. Looks like the Marlboro man, she says. Throws her up against the wall and down the stairs, and she can't stop phoning him. Phones every night. Says she's trying to get him to feel some remorse. No luck yet. See that dark, youngish guy, working-class? Two tables to your left. A glazier. Sweet guy. Wife hates his family and won't let him take the children to see them. Wanders around all day talking to himself. 'It's useless . . . it's hopeless . . . it's never going to change . . . the shouting . . . the scenes . . . can't take it.' All you hear in the morning are people crying in their rooms, crying and saying 'I wish I were dead.' See the guy there? Tall, bald, big-nosed guy? In the silk robe? Gay. Room full of perfumes. Wears his robe all day. Always carrying a book. Never comes to program. Tries to kill himself every September. Comes here every October. Goes home every November. He's the only man in Roderick. One morning I passed his room and heard him sobbing inside. I went in and sat down on the bed. He told me his story. His mother died three weeks after he was born. Rheumatic heart. He didn't know how she died until he was twelve. She was warned beforehand about pregnancy but had him anyway and died. He thought he killed her. His first memory is of sitting in a car with his father, being driven from one home to another. They changed residences all the time. When he was five his father moved in with a couple, friends. His father stayed there thirty-two years. Had a secret affair with the wife. The couple had two daughters he considers his sisters. One *is* his sister. He's an architectural draftsman. Lives by himself. Sends for pizza every night. Eats it watching television. Saturday nights he makes himself something special, a veal dish. He stammers. You can barely hear him when he speaks. I held his hand for about an hour. He was crying and crying. Finally he says, 'When I was seventeen, my mother's brother came, my uncle, and he . . .' But he couldn't finish.

He can't tell anybody what happened when he was seventeen. Still can't, and he's fifty-three. That's Ray. One person's story is worse than the next. They want internal quiet and all they get's internal noise."

So she continued till they had finished their ice cream, whereupon she jumped to her feet, and together they headed for her father's letters.

Walking rapidly beside her down the drive to the parking lot, Sabbath spotted a modern building of glass and pink brick on a crest off to the back of the Mansion. "The lockup," Roseanna told him. "It's where they detox the ones that come in with d.t.'s. It's where they give you shock. I don't even like to look at it. I said to my doctor, 'Promise me you'll never send me to the lockup. You can't ever send me to the lockup. I couldn't take it.' He said, 'I cannot make you any such promise.'"

"Surprise," said Sabbath. "They only stole the hubcaps."

He opened the car door, and the moment he took the binder (with the thick elastic bands back in place) out from under the front seat and handed it to her, she was sobbing again. Somebody else every two minutes. "This is *hell*," said Roseanna, "the turbulence doesn't *stop*!" and, turning away from him, she ran back up the hill, clutching the binder to her chest as though it alone would spare her from the lockup. Should he spare her the further agony of his presence? If he left now he'd be home before ten. Too late to get to Drenka, but how about Kathy? Take her to the house, dial S-A-B-B-A-T-H, listen to the tape while they went down on each other.

It was twenty to seven. Roseanna's meeting began in the Mansion "lounge" at seven and ran until eight. He strolled across the green bowl of the lawn, still impersonating—though for how much longer who could tell?—a guest. By the time he had got to Roderick, Roseanna had called the nurse on duty from a Mansion phone to ask her to tell him to wait in the room until she got back from AA. But that had been his plan, whether he was invited or not, ever since he'd seen on her desk the composition notebook in which she was readying her revelation for the next night.

Maybe Roseanna had forgotten where she'd left it; maybe from merely having to lay eyes on him again (and here, without

the helping hand of the drink whose beneficent properties as a
marital booster are celebrated even in Holy Scripture*), she'd
been unable to think straight and had left a message with the
nurse that made no sense at all. Or maybe she actually wanted
him to sit alone in her room and read all that her agony had
written there. But to get him to see what? She had wanted him
to provide her with this while she provided him with that, and,
of course, he had no intention of being party to any such
arrangement, because, as it happened, he had wanted her to
provide him with that while he provided her with this. . . .
But why, then, remain married? To tell the truth, he didn't
know. Sitting it out for thirty years is indeed inexplicable until
you remember that people do it all the time. They were not
the only couple on earth for whom mistrust and mutual aversion furnished the indestructible foundation for a long-standing union. Yet, how it seemed to Rosie, when her endurance
had reached its limit, was that they *were* the only ones with
such wildly contradictory cravings, they *had* to be: the only
couple who found each other's behavior so tediously antago-
nizing, the only couple who deprived each other of everything
each of them most wanted, the only couple whose battles over
differences would never be behind them, the only couple whose
reason for coming together had evaporated beyond recall, the
only couple who could not sever themselves one from the
other despite ten thousand grievances apiece, the only couple
who could not believe how much worse it got from year to
year, the only couple between whom the dinner silence was
freighted with such bitter hatred. . . .

He had imagined her journal as mostly a harangue about him.
But there was nothing about him. The notes were all about the
other him, the professor in the starched collar whose picture
she was forcing herself to face in the morning when she awoke
and at night when she went to sleep. There was something in
her existence worse than Kathy Goolsbee—Sabbath *himself*
was beside the point. The last thirty *years* were beside the
point, so much futile churning about, so much festering of the

---

*"Give strong drink unto him that is perishing, and wine unto the dis-
tressed in soul: Let him drink and forget his misery and remember his sorrow
no more!" (Proverbs 31.6–7)

wound by which—as she portrayed it here—her soul had been permanently disfigured. He had his story; this was Roseanna's, the official in-the-beginning story, when and where the betrayal that is life was launched. *Here* was the frightful lockup from which there was no release, and Sabbath was not mentioned once. What a bother we are to one another—while actually nonexistent to one another, unreal specters compared to whoever originally sabotaged the sacred trust.

We had different women, housekeepers, who would live with us, that would help to make the dinner. My father also did the cooking. A little bit vague in my memory. The housekeeper would sit with us too. I don't remember the dinners that well.

He was not there after school. I had a key. I would go to the store and buy myself some food. Pea soup. Cake and cookies that I liked. My sister would be home. We would take a snack in the afternoon, and then we would go out and play with our friends.

Recollection of his snoring loudly. Had to do with his drinking. Find him in the morning fully dressed, sleeping on the floor. So drunk he would miss the bed.

He wouldn't drink during the week but on weekends. We had a sailboat for a while and we would go out in the summertime on the boat. He was overpowering. Wanted his way. And he wasn't a terrific sailor. As he got a little bit more drunk he would lose control and walk and turn his pockets inside out to show us he had no money. And then he would be clumsy, and if we had a friend along, he embarrassed me terribly. Very disgusted by him physically when he did these things.

I needed clothes so he would take me to the clothing store. I was very embarrassed by having a father to do that. He didn't have the taste for it and sometimes he made me buy clothes that I didn't like and forced me to wear them. I remember a loden jacket that I hated. I hated it with a passion. I felt very tomboyish because I didn't have women who could take care of me and give me advice. That was very hard.

He would have the housekeepers and several of them wanted to marry him. I remember one who was an educated woman and she cooked very well and she wanted so much to marry the professor. But it always ended in catastrophe. Ella and I would listen through the doors to follow the romantic developments. We knew exactly when they were fucking. I don't imagine he was a good fuck, drunk as he was. But we would always listen from behind the door and were aware of everything going on. But then the reality set in, his bossing them around, telling them even how to do the dishes. He was a professor of geology and so he knew how to wash the dishes better than they did. There would be arguments and screaming, and I don't think he hit the women but there was always an unpleasant ending. When they left it was always a crisis. And for me there was always the expectation of the crisis. And when I was twelve and thirteen and grew more interested in going out and meeting boys, and I had a gang of girlfriends, he took that very hard. He would sit drinking his gin by himself and fall asleep that way. I can't think of him, that isolated person who could not manage by himself, without crying, as I am doing now.

She left in 1945, when I was eight years old. I don't remember when she left, I just remember being left. And then I remember when she came back the first time, 1947, at Christmas. She brought some toy animals that made noises. My sense of desperation. I wanted my mother back. Ella and I were again listening, now to what she and our father were talking about behind the doors. Maybe they were fucking too. I don't know. But what went on behind the doors we tried to listen to. There were intense whispers and sometimes very loud arguments. My mother was there for two weeks and it was a great relief when she left because the tension was so awful. She was a striking-looking woman, well dressed, so worldly to me from living in Paris.

He used to have a locked desk. Ella and I knew how to open it with a knife, so we always had access to his secrets. We found letters from the different women. We laughed and thought it was a big joke. One night my father came into my room and he said, "Oh, I'm falling in love." I pretended that I knew nothing. He said he was going to get married. I thought, "Wonderful, now I can be relieved of my duty of caring for him." She was a widow, already sixty, and he thought she had some money. No sooner had they married than the arguments started, the same as with the other women. This time I felt myself in the middle of the whole thing, responsible for the fact that they had married! My father came to me and said it was terrible because she was older than she said and she didn't have the money she said she had. An enormous calamity. And she began bad-mouthing me. Complaining that I didn't study, that I was spoiled, I wasn't reliable, I was messy, I didn't clean up my room, a hopeless brat and I never told the truth or listened to what she said.

I was taking a bath in my mother's place and the phone rang and I heard my mother screaming. My first thought was that my father had killed my stepmother. But my mother came into the bathroom and she said, "Your father is dead. I have to go Cambridge." I said, "What about me?" She said, "You have to study and I don't think you should go." But I insisted that this was important for me and so she let me come with her. Ella didn't want to come, she was afraid to, but I made her come. He had left a letter to Ella and me. I still have that letter. I have all the letters he sent me when I went to live with my mother. I haven't read them since he died. When I got them in the mail I couldn't read them. To receive a letter from my father made me nauseated all day. My mother would finally make me open it. I would read it in her presence or she would read it to me. "Why haven't you written your father who misses you?" In the third person. "Why haven't you written to your father who loves you so much? Why did you lie to me about the money?" Then the next day, "Oh, my beloved Roseanna, I did receive a letter from you and I'm so happy."

I didn't hate him but he was a giant discomfort for me. He had gigantic power over me. He wasn't drunk every day because he had to teach. It was when he was drunk that he would come into my room late at night and lie in bed beside me.

In February '50 I moved into my mother's apartment with Ella. I saw my mother as my rescuer. I adored her and looked up to her. I thought she was beautiful. My mother made me into a doll. Overnight I became a popular young girl, with all the boys after me, and I got tall practically overnight. There was even a "Roseanna Club," the boys told me. But the attention I got, I couldn't take in. I wasn't there. I was someplace else. It was hard. But I do remember that I suddenly became very prim-looking, striped little dresses, and petticoats, and a rose in my hair for parties. My mother's mission in life was to justify her leaving. She said he would have killed her. Even when she picked up the phone to talk to him, she was afraid of him— her veins would stick out and she'd go white. I think I heard it every day, one way or another, her justification for running away. She too hated when his letters would come but she was too afraid of him not to make me read them. And there was a struggle over money. He didn't want to pay if I didn't live with him. It was always me, never

Ella. I had to live with him or he wouldn't pay for me. I don't know how they resolved it, all I know is that there was always a struggle over money and me.

There was something physically disgusting about him. The sexual part. I had then and I have still a strong physical distaste for him. For his lips. I thought they were ugly. And the way he held me, even in public, like a woman he loved instead of like a young girl. When he took me on his arm to take a walk, I felt I was in a grip I could never get out of.

I got so frantic and busy doing other things that I was able for a while to forget about him. I went to France that next summer after his death and at fourteen I had a love affair. I stayed with a friend of my mother's and there were all these boys . . . so I did forget him. But I was in a daze for years. I've been in a daze always. I don't know why he comes to haunt me now that I'm a woman in her fifties, but he does.

I prepared myself to read his letters last summer by picking some flowers and making it pleasant and when I started reading I had to stop.

I drank to survive.

On the page following, every line of her handwriting had been scratched out so heavily that barely anything remained legible. He searched for the words to amplify "It was when he was drunk that he would come into my room late at night and lie in bed beside me," but all he could distinguish, even with microscopic scrutinizing, were the words "white wine," "my mother's rings," "a torture day" . . . and these were part of no discernible sequence. What she'd written here was not for the ears of the patients at that meeting or for the eyes of any-one, herself included. But then he turned the page and found some kind of exercise written out quite legibly, perhaps one she had been assigned by her doctor.

Reenactment of leaving my father at age thirteen, 39 years ago, in February. First as I remember it and then as I would have liked it to happen.

As I remember it: My father had picked me up at the hospital where I'd checked in a few days earlier to have a tonsillectomy. In spite of all my fear of him, I could tell that he was very happy to have me home, but I felt as I often did with him—I can't quite pinpoint it, but made terribly uncomfortable by his breathing and his lips. I have no recollection of the act itself. Just the vibrations set off in me by his breathing and his lips. I never told Ella. I haven't to this day. I have told no one.

Daddy told me that he and Irene did not get along very well. That she continued to complain about me, that I was a slob and didn't study or listen to what she had to say. Best for me to stay away from her as much as possible. . . . Daddy and I were sitting in the living room after lunch. Irene was cleaning up in the kitchen. I felt weak and tired but determined. I had to tell him now that I was leaving him. That everything was already planned. My mother had agreed to take me as long as—she stressed this repeatedly—it was my will to come and not her coercion that had made me. Legally my father had custody over us. Rather unusual at that time. My mother had given up all claims on us, since she felt we children should not be separated and she had few resources to bring us up. Besides, Daddy was likely to kill us all if we all left him. It's true that he had commented after reading in the newspaper about family tragedies where a husband actually killed everyone, including himself, that that was the right thing to do.

I remember my father standing in front of me looking much older than fifty-six, bushy white hair and a worn face, slightly stooped over but still tall. He was pouring coffee into a cup. I told him boldly that I was leaving. That I had talked to my mother and she had agreed to let me come to her. He almost dropped his cup and his face became ashen. Everything went out of him. He sat down, speechless. He did not frighten me by getting angry, which I had feared. Although I often defied him, I was always deadly afraid of him. But not this time. I knew I had to get out of there. If I didn't, I was dead. All he could say was, "I understand, but we must not let Irene know. We will only tell her that you are going to your mother to recuperate." Less than six months later he hanged himself. How could I not believe I was responsible?

As I would have liked it to happen: Feeling rather weak but happy that the surgery was over, I was glad to be going home. My father had picked me up at the hospital. It was a sunny January day. Daddy and

I sat in the living room after finishing lunch. With my sore mouth I could only drink liquids. I had no appetite and I was also worried about starting to bleed. I had gotten scared in the hospital seeing other patients being readmitted because of slow bleeding. I was told you could bleed to death if it wasn't discovered in time. Daddy sat next to me on the sofa. He told me that he wanted to talk to me. He told me that my mother had called and told him that I might want to move to her now that I was a grown girl. Daddy said that he understood I was having a hard time. This had been a difficult year for everyone. There had been a lot of unhappiness between him and Irene and he knew it had spilled over on me. His marriage was not working out the way he hoped, but I, who was his daughter and still a child—now a teenager but still a child—had absolutely no responsibility for the way things were at home. He told me that it was unfortunate that I had been in the middle, with Irene coming to complain about him and he coming to complain about her. He felt guilty about this, and therefore, though it was hard for him to see me go since he loved me dearly, he felt that should I want to go it was probably a good idea. Of course he would pay child support for me if I moved to mother. He truly wanted what was best for me. He went on to tell me that he had not been feeling well for a long time, often suffering from insomnia. I felt enormously relieved that he understood my problems. I would now at last have a mother to guide me. Also I could come back any time I wanted, my room would always be there.

Dear Father,

Today, while waiting for your letters to me to arrive at the hospital, I've decided to write a letter to you. The pain I felt then, the pain I feel now—are they the same? I would hope not. Yet they feel identical. Except today I am tired of hiding from my pain. My old hiding skill (being drunk) won't ever work again. I am *not* suicidal, the way you were. I only wanted to die because I wanted the past to leave me alone and go away. Leave me alone, Past, let me just sleep!

So here I am. You have a daughter in a mental hospital. You did it. Outside it is a beautiful fall day. Clear blue sky. The leaves changing. But within I am still terrified. I will not say that my life has been wasted but do you know that I was robbed by you? My therapist and I have talked about it and I know now that I was robbed by you of the ability to have a normal relationship with a normal man.

Ella used to say that the best thing you did was to commit suicide. That's how simple it is for Ella, my unmolested sister with all her lovely children! What a strange family I come from. Last summer when I was at Ella's I visited your grave. I had never been back since your funeral. I picked some flowers and put them on your stone. There you lay next to Grandpa and Grandma Cavanaugh. I wept for you and for the life that ended so horribly. You nebulous figure, so abstract and yet so crucial to me, please let God watch over me when I have to undertake my task tomorrow night!

Your daughter in a mental hospital,

Roseanna

By eight-ten he had read everything three times over and she still had not returned to the room. He studied the father's photo, looking in vain for a visible sign of the damage done him and the damage he'd done. In the lips she hated he could see nothing extraordinary. Then he read as much as he could stand of *A Step-by-Step Guide for Families of Chemically Dependent Persons*, a paperback book on the table beside her pillow that was undoubtedly intended to brainwash him once she had returned home to displace Drenka from their bed. Here he was introduced to Share and Identify, who soon were to become household helpers, like Happy or Sleepy or Grumpy or Doc. "Emotional pain," he read, "can be broad and deep. . . . It hurts to become involved in arguments. . . . And what about the future? Will things keep getting worse?"

He left on the desk the file cabinet key that he'd found in her riding boot. But before he went down to the nurse's station to ask where Roseanna might be, he returned to her notebook and took fifteen more minutes to make a contribution of his own directly below the letter she had written to her late father earlier that day. He did nothing to disguise his handwriting.

Dear little Roseanna!

Of course you are in a mental hospital. I warned you again and again about separating yourself from me and separating me from pretty little Helen Kylie. Yes, you are mentally ill, you have completely lost yourself to drink and cannot retrieve yourself on your own, but your letter today still gave me a real shock. If you want to take legal action, go ahead, even though I am dead. I never did expect that death would bring me any peace. Now, thanks to you, my beloved little darling, being dead is as awful as being alive was. *Take* legal action. You who abandoned your father have no position at all. For five years I lived entirely for you. Because of the expenses of your education and your clothes, etc., I was never able to be secure on a professor's salary. For my own part, during those years I bought nothing, not even clothes. I even had to sell the boat. Nobody can say that I did not sacrifice everything to taking loving care of you, even though one can argue about different methods of upbringing.

I don't have time to write any more. Satan is calling me to my session. Dear little Roseanna, cannot you and your husband be happy in the end? If not, the fault is entirely your mother's. Satan agrees. He and I have talked in therapy about the husband you chose and I know for sure that I have nothing to be guilty about. If you did not marry a normal man it is entirely your mother's fault for sending you to a coeducational school during the dangerous years of puberty. All the pain in your life is entirely her responsibility. My anxiety, which has its roots way back when I was alive, will not disappear even here, because of what your mother did to you and what you did to me. In our group there is another father who had an ungrateful daughter. He shared about his agony and we identified. It was very helpful. I learned that I cannot change my ungrateful daughter.

Only how much farther do you want to push me, my little one? Didn't you push me far enough? You judge me entirely by your pain, you judge me entirely by your holy feelings. But why don't you judge me for a change by *my* pain, by *my* holy feelings? How you cling to your grievance! As though in a world of persecution you alone have a grievance. Wait till you're dead—death is grievance and only grievance. Perennial grievance. It is despicable of you to continue this attack on your dead father—I will be in therapy here forever because of you. Unless, unless, dear little Roseanna, you were somehow to find it in you to write just a few thousand pages to grieving Papa to tell him how remorseful you are for everything you did to ruin his life.

Your father in Hell,

Dad

"Probably still at the Mansion," said the nurse, consulting her watch. "They hang around to smoke. Why don't you go over there? If she's headed this way, you'll pass her on the drive."

But at the Mansion, where smokers were indeed gathered once again outside the main door, he was told that Roseanna had gone to the gym with Rhonda to take a swim. The gym was a low, sprawling building down the lawn and across the road—they told him he could see the pool through the windows.

There was no one swimming there. It was a big, well-lit

pool, and, after peering through the misty windows, he went inside to see if perhaps she was at the bottom of it, dead. But the young woman attendant, sitting at a desk next to a pile of towels, said no, Roseanna hadn't been there tonight. She'd done her hundred laps that afternoon.

He proceeded back up the dark hill to the Mansion to look in the lounge where the meeting had been held. He was guided to it by the glazier, who'd been reading a magazine in the parlor while someone at the piano—the Wellesley girl-friend of the Marlboro man—was tapping out "Night and Day" with one hand. The lounge was along a broad corridor with a pay phone at either end. Standing at one of them was a small, skinny Hispanic kid of about twenty who Roseanna had told him at dinner was an addict who dealt cocaine. She was wearing a colorful nylon sweat suit and had a headset over her ears even as she loudly argued over the phone in what Sabbath figured to be either Puerto Rican or Dominican Spanish. From what he understood, she was telling her mother to fuck herself.

In the lounge, a large room with a television screen at the far end, there were couches and lots of easy chairs scattered about, but it was empty now except for two elderly women quietly playing cards at a table beside a standing lamp. One was a gray-haired patient, dumpy but with a becoming air of antique jadedness, whom several of the patients had jokingly applauded when she'd appeared, twenty minutes late, in the dining room doorway. "My public," she had said grandly in her high-born New England accent, and curtsied. "This is the P.M. performance," she announced, fluttering into the room on her toes. "If you're lucky you can come to the A.M. perfor-mance." The woman playing cards with her was her sister, a visitor, who must also have been in her late seventies.

"Have you seen Roseanna?" Sabbath called over to them.

"Roseanna," replied the patient, "is seeing her doctor."

"It's eight-thirty at night."

"The suffering that is the hallmark of human affairs," she in-formed him, "does not diminish at eventide. To the contrary. But you must be the husband who is of such importance to her. Yes. Yes." Cannily sizing him up—girth, height, beard, baldness, costume—she said with a gracious smile, "That you are a very great man is unmistakable."

On the second floor of the Mansion, Sabbath made his way past a row of patients' rooms to the end of the corridor and a nurse's station that was about twice the size of the one at Roderick, a lot less bright and cheery, but mercifully without the "Peanuts" posters. Two nurses were doing some paperwork, and atop a low file cabinet, swinging his legs and drinking what looked from both the plastic sack full of Pepsis at his side and the wastebasket at his feet to be his sixth or seventh soda, sat a muscular young man with a dark chin beard wearing black jeans, a black polo shirt, and black sneakers, who vaguely resembled the Sabbath of some thirty years ago. He was expounding to one of the nurses in an impassioned voice; from time to time she glanced up to acknowledge what he was saying but then went right back to her paperwork. She herself couldn't have been more than thirty, chunky, robust, clear-eyed, with dark hair clipped neatly short, and she gave Sabbath a friendly wink when he appeared at the door. She was one of the two nurses who had searched Rosie's suitcases the afternoon they arrived.

"Ideological idiots!" proclaimed the young man in black. "The third great ideological failure of the twentieth century. The same stuff. Fascism. Communism. Feminism. All designed to turn one group of people against another group of people. The good Aryans against the bad others who oppress them. The good poor against the bad rich who oppress them. The good women against the bad men who oppress them. The holder of the ideology is pure and good and clean and the other is wicked. But do you know who is wicked? Whoever imagines himself to be pure is wicked! I am pure, you are wicked. How can you swallow that stuff, Karen?"

"I don't, Donald," the young nurse replied. "You know I don't."

"*She* does. My ex-wife does!"

"I am not your ex-wife."

"There *is* no human purity! It does not exist! It cannot exist!" he said, kicking the file cabinet for emphasis. "It must not and *should* not exist! Because it is a lie! Her ideology is like all ideologies—founded in a lie! Ideological tyranny. It's the disease of the century. The ideology *institutionalizes* the pathology. In twenty years there will be a new ideology. People against dogs. The dogs are to blame for our lives as people. Then after dogs there will be what? Who will be to blame for corrupting our purity?"

"I hear where you're coming from," mumbled Karen while attending to the work on her desk.

"Excuse me," said Sabbath. He leaned into the room. "I don't mean to interrupt a man whose aversions I wholeheartedly endorse, but I am looking for Roseanna Sabbath and I have been told she is seeing her doctor. Any way this can be established as fact?"

"Roseanna's in Roderick," said the Donald in black.

"But she's not there now. I can't find her. I came all this way and I've lost her. I am her husband."

"Are you? We've heard so many wonderful things about you in group," Donald said, again whacking both sneakers against the file cabinet and reaching into the plastic sack for a Pepsi. "The great god Pan."

"The great god Pan is dead," a deadpan Sabbath informed him. "But I see"—stentorian now—"that you are a young fellow unafraid of the truth. What are you doing in a place like this?"

"Trying to leave," said Karen, rolling her eyes like an exasperated kid. "Donald's been trying since nine this morning. Donald's been graduated but he can't go home."

"I have no home. The bitch destroyed my home. Two years ago," he told Sabbath, who by now had come into the room and taken the empty chair beside the wastebasket. "I came back from a business trip one night. My wife's car isn't in the driveway. I go into the house and it's empty. All the furniture is gone. All she left was the album with the wedding pictures. I sat on the floor and looked at the wedding pictures and cried. I came home from work every day and looked at the wedding pictures and cried."

"And like a good boy, drank your dinner," said Karen.

"The booze was only to quell the depression. I got over that. I'm in the hospital," he told Sabbath, "because she is getting married today. *Got* married today. She married another woman. A *rabbi* married them. And my wife is not Jewish!"

"Ex," said Karen.

"But the other woman is Jewish?" asked Sabbath.

"Yeah. The rabbi was there to please the other woman's family. How's that?"

"Well," said Sabbath gently, "rabbis occupy an exalted position in the Jewish mind."

"Fuck that. *I'm* Jewish. What the fuck is a rabbi doing marrying two lesbos? You think in Israel a rabbi would do it? No, only in Ithaca, New York!"

"To embrace humanity in all its glorious diversity," asked Sabbath, professorially stroking his beard, "is that a long-standing peculiarity of the Ithaca rabbinate?"

"Fuck no! They're rabbis! They're assholes!"

"Language, Donald." It was the other nurse speaking now, clearly a tough one—seasoned, hardened, and tough. "It's time for vital signs, Donald. It'll be time for meds soon. We're going to get busy here. What are your plans? Have you made any plans?"

"I'm leaving, Stella."

"Good. When?"

"After vital signs. I want to be sure to say good-bye to everybody."

"You have been saying good-bye to everybody all day long," Stella reminded him. "Everybody in the Mansion has taken you for a walk and told you you can make it. You *can* make it. You are *going* to make it. You won't stop at a bar to have a drink. You will drive straight to your brother's in Ithaca."

"My wife is a lesbian. Some asshole rabbi married her today to another woman."

"You don't know this for sure."

"My sister-in-law was *there*, Stella. My ex-wife stood under the *chuppa* with this broad, and when the time came she broke the glass. My wife is a shiksa. The two of them are lesbians. This is what Judaism has come to? I can't believe it!"

"Donald, be kind," said Sabbath. "Don't disparage the Jews for wanting to be with it. Even the Jews are up against it in the Age of Total Schlock. The Jews can't win," Sabbath said to Stella, who looked to be Filipino and was, like himself, an older and wiser person. "Either they're mocked because they're still wearing their beards and waving their arms in the air or they are ridiculed by people like Donald here for being up-to-the-minute servants of the sexual revolution."

"What if she'd married a zebra?" Donald asked indignantly. "Would a rabbi have married her to a zebra?"

"Zebra or *zebu*?" asked Sabbath.

"What's a zebu?"

"A zebu is an east Asian cow with a large hump. Many women today are leaving husbands for zebus. Which did you say?"

"Zebra."

"Well, I think not. A rabbi wouldn't touch a zebra. Can't. They don't have cloven hooves. For a rabbi to officiate at the marriage of a person to an animal, the animal has to chew its cud *and* have a cloven hoof. A camel. A rabbi can marry a person to a camel. A cow. Any kind of cattle. Sheep. Can't marry someone to a rabbit, however, because even though a rabbit chews its cud, it doesn't have a cloven hoof. They also eat their own shit, which, on the face of it, you might think a point in their favor: chew their food *three* times. But what is required is *twice*. That's why a rabbi can't marry a person to a pig. Not that the pig is unclean. That's not the problem, never has been. The problem with the pig is, though it has a cloven hoof, it doesn't chew its cud. A zebra may or may not chew its cud—I don't know. But it doesn't have a cloven hoof, and with the rabbis, one strike and you're out. The rabbi can marry a person to a bull, of course. The bull is like a cow. The divine animal, the bull. The Canaanite god El—which is where the Jews got El-o-him—is a bull. Anti-Defamation League tries to downplay this, but like it or not, the El in Elohim, a bull! Basic religious passion is to worship a bull. Damn it, Donald, you Jews ought to be *proud* of that. *All* the ancient religions were obscene. Do you know how the Egyptians imagined the origins of the universe? Any kid can read about it in his encyclopedia. God masturbated. And his sperm flew up and created the universe."

The nurses did not look happy with the turn given to the conversation by Sabbath, and so the puppeteer decided to address them directly. "God's jerking off alarms you? Well, gods are alarming, girls. It's a god who commands you to cut off your foreskin. It's a god who commands you to sacrifice your firstborn. It's a god who commands you to leave your mother and father and go off into the wilderness. It's a god who sends

you into slavery. It's a god who *destroys*—it's the spirit of a god
that comes down to *destroy*—and yet it's a god who gives life.
What in all of creation is as nasty and strong as this god who
gives life? The God of the Torah embodies the world in all its
horror. And in all its truth. You've got to hand it to the Jews.
Truly rare and admirable candor. What other people's national
myth reveals their God's atrocious conduct *and* their own?
Just read the Bible, it's all there, the backsliding, idolatrous,
butchering Jews and the schizophrenia of these ancient gods.
What is the archetypal Bible story? A story of betrayal. Of
treachery. It's just one deception after another. And whose is
the greatest voice in the Bible? Isaiah. The mad desire to obliterate all! The mad desire to save all! The greatest voice in the
Bible is the voice of somebody who has lost his mind! And that
God, that Hebrew God—you can't escape Him! What's shocking is not His monstrous features—plenty of gods are monstrous, it seems almost to have been a prerequisite—but that
there's no recourse from Him. No power beyond *His*. The
most monstrous feature of God, my friends, is the *totalitari-
anism*. This vengeful, seething God, this punishment-ordaining
bastard, is *ultimate*! Mind if I have a Pepsi?" Sabbath inquired
of Donald.

"Awesome," said Donald, and thinking perhaps, as Sabbath
was thinking, that this was the way people in a madhouse were
supposed to talk, he took a cold can out of the plastic sack and
even opened the tab for Sabbath before handing it on to him.
Sabbath took a long swig just as the baby cocaine dealer came
in to have her vital signs checked. She was listening to the
music on her headset and singing along with the lyrics in a flat-
tish, unvarying, throaty tone. "Lick it! Lick it! Lick it, baby,
lick it, lick it, lick it, lick it!" When she saw Donald, she said,
"Ain't you goin'?"

"I wanted to see them take your blood pressure one last time."

"Yeah, that make you hot, Donny?"

"What *is* her pressure?" asked Sabbath. "What would you
think?"

"Linda? Doesn't make much difference to Linda. Her pressure isn't the big thing in Linda's life."

"How do you feel, Linda?" Sabbath asked her. "Estas siempre enfadada con tu mama?"

"La odio."

"Por qué, Linda?"

"Ella me odia a *mí*."

"Her pressure's 120 over 100," said Sabbath.

"Linda?" said Donald. "Linda's a kid. 120 over 70."

"Wanna bet the spread?" said Sabbath. "A buck on the spread, another buck if you hit the diastolic or the systolic, three if you nail 'em both." He took a wad of singles out of his pants pocket, and when he smoothed them into a pile on the palm of one hand, Donald took some bills out of his wallet and said to Karen, who was standing holding the blood pressure cuff beside the chair where Linda was seated, "Go ahead. I'll play him."

"What's going on here?" Karen asked. "Play *what*?"

"Go ahead. Take her pressure."

"Jesus," Karen said and put the cuff on Linda, who was singing along with the tape again.

"Shut *up*," said Karen. She listened through the stethoscope, made a recording in the ledger, and then took Linda's pulse.

"What was it?" said Donald.

Karen was silent as she entered the pulse rate in the ledger.

"Oh fuck, Karen—what *was* it?"

"120 over 100," Karen said.

"Shit."

"Four bucks," said Sabbath, and Donald peeled off the money and gave it to him. "Next." Sciarappa the barber, back in Bradley.

In the doorway was Ray in his silk robe. He went silently to the chair and rolled up his left sleeve.

"140 over 90," said Sabbath.

"160 over 100," said Donald.

Ray nervously tapped the book in his hand until Karen touched his fingers and made him relax them. Then she took his pressure. Linda, leaning against the door frame, was waiting to see who was going to win all the money. "This is great," she said. "This is crazy."

"150," said Karen, "over 100."

"I got you on the spread," said Sabbath, "you got me on the diastolic. It's a wash. Next."

His next was the young woman with the scar on her wrist,

the tall, pretty blond who slouched and who had given Sabbath directions to Roderick House before dinner. She said to Donald, "Aren't you ever leaving?"

"If you come with me, Madeline. You look good, honey. You're almost standing straight."

"Don't get alarmed—it's the same old me," she said. "Listen to what I found in the library today. I was reading the journals. Listen." She took a piece of paper out of the pocket of her jeans. "I copied it from a journal. Word for word. *Journal of Medical Ethics*. 'It is proposed that *happiness*'"—glancing up, she said, "Their italics"—"'it is proposed that *happiness* be classified as a psychiatric disorder and be included in future editions of the major diagnostic manuals under the new name: major affective disorder, pleasant type. In a review of the relevant literature it is shown that *happiness* is statistically abnormal, consists of a discrete cluster of symptoms, is associated with a range of cognitive abnormalities, and probably reflects the abnormal functioning of the central nervous system. One possible objection to this proposal remains—that *happiness* is not negatively valued. However, this objection is dismissed as scientifically irrelevant."

Donald looked pleased, proud, beguiled, as though the reason for his stalling around was indeed to run off with Madeline. "You make that up?"

"If I'd made it up it would be clever. Nope. A psychiatrist made it up. That's why it's not."

"Oh bullshit, Madeline. Saunders isn't stupid. He used to be an analyst," he told Sabbath, "the guy who runs the place, and now he's, like, this cool-guy psychiatrist who tries to be relaxed about everything—not too analytic. He's into this big cognitive behavioral thing. Trying to make yourself stop if you're having obsessive ruminations. Just train yourself to say 'Stop!'"

"That's not stupid?" asked Madeline. "And meanwhile, what am I supposed to do about my rage and having no confidence? Nothing is easy. Nothing is pleasant. What am I supposed to do about this idiotic therapist I had this morning for Assertiveness Training? I had her again this afternoon—we had to sit through a videotape on medical aspects of addiction and afterwards she led the discussion. And I raised my hand, I said, 'There are some things that I don't understand about this tape. You know, when they have the experiment on the two different mice—' And the idiot therapist says, 'Madeline, this is not a discussion about that. This is a discussion about your feelings. How did the tape make you feel about your alcoholism?' I said, 'Frustrated. It raised more questions than it answered.' 'Okay,' she said in that perky way she has, 'Madeline feels frustrated. Anyone else? What do *you* feel, Nick?' So we go around the room, and so I raise my hand again and I said, 'If we could ever just for a minute shift the discussion from the level of feelings to the level of information—' 'Madeline,' she says, 'this is a discussion of people's feelings in response to this tape. If you have a need for information, I suggest you go to the library and look things up.' That's how I wound up in the library. My feelings. Who *cares* how I feel about my addiction?"

"If you will only keep monitoring your feelings," said Karen, "that is what is going to keep you from *being* addicted."

"It's not worth it," said Madeline.

"It is," said Karen.

"Yeah," said Donald, "you're an addict, Madeline, because you're not connected to people, and you're not connected to people because you haven't told them your *feelings*."

"Oh, why can't things just be nice?" asked Madeline. "I just want to be told what to do anyway."

"I like when you say that," said Donald. "'I just want to be told what to do.' It's a turn-on in that little voice."

"Ignore his negativity, Madeline," Karen the nurse told her. "He's just pulling your chain."

But Madeline appeared unable to ignore anything. "Well," she said to Donald, "in certain situations I do like to be told what to do. And in certain other situations I like to make demands."

"So there you go," said Donald. "It's all too fucking complicated."

"I had art therapy this afternoon," Madeline told him.

"Did you draw a picture, dear?"

"I did a collage."

"Somebody interpret it for you?"

"They didn't need to."

Donald, laughing, started on another Pepsi. "And how's your crying going?"

"I'm in a real slump of a day. I woke up crying this morning. I cried all morning long. I cried in Meditation. I cried in group. You'd think it would dry up."

"Everybody cries in the morning," Karen said. "Just part of getting under way."

"I don't know why today should be worse than yesterday," Madeline told her. "I think all the same dark thoughts but they're not any darker today than they were yesterday. In Meditation, guess who we read from in our little daily meditation book? Shirley MacLaine. And this morning I went to the sharps nurse to get my tweezers. I said, 'I need my tweezers out of the sharps closet.' And she said, 'You have to use them here, Madeline. I don't want you to take them back to your room.' And so I said, 'If I'm going to kill myself, I'm not going to do it with my *tweezers.*'"

"Tweeze yourself to death?" said Donald. "Hard to do. How do you do that, Karen?"

Karen ignored him.

"I got very angry," said Madeline. "I told her, 'I can crack the light bulb and swallow it, too. Give me my tweezers!' But she wouldn't, just because I was crying."

"At AA," Donald said to Sabbath, "they go around at the beginning of the meeting. Everybody has to introduce himself. 'Hi, my name is Christopher. I'm an alcoholic.' 'Hi, my name is Mitchell. I'm an alcoholic.' 'Hi, I'm Flora. I'm cross-addicted.'"

"Cross-addicted?" Sabbath asked.

"Who knows—some Catholic thing. I think she's in the wrong group. Anyway, they get to Madeline. Madeline gets up. 'My name is Madeline. What's your red wine by the glass?' How's your smoking?" he asked her.

"I am basically smoking like a fiend."

"Tsk-tsk," said Donald. "Smoking is just another of your defenses against intimacy, Madeline. You know nobody wants to kiss a smoker anymore."

"I'm smoking even more than when I came in. A couple months ago I really thought I had it . . ."

"*Licked?*" said Donald. "Could the word be *licked?*"

"I was going to, but I thought, I'm just not using that word around him. You know, nothing *is* easy—*nothing*. And it's making me nervous. Press 1 for this, press 2 for that. What am I supposed to do about being left on hold all day? Everything is such a fight. I'm still fighting my managed care from the first time I was here. They keep telling me I should have called them when I was admitted to the Poughkeepsie ICU. I was in a fucking *coma*. It's hard to push 1 and push 2 when you're in a coma. And even if you could, they don't *have* phones in the ICU."

"You were in a coma?" asked Sabbath. "What is that like?"

"You're in a coma. You're out," said Madeline in the voice that *didn't* sound as though it had seen much change since she was a ten-year-old. "You're unresponsive. It's not like anything."

"This gentleman is Roseanna's husband," Donald said to her.

"Ah," said Madeline, her eyes widening.

"Madeline is an actress. When she's not in a coma she's in the soaps. She's a very wise girl who wants from life no more than to die by her own hand. She left her family an endearing suicide note. Ten words. 'I don't know what I did to deserve this gift.' Mr. Sabbath wants to bet on your blood pressure."

"Under the circumstances, that is very kind of him," she replied.

"120 over 80," said Sabbath.

"And what do you bet?" Madeline asked Donald.

"I bet low, honey. I bet 90 over 60."

"Hardly living," said Madeline.

"Wait a minute," said Stella, the Filipino nurse. "What *is* this?" She got up from the desk to confront the gamblers. "Usher is a *hospital*," she said, glaring directly at Sabbath. "These people are *patients*. . . . Donald, show a little mental toughness, Donald. Get in your car and go home. And you, did you come here to play games, or did you come here to see your wife?"

"My wife is hiding from me."

"You get out. You leave."

"I can't find my wife."

"Beat it," she told him. "Go reside with the gods."

Sabbath waited around the corner from the nurse's station until Madeline's blood pressure had been taken and she appeared in the corridor alone. "Can you lead me to Roderick House again?" he asked her.

"Sorry, I can't go outside."

"If you could just get me aimed in the right direction . . ."

Together they walked down the staircase to the first floor; she went as far as the porch, where, from the top of the steps, she pointed to the lights of Roderick House.

"It's a beautiful fall night," said Sabbath. "Walk me there."

"I can't. I'm a high-risk person. For a psychiatric hospital you have a lot of freedom here. But after dark I'm not allowed outside. I'm only a week out of ACU."

"What's ACU?"

"Acute care unit."

"The place on the hill?"

"Yeah. A Holiday Inn you can't get out of."

"Were you the most acute person there?"

"I don't really know. I wasn't paying much attention. They won't let you have caffeine after breakfast so I was busy storing up tea from morning. So pathetic. I was too busy working out the caffeine smuggling to make many friends."

"Come. We'll find you a Lipton's tea bag to suck on."

"I can't. I have program tonight. I think I have to go to Relapse Prevention."

"Aren't you a bit ahead of yourself?"

"Actually, no. I've been planning my relapse."

"Come with me."

"I really should go and work on my relapse."

"Come on."

She hurried down the steps and started with him along the dark drive to Roderick House. He had to move fast.

"How old are you?" Sabbath asked.

"Twenty-nine."

"You look ten."

"And I tried not to look too young tonight. Didn't it work? I get carded all the time. They're always asking for my ID. Whenever I have to wait in a doctor's office, the receptionist gives me a copy of *Seventeen*. Aside from how I look, I act younger than I am, too."

"That you can expect to get worse."

"Whatever. The harsh reality."

"Why did you try to kill yourself?"

"I don't know. The only thing that doesn't bore me. The only thing worth thinking about. Besides, by the middle of the day I think the day has just gone on long enough and there's only one way to make the day go away, and that is either booze or bed."

"And that does it?"

"No."

"So next you try suicide. *The* taboo."

"I try it because I'm confronting my own mortality *ahead* of my time. Because I realize it's the critical question, you see. The messiness of marriage and children and career and all that —I've already realized the futility of it all without having had to go through it all. Why can't I just be fast-forwarded?"

"You've got a mind, don't you? I like the mosaic it makes."

"I'm wise and mature beyond my years."

"Mature beyond your years and immature beyond your years."

"What a paradox. Well, you can only be young once, but you can be immature forever."

"The too-wise child who doesn't want to live. You're an actress?

"Of course not. Donald's humor—Madeline's life is soap opera. I think he anticipated something of a romantic nature between us. There was an element of seduction, which was sort of touching in its own little way. He said lots of glowing and flattering things about me. Intelligent. Attractive. He told me I should stand up straight. To do something about my shoulders. 'Elongate, honey.'"

"What happens when you stand up straight?"

Her voice was soft and the answer that she muttered now he couldn't even hear. "You must speak up, dear."

"I'm sorry. I said nothing happens."

"Why do you speak so quietly?"

"Why? That's a good question."

"You don't stand up straight and you don't speak loud enough."

"Oh, just like my father. My high, squeaky voice."

"Is that what he tells you?"

"All my life."

"Another one with a father."

"Yes indeed."

"How tall *are* you when you stand up straight?"

"Just under five ten. But it's hard to stand up straight when you're at the lowest point of your life."

"Also hard when you went through high school not only five ten, not only with a conspicuously active mind, but flat-chested to boot."

"Golly, a man understands me."

"Not you. Tits. I understand tits. I have been studying tits since I was thirteen years old. I don't think there's any other organ or body part that evidences so much variation in size as women's tits."

"I *know*," replied Madeline, openly enjoying herself suddenly and beginning to laugh. "And why is that? Why did God allow this enormous variation in breast size? Isn't it amazing? There are women with breasts ten times the size of mine. Or even more. True?"

"That is true."

"People have big noses," she said. "I have a small nose. But are there people with noses ten times the size of mine? Four or five, max. I don't know why God did this to women."

"The variation," Sabbath offered, "accommodates a wide variety of desires, perhaps. But then," he added, thinking again, "breasts, as you call them, are not there primarily to entice men—they're there to feed children."

"But I don't think size has to do with milk production," said Madeline. "No, that doesn't solve the problem of what this enormous variation is *for*."

"Maybe it's that God hasn't made up his mind. That's often the case."

"Wouldn't it be more interesting," asked Madeline, "if there were different *numbers* of breasts? Mightn't that be more interesting? You know—some women with two, some with six . . ."

"How many times have you tried to commit suicide?"

"Only twice. How many times has your wife tried?"

"Only once. So far."

"Why?"

"Forced to sleep with her old man. As a kid, her father's girl."

"Was she really? They all say that. The simplest story about yourself that explains everything—it's the house specialty. These people read more complicated stories in the newspaper every day, and then they're handed this version of their lives. In Courage to Heal they've been trying for three weeks to get me to turn in my dad. The answer to every question is either Prozac or incest. Talk about boring. All the false introspection. It's enough in itself to make you suicidal. Your wife is one of the two or three I can even stand to listen to. She's elegant-minded by comparison with the others. Her desire is passionate to face the losses. She doesn't back away from the excavation. But you, of course, find nothing redeeming in these reflections back on origins."

"Don't I? I wouldn't know."

"Well, they're trying to confront this awful stuff with their raw souls, and it's way, way beyond them, and so they say all those stupid things that don't sound much like 'reflections.' Still, there's something about your wife that, in its own way, has a certain heroism. The way she stood up to an excruciating detox. There's a kind of deliberateness to her that I sure don't have: running around here collecting the shards of her past, struggling with her father's letters. . . ."

"Don't stop. *You* get more and more elegant-minded by the moment."

"Look, she's a drunk, drunks drive people nuts, and to the husband that's the crux. Fair enough. She's putting up a struggle that you disdain for its lack of genius. She doesn't have your wit and so forth and so she can't have the penetrating cynicism. But she has as much nobility as someone can within the limits of her imagination."

"How do you know she does?"

"I don't. I just made it up. I make it up as I go along. Doesn't everyone?"

"Roseanna's heroism and nobility."

"I mean it's clear to me that she did suffer a great blow and that she earned her pain, that's all. She came by her pain honestly."

"How?"

"Her father's suicide. The awful way in which he suffocated

her. Her father's effort to become the great man in her life. And then the suicide. Wreaking that vengeance on her just for saving her own life. That was a huge blow for a young girl. You couldn't really ask for a bigger one."

"So you believe he fucked her or you don't?"

"I don't. I don't believe it, because it's not necessary. She had enough without it. You're talking about a little girl and her father. Little girls love their fathers. There's enough going on there. The courting is all you need. It doesn't require a se-duction. Could be he killed himself not because they had con-summated it but so that they wouldn't. A lot of suicides, gloomy people with guilty ruminations, think their families would be better off without them."

"And did you think like that, Madeline?"

"Nope. I thought I might be better off without my family."

"If you know all this," said Sabbath, "or know enough to make it up, how come I'm meeting you here?"

"You're meeting me here *because* I know all this. Guess who I'm reading in the library? Erik Erikson. I'm in the intimacy-versus-isolation stage, if I understand him correctly, and I think really not coming out ahead. You are in the generativity-versus-stagnation stage, but you are very quickly approaching the integrity-versus-despair stage."

"I have no children. I haven't generated shit."

"You'll be relieved to learn that the childless can generate through acts of altruism."

"Unlikely in my case. What is it, again, I have to look for-ward to?"

"Integrity versus despair."

"And how do things look for me, from what you've read?"

"Well, it depends whether life is basically meaningful and purposeful," she said, bursting out laughing.

Sabbath laughed too. "What's so funny about 'purposeful,' Madeline?"

"You do ask tough questions."

"Yeah, well, it's amazing what you find out when you ask."

"Anyway, I don't have to worry yet about generativity. I told you: I'm in intimacy versus isolation."

"And how are you doing?"

"I think it's questionable how I'm doing on the intimacy question."

"And on the isolation one?"

"I get the feeling they're somewhat meant by Dr. Erikson to be polar opposites. If you're not doing well in one, you must be scoring fairly high in the other."

"And you are?"

"Well, I guess mainly in the romantic arena. I didn't realize, until I read Dr. Erikson, that this was my 'developmental goal,'" she said, starting to laugh again. "I guess I haven't achieved it."

"What's your developmental goal?"

"I suppose a stable little relationship with a man and all his fucking complex needs."

"When was the last time you had that?"

"Seven years ago. It hasn't been an *abysmal* failure. I can't really tell objectively how sorry I should feel for myself. I don't give the same credibility to my being that other people give to theirs. Everything feels acted."

"Everything *is* acted."

"Whatever. With me there's some glue missing, something fundamental to everyone else that I don't have. My life never seems real to me."

"I have to see you again," Sabbath said.

"So. This *is* a flirtation. I wondered but couldn't believe it. Are you always attracted to damaged women?"

"I didn't know there were any other kind."

"Being called damaged is a lot worse than being called cuckoo, isn't it?"

"I believe you were called damaged by yourself."

"Whatever. That's the risk you take talking. In high school I was called ditsy."

"What's 'ditsy' mean?"

"Kind of an airhead. Call Mr. Kasterman, my math teacher. He'll tell you. I'd always be coming in from cooking class with flour all over me."

"I never slept with a girl who tried to commit suicide."

"Sleep with your wife."

"*That* is ditsy."

Her laugh was very sly now, a delightful surprise. A delightful person, suffused by a light soulfulness that wasn't at all juvenile, however juvenile she happened to look. An adventurous mind with an intuitive treasure that her suffering hadn't shut down, Madeline displayed the bright sadder-but-wiser outlook of an alert first grader who'd discovered the alphabet in a school where Ecclesiastes is the primer—life is futility, a deeply terrible experience, but the really serious thing is *reading*. The sliding about of her self-possession was practically visible as she spoke. Self-possession was not her center of gravity, nor was anything else of hers that was on display, other perhaps than a way of saying things that was appealing to him for being just a little impersonal. Whatever had denied her a woman's breasts and a woman's face had made compensation of sorts by charging her mind with erotic significance—or so at least its influence swept over Sabbath, ever vigilant to all stimuli. A sensual promise that permeated her intelligence disarranged pleasantly his hard-on's time-worn hopes.

"What would it be like for you," she asked him, "sleeping with me? Like sleeping with a corpse? A ghost? A corpse resurrected?"

"No. Sleeping with somebody who took the thing to the final step."

"The adolescent romanticism makes you look like an asshole," said Madeline.

"I've looked like an asshole before. So what? What are you so bitter about at your age?"

"Yes, my retrospective bitterness."

"What's it about?"

"*I* don't know."

"But you do."

"You just like to dig right on in there, don't you, Mr. Sabbath? What am I bitter about? All those years I worked and planned for things. It all seems . . . I'm not sure."

"Come down to my car."

She gave the suggestion serious consideration before she replied, "For a quart of vodka?"

"A pint," he said.

"In return for sexual favors? A quart."

"A fifth."

"A quart."

"I'll get it," he said.

"You do that."

Sabbath ran to the parking lot, in a frenzy drove the three miles to Usher, found a liquor store, bought *two* quarts of Stolichnaya, and drove back to the parking lot, where Madeline was to be waiting. He'd done the whole thing in twelve minutes but she wasn't there. She wasn't among the smokers outside the Mansion, she wasn't in the Mansion lounge playing cards with the two old ladies or in the parlor, where the battered Wellesley girl was now doggedly trying her luck with "When the Saints Go Marching In," and, when he retraced their steps, she was not anywhere along the route to Roderick House. So there he was, alone in the shadows on a beautiful fall night, two quarts of the best hundred-proof Russian vodka in a brown paper bag beneath his arm, stood up by someone whom he'd had every reason to trust, when a guard appeared behind him—a very large black man in a blue security officer's uniform and carrying a walkie-talkie—and asked him politely what his business was. The explanation having proved inadequate, two more guards appeared, and though no one assaulted him physically, there were insults to be endured from the youngest and most vigilant of the guards while Sabbath voluntarily allowed himself to be escorted to his car. There the three examined his license and registration by flashlight, wrote down his name and his out-of-state license number, and then took the car keys and got in the car, two in the back with Sabbath and the Stolichnaya and one up front to drive the car off the grounds. Mrs. Sabbath would be questioned before she went to bed and a report filed with the chief doctor (who happened to be Roseanna's doctor) first thing in the morning. If the patient had arranged for her visitor to bring her the alcohol, his wife would be ejected on the spot.

He arrived in Madamaska Falls close to one A.M. Exhausted as he was, he drove to the lake and then followed Fox Run Crossing up past the inn to where the Baliches lived atop the hill overlooking the water, in a new house as spacious and lavish as any on the mountain. The house was the realization for Matija of a dream—the dream of a grand family castle that was a country unto itself—and the dream dated back to elementary school, when, for homework, he had to write about his parents and tell the teacher truthfully, like a good Pioneer, what their relationship was to the regime. Matija had even brought a blacksmith over from Yugoslavia, an artisan from the Dalmatian coast, to stay for six months in the inn's annex and work at a forge near Blackwall where he made the outdoor railings for the vast green terrace that looked onto the sunsets staged at the western end of the lake, the indoor banisters for the wide central staircase that twisted up toward a dome ceiling, and the filigreed iron entrance gates operated electronically from the house. The iron chandelier had come by sea from Split. Matija's brother was a contractor and he had bought it from gypsies who sold all that kind of antique stuff. The chain forged for the chandelier by the resident blacksmith hung menacingly down the two stories from the sky-blue dome into a foyer where there were leaded stained-glass window panels to either side of a mahogany double door. Through the doorway you could have driven a horse-drawn carriage onto the marble floor (cut especially for the house after Matija had gone to Vermont to inspect the quarry). It seemed to Sabbath—the first day that Matija had taken Silvija to see the sights, and Drenka was fucked on Silvija's bed in Silvija's dirndl—that no two rooms in the house were level with each other but had to be reached by going up or down three, four, or five highly varnished, broad steps. And there were wood carvings of kings on pedestals beside the stairways between the rooms. A Boston antiques dealer had found them in Vienna—seventeen medieval kings who, together, had to have beheaded at least as many of their subjects as Matija had beheaded chickens for his popular chicken paprikash with noodles. There were six beds in the house, all with brass frames. The pink marble Jacuzzi could seat six. The modernistic kitchen with the state-of-the-art cooking island at its heart could seat sixteen. The dining room with the tapestried walls could seat thirty. Nobody, however, used the Jacuzzi or entered the dining room, the Baliches slept in just one claustrophobic bed, and the prepared food they carried up from the inn late at night, they ate in front of a TV console installed on four empty egg crates in a room as barren and humble as any you could have found in a worker's housing block built by Tito.

Because Matija was fearful lest his good fortune arouse envy in his guests no less than in his staff, the house had deliberately been situated behind a triangular expanse of firs said to be as old as any in New England. The stand of trees pointed dramatically heavenward, stately schooner masts that had been spared the colonial ax, and yet the roof lines of Matija's million-dollar house—conforming to his fanciful immigrant aim—looked at first glance to be going in every direction *except* up. Strange. The tamed, abstemious, frugal foreigner, beneficiary not merely of his own dedicated hard work but of the fat-cat blowout of the eighties, conceives for himself a palace of abundance, as grand a manifestation as he can imagine of his personal triumph over Comrade Tito, while his wife's intemperate lover, the native-born American hog, lives in a four-room little box built without a basement in the 1920s, a pleasant enough house by now but one that only Roseanna's ingenuity with a paintbrush and a sewing machine, and a hammer and nails, had been able to salvage from the dank Tobacco Road horror it was when, in the mid-sixties, Roseanna came up with the bright idea of domesticating Sabbath. Home and Hearth. The woods, the streams, the snow, the thaw, the spring, New England's spring, that surprise that is among the greatest reinvigorators of humankind on record. She pinned her hopes on the mountainous north—and a child. A family: a mother, a father, cross-country skis, and the kids, a lively, healthy band of shrieking kids, running unmenaced all over the place, enabled, by the very air they breathed, to avoid growing up like their malformed parents, entirely at the mercy of living. Rural domestication, the city dweller's old agrarian dream of "Live Free or Die" license plates on the Volvo, was the purifying rubric not simply by which she hoped and prayed she could put to rest her father's ghost but by which Sabbath could silence Nikki's. Little wonder Roseanna was in orbit from there on out.

There were no lights on at the Baliches', at least not that Sabbath could see through the fir-tree wall. He tapped twice on the horn, waited, tapped twice, and then sat for ten minutes till it was time to tap the horn once again and allow her five minutes more before driving away.

Drenka was a light sleeper. She'd become a light sleeper

when she became a mother. The smallest noise, the tiniest cry of distress from little Matthew's room, and she was out of the bed and had him in her arms. She told Sabbath that when Matthew was a baby she would lie down and sleep on the floor beside his crib to be certain that he didn't stop breathing. And even when he got to be four and five, she would sometimes be seized in her bed by fears for his safety or his health and spend the night on the floor of his room. She had done her mothering the way she did everything, as though she were breaking down a door. Lead her into temptation, into motherhood, into software, you got the impress of all of her, all that rash energy without a single restraint. In full force this woman was extraordinary. To whatever was demanded, she had no aversion. Fear, of course, plenty of fear; but aversions, none. An amazing experience, this thoroughly unaloof Slav for whom her existence was a great experiment, the erotic light of his life, and he had found her not dangling a little key from her finger on Rue St. Denis between Châtelet and the archway of the Porte St. Denis but in Madamaska Falls, capital of caution, where the local population is content to be in raptures about changing the clock twice a year.

He rolled down the window and heard the Baliches' horses breathing in the paddock across the road. Then he saw two of them looming up by the fence. He opened a Stolichnaya bottle. He'd been drinking some since he went to sea but never like Roseanna. That moderation—and circumcision— were about all he had to show for being a Jew. Which was probably the best of it, anyway. He took two drinks and there she was, in her nightgown, with a shawl drawn around her shoulders. He reached out the window and there *they* were. Two hundred and sixty miles round-trip, but it was worth it for Drenka's breasts.

"What is it? Mickey, what's wrong!"

"Not much chance of a blow job, I guess."

"Darling, *no.*"

"Get in the car."

"No. No. Tomorrow."

He took her flashlight out of her hand and shined it into his lap.

"Oh, it's so big. My darling! I can't now. Maté—"

"If he wakes up before I come, fuck it, we'll run away, we'll do it—I'll just turn on the motor and off we go like Vronsky and Anna. Enough of this hiding-out shit. Our whole *lives* are hiding."

"I mean Matthew. He's working. He could come by."

"He'll think we're kids necking. Get in, Drenka."

"We *can't*. You're crazy. Matthew knows the car. You're drunk. I have to go back! I love you!"

"Roseanna may be out tomorrow."

"But," she exclaimed, "I thought two more *weeks*!"

"What am I supposed to do with this thing?"

"You know what." Drenka leaned in through the open window, squeezed it, jerked it once—"Go *home*," she pleaded and then ran for the path back to the house.

On the fifteen-minute drive to Brick Furnace Road, Sabbath saw only one other vehicle on the road, the state police cruiser. That's why she was up—listening to the scanner. Warming to the biblical justice of being taken in for adulterous sodomy by her son, he sounded his horn and flashed his brights; but for the time being, the run of bad luck appeared to have ended. Nobody came tearassing after the county's leading sex of-fender and had him pull over to surrender his license and reg-istration; no one invited him to justify how he came to be driving with a vodka bottle in his steering hand and a dick in the other, his focus not at all on the highway, not even on Drenka, but on that child's face that masked a mind whose core was all clarity, on that lanky blond with the droopy shoul-ders and the delicate voice and the freshly sliced wrist, who was just three weeks clear of going completely off the rails.

"'Pray, do not mock me. / I am a very foolish fond old man, / Four score and upward, not an hour more nor less, / And, to deal plainly, / I fear I am not in my perfect mind. / Methinks . . .'"

Then he lost it, one stop north of Astor Place went com-pletely dry. Yet remembering even that much while begging in the subway on the way to Linc's funeral after the soft-porn drama with the Cowans' Rosa was a huge mnemonic surprise. Methinks what? Methinking methoughts shouldn't be hard. The mind is the perpetual motion machine. You're not ever free of anything. Your mind's in the hands of *everything*. The

personal's an immensity, nuncle, a constellation of detritus
that doth dwarf the Milky Way; it pilots thee as do the stars the
blind Cupid's arrow o' wild geese that o'erwing the Drenka
goose'd asshole as, atop thy cancerous Croatian, their coarse
Canadian honk thou libid'nously mimics, inscribing 'pon her
malignancy, with white ink, thy squandered chromosomal
mark.

Back up, back way, way up. Nikki says, "Sir, do you know
me?" Lear says, "You are a spirit, I know. Where did you die?"
Cordelia says blah, blah; the doctor says blah, blah; I say,
"Where have I been? Where am I? Fair daylight? I am mightily
abused . . . blah, blah, blah." Nikki: "O look upon me, sir, /
And hold your hand in benediction o'er me. / No, sir, you
must not kneel." And Lear says it was a Tuesday in December
1944, I came home from school and saw some cars, I saw my
father's truck. Why is that there? I knew something was
wrong. In the house I saw my father. In terrible pain. In terrible pain. My mother hysterical. Her hands. Her fingers. Moaning. Screaming. People there already. A man had come to the
door. "I'm sorry," he said and gave her the telegram. Missing
in action. Another month before the second telegram arrived,
a tentative, chaotic time—hope, fear, searching for any story
we could get, the phone ringing, never knowing, stories reaching us that he had been picked up by friendly Filipino guerrillas, someone in his squadron said he passed him in the flight,
he was going on the last run, the flak got very bad and Morty's
plane went down, but in friendly territory . . . and Lear
replies, "You do me wrong to take me out o' the grave," but
Sabbath is remembering the second telegram. The month
before was terrible but not as terrible as this: the death notice
was like losing *another* brother. Devastating. My mother in
bed. Thought *she* was dying, afraid she was going to die too.
Smelling salts. The doctor. The house filling up with people.
It's hard to be clear about who was there. It's a blur. Everybody was there. But life was over. The family was finished. I
was finished. I gave her smelling salts and they spilled and I
was afraid I killed her. The tragic period of my life. Between
fourteen and sixteen. Nothing to compare with it. It didn't
just break her, it broke us all. My father, for the rest of his life,
completely changed. He was a reassuring force to me, because

of his physique and because he was so dependable. My mother was always the more emotional one. The sadder one, the happier one. Always whistling. But there was an impressive sobriety in my father. So to see *him* fall apart! Look at my emotions now—I'm fifteen remembering this stuff. Emotions, when they're revved up, don't change, they're the same, fresh and raw. Everything passes? *Nothing* passes. The same emotions are here! He was my *father*, a hardworking guy, out in the truck to the farmers at three in the morning. When he came home at night he was tired and we had to be quiet because he had to get up so early. And if he was ever angry—and that was rare—but if he was ever angry, he was angry in Yiddish and it was terrifying because I couldn't even be sure what he was angry about. But after, he was never angry again. If only he had been! After, he became meek, passive, crying all the time, crying everywhere, in the truck, with the customers, with the Gentile farmers. This fucking thing *broke* my father! After the *shiva* he went back to work again, after the year of official mourning he stopped crying, but there was always that personal, private misery that you could see a mile away. And I didn't feel so terrific myself. I felt I lost a part of my body. Not my prick, no, can't say a leg, an arm, but a feeling that was physiological and yet an interior loss. A hollowing out, as though I'd been worked on with a chisel. Like the horseshoe-crab shells lying along the beach, the armature intact and the inside empty. All of it gone. Hollowed out. Reamed out. Chiseled away. It was so oppressive. And my mother going to bed—I was *sure* I was going to lose my mother. How will she survive? How will any of us survive? There was such an emptiness everywhere. But I had to be the strong one. Even *before* I had to be the strong one. Very tough when he went overseas and all we knew was his APO number. The anxiety. Excruciating. Worried all the time. I used to help my father with the deliveries the way Morty did. Morty did things that nobody in his right mind would have done. Clambering around up on the roof fixing something. On his back, shimmying all the way into the dark crud under the porch, wiring something. Every week he washed the floors for my mother. So now I washed the floors. I did a lot of things to try to calm her down after he shipped out to the Pacific. Every week we used to go to the movies. They wouldn't go near a war movie. But even during an ordinary movie, when something suddenly cropped up about the war or somebody just said something about somebody overseas, my mother would get upset and I would have to calm her down. "Ma, it's just a movie." "Ma, let's not think about it." She would cry. Terribly. And I'd leave with her and walk her around. We used to get letters through the APO. He'd do little cartoons on the envelope sometimes. I'd looked forward to the cartoons. But the only one they cheered up was me. And once he flew over the house. He was stationed in North Carolina and he had to make a flight to Boston. He told us, "I'm going to fly over the house. In a B-25." All the women were outside in the street in their aprons. In the middle of the day my father came home in the truck. My friend Ron was there. And Morty did it—flew over and dipped his wings, those flat gull wings. Ron and I were waving. What a hero he was to me. He was incredibly gentle with me, five years younger—he was just so gentle. He had a real physique. A shot-putter. A track star. He could heave a football almost the whole length of the field; he had a tremendous capacity to toss a ball or to put the shot—to throw things, that was his skill, to throw them far. I would think of that after he was missing. In school I would be thinking that throwing things far might help him survive in the jungle. Shot down on the twelfth of December and died of wounds on the fifteenth. Which was another misery. They had him in a hospital. The rest of the crew was killed instantly, but the plane was shot down over guerrilla territory and the guerrillas got him out and to a hospital and he lived for three days. That made it even worse. *The crew was killed immediately and my brother lived three more days.* I was in a stupor. Ron came. Usually he as good as lived at our house. He said, "Come on out." I said, "I can't." He said, "What happened?" I couldn't talk. It took a few days before I could tell him. But I couldn't tell people at school. I couldn't do it. Couldn't *say* it. There was a gym teacher, a big, strong guy who had wanted Morty to give up track and train as a gymnast. "How's your brother?" he would ask me. "Fine," I'd say. I couldn't say it. Other teachers, his shop teacher, who always gave him A's: "How's your brother doing?" "Fine." And then they finally knew, but I never told them. "Hey, how's Morty doing?" And I perpetuated the lie. This went on and on with the people who hadn't heard. I was in my stupor for a year at least. I even got scared for a while of girls' having lipstick and having tits. Every challenge was suddenly too great. My mother gave me his watch. It nearly killed me, but I wore it. I took it to sea. I took it to the Army. I took it to Rome. Here it is, his GI Benrus. Wind it daily. All that's changed is the strap. Stop function on the second hand still working. When I was on the track team I used to think about his ghost. That was the first ghost. I was like my father and him, always strong up top. Besides, Morty threw the shot, so I *had* to. I *imbued* myself with him. I used to look up at the sky before I threw it and think that he was looking over me. And I called for strength. It was a state meet. I was in fifth place. I knew the unreality of it but I just kept praying to him and I threw it farther than I ever did before. I still didn't win, but I had got his strength!

I could use it now. Where is it? Here's the watch, but where's the strength?

In the seat to the right of where Sabbath had gone blank on "Methinks . . ." was what had caused him to go blank: no more than twenty-one or -two, sculpted entirely in black—turtleneck sweater, pleated skirt, tights, shoes, even a black velvet headband keeping her shining black hair back from her forehead. She had been gazing up at him, and it was the gaze that had stopped him, its meek, familiar softness. She sat with one arm resting on the black nylon backpack by her side, silently watching as he worked to recall the last scene of act four: Lear is carried sleeping into the French camp—"Ay, madam; in the heaviness of sleep / We put fresh garments on him"—and there to wake him is Cordelia—"How does my royal lord? How fares your majesty?" And it is then Lear replies, "You do me wrong to take me out o' the grave. . . ."

The girl with the gaze was speaking, but so softly at first that he couldn't hear her. She was younger than he'd thought, probably a student, probably no more than nineteen.

"Yes, yes, speak up." What he was always telling Nikki whenever she said something she was afraid to say, which was half the time she spoke. She had driven him crazier with each passing year, saying things so that he couldn't hear them. "What did you say?" "It doesn't matter." Drove him *nuts*.

" 'Methinks,' " she said, quite audibly now, " 'I should know you, and know this man. . . .' " She'd given him the line! A drama student, on her way uptown to Juilliard.

He repeated, " 'Methinks I should know you, and know this man,' " and then on his own momentum proceeded. " 'Yet I am doubtful; for I am mainly ignorant / What place this is; and all the skill I have . . .' " Here he *pretended* not to know what was next. " 'And all the skill I have . . .' " Feebly, twice, he repeated this and looked to her for assistance.

" 'Remembers not these garments,' " prompted the girl, " 'nor I know not . . .' "

She stopped when, with a smile, he indicated that he believed he could himself once again pick up from there. She smiled back. " 'Nor I know not / Where I did lodge last night. Do not laugh at me, / For, as I am a man, I think this lady . . .' "

Is Nikki's daughter.

Not impossible! Nikki's beautifully imploring eyes, Nikki's perplexingly, perpetually uncertain voice . . . no, she was not merely some tenderhearted, overimpressionable kid who would excitedly tell her family tonight that a white-bearded old bum had been reciting to her from *Lear* on the Lexington IRT and that she had dared to help him remember the lines— *she was Nikki's daughter*. The family she was going home to tonight was *Nikki's*! Nikki was alive. Nikki was in New York. This girl was hers. And if hers, somehow his, whoever the father might be.

Sabbath was hovering directly above her now, his emotions an avalanche rolling across him, sweeping him beneath them, uprooting the little rootedness still holding him to himself. What if they were *all* alive and at Nikki's house? Morty. Mom. Dad. Drenka. Abolishing death—a thrilling thought, for all that he wasn't the first person, on or off a subway, to have it, have it desperately, to renounce reason and have it the way he did when he was fifteen years old and they *had* to have Morty back. Turning life back like a clock in the fall. Just taking it down off the wall and winding it back and winding it back until your dead all appear like standard time.

" 'For, as I am a man,' " he said to the girl, " 'I think this lady / To be my child Cordelia.' "

" 'And so I am, I am.' " Undesigning Cordelia's unguarded response, the poignantly simple iambic trimeter that Nikki had uttered in a voice one-tenth a lost orphan's and the rest a weary, teetering woman's, spoken by the girl whose gaze was Nikki's exactly.

"Who is your mother?" Sabbath whispered to her. "Tell me who your mother is."

The words made her go pale; her eyes, Nikki's eyes, which could hide nothing, were like those of a child who's just been told something terrible. All her horror of him came right up to the surface, as it would, sooner or later, in Nikki, too. To have been moved by this mad monstrosity because he could quote Shakespeare! To have become entangled on the subway with someone unmistakably crazy, capable of *anything*—how could she be so idiotic!

Simple as it was to read her thoughts, Sabbath declaimed, no less brokenly than Lear, "You are the daughter of Nikki Kantarakis!"

Frantically pulling open the straps of her knapsack, the girl tried to locate her purse and find money to give him, money to make him *go away*. But Sabbath had to see once more the fact that was indisputable—that Nikki lived—and turning her face with his crippled hand, *feeling Nikki's living skin*, he said, "Where is your mother hiding from me?"

"Don't!" she screamed, "don't touch me!" and was swatting at his arthritic fingers as though a swarm of flies had attacked her when somebody came up from behind him and with jarring force hooked Sabbath under the arms.

A business suit was all he could see of his powerful captor. "Calm down," he was being told, "calm down. You shouldn't drink that stuff."

"What *should* I drink? I'm sixty-four years old and I've never been sick a day in my life! Except my tonsils as a child! *I drink what I want!*"

"Calm *down*, Mac. Cut it out, calm down, and get yourself to a shelter."

"I caught lice in the shelter!" Sabbath boomed back. " 'Do not abuse me'!"

"*You* abuse *her*—you're the abuser, chief!"

The train had reached Grand Central. People rushed for the open doors. The girl was gone. Sabbath was freed. "'Pray you now,'" shouted Sabbath as he wandered off the train alone, looking in all directions for Nikki's daughter. "'Pray you now,'" he exclaimed to those standing back from him as he strode majestically along the platform, shaking his cup out before him, "'pray you now . . .'" and then, without even Nikki's daughter to prompt him, he remembered what is next, words that could have meant nothing at all to him in the theater of the Bowery Basement Players in 1961: "'Pray you now, forget and forgive. I am old and foolish.'"

This was true. It was hard for him to believe that he was simulating any longer, though not impossible.

> Thou'lt come no more;
> Never, never, never, never, never.

Destroy the clock. Join the crowd.

IT WAS Michelle Cowan, Norman's wife, who'd got the fifty tablets of Voltaren sent over from a pharmacy on Broadway and written him a prescription for four refills, and so he was in great form over dinner that evening because he knew that he'd soon be getting some relief from the pain in his hands, and also because Michelle was nothing like so gaunt as she'd looked in the Polaroid photos hidden beneath her lingerie along with that envelope of a hundred hundred-dollar bills. She was a nicely fleshed-out woman very much in the mold of Drenka. And she laughed so easily—so quick to be amused and entertained by him. And she'd done nothing at all to indicate distress after he stealthily hunted down beneath the table her unshod foot and lightly laid upon it the sole of his slipper.

The slippers were on loan from Norman. Norman had also sent his secretary out to an army-navy store to buy Sabbath a change of clothes. Two pairs of khakis, a couple of work shirts, some socks, undershirts, and briefs were all in a big paper bag on Debby's bed when they got home from the funeral. Even handkerchiefs. He looked forward to organizing his new things in among Debby's later that night.

Michelle's hidden Polaroids had to be at least five years old. Mementos of an old affair. Ready for a new one? She looked ripish all right, though maybe because she'd let herself go, gotten heavier, figuring it was over with men. Probably about Drenka's age but living with a husband who, of course, in no way resembled Drenka's Matija. Though sooner or later all husbands resemble Drenka's Matija, do they not?

The previous night Norm had described the antidepressant he was taking as not a "dick-friendly" drug. So here there was nobody fucking her, that much was clear. Not that Sabbath was about to take up the slack if she was getting a thousand bucks a shot. Though maybe it wasn't men who gave her the money but Michelle who gave money to men. Young men. In her laugh was the lowdown trace of a coarse rumble that made him want to believe that. Or maybe the cash was for the day she packed up and left.

The plan to leave. Who didn't have one? It evolves as tortuously as the wills of propertied people, rewrites and revisions every six months. I'll go stay with this one; no, I'll go stay with that one; this hotel, that hotel, this woman, that woman, two different women, with *no* woman, no woman ever again! I'll open a secret account, hock the ring, sell the bonds. . . . Then they get to be sixty, sixty-five, seventy, and what difference does it make anymore? They're going to leave all right, but this time they're *really* going to leave. For some people this is the best thing to be said for death: finally out of the marriage. And without having to wind up in a hotel. Without having to live through those miserable Sundays alone in a hotel. It's the Sundays that keep these couples together. As if Sundays alone could be any worse.

No, this is not a good marriage. You wouldn't be far off guessing that much no matter whose table you happened to be eating at, but Sabbath could tell from that laugh—if not from the fact that he was being permitted to play footsie with her only ten minutes into the meal—that something had turned out wrong. In her laugh was the recognition that she was no longer in charge of the forces at work. In her laugh was the admission of her captivity: to Norman, to menopause, to work, to aging, to everything that could only deteriorate further. Nothing unforeseen that happens is likely ever again to be going to be good. What is more, Death is over in its corner doing deep knee bends and one day soon will leap across the ring at her as mercilessly as it leaped upon Drenka—because even though she's at her heaviest ever, weighing in at around one thirty-five, one forty, Death is Two-Ton Tony Galento and Man Mountain Dean. The laugh said that everything had shifted on her while her back was turned, while she was facing the other way, the *right* way, her arms open wide to the dynamic admixture of demands and delights that had been the daily bread of her thirties and forties, to all that assiduous activity, all the extravagant, holidaylike living—so inexhaustibly *busy* . . . with the result that in no more time than it took for the Cowans to cross the ocean on the Concorde for a long weekend in Paris, she was fifty-five and seared with hot flashes, and her daughter's was now the female form exuding the magnetic currents. The laugh said that she was sick of staying, sick of plotting leaving, sick of unsatisfied dreams, sick of satisfied dreams, sick of adapting, sick of not adapting, sick of just about everything except existing. Exulting in existing while being sick of everything—*that's* what was in that laugh! A semidefeated, semiamused, semiaggrieved, semiamazed, seminegative, hilarious big laugh. He liked her, he liked her enormously. Probably just as insufferable a mate as he was. He could discern in her, whenever her husband spoke, the desire to be just a little cruel to Norman, saw her sneering at the best of him, at the very best things in him. If you don't go crazy because of your husband's vices, you go crazy because of his virtues. He's on Prozac because he can't win. Everything is leaving her except for her behind, which her wardrobe informs her is broadening by the season—and except for this steadfast prince of a man marked by reasonableness and ethical obligation the way others are scarred by insanity or illness. Sabbath understood her state of mind, her state of life, her state of suffering: dusk is descending, and sex, our greatest luxury, is racing away at a tremendous speed, *everything* is racing off at a tremendous speed and you wonder at your folly in having ever turned down a single squalid fuck. You'd give your right arm for one if you are a babe like this. It's not unlike the Great Depression, not unlike going broke overnight after years of raking it in. "Nothing unforeseen that happens," the hot flashes inform her, "is likely ever again to be going to be good." Hot flashes mockingly mimicking the sexual ecstasies. Dipped, she is, in the very fire of fleeting time. Aging seventeen days for every seventeen seconds in the furnace. He clocked her on Morty's Benrus. Seventeen seconds of menopause oozing out all over her face. You could baste her in it. And then it just stops like a tap that's been shut. But while she is in it, he can see how it seems to her that there's no bottom to it—that this time they're out to cook her like Joan of Arc.

Nothing quite touches Sabbath like these aging dishes with the promiscuous pasts and the pretty young daughters. Especially when they've still got it in them to laugh like this one. You see all they once were in that laugh. I am what's left of the famous motel fucking—hang a medal on my drooping boobs. It's no fun burning on a pyre at dinner.

And Death, he reminded her by evenly pressing down on

her naked instep with the ball of his foot, on top of us, over us, ruling us, Death. You should have seen Linc. You should have seen him all quieted down like a good little boy, a good little boy with green skin and white hair. Why was he green? He wasn't green when I knew him. "It's frightening," Norman had said after quickly identifying the corpse. They walked out into the street and over to a coffee shop for a Coke. "It's spooky," said Norman, with a shudder. Yet Sabbath enjoyed it. Exactly what he'd driven all this way to see. Learned a lot, Michelle. You lie in there like a good little boy who does what he is told.

And as if pressing Michelle Cowan's foot beneath his own wasn't sufficient reason to live, there were his new khaki trousers and his new Jockey briefs. A big bagful of clothes such as he had not thought to buy for himself in years. Even handkerchiefs. Long time between handkerchiefs. All the tattered shit he wore, the T-shirts yellowing under the arms, the boxer shorts with the elasticity shot, the unmatched remnants that were his socks, the big-tipped boots he sported like Mammy Yokum twelve months a year. . . . Were the boots what they call a "statement"? This fucking way they talk made him feel like a curmudgeon. Diogenes in his tub? Making a statement! He'd noticed that the college girls down in the valley were all now wearing clodhoppers not unlike his own, kind of lace-up construction boots, along with lacy maiden-aunt dresses. Feminine in the dress but not conventionally feminine, because there's something else there in the shoes. The shoes say, "I'm tough. Don't mess with me," while the lacy, long, old-fashioned dress says . . . so that altogether we've got ourselves a *statement*, something like, "If you would be kind enough, sir, to try to fuck me, I'll kick your fucking head in." Even Debby, with her low self-esteem, gets burnished up like Cleopatra. Haute couture has been passing me by, along with everything else. Wait'll I hit the streets in my khakis. Manhattan, let me in!

He was sublimely effervescent about not being the good little boy in the box doing what he was told. Also over not having been turned in by Rosa. She'd said nothing to anyone about their morning. The mercy there is in life, and none of it deserved. All our crimes against each other, and still we get another shot at it in a new pair of pants!

Outside the funeral home, after the service, Linc's eight-year-old grandson, Joshua, had said to his mother—whose hand was in Norman's—"Who were the people talking about?"

"Grandpa. Linc was his name. You know that. Lincoln."

"But that wasn't Grandpa," the boy said. "That wasn't what he was like."

"Wasn't it?"

"No. Grandpa was like a baby."

"But not always, Josh. When he got sick he became like a baby. But before, he was just as all his friends described him."

"That wasn't Grandpa," he replied, determinedly shaking his head. "Sorry, Mom."

Linc's littlest grandchild named Laurie. A tiny, energetic girl with large, dark, sensual eyes who raced up to Sabbath on the pavement after the service and said, "Santa, Santa, I'm three! They put Grandpa in a box!"

The box that never failed to impress. Whatever your age, the sight of that box never lost its power. One of us takes up no more room than that. You can store us like shoes or ship us like lettuce. The simpleton who invented the coffin was a poetic genius and a great wit.

"What would you like for Christmas?" Sabbath asked the child, kneeling to satisfy her desire to touch his beard.

"Chanukah!" Laurie shouted with great excitement.

"It's yours," he told her and restrained the impulse to touch .with a crooked finger her clever little mouth and thereby wind up where he began.

Where he began. That indeed was the subject. The obscene performance with which he'd begun.

It was Norman who'd started it off, describing for Michelle the skit that had got Sabbath arrested out in front of the gates of Columbia back in 1956, that skit in which the middle finger of his left hand would beckon a pretty young student right up to the screen and then enter into conversation with her while the five fingers of the other hand had begun deftly to unbutton her coat.

"Describe it, Mick. Tell Shel how you got arrested."

Mick and Shel. Shel and Mick. A duo if ever there was one. And Norman seemed to recognize that already, to understand after less than half an hour at the dinner table that in Sabbath's down-and-outness there might be more to stir his wife than in all his own orderly success. There was in the aging Sabbath's failure a threat of disarray not unlike the danger there used to be to Norman in young Sabbath's eruptive-disruptive vitality. My misbehaving always imperiled him. He should know what it's done to me. This mighty fortress built to withstand the remotest intimation of mayhem, and yet here near the end, as at the beginning, he continues to be humbled by the stinky little mess I make of things. I frighten him. As my father said, "*Bolbotish.*" This generous, lovely, *bolbotish* success continues to kowtow to a putz. You'd think I'd burst forth in a boiling blaze, incandescent from Pandemonium, instead of having driven down 684 in an ancient Chevy with a busted tailpipe.

"How I got arrested," Sabbath said. "Four decades, Norm. Almost forty years. I don't know that I remember anymore how I got arrested." He did, of course. Had never forgotten any of it.

"You remember the girl."

"The girl," he repeated.

"Helen Trumbull," Norman said.

"That was her name? Trumbull? And the judge?"

"Mulchrone."

"Yes. Him I remember. Gave a great performance. Mulchrone. The cop was Abramowitz. Right?"

"Officer Abramowitz, yes."

"Yes. The cop was a Jew. And the prosecutor another Irishman. That kid with the crew cut."

"Just out of St. John's," said Norman. "Foster."

"Yes. Very disagreeable, Foster. Didn't like me. Outraged. Genuinely outraged. How can anyone do this? Yes. Guy from St. John's. That's right. Crew cut, rep tie, his father's a cop, he never thinks he'll earn more than ten thousand dollars a year and he wants to send me up for life."

"Tell Shelly."

Why? What's he up to, showing me in my best light or in my worst? Turning her on to me or turning her off? It had to be off, because before dinner, alone in the living room with Sabbath, he had lavished on his wife and her work a uxorious deluge of admiration—what Roseanna had been dying for, thirsting for, all her married life. While Michelle was shower-

ing and changing for dinner, Norman had shown him, in a recent alumni magazine from the University of Pennsylvania
dental school, a photograph of Michelle and her father, an old
man in a wheelchair, one of several pictures illustrating a story
about parents and children who were Penn dental school graduates. Before his stroke and well into his seventies, Michelle's
father had been a dentist in Fairlawn, New Jersey, according to
Norman an overbearing bastard whose own father had been a
dentist and who had pronounced at Michelle's birth, "I don't
give a shit that she's a girl—this is a dental family, and she's
going to be a dentist!" As it turned out, she had not merely
gone to his dental school but outdone the hard-driving son of
a bitch by taking two more years to become a periodontist and
ending up at the top of her class. "I can't tell you," said Norman, nursing the evening glass of wine he said he was allowed
while on Prozac, "what a physical trial being a periodontist is.
Most days she gets home just like tonight, beat. Imagine going
with an instrument and trying to clean the back outer corner
of an upper second or third molar and trying to get up in that
pocket there, up in the gum. Who can see? Who can *reach*?
She's physically amazing. Over twenty years of this. I've said to
her, why don't you think of cutting the practice back to three
days a week? With periodontal disease you see your patients
year after year, forever—her patients will wait for her. But no,
she's out every morning at seven-thirty and isn't home until
seven-thirty, and some weeks she's even in there on Saturdays." Yes, Saturday, Sabbath was thinking, must be a big day
for Shelly . . . while Norman was explaining, "If you're
meticulous in the way that Michelle is, and you've got to do a
cleaning around every surface of every tooth in unreachable
places . . . Granted, she's got instruments with curves that
help; she's got these instruments she cleans these roots with
called scalers and curettes, because she's not just dealing with
the crown portion like a hygienist. She's got to do this up to
the root surfaces if there are pockets, if there is bone loss—"
How he praises her! How much he cares! How much he
knows—and doesn't. Before dinner, Sabbath had been wondering whether the encomium was designed to keep him at
bay or whether it was the drug speaking. I may be listening to
Prozac. Or maybe I am merely listening to his wife's elaborate

excuses for Working Late at the Office—to somebody lamely repeating, as if he believed it, something somebody else told them to believe about them. "Because up there," Norman continued, "is where the action is. It's not just to shine the enamel and make pretty teeth. It's to pick the tartar, which can be very adherent—and I've seen her come home *limp* after a day of this stuff—it's to snap the tartar off the roots. Sure, there are ultrasonic instruments that help. They use an ultrasonic device, runs on an electrical current, emits ultrasonic energy, goes up into the pocket there to help crack off all the crap. But so it doesn't overheat, there's of course a water spray, and it's like living in a fog, with that water spray. Living in the mist. It's like spending twenty years in the rain forest. . . ."

So she was an Amazon, was that it? Daughter of a once-terrifying tribal chief whom she had conquered and gone beyond, an Amazon warrior, emitting ultrasonic energy, armed against barnacled tartar with stainless steel scalers and curving curettes . . . what *was* Sabbath to conclude? That she was too much for Norman? That he was as perplexed by her as he was proud of her—and overpowered? That now that the youngest child was off at college and it was just him and the dental dynasty heiress alone together side by side . . . Sabbath didn't know what to think in the living room, before dinner, any more than he did at the table, with Norman urging him to tell the story of the defiant outsider that he'd been in his twenties, so unlike Norman himself starting out, the well-groomed, well-mannered Columbia-educated son of the jukebox distributor whose croaking voice and crude success had shamed Norman throughout his youth. The son and the daughter of two brutes. Only I had the gently loving father, and look how it all turned out.

"Well, so there I am. 1956. On 116th and Broadway, just by the university gates there. Twenty-seven years old. The cop has been standing around for days watching. There are usually about twenty, twenty-five students. Some passersby, but mostly students. Afterward I pass the hat. The whole thing takes less than thirty minutes. I think I got a breast out once before. To get a kid to go that far with me, rare in those days. I didn't expect it. The idea of the act was that I *couldn't* get that far. But this time it happened. The tit is out. It's out. And the cop comes up and he says, 'Hey, you, you can't do that.'

He's calling this down to me back of the screen. 'It's all right, Officer,' I tell him, 'it's part of the show.' I stayed down and the middle finger said it to him, the one that had been talking to the girl. I figure, 'Great, now I've got a cop in the show.' The kids watching aren't sure he *isn't* part of the show. They start laughing. 'You can't do that,' he tells me. 'There are children here. They can see the breast.' 'There aren't any children here,' the finger says. 'Get up,' he tells me, 'stand up. You can't expose that breast on the street. You can't have a breast exposed in the middle of Manhattan at twelve-fifteen at 116th Street and Broadway. And also, you're taking advantage of this young woman. Do you want him to do this to you?' the cop asks her. 'Is there a sexual molestation charge here?' 'No,' she says, 'I permitted him to do it.'"

"The girl's a student," Michelle said.

"Yep. Barnard student."

"Brave," said Michelle. "'I permitted him to do it.' What'd the policeman do?"

"He says, 'Permitted? You were hypnotized. This guy hypnotized you. You didn't know he was doing it to you.' 'No,' she says to him defiantly, 'it was okay.' She was frightened when the cop came but there she was with all the other students, and students are generally anti-cop, so she just picked up the mood and she went with it. She said, 'It's all right, Officer—leave him alone. He wasn't doing anything wrong.'"

"Sound like Debby?" Michelle said to Norman.

Sabbath waited to see how the Prozac would field that one. "Let him go on," Norman said.

"So the cop says to the girl, 'I can't leave him alone. There could be kids here. What would people say about the police if they just allowed blouses to be opened and breasts to be out on the street and someone publicly twisting a nipple? You want me to let him do it in Central Park? Have you done it,' he asks me, 'in Central Park?' 'Well,' I said, 'I have my show in Central Park.' 'No, no,' he says to me, 'you can't do this. People are complaining. The guy who owns the drugstore over there is complaining, get these people away from here, it's not good for his business.' I told him I wasn't aware of that—if anything, I felt the drugstore hurt *my* business. This got a rise from the kids, and now he's getting pissed off. 'Listen, this young woman didn't want her breast out and she wasn't even aware of it until I pointed it out to her. She was hypnotized by you.' 'I *was* aware of it,' the girl says, and all the kids applaud her—they're really impressed by her. 'Officer, listen,' I said, 'what I did was okay. She agreed to it. It was just fun.' 'It was not fun. It's not my idea of fun. It's not that druggist over there's idea of fun. You can't use that kind of behavior here.' 'Okay, so okay,' I said, 'now what are you going to do about it? I can't stand around talking all day. I got a living to make.' The kids love this, too. But the cop remains decent, given the circumstances. All he says is, 'I want you to tell me you're not going to do it again.' 'But it's my act. It's my art.' 'Oh, don't give me that shit about your art. What does playing with a nipple have to do with art?' 'It's a new art form,' I tell him. 'Oh, bullshit, bullshit, you bums are always telling me about your art.' 'I'm not a bum. This is what I do for my livelihood, Officer.' 'Well, you're not doing this livelihood in New York. You have a license?' 'No.' 'Why don't you have a license?' 'You can't get a license for it. I'm not selling potatoes. There is no license for a puppeteer.' 'I don't see puppets.' 'I carry my puppet between my legs,' I said. 'Watch it, shorty. I don't see puppets. I just see fingers. And there *is* a license for a puppeteer— there's a street license for acting—' 'I can't get that.' 'Of course you can get it,' he tells me. 'I *can't*. And I can't go down there and wait four or five hours to find out I can't.' 'Okay,' says the cop, 'so you're vending without a license.' 'There's no vending license,' I tell him, 'for touching women's breasts on the street.' 'So you *admit* that's what you do.' 'Oh, shit,' I say, 'this is ridiculous.' And the whole thing starts to get belligerent and he tells me he's going to take me in."

"And the girl?" Michelle again.

"The girl's good. The girl says, 'Hey, leave him alone.' And the cop says, 'You trying to interfere with this arrest?' 'Leave him alone!' she tells him."

"This *is* Debby," Michelle laughed. "Absolutely Deborah."

"Is it?" Sabbath asked.

"To a T." She's proud.

"The cop grabs me because I'm starting to be a real pain in the ass. I say, 'Hey, I'm not going in. This is silly,' and he says, 'You are,' and the girl says, 'Leave him alone,' and he says, 'Listen, if you keep doing this, I'll take you in also.' 'This is crazy,' the girl says, 'I just came from my physics class. I didn't do anything.' Things get out of control and the cop pushes her out of the way, and so I start shouting, 'Hey, don't push her.' 'Oh,' he says to me, 'Sir Galahad.' In 1956 a cop could still say something like that. This was before the decline of the West spread from the colleges to the police departments. Anyway, he takes me in. He lets me get all my apparatus together and he takes me in."

"With the girl," Michelle said.

"No. Just took me. 'I want to book this guy,' he tells the booking officer. The precinct station on 96th Street. I got scared, of course. When you walk into a station, there's a big desk up front with a booking officer, and this big desk scares you. I said, 'This is absolutely *bullshit*,' but when Abramowitz says, 'This guy should be booked for vending without a license, disorderly conduct, harassment, assault, and obscenity. And resisting arrest. And obstruction of justice,' when I heard this, I think I'm going to serve for the rest of my life and I went nuts. 'This is all bullshit! I'll get the ACLU! This'll be the end of you!' I tell the cop. I'm shitting my pants but that's what I'm shouting. 'Yeah, the ACLU,' Abramowitz says, 'those Red bastards. Great.' 'I'm not going to say anything till I get a lawyer from the ACLU!' Now the cop is shouting, 'Fuck them. Fuck you. We don't need a lawyer. We're just going to arrest you now, shorty—you bring a lawyer here when you got to be in court.' The desk sergeant is listening to all this. He says to me, 'Tell me what happened, young man.' I don't know from shit what it means, but I just say again and again, 'I'm not going to tell you till I get a lawyer!' And Abramowitz is now deep in the fuck-you mode. But the other guy says, 'What happened, son?' I think, Tell him; he's not a bad guy. So I said, 'Listen, this is all that happened. And he went crazy. He went crazy because he saw a breast. It happens all the time. Kids are making out on the street. This guy lives in Queens—he doesn't know what's happening. Does he ever see the way girls walk around here in the summer? Everybody on the street knows except this guy who lives in Queens. An exposed breast is no big deal.' So Abramowitz says, 'It's not just an exposed breast. You don't know her, you never met her, you unnippled it, you unbuttoned it, she really didn't know what was going on, you were distracting her with the finger and you hurt her.' '*I* didn't hurt her—*you* hurt her. You *pushed* her.' The desk sergeant says, 'You mean to say you totally undressed a woman on Broadway?' 'No! No! All I did was this.' And I explained again. The guy was fascinated. 'How could you, on an open street, with a woman you never met before?' 'My art, Sergeant. That's my art.' This breaks him up," said Sabbath, seeing it breaking Michelle up, too. And Norman, so happy! Watching from a foot away while I seduce his wife. This Prozac is some drug.

" 'Harry,' the desk sergeant says to Abramowitz, 'why don't you leave the kid alone? He's not a bad kid. All he did was his art.' He's still laughing. 'Finger painting. Baby shit. What's the difference? He has no record. He's not going to do it again. If the kid had seventeen molestation charges . . .' But Abramowitz is furious now. 'No! That's my street. Everybody knows me there. He was abusive to me.' 'How?' 'He pushed me away.' 'He touched you? He touched a police officer?' 'Yeah. He touched me.' So now I'm not up for touching the girl; now I'm up for touching the cop. Which I never did, but of course the desk sergeant, after trying to placate Harry, switches and goes over to Harry's side. To the arresting officer's side. And so they charge me with all this stuff. The cop makes out an affidavit as to what happened. And a complaint is issued against me. Seven charges. I can get a year for each. I'm commanded to appear at Sixty Centre Street—that it, Norm? Sixty Centre?"

"Sixty Centre Street, in Part Twenty-two, at two-thirty in the afternoon. You remember everything."

"So how did you get a lawyer?" Michelle asked him.

"Norman. Norman and Linc. I got a phone call, either from Norm or Linc."

"Linc," said Norman. "Poor Linc. In that box."

Got him, too. And it's only a box. Never seems to become clichéd.

"Linc said, 'We understand you got arrested. We've got a lawyer for you. Not a little shmegeggy just out of law school but some guy who's been around for a while. Jerry Glekel.

He's done fraud cases, assault and battery, robbery, burglary. He does organized-crime work. It pays very well but the work is not marvelous, and this he's willing to do as a favor to me.' Right, Norm? A favor to Linc, whom he somehow knows. Glekel says this is all bullshit and in all probability it'll be dismissed. I talk to Glekel. I'm still hot on the ACLU, so he goes to the Civil Liberties Union and tells them this is a case he thinks they should support. I'll represent him, he says. You should support him, submit an amicus brief. We'll make it an ACLU-sponsored case. Glekel's got it all figured out. What it deals with really is artistic freedom on the streets, arbitrary control by the police of the streets. Who controls the streets? The people or the police force? Two people doing something that's innocuous, that's playful—the defenses are all obvious, just another case of police abuse. Why should a kid like this have to spend X and Y and Z, et cetera? So we came to trial. About twenty-two people show up at the trial. Lost in the big courtroom. The civil rights student group from Columbia. About twelve kids and their adviser. Somebody from the *Columbia Spectator*. Somebody from the Columbia radio station. They're not there because of me. They're there because this girl, Helen Trumbull, is saying that I did nothing wrong. In 1956, this creates a tiny stir. Where'd she get the guts? This is still years before Charlotte Moorman is playing the cello barebreasted down in the Village, and this is just a kid, not a performer. There's even somebody sitting there from the *Nation*. They got wind of it. And there's the judge. Mulchrone. Old Irish guy, former prosecutor. Tired. Very tired. He doesn't want to hear this shit. He doesn't care. There are murders and killings in the street, and here he is wasting his time with a guy who twisted a nipple. So he's not in the best of moods. The prosecutor is the young boy from St. John's, who wants to put me behind bars for life. The trial starts at two, two-thirty, and about an hour before, he has the witnesses down in his office running them through the lies. And then they get on the stand and they do their stuff. Three of them, as I remember it. Some old lady who says the girl kept trying to push my hand away but I wouldn't stop. And the druggist, the Jewish druggist, humanistically outraged as only a Jewish druggist can be. He could only see the back of the woman but he testified that she was upset. Glekel cross-examines him, contending that the druggist couldn't have seen it, because the girl had her back to him. Twenty minutes of his Jewish druggist lies. And the cop testifies. He's called at the beginning. He testified, and I'm nuts—I'm angry, I'm squirming, I'm furious. Then I got up and testified. The prosecutor asks me, 'Did you ever ask the woman if you could unbutton her shirt?' 'No.' '*No*? Did you know who was in the audience at the time?' 'No.' 'Did you know that there were kids in the audience?' 'There were no kids in the audience.' 'Can you state under oath, as a matter of certainty, that there were no kids in the audience? You're down *there* and they're up *here*. Didn't you see seven kids walking at the back there?' And the druggist, you see, will testify that there were seven kids, and the old lady, too, all of them, you see, they all want to hang me because of the tit. 'Look, this is a form of art.' This gets a rise every time. The kid from St. John's makes a face. 'Art? What you did was you unbuttoned a woman's breast, and that's art? How many other women's dresses have you unbuttoned?' 'Actually it rarely has ever happened that I've got that far. Unfortunately. But that's the art. The art is being able to get them into the act.' The judge, Mulchrone, the first thing he says, he says now. Flat voice. 'Art.' Like he's just been wakened from the dead. 'Art.' The prosecutor won't even get into the dialogue, it's so absurd. Art! He says to me, 'You have any kids?' 'No.' 'You don't care about kids. You have a job?' 'This is my job.' 'You don't have a job. Have a wife?' 'No.' 'Ever had a job that lasted more than six months?' 'Merchant seaman. U.S. Army. GI Bill in Italy.' So he's got me nailed. He delivers his shot. 'You call yourself an artist. I call you a drifter.' Then my lawyer calls the professor from NYU. Big mistake. This was Glekel's idea. They had professors to argue the *Ulysses* case, they had professors to argue the 'Miracle' case—why shouldn't we have a professor to argue *your* case? I didn't want it. The professors are as full of shit on the stand as the druggist and the cop. Shakespeare was a great street artist. Proust was a great street artist. And so on. He was going to compare me and my act to Jonathan Swift. The professors are always schlepping in Swift to defend some *farshtunkeneh* nobody. Anyway, in about two seconds the judge learns he's not a witness—he's an *expert* witness. To Mulchrone's credit, he is baffled. 'What's he an expert on?' 'That street art is a valid form of art,' my lawyer says, 'and what they were doing, this interplay on the streets, is traditional.' The judge covers his face. It's three-thirty in the afternoon and the man has heard a hundred and twelve cases before me. He is seventy years old and he has been on the bench all day. He says, 'This is absolute nonsense. I'm not going to listen to a professor. He touched a breast. What happened is he touched a breast. I don't need any testimony from a professor. The professor can go home.' Glekel: 'No, Your Honor. There is a larger perspective to this case. And the larger perspective is that there is legitimate street art and what happens in street art is that you can engage people in a way that you can't engage them in a theater.' And all the time Glekel is speaking, the judge is still covering his face. The judge covers his face even when he himself is speaking. The whole of *life* makes him want to cover his face. He's right, too. He was a wonderful man, Mulchrone. I miss him. He knew the score. But my lawyer goes on, Glekel goes on. Glekel is sick of doing organized-crime work. He has higher aspirations. I think mostly now he is directing his argument to the reporter from the *Nation*. 'It's the intimacy of street art,' he says, 'that makes it unique.' 'Look,' Mulchrone says, 'he touched a breast on the street in order to get some laughs or in order to get some attention. Isn't that right, sonny?' So the prosecutor has three witnesses and the cop against me, and we don't have the professor, but we've got the girl. We've got Helen Trumbull. The wild card is this girl. It was unusual that she should come down there. Here's the alleged victim testifying for the perpetrator. Though Glekel is saying this is a victimless crime. In fact, the victim, if there even is one, is coming his way, but the prosecutor says no, the victim is the public. The poor public, getting the shaft from this fucking drifter, this *artist*. If this guy can walk along the street, he says, and do this, then little kids think it's permissible to do this, and if little kids think it's permissible to do this, then they think it's permissible to blah blah banks, rape women, use knives. If seven-year-old kids—the seven nonexistent kids are now seven seven-year-*old* kids—are going to see that this is fun and permissible with strange women . . ."

"And what happened with the girl?" Michelle asked. "When she testified."

"What do you want to have happened?" Sabbath asked her.

"How did she hold up?"

"She's a middle-class girl, a nervy girl, a terrific, defiant girl, but once she gets in the court, how do you expect she held up? She gets scared. Out on the street, she was a good kid, she had guts—116th Street and Broadway is a young people's world—but here in the courtroom, the alliance is the cops, the prosecutor, and the judge . . . it's their world, they believe each other, and you've got to be blind not to see it. So how does she testify? In a scared voice. Goes there meaning to help me, but once she walks into the courtroom, a big room, big walls, JUSTICE FOR ALL written up there in wood—she gets scared."

"Debby," said Michelle.

"The girl testifies that she didn't scream. The druggist said she screamed and she says she never screamed. 'You mean to say a man is touching your breast, in the middle of Manhattan, doing this, and you didn't scream out?' See, sounds like she's a whore. That's what he wants to establish, that Debby," says Sabbath, altogether deliberately, but pretending not even to have heard his own error, "is a whore." Nobody corrects him. "'How often do men touch your breasts in the middle of the Street?' 'Never.' 'Were you surprised, were you upset, were you shocked, were you this, were you that?' 'I didn't notice.' 'You didn't *notice*?' The kid is getting nervous as hell but she hangs in. 'It was part of the game.' 'Do you generally have men play games with your breasts in the middle of the street? A man you didn't know, a man you'd never spoken to, a man whose face you couldn't see?' 'But he testified I screamed,' Debby says; 'I *never* screamed.'"

"Helen," Norman said.

"Trumbull," Sabbath said. "Helen Trumbull."

"You said Debby."

"No, I said Helen."

"It doesn't matter," Michelle said. "What happened to her?"

"Well, he really goes to work on her. For old St. John's. For

his father the cop. For morality. For America. For Cardinal
Spellman. For the Vatican. For Jesus and Mary and Joseph and
all the gang there in the manger, for the donkeys and the cows
there in the manger, for the wise men and the myrrh and the
frankincense, for the whole fucking Catholic schmeer that we
all need like a fucking hole in the head, this kid from St. John's
really tears into Debby's ass. He brutalizes her. He kicks her
every fucking which way. I twist nipples out on the street, but
this guy goes right for the cunt. Remember? Yeah, I remember, Norm. A real clitorectomy, the first I ever had the privilege to see. He cut her little fucking weenie right off her, right
there, right under where it says JUSTICE FOR ALL, and the
judge and the cop and the druggist ate it up. Yeah, he really
broke her down. 'Have you ever walked into class with your
breasts exposed?' 'No.' 'When you were at Bronx Science high
school, before you came to Barnard to become a defender of
artistic freedom, did anybody at Bronx Science ever touch
your breasts in full view of the other students?' 'No.' 'But
weren't some of those students friends of yours? Isn't it less
embarrassing to do it in front of friends than in front of
strangers in the street?' 'No. Yes. I don't know.' Uh-oh—score
this round for the gang in the manger. He's finally got her
thinking that she may be *in the wrong*. Have you ever exposed
your breasts on 115th Street, 114th Street, 113th Street—and
what about the little kids who were watching? 'There *were* no
little kids.' 'Listen, you're standing *here*, this guy is performing
there—this whole thing took a minute and a half. Did you see
who was walking behind you during that minute and a half?
Yes or no?' 'No.' 'It's noon. Kids are on lunch hour. You have
kids from the music school up there, you have kids from private schools. Do you have a brother or a sister?' 'Yes. Both.'
'How old are they?' 'Twelve and ten.' 'Your sister is ten. How
would you like your ten-year-old sister to know what you allowed a man you didn't know to do to you in full view of 116th
Street and Broadway, with dozens of cars passing, hundreds of
people walking around? For you to be standing there while
this man is twisting your nipple—how do you feel about
telling that to your sister?' Debby tries to brazen it out. 'I
wouldn't mind.' I wouldn't mind. What a girl! If I could find
her today and if she would let me, I'd get down on 116th Street

and Broadway and lick the soles of her feet. *I wouldn't mind.* In 1956. 'And how about if he did it to your sister?' This gets her back up. 'My sister's only ten,' she says. 'Have you told this to your mother?' 'No.' 'Have you told this to your father?' 'No.' 'No. And so isn't it true, then, that the reason you're testifying for him is that you feel sorry for him? It's not because you think what he did was right, is it? Is it? Is it, Debby?' Well, by now she's in tears. They did it. They've done it. They've pretty well proved that this girl is a whore. I went nuts. Because the basic lie in this case is that there are kids there. And what if there even were? I stood up, I screamed, 'If there are so many kids, why aren't there any kids testifying here!' But the prosecutor likes that I screamed. Glekel is trying to get me to sit down but the prosecutor says to me, and the voice is *very* holy, he says, 'I wasn't going to drag kids in here and expose them to this. I'm not you.' 'Fuckin' A, you're not! And if kids wander by, what are they going to do—drop dead? *This is part of the show!*' Well, shouting like that, I didn't do my cause much more good than the girl did. She goes off in tears, and the judge asks if anybody has any more witnesses. Glekel: 'I'd like to sum up, Your Honor.' The judge: 'I don't need it. It's not that complicated. You're telling me that, if this guy is having intercourse with her in the middle of the street, that's also art? And I can't do anything about it because it has antecedents in Shakespeare and the Bible? Come on. Where do you draw the line between this and intercourse in the street? Even if she consents.' So I got convicted."

"On which grounds?" Michelle asked. "All of them?"

"No, no. Disorderly conduct and obscenity. Obscene performance on the street."

"What *is* 'disorderly conduct' anyway?"

"I am disorderly conduct. The judge can sentence me anywhere up to a year for each offense. But he's not a bad guy. It's almost four o'clock now in the afternoon. He looks out into the courtroom and he's got twelve more cases out there, or twenty, and he wants to go home and have a drink in the worst way. He looks like he's four hundred miles southwest of the nearest drink. He does not look good. I didn't know what arthritis was then. Today my heart goes out to him. He's got it all over and the pain is driving him nuts, but still he says to me,

'Are you going to do this again, Mr. Sabbath?' 'It's how I make my living, Your Honor.' He covers his face and tries me a second time. 'Are you going to do this again? I want you to promise me that, if I don't put you in jail, you won't do this and you won't touch that and you won't touch this.' 'I can't,' I say. St. John's sneers. Mulchrone: 'If you're telling me that you committed a crime and you're going to do it again, I'm going to give you thirty days in jail.' Here Jerry Glekel, my ACLU lawyer, whispers in my ear, 'Say you won't do it. Fuck him. Just say it.' Jerry leans over and says, 'Fuck him—let's get out of here.' 'Your Honor, I won't do it.' 'You won't do it. That's wonderful. Thirty days, sentence suspended. A fine of one hundred dollars, payable now.' 'I have no money, Your Honor.' 'What do you mean, you don't have any money? You have a lawyer, you pay for a lawyer.' 'No, the ACLU gave me this lawyer.' 'Your Honor,' Jerry says, 'I'll put up the hundred dollars, I'll pay the hundred dollars, and we all go home.' And then on the way out, St. John's passes by us and says, so nobody but us can hear, 'And which of you gets to screw with the girl?' I said to him, 'You mean, which of us Jews? We all do. We all get to screw the girl. Even my old *zaydeh* gets to screw her. My rabbi gets to screw her. Everybody gets to screw her except you, St. John's. You get to go home and screw your wife. That's what you're sentenced to—screwing for life Mary Elizabeth, who worships her older sister, the nun.' So there was the flare-up, a fight mercifully cut short by Linc and Norm and Glekel, and this cost another hundred bucks, which Glekel paid, and then Linc and Norm paid Glekel back, and in all I got off lucky. It didn't have to be an Enlightenment philosopher like Mulchrone up there. I could have got Savonarola."

I did, thought Sabbath. Thirty-three years later, I got Savonarola dressed up to look like a Japanese woman. Helen Trumbull. Kathy Goolsbee. The Savonarolas break them down. They don't want my foot on hers or on anyone else's. They want my foot like Linc's in the casket, touching nothing and dead to the touch.

Not for a second had Sabbath let her foot be. So close already to copulation! Not once throughout the entire performance did he lose her—unlike Norman, she was too entertained by him to seize up even momentarily each time he called Helen Debby or when, for her benefit, he put in the bit about licking the girl's feet. She was right at his side, from the farce out on the street to the playground finale in Mulchrone's courtroom, her large, plump laugh filled half with her earthy happiness and half with her wild distress. She was thinking, like Lear, "Let copulation thrive!" She was thinking (thought Sabbath) that in cahoots with this loathsome freak there might yet be a use to which she might put her old propensities and her pendulating breasts, still a chance for the old juicy way of life to make one big, last thumping stand against the inescapable rectitude, not to mention the boredom, of death. Linc did look bored. Good and green and bored. Don't admonish me, Drenka—you'd do it in a shot. This is the crime we were wedded to. I'll be as bored as you and Linc soon enough.

Everybody went to bed early. Sabbath knew enough not to get right into Debby's things, and sure enough, only ten minutes after the dinner dishes had been cleared away and they'd all said good night, Norman had knocked at the door to give him a bathrobe and to ask if he wanted to see last Sunday's *Times* before they threw it away. Had numerous sections of it clutched in his arms, and Sabbath decided to accept them, if for no other reason than so Norman could deceive himself, assuming he was so inclined, into thinking that the *chazerai* in the Sunday papers was the soporific his guest was using to put himself to sleep. It was probably no less dependable than ever, but Sabbath had a better idea. "I haven't seen last Sunday's *Times* for over thirty years," Sabbath said, "but why not?" "Don't you get the New York papers up there?" "I don't get anything up there. If I read the New York papers, I'd be on Prozac too." "Can you at least get a bagel on a Sunday morning?" "Any morning. We were a bagel-free zone for a very long time. One of the last. But now, except for a county in Alabama where the citizens voted no on a referendum, I believe the poor goy cannot elude the bagel anywhere in America. They're everywhere. They're like guns." "And you don't read the papers, Mickey? This is unimaginable to me," Norm said. "I gave up reading the papers when I found that every day there was another story about the miracle of Japan. I can't take the photographs of all those Japs wearing suits.

What happened to their little uniforms? They must do a quick change for the photographer. When I hear the word *Japan*, I reach for my thermonuclear device." Now that should send him packing . . . but no, he'd gone so far as to cause Norman to worry again. They were in the doorway of Debby's room still and Sabbath could see that Norman, tired as he was, was about to come in now and have a talk—probably again about going to Graves. The guy's name was Graves. Sabbath had begged off after the funeral, said he'd think about seeing the doctor another day. "I know what you're wondering," Sabbath quickly put in, "you're wondering where do I get my news from—from television? No. Can't. They've got Japs on TV too. All over the screen, little Japs holding elections, little Japs buying and selling stock, little Japs even shaking hands with our president—with the president of the United States! In his grave Franklin Roosevelt is spinning like an atomic dreydl. No, I prefer to live without the news. I got all the news I need about those bastards a long time ago. Their prosperity creates difficulties for my sense of fair play. The Land of the Rising Nikkei Average. I'm proud to say I still have all my marbles as far as racial hatred is concerned. Despite all my many troubles, I continue to know what matters in life: profound hatred. One of the few remaining things I take seriously. Once, at my wife's suggestion, I tried to go a whole week without it. Nearly did me in. Week of great spiritual tribulation that was for me. I'd say hating the Japanese plays a leading role in every aspect of my life. Here, of course, in New York, you New Yorkers love the Japanese because they brought you raw fish. The great bonanza of raw fish. They serve raw fish to people of our race, and, as though we were prisoners on the Bataan death march who have no choice, who would starve to death otherwise, the people of our race eat it. And pay for it. Leave *tips*. I don't get it. After the war was over we shouldn't have allowed them ever to fish again. You lost the right to fish, you bastards, on December 7, 1941. Catch one fish, *one*, and we will show you the *rest* of the arsenal. Who else would so relish eating fish raw? Between their cannibalism and their prosperity, they affront me, you know? His Highness. Do they still have 'His Highness'? Do they still have their 'glory'? Are they still glorious, the Japanese? I don't know, for some reason all my racial hatred leaps to the fore just thinking about how glorious they are. Norman, I have so much to put up with in life. Professional failure. Physical deformity. Personal disgrace. My wife is a recovering alcoholic who goes to AA to learn how to forget to speak English. Never blessed with children. Children never blessed with me. Many, many disappointments. Do I have to put up with the prosperity of the Japanese, too? That could really push me over the edge. Maybe it's what did it to Linc. What the yen has done to the dollar, who knows if that didn't do it to him. Me it kills. Oh, it kills me so much I wouldn't mind—what's the expression they use now when they want to bomb the shit out of someone? 'Send them a message.' I'd like to send them a message and rain just a little more terror down on their fucking heads. Still great believers, are they, in taking things by force? Still inspired, are they, by the territorial imperative?—" "Mickey, Mickey, Mickey—whoa, slow down, cool it, Mick," pleaded Norman. "Do they still have that fucking flag?" "Mick—" "Just answer that. I'm asking a guy who reads the New York *Times* a question. You read the 'News of the Week in Review.' You watch Peter Jennings. You're an up-to-the-minute guy. Do they still have that flag?" "Yes, they have that flag." "Well, they shouldn't have a flag. They shouldn't be allowed to fish and they shouldn't have a flag, and they shouldn't come over here and shake *anybody's* hand!" "Kid, you're off and runnin' tonight, you haven't stopped," Norman said, "you're—" "I'm fine. I'm just telling you why I gave up on the news. The Japs. That's it in a nutshell. Thanks for the paper. Thanks for everything. The dinner. The handkerchiefs. The money. Thanks, buddy. I'm going to sleep." "You should." "I will. I'm beat." "Good night, Mick. And slow down. Just slow down and get some sleep."

Sleep? How could he ever sleep again? *There they are.* Sabbath tossed the heap of paper onto the bed, and what slides out of the center but the business section—and there they are! Big headline running across all but one column of the page: "The Men Who Really Run Fortress Japan." *That* can gall ya! Fortress Japan! And under it, "Bad news for business: The Prime Minister is quitting. But the bureaucrats not." Headlines, photos, paragraph after infuriating paragraph not only dominating the front of the business section but running over

and taking up most of page 8, where there's a graph, and another photo of another Jap, and that headline again, ending
with "Fortress Japan." Three of them on the front page, each
with his own picture. None of them wearing their little uniforms. All of them in ties and shirts, pretending to be ordinary
peace-loving people. They've got mock-ups of offices behind
them, so as to make the readers of the *Times* think they work
in offices like human beings and aren't flying around conquer-
ing countries in their fucking Zeroes. "They are among an intellectually nimble, hard-working elite of 11,000 sitting atop
Japan's million or so national civil servants. They oversee perhaps the most closely regulated economy in . . ." The caption
beneath one of the photographs—Sabbath could not believe
it. According to the caption, the Jap in the photograph "says
he was burned by U.S. negotiators. . . ." Burned? His skin
burned? How much of it? Morty's burns covered eighty percent of his body. How much of his body did the U.S. negotiators burn on this son of a bitch? Doesn't look very burned to
me. I don't see any burns at all. We've got to give our negotiators more kerosene—we've got to get negotiators who know
how to build a fire under these bastards! "What has gone
wrong? Japanese officials say that the United States has demanded too much. . . ." Oh, you fuckers, you filthy, fanati-
cal, fucking imperialist Jap fuckers . . .
    His speaking aloud must have been what prompted the
knock on the door. But when he opened it once again to assure Norman that he was fine, just reading the Japanese papers,
there was Michelle. At dinner she'd been wearing black tights
and a narrow rust-colored velvety top that came down to her
thighs: sham waifdom. Intended to awaken what fantasy in
me? Or maybe she was confiding in him an original of her
own: I am Robin Hood; I give to the poor. At any rate, she
had changed now into—Christ, a kimono. Flowers all over it.
Those wide sleeves. Into a Japanese kimono down to her feet.
Yet the abhorrence inflamed by that paper's contemptible
paean to Fortress Japan was subsumed instantaneously in his
excitement. Beneath the kimono there appeared to be only her
biography. He liked the extreme boyish way her hair was cut.
Big tits and a boy's short haircut. And a well-worn woman's
lines around the eyes. This look took a firmer hold on him

than the first, the Central Park West Peter Pan. Something French now wafting around her. You get this look in Paris. You get this in Madrid. You get this in Barcelona, in the really classy places. There were a few times in my life, in Paris and other places, where I liked her so well that I gave her my number and my address and I said, "Anytime you come to America, look me up." I remember one said she was going to do some traveling. I've been waiting for that whore to call ever since. Michelle's family background was, in fact, French—Norman had told him so before dinner. Maiden name Boucher. And she looked it now, too, whereas in the dirty pictures, with her hair tautly back and the body unsurpassingly gaunt, she had looked to him like some rich Jewish husband's Canyon Ranch Carmen. The middle-aged dieters from the spa down in Lenox sometimes came to Madamaska Falls to visit the Indian sites when they were bored with their tofu at a hundred smackers a plate. Some ten years back he'd made a stab at picking up two of them who'd driven all the way out from Canyon Ranch for an afternoon of sightseeing. But when he offered—admittedly, early in the game—to guide them along the falls to the ridge where the Madamaskas used to initiate their maidens into the sacred mysteries with a gourd, all their anthropological ignorance was glaringly revealed and they drove off. "It wasn't my idea," he called after the Audi, "it was *theirs*, the Native Americans'!" He'd be hearing from those two when he heard from that whore.

But here was the former Mademoiselle Boucher, New Jersey's Colette, brimming over with boredom. She did not love her husband and she had come to a decision. Thus the kimono. Nothing Japanese about it at all—it was the most scandalous thing she could get away with in the circumstances. She was shrewd. He knew her lingerie drawer. He knew she could do better. He knew she would, too. Isn't it something the way the course of a life can change overnight? Never, never would he voluntarily depart this stupendous madness over fucking.

She said she had forgotten earlier to give him the prescription for Zantac. Here it was. Zantac was what he took to try to control the stomach pains and the diarrhea produced by the Voltaren that lessened the pain in his hands, providing he didn't use a knife and fork, drive a car, tie his shoelaces, or wipe his ass. If only he had the money, he could go out and hire some enterprising Jap to wipe his ass, one of the intellectually nimble, hard-working elite of 11,000 sitting atop— "sitting atop." They know how to write in those enlightened papers. I should start taking the *Times.* Hep me with learn Engwish so no more get me burn by U.S. My brother's legs were two charred timbers. Had he even lived, he would have been legless. The legless track star of Asbury High.

Pills and pain. Aldomet for my blood pressure and Zantac for my gut. A to Z. Then you die.

"Thanks," he said. "Never before received a prescription from a doctor in a kimono."

"Our era has lost much to commercial inelegance," she replied, pleasing him no end with a geisha bow. "Norman thinks you might want to have those pants of yours dry-cleaned." She pointed to his corduroys. "And that jacket, the mackinaw, that odd thing you wear with the pockets."

"The Green Torpedo."

"Yes. Maybe the Green Torpedo could use a cleaning."

"You want the trousers now?"

"We are not children, Mr. Sabbath."

He retreated into Debby's bedroom and slipped off his pants. Norman's robe, a colorful full-length velour robe with a belt long enough to hang himself, was still where he'd dropped it beside his jacket on the carpet. He returned to her, enwrapped in the robe, to make an offering of his dirty clothes. The robe trailed behind him like a gown. Norman was six two.

She took the clothes without a word, without the slightest manifestation of the squeamishness she had every right to feel. Those pants had had an active life during the last several weeks, a real full life such as would leave an ordinary person exhausted. Every indignity he had ever suffered seemed collected and preserved in the loose-fitting seat of those old pants, their cuffs encrusted with mud from the cemetery. But they did not appear to repel her, as he had momentarily feared while undressing. Of course not. She deals with dirt all day. Norman had narrated the whole saga. Pyorrhea. Gingivitis. Swollen gums. One *schmutzig* mouth after another. *Schmutz* is her métier. Crud is what she works away at with her instruments. Drawn not to Norman but to crud. Scrape the tartar.

Scrape the pockets. . . . Seeing Michelle so enthrallingly kimono'd, his *schmutzig* clothes balled up under her arm—and
with her geisha boy haircut lending just the right touch of trans-
sexual tawdriness to the whole slatternly picture—he knew he
could kill for her. Kill Norman. Push him out the fucking
window. All that marmalade, mine.

So. Here we are. The moon is high, somewhere there's
music, Norman's dead, and it's just me and this betitted
pretty-boy in his flowered kimono. Missed my chance with a
man. That Nebraska guy who gave me the books on the
tanker. Yeats. Conrad. O'Neill. He would have taught me
more than what to read if I'd let him. Wonder what it's like.
Ask her, she'll tell you. The only other people who fuck men
are women.

"Why do you like to look this way?" she asked, patting the
dirty clothes.

"What other way is there to look?"

"Norman says that, when you were young, to look at you
was to die. He says Linc used to say, 'There's a bull in Sabbath.
He goes all out.' He says people couldn't take their eyes off of
you. A force. A free spirit."

"Why would he say that? To justify having seated at your
dinner table a nobody nobody can possibly take seriously?
Who of your social class can take seriously someone like me,
steeped in selfishness, and with my terrible level of morality,
and lacking all the appurtenances that go with all the right
ideals?"

"You have great eloquence at your command."

"I learned early on that people seem more easily to pass over
how short I am when I am linguistically large."

"Norman says you were the most brilliant young fellow he
ever met."

"Tell him he doesn't have to."

"He adored you. He still has a lot of feeling for you."

"Yeah, well, a lot of well-bred people need their real-lifer.
Normal enough. I'd been to sea. I'd been to Rome. Whores
on more than one continent—a laudable achievement in those
years. Showed 'em I'd escaped the bourgeois trammels. Educated bourgeoisie like to admire someone who's escaped the

bourgeois trammels—reminds them of their college ideals. When I got written up in the *Nation* for taking a tit out on the street I was their noble savage for a week. Today they'd excoriate my balls off for so much as thinking about it, but in those days that made me heroic to all right-thinking people. Dissenter. Maverick. Menace to society. Great. I would bet you that even today part of being a cultivated millionaire in New York is having an interest in a disgraceful person. Linc and Norm and their friends got a big kick then out of just saying my name. Gave them a spacious feeling of being illegit. A puppeteer who takes tits out on the street—like knowing a boxer, like helping a convict publish his sonatinas. To add to the fun I had a crazy young wife. An actress. Mick and Nikk, their favorite pathological couple."

"And she?"

"I murdered she."

"Norman says she disappeared."

"No. I murdered her."

"How much does this act cost you? How much of an act do you really need?"

"What other way is there for me to be? If you know, I'd like you to tell me. There is no stupidity that fails to interest me," he said, feigning anger only a little—the "really" had been a cheap shot. "What other way is there to act?"

He liked that she did not appear intimidated. Refused to back off. That was good. Well schooled by her old man. Nonetheless, suppress the inclination to undo the kimono. Not yet.

"You'll do anything," she said, "not to be winning. But why *do* you behave this way? Primal emotions and indecent language and orderly complex sentences."

"I'm not big on oughts, if that's what you mean."

"I don't entirely believe that. As much as he wants to be the Marquis de Sade, Mickey Sabbath is not. The degraded quality is not in your voice."

"Neither was it in the Marquis de Sade's. Neither is it in yours."

"Freed from the desire to please," she said. "A giddy feeling. What has it got you?"

"What has it got *you?*"

"*Me?* I'm pleasing people all the time," she said. "I've been pleasing people since I was born."

"Which people?"

"Teachers. Parents. Husband. Children. Patients. All people."

"Lovers?"

"Yes."

Now.

"Please me, Michelle," and, taking her by one wrist, he tried to pull her into Debby's room.

"Are you crazy?"

"Come on, you've read Kant. 'Act as if the maxim from which you act were to become through your will a universal law.' *Please me.*"

Her arms were strong from scraping all that crud away and his were no longer a seaman's. No longer even a puppeteer's. He could not budge her.

"Why were you pressing Norman's foot throughout dinner?"

"No."

"Yes," she whispered—and that laugh, that laugh, a mere *tendril* of it was marvelous! "You were playing footsie with my husband. I expect an explanation."

"No."

And now she gave over the whole provocative thing—softly, because they were only down the hall from the conjugal bed, but the whole branching tangle of contradictions that was her laugh. "Yes, yes." The kimono. The whispering. The haircut. The laugh. And so little time left.

"Come *in.*"

"Don't be insane."

"You're great. You're a great woman. *Come inside.*"

"Unbridled excess knows no limit in you," she said, "but I suffer from a severe predilection not to ruin my life."

"What did Norman say about my foot? How come he didn't just throw me out?"

"He thinks you're having a breakdown. He thinks you're cracking up. He thinks you don't know what you're doing or why you're doing it. He's intent on getting you to his psychiatrist. He says you need help."

"You're all I thought you were. You're more, Michelle. Norman told me the whole story. Those upper third molars. Like cleaning windows at the top of the Empire State Building."

"Your mouth could *use* a little going-over. The interdental papilla? That little piece of flesh that sticks out between each tooth? Red. Swollen. Might want to investigate that further."

"Then come in, for God's sake. Investigate the papilla. Investigate the molars. Pull 'em out. Whatever makes you happy. I want to make you happy. My teeth, my gums, my larynx, my kidneys—if it works and you like it, take it, it's yours. I cannot believe that I was playing with Norman's foot. It felt so good. Why didn't he say anything? Why didn't he get down there under the table and pick it up and place it where it was supposed to be? I thought he was such a great host. I thought he had all this feeling for me. Yet he placidly sits there and allows my foot *not* to be where he knows full well I *want* it to be. And at *his* dinner table. Where I am an invited guest. I didn't beg to eat here, he *asked* me to. I'm really surprised at him. I want *your* foot."

"Not now."

"Don't you find that the simplest formulations in English are barely endurable? 'Not now.' Say that again. Treat me like shit. Temper me like steel—"

"Calm down. Control yourself. Quiet, *please*."

"Say it again."

"Not now."

"When?"

"Saturday. Come to my office Saturday."

"Today's Tuesday. Wednesday, Thursday, Friday—no, no. Absolutely not. I'm sixty-four years old. Saturday's too late."

"*Calm*."

"If Yahweh wanted me to be calm, he would have made me a goy. Four days. No. *Now*."

"We *can't*," she whispered. "Come Saturday—I'll give you a periodontal probe."

"Oh, okay. You've got a customer. Saturday. Okay. Wonderful. How do you do it?"

"I've got an instrument for it. I stick my instrument into your periodontal pocket. I enter the gingival crevice."

"More. More. Speak to me about the business end of your instrument."

"It's a very fine instrument. It won't hurt. It's slender. It's flat. It's about a millimeter wide. Perhaps ten millimeters long."

"You think metrically." Drenka.

"It's the only area in which I think metrically."

"Will I bleed?" he asked.

"Just a drop or two."

"That's all?"

"Christ . . ." she said and allowed her forehead to fall forward onto his. To rest there. It was a moment unlike any he'd had all day. Week. Month. Year. He calmed down.

"How," she asked, "did we arrive at this so soon?"

"It's a consequence of living a long time. There isn't forever to fuck around."

"But you are a maniac," she said.

"Oh, I don't know. It takes two to tangle."

"You do a lot of things that most people don't do."

"What do I do that you don't do?"

"Express yourself."

"And you don't do that?"

"Hardly. You have the body of an old man, the life of an old man, the past of an old man, and the instinctive force of a two-year-old."

What is happiness? The substantiality of this woman. The compound she was. The wit, the gameness, the shrewdness, the fatty tissue, the odd indulgence in high-flown words, that laugh marked with life, her responsibility to everything, not excluding her carnality—there was stature in this woman. Mockery. Play. The talent and taste for the clandestine, the knowledge that everything subterranean beats everything terranean by a mile, a certain physical poise, the poise that is the purest expression of her sexual freedom. And the conspiratorial understanding with which she spoke, her terror of the clock running down . . . Must everything be behind her? No! No! The ruthless lyricism of Michelle's soliloquy: and no I said no I will No.

"Adultery is a tough business," he whispered to her. "The main thing is to be clear about wanting it. The rest is incidental."

"Incidental," she sighed.

"God, I'm fond of adultery. Aren't you?" He dared to take her face in his crippled hands and to trace the boyish haircut around at the neckline with that middle finger for which they had once arrested him, the middle finger whose sweet talk was thought to have traumatized or hypnotized or tyrannized Helen Trumbull. Yeah, they had it all figured out in 1956. They still have. "The softness it brings to the hardness," he went on. "A world without adultery is unthinkable. The brutal inhumanity of those against it. Don't you agree? The sheer fucking depravity of their views. The *madness*. There is no punishment too extreme for the crazy bastard who came up with the idea of fidelity. To demand of human flesh fidelity. The cruelty of it, the mockery of it, is simply unspeakable."

He would never let her get away. Here was Drenka, only instead of the colloquialisms that she fucked up in her ardor to engage the teacher and enjoy his games, speaking charmingly humorous, delectable English. Drenka, it's *you*, only from suburban New Jersey instead of Split. I know because this high degree of excitement I experience with no one *but* you—this is your warm body resurrected! Out o' the grave. Morty next.

He chose then to undo his own robe rather than hers—the six-footer's velour robe, with the Paris label, that made him look like the Little King in the old comic strip—to introduce her to his hard-on. They should meet. "Behold the arrow of desire," said Sabbath.

But one glimpse caused her to recoil. "Not *now*," she warned again, and this breathy utterance won his heart. Even better was watching her run off. Like a thief. Running but willing. Running but ready.

He had a reason to live until Saturday. A new collaborator to replace the old one. The vanishing collaborator, indispensable to Sabbath's life—it wouldn't have been Sabbath's life otherwise: Nikki disappearing, Drenka dying, Roseanna drinking, Kathy indicting him . . . his mother . . . his brother. . . . If only he could stop replacing them. Miscasting them. Since the latest loss, he'd really been out there calibrating the dread. And to think that as a puppeteer he could do it without even a puppet, a full life with just his fingers.

Saturday, he decided, we'll make the quick reassessment. No shortage of sharp objects lying about in her dental tray. He'd swipe a curette, end it that way, if, that is, it all went nowhere. Let the adventure occur, O Lord Dionysus, Noble Bull, Mighty Maker of the Sperm of All Male Creatures. It's not life repossessed that I expect to encounter. That exaltation is long gone. It's more what Krupa used to call to Goodman when Benny was ridin' solo, on "China Boy." "Take one more, Ben! Take one more!"

Providing she doesn't come to her senses, the last of the collaborators. Take one more.

Of the second night that Sabbath spent in Debby's room, suffice it to say—before moving on to the crisis of the morning—that his thoughts were of both mother and daughter, singly and together. He was under the spell of the tempter whose task it is to pump the hormone preposterone into the male bloodstream.

In the morning, after a leisurely bath in Debby's tub, he took a wonderful crap in her toilet—satisfying stools easily urged forth, density, real dimension, so unlike the sickbed stuff that, on an ordinary day, streamed intermittently out of him because of the agitating action of Voltaren. He bequeathed unto the bathroom a big, trenchant barnyard bouquet that filled him with enthusiasm. The robust road again! I have a mistress! He felt as overcome and nonsensical as Emma Bovary out riding with Rodolphe. In the masterpieces they're always killing themselves when they commit adultery. He wanted to kill himself when he couldn't.

After meticulously returning to the dresser and the closet every stitch of Debby's he'd venerated during the night, adorned for the first time in decades in all new clothes, he came stomping into the kitchen to find the party was over. Norman had delayed his departure to tell Sabbath that he was to get out after breakfast. Michelle was off at work but her instructions were that Sabbath be ejected immediately. Norman told him to go ahead and have breakfast but to leave after that. In the jacket Sabbath had given Michelle to send to the cleaners, she'd found a bag of crack, which Norman had in front of him on the table. Sabbath remembered having bought it the morning before on the streets of the Lower East Side,

bought it for a joke, for no reason at all, because he was getting a kick out of the dealer.

"And these. In your trousers."

The father was holding in his hand the daughter's floral
underpants. During all of the day's excitements and difficulties, when exactly had Sabbath forgotten that the panties were
in his pocket? He could clearly remember, at the funeral, rolling them around in his pocket through the two-hour amusement of the eulogies. Who wouldn't have? Overflow crowd.
Broadway and Hollywood people—Linc's most famous friends
—each in turn recollecting the corpse. The predictable torrent
of claptrap. The two sons spoke and the daughter—the architect, the lawyer, the psychiatric social worker. I knew nobody
and nobody knew me. Except Enid, heavyset, white-haired,
dowagerly, as unrecognizable to him at first as he was to her.
"It's Mickey Sabbath," Norm had said to her. He and Sabbath, after identifying Linc's body, had come back to the anteroom where Enid sat alone with the family. "He drove down
from New England." "My God," said Enid, and clutching
Sabbath's hand she began to cry. "And I haven't shed a tear all
day," she told Sabbath with a helpless laugh. "Oh, Mickey,
Mickey, I did a terrible thing just three weeks ago." Hadn't
seen Sabbath in over thirty years, and yet to him she confessed
the terrible thing she had done. Because he knew what it was
to do terrible things? Or because terrible things had been done
to him? Most likely the former. Reaching into my pocket,
knowing they were there; silk putty to knead painfully while
each of the eulogists stood across from the coffin and described the suicide's comic antics, how he loved to play with
children, how everybody's kids loved him, how endearingly,
wonderfully eccentric he was. . . . Then the young rabbi.
Take the beauty out of the tragedy. Half an hour to explain to
us how that's done. Lincoln isn't really dead, in our hearts this
love lives on. True, true. Yet at the open coffin, when I asked,
"Linc, what would you like for dinner tonight?" I got no answer. That proves something, too. Guy next to me, without a
pocketful of panties to ease the pain, couldn't resist the anti-
clerical aperçu. "He plays it a little girlish for my taste." "I
think he's auditioning," I replied. He liked that. "I'm not

going to mind never seeing him again," the guy whispered. I thought he meant the rabbi, only out on the street realized that he'd meant the deceased. A young TV star gets up, sleek in a black sheath dress, smiling to beat the band, and she tells everybody to hold hands with everybody else and observe a minute of silence remembering. Linc. I held the hand of the nasty guy next to me. Had to take a hand out of my pocket to do it—and *that's* when I forget the underpants! Then Linc: green. The man was green. Then my hideous fingers clasped in Enid's while she confessed the terrible thing she'd done. "I couldn't take the tremor any longer and I hit him. I hit him, with a book, and I shouted, 'Stop shaking! Stop shaking!' There were some times when he *could* stop—he would bring all his strength to bear on it and the shaking would stop. He'd hold out his hands for me to see. But if he succeeded in doing that, he couldn't do anything else. All his systems had to be recruited to stop shaking. The result was he couldn't talk, he couldn't walk, he couldn't answer the simplest question." "Why was he shaking?" I asked her, because just that morning, in Rosa's embrace, I'd been shaking myself. "Either the medication," she said, "or the fear. They released him from the hospital when he could eat again and sleep again, and they said he was no longer suicidal. But he was still depressed and frightened and crazy. And he had the tremor. I couldn't live with him any longer. I moved him to an apartment around the corner a year and a half ago. I phoned him every day, but this last winter three months went by when I didn't see him. He phoned me. Sometimes ten times a day he phoned me. To see if I was all right. He was terrified that I was going to get sick and disappear. When he saw me he'd burst into tears. He was always the crier in the family, but this was something else. This was ultrahelplessness. He cried from the pain—from the terror. It never let up. But still I thought he was going to get better. I thought, Someday it's going to be the way it used to be. He'll make us all laugh." "Enid, do you know who I am," asked Sabbath, "who you are telling all this to?" But she did not even hear his words, and Sabbath understood that she was telling this to everyone. He was just the last one to hit the anteroom. "Three months in the hospital with a lot of crazy people," she said. "But after the first week he felt safe there.

The first night they put him in bed next to a man who was dying—it terrorized him. Then in a room with three others, truly screwy people. Near the end of his stay I took him out to lunch twice, but apart from that he never left the hospital. Bars on the windows. The suicide watch. Seeing his face behind the barred windows, waiting for us to come—" She told him so much, she held him to her so long, that in the end he forgot what in his pocket he had been clinging to. Then at dinner he started telling *his* story. . . .

So, during the night, lust and treachery gunned down by her prudence, by foresight—by her brains. *That's* what happened. Don't blame Enid. Nor was it jealousy of the kid. If she'd wanted to probe his papilla on Saturday, the kid's stolen panties would only have turned her on more. She would have worn them for him. She would have got herself up in Debby's stuff for him. She's done it before, along with everything else. But she was using the underpants to get him out before he ruined everything she had going for her. The underpants to inform him that there would be no wavering, that should he try to bring pressure there'd be an even more resourceful authority than Officer Abramowitz to crush him. It wasn't the underpants, the crack, even the Green Torpedo—it was *Sabbath*. Maybe he could still tell a story, but otherwise nothing remotely alluring left, not even the hard-on he'd showed her. All that remained of his *going all out* was repellent to her. Crude she was herself, besmirched, wily, connubially half-crazed, but not yet uncontrollably desperate. Hers was the ordinary automatic dishonesty. She was a betrayer with a small *b*, and small-*b* betrayals are happening all the time—by now Sabbath could pull them off in his sleep. That wasn't what was at the center for him: this guy is *spinning*; he wants *to die*. Michelle had enough equilibrium to reach a sensible decision. The maniacal intoxicant to put the enchantment back in life is not me. She will be better off shopping around, scenting out somebody less clamorously kaput. And he'd thought he was going to gorge himself. It was bursting time again. You great big infant. That you could still believe that it could go on forever. Maybe now you've got a better picture of what's up. Well, let it come. I know what's up. Let it come.

Eat breakfast and go. This is an amazing moment. *It's over.*

"How could you take Debby's underwear?" Norman asked.

"How could I not is the question."

"It was irresistible to you."

"What a strange way to put it. Where does resistance even enter in? We're talking about thermodynamics. Heat as a form of energy and its effect on the molecules of matter. I am sixty-four, she is nineteen. It's only natural."

Norman was dressed like the connoisseur of fine living that he was: double-breasted chalk-stripe suit, maroon silk tie with matching breast-pocket handkerchief, pale blue shirt monogrammed at the pocket NIC. All of his considerable dignity was on display, not simply in his clothing, but in his distinctive face, a lean, long, intelligent face with gentle dark eyes and a becoming kind of baldness. That he had less hair even than Sabbath made him a thousand times more attractive. Without the hair you saw unveiled all the mind in that skull, the introspection, the tolerance, the acuity, the reason. And a manly skull it was, finely made yet almost ostentatiously determined —none of its delicacy suggested weakness of will. Yes, the whole figure emanated the ideals and scruples of humanity's better self and it wouldn't have been hard for Sabbath to believe that the office for which Norman shortly would be leaving in a limo had spiritual aims loftier even than those of a theatrical producer. Secular spirituality, that's what he exuded —maybe they all did, the producers, the agents, the mega-deal lawyers. With the aid of their tailors, Jewish cardinals of commerce. Yeah, now that I think of it, very much like them sharpies surrounding the pope. You'd never guess that the jukebox distributor who paid for it all dealt at the edges of the Mob. You're not supposed to guess. He'd made himself into that impressive American thing, a nice guy. It all but says he's one on his shirt. A nice rich guy with some depth, and dynamite on the phone at the office. What more can America ask of its Jews?

"And at dinner last night," Norman said, "was it only natural to want to play with Michelle's foot under the table?"

"I didn't want to play with Michelle's foot under the table. I wanted to play with your foot under the table. *Wasn't* that your foot?"

He registers neither antipathy nor amusement. Is it because

he knows where we're headed or because he doesn't know? I surely don't know. Could be anywhere. I'm beginning to smell Sophocles in this kitchen.

"Why did you tell Michelle you killed Nikki?"

"Should I try to hide it from her instead? Am I supposed to be ashamed of that too? What is this shame kick you're on?"

"Tell me something. Tell me the truth—tell me if you believe that you murdered Nikki. Is this something you *believe*?"

"I see no reason why I shouldn't."

"I do. I was there. I do because I was with you when she disappeared. I saw what you went through."

"Yeah, well, I'm not saying it was easy. Going to sea doesn't prepare you for everything. The color she turned. That came as a surprise. Green, like Linc. With strangulation the primitive satisfactions are all built in, of course, but if I had it to do over again I'd opt for one of the more expeditious modes. I'd have to. My hands. How do you plan to kill Michelle?"

Some emotion stirred up by Sabbath's question made Norman look to Sabbath as though he were afloat or flying, drifting away from the entire orientation of his life. An exciting silence ensued. But in the end Norman did no more than to put Debby's underpants into the pocket of his own pants. The words he next spoke were not without a tinge of menace.

"I love my wife and children more than anything in this world."

"I take that for granted. But how do you plan to kill her? When you find out she is fucking your best friend."

"Don't. Please. We all know how you are a man on the superhuman scale, who has no fear of verbal exaggeration, but not everything is worth saying, even to a successful person like me. Don't. Not necessary. My wife found our daughter's underpants in your pocket. What do you expect her to do? How do you expect her to respond? Don't degrade yourself further by defiling my wife."

"I wasn't degrading myself. I wasn't defiling your wife. Norman, aren't the stakes too high for us to bow to convention? I was just wondering how you think about killing her when you think about killing her. Okay, let's change the subject. How do you think she thinks about killing you? Do you imagine her content, when you fly off to L.A., just to kind of hope American Airlines will take care of it for her? Too mundane for a Michelle. The plane will crash and I'll be free? No, that's how the secretaries solve their problems on the subway. Michelle's a doer, her father's daughter. If I know anything about periodontists, she's thought of strangling you more than once. In your sleep. And she could do it. Got the grip for it. So did I once upon a time. Remember my hands? My old hands? All day you work as a seaman on deck, chipping, chipping, chipping—the constant work of the ship. A metal drill, a hammer, a chisel. And then the puppets. The *strength* in those hands! Nikki never knew what hit her. She was a long time looking up at me with those imploring eyes, but actually I would think a coroner would have said that she was brain-dead in sixty seconds."

Leaning back in his chair at the breakfast table, Norman crossed an arm over his chest and, with the other arm resting on it, let his forehead drop forward onto his fingertips. Exactly how Michelle's forehead dropped onto mine. I can't believe the panties did it. I can't believe this truly superior aging woman could have been daunted by that. This isn't happening! This is a fairy tale! This is *true* depravity, this genteel shit!

"What the hell has become of your mind?" Norman said. "This is awful."

"What is awful?" Sabbath asked. "The kid's underpants wrapped around my dick to help me through the night after the day that I'd been through? That's so awful? Come off it, Norm. Panties in my pocket at a funeral? That's *hope*."

"Mickey, where are you going to go after you leave here? Are you going to drive home?"

"It's always been hard for you, Norman, hasn't it, to imagine me? How does he do it without protection? How do any of them do it without protection? Baby, there *is* no protection. It's all wallpaper, Norman. Look at Linc. Look at Sabbath. Look at Morty. Look at Nikki. *Look*, tiresome and frightening as looking may be. What we are in the hands of *is not protection*. When I was on the ships, when we got to port, I always liked to visit the Catholic churches. I always went by myself, sometimes every day we were in port. You know why? Because I found something terrifically erotic about watching kneeling maidens at prayer, asking forgiveness for the wrong things altogether. Watching them seeking protection. It made me very hot. Seeking protection against the other. Seeking protection against themselves. Seeking protection against everything. *But there isn't any.* Not even for you. Even you are exposed—what do you make of that? Exposed! Fucking naked, even in that suit! The suit is futile, the monogram is futile—nothing will do it. *We have no idea how it's going to turn out.* Christ, man, *you* can't even protect a pair of your daughter's—"

"Mickey," he said softly, "I take your point. I get the philosophy. It's a fierce one. You're a fierce man. You've let the whole creature out, haven't you? The deeper reasonability of seeking danger is that there is, in any event, no escaping it. Pursue it or be pursued by it. Mickey's view, and, in theory, I agree: there *is* no escaping it. But in practice I proceed differently: if danger's going to find me anyway, I needn't pursue it. That the extraordinary is assured Linc has convinced me. It's the ordinary that escapes us. I do know that. But that doesn't mean I care to abandon the portion of the ordinary I've been lucky enough to corral and hold on to. I want you to go. It's time for you to go. I'm getting your things out of Debby's room and then you're to go."

"With or without breakfast?"

"I want you *out* of here!"

"But what's eating you? It can't just be the underwear. We go too far back for that. Is it that I showed my dick to Michelle? Is that the reason I can't have my breakfast?"

Norman had risen from the table—he was not as yet shaking like Linc (or Sabbath with Rosa), though there *was* a seizure of sorts in his jaw.

"Didn't you know? I can't believe she didn't tell you. 'There's a bull in Sabbath. He goes all out.' The underpants are nothing. I just thought the only fair thing was to take it out. Before we met on Saturday. In case it wasn't to her taste. She invited me Saturday for a periodontal probe. Don't tell me you didn't know that either. Her office. Saturday." When Norman remained, without moving, on his side of the table, Sabbath added, "Just ask her. That was the plan. We had it all set up. That's why, when you said I couldn't stay to have breakfast, I figured it was because I was going to her office on

Saturday to fuck her. *Plus* my taking out my dick. That it's only the panties . . . no, I don't buy that."

And this Sabbath meant. The husband understood the wife better than he let on.

Norman reached up to one of the cabinets above the serving counter and took down a package of plastic garbage sacks. "I'm going to get your things."

"Whatever you say. *May* I eat the grapefruit?"

Without again bothering to respond, Norman left Sabbath alone in the kitchen.

The half grapefruit had been segmented for Sabbath. The segmented grapefruit. Fundamental to their way of life—as fundamental as the Polaroids and the ten thousand bucks. Do I have to tell him about the money, too? No, he knows. Bet he knows everything. I do like this couple. I think the more I come to understand the chaos churning about here, the more I admire how he holds it together. The soldierly way he stood there while I briefed him on last night. He knows. He's got his hands full. There is something in her that is always threatening to undo it all, the warmth, the comfort, the whole wonderful eiderdown that is their privileged position. Having to deal with all that she is while holding to his civilized ideals. Why does he bother? Why does he keep her? The past, for one thing. So much of it. The present—so much of *it*. The machine that it all is. The house on Nantucket. The weekends at Brown as Debby's parents. Debby's grades would tailspin if they split up. Call Michelle a whore, throw her the hell out, and Debby would never make it to med school. And there's the *fun* besides: the skiing, the tennis, Europe, the small hotel they love in Paris, the Université. The repose when all is well. Somebody there while you wait for the biopsy report to come back from the lab. No time left for settlements and lawyers and starting again. The courage of putting up with it instead—the "realism." And the dread of no one at home. All these rooms at night and no one else home. He's fixed in this life. His *talent* is for this life. You can't start dating at the twilight of life. And then menopause is on his side. If he continues to let her get away with it, if he never goes the distance with being fed up, it's because soon enough menopause will do her in anyway. But neither does Michelle go the distance—because she's not just one thing, either. Norman understands (if menopause doesn't do it, that understanding of his will)—minimize, minimize. I never learned that: work it out, ride it out, cool it down. She is as indispensable to the way of life as the segmented grapefruit. She *is* the segmented grapefruit: the partitioned body and the piquant blood. The unholy Hostess. The holy Hotness. This is as close to eating Michelle as I will come. It's over. I am a *meshuggeneh* cast-off shoe.

"You live in the world of real love," he said when Norman came back into the kitchen holding in one hand the sack stuffed with everything except for Sabbath's jacket. The Green Torpedo Norman handed to him at the table.

"And what do you live in?" Norman inquired. "You live in the failure of this civilization. The investment of everything in eroticism. The final investment of everything in sex. And now you reap the lonely harvest. Erotic drunkenness, the only passionate life you can have."

"And is it even that passionate?" asked Sabbath. "You know what Michelle would have told her therapist had we gone ahead and got it off? She would have said, 'A nice enough man, I suppose, but he has to be kept fresh by ice.'"

"No, kept fresh by provoking. Kept fresh by means of anarchic provocation. We are determined by our society to such an extent that we can only live as human beings if we turn anarchic. Isn't that the pitch? Hasn't that always been the pitch?"

"You're going to feel dashed by this, Norman, but on top of everything else I don't have, I don't have a pitch. You have kind-hearted liberal comprehension but I am flowing swiftly along the curbs of life, I am merely debris, in possession of nothing to interfere with an objective reading of the shit."

"The walking panegyric for obscenity," Norman said. "The inverted saint whose message is desecration. Isn't it tiresome in 1994, this role of rebel-hero? What an odd time to be thinking of sex as rebellion. Are we back to Lawrence's gamekeeper? At this late hour? To be out with that beard of yours, upholding the virtues of fetishism and voyeurism. To be out with that belly of yours, championing pornography and flying the flag of your prick. What a pathetic, outmoded old crank you are, Mickey Sabbath. The discredited male polemic's last gasp. Even as the bloodiest of all centuries comes to an end, you're out working day and night to create an erotic scandal. You fucking relic, Mickey! You fifties antique! Linda Lovelace is already light-years behind us, but you persist in quarreling with society as though Eisenhower is president!" But then, almost apologetically, he added, "The immensity of your isolation is horrifying. That's all I really mean to say."

"And there you'd be surprised," Sabbath replied. "I don't think you ever gave isolation a real shot. It's the best preparation I know of for death."

"Get out," Norman said.

Deep in the corner of one of his front pockets, those huge pockets in which you could carry a couple of dead ducks, Sabbath came upon the cup that he'd pushed in there before entering the funeral home, the beggar's cardboard coffee cup, still containing the quarters, nickels, and dimes that he'd managed to panhandle down in the subway and on the street. When he'd given his stuff over to Michelle to send out with the dry cleaning, he'd forgotten the cup, too.

The cup did it. Of course. The beggar's cup. That's what terrified her—the begging. Ten to one the panties took her to a new edge of excitement. It's the cup that she shrank from; the social odium of the cup went beyond even her impudence. Better a man who didn't wash than a man who begged with a cup. That was farther out than even she wished to go. There was stimulation for her in many things that were scandalous, indecent, unfamiliar, strange, things bordering on the dangerous, but there was only steep effrontery in the cup. Here at last was degradation without a single redeeming thrill. At the beggar's cup Michelle's daring drew the line. The cup had betrayed their secret hallway pact, igniting in her a panicked fury that made her physically ill. She pictured in the cup all the lowly evils leading to destruction, the unleashed force that could wreck everything. And probably she wasn't wrong. Stupid little jokes can be of great moment in the struggle not to lose. Was how far he had fallen with that cup entirely clear to *him*? The unknown about any excess is how excessive it's been. He really couldn't detest her as much for throwing him out because of the cup as he had when he'd thought that to her the treacherous villainy was jacking off in the panties, a natural enough human amusement and surely, for a houseguest, a minor misdemeanor.

At the thought that he had lost his last mistress before he'd even had the chance of wholeheartedly appropriating her secrets—and all because of the magical lure of begging, not just the seductiveness of a self-mocking joke and the irresistible theatrical fun in that but the loathsome rightness of its exalted wrongness, the grand *vocation* of it, the opportunity its encounters offered his despair to work through to the unequivocal end—Sabbath fell faint to the floor.

The fainting was a little like the begging, however, neither wholly rooted in necessity nor entirely unentertaining. At the thought of all that the cup had destroyed, two broad black strokes did indeed crisscross his mind from one edge of the canvas to the other—yet there was also in him the *wish* to faint. There was craft in Sabbath's passing out. The tyranny of fainting did not escape him. That was the last observation integrated into his cynicism before he hit the floor.

Things wouldn't have worked better had he planned them down to the smallest detail—a "plan" wouldn't have worked at all. He found himself laid out, still living, amid the pale plaids of the Cowans' room. It was criminal for his un-dry-cleaned beggar's jacket to be flush with their bedcover, but then, it was Norman who had put him there. Drizzle beading the big windows and a mist whose milkiness obliterated everything above the treetops of the park: a rumble not quite so low as the rumble in Michelle's laugh rolled in from beyond the windows, thunder summoning up for Sabbath his years and years of exile beside the Madamaskas' sacred falls. The haven of the Cowans' bed made him feel oddly lonely for Debby's and the barely discernible (perhaps even imaginary) impress of her torso along the mattress's spine. Only a day, and Debby's bed had become a home away from home. But her room was shut down like La Guardia. No more flying in and out.

Sabbath could hear Norman on the phone with Dr. Graves, talking about getting him into the hospital, and it did not sound as though he was encountering opposition. Norman couldn't bear to see what he was seeing, this guy now on the heels of Linc. . . . Sounded as though he'd set his mind to taking charge of Sabbath's deformities and restoring to him a harmonious being such as Sabbath had last known in third grade. Forgiving, compassionate, determined, indefatigable, almost irrationally humane—every person should have a friend like Norman. Every wife should have a husband like Norman, revere a husband like Norman instead of battering on his decency with her low-minded delights. Marriage is not an ecstatic union. She must be taught to renounce the great narcissistic illusion of rapture. Her lease on rapture as hereby revoked. She must be taught, before it's too late, to renounce this callow quarrel with life's limits. Sabbath owed Norman no less than that for sullying the Cowan home with his piddling vices. He must think selflessly only of Norman now. Any attempt to save Sabbath would plunge Norman into an experience he hardly deserved. The man to save was Norman—he was the indispensable one. And the power to save him is mine. The deed will crown my visit here, repaying as straightforwardly as I know how my debt for all the unwise ardor with which he invited me in. I am called to enter the realm of virtue.

Nothing was clearer to Sabbath than that Norman must never lay eyes on those Polaroids. And if ever he were to come upon the cash! On the heels of this friend's suicide and that friend's collapse, finding the pictures or the money or both would turn the last of his illusions to ashes, smash his orderly existence to bits. Ten thousand in cash. For buying what? For selling what? Who and what is she working for? Her pussy photographed for posterity by whom? Where? Why? To commemorate what? No, Norman must never know the answers, let alone get round to the questions.

The maneuverings necessary to hospitalize Sabbath were being finalized on the phone when he crossed the carpet to Michelle's dresser, reached into the bottom drawer and, from beneath the lingerie, removed the manila envelopes. He stuffed both into his jacket's big, waterproof interior pocket and, in their place, stowed his beggar's cup, change and all. When she next wished to bestir herself with a reminder of the other half of her story, it would be his cup that she'd find secreted in her drawer, his cup to shock her with the horrors she'd been spared. She'd count her blessings when she saw that cup . . . and cleave unto Norman, as she ought.

Seconds later, speeding out the apartment door, he ran into Rosa arriving for the day. He pressed his fingertip to the raised curve of her lips and signaled with his eyes that she should be quiet—the *señor* was home, on the phone, important *trabajo*. How she must love Norman's suave civility—and hate Michelle's betrayal of him. Hates her for everything. "Mi linda muchacha—adiós!" and then, even while Norman was nailing down a bed in Payne Whitney for him, Sabbath made haste for his car and the Jersey shore, to arrange there for his burial.

TUNNEL, turnpike, parkway—the shore! Sixty-five minutes south and there it was! But the cemetery had disappeared! Asphalt laid over the graves and the cars *parking* there! A cemetery plowed under for a supermarket! *People were shopping at the cemetery.*

His agitation did not compel the manager's attention when he rushed through the outer door and made directly past the long daisy chain of empty shopping carts (the century was nearing its end, the century that had virtually reversed human destiny, but the shopping cart was what still signified to Sabbath the passing of the old way of life) for the crow's nest office overseeing the registers, to find out who was responsible for this insane desecration. "I don't know what you're talking about," the manager said. "What are you shouting for? Look in the yellow pages."

But it was a *cemetery*, didn't have a phone. A phone at a cemetery would be ringing off the hook. If you could get them on the *phone* . . . Besides, my family lies beneath that spit where you are roasting chickens. "Where the hell did you put them?"

"Put who?"

"The dead. I am a mourner! Which aisle?"

He drove in circles. He stopped to inquire at gas stations, but he didn't even know the place's name. Not that B'nai This or Beth That would have enlightened the black kids manning the pumps. He only knew where it was—and there it wasn't. Here, at the outlying frontier of the county, where as recently as when his mother had died there'd been miles of sea-level brush, there was now risen everywhere something with which somebody hoped to advance his interest, and nothing that didn't say, "Of all our ideas, this is the worst," nothing that didn't say, "The human love for the hideous—there is no keeping up with it." Where'd they put them? What a demented civic project, to relocate the dead. Unless they'd obliterated them totally, to end the source of all uncertainty, to dispose of the problem entirely. Without them around, maybe it won't be so lonely. Yes, it's the dead who are standing in our way.

Only through the lucky accident of getting caught in a turning lane behind a car full of Jews on their way to bury someone did Sabbath find it. The chicken farmers were gone—that explained how he'd got so lost—and the triangular site half the size of an oil tanker was now bounded along its hypotenuse by a sprawling one-story "colonial" warehouse erected back of a high chain fence. An ominous conglomeration of pylons and power cables had been massively raised along the second side, and on the third a final resting place had been established by the local populace for box springs and mattresses that had met a violent end. Other household remains were scattered across the field or lying, just dumped there, at the edge of it. And it hadn't stopped raining. Mist and a drizzling rain to ensure the picture's permanent place in the North American wing of his memory's museum of earthly blight. The rain bestowed more meaning than was necessary. That was realism for you. More meaning than was necessary was in the nature of things.

Sabbath parked close beside the rusted picket fence opposite the pylons. Beyond a low iron gate hanging half off its hinges there stood a red brick house, a tilting little thing with an air conditioner that looked itself to be somebody's tomb.

ATTENTION GRAVEOWNERS
Leaning or incorrectly
set headstones are
DANGEROUS

Repairs must be made or
headstones will be removed

WARNING
Lock your car and protect your
valuables while visiting cemetery

Two dogs were chained to the house, and the men standing and talking beside them were all three wearing baseball caps, maybe because it was a Jewish cemetery or maybe because that is what gravediggers wear. One, who was smoking, threw away his cigarette as Sabbath approached—gray hair brutally cut, a green work shirt and dark glasses. His tremor suggested that he needed a drink. A second guy, in Levi's and a red and black flannel shirt, couldn't have been more than twenty, a kid with the big-eyed, sad-eyed Italian face of all the Casanova types at Asbury High, the lovers in the Italian crowd who probably wound up selling rubber tires for a living. They considered it a great coup to grab a Jewish girl, all the while the Asbury High Jewboys were thinking, "The little wop girls, the ginzo cheerleaders, those are the hot ones, the ones that, if you're lucky . . ." The Italians used to call the colored kids *moolies*, *moolenyams*—Sicilian dialect, Calabrian maybe, for eggplant. Hadn't been tickled by the comical dumbness of that word for years, not until he'd pulled up at the Hess station to ask where there was a Jewish cemetery nearby, an inquiry the mooly working there had taken for some bearded white guy's weirdo joke.

The boss was obviously the big older man with the belly, who walked with a limp and waved his arms about in dismay and whom Sabbath asked, "How do I find Mr. Crawford?" A. B. Crawford was the name affixed to the two warning signs nailed up on a post by the gate. Identified as "Superintendent."

The dogs had begun needling Sabbath as soon as he entered the cemetery and didn't let up while he spoke. "Are you A. B. Crawford? I'm Mickey Sabbath. My parents are over there somewhere"—he pointed to a distant corner across from the dump where the paths were wide and grassy and the stones didn't yet look weatherworn—"and my grandparents are over in there." Here he motioned to the other end of the cemetery, backing now onto the storage facility across the road. The graves in that section were laid out in tightly interlaced, unbroken rows. The detritus, if that, of the shore's first Jews. Their stones had darkened decades ago. "You've got to find a place for me."

"You?" said Mr. Crawford. "You're young yet."

"Only in spirit," replied Sabbath, feeling suddenly very much at home.

"Yeah? I've got sugar," Crawford told him. "And this place is the worst place in the world for it. Constant aggravation. This is the worst winter we ever, ever put in."

"Is that right?"

"The frost in the ground was sixteen inches deep. *This*," he gestured dramatically across his domain, "was a sheet of ice. You couldn't get to a grave over there that somebody'll fall down."

"How did you bury people?"

"We buried 'em," he answered wearily. "They gave us a day to knock out the frost and then we bury them the next day. Jackhammers and stuff. Rough, rough winter. And water in the ground? Forget it." Crawford was a sufferer. The métier made no difference. Someone who cannot get out from under. A problem of disposition. Unalterable. Sabbath sympathized.

"I want a plot, Mr. Crawford. The Sabbaths. That's my family."

"You hit me at a bad time because I'm gonna have a funeral pretty soon."

The hearse had arrived and people were assembling around it. Umbrellas. Women carrying infants. Men with yarmulkes on. Children. Everyone waiting back in the street only yards away from the cables and pylons. Sabbath heard a chuckle from the crowd, somebody saying something funny at a funeral. It always happens. The small man who'd just arrived must be the rabbi. He was holding a book. Immediately he was offered shelter beneath an umbrella. Another chuckle. Hard to tell what that meant about the person who died. Nothing probably. It was just that the living were living and couldn't help it. Wit. As delusions go, not the worst.

"Okay," said Mr. Crawford, quickly estimating the size of the crowd, "they're still coming. Let's take a walk. Rufus," he called to the trembling drunk, "watch the dogs, huh?" But the going-over they'd been giving Sabbath erupted into vicious snapping when their master limped off with him. Crawford swiftly turned back and aimed a threatening finger toward the sky. "*Stop it!*"

"Why do you have dogs?" Sabbath asked as they resumed along a path that led around the gravestones to the Sabbath plot.

"They broke into the building four times already. To steal equipment. They robbed all the tools. Machinery that costs three, four hundred dollars. Gasoline-driven hedge shears and all that other kind of stuff that's over there."

"Don't you have insurance?"

"No. No insurance. Forget about that. It's me!" he said excitedly. "It's me! It's out of my pocket! I buy all the equipment and all that. This association here gives me nine hundred dollars a month—see? I have to pay all the help out of that—see? In the meantime, I just turned seventy and I dig all the graves, I put in all the foundations, and it's an absolute joke. The help you get today—you have to tell them every goddarn thing to do. And nobody wants to do this work anymore. I'm one man short. I'm going over to Lakewood and bringing a Mexican down here. You got to get a Mexican. It's a joke. Six months ago somebody was up here visiting a grave and a *schvartze* goes ahead and puts a gun to the people's head. Ten o'clock in the morning! That's why I got the dogs over here—they warn me if somebody is outside, if you're sittin' here by yourself."

"How long have you been here?" Sabbath asked, though he knew the answer already: long enough to learn to say *schvartze*.

"Too long," replied Crawford. "I been here I would say maybe close to forty years. I've had it right to here. The cemetery is broke. I know they're broke. There ain't no money in the cemetery business. The money is in the monument business. I got no pension. Nothin'. I just juggle back and forth. When I have a funeral, see, that you get a few extra dollars, and that goes toward the payroll, but it's just a, just a . . . I don't know, a problem."

Forty years. Missed Grandma and Morty, but got everybody else. And now he gets me.

Crawford was lamenting, "And nothing to show for it. Nothin' in the bank. *Nothin'*."

"There's a relative of mine right there." Sabbath pointed to a stone marked "Shabas." Must be Cousin Fish, who'd taught him to swim. "The old-timers," he explained to Crawford, "were Shabas. They wrote it all kinds of ways: Shabas, Shabbus, Shabsai, Sabbatai. My father was Sabbath. Got it from relatives up in New York when he came to America as a kid. We're over here, I think."

In search of the graves he was growing excited. The last forty-eight hours had been replete with theatrics, confusion, disappointment, adventure, but nothing with a power as primary as this. His heart had not sounded as loud even while he was stealing from Michelle. He felt himself at last inside his life, like someone who, after a long illness, steps back into his shoes for the first time.

"One grave," Crawford said.

"One grave."

"For yourself."

"Right."

"Where did you want this grave?"

"Near my family."

Sabbath's beard was dripping, and after wringing it out with one hand, he left it looking like a braided candlestick. Crawford said, "Okay. Now where is your family?"

"There. There!" and walls of embitterment were crashing down; the surface of something long unexposed—Sabbath's soul? the film of his soul?—was illuminated by happiness. As close as a substanceless substance can come to being physically caressed. "They're *there*!" All in the ground *there*—yes, living together there like family of field mice.

"Yeah," said Crawford, "but you need a single. This here is the single section. Against the fence here." He was pointing along a portion of badly neglected wire-mesh fence across the road from the worst of the dump. You could crawl through the fence, step right over it, or, without even wire cutters or a pliers, just peel away with your hand what remained affixed to the railings. A standing lamp had been pushed out of a car across the way, so that the lamp was not even in the dump but lying in the gutter like somebody gunned down in his tracks. Probably it needed nothing more than new wiring. But its owner obviously hated that lamp and drove it out to do it in across from the Jews' cemetery.

"I don't know if I can give you a grave here or not. This last one by the gate here is the only space I see and it could be reserved, you know. And from here on, the other side of the gate, there's four-grave plots. But maybe you got a grave over with your folks and don't even know it."

"That's possible," said Sabbath, "yes," and now that Crawford had raised that possibility he remembered that when they buried his mother there *was* an empty plot beside her.

There had been. Occupied. According to the dates on the

stone, two years back they had put Ida Schlitzer in the family's
fourth plot. His mother's maiden sister from the Bronx. In the
whole of the Bronx no room left, not even for a half-pint like
Ida. Or had everybody forgotten the second son? Maybe they
thought he was still at sea or already dead because of his way of
life. Buried in the Caribbean. In the West Indies. Should have
been. On the island of Curaçao. Would have liked it down
there. No deep-water port in Curaçao. There was a long, long
pier, seemed like a mile long then, and at the end of it the
tanker tied up. Never forget it, because there were horses and
there were runners—pimps, if you like—but they were kids,
little kids who had the horses. And they swat the goddamn
horse and the horse takes you right to the whorehouse. Curaçao was a Dutch colony, the port called Willemstad, a bourgeois colonial port, men and women in tropical gear, white
people in pith helmets, a pleasant little colonial town, and the
cemetery just down from those beautiful hills where there was
a complex of whorehouses bigger than any I had ever seen in
all my days at sea. The crews of God knows how many ships
tied up at this port, and all of them up there fucking. And the
good men of the town up there fucking. And me asleep in the
pretty cemetery below. But I missed my chance at Willemstad
by giving up the whores for puppets. And so now Aunt Ida,
who never dared say boo to, anyone, has screwed me out of
my plot. Displaced by a virgin who typed all her life for the
Department of Parks and Recreation.

> Beloved son and brother
> Killed in Action in the
> Philippines
> April 13, 1924—December 15, 1944
> Always in our hearts
> Lt. Morton Sabbath

Dad to one side of him, Mother to the other, and, to
Mother's side, Ida instead of me. Not even the memories of
Curaçao could compensate for this. King of the kingdom of
the unillusioned, emperor of no expectations, crestfallen man-
god of the double cross, Sabbath had *still* to learn that nothing
but *nothing* will ever turn out—and this obtuseness was, in itself, a deep, deep shock. Why does life refuse me even the

grave I want! Had I only marshaled my abhorrence in a good cause and killed myself two years ago, that spot next to Ma's would be mine.

Looking over the Sabbath burial plot, Crawford suddenly announced, "Oh, I know them. Oh, they were good friends of mine. I knew your family."

"Yes? You knew my old man?"

"Sure, sure, sure, a good guy. A real gentleman."

"That he was."

"In fact, I think the daughter or someone comes out. You have some daughters?"

No, but what was the difference? He was only salving emotional wounds and trying to pick up a few bucks on the side. "Sure," said Sabbath.

"Well, yeah, she comes out a lot. See that," said Crawford, pointing to the shrubbery thickly covering all four graves, evergreen crew-cut to about six inches high, "you don't need work on that plot, no sir."

"No, that's nice. It looks very nice."

"Look, the only possible thing is if I can give you a grave over there." Where the triangle came to a point and the two potholed streets beyond intersected, there was an empty expanse within the sagging wire fence. "See? But you'd have to go for two graves up there. Anyplace but the single section you have to buy at least two graves. Want me to show you where the two-graves are?"

"Sure, why don't we do that, since I'm here now and you've got the time."

"I ain't got the time but I'll make the time."

"That's good, that's kind of you," Sabbath said, and together they started off through the drizzle toward where the cemetery looked like an abandoned lot, already in mid-April choked with unmown weeds.

"This is a nicer section," Crawford told him, "than with the singles. You'd be facing the road. Somebody going past would see your stone. Two roads join up there. Traffic from two directions." Banging the wet ground with the muddy boot on his good leg, he proclaimed, "I would say *right here*."

"But my family is way over there. And my back would be to them, right? I'm facing the wrong way here."

"Then take the other, with the singles. If it's not reserved."

"I don't have that good a shot at them from there either, frankly."

"Yeah, but you're across from a very fine family. The Weizmans. You're looking onto a very good family over there. Everybody's proud of the Weizmans. That woman that's in charge of this cemetery, her name is Mrs. Weizman. We just put her husband in here. Her whole family is buried in there. We just buried her sister in there. It's a good section, and right across from them is the single section."

"But how about along the fence over there, where it's not that far from my family? You see where I mean?"

"No, no, no. Them graves is sold to somebody already. And that's a *four*-grave section. You follow me?"

"Okay, I do," said Sabbath. "The single section, the two-graves, and the rest is all four-grave plots. I get the picture. Why don't you look and see whether that single is reserved or not? Because that's a little closer to my folks."

"Well, I can't do it now. I got a funeral."

Together they worked their way back through the rows of graves toward the little brick house where the dogs were chained up.

"Well, I'll wait," said Sabbath, "till the funeral is over. I can visit with my family, and you can tell me after if it's available and what the cost is."

"The cost. Yeah. Yeah. They ain't really that much. How much could it be? Four hundred, something like that. The most it could be. Maybe four fifty. I don't know. I have nothing to do with selling the graves."

"Who does?"

"The lady at the organization. Mrs. Weizman."

"And that's who pays you, the organization?"

"Pay me," he said in disgust. "It's a joke what they pay me. A hundred and a quarter a week I clear for myself. And from there over to there, it takes a man three days to cut the grass without anything else. For a hundred and a quarter a week, that's all. I've got no pension. I got sugar and no pension and all this aggravation. Social Security and that's all. So what do you want, do you think—the one grave or the two? I would rather see you up with the two. You won't be crammed in up there. It's a nicer section. But it's up to you."

"There's definitely more legroom," said Sabbath, "but it's so far from everyone. And I'm going to be lying there a long time. Look, see what's available. We'll talk together after you're done. Here," he said, "thanks for making time." He'd changed a hundred of Michelle's to get gas from the moolies, and he handed Crawford twenty bucks. "And," he said, slipping him a second twenty, "for taking good care of my family."

"My pleasure. Your father was a real gentleman."

"So are you, sir."

"Okay. You just look around and see where you'll be comfortable."

"That's what I'll do."

The lone plot that might or might not be available to him in the single section was beside a tombstone with a large Star of David carved at the top and four Hebrew words beneath it. Interred there was Captain Louis Schloss. "Holocaust Survivor, VFW, Mariner, Businessman, Entrepreneur. In Loving Memory Relatives and Friends May 30, 1929–May 20, 1990." Three months my senior. Ten days shy of sixty-one. Survived the Holocaust but not the business. A fellow mariner. Mickey Sabbath, Mariner.

They were rolling the plain pine box in now, Crawford pulling at the front, in the lead, limping at a rapid pace, and the two helpers at either side steering, the drunk with the green work shirt checking his pockets for the cigs. It hasn't even begun and he can't wait till it's over to light up. The smallish rabbi, his hands in front of him holding the book, was talking to Mr. Crawford as he hastened to keep abreast of him. They brought the box up to the open grave. Very clean, that wood. Must put in my order. Pay for that today. Plot, coffin, even a monument—get everything in order, courtesy of Michelle. Buttonhole this rabbi before he leaves and slip him a hundred to come back for me and read from that book. Thus do I cleanse her money of its frivolous history of illicit gratification and reintegrate this stash of bills into the simple and natural business of the earth.

The earth. Very much in evidence here today. Only a few

steps behind him there was a raw mound of the earth piled up where somebody had recently been buried in it, and across the way from that were two graves freshly dug into the earth, side by side. Expecting twins. He walked over to take a look inside one, a little window-shopping. The clean way each was cut into the ground smacked of a solid achievement. The sharp spaded corners and the puddly bottom and the ripply deep sides—you had to hand it to the drunk, the Italian kid, and Crawford: there was the magnificence of centuries in what they did. This hole goes all the way back. As does the other. Both dark with mystery and fantastic. The right people, the right day. This weather told no lies about his situation. It put to him the grimmest of questions about his intentions, to which his answer was "Yes! Yes! Yes! I will emulate my failed father-in-law, a successful suicide!"

But am I playing at this? Even at this? Always difficult to determine.

In a wheelbarrow left out in the rain (more than likely by the drunk—Sabbath knew this from living with one) there was a conical pile of wet dirt. Sabbath, with a tinge of ghoulish pleasure, forced his fingers through the gritty goop until they all disappeared. If I count to ten and then extract them, they'll be the old fingers, the old, provocative fingers with which I pulled their tail. Wrong again. Have to go down in the dirt with more than these fingers if I hope ever to make straight in me all that is crooked. Have to count to ten ten billion times, and he wondered how high Morty had counted by now. And Grandma? And Grandpa? What is the Yiddish for zillion?

Getting to the old graves, to the burial ground established in the early days by the original seashore Jews, he gave the funeral in progress a wide berth and was careful to steer clear of the watchdogs when he passed the little red house. These dogs had not yet been made conversant with the common courtesies, let alone the ancient taboos that obtain in a Jewish cemetery. Jews guarded by dogs? Historically very, very wrong. His alternative was to be buried bucolically on Battle Mountain as close to Drenka as he could get. This had occurred to him long before today. But whom would he talk to up there? He had never found a goy yet who could talk fast enough for him.

And there they'd be slower than usual. He would have to swallow the insult of the dogs. No cemetery is going to be perfect.

After ten minutes of rambling about in the drizzle, searching for his grandparents' graves, he saw that only if he traveled methodically up and down, reading every headstone from one end of each row to the other, could he hope to locate Clara and Mordecai Sabbath. Footstones he could ignore—they mostly said "At Rest"—but the hundreds upon hundreds of headstones required his concentration, an immersion in them so complete that there would be nothing inside him but these names. He had to shrug off how these people would have disliked him and how many of them he would have despised, had to forget about the people they had been alive. Because you are no longer insufferable if you are dead. Goes for me, too. He had to drink in the dead, down to the dregs.

Our beloved mother Minnie. Our beloved husband and father Sidney. Beloved mother and grandmother Frieda. Beloved husband and father Jacob. Beloved husband, father, and grandfather Samuel. Beloved husband and father Joseph. Beloved mother Sarah. Beloved wife Rebecca. Beloved husband and father Benjamin. Beloved mother and grandmother Tessa. Beloved mother and grandmother Sophie. Beloved mother Bertha. Beloved husband Hyman. Beloved husband Morris. Beloved husband and father William. Beloved wife and mother Rebecca. Beloved daughter and sister Hannah Sarah. Our beloved mother Klara. Beloved husband Max. Our beloved daughter Sadie. Beloved wife Tillie. Beloved husband Bernard. Beloved husband and father Fred. Beloved husband and father Frank. My beloved wife our dear mother Lena. Our dear father Marcus. On and on and on. Nobody beloved gets out alive. Only the very oldest recorded all in Hebrew. Our son and brother Nathan. Our dear father Edward. Husband and father Louis. Beloved wife and mother Fannie. Beloved mother and wife Rose. Beloved husband and father Solomon. Beloved son and brother Harry. In memory of my beloved husband and our dear father Lewis. Beloved son Sidney. Beloved wife of Louis and mother of George Lucille. Beloved mother Tillie. Beloved father Abraham. Beloved mother and grandmother Leah. Beloved husband and father Emanuel.

Beloved mother Sarah. Beloved father Samuel. And on mine, beloved what? Just that: Beloved What. David Schwartz, beloved son and brother died in service of his country 1894–1918. 15 Cheshvan. In memory of Gertie, a true wife and loyal friend. Our beloved father Sam. Our son, nineteen years old, 1903–1922. No name, merely "Our son." Beloved wife and dear mother Florence. Beloved brother Dr. Boris. Beloved husband and father Samuel. Beloved father Saul. Beloved wife and mother Celia. Beloved mother Chasa. Beloved husband and father Isadore. Beloved wife and mother Esther. Beloved mother Jennie. Beloved husband and father David. Our beloved mother Gertrude. Beloved husband, father, brother Jekyl. Beloved aunt Sima. Beloved daughter Ethel. Beloved wife and mother Annie. Beloved wife and mother Frima. Beloved father and husband Hersch. Beloved father . . .

And here we are. Sabbath. Clara Sabbath 1872–1941. Mordecai Sabbath 1871–1923. There they are. Simple stone. And a pebble on top. Who'd come to visit? Mort, did you visit Grandma? Dad? Who cares? Who's left? What's in there? The box isn't even in there. You were said to be headstrong, Mordecai, bad temper, big joker . . . though even you couldn't make a joke like this. Nobody could. Better than this they don't come. And Grandma. Your name, the name also of your occupation. A matter-of-fact person. Everything about you—your stature, those dresses, your silence—said, "I am not indispensable." No contradictions, no temptations, though you were inordinately fond of corn on the cob. Mother hated having to watch you eat it. The worst of the summer for her. It made her "nauseous." I loved to watch. Otherwise you two got along. Probably keeping quiet was the key, letting her run things her way. Openly partial to Morty, Grandpa Mordecai's namesake, but who could blame you? You didn't live to see everything shatter. Lucky. Nothing big about you, Grandma, but nothing small either. Life could have marked you up a lot worse. Born in the little town of Mikulice, died at Pitkin Memorial. Have I left anything out? Yes. You used to love to clean the fish for us when Morty and I came home at night from surf casting. Mostly we came home with nothing, but the triumph of walking home from the beach with a couple of big blues in the bucket! You'd clean them in the kitchen. Fillet knife right at the opening, probably the anus, slit it straight up the center till you got behind the gills, and then (I liked watching this part best) you would just put your hand in and grab all the good stuff and throw it away. Then you scaled. Working against the scales and somehow without getting them all over the place. It used to take me fifteen minutes to clean it and half an hour to clean up after. The whole *thing* took you ten minutes. Mom even let you cook it. Never cut off the head and the tail. Baked it whole. Baked bluefish, corn, fresh tomatoes, big Jersey tomatoes. Grandma's meal. Yes, yes, it was something down on the beach at dusk with Mort. Used to talk to the other men. Childhood and its terrific markers. From about eight to thirteen, the fundamental ballast that we have. It's either right or it's wrong. Mine was right. The original ballast, an attachment to those who were nearby when we were learning what feeling was all about, an attachment maybe not stranger but stronger even than the erotic. A good thing to be able to contemplate for a final time—instead of racing through with it and getting out of here—certain high points, certain human high points. Hanging out with the man next door and his sons. Meeting and talking in the yard. Down on the beach, fishing with Mort. Rich times. Morty used to talk to the other men, the fishermen. Did it so easily. To me everything he did was so authoritative. One guy in brown pants and a short-sleeve white shirt and with a cigar always in his mouth used to tell us he didn't give a shit about catching fish (which was lucky, since he rarely pulled in more than a sand shark)—he told us kids, "The chief pleasure of fishing is getting out of the house. Gettin' away from women." We always laughed, but for Morty and me the bite was the thrill. With a blue you get a big hit. The rod jolts in your hand. Everything jolts. Morty was my teacher fishing. "When a striper takes the bait, it'll head out. If you stop the line from paying out it'll snap. So you just have to let it out. With a blue, after the hit, you can just reel in, but not with a striper. A blue is big and tough, but a striper will fight." Getting blowfish off the hook was a problem for everybody but Mort—spines and quills didn't bother him. The other thing that wasn't much fun to catch was rays. Do you remember when I was eight how I wound up in the hospital? I was out on the jetty and I caught a huge ray and it bit me and I just passed out. Beautiful, undulating swimmers but predatory sons of bitches, very mean with their sharp teeth. Ominous. Looks like a flat shark. Morty had to holler for help, and a guy came and they carried me up to the guy's car and rushed me to Pitkin. Whenever we went out fishing, you couldn't wait for us to get back so you could clean the catch. Used to catch shiners. Weighed less than a pound. You'd fry four or five of them in a pan. Very bony but great. Watching you eat a shiner was a lot of fun, too, for everyone but Mother. What else did we bring you to clean? Fluke, flounder, when we fished Shark River inlet. Weakfish. That's about it. When Morty joined the Air Corps, the night before he left we went down to the beach with our rods for an hour. Never got into the gear as kids. Just fished. Rod, hooks, sinkers, line, sometimes lures, mostly bait, mostly squid. That was it. Heavy-duty tackle. Big barbed hook. Never cleaned the rod. Once a summer splashed some water on it. Keep the same rig on the whole time. Just change the sinkers and the bait if we wanted to fish on the bottom. We went down the beach to fish for an hour. Everybody in the house was crying because he was going to war the next day. You were already here. You were gone. So I'll tell you what happened. October 10, 1942. He'd hung around through September because he wanted to see me bar mitzvahed, wanted to be there. The eleventh of October he went to Perth Amboy to enlist. The last of the fishing off the jetties and the beach. By the middle, the end of October, the fish disappear. I'd ask Morty—when he was first teaching me off the jetties with a small rod and reel, one made for fresh water—"Where do the fish go to?" "Nobody knows," he said. "Nobody knows where the fish go. Once they go out to sea, who knows where they go to? What do you think, people follow them around? That's the mystery of fishing. Nobody knows where they are." We went down to the end of the street that evening and down the stairs and onto the beach. It was just about dark. Morty could throw a rig a hundred and fifty feet even in the days before spin casting. Used the open-faced reels. Just a spool with a handle on it. Rods much stiffer then, much less adroit reel and a stiffer rod. Torture to cast for a kid. In the beginning I was always snarling the line. Spent most of the time getting it straightened out. But eventually I got it.

Morty said he was going to miss going out fishing with me.
He'd taken me down to the beach to say so long to me without the family carrying on around us. "Standing out here," he
told me, "the sea air, the quiet, the sound of the waves, your
toes in the sand, the idea that there are all those things out
there that are about to bite your bait. That thrill of something
being out there. You don't know what it is, you don't know
how big it is. You don't even know if you'll ever see it." And
he never did see it, nor, of course, did he get what you get
when you're older, which is something that mocks your opening yourself up to these simple things, something that is formless and overwhelming and that probably is dread. No, he got
killed instead. And that's the news, Grandma. The great gen-
erational kick of standing down on the beach in the dusk with
your older brother. You sleep in the same room, you get very
close. He took me with him everywhere. One summer when
he was about twelve he got a job selling bananas door-to-door.
There was a man in Belmar who sold only bananas, and he
hired Morty and Morty hired me. The job was to go along the
streets hollering, "Bananas, twenty-five cents a bunch!" What
a great job. I still sometimes dream about that job. You got
paid to shout "Bananas!" On Thursdays and Fridays after
school let out for the day, he went to pluck chickens for the
kosher butcher, Feldman. A farmer from Lakewood used to
call on Feldman and sell him chickens. Morty would take me
along to help him. I liked the worst part best: spreading the
Vaseline all the way up our arms to stymie the lice. It made me
feel like a little big shot at eight or nine not to be afraid of
those horrible fucking lice, to be, like Mort, utterly contemptuous of them and just pluck the chickens. And he used to protect me from the Syrian Jews. Kids used to dance on the
sidewalk in the summertime outside Mike and Lou's. Jitterbug
to the jukebox music. I doubt you ever saw that. When Morty
was working at Mike and Lou's one summer he'd bring home
his apron and Mom would wash it for him for the next night.
It would be stained yellow from the mustard and red from the
relish. The mustard came right with him into our room when
he came into our room at night. Smelled like mustard, sauerkraut, and hot dogs. Mike and Lou's had good dogs. Grilled.
The Syrian guys used to dance outside Mike and Lou's on the

sidewalk, used to dance by themselves like sailors. They had a little kind of Damascus mambo they did, very explosive steps. All related they were, clannish, and with very dark skin. The Syrian kids who joined our card games played a ferocious blackjack. Their fathers were in buttons, thread, fabrics then. Used to hear Dad's crony, the upholsterer from Neptune, talking about them when the men played poker in our kitchen on Friday nights. "Money is their god. Toughest people in the world to do business with. They'll cheat you as soon as you turn around." Some of these Syrian kids made an impression. One of them, one of the Gindi brothers, would come up to you and take a swing at you for no reason, come up and kill you and just look at you and walk away. I used to be hypnotized by his sister. I was twelve. She and I were in the same class. A little, hairy fireplug. Huge eyebrows. I couldn't get over her dark skin. She told him something that I said, so once he started to rough me up. I was deathly afraid of him. I should never have looked at her, let alone said *anything* to her. But the dark skin got me going. Always has. He started to rough me up right in front of Mike and Lou's, and Morty came outside in his mustard-stained apron and told Gindi, "Stay away from him." And Gindi said, "You gonna make me?" And Morty said, "Yes." And Gindi took one shot at him and opened up Morty's whole nose. Remember? Isaac Gindi. His form of narcissism never enchanted me. Sixteen stitches. Those Syrians lived in another time zone. They were always whispering among themselves. But I was twelve, inside my pants things were beginning to reverberate, and I could not keep my eyes off his hairy sister. Sonia was her name. Sonia had another brother, as I recall, Maurice, who was not human either. But then came the war. I was thirteen, Morty was eighteen. Here's a kid who never went away in his life, except maybe for a track meet. Never out of Monmouth County. Every day of his life he returned home. Endlessness renewed every day. And the next morning he goes off to die. But then, death is endlessness par excellence, is it not? Wouldn't you agree? Well, for whatever it is worth, before I move on: I have never once eaten corn on the cob without pleasurably recalling the devouring frenzy of you and your dentures and the repugnance this ignited in my mother. It taught me about more than mother-in-laws and daughter-in-laws; it taught me everything. This model grandmother, and Mother had all she could do not to throw you out into the street. And my mother was not unkind—you know that. But what affords the one with happiness affords the other with disgust. The interplay, the ridiculous interplay, enough to kill all and everyone.

Beloved wife and mother Fannie. Beloved wife and mother Hannah. Beloved husband and father Jack. It goes on. Our beloved mother Rose. Our beloved father Harry. Our beloved husband, father, and grandfather Meyer. People. All people. And here is Captain Schloss and there . . .

In the earth turned up where Lee Goldman, another de-voted wife, mother, and grandmother, had just been united with one of her family, a beloved one as yet unidentified, Sab-bath found pebbles to place on the stones of his mother, his father, and Morty. And one for Ida.

Here I am.

Crawford's office was barren of everything except a desk, a phone, a couple of battered chairs, and, inexplicably, a con-tentless vending machine. A smell of wet dog fur soured the air, and there was no reason not to think that the desk and two chairs had been culled from the inventory of the improvised dump across the way. On the desk a piece of glass, crisscrossed with masking tape to hold it together, served the cemetery superintendent as a writing surface; a slew of old business cards had been pushed beneath the glass along its four edges. The card that Sabbath saw first read, "The Good Intentions Paving Company, 212 Coit Street, Freehold, New Jersey."

To enter the brick tomblike building, Sabbath had had to shout for Crawford to come out and calm the dogs. April 13, 1924–December 15, 1944. Morty would be seventy. Today would be his seventieth birthday! He'll be dead in December *fifty years*. I won't be here for the commemoration. Thank God none of us will.

The funeral was by then long over and the rain had stopped. Crawford had phoned Mrs. Weizman to get the costs for Sab-bath and to see if the single was reserved, and for nearly an hour now he had been waiting for Sabbath to come to the office so he could report her prices, as well as the good news about the single. But each time Sabbath started away from the family plot, he'd turn around and go back. He didn't know whom he would be depriving of what by walking away after ten minutes of standing there, but he couldn't do it. The repeated leaving and returning did not escape his mockery, but he could do nothing about it. He could not go and he could not go and he could not go, and then—like any dumb creature who abruptly stops doing one thing and starts doing another and about whom you can never tell if its life is all freedom or no freedom—he could go and he went. And no lucidity to be derived from any of this. Rather, there was a distinctly assertive quickening of the great stupidity. If there was ever anything to know, now he knew he never had known it. And all this while his fists had been clenched, causing arthritic agony.

Crawford's face didn't make as much sense indoors as it had outside. Without his Phillies cap, he was revealed to be all burgeoning chin, bridgeless nose, and narrow expanse of forehead —it was as though, having given him this chin curved unmistakably in the shape of a shovel, God had marked baby Crawford at birth as a cemetery superintendent. It was a face on the evolutionary dividing line between our species and the subspecies preceding ours, and yet, from behind the desk with the fractured legs and the broken glass top, he established quickly a professional tone appropriate to the gravity of the transaction. To keep pictorially at the forefront of Sabbath's mind all the impertinences in store for his carcass, there was the wild snarling of the dogs. Rattling their chains beneath Crawford's window, they sounded all stoked up with Jew-hating dreams. Moreover, there were dog chains and leashes scattered about on the unswept, beat-up floor of dark checkerboard linoleum, and on Crawford's desk, to hold his pencils, his pens, his paper clips, and even some paperwork, he used the empty Pedigree dog food cans from which the dogs had been fed. A carton half full of unopened dog food had to be removed from the seat of the room's other chair before Sabbath could sit down across from Crawford's. Only then did he notice the transom over the front door, a rectangular window of colored glass scribed with the Star of David. This place had been built as the cemetery prayer house where the mourners gathered with the casket. It was a doghouse now.

"They want six hundred dollars for the single," Crawford told him. "They want twelve hundred for the two graves over there, and I chopped them down to eleven hundred. And I would suggest that the two graves would be the best thing for you over there. A nicer section. You'll be better off. The other you got the gate swinging next to you, you got the traffic in and out there—"

"The two graves are too far away. Give me the one next to Captain Schloss."

"If you think you'll be better off . . ."

"And a monument."

"I don't sell 'em. I told you."

"But you know somebody in the business. I want to order a monument."

"There are a million kind."

"Just like Captain Schloss's will do. A simple monument."

"That's not a cheap stone. That's about eight hundred. In New York they would charge you twelve hundred. More. There is a matching base. There is the foundation fee—concrete feet. The lettering I gotta bill you separate, a separate charge."

"How much?"

"Depends how much you want to say."

"As much as Captain Schloss says."

"He's got a lot written there. That's gonna cost you."

Sabbath removed from his interior pocket the envelope with Michelle's money, feeling to be sure the envelope of Polaroids was still there as well. From the money envelope he took six hundred for the plot and eight for the stone and put the bills on Crawford's desk.

"And three hundred more," asked Sabbath, "for what I want to say?"

"We're talkin' over fifty letters," said Crawford.

Sabbath counted out four hundred-dollar bills. "One is for you. To take care that everything is done."

"You want planting? On top of you? Yeco trees is two hundred and seventy-five dollars, for the trees and the work."

"Trees? I don't need trees. I never heard of yeco trees."

"That is what is on your family plot. That is yeco trees."

"Okay. Give me the same as theirs. Give me some yeco trees."

He reached in for three more of the hundreds. "Mr. Crawford, all my next of kin are here. I want you to run the show."

"You're ill."

"I need a coffin, buddy. One like I saw today."

"Plain pine. That one was four hundred. I know a guy can do the same for three fifty."

"And a rabbi. That short guy will do. How much?"

"Him? A hundred. Let me find you somebody else. I'll get you somebody just as good for fifty."

"A Jew?"

"Sure a Jew. He's old, that's all."

The door beneath the Star of David transom was pushed open, and just as the Italian kid came walking in, one of the dogs darted in alongside him and surged on his chain to within inches of Sabbath.

"Johnny, for Christ's sake," said Crawford, "shut the door and keep the dog outside."

"Yeah," said Sabbath, "you wouldn't want him to eat me yet. Wait'll I sign on."

"No, this one here won't bite you," Crawford assured Sabbath. "The other one, he can jump on you, but not this one. Johnny, get the dog out!"

Johnny dragged the dog backward by the chain and forced him, still snarling at Sabbath, out the door.

"The help. You can't sit here and say, 'Here, go do this job over there.' They don't know how. And now I'm going to have to get a Mexican? And he's gonna be any better? He's gonna be worse. Did you lock your car?" he asked Sabbath.

"Mr. Crawford, what am I leaving out of my plans?"

Crawford looked down at his notes. "Burial costs," he said. "Four hundred."

Sabbath counted out four hundred more and added the bills to the stack already on the desk.

"The instructions," Crawford told him. "What you want on the monument."

"Give me paper. Give me an envelope."

While Crawford prepared the bills—everything with carbon and in triplicate—Sabbath outlined on the back of Crawford's paper (the front was an invoice form, "Care of Grave," et cetera) the shape of a monument, drew it as naively as a child draws a house or a cat or a tree and felt very much the child while he did it. Within the outline he arranged the words of his epitaph as he wished them to appear. Then he folded the paper in thirds and slipped it into the envelope and sealed it. "Instructions," he wrote across the face of the envelope, "for inscription on the monument of M. Sabbath. Open when necessary. M.S. 4/13/94."

Crawford, contemplative, was a long time completing the paperwork. Sabbath enjoyed watching him. It was a good show. He formed every letter of every word on every document and receipt as though each were of the utmost importance. Suddenly he seemed to be inspired by a profound reverence, perhaps only for the money he had overcharged Sabbath but perhaps a little for the ineluctable meaning of the formalities. So these two shrewdies sat across that battered desk from each other, aging men mistrustfully interlinked—as one is, as we are —each of them drinking whatever still bubbled into his mouth out of the fountain of life. Mr. Crawford carefully rolled up the office copies of the invoices and filed the neat cylinder of papers in an empty dog food can.

Sabbath returned one last time to stand at the family plot, his heart both leaden and leaping, and tearing from within him the last of his doubt. *At this I will succeed. I promise you.* Then he went to look at his own plot. On the way there, he passed two gravestones he hadn't seen before. Beloved son and dear brother killed in action at Normandy July 1, 1944 age 27 years you will always be remembered Sergeant Harold Berg. Beloved son and brother Julius Dropkin killed in action Sept. 12, 1944 in southern France age 26 years always in our heart. They got these boys to die. They got Dropkin and Berg to die. He stopped and cursed on their behalf.

Despite the dump across the street and the damaged fence to the back and the corroded, fallen-down iron gate to one side, pride of ownership welled up in him, however mean and paltry that sandy bit of soil happened to look, there at the edge of the line of singles consigned to the cemetery's fringe. They can't take that away from me. So pleased was he with a prudent morning's work—the scrupulous officializing of his decision, the breaking of bonds, the shedding of fear, the bidding adieu—he whistled some Gershwin. Maybe the other section *was* nicer, but if he stood on his toes he could see through from here to his family's plot, and there were all the inspiring Weizmans just across the path, and immediately to the right of him—to his left, lying down—was Captain Schloss. He slowly read once again the substantial portrait of his eternal neighbor-to-be. "Holocaust Survivor, VFW, Mariner, Businessman, Entrepreneur. In Loving Memory Relatives and Friends May 30, 1929–May 20, 1990." Sabbath remembered only some twenty-four hours earlier reading the sign in the window of the salesroom abutting the funeral home where Linc had been eulogized. A nameless gravestone stood on display, beside it was a sign, headed "What Is a Monument?" and, beneath that, simple, elegant script avowing that a monument "is a symbol of devotion . . . a tangible expression of the noblest of all human emotions—LOVE . . . a monument is built because there was a life, not a death, and with intelligent selection and proper guidance, it should inspire REVERENCE, FAITH and HOPE for the living . . . it should speak out as a voice from yesterday and today to the ages yet unborn. . . ."

Beautifully put. I'm glad they have clarified for us what is a monument.

Beside the monument to Captain Schloss, he envisioned his own:

Morris Sabbath
"Mickey"
Beloved Whoremonger, Seducer
Sodomist, Abuser of Women,
Destroyer of Morals, Ensnarer of Youth,
Uxoricide,
Suicide
1929–1994

. . . and that was where Cousin Fish lived—and that finished the tour. The hotels were gone, replaced along the oceanfront by modest condos, but back down the streets the little houses still squarely stood, the wooden bungalows and stucco bungalows where everyone had lived, and as though on the recommendation of the Hemlock Society, he had driven past them all, final remembrance and farewell. But now he could think of

no further procrastination that he might construe as a symbolic act of closure; now it was time to get a move on and get
the damn thing done, the great big act that will conclude my
story . . . and so he was leaving Bradley Beach forever when
there on Hammond Avenue materialized the bungalow that
had been Fish's.

Hammond ran parallel to the ocean but up by Main Street
and the railroad tracks, a good mile or so from the beach. Fish
must be dead many years now. His wife got the tumor when
we were boys. A very young woman—not that we grasped that
then. On the side of her head, a potato growing beneath the
soil of her skin. She wore kerchiefs to hide the unsightliness,
but even so, a sharp-eyed kid could see where the potato was
flourishing. Fish sold us vegetables from his truck. Dugan for
cake, Borden for milk, Pechter for bread, Seaboard for ice,
Fish for vegetables. When I saw the potatoes in the basket, I
would think of you-know-what. A dead mother. Inconceivable. For a while I couldn't eat a potato. But I got older and
hungrier and it passed. Fish raised the two kids. Brought them
with him to the house the nights the men played cards. Irving
and Lois. Irving collected stamps. Had at least one from every
country. Lois had boobs. At ten she had them. In grade
school, boys used to throw her coat over her head, squeeze
'em, and run. Morty told me I couldn't do it, because she was
our cousin. "*Second* cousin." But Morty said no, it was against
some Jewish law. Our last names were all but the same. Thanks
to the alphabet, I sat a mere eighteen inches away from Lois.
Very trying, those classes. The pleasure was difficult—my first
lesson in that. At the end of the hour I had to carry my notebook in front of my pants while leaving the room. But Morty
said not to—even at the height of the sweater era, no. The last
person I ever listened to in that department. Should have told
him off at the cemetery: "What Jewish law? You made it up,
you son of a bitch." Would have handed him a laugh. Rapture
itself, to reach out my hand and give him a laugh, a body, a
voice, a life with some of the fun in it of being alive, the fun of
existing that even a flea must feel, the pleasure of existence,
pure and simple, that practically anyone this side of the cancer
ward gets a glimmer of occasionally, uninspiring as his fortunes
overall may be. Here, Mort, what we call "a life," the way we

call the sky "the sky" and the sun "the sun." How nonchalant we are. Here, brother, a living soul—for whatever it's worth, take mine!

Okay. Time to marshal the state of mind necessary to carry it off. That it would require of him a state of mind and *more*—littleness, greatness, stupidity, wisdom, cowardice, heroism, blindness, vision, everything in the arsenal of his two opposing armies united as one—this he knew. Swill about the fun that even a flea must feel was not going to make it any easier. Stop thinking the wrong thoughts and think *the right one*. And yet Fish's house—of all the houses! His own family's house, fussily kept up now by a Hispanic couple whom he had seen gardening on their knees along the edge of the driveway (no longer sand but asphalt), had worked beautifully on his resolve, causing all his misery to cohere around his decision. The new stuff, the glass sunporch and the aluminum siding and the scalloped metal shutters, made it ludicrous to think of the house as *theirs*, as ludicrous as to think that the cemetery was *theirs*. But *this* ruin, Fish's, had significance. That unaccountable exaggeration, significance: in Sabbath's experience invariably the prelude to missing the point.

Where there were shades, they were torn; where there were screens still hanging, they were rent and slit; and where there were steps, they did not look as though they could support a cat. Fish's badly dilapidated house looked to be uninhabited. How much, Sabbath wondered—before committing suicide—to buy it? He did have seventy-five hundred dollars left—and he had *life* left, and where there's life there's mobility. He got out of the car, and, grasping a railing that looked to be adhering to the steps by nothing more solid than a thought, he made his way to the door. Cautiously—lacking utterly the freedom of a man for whom the preservation of life and limb had ceased to be of concern.

Like Mrs. Nussbaum from the old *Fred Allen Show*—Fish's favorite—he called out, "Hello, is anybody?" He knocked on the living room windows. It was difficult to see inside because of the dreary day and because hanging across each window were mummy wrappings that had once been the curtains. He went around to the side and into the backyard. Splotches of grass and weed, nothing there but a beach chair, a sling beach chair that looked as though it had not been taken in out of the weather since the June afternoon he'd gone over to see Irving's stamps (purportedly) and from Irving's upstairs window watched Lois sunning below in her swimsuit, her body, her body, the vineyard that was her body taking up every inch of that very chair. The sun cream. Come from a tube. She rubbed it all over herself. It looked like come to him. She had a husky voice. Covered with come. His cousin. When someone only twelve has to live with all that, it is almost too much to ask. There was no Jewish law, you bastard.

He came around to the front to look for a For Sale sign. Where could he inquire about the house? "Hello?" he shouted from the bottom step, and from across the street he heard a voice call back, a woman's voice, "You looking for the old man?"

There was a black woman waving at him—youngish, smiling, nice and round in a pair of jeans. She was standing on the top step of the porch, where she'd been listening to the radio. When Sabbath was a boy the few blacks he saw were either in Asbury or over in Belmar. The blacks in Asbury were mostly dishwashers at the hotels, domestic servants, menial odd-jobs people, living over by Springwood Avenue, down from the chicken markets, the fish markets, and the Jewish delis where we went with an empty jar my mother gave us and they filled it up with sauerkraut when it was in season. A black bar there, too, a hot place during the war, Leo's Turf Club, full of bimbos and dandies in zoot suits. The guys stepped out in their fine duds on Saturday night and got *shicker*. The best music around at Leo's. Great sax players, according to Morty. Blacks weren't antagonistic to whites in Asbury then, and Morty got to know some of the musicians and took me there a couple of times when I was still a kid to hear that jivey jazz stuff. My appearance used to crack up Leo, the big Jewish guy who owned the place. He'd see me coming in and he'd say, "What the hell are you doin' in here?" There was a black saxophonist who was the brother of the star hurdler on the Asbury track team that Morty threw the discus and the shot for. He'd say, "What's happenin', Mort? What's up wit *dju*?" Dju! I loved *dju* for every possible reason and drove Morty crazy repeating it all the way home. The other black bar had the dreamier name—The Orchid Lounge—but it didn't have live music, only a jukebox, and we never went inside. Yes, Asbury High in Sabbath's day was Italian, some djus, these few blacks, and a smattering of what the hell do you call 'em, Protestants, white Protestants. Long Branch strictly Italian then. Longa Branch. Over in Belmar a lot of the blacks worked at the laundry and lived around 15th Avenue, 11th Avenue. There was a black family across the street from the synagogue in Belmar who came over for Shabbos to turn the lights on and off. And there was a black iceman around for a few years, before Seaboard monopolized the summer trade. He always puzzled Sabbath's mother, not so much because he was a Negro selling ice, the first and last anyone ever saw, but because of how he sold it. She would ask for a twenty-five-cent piece of ice and he would cut a piece and put it on the scale and say, "Dat's it." And she would bring it inside and over dinner that evening she would say to the family, "Why does he put it on the scale? I never see him add a piece or chop off a piece. Who is he fooling putting it on the scale?" "You," Sabbath's father said. She would get ice from him twice a week until one day he just disappeared. Maybe this is his granddaughter, the granddaughter of the iceman Morty and called Dat's It.

"We ain't seen him in a month," she said. "Somebody ought to check him. You know?"

"That's what I'm here to do," Sabbath said.

"He can't hear. You got to bang real hard. Don't stop bangin'."

He did better than bang hard and long—he pulled open the rusted screen door and turned the knob of the front door and walked inside. Unlocked. And there was Fish. There was Cousin Fish. Not at the cemetery under a stone but sitting on a sofa by the side window. Clearly he neither saw nor heard Sabbath enter. Awfully small for Cousin Fish but that was who it was. The resemblance to Sabbath's father was still there in the wide bald skull, the narrow chin, the big ears, but more so in something not so easily describable—the family look that that whole generation of Jews had. The weight of life, the simplicity to bear it, the gratitude not to have been entirely crushed, the unwavering, innocent trust—none of that had left his face. Couldn't. Trust. A great endowment for this mortuary world.

I should go. He looks as though to extinguish him it wouldn't take more than a syllable. Whatever I say is liable to kill him. But this is Fish. Back then I thought that he got his name because he sometimes dared to go out at night on the party boats with the working-class goyim to fish. Not many Jewish guys with accents went out with those drunks. Once, when I was a little kid, he took Morty and me. Fun to go out with a grown man. My father didn't fish *or* swim. Fish did both. *Taught* me to swim. "Fishing you usually don't catch," he explained to me, the smallest person on the boat. "You don't catch more than you catch. Every once in a while you get a fish. Sometimes you get a school and you get a lot of fish. But that don't happen much." One Sunday early in September there was a terrific thunderstorm, and as soon as it was over, Fish raced up in the empty vegetable truck with Irving and told Morty and me to get in the back with our rods, and then he drove like mad down to Newark Avenue beach—he knew just which beach to go to. In the summertime, when there's a thunderstorm and the water temperatures change and the water gets very turbulent, the schools come in after the minnows and you can see the fish; they're right out there in the waves. And they were. And Fish knew. See them on the waves coming out of the water. Fish caught fifteen fish in thirty minutes. I was ten, and even I caught three. 1939. And when I was older—this was after Morty went away; I was about fourteen —I was missing Morty, and Fish learned about it from my father and took me out on the beach for the whole night with him one Saturday. After blues. He had a thermos of tea that we shared. I cannot commit suicide without saying good-bye to Fish. If my speaking up startles him and he drops dead, they can just carve "Geriacide" on the stone.

"Cousin Fish—remember me? I'm Mickey Sabbath. I'm Morris. My brother was Morty."

Fish hadn't heard him. Sabbath would have to approach the sofa. He'll think, when he sees the beard, that I'm Death, I'm a thief, a burglar with a knife. And I have not felt less sinister since I was five. Or happier. This is Fish. Uneducated, well mannered, something of a jokester, but stingy, oh so stingy, said my mother. True. The dread about money. But the men had that. How could they not, Mom? Intimidated, outsiders in the world, yet with wellsprings of resistance that were a mystery even to them, or that would have been, had they not been mercifully spared the terrible inclination to think. Thinking was the last thing they felt to be missing from their lives. It was all more basic than that.

"Fish," he said, advancing with his arms extended, "I'm Mickey. It's Mickey Sabbath. Your cousin. The son of Sam and Yetta. Mickey Sabbath." His shouting got Fish to look up from two pieces of mail that he was fiddling with in his lap. Who mailed him anything? I hardly get mail. More proof he's not dead.

"You? Who are you?" Fish asked. "Are you from the newspaper?"

"I'm not from the newspaper. No. I'm Mickey Sabbath. *Sabbath.*"

"Yes? I had a cousin Sabbath. On McCabe Avenue. That's not him, is it?"

The accent and syntax the same, but no longer the muscular voice for shouting from the street into the houses and all the way back to the yards, "Veg-e-tables! Fresh veg-e-tables, ladies!" In the tonelessness, the hollowness, you heard not only how deaf he was and how alone he was but that this was not one of his life's great days. A mere mist of a man. And at those card games, when he won, the delight was violent— repeatedly he smacked the oilcloth of the kitchen table as he laughed and raked in the dough. Later my mother explained that this was because of how greedy he was. Flypaper dangled from the kitchen fixture. The short-circuited *bzzz* of a fly fitfully dying over their heads was all that was to be heard in the kitchen while they concentrated on what they'd been dealt. And the crickets. And the train, that not very sonorous sound which can strip a youngster in his bed right out of his skin and down to his nerve endings—in those days, at least, peel a boy down to expose every inch of him to living's high drama and mystery—the whistle in the dark of the Jersey Shore freight line tearing through the town. And the ambulance. In the summertime, when the old people were in for their week to escape the North Jersey mosquitoes, the ambulance siren every night. Two blocks south, over at the Brinley Hotel, somebody dying about every night. Splashing with the grandchildren by water's edge at the sunny beach and, at night, talking in Yiddish on the benches at the boards and then, stiffly, together, back to the kosher hotels, where, while getting ready for bed, one of them would keel over and die. You'd hear it on the beach the next day. Just keeled over on the toilet and died. Only last week he saw one of the hotel employees shaving on Saturday and complained to the owner—and today he's gone! At eight and nine and ten I couldn't stand it. The sirens terrified me. I'd sit up in bed and holler, "No! No!" This would wake Morty in the twin bed beside mine. "What is it?" "I don't want to die!" "You won't. You're a kid. Go to sleep." He'd get me through it. Then *he* died, a kid. And what in Fish so antagonized my mother? That he could survive and laugh without a wife? Maybe there were girlfriends. Mingling on the street with the ladies all day long, bagging vegetables, maybe he bagged a couple of them ladies. This could explain why Fish is still here. A gonadal disgrace can be a dynamic force, hard to stop.

"Yes," said Sabbath. "That was my father. On McCabe. That was Sam. I'm his son. My mother was Yetta."

"They lived on McCabe?"

"That's right. The second block. I'm their son Mickey. Morris."

"The second block on McCabe. I swear I don't remember you, honest."

"You remember your truck, don't you? Cousin Fish and his truck."

"The truck I remember. I had a truck then. Yes." He seemed to understand what he'd said only after he said it. "Hah," he added—some wry recognition of something.

"And you sold vegetables from the truck."

"Vegetables. Vegetables I know I sold."

"Well, you sold them to my mother. Sometimes to me. I

came out with her list and you'd sell them to me. Mickey. Morris. Sam and Yetta's son. The younger son. The other was Morty. You used to take us fishing."

"I swear I don't remember."

"Well, that's all right." Sabbath came around the coffee table and sat beside him on the sofa. His skin was very brown, and behind large horn-rimmed glasses, the eyes looked to be getting signals from the brain—up close Sabbath saw more clearly that somewhere back there things still converged. This was good. They could actually talk. To his surprise, he had to overcome a desire to take Fish and pick him up and put him on his lap. "It's wonderful to see you, Fish."

"Nice to see you, too. But I still don't remember you."

"It's okay. I was a boy."

"How old were you then?"

"At the vegetable truck? It was before the war. I was nine, ten years old. And you were a young fellow in your forties."

"And I used to sell vegetables to your mother, you said?"

"That's right. To Yetta. It doesn't matter. How do you feel?"

"Pretty good, thank you. All right."

That politeness. Must have got the ladies, too, a virile specimen with muscles, manners, and a couple of jokes. Yes, that's what made my mother angry, no doubt about it. The ostentatious virility.

Fish's pants were streaked with urine stains and his cardigan sweater was a color that was indescribable where it was thickly caked with food at the front—particularly rich it was along the ribbon of the buttonholes—but his shirt seemed fresh and he did not smell. His breath, astonishingly, was sweet: the smell of a creature that survives on clover. But could those big, crooked teeth be his own? Had to be. They don't make dentures that look like that except maybe for horses. Sabbath again overcame the impulse to bodily lift him onto his lap and contented himself with swinging an arm around the back of the sofa so that it rested partly on Fish's shoulder. The sofa had much in common with the cardigan. Impasto, the painters call it. The way a young girl might present her lips—or did in a fashion long out-of-date—Fish offered his ear up to Sabbath, the better to hear him when he spoke. Sabbath could have eaten it, hairs and all. He was getting steadily happier by the moment. The ruthless hunger to win at cards. Fondling a customer behind the truck. The gonadal disgrace with the teeth of a horse. The incapacity to die. Sitting it out instead. This thought made Sabbath intensely excited: *the perverse senselessness of just remaining, of not going.*

"Can you walk?" Sabbath asked him. "Can you take a walk?"

"I walk around the house."

"How do you eat? You make your own food?"

"Oh, yeah. I cook myself. Sure. I make chicken . . ."

They waited while Fish waited for something to come after "chicken." Sabbath could have waited forever. I could move in here and feed him. The two of us having our soup. That black girl from across the street coming over for dessert. Don't stop bangin'. Wouldn't mind hearing that from her every day.

"I have, what you call it. Applesauce I have. For dessert."

"What about breakfast? Did you eat breakfast this morning?"

"Yeah. Breakfast. I made my cereal. Cook my cereal. I make oatmeal. The next day I make . . . what you call it. Cereal— what the hell you call it?"

"Cornflakes?"

"No, I don't have cornflakes. No, I used to have cornflakes."

"And Lois?"

"My daughter? She died. You knew her?"

"Of course. And Irv?"

"My son, he passed away. Almost a year ago. He was sixty-six years old. Nothing. He passed away."

"We were in high school together."

"Yes? With Irving?"

"He was a little ahead of me. He was between my brother and me. I used to envy Irving, running from the truck to carry the bags for the ladies right to their doors. When I was a kid, I thought Irving was somebody because he worked with his father up on the truck."

"Yes? You live here?"

"No. Not now. I did. I live in New England. Up north."

"So what made you come down here?"

"I wanted to see people I knew," Sabbath said. "Something told me you were still alive."

"Thank God, yes."

"And I thought, 'I would like to see him. I wonder if he remembers me or my brother. My brother, Morty.' Do you remember Morty Sabbath? He was your cousin too."

"A poor memory. I remember little. I been here about sixty years. In this house. I bought it when I was a young man. I was about thirty. Then. I bought a home and here it is, the same place."

"Can you still manage stairs by yourself?" At the other end of the living room, by the door, was a stairway Sabbath used to race up with Irving so he could look down from the back bedroom on Lois's body. Sea & Ski. Was that what she squirted out of the tube, or was Sea & Ski later? It's a shame she didn't live to know how it nearly killed me to watch her rub it on. Bet she'd like to hear it now. Bet our friend decorum doesn't mean much to Lois now.

"Oh, yeah," Fish said. "I manage. I go upstairs, sure. I manage to walk up. My bedroom is upstairs. So I gotta go upstairs. Sure. I go up once a day. I go up and come down."

"Do you sleep much?"

"No, that's my trouble. I'm a very poor sleeper. I hardly sleep. I never slept in my life. I can't sleep."

Could this be everything that Sabbath thought it was? It wasn't considered characteristic of him to extend himself this way. But he hadn't had as interesting a conversation—barring last night's in the hallway with Michelle—in years. The first man I've met since going to sea who doesn't bore me stiff.

"What do you do when you don't sleep?"

"I just lie in bed and think, and that's all."

"What do you think about?"

A bark came out of Fish, sounding like a noise coming out of a cave. Must be what he remembers of a laugh. And he used to laugh a lot, laugh like mad whenever he won that pot. "Oh, different things."

"Do you remember anything, Fish, about the old days? Do you remember the old days at all?"

"Such as what?"

"Yetta and Sam. My parents."

"They were your parents."

"Yes."

Fish was trying hard, concentrating like a man at stool. And some shadowy activity did appear momentarily to be transpiring in his skull. But finally he had to reply, "I swear I don't remember."

"So what do you do all day, now that you don't sell vegetables?"

"So I walk around. I exercise. I walk around the house. When the sun is out, I'm outdoors in the sun. Today is the thirteenth of April, right?"

"Right. How do you know the date? Do you follow the calendar?"

The indignation was genuine when he said, "No. I just *know* today's the thirteenth of April."

"Do you listen to the radio? You used to listen to the radio with us sometimes. To H. V. Kaltenborn. To the news from the front."

"Did I? No, I don't. I got a radio in there. But I don't bother with it. My hearing is bad. Well, I'm getting on in years. How old do you think I am?"

"I know how old you are. You're a hundred years old."

"So how do you know?"

"Because you were five years older than my father. My father was your cousin. The butter-and-egg man. Sam."

"He sent you over here? Or what?"

"Yeah. He sent me over here."

"He did, eh? He and his wife, Yetta. Do you see them often?"

"Occasionally."

"He sent you over to me?"

"Yes."

"Isn't that remarkable?"

The word gave Sabbath an enormous boost. If he can deliver "remarkable," then it, the brain, can come up yet with the things I want. You are dealing with a man on whom his life has left an impression. It's in there. It's just a matter of staying on him, staying with him, until you can take an impression of the impression. To hear him say, "Mickey. Morty. Yetta. Sam," to hear him say, "I was there. I swear I remember. We all were alive."

"You look pretty good for a man who's a hundred years old."

"Thank God. Not bad, no. I feel all right."

"No aches or pains?"

"No, no. Thank God, no.

"A lucky man you are, Fish, not to have pain."

"Thank God, sure. I am."

"So what do you enjoy to do now? Do you remember the card games with Sam? Do you remember the fishing? From the beach? From the boat with the goyim? It used to give you pleasure to visit our house at night. You would see me sitting there and you would squeeze my knee. You would say, 'Mickey or Morris, which is it?' You don't remember any of this. You and my father used to speak Yiddish."

"*Vu den?* I still speak Yiddish. I never forgot that."

"That's good. So you speak Yiddish sometimes. That's good. What else do you do that gives you pleasure?"

"For pleasure?" He is astonished that I can ask such a question. I ask about pleasure and for the first time it occurs to him that he may be dealing with a crazy person. A madman has come into the house and there is reason to be terrified. "What kind of pleasure?" he said. "I'm just around the house and that's all. I don't go to see no movies or anything like that. I can't. I wouldn't be able to see anything anyway. So what's the use?"

"Do you see any people?"

"Ummm." People. There is a big blot there, obscuring the answer. People. He thinks, though what that entails I have no idea—like trying to get wet kindling to light. "Hardly," he says at last. "I got my neighbor next door I see. He's a goy. A Gentile."

"Is he a nice fellow?"

"Yeah, yeah, he's nice."

"That's good. As it should be. They're taught to love their neighbors. You're probably lucky it's not a Jew. And who cleans for you?"

"I have a woman cleaning up a couple of weeks ago."

Yeah, well, she is out on her ass when I take over. The filth. The dirt. The living room is little more than a floor—besides the sofa and the coffee table there is only a broken, armless upholstered chair by the stairs—and the floor is like the floor of a monkey's cage I once saw in a zoo in a town in the boot of Italy, a zoo I've never forgotten. But the debris and the dust are the least of it. Either the woman is blinder than Fish or she is a crook and a drunk. She goes.

"There's nothing here to clean," Fish said. "The bed, it's in good shape."

"And who does your washing? Who washes your clothes for you?"

"The clothes . . ." That's a hard one. They're getting harder. Either he is tiring or he is dying. If it's death, Fish's long-deferred death, it wouldn't be inappropriate if what he hears last is "Who washes your clothes?" Tasks. These men *were* tasks. The men and the tasks were one.

"Who does your laundry?"

"Laundry" works. "A few little things. I do it myself. I haven't got much laundry. Just an undershirt and the shorts, and that's all. There isn't much to do. I wash it out in the basin, in the sink. And hang it on the line. And—it dries!" For comic effect, a pause. Then triumphantly—"it dries!" Yes, Fish is coming over; he always says something to make Mickey laugh. It didn't take much, but there was humor in him, all right, about the miracles and the gifts. It dries! "But he's so stingy. Before she passed away, poor woman, he never bought her a thing." "Fischel is a lonely man," my father says; "let him enjoy a family for ten minutes at night. He loves the boys. More than his own. I don't know why it's so, but he does."

"You ever go and take a look at the ocean?" Sabbath asked.

"No. I can't go anymore. That's out now. Too far to walk. Good-bye, ocean."

"Your mind's all right, though."

"Yeah, my mind is all right. Thank God. It's okay."

"And you still have the house. You made a good living selling vegetables."

Indignant again. "No, it *wasn't* a good living, it was a *poor* living. I used to peddle around. Asbury Park. Belmar. Belmar I used to go. In my truck. I had an open truck. All the baskets lined up. Used to be a market here. A wholesale market. And then years ago there used to be farmers. The farmers used to come in. It's a long time ago. I forgot about it even."

"You spent your whole life being a vegetable man."

"Mostly, yes."

Push. It's like single-handedly freeing a car from the

banked-up snow, but the spinning tires are taking hold, so *push*. Yes, I remember Morty. Morty. Mickey. Yetta. Sam. He can say it. Get him to do it.

Do what? What can be done for you at this late hour?

"Do you remember your mother and father, Fish?"

"If I remember them? Sure. Oh, yes. Of course. In Russia. I was born in Russia myself. A hundred years ago."

"You were born in 1894."

"Yeah. Yeah. You're right. How did you know?"

"And do you remember how old you were when you came to America?"

"How old I was? I remember. Fifteen or sixteen years old. I was a young boy. I learned English."

"And you don't remember Morty and Mickey? The two boys. Yetta and Sam's boys."

"You're Morty?"

"I'm his kid brother. You remember Morty. An athlete. A track star. You used to feel his muscles and whistle. The clarinet. He played the clarinet. He could fix things with his hands. He used to pluck chickens for Feldman after school. For the butcher who played cards with you and my father and Kravitz the upholsterer. I would help him. Thursdays and Fridays. You don't remember Feldman either. It doesn't matter. Morty was a pilot in the war. He was my brother. He died in the war."

"During the war it was? The Second World War?"

"Yes."

"That was quite a few years ago, isn't it?"

"It's fifty years, Fish."

"That's a long time."

A dining room opened out back of the living room, and its windows looked onto the yard. In the winter, on weekends, they used to catalog Irving's stamps on the dining room table, study the perforations and watermarks for as many centuries as it took before Lois came into the house and went up the stairs to *her room*. Sometimes she went to *the toilet*. The sounds of the water flowing through the pipes overhead Sabbath studied harder than he studied the stamps. The dining room chairs on which he and Irv sat were now buried away beneath clothing, draped with shirts, sweaters, pants, coats. Too blind for closets, the old man maintained his wardrobe here.

Against the length of one wall there was a sideboard that Sabbath, who had been staring at it intermittently ever since sitting down beside Fish, at last recognized. Maple veneer with rounded corners—it was his mother's, his own mother's treasured sideboard, where she kept the "good" dishes they never ate from, the crystal goblets they never drank from; where his father kept the tallis he used twice a year, the velvet bag of tefillin he never prayed with; and where once Sabbath had found, beneath the pile of "good" tablecloths too good for the likes of them to eat off of, a book bound in blue cloth consisting of instructions on how to survive the wedding night. The man was to bathe, powder himself, wear a soft robe (preferably silk), shave—even if he had already shaved in the morning—and the woman was to try not to pass out. Pages and pages, nearly a hundred of them, in which Sabbath could not find a single word he was looking for. The book was mostly about lighting, perfume, and love. Must have been a great help to Yetta and Sam. I only wonder where they got the cocktail shaker. No smells were involved, according to this book—not a single smell listed in the index. He was twelve. The smells he would have to come by beyond his mother's sideboard, sometimes grandly called the credenza.

When, four years before her death, his mother had gone into the rest home and he'd sold the house, the stuff must have been distributed around or stolen. He'd thought that lawyer had arranged an auction to pay the bills. Maybe Fish had bought the piece. Out of feeling for those evenings in our house. He would already have been ninety. Maybe for twenty bucks Irving had bought the sideboard for him. Anyway, here it is. Fish here, the sideboard here—what more is here?

"Remember, Fish, how during the war the lights were out on the boardwalk? Remember they had the blackout?"

"Yeah. The lights were out. I also remember when the ocean was so rough it picked up the whole boardwalk and put it on Ocean Avenue. It raised it up twice in my life. A big storm."

"The Atlantic is a powerful ocean."

"Sure. Picked up the whole boardwalk and put it on Ocean Avenue. Happened twice in my life."

"You remember your wife?"

"Of course I remember her. I came down here. I got married. A very fine woman. She passed away, it's about thirty, forty years ago. Since then I'm alone. It's no good to be alone. It's a lonely life. So what are you going to do? Nothing you can do about it. Make the best of it. That's all. When it's sunny out, the sun, I go out in the back. And I sit in the sun. And I get nice and brown. That's my life. That's what I love. The outdoor life. My backyard. I sit there mostly all day when the sun is out. You understand Yiddish? 'You're old, you're cold.' Today it's raining."

To get over to that sideboard. But by now Fish has put his hands on my thighs, they are resting on me while we talk, and not even Machiavelli could have got up at that moment, even if he knew, *as I did*, that inside that sideboard was everything he had come looking for. I knew this. Something is there that is not my mother's ghost: she's down in the grave with her ghost. Something is here as important and as palpable as the sun that turns Fish brown. Yet I couldn't move. This must be the veneration that the Chinese have for the old.

"You fall asleep out there?"

"Where?"

"In the sunshine."

"No. I don't sleep. I just look. I close my eyes and I look. Yeah. I can't sleep there. I told you before. I'm a very poor sleeper. I go upstairs in the evening, about four or five o'clock. I go to bed. So I rest in the bed, but I don't sleep. A very poor sleeper."

"Do you remember when you first came down the shore by yourself?"

"When I came to the shore? What do you mean, from Russia?"

"No. After New York. After you left the Bronx. After you left your mother and father."

"Oh. Yeah. I came down here. You're from the Bronx?"

"No. My mother was. Before she married."

"Yes? Well, I just got married and I came down here. Yeah. I married a very fine woman."

"How many children did you have?"

"Two. A boy and a girl. My son, the one who died not long

ago. An accountant. A good job. With a retail concern. And Lois. You know Lois?"

"Yes, I know Lois."

"A lovely child."

"That she is. It's very nice to see you, Fish." Taking his hands in mine. About time.

"Thank you. It's a pleasure seeing you, I'm sure."

"You know who I am, Fish? I'm Morris. I'm Mickey. I'm Yetta's son. My brother was Morty. I remember you so well, on the street with the truck, all the ladies coming out of the houses—"

"To the truck."

He's with me, he's back there—and squeezing my hands with a strength greater even than what I have left in my own! "To the truck," I said.

"To buy. Isn't that remarkable?"

"Yes. That's the word for it. It was all remarkable."

"Remarkable."

"All those years ago. Everyone alive. So can I look around your house at the photographs?" There were photographs arranged along the top of the sideboard. No frames. Just propped up against the wall.

"You want to take a picture of it?"

I *did* want to take a picture of the sideboard. How did he know? "No, I just want to look at the photographs."

I lifted his hands from my lap. But when I got up, he got up and followed me into the dining room, walked very well, right at my heels, followed me to the sideboard like Willie Pep chasing some little *pisher* around the ring.

"Can you see the pictures?" he asked.

"Fish," I said, "this is you—with the truck!" There was the truck, with the baskets lined up along the slanting sides and Fish on the street next to the truck, standing at military attention.

"I think so," he said. "I can't see. It looks like me," he said when I held it up directly in front of his glasses. "Yes. That's my daughter there, Lois."

Lois had lost her looks later in life. She too.

"And who is this man?"

"That's my son, Irving. And who is this?" he asked me,

picking up a photograph that was lying flat on the sideboard. They were old, faded photographs, water-stained around the edges and some sticky to the touch. "That's me," he asked, "or what?"

"I don't know. Who is this? This woman. Beautiful woman. Dark hair."

"Maybe it's my wife."

Yes. The potato then probably no more than a bud. I can't remember any of those women approaching the beauty of this one. And she's the one who died.

"And is this you? With a girlfriend?"

"Yeah. My girlfriend. I had her then. She passed away already."

"You outlive everybody, even your girlfriends."

"Yeah. I had a few girlfriends. I had a few, in my younger years after my wife passed away. Yeah."

"Did you enjoy that?"

The words have no meaning for him at first. In this question he seems to have met his match. We wait, my crippled hands on my mother's sideboard, which is thick with grease and dirt. The tablecloth on the dining room table bears every stain imaginable. Nothing else here is quite so fetid and foul. And I'll bet it's one of the cloths we never got to use ourselves.

"I asked if you enjoyed the girls."

"Well, yes," he suddenly replied. "Yes. It was all right. I tried a few."

"But not recently."

"What reason?"

"Not *recently*."

"What do you mean what reason?"

"Not *lately*."

"Lately? No, too old for that. Finished with that." He waves a hand almost angrily. "That's *done*. That's *out*. Good-bye, girlfriends!"

"Any more photos? You have a lot of nice old photographs. Maybe there are more inside."

"Here? Inside here? Nothing."

"You never know."

The top drawer, where once one would have found a bag of

tefillin, a tallis, a sex manual, the tablecloths, reveals itself, when opened, to be indeed empty. Her whole life was devoted to keeping things in drawers. Things to call ours. Debby's drawers, too, things to call hers. Michelle's drawers. All the existence, born and unborn, possible and impossible, in drawers. But empty drawers looked at long enough can probably drive you mad.

I kneel to open the door to the tall middle drawer. There is a box. A cardboard carton is there. *Not* nothing. On top of the box is marked "Morty's Things." My mother's writing. On the side, again in her writing, "Morty's Flag & things."

"No, you're right. Nothing here," and shut the sideboard's lower door.

"Oh, what a life, what a life," muttered Fish as he led me back to the living room sofa.

"Yeah, was it good, life? Was it good to live, Fish?"

"Sure. Better than being dead."

"So people say."

But what I was thinking really was that it all began with my mother's coming to watch over my shoulder what I did with Drenka up at the Grotto, that it was her staying to watch, however disgusting it was to her, it was her seeing me through all those ejaculations leading nowhere, that led me to here! The goofiness you must get yourself into to get where you have to go, the extent of the mistakes you are required to make! If they told you beforehand about all the mistakes, you'd say no, I can't do it, you'll have to get somebody else, I'm too smart to make all those mistakes. And they would tell you, we have faith, don't worry, and you would say no, no way, you need a much bigger schmuck than me, but they repeat they have faith that you are the one, that you will evolve into a colossal schmuck more conscientiously than you can possibly begin to imagine, you will make mistakes on a scale you can't even dream of now—*because there is no other way to reach the end.*

The coffin came home in a flag. His burned-up body buried first on Leyte, in an Army cemetery in the Philippines. When I was away at sea the coffin came back; they sent it back. My father wrote me, in his immigrant handwriting, that there was a flag on the coffin and after the funeral "the Army guy folded it up for mother in the offishul way." It's in that carton in the sideboard. It's fifteen feet away.

They were back together on the sofa holding hands. And he has no idea who I am. No problem stealing the carton. Just have to find the moment. It'll be best if Fish doesn't have to die in the process.

"I think, when I think of dying," Fish happened to be saying, "I think I wish I was never born. I wish I was never born. That's right."

"Why?"

"Cause death, death is a terrible thing. You know. Death, it's no good. So I wish I was never born." Angrily he states this. *I* want to die because I don't have to, *he* doesn't want to die because he does have to. "That's my philosophy," he says.

"But you had a wonderful wife. A beautiful woman."

"Oh, yeah, that I did."

"Two good children."

"Yeah. Yeah. Yes." The anger subsides, but only slowly, by degrees. He's not to be easily convinced that death can be redeemed by anything.

"You had friends."

"No. I didn't have too many friends. I didn't have time for friends. But my wife, she was a very nice woman. She passed away forty or fifty years ago already. Nice woman. As I say, I met her through my . . . wait a minute . . . her name is Yetta."

"You met her through Yetta. That's right. You met her through my mother."

"Her name was Yetta. Yes. I was introduced to her from the Bronx. I still can remember that. They were walking across the park. I took a walk. And I met them on the way. And they introduced me to her. And that's the girl I fell in love with."

"You have a good memory for a man your age."

"Oh, yeah. Thank God. Yes. What time is it now?"

"Almost one o'clock."

"Is it? It's late. It's time to put up my lamb chop. I make a lamb chop. And I have applesauce for dessert. It's almost one, you say?"

"Yeah. Just a few minutes to one."

"Oh, yeah? So I'm gonna put up, I call it my dinner."

"You cook the lamb chop yourself?"

"Oh, yeah. I put it in the oven. Takes about ten, fifteen minutes and it's done. Sure. I got Delicious apples. I put in an apple to bake. So that's my dessert. And then I have an orange. And that's what I call a good meal."

"Good. You take good care of yourself. Can you bathe yourself?" Get him in the bath, then walk off with the carton.

"No. I take a shower."

"And it's safe for you? You hold on?"

"Yeah. It's a closed shower, you know, with a curtain. I got a shower there. So that's where I shower. No problem at all. Once a week, yeah. I take a shower."

"And nobody ever drives you down to look at the ocean?"

"No. I used to love the ocean. I used to go bathing in the ocean. Many years ago already. I was a pretty good swimmer. I learned in this country."

"I remember. You were a member of the Polar Bear Club."

"What?"

"The Polar Bear Club."

"I don't remember that."

"Sure. A group of men who went swimming on the beach in the cold weather. They were called the Polar Bear Club. You would go out in the cold water in a bathing suit, go in the water, come right out. In the twenties. In the thirties."

"The Polar Bear Club, you say?"

"Yes."

"Yes. Yes. I do. I think I do remember that."

"Did you enjoy that, Fish?"

"The Polar Bear Club? I hated it."

"Why did you do it then?"

"I swear to God, I don't remember why I did it."

"You taught me, Fish. You taught me to swim."

"I did? I taught Irving. My son was born in Asbury Park. And Lois was born right here, upstairs in this house. In the bedroom. In the bedroom where I sleep now, she was born. Lois. The baby. She passed away."

In the corner of the living room that is back of Fish's head, there is an American flag rolled around a short pole. Fresh from reading the words "Morty's Flag & things," Sabbath

only now sees it for the first time. Is that it? Is there just the
carton there empty, in it none of Morty's things any longer,
and the flag from his coffin tacked to this pole? The flag looks
as washed out as the beach chair in the yard. If this cleaning
lady were interested in cleaning, she would have torn it up for
rags long ago.

"How come you have an American flag?" Sabbath asked.

"I got it quite a few years already. I don't know how I got it,
but I got it. Oh, wait a minute. I think it was from the Belmar
bank. When I piled up money, they gave me this flag. This
American flag. In Belmar I used to be a depositor. Now, good-
bye, deposits."

"Do you want to have your dinner, Fish? Do you want to
go in and make your lamb chop? I'll sit right here if you want
me to."

"It's all right. I got time. It wouldn't run away."

Fish's laughing getting more and more like a laugh.

"And you still have a sense of humor," said Sabbath.

"Not much."

So, even if nothing is left in the carton, I will come away
having learned two things today: the fear of death is with you
forever and a shred of irony lives on and on even in the simplest Jew.

"Did you ever think that you would live to be a man a hundred years old?"

"No, I really didn't. I heard about it in the Bible, but I really
didn't. Thank God, I made it. But how long I'm going to last,
God knows."

"How about your dinner, Fish? How about your lamb
chop?"

"What is this here? Can you see this?" In his lap again are
the two pieces of mail he was fiddling with when I came in.
"Will you read it to me? It's a bill, or what?"

" 'Fischel Shabas, 311 Hammond Avenue.' Let me open it up.
Comes from Dr. Kaplan, the optometrist."

"Who?"

"Dr. Kaplan, the optometrist. In Neptune. Inside is a card.
I'll read it. 'Happy Birthday.' "

"Oh!" The recognition pleases him inordinately. "What's
his name here?"

"Dr. Benjamin Kaplan, the optometrist."

"The optometrist?"

"Yeah. 'Happy Birthday to a Wonderful Patient.'"

"Never heard of him."

"'Hope your birthdays are as special as you are.' Did you have a birthday recently?"

"Yeah, sure."

"When was your birthday?"

"The first of April."

Right. April Fool's Day. My mother always thought this appropriate for Fish. Yes, that distaste of hers was for his pecker. Unfathomable otherwise.

"So this is a birthday card."

"A birthday card? The name is what?"

"Kaplan. A doctor."

"That's a doctor I never heard of. Maybe he heard about my birthday. And the other one?"

"Shall I open it up?"

"Yeah, sure, go ahead."

"From the Guaranty Reserve Life Insurance Company. I don't think it's anything."

"What does he say there?"

"They want to sell you a life insurance policy. It says, 'Life insurance policy available to ages forty to eighty-five.'"

"You can throw it out."

"So that's the only mail there is."

"The heck with that."

"No, you don't need that. You don't need a life insurance policy."

"No, no. I got one. I think about five thousand dollars or something. My neighbor, he pays for it all the time. That's the policy. I never carry big insurance. For who? For what? Five thousand dollars is enough. So he takes care of that. After my death it'll bury me, and he gets the rest." He pronounces "death" like "debt."

"Who knows," Fish says, "how much longer have I got to live? The time is running out. Sure. How much more can I live after a hundred years? Very little. If I have a year or two I'll be lucky. If I have an hour or two I'll be lucky."

"How about your lamb chop?"

"A guy is supposed to come from the Asbury Park *Press* to interview me. At noon."

"Yes?"

"I left the door open. He didn't show up. I don't know why."

"To interview you about being a hundred?"

"Yeah. For my birthday. At noon. Maybe he got cold feet or something. What is your name, Mister?"

"My first name is Morris. Mickey is what they've called me since I was a boy."

"Wait a minute. I knew a Morris. From Belmar. Morris. It'll come to me."

"And my last name is Sabbath."

"Like my cousin."

"That's exactly right. On McCabe Avenue."

"And the other guy, the name is also Morris. Oh, gee. Morris. Huh. It'll come to me."

"It'll come to you after you eat your lamb chop. Come on, Fish," I said, and here I lifted him onto his feet. "You are going to eat now."

Sabbath never got to see him make the lamb chop. He would have liked to. He would very much have liked to see the lamb chop itself. It would have been fun, thought the puppeteer, to watch him make the lamb chop and then, when he turned around, take the lamb chop quickly and eat it. But as soon as he got Fish into the kitchen, he excused himself to go upstairs to use the bathroom and returned to the dining room, where he lifted the carton out of the sideboard—it was not empty—and carried it out of the house.

The black woman was still on the top step of the porch, sitting there now and watching the rain come down as she listened to the music on the radio. Awfully happy. Another one on Prozac? Features that could be part Indian. Young. Ron and I were taken by the other sailors to a district on the outskirts of Veracruz. A kind of nightclub that's half outside, sleazy and shabby, in a honky-tonk district with strings of lights and dozens and dozens of young women and sailors at crude tables. As they made their bargains and finished their drinking, they retired to a low-slung row of houses where there were the rooms. All the girls were a mixture. We're on the Yucátan peninsula—the Mayan past is not far away. Admixture of races, always mystifying. Takes a person to the depths of living. This girl was a sweetheart with a lovely personality. Very dark. Decent, smiling, engaging, warm in every way. Probably twenty or under. She was lovely, there was no hurry, there was no rush. I remember her using some kind of ointment on me afterward that stung. Maybe this astringent stuff was supposed to forestall any disease. Very nice girl. Just like her.

"How's the old man?"

"Eatin' his lamb chop."

"Yipp*ee*," she cried.

Christ, I'd like to meet her! Don't stop bangin'. No. Too old. Finished with that. That's *done*. That's *out*. Good-bye, girlfriends.

"You from Texas? Where'd you get that yippee? Yippee-ki-yo-ki-yay."

"That's only when cattle's involved," she said, laughing with her mouth open wide. "Whoopee ti-yi-yo, git along, little dogies!"

"What is a dogie, anyway?"

"A little stunted calf whose mother's left it. A dogie's a calf that's lost its mom."

"You're a real cowpuncher. I took you first for an Asbury girl. I like you, ma'am. I hear your spurs ajinglin'. What do they call you?"

"Hopalong Cassidy," she told him. "What do they call you?"

"Rabbi Israel, the Baal Shem Tov—the Master of God's Good Name. The boys at the shul here call me Boardwalk."

"Nice to meet ya."

"Let me tell you a tale," he said, brushing his beard with a raised shoulder while, by the side of his car, cradling in his two arms the box of Morty's things. "Rabbi Mendel once boasted to his teacher, Rabbi Elimelekh, that evenings he saw the angel who rolls away the light before the darkness, and mornings the angel who rolls away the darkness before the light. 'Yes,' said Rabbi Elimelekh, 'in my youth I saw that, too. Later on you don't see those things anymore.'"

"I don't get Jewish jokes, Mr. Boardwalk." She was laughing again.

"What kind of jokes *do* you get?"

But from within the carton, Morty's American flag—which I know is folded there, at the very bottom, in the official way—tells me, "It's against some Jewish law," and so, on into the car he went with the carton, and then he drove it down to the beach, to the boardwalk, which was no longer there. The boardwalk was gone. Good-bye, boardwalk. The ocean had finally carried it away. The Atlantic is a powerful ocean. Death is a terrible thing. That's a doctor I never heard of. Remarkable. Yes, that's the word for it. It was all remarkable. Good-bye, remarkable. Egypt and Greece good-bye, and good-bye, Rome!

Here's what Sabbath found in the carton on that rainy, misty afternoon, Morty's birthday, Wednesday, April 13, 1994, his car, with the out-of-state plates, the only car on Ocean Avenue by the McCabe Avenue beach, parked diagonally, all by itself, looking toward the sloshing-unimpressively-about sea god as it grayly swept southward in the tail end of the storm. There was nothing before in Sabbath's life like this carton, nothing approached it, even going through all of Nikki's gypsy clothes after there was no more Nikki. Awful as that closet was, by comparison with this box it was nothing. The pure, monstrous purity of the suffering was new to him, made any and all suffering he'd known previously seem like an imitation of suffering. This was the passionate, the violent stuff, the worst, invented to torment one species alone, the remembering animal, the animal with the long memory. And prompted merely by lifting out of the carton and holding in his hand what Yetta Sabbath had stored there of her older son's. This was what it felt like to be a venerable boardwalk jerked from its moorings by the Atlantic, a worn, well-made, old-fashioned boardwalk running the length of a small oceanside town, immovably bolted onto creosoted piles as thick around as a strong man's chest and, when the familiar old waves turn on the coast, jiggled up and out like a child's loose tooth.

Just things. Just these few things, and for him they were the hurricane of the century.

Morty's track letter. Dark blue with the black trim. A winged sneaker on the crossbar of the *A*. On the back a tiny tag: "The Standard Pennant Co. Big Run, Pa." Wore it on the light blue letter sweater. The Asbury Bishops.

Photo. Twin-engine B-25—not the J he went down in but the D he trained in. Morty in undershirt, fatigue pants, dog tags, officer's cap, parachute straps. His strong arms. A good kid. His crew, five altogether, all of them on the airstrip, mechanics servicing one engine behind them. "Fort Story, Virginia" stamped on back. Looking happy, sweet as hell. The watch. My Benrus. This watch.

Portrait photo taken by La Grotta of Long Branch. A boy in cap and uniform.

Photo. Throwing the discus at the stadium. Getting ready to make his circle, arm back behind him.

Photo. Action shot. The discus released, five feet out in front of him. His mouth open. The dark undershirt with the *A* emblem, the skimpy blue shorts. Pale color photo. Runny like watercolor. His open mouth. The muscles.

Two little recordings. No memory of these at all. One addressed from him at 324 C.T.D. (Air Crew), State Teachers College, Oswego, New York. "This living record was recorded at a USO Club operated by the YMCA." His voice is on this record. Addressed to "Mr. and Mrs. S. Sabbath and Mickey."

A metal backing on the second record. "This 'letter-on-record' is one of the many services enjoyed by the men of the armed forces as they use the USO 'A HOME AWAY FROM HOME.'" VOICE-O-GRAPH. Automatic Voice Recorder. To Mr. and Mrs. S. Sabbath and Mickey. He always included me.

Isosceles triangles of red, white, and blue satin, stitched together to make a yarmulke. White triangle at the front shows a *V*, below the *V* dot-dot-dot-dash—the Morse code for *V*. "God Bless America" beneath that. A patriot's yarmulke.

A miniature Bible. *Jewish Holy Scriptures.* Inside, in light-blue ink, "May the Lord bless you and keep you, Arnold R. Fix, Chaplain." Opening page headed "The White House." "As Commander-in-Chief I take pleasure in commending the reading of the Bible to all who serve . . ." Franklin Delano Roosevelt commends "the reading of the Bible" to my brother. The way they got these kids to die. Commends.

Abridged Prayer Book for Jews in the Armed Forces of the United States. A brown palm-size book. In Hebrew and

English. Between two middle pages, sepia snapshot of the family. We're in the yard. His hand on my father's shoulder. My father in his suit, vest, even a pocket hankie. What's up? Rosh Hashanah? I'm dressed to kill in a "loafer" jacket and slacks. My mother in coat and a hat. Morty in a sports jacket but no tie. Year he went in. Took it along with him. Look at what a good kid he is. Look at Dad—like Fish, a camera and he's frozen stiff. My little mother under her veiled hat. Carried our picture in his prayer book for Jews in the armed forces of the United States. But he didn't die because he was a Jew. Died because he was an American. They killed him because he was born in America.

His toilet case. Brown leather engraved "MS" in gold. About six by seven by three. Two packets of capsules inside. Sustained-release capsules. Dexamyl. To relieve both anxiety and depression. Dexedrine 15 mg. and amobarbital 1½ gr. (Amobarbital? Morty's or Mom's? Did she use his case for her own stuff when she went nuts?) Half a tube of Mennen brushless shave. Little green and white cardboard pepper shaker of Mennen talcum for men. Shasta Beauty Shampoo, a gift from Procter & Gamble. Nail scissors. Tan comb. Mennen Hair Creme for Men. Still smells. Still creamy! One unlabeled bottle, contents dried up. Imitation enamel box, bar of Ivory soap inside, unopened. A black Majestic Dry Shaver in a small red box. With cord. Hairs in the head of it. The microscopic hairs of my brother's beard. That is what they are.

A black leather money belt, supple from being worn next to his skin.

Black plastic tube containing: Bronze medal inscribed "Championship 1941 3rd Senior Discus." Dog tag. "A" for blood type, "H" for Hebrew. Morton S Sabbath 12204591 T 42. Mother's name beneath his. Yetta Sabbath 227 McCabe Ave Bradley Beach, NJ. A round yellow pin that says "Time for Saraka." Two bullets. A red cross on a white button and the words "I Serve" at the top. Second lieutenant bars, two sets. Bronze wings.

A red and gold tea chest the size of a small brick. Swee-Touch-Nee Tea. (From the house, wasn't it, to put doodads in, wire, keys, nails, picture hangers? Morty take it with him or

did she just put his things there when they came back?)
Patches. The Air Apaches. The 498th Squadron. The 345
Bomb Group. I can still tell which is which. Ribbons. The
wings from his cap.

Clarinet. In five pieces. The mouthpiece.

A diary. The Ideal Midget Diary Year 1939. Only two entries.
For August 26: "Mickey's birthday." For December 14: "Shel
and Bea got married." Our cousin Bea. My tenth birthday.

A GI sewing kit. Mildewed. Pins, needles, scissors, buttons.
Some khaki-colored thread still left.

Document. American eagle. *E pluribus unum.* In grateful
memory of Second Lieutenant Morton S. Sabbath, who died
in the service of his country in the southwest Pacific area December 15, 1944. He stands in the unbroken line of patriots
who have dared to die that freedom might live, and grow, and
increase its blessings. Freedom lives, and through it, he lives—
in a way that humbles the undertakings of most men. Franklin
Delano Roosevelt, President of the United States of America.

Document. Purple Heart. The United States of America, to
all who shall see these presents, Greetings: This is to certify
that the President of the United States of America pursuant to
authority vested in him by Congress has awarded the Purple
Heart established by General George Washington at New-
burgh, N.Y., August 7, 1782, to Second Lieutenant Morton
Sabbath AS#0-827746, for military merit and for wounds received in action resulting in his death December 15, 1944,
given under my hand in the city of Washington the sixteenth
day of June 1945, Secretary of War Henry Stimson.

Certificates. Trees planted in Palestine. In Memory of Morton Sabbath, Planted by Jack and Berdie Hochberg. Planted
by Sam and Yetta Sabbath. For the Reforestation of Eretz Yis-
rael. Planted by the Jewish National Fund for Palestine.

Two small ceramic figures. A fish. The other an outhouse
with a kid sitting on the seat and another kid waiting his turn
around the corner. *We* were kids. We won it one night at the
Pokerino on the boards. Our joke. The Crapper. Morty took it
with him to the war. With the ceramic bluefish.

At the bottom, the American flag. How heavy a flag is! All
folded up in the official way.

He took the flag down with him onto the beach. There he unfurled it, a flag with forty-eight stars, wrapped himself in it, and, in the mist there, wept and wept. The fun I had just watching him and Bobby and Lenny, watching him with his friends, watching them just fool around, kid, laugh, tell jokes. That he included me in the address. That he always included me!

Not until two hours later, when he returned from tramping the beach wrapped in that flag—up through the sand to the Shark River drawbridge and back, crying all the way, rapidly talking, then wildly mute, then chanting aloud words and sentences inexplicable even to himself—not until after two solid hours of this raving about Morty, about the brother, about the one loss, he would never bull his way through, did he return to find in the car, on the floor beside the brake pedal, the packet of envelopes addressed in Morty's easy-to-read hand. They had dropped out of the carton while he was unpacking it, but he'd been too emotional to pick them up, let alone to read them.

And he'd come back because after two hours of staring into the sea and up at the sky and seeing nothing and everything and nothing, he'd thought that the frenzy was over and that he had regained possession of 1994. He figured the only thing that could ever swallow him up like that again would have to be the ocean. And all from only a single carton. Imagine, then, the history of the world. We are immoderate because grief is immoderate, all the hundreds and thousands of kinds of grief.

The return address was Lieutenant Morton Sabbath's APO number in San Francisco. Six cents via airmail. Postmarked November and December 1944. In a brittle rubber band that broke into bits the moment Sabbath slipped his finger beneath it, five letters from the Pacific.

To get a letter from him was always powerful. Nothing mattered more. The insignia of the U.S. Army at the top of the page and Morty's handwriting underneath, like a glimpse of Morty himself. Everybody read them ten times, twenty times, even after his mother had read them aloud at the dinner table. "There's a letter from Morty!" To the neighbors. Over the phone. "A letter from Morty!" And these were the last five.

Dec. 3, 1944

Dearest Mom, Dad & Mickey,

Hello everyone, how is every little thing at home. Some mail came in today & I thought sure that I had some however I was wrong. I think someone screwed up somewhere and I think I will try to locate it. If I can I am going to fly to New Guinea and check up.

I awoke at 9:20 this morning and shaved and then made some breakfast. It began raining again so I went down to my navigator tent and painted our Group insignia on my B.4 bag. It is an indian head and I am going to print the name Air Apaches. If you ever read about the Air Apaches you will know that it is our Group. I spent most of the afternoon painting and then we brewed up some tea and cookies for a "nosh."

Mom has anything ever been cut of my letters that I have been writing. I ate supper and then checked to see whether I was flying for tomorrow.

We played cards tonight and listened to the radio. We got some jazz. Incidently we won the game.

I got a bread from the mess hall and we have grape jelly so we made hot chocolate & ate bread & jelly this evening.

Well folks I guess thats about all for now so I will sign off with all my love. Don't work too hard & take good care of yourselves. Give everyone my love & Be Good.

May God Bless & keep you well.

Your loving son,
Mort

Dec. 7, 1944

Dearest Mom, Dad & Mickey,

Hi folks well another day is almost over and I am operations officer tonight. We have been flying pretty often around here as you probably have been reading in the newspaper.

There isn't much new around here that I haven't already told you. By the way if you read about the "Air Apaches" thats our Group so you will know that it was us on the mission. The war began three years ago today.

We put up our tent today and tomorrow I am going to try and put a wooden floor in. Wood is scarce around here but if you know where to go you can usually get some. We are fixing up a shower and a lot of odds and ends to make it homelike. The natives are eager to help us. They haven't much clothes for the Japs took most of it so we give them a few articles of clothes & they will do almost anything for us.

We have air raids quite often but they don't amount to much.

How are things going at home? The food here has gotten better & we had turkey for dinner & get plenty of vegetables.

Well folks since there isn't much more to write about so I will sign off for tonight. Take good care of yourselves & May God Bless you. I love you very much & think of home always.

Heres a big hug a kiss folks.

Good night.

Your loving son,
Mort

Dec. 9, 1944

Dearest Mom, Dad & Mickey,

Hi folks I received your v-mail the other day dated the 17th of Nov. and it sure was grand hearing from you. Mom don't use v-mail for it takes longer to get here then air-mail letters and you can write more in a letter. Your mail comes through now in a little over 14 days so things have straightened out. Let me know where Sid L. is as soon as you find out for if he comes over here I would like to look him up. As yet I haven't received your packages but they should arrive soon.

A few days ago I flew back to our old field to bring back a new plane. I have been here two days waiting and I again looked up Gene Hochberg and we had a good time seeing each other. I bought a new pair of GI shoes and mattress covers that I needed. I found my clothes here and picked up the laundry that I left when I went. Everything was intact and I bought more articles while here. I also purchased a case of grapefruit juice for they are good on a mission when you are thirsty. Last night I saw "When Irish Eyes are smiling" and it was very enjoyable. It rained last night and I was lazy and didn't get up until 10:30 AM.

I am glad to hear that everyone at home is feeling fine. I think I will see how Eugene is doing today. I gave him a wooden floor for his tent yesterday.

Well folks thats about all the bull for now. Be good & May God Bless you. I think of you always.

Your loving son,
Mort

Dec. 10, 1944

Dearest Mom, Dad, & Mickey,

Hello folks well we are still waiting for a new airplane. Yesterday I went to see Gene but I didn't stay long for I had to bring the jeep back to the squadron. I read Bob Hopes book "I never left home" and it was very good. It began to rain about then and kept up until chow time. I went to a friends tent and we played bridge for a few hours. Then we cooked up a little "nosh" of ham & eggs & onions & bread & hot chocolate.

I went to sleep quite late and got up for breakfast at 7:10 AM. Most of the morning I spent cleaning my moccasins with oil and then my co-pilot and I took our pistols and practiced firing at bottles and cans. When I returned I took my gun apart and oiled it. I finished reading my book and then ate dinner. I practised my clarinet.

In the evening I went to see one of our boys who is in the hospital and he should be getting out in a few days. Right now I am listening to the radio and writing to you.

How are things going at home? I sent home about $222 about a month ago and you haven't said anything about receiving the money-orders. If you received them let me know. And also if you are getting my bonds and $125 allotment every month.

Well folks be good, and take good care of yourselves. I miss you a lot & sure hope the war ends soon.

Good night and May God Bless you.

Your loving son,
Mort

Dec. 12, 1944

Dearest Mom, Dad & Mickey,

Well I finally returned today and I ferried a new ship here. I saw a good movie last night and when I returned to my tent we shot the bull for a few hours and hit the sack. I packed our ship in the morning and took off. We flew formation up and the new ships are a lot faster than the others.

The food here is very good and we are still working on our tent. We should have a wooden floor in soon.

We had fresh lamb for supper and good coffee. I picked up a lot of equipment for our tent while at our old field. Things are going quite well around here and I guess you read about the invasion up here. Naturally we participated in it.

How are things going at home? I haven't received mail for the last few days but there should be some tomorrow.

I'm sure glad to hear that Mickey is doing so well with the discus and the shot. Just keep after him and make him practice and who knows he might be in the Olympics.

Let me know whether you have received my money-order of $222 and war bond.

I guess we will be going on leave in a few months.

Well folks that's about all for now. I will keep on writing as often as I can when I have something to write.

Well Good night and May God Bless you. I think of you all often and hope to see you soon.

Your loving son,
Mort

The Japs shot him down the next day. He would be seventy. We would be celebrating his birthday. Only for a while was all this his, a very little while.

THE B-25D had a maximum speed at 15,000 feet of 284 miles per hour. It had a range of 1,500 miles. Empty it weighed 20,300 pounds. Wingspan of those flat gull wings 67 feet 7 inches. Length 52 feet 11 inches. Height 15 feet 10 inches. Two .5-inch nose guns and twin .5-inch guns in both the dorsal and the retractable ventral turrets. The normal bomb load was 2,000 pounds. Maximum permissible overload 3,600 pounds.

There was nothing Sabbath hadn't known about the North American Mitchell B-25 medium bomber and little that he couldn't remember, and remember precisely, while driving north in the dark with Morty's things beside him on the passenger seat. He remained wrapped in the American flag. Never take it off—why should he? On his head, the red, white, and blue *V* for Victory, God Bless America yarmulke. Dressing like this made not a scrap of difference to anything, transformed nothing, abated nothing, neither merged him with what was gone nor separated him from what was here, and yet he was determined never again to dress otherwise. A man of mirth must always dress in the priestly garb of his sect. Clothes are a masquerade anyway. When you go outside and see everyone in clothes, then you know for sure that nobody has a clue as to why he was born and that, aware of it or not, people are perpetually performing in a dream. It's putting corpses into clothes that really betrays what great thinkers we are. I liked that Linc was wearing a tie. And a Paul Stuart suit. And a silk handkerchief in his breast pocket. Now you can take him anywhere.

Jimmy Doolittle's raid. Sixteen B-25s, land-based planes, taking off from a carrier to drop their bombs 670 miles away. From the USS *Hornet*, April 18, 1942, fifty-two years ago next week. Six minutes over Tokyo, followed by hours of pandemonium in our house, two glasses of schnapps for Sam, the annual intake in a single night. Flew right over the palace of the God Emperor (who could have stopped his nutty admirals before it even began if God had given God Emperor just an

ordinary commoner's pair of balls). Only four months after
Pearl Harbor, first raid on Japan of the war—ten, eleven tons
of a medium-range bomber lifting off the deck sixteen times.
Then in February and March '45, the B-29s, the Super-
fortresses, out of the Marianas, burning them to a crisp at
night: Tokyo, Nagoya, Osaka, Kobe—but the biggest and best
of the B-29s, which did in Hiroshima and Nagasaki, were eight
months too late for us. The date to end the fucking thing was
Thanksgiving 1944—*that* would have been something to be
thankful for. We played cards tonight and listened to the radio.
We got some jazz. Incidentally we won the game.

The Jap bomber was the Mitsubishi G4M1. Their fighter
was the Mitsubishi Zero-Sen. Sabbath worried every night in
bed about the Zero. A math teacher at school who'd flown in
World War I said the Zero was "formidable." In the movies
they called it "deadly," and when he lay alone in the dark
beside Morty's empty bed, he couldn't do anything to get
"deadly" out of his head. The word made him want to scream.
The Jap carrier plane at Pearl Harbor had been the Nakajima
B5N1. Their high-altitude fighter was the Kawasaki Hien, the
"Tony" that gave the B-29s a hard time until LeMay moved
from Europe to XXI Bomber Command and switched from
day to nighttime fire raids. Our carrier planes: Grumman F6F,
Vought 54U, Curtiss P-40E, Grumman TBF-1—the Hellcat,
the Corsair, the Warhawk, the Avenger. The Hellcat, at 2,000
horsepower, *twice* as powerful as the Zero. Sabbath and Ron
could identify from cutout models the silhouettes of every
plane the Japs put up against Morty and his crew. The P-40
Warhawk, Ron's favorite American fighter, had a shark's
mouth painted under its nose when they used them as Flying
Tigers in Burma and China. Sabbath's favorite was Colonel
Doolittle's plane and Lieutenant Sabbath's, the B-25: two
1,700-horsepower Wright R-2600-9 fourteen-cylinder radial
engines, each driving a Hamilton-Standard propeller.

How could he kill himself now that he had Morty's things?
Something always came along to make you keep living, god-
damnit! He was driving north because he didn't know what
else to do but take the carton home, put it in his studio, and
lock it up there for safekeeping. Because of Morty's things he
was headed back to a wife who had nothing but admiration for

a woman in Virginia who had cut off her husband's dick in his sleep. But was the alternative to return the carton to Fish and then go back down to the beach and charge out into the rising tide? The blade head of the electric shaver contained particles of Morty's beard. In the case with the clarinet pieces was the reed. The reed from Morty's lips. Only inches from Sabbath, in the toilet case stamped "MS," was the comb with which Morty had combed his hair and the scissors with which Morty had clipped his nails. And there were recordings, two of them. On each, Morty's voice. And in his Ideal Midget Diary Year 1939, under August 26, "Mickey's birthday" written in Morty's hand. I cannot walk into the waves and leave this stuff behind.

Drenka. *Her* death. No idea that would be her last night. Every night saw pretty much the same picture. Got used to it. Visiting hours over at eight-thirty. Get there a little after nine. Wave to the night nurse, a good-natured buxom blond named Jinx, and just keep going down the hall to Drenka's darkened room. It's not allowed, but it is allowed if the nurse allows it. The first time Drenka asked, and after that nothing more had to be said. "I'm leaving now." Always mouthed this to the nurse on the way out: meaning, *There's no one with her now.* Sometimes when I left, she'd already be asleep from the morphine drip, her dried-out lips open and her eyelids not completely closed. Could see the whites of her eyes. Either leaving or coming I was sure that she was dead when I saw that. But the chest was moving. It was just the drugged-out state. The cancer everywhere. But her heart and her lungs were still okay, and I never dreamed she would go that night. Got used to the oxygen prong in her nose. Got used to the drainage bag pinned to the bed. Her kidneys were failing, yet there was always urine there when I checked the bag. Got used to that. Got used to the IV pole and the morphine drip hooked to the pump. Got used to the upper part of her no longer looking like it belonged to the bottom part. Emaciated from a little above the waist, and from the waist down—boy, oh boy— bloated, edemic. The tumor pressing on the aorta, decreasing the blood flow—Jinx explained it all, and he got used to the explanations. Under the blanket, out of sight, a bag so that the shit could come out somewhere—ovarian cancer hits the colon and bowel fast. If they'd operated she'd have bled to death.

Cancer too widespread for surgery. I'd got used to that, too.
Widespread. Okay. We can live with widespread. I'd show up,
we'd talk, I'd sit and watch her breathing through that open
mouth, asleep. Breathing. Yes, oh yes, how I had got used to
Drenka breathing! I'd come in, and if she was awake she'd say,
"My American boyfriend is here." Eyes and cheekbones beneath a gray turban appeared to be what was speaking to him.
Patches of hair all that was left. "I failed chemotherapy," she
told him one night. But he'd got used to that. "Nobody passes
everything," he told her. She'd just go on sleeping a lot with
her mouth open and her eyelids not completely closed, or
she'd be waiting, propped up on her pillow, comfortable on
the morphine drip—until she suddenly wasn't and she needed
a booster. But he'd got used to the booster. It was always
there. "She needs a little morphine booster," and Jinx was
always there to say, "I have your morphine, honey," and so
that was taken care of, and we could go on like this forever,
couldn't we? When she had to be turned and moved, Jinx was
always there to move her, and he was there to help, cupping
the tiny cup of cheekbones and eyes, kissing her forehead,
holding her shoulders to help move her; and when Jinx lifted
the blankets to turn her, he saw that the sheets and the pads
were all yellow and wet, the fluid just seeping out of her. When
Jinx turned her, to move her onto her back, onto her side, the
indentations of her fingers showed on Drenka's flesh. He'd
even got used to that, to that's being Drenka's flesh. "Something happened today." Drenka always told them a story while
they were repositioning her. "I thought I saw a blue teddy
bear playing with the flowers." "Well," laughed Jinx, "it's just
the morphine, honey." After the first time, Jinx whispered to
Sabbath in the hallway, to calm him down. "Hallucinating. A
lot of them do." The flowers where the blue teddy bears
played were from clients of the inn. There were so many bou-
quets the head nurse wouldn't allow them all in the room.
There were often flowers without cards. From the men. From
everybody who had ever fucked her. The flowers never
stopped coming. He'd got used to *that*.

Her last night. Jinx calling the next morning, after Rosie
had left for work. "She threw a clot—a pulmonary embolus.
She's dead." "How? How can that happen!" "Her blood work

was all out of kilter, the bed rest—look, it's a nice way to go. A very merciful killing." "Thanks, thanks. You're a good scout. Thanks for calling me. What time did she die?" "After you left. About two hours after." "Okay. Thanks." "I didn't want you to not know and to show up tonight." "Did she say anything?" "In the end she said something, but it was in that Croatian." "Okay. Thanks."

Driving Morty's things north for safekeeping, wrapped in his flag and wearing his yarmulke, driving in the dark with Morty's things and Drenka and Drenka's last night.

"My American boyfriend."

"Shalom."

"My secret American boyfriend." Her voice wasn't that weak, but he pulled the chair close to the bed, beside the irrigation bag, and held her hand in his. This was the way they did it now, night after night. "To have a lover of the country . . . I was thinking this all day, to tell you, Mickey. To have a lover of the country which one . . . it gave me the feeling of having the opening of the door. I was trying to remember this all day."

"The opening of the door."

"The morphine is bad for my English."

"We should have put your English on morphine long ago. It's better than ever."

"To have the lover, Mickey, to be very close that way, to be accepted by you, the American boyfriend . . . it made me less fearful about not understanding, not going to school here. . . . But having the American boyfriend and seeing the love from your eyes, it's all all right."

"It's all all right."

"So I don't get so fearful with an American boyfriend. That's what I was thinking all day."

"I never thought of you as fearful at all. I thought of you as bold."

She laughed at him, though with her eyes alone. "Oh my," she said. "So fearful."

"Why, Drenka?"

"Because. Because of everything. Because I don't have the intuition, the intuitive feeling about it. I've been working in this society so long and I had a child who grew up here and in the school system here . . . but in my own country I could have sorted it out with my fingertips. It was all a lot of work for me here, overcoming my inferiority complex at being the outsider. But all the small things I could understand, because of you."

"What small things?"

"'I pledge a legion to the flag.' It had no meaning. And the dancing. Remember? At the motel."

"Yes. Yes. The Bo-Peep-Lysol."

"And it isn't 'nuts and bulbs,' Mickey."

"What isn't?"

"The expression in English. Jinx said today, 'nuts and bolts,' and I thought, 'Oh God, it isn't "nuts and bulbs."' Matthew was right—it is 'nuts and *bolts.*'"

"It is? It can't be."

"You are a wicked boy."

"Call me practical."

"I was thinking today that I was pregnant again."

"Yes?"

"I was thinking I was back in Split. I was pregnant. Other people from the past were present."

"Who? Who was present?"

"In Yugoslavia I had fun, too, you know. In my city I had fun when I was young. A Roman palace is there, you know. An old palace that's in the central part of the place."

"In Split, yes, I do know. You told me years ago. Years and years ago, Drenka dear."

"Yes. The Roman guy. The emperor. Dioklecijan."

"It's an old Roman town on the sea," said Sabbath. "We both grew up by the sea. We both grew up loving the sea. *Aqua femina.*"

"Next to Split is a smaller place, a sea resort."

"Makarska," said Sabbath. "Makarska and Madamaska."

"Yes," said Drenka. "What a coincidence. The two places where I had the most fun. It *was* fun. We swim there. We spend all day on the beach. Dance in the evening. My first fuck was there. We sometimes have dinner. They would be serving this soup in these little bowls, and they would go and they would spill over you because they are not experienced, the waiters. They would come with a whole tray and they would carry it; they would come and they would serve it and they would spill it. America was so far away. I couldn't even dream of it. Then to be able to dance with you and hear you sing the music. I suddenly step that close to it. To America. I was dancing with America."

"Sweetheart, you were dancing with an unemployed adulterer. A guy with time on his hands."

"You *are* America. Yes, you are, my wicked boy. When we flew to New York and drove in on the highway, whatever the highway is, and those graveyards that are surrounded by cars and the traffic, and that was very confusing and frightening to me. I said to Matija, 'I don't like this.' I was crying. Motorized America with all the endless cars that never stop, and then, suddenly, the place of rest is between *that*. And they are thrown a little here and a little there. It's so very scary to me, so extremely opposite and different that I couldn't understand it. Through you it is all different now. Do you know? Through you I can think of those stones with understanding now. I only wish now I went places with you. I was wishing today, all day, thinking of the places."

"Which places?"

"To where you were born. I would have liked to go to the Jersey shore."

"We should have gone. I should have taken you."

Shoulda, Woulda, Coulda. The three blind mice.

"Even to New York City. To show it to me through your eyes. I would have liked that. Wherever we went, we always went to hide. I hate hiding. I wouldn't mind to go to New Mexico with you. To California with you. But mainly to New Jersey, to see the sea where *you* grew up."

"I understand." Too late, but I understand. That we don't perish of understanding everything too late, that is a miracle. But we *do* perish of that—of *just* that.

"If only," said Drenka, "we could have gone for a weekend to see the Jersey shore."

"You wouldn't need a weekend. From Long Branch to Spring Lake and Sea Girt, it's about eleven miles. You're driving in Neptune, down Main Street, and before you know it you're in Bradley Beach. You drive eight blocks in Bradley and you're in Avon. It was all pretty small."

"Tell me. Tell me." At the Bo-Peep too, she had always begged him to tell her, to tell her, to tell her. But to come up with something he hadn't told her, he'd have to think pretty hard. And suppose he should repeat himself? Did that matter to a dying person? To a dying person you can repeat yourself forever. They don't care. Just so they can still hear you talking.

"Well, it was small-town stuff. Drenka, you know that."

"Tell me. Please."

"Nothing very exciting ever happened to me. I was never quite in with the right kids, you know. Uncouth little runt, family didn't even belong to a 'beach club'—the rich broads from Deal weren't falling over one another pursuing me. I did manage somehow to get a couple hand-jobs in high school, but that was a fluke, didn't really count for much. Mostly we sat around and talked about what we would give if we could get laid. Ron, Ron Metzner, who nobody looked at back then because of his skin, used to try to console himself by saying to me, 'It has to happen sooner or later, doesn't it?' We didn't care who it was or even what it was, we just wanted to get laid. Then I got to be sixteen and all I wanted was to bust out."

"You went to sea."

"No, the year before that. The summer I was a lifeguard during the day. Had to be—on the beach were the dramatically endowed Jewish girls from North Jersey. And so I worked nights to supplement my shitty lifeguard pay. Had all kinds of after-school jobs, summer jobs, Saturday jobs. Ron's uncle had an ice cream franchise business. They'd come along like Good Humor, ding-a-ling. Blanketed the shore. I worked for him once, hawking Dixie cups from a bicycle truck. I had two, three jobs going in a single summer. Ron's father had a job with a cigar company. Salesman for Dutch Masters cigars. Colorful character to a hick kid. Grew up in South Belmar, the son of the cantor and mohel there, who in those days had a horse, a cow, and an outhouse, and a well in the backyard. Mr. Metzner was the size of a city block. Enormous man. Loved dirty jokes. Salesman for Dutch Masters cigars and he had opera on the radio on Saturday afternoons. Carried off by a heart attack as big as the Ritz when we were in our last year of high school. Why Ron went to sea with me—fleeing selling Popsicles for the rest of his life. Dutch Masters had their place up in Newark then. Mr. Metzner used to go up there twice a week to pick up cigars. During the winter, on Saturdays, when gas was rationed during the war, Ron and I made deliveries all over the county for him on our bikes. One winter I worked in ladies' shoes at Levin's Department Store in Asbury. Pretty good-size store. Asbury was a busy town. On Cookman Avenue alone, five or six shoe stores. I. Miller and so on. Tepper's. Steinbach's. Yep, Cookman was a great street before the riots carried it away. Ran from the beach right to Main Street. But did I never tell you that I was a ladies' shoes specialist as young as fourteen? The wonderful world of perversity, discovered it right there at Levin's in Asbury Park. The old salesguy used to lift the ladies' legs when he tried the shoes on them so I could see up their dresses. He used to take their shoes, when a customer came in, and put 'em far away where they couldn't reach 'em. Then the fun began. 'Now this shoe,' he'd tell them, 'is a genuine *shmatte*,' and all the time raising their leg up just a little higher. In the stockroom I'd smell the inner soles after they'd tried them on. A friend of my father's used to peddle socks and work pants to the farmers around Freehold. He'd go into the wholesalers in New York and then come back and I'd go out with him on a Saturday in his truck—when the truck started— and I'd sell and get to keep five dollars for myself at the end of the day. Yeah, a variety of jobs. A lot of the people I worked for would be quite surprised to know that I grew up to be a rocket scientist. That didn't look to be in the cards back then. The job where I could really pick up bucks was parking cars for Eddie Schneer. At night, down by the amusement area in Asbury, Ron and me, that summer I was a lifeguard. We'd park one car for Eddie and put a buck in his pocket, the other car for us and put a dollar in this pocket. Eddie knew, but my brother used to work for him, and Eddie loved Morty because he was a Jewish athlete and didn't hang around with the nutty, bummy-type hot-shot stars but came right home after practice to help his father. Besides, Eddie was in politics and real estate and a thief bastard himself, and he was making so much money he didn't even care. But he liked to scare me. His brother-in-law used to sit across the street and spot."

"What's 'spot'?"

"Bernie, the brother-in-law, would spot a hundred cars in

your area and you were supposed to have a hundred bucks in your pocket. Eddie had a big Packard and he would drive down to the area where I was working. He'd pull up, and out the car window he'd say to me, 'Bernie's been spotting you. He doesn't think you've been giving me my fair share. He thinks you're screwing me too much.' 'No, no, Mr. Schneer. None of us is screwing you too much.' 'How much do you take, Sabbath?' 'Me? I'm down to only half.' "

He'd done it—a laugh came from back in her throat, and her eyes were Drenka's! Drenka a-laughing. "You are the easiest shiksa to make laugh that ever was. Mr. Mark Twain said that. Yep, the summer before my brother got killed. Everybody was worried that because of Morty's being away I was getting in with the wrong crowd. Then he got killed in December, and the *next* year I went to sea. And *that's* when I got in with the wrong crowd."

"My American boyfriend." Now she was in tears.

"Why do you cry?"

"Because I couldn't be on that beach when you were a lifeguard. In the beginning here, before I met you, I was always crying about Split and Brač and Makarska. I was crying about my city with the narrow streets, the medieval streets, and all the old women all in black. I was crying for the islands and the inlets of the coastline. I was crying for the hotel on Brač, when I was a bookkeeper still with the railway and Matija was the handsome waiter dreaming of his inn. But then we began to make all the money. Then Matthew came. Then we began to make all the money. . . ." She was lost and took refuge behind her closed eyes.

"Is it pain? Are you in pain?"

Her eyes fluttered open. "I'm all right." It had been not pain but terror. But he had got used to that, too. If only she could. "They said about Americans that they are naive and not good lovers." Bravely Drenka went on. "This nonsense. Americans are more puritanistic. They don't like to show themselves naked. American men, they weren't able to talk about fucking. All this European cliché. I certainly learned that 'ain't' the case."

"Ain't. Very good. Excellent."

"See, American boyfriend? Eventually I am not so stupid a Croatian Catholic shiksa woman. I even learn to say 'ain't.'"

She'd also learned to say "morphine," a word it had never occurred to him to teach her. But without the morphine she felt as though she were being torn apart alive, as though a flock of black birds, huge birds, she said, were walking all over her bed and her body, tugging violently with their beaks inside her belly. And the sensation, she used to tell him . . . yes, she, too, loved the telling . . . the sensation of your coming inside me. I don't really feel the squirting, I can't, but the pulsation of the cock, and my contractions at the same time, and the whole thing so totally wet, I never know if it is my juice or your juice, and I am dripping from the cunt and I am dripping from the ass and I feel the drops coming down my legs, oh Mickey, so much juice, Mickey, all over, all so juicy, such an enormous wet sauce. . . . But lost now was the wet sauce, the pulsation, the contractions; lost to her now were the trips we never took, lost to her was *all of it*, her excesses, her willfulness, her wiliness, her recklessness, her amorousness, her impulsiveness, her self-division, her self-abandon—the sardonic and satiric cancer turning to carrion the female body that for Sabbath had been the most intoxicating of them all. The yearning to go endlessly on being Drenka, to go on and on and on being hot and healthy and herself, everything trivial and everything stupendous consumed now, organ by organ, cell by cell, devoured by the hungry black birds. Just the shard of the story now and the shards of her English, just bits of the core of the apple that was Drenka—only that was left. The juice flowing out of her was yellow now, oozing out of her yellow onto the pads, and yellow-yellow, concentrated yellow, into the irrigation bag.

There was a smile on her face after the morphine boost. Why, this little bit left of her looked almost sexy! Amazing. And she had a question to ask.

"Go ahead."

"Because I am almost blocked out about it. I could not remember today. Maybe you said, 'Yes, I want to piss on you, Drenka,' and whether I really wanted it, I don't think I really pondered so much upon that, how would it be, but I would say that to you, yes, you could, to make you hot and to make you happy, to do things that work for you, or something . . ."

Immediately after the morphine it was never easy to follow her. "And the question is what?"

"Who started? Was it that you took your dick out and said, 'I want to piss on you, Drenka. May I? I want to piss on you, Drenka'? Is that how it started?"

"Sounds like me."

"And then I thought, 'Oh well, this transgression, why not? Life is so crazy anyway.'"

"And why were you thinking about that today?"

"I don't know. They were changing my bed. The idea of tasting somebody else's piss."

"It was harrowing?"

"The idea? It was both harrowing and the idea was exciting. So then I remember you stood there, Mickey. In the stream. In the woods. And I was in the stream on the rocks. And you stood there, over me, and it was very hard for you to start getting it out, and finally there came a drop. Ohhh," she said, recalling that drop.

"Ohhh," he muttered, his grip tightening on her hand.

"It came down, and as it came upon me, I realized that it was warm. Do I dare to taste it? And I started with my tongue to lick around my lips. And there was this piss. And the whole idea that you were standing above me, and at first you strained to get it out, and then suddenly came this enormous piss, and it just came into my face and it was warm and it was just fantastic; it was exciting and everywhere and it was like a whirlwind, what I was feeling, the emotions. I don't know how to describe it more than that. I tasted it, and it tasted sweet, like beer. It had that kind of taste to it, and just something forbidden that made it so wonderful. That I could be allowed to do this that was so forbidden. And I could drink it and I wanted more as I was lying there and I wanted more, and I wanted it on my eyes and I wanted it in my face, I wanted lots of it in my face, I wanted to be showered by it in my face, and I wanted to drink it, and then, I wanted it all the way then, once I allowed myself to let go. And so I wanted everything of it, I wanted it on my tits. I remember you were standing over me, and you did it on my cunt also. And I started playing with myself as you were doing it, and you made me come, you know; I was coming while you were just squirting it over my cunt. It was very warm, it was so warm, I just felt totally . . . I don't know—taken by it. Then I come home afterward and I was sitting in the kitchen, remembering it, because I had to sort it through —did I like it or not—and I realized that, yes, it was like we had a pact; we had a secret pact that tied us together. I'd never done that before. I didn't expect to do it with anyone else, and today I was thinking I never will. But it really made me have a pact with you. It was like we were forever united in that."

"We were. We are."

Both crying now.

"And pissing on me?" he asked her.

"It was funny. I was unsure. Not so much that I wouldn't want to do it. But to let go of my own, you know—would you like my piss, the idea of abandoning myself in that way to you, because I was sort of, not that I wouldn't like it, but how would you react to it, my own piss in your face? You wouldn't like the way it tasted, or that I would offend you. So I was shy about it at first. But once I started doing it, and I realized that it was okay, that I didn't have to be frightened, and seeing your reaction—you took some of it, you even drank some of it . . . and . . . and . . . I like it. And I had to stand above you, and so it made me feel that I can do anything, anything with you, and anything is all right. We're in this together, and we can do anything together, everything together, and, Mickey, it was just wonderful."

"I have a confession to make."

"Oh? Tonight? Yes? What?"

"I was not so delighted to drink it."

A laugh came out of that tiny face, a laugh a lot bigger than the face.

"I wanted to do it," Sabbath told her. "And when it first began to come out of you, it came out in a little trickle. That was okay. But then when it came the full stuff—"

" 'But then when it came the full stuff'? You are talking like me! I have made you speak translated Croatian! I taught you, too!"

"You sure did."

"So tell me, tell me," she said excitedly. "So what happened when it began to come out the full stuff?"

"The warmth. I was astonished by it."

"Exactly. But it's very pleasant that it's warm."

"And there I was, between your legs, and I had to take it in my mouth. And Drenka, I wasn't sure I wanted to."

She nodded. "Uh-huh."

"You could tell?"

"Yes. Yes, darling."

"It thrilled me mostly because I could see it was thrilling you."

"And it really was. It was."

"I could see that. And that was enough for me. But I couldn't abandon myself to drinking it quite the way you could."

"You. How strange," she said. "Tell me about that."

"I guess I have idiosyncrasies, too."

"How did it taste to you? Was it sweet? Because yours was very sweet. Beer and sweet together."

"Do you know what you said, Drenka? When you finished the first time?"

"No."

"You don't remember? When you finished pissing on me?"

"Do you remember?" she asked.

"Could I forget? You were radiant. You were glowing. You said, triumphantly, 'I did it! I did it!' It made me think, 'Yes, Roseanna drank all the wrong stuff.'"

"Yes," she laughed, "yes, I think maybe I did. Yes, you see, that fits what I told you, that I was so shy. Exactly. It was like I passed a test. No, not to pass a test. As though . . ."

"As though what?"

"Maybe what I was worried about was that I would regret it. There are many times when one has ideas to do things or maybe you get led in to do something, and afterward there's a sense of shame. And I wasn't sure—would I have shame for it? That was what was so incredible about it. And now I even love to talk about it with you. It was a lustful feeling . . . and a feeling of giving, also. In a way that I could not do to anyone else."

"By pissing on me?"

"Yes. And allowing you to piss on me. I feel that, I felt that—you were totally with me then. In all senses, as I was lying there afterward in the stream with you, holding you in the stream, in all senses, not just as my love; as my friend, as someone, you know, when you are sick I can help you, and as my total blood brother. You know, it was a rite, a passage of a rite or something."

"Rite of passage."

"Yes. Rite of passage. Very definitely. That's true. It's so forbidden and yet it has the most innocent meaning of anything."

"Yes," he said, looking at her dying, "how innocent it is."

"You were my teacher. My American boyfriend. You taught me everything. The songs. Shit from Shinola. To be free to fuck. To have a good time with my body. To not hate having such big tits. You did that."

"About fucking you knew before you met me, Drenka dear, at least a little something."

"But in my life, married, I didn't have many outlets in this regard."

"You did all right, kid."

"Oh, Mickey, it was wonderful, it was fun—the whole kitten and kaboozle. It was like *living*. And to be denied that whole part would be a great loss. You gave it to me. You gave me a double life. I couldn't have endured with just one."

"I'm proud of you and your double life."

"All I regret," she said, crying again, crying with him, the two of them in tears (but he had got used to that—we can live with widespread and we can live with tears; night after night, we can live with *all* of it, as long as it doesn't stop), "is that we couldn't sleep together too many nights. To commingle with you. Commingle?"

"Why not."

"I wish tonight you could spend the night."

"I do, too. But I'll be here tomorrow night."

"I meant it up at the Grotto. I didn't want to fuck any more men, even without the cancer. I wouldn't do that even if I was alive."

"You are alive. It is here and now. It's tonight. You're alive."

"I wouldn't do it. You're the one I always loved fucking. But I don't regret that I have fucked many. It would have been a great loss to have had otherwise. Some of them, they were sort of wasted times. You must have that, too. Haven't you? With women you didn't enjoy?"

"Yes."

"Yes, I had experiences where the men would just want to fuck you whether they cared about you or not. That was always harder for me. I give my heart, I give my self, in my fucking."

"You do indeed."

And then, after just a little drifting, she fell asleep and so he went home—"I'm leaving now"—and within two hours she threw a clot and was dead.

So those were her last words, in English anyway. I give my heart, I give my self, in my fucking. Hard to top that.

To commingle with you, Drenka, to commingle with you now.

Amid the dark fields, halfway up the hill, the living room lights were softly burning. From the bottom of the steep drive, where he paused to reconsider what he was doing—what he had already half-thinkingly done—the lights made the house look cozy enough for him to call the place home. But from outside, at night, they all look cozy. Once you're no longer outside looking in but inside looking out . . . Still, the closest he had to a home was this one, and because he couldn't leave what was left of Morty nowhere, here was where he'd come with Morty's things. Had to. He was not a beggar any longer, not a mischievous intruder nor was he washing in toward shore somewhere south of Point Pleasant, nor at dawn would someone out for a jog along the beach with the Lab find his remains among the night's debris. Nor was he boxed in beside Schloss. He was custodian of Morty's things.

And Rosie? I'll bet I can keep her from cutting off my dick. Start there. Set modest goals. See if you can get through the rest of April without her cutting it off. After that, you can raise your sights a little. But begin with just that and see if it's doable. If it's not, if she does cut it off, well, then you'll have to rethink your position. Then you and Morty's things will have to find a home elsewhere. In the meantime, display to her not the least apprehension about being mutilated in your sleep.

And don't forget the benefits of her stupidity. One of the first rules of any marriage. (1) Don't forget the benefits of her (his) stupidity. (2) She (he) cannot be taught anything by you, so don't try. There were ten of these he'd worked up for Drenka to help her through a stretch with Matija when just the meticulous way Matija double-tied his shoelaces made her see life as nothing but blackness. (3) Take a vacation from your grievances. (4) The regularity of it isn't totally worthless. Et cetera.

You could even fuck her.

Now, this was an odd thought to have. He could not, on reflection, remember thinking anything more aberrant in his entire life. When they'd moved up north, of course, he used to fuck Rosie all the time, into her up to the hilt all the time. But when they'd come up here, she was twenty-seven. No, first thing was to keep her from cutting off his dick. Trying to fuck her could even work against him. Modest goals. You're just looking for a home for you and Mort.

In the living room she would be reading, in there with a fire going, stretched out on the sofa, reading something somebody at the meeting had given her. That's all she read now—the Big Book, the Twelve-Step Book, meditation books, pamphlets, booklets, an endless supply of them; not since leaving Usher had she stopped reading a new one that was just like the old one that she could not live without. First the meeting, then the booklets by the fire, then in bed with Ovaltine and the "Personal Story Section" of the Big Book, alcoholics' anecdotes with which she put herself to sleep. He believed that when the lights were out she prayed some AA prayer in bed. At least she had the decency, in his presence, never to mutter the thing aloud. Though sometimes he gave it to her anyway—who could resist? "You know what my Higher Power is, Rose-anna? I've figured out what my Higher Power is. It's *Esquire* magazine." "Couldn't you be more respectful? You don't understand. This is a very serious business for me. I'm in recovery." "And how long is that going to last again?" "Well, it's a day at a time, but it will be forever. It isn't something that you can just put aside. You have to keep going." "I guess I won't see the end of it, will I?" "You can't. Because it's a constant process." "All your art books on those shelves. You never look at one. You never look at a picture in any of them." "I don't feel guilty, Mickey. I don't need art. I need this. This is my medicine." "*Came to Believe. Twenty-four Hours. The Little Red Book.* It's an awfully tiny aperture onto life, my dear." "I'm trying to get some peace. Some inner peace. Serenity. I'm getting in touch with my inner self." "Tell me, whatever happened to the Roseanna Cavanaugh who could think for herself?" "Oh, her? She married Mickey Sabbath. That took care of that."

In her robe, reading that shit. He imagines her, robe undone, holding her book with her right hand while diddling herself idly with the left. Ambidextrous, but happens to feel more comfortable playing around with the left. Reading and not even aware for a while that she is starting up. A bit distracted by the reading. Tends to like to have some cloth between her hand and her pussy. Nightgown, robe—tonight, panties. The material turns her on; why that is she doesn't quite know. Uses three fingers: outer fingers on the lips, middle finger pressing the button. Circular movement of the fingers, and soon the pelvis in a circular movement, too. Middle finger on the button—not the tip of the finger, the ball of the finger. First a very light pressure. Knows automatically where the button is, of course. Then a little pause, because she's still reading. But it's getting more difficult to concentrate on what she is reading. Not sure she wants to do it yet. The pressure of the ball of the two fingers surrounding the button. As she gets more excited, the ball of one finger is right on the button yet the feeling is somehow spread by the other fingers. Finally she puts the book down. Intermittently now, her fingers are still while her pelvis does the moving. Then back on the button, round and round, the other hand on her breast, on her nipples, squeezing. She has now decided that she is not going to be reading for a while. Takes her right hand down from her breast and rubs the whole thing forcefully with both hands, still outside the material. Three fingers next, over where the button is. Always knows exactly where it is, which is better than I can say for myself. Nearly fifty years on the job, and still the damn thing is there and then it's here and then it's gone and you can spend half a minute looking everywhere before kindly her hands reposition you. "There! No, *there*! Right there! Yes! Yes!" And now she stretches her legs straight out, a long cat stretch, her hands pressed tight between her thighs. Squeezing. Manages a pre-come that way, a *forshpeis*, squeezing the whole cunt hard as she can, and now she has decided: she doesn't want to stop. Sometimes she does it through the cloth the whole way; tonight she wants her fingers on the inside of the lips and she pushes the panties aside. Going up and down now, straight up and down, and not in a circular motion. And faster, going much faster. Then, using the other hand, she slips her middle finger (elegant long finger it is, too) into her cunt. Very fast with it, until she feels the first premonitory convulsions. Moves her legs back up now, spreading the legs apart while bending the knees and bringing the feet together so that, almost beneath her buttocks, the toes are touching. Opens herself up all the way. Wide open now. And constant contact with two fingers on the cut, the middle finger and the ring finger. Up and down. Tensing herself. Buttocks up now, raising herself up on her bent legs. Now she slows down a little. Stretches her legs out to slow it down, bringing it all almost to a stop. Almost. And now she bends her legs up again. This is the position in which she wants to come. Here begins the muttering. "Can I? Can I?" All the while she is making the decision *when*, she is muttering aloud, "Can I? Can I? Can I come?" Whom does she ask? The imaginary man. Men. The whole lot of them, one of them, the leader, the masked one, the boy, the black one, asking herself maybe or her father, or asking no one at all. The words alone are enough, the begging. "Can I? Can I come? Please, can I?" And now she is keeping the pressure even, now a little harder, increasing the pressure, constant pressure, *just right there*, and now she feels it, she feels it, now she's got to keep going— "Can I? Can I? Please?"—and here are the noises, ladies and gentlemen, in combinations peculiar to each woman alone, the noises that could serve as well as fingerprints to individualize the whole sex for the FBI—ohh, ummmm, ahhh—because now she's started, she's coming, and the pressure is harder but not extremely hard, not so hard that it hurts, two fingers up and down, wide pressure, she wants *wide pressure* because she wants to come again, and now the feeling is moving down toward the cunt, and she puts her finger in, and now she

thinks she could enjoy having a dildo there, but she's got her
finger there, and that's, that's IT! And so she goes up and
down with her finger as though somebody were fucking her,
and voluntarily now she tightens her cunt to increase the feeling, squeezes tight to give herself more feeling, up and down,
while still working the clit. It changes what she feels when she
introduces her finger into her cunt—on the button it's very
precise, but with the finger in her cunt the feeling is distributed, and that's what she wants: *the distribution of the feeling.*
Though it's physically not easy to coordinate the two hands,
with supreme concentration she works to overcome the difficulty. And does. Ohhhh. Ohhhh. Ohhhh. And then she lies
there and she pants for a while, and then she picks up the book
and goes back to her reading, and, in all, there is much here to
be compared with Bernstein conducting Mahler's Eighth.

Sabbath felt like offering a standing ovation. But seated in
the car at the foot of the long dirt drive leading up nearly a
hundred yards to the house, he could only stamp his feet and
cry, "Brava, Rosie! Brava!" and lift his God Bless America yarmulke in admiration of the crescendos and, the diminuendos,
of the floating and the madness, of the controlled uncontrol-
lableness, of the sustained finale's driving force. Better than
Bernstein. His wife. He'd forgotten all about her. Twelve, fifteen years since she let me watch. What *would* it be like to fuck
Roseanna? A percentage of guys still do it to their wives, or so
the pollsters would have us believe. Wouldn't be totally freak-
ish. Wonder what the smell is like. If she even. The swampy
scent Roseanna exuded in her twenties, most unique, not at all
fishy but vegetative, rooty, in the muck with the rot. Loved it.
Took you right to the edge of gagging, and then, in its depths
something so sinister that, boom-o, beyond repugnance into
the promised land, to where all one's being resides in one's
nose, where existence amounts to nothing more or less than
the feral, foaming cunt, where the thing that matters most in
the world—*is* the world—is the frenzy that's in your face.
"There! No—*there!* Right . . . *there!* There! There! There!
Yes! There!" Their ecstatic machinery would have dazzled
Aquinas had his senses experienced its economy. If anything
served Sabbath as an argument for the existence of God, if
anything marked creation with God's essence, it was the thou-

sands upon thousands of orgasms dancing on the head of that pin. The mother of the microchip, the triumph of evolution, right up with the retina and the tympanic membrane. I wouldn't mind growing one myself, in the middle of my forehead like Cyclops's eye. Why do they need jewelry, when they have that? What's a ruby next to that? There for no reason other than the reason that it's there for. Not to run water through, not to spread seed, but included in the package like the toy at the bottom of the old Cracker Jack box, a gift to each and every little girl from God. All hail the Maker, a generous, wonderful, fun-loving guy with a real soft spot for women. Much like Sabbath himself.

There was a home, inside it a wife; in the car were things to revere and protect, replacing Drenka's grave as the meaning and the purpose of his life. He need never lie down weeping on her grave again, and, thinking that, he was seized by the miracle of having survived all these years in the hands of a person like himself, astonished at having discovered amid Fish's squalor a reason to go on at the mercy of the inexplicable experience that he was and astonished by the nonsensical thought that he wasn't, that he hadn't survived himself, that he had perished down there in Jersey, very likely by his own hand, and that he was at the foot of the drive of the afterlife, entering that fairy tale freed at last from the urge that was the hallmark of his living: the overwhelming desire to be elsewhere. He *was* elsewhere. He had achieved the goal. Now it was clear to him. If that little house halfway up that hill on the outskirts of this little village where I am the biggest scandal around, if that isn't elsewhere, nothing is. Elsewhere is wherever you are; elsewhere, Sabbath, is your home and no one is your mate, and if ever anyone was no one it's Rosie. Search the planet and you will not find at any latitude a setup more suitable than this one. This is your niche: the solitary hillside, the cozy cottage, the Twelve-Step wife. *This* is Sabbath's Indecent Theater. Remarkable. As remarkable as the women coming out of their houses and onto the street to buy their stringbeans from Fish's truck. Hello, remarkable.

But nearly an hour after the lights had gone out at the front of the house and come on again in their bedroom around to the side by the carport, Sabbath was still a hundred yards away, down at the bottom of the drive. Was the afterlife really for him? He was having serious second thoughts about having killed himself. All he'd had to struggle through before was the prospect of oblivion. Alongside fellow mariner Schloss, across from the esteemed Weizmans, a stone's throw from all the family, but oblivion is oblivion nonetheless, and getting himself ready for it had not been simple. What he could never have imagined was that, after being left there to rot overseen by those dogs, he would find himself not in oblivion, oblivious, but in Madamaska Falls; that instead of facing the eternal nothing he would be back in that bed with Rosie beside him, forever seeking inner peace. But then, he had never figured on Morty's things.

He took the driveway curves just as slowly as the car could negotiate them. If he was years in reaching the house it would make no difference now. He was dead, death was changeless, and there was no longer the illusion of ever escaping. Time was endless or it had stopped. Amounted to the same thing. All the fluctuation's gone—that's the difference. No flux, and flux was human life all over.

To be dead and to know it is a bit like dreaming and knowing it, but, oddly, everything was *more* firmly established dead. Sabbath didn't feel spectral in any way: his sense couldn't have been *sharper* that nothing was growing, nothing altering, nothing aging; that nothing was imaginary and nothing was real, no longer was there objectivity or subjectivity, no longer any question as to what things are or are not, everything simply held together by death. No way around his knowing that he was no longer on a day-to-day basis. No worry about suddenly dying. Suddenness was over. Here for good in the nonworld of no choice.

Yet if this was death, whose pickup truck was parked in the carport beside Rosie's old jeep? A rippling American flag was resplendently painted across the width of its tailgate. Local plates. If all flux was gone, what the fuck was this? Somebody with local plates. There was more to death than people realized —and more to Roseanna.

In bed, they were watching television. That's why nobody

heard him drive up. Though he got the feeling—looking at the two of them nestled together, taking turns biting into a plump green pear, whose juice they licked from each other's taut bellies whenever it dribbled from their mouths—he got the feeling that nothing might have pleased Rosie more than knowing that her husband was back and couldn't miss finding out what had been happening while he was gone. In a corner of the bedroom all his clothes had been dumped on the floor, everything of his removed from the closet and the bureau drawers and piled in the corner, waiting to be bagged or cartoned or, when the weekend came, dragged up the hill to the ravine and pushed by the bedmates over the side.

Dispossessed. Ida had usurped his plot at the cemetery, and Christa from the gourmet shop—whose tongue Drenka had held in such high esteem and whom Rosie had waved hello to in town, just someone she knew from AA—had taken his place in the house.

If this was death, then death was just life incognito. All the blessings that make this world the entertaining place that it is exist no less laughably in the nonworld, too.

They watched television while, from the dark beyond the window, Sabbath watched them.

Christa would by now be twenty-five, but the only change that he could see was that the close-clipped blond hair had grown in black and that it was her cunt that had been shaved. Not the model child—never that, far from that—but the child model most provocatively. The hair fell elfinly in ragged little points about her head, as though an eight-year-old had scissored Christa an upside-down crown. The mouth was still no gaping thing, but the cold opening of a German slot machine, and yet the violet surprise of her eyes and the glazed Teutonic snowdrift of her ass, the sweet lure of those uncorroded curves, made her no less pleasant to ogle than when he'd faithfully stood by as assistant tool handler and she worked her lesbian magic on Drenka. And Roseanna, though nearly a foot taller than Christa—even Sabbath was taller than Christa—could hardly have been taken for more than twice Christa's age: even more slender than Christa, small-breasted like her, the breasts probably shaped much the same as when she moved to her mother's at thirteen. . . . Four years of no booze, followed by forty-eight hours without him, and his childless wife, in her sixth decade of life, miraculously looked to be still in bud.

The program they had on was about gorillas. Occasionally Sabbath got a glimpse of the gorillas knuckle-walking around in the tall grass or sitting about, scratching their heads and their asses. He discovered that gorillas do a lot of scratching.

When the program was over, Rosie switched off the set and, without a word, began to pretend that she was a mother gorilla grooming her little one, who was Christa. Watching from the window while they passed themselves off as gorilla mom and child, he began to remember how extensive a talent Rosie once displayed for following his lead when he was trying out stage voices at the dinner table or amusing her along these lines in bed, lipsticking a beard and cap onto the head of his prick and using his hard-on for a puppet. After the show she got to play with the puppet, every child's dream. The real ring of openness in her laughter then—spunky, heedless, a little wicked, nothing to hide (except everything), nothing to fear (except everything) . . . yes, distantly he could remember her enjoying his foolishness very much.

Nothing could have been more serious than the attention Rosie gave to Christa's gorilla coat. It was as though she were not only cleansing her of insects and lice but purifying both of them through this studious contact. All the emotions were invisible, and yet not a lifeless second passed between them. Rosie's gestures were of such delicacy and precision that they appeared to be in the conscientious service of some pure religious idea. Nothing was going on other than what was going on, but to Sabbath it seemed tremendous. Tremendous. He had arrived at the loneliest moment of his life.

Under his eyes, Christa and Rosie developed complete gorilla personalities—the two of them living in the gorilla dimension, embodying the height of gorilla soulfulness, enacting the highest act of gorilla rationality and love. The whole world was the other one. The great importance of the other body. Their unity: giver the taker, taker the giver, Christa perfectly confident of Rosie's hands grazing her, a map on which Rosie's fingers trace a journey of sensual tact. And between them that liquid, intensely wordless gorilla look, the only noises rising from the bed Christa's chicken-like baby-gorilla clucks of comfort and contentment.

Roseanna Gorilla. I am nature's tool. I am the fulfiller of every need. If only the two of *them*, husband and wife, had pretended to be gorillas, nothing but gorillas all the time! Instead they had pretended, only too well, to be being human beings.

When the two had had enough, they fell into a laughing embrace, each gave the other a juicy, demonstrably human kiss, and the lights were flicked off at either side of the bed. But before Sabbath could size up the situation and decide what to do next—move on or move in—he heard Rosie and Christa reciting together. A prayer? Of course! "Dear God . . ." Rosie's nightly AA prayer—he was finally to hear it spoken aloud. "Dear God . . ."

The duet was faultlessly rendered, neither of them groping for either the words or the feeling, two voices, two females, harmoniously interlaced. Young Christa was the ardent one, whereas Roseanna's recitation was marked by the careful thought that she had clearly given every word. There was in her voice both gravity and mellowness. She had battled her way to that inner peace so long unattainable; the agony of that childhood—deprivation, humiliation, injustice, abuse—was behind her, and the tribulation of the—for her—inescapable adulthood with a stand-in savage for her father was behind her, and the relief from the pain was audible. Her utterance was quieter and calmer than Christa's, but the effect was of a communion profoundly absorbed. New beginning, new being, new beloved . . . although, as Sabbath could virtually guarantee her, formed from more or less the same mold as the old beloved. He could envision the letter posted to Hell the day after Christa took off with Roseanna's mother's antique silver. *If Mother hadn't had to run for her life, if I hadn't had to attend that girls' school until she returned, if you hadn't forced me to wear that loden jacket, if you didn't scream at the housekeepers, if you didn't* fuck *the housekeepers, if you hadn't married that monstrous Irene, if you hadn't written me those crazy letters, if you hadn't had those disgusting lips and hands that gripped me*

like a vise . . . Father, you've done it again*! You rob me of a
normal relationship with a normal man, you rob me of a normal
relationship with a normal woman! You rob me of everything!*

"Dear God, I have no idea where I am going. I do not see
the road ahead of me. I cannot know for certain where it will
end. Nor do I really know myself, and the fact that I think I
am following Your will does not mean that I am actually doing
so. But I believe this. I believe . . ."

In Sabbath their prayer encountered no resistance. If only
he could get everything else he detested to leave not so much
as a pinhole in his brain. He himself prayed that God was om-
niscient. Otherwise He wasn't going to know what the fuck
these two were talking about.

"I believe that the desire to please You does in fact please
You. I hope I have that desire in everything I do. I hope I
never do anything apart from that desire. And I know that if I
do this You will lead me by the right road though I may know
nothing about it at the time. Therefore I will trust You always
though I may seem to be lost, and in the shadow of death, I
will not be afraid because I know You will never leave me to
face my troubles alone."

And here began the bliss. Stirring each other up took no
time at all. These weren't the cluckings of two contented gorillas Sabbath was overhearing now. The two of them were no
longer playing at anything; there was nothing nonsensical any
longer about a single sound they made. No need for dear God
now. They had taken unto themselves the task of divinity and
were laying bare the rapture with their tongues. Amazing organ, the human tongue. Take a good look at it someday. He
himself well remembered Christa's—the muscular, vibrating
tongue of the snake—and the awe it inspired in him no less
than in Drenka. Amazing all a tongue can say.

A digital clock face, aglow, green, was the sole object Sabbath could discern in the room. It was on the unseen table at
the side of the unseen bed that previously had been his side.
He believed he still had some of his death books piled there,
unless they were in among the clothes dumped in the corner.
He felt as though he had been expelled from an enormous
cunt whose insides he'd been roaming freely all his life. The
very house where he had lived had become a cunt into which

he could never insert himself again. This observation, arrived at independently of the intellect, only intensified as the odors that exist only within women wafted out of them and through the opening of the window, where they enveloped the flag-draped Sabbath in the violent misery of everything lost. If irrationality smelled, it would smell like this; if delirium smelled, it would smell like this; if anger, impulse, appetite, antagonism, ego . . . Yes, this sublime stink of spoilage was the smell of everything that converges to become the human soul. Whatever the witches were cooking up for Macbeth must have smelled just like this. No wonder Duncan doesn't make it through the night.

It seemed for a long while as though they would never be finished and that, consequently, on this hillside, at this window, hidden behind this night, he was to be chained to his ridiculousness forever. They could not seem to find what they needed. A piece or a fragment of something was missing, and they were speaking fluently together, purportedly about the missing piece, in a language consisting entirely of gasps and moans and exhalations and shrieks, a musical miscellany of explosive shrieks.

First one of them seemed to imagine she had found it and the other seemed to imagine *she* had found it, and then, in the voluminous blackness of their house of cunt, in the same immense instant, they landed on it together, and never before had Sabbath heard in any language anything like the speech pouring out of Rosie and Christa upon discovering the whereabouts of that little piece that made the whole picture complete.

In the end, she had been satisfying herself in a way that, were she Drenka, he might have enjoyed. It wasn't that he felt shut out and tragically abandoned because Roseanna was doing anything that, from another tangent, might not actually have stirred him to fellow feeling. Why should he regard as other than resonant with his own greatest creations her creation of an orgasmic haven apart from him? Roseanna's roundabout journey had, from all appearances, carried her back to where they'd begun as insatiable lovers hiding from Nikki in his puppet studio. In fact, his entire fantasy of her masturbating was precisely what he'd been conning himself with as a part of his getting ready to go back and try to . . . try to what? To reassert what? To recover what? To reach back into the past for what? For the residue of what?

And that's when he erupted. When male gorillas get angry, it's terrifying. The largest and heaviest of the primates, they get angry on a very grand scale. He had not known that he could open his mouth so wide, nor had he ever before realized, even as a puppet performer, what a rich repertoire of frightening noises he was able to produce. The hoots, the barks, the roars—ferocious, deafening—and all the while jumping up and down and pounding his chest and tearing out by the roots the plants growing at the foot of the window, and then dashing to and fro, and at last hammering his crippled fists on the window until the frame gave way and went crashing into the room, where Rosie and Christa were screaming hysterically.

Beating a tattoo on his chest he enjoyed the most. All these years he'd had the chest for it, and all these years he had let it go to waste. The pain in his hands was excruciating but he did not desist. He was the wildest of the wild gorillas. Don't you dare to threaten me! Thumping and thumping his large chest. Breaking apart the house.

In the car, he flipped on the headlights and saw that he had frightened the raccoons off as well. They had been out working the garbage cans back of the kitchen. Rosie must have forgotten to latch shut the slatted wooden cover to the rack where the four cans were stored, and though the raccoons were now gone, there was garbage strewn everywhere. That explained the smell of spoilage that, standing outside the window, he had attributed to the women on the bed. He should have known they didn't have it in 'em.

He parked at the entrance to the cemetery, not thirty yards from Drenka's grave. On the back of a garage repair bill that he dug out of the glove compartment, he composed his will. He worked by the gleam from the dashboard and the overhead lamp. His flashlight batteries had petered out—juice enough for just a pinprick of light, but then, he'd been going on these batteries since she died.

Outside the car the blackness was immense, shocking, a night as challenging to the mind as any he had ever known at sea.

I leave $7,450 plus change (see envelope in jacket pocket) to establish a prize of $500 to be awarded annually to a female member of the graduating class of any of the colleges in the four-college program—500 bucks to whoever's fucked more male faculty members than any other graduating senior during her undergraduate years. I leave the clothes on my back and in the brown paper bag to my friends at the Astor Place subway station. I leave my tape recorder to Kathy Goolsbee. I leave twenty dirty pictures of Dr. Michelle Cowan to the State of Israel. Mickey Sabbath, April 13, 1944.

Ninety-four. He crossed out 44. 1929–1994.

On the back of another repair bill he wrote, "My brother's things are to be buried with me—the flag, the yarmulke, the letters, everything in the carton. Lay me unclothed in the coffin, surrounded by his things." He slipped this in with Mr. Crawford's receipts and marked the envelope "Additional Instructions."

Now, the note. Coherent or incoherent? Angry or forgiving? Malevolent or loving? High-flown or colloquial? With or without quotations from Shakespeare, Martin Buber, and Montaigne? Hallmark should sell a card. All the great thoughts he had not reached were beyond enumeration; there was no bottom to what he did not have to say about the meaning of his life. And something funny is superfluous—suicide *is* funny. Not enough people realize that. It's not driven by despair or revenge, it's not born of madness or bitterness or humiliation, it's not a camouflaged homicide or a grandiose display of self-loathing—it's the finishing touch to the running gag. He would count himself an even bigger washout to be snuffed out any other way. For anybody who loves a joke, suicide is indispensable. For a puppeteer particularly there is nothing more natural: disappear behind the screen, insert the hand, and instead of performing as yourself, take the finale as the puppet. Think about it. There is no more thoroughly amusing way to go. A man who wants to die. A living being choosing death. That's entertainment.

No note. The notes are a sham, whatever you write.

And so now for the last of last things.

He stepped out of the car into the black granite world of the blind. Unlike suicide, seeing nothing was not amusing, and, proceeding with his arms before him, he felt as old a wreck as his Tiresias, Fish. He tried to picture the cemetery, but his five-month-long familiarity with it did not prevent him from wandering off almost immediately in among the graves. Soon he was breathless from stumbling and falling and getting back to his feet, despite the cautious tiny steps he was taking. The ground was drenched from the day's heavy rain and her grave was up the hill, and it would be a shame, having come this far, if a coronary beat him to the punch. To die of natural causes would be the unsurpassable insult. But his heart had had enough and would haul the load no more. His heart was not a horse, and it informed him of this, malevolently enough, by kicking him in the chest with its hooves.

So Sabbath ascended unassisted. Imagine a stone carrying itself, and that should give you some idea of how he struggled to reach Drenka's grave, where, in what was to be his grand farewell to the farfetched, he proceeded to urinate on it. The stream was painfully slow to start, and he was fearful at first that he was asking of himself the impossible and that there was, in him, nothing left of him. He imagined himself—a man who did not get through a night without three trips to the toilet—standing there into the next century, unable to draw a drop of water with which to anoint this sacred ground. Could what was impeding the urine flow be that wall of conscience that deprives a person of what is most himself? What had happened to his entire conception of life? It had cost him dearly to clear a space where he could exist in the world as antagonistically as he liked. Where was the contempt with which he had overridden their hatred; where were the laws, the code of conduct, by which he had labored to be free from their stupidly harmonious expectations? Yes, the strictures that had inspired his buffoonery were taking their vengeance at last. All the taboos that seek to abate our monstrosity had shut his water down.

Perfect metaphor: empty vessel.

And then the stream began . . . a trickle at first, just some feeble dribbling, as when your knife slices open an onion and the weeping consists of a tear or two sliding down either cheek. But then a spurt followed that, and a second spurt, and then a flow, and then a gush, and then a surge, and then Sabbath was peeing with a power that surprised even him, the way strangers to grief can be astounded by the unstoppable copiousness of their river of tears. He could not remember when he had peed like this last. Maybe fifty years ago. To drill a hole in her grave! To drive through the coffin's lid to Drenka's mouth! But he might as well try, by peeing, to activate a turbine—he could never again reach her in any way. "I did it!" she cried, "I did it!" And never had he adored anyone more.

He did not stop, however. He couldn't. He was to urine what a wet nurse is to milk. Drenchèd Drenka, bubbling spring, mother of moisture and overflow, surging, streaming Drenka, drinker of the juices of the human vine—sweetheart, rise up before you turn to dust, come back and be revived, oozing all your secretions!

But even by watering all spring and summer the plot that all her men had seeded, he could not bring her back, either Drenka or anyone else. And did he think otherwise, the anti-illusionist? Well, it is sometimes hard even for people with the best intentions to remember twenty-four hours a day, seven days a week, three hundred and sixty-five days a year that nobody dead can live again. There is nothing on earth more firmly established, it's all that you can know for sure—and no one wants to know it.

"Excuse me! Sir!"

Someone tapping from behind, someone at Sabbath's shoulder.

"Stop what you are doing, sir! *Stop now!*"

But he was not finished.

"You are pissing on my mother's grave!"

And ferociously, by his beard, Sabbath was swung around, and when the light of a powerful lamp was turned on his eyes, he threw up his hands as though something that could pierce his skull was flying into his face. The light passed down the length of his body and then upward from his feet to his eyes. He was painted like this, coat upon coat, six or seven times, until at last the beam illuminated the prick alone, seemingly keeping an eye out from between the edges of the flag, a spout without menace or significance of any kind, intermittently dripping as though in need of repair. It did not look like anything that would have inspired the mind of mankind, over the

millennia, to give it five minutes of thought, let alone to conclude that, were it not for the tyranny of this tube, our species'
story here on earth would be altered beyond recognition,
beginning, middle, and end.

"Get it out of my sight!"

Sabbath could easily have tucked himself into his trousers
and pulled up the zipper. But he wouldn't.

"Stash it!"

But Sabbath did nothing.

"What *are* you?" Sabbath was asked, the light blinding him
once again. "You desecrate my mother's grave. You desecrate
the American flag. You desecrate your own people. With your
stupid fucking prick out, wearing the skullcap of your own religion!"

"This is a religious act."

"Wrapped in the flag!"

"Proudly, proudly."

"*Pissing!*"

"My guts out."

Matthew now began to wail. "My mother! That was my
mother! My mother, you filthy, fucking creep! You depraved
my mother!"

"Depraved? Officer Balich, you are too old to idealize your
parents."

"She left a diary! My father has read the diary! He read the
things you made her do! Even my *cousin*—my little kid *cousin*!
'Drink it, Drenka! Drink it!'"

And so swept away was he by his own tears that he was no
longer even lighting up Sabbath's face. The beam pointed,
rather, to the ground, illuminating the puddle at the foot of
the grave.

Barrett's head had been smashed open. Sabbath was expecting worse. Once he realized by whom he had been apprehended, he did not believe that he was going to walk away alive.
Nor did he want to. It was played out, that thing which allowed him to improvise endlessly and which had kept him
alive. The nutty tawdriness is over.

Yet once again did he walk away, as he had from hanging
himself at the Cowans', as he had from drowning himself at
the shore—walked away, leaving Matthew sobbing at the

grave, and, propelled still by the thing that allowed him to improvise endlessly, stumbled through the blackness down the
hill.

Not that he didn't want to hear more from Matthew about
Drenka's diary, not that he wouldn't have greedily read every
word. It had never occurred to him that Drenka was writing
everything down. In English or in Serbo-Croatian? Out of
pride or incredulity? To trace the course of her daring or of her
depravity? Why hadn't she warned him in the hospital that
there was this diary? Too sick by then to think of it? Had leaving it to be found been inadvertent, an oversight, or the boldest thing she had ever done? I did it! I did it! This was who was
living under all the nice clothes—and none of you ever knew!

Or had she left it behind because she had not the strength to
throw it out? Yes, such diaries have a privileged place among
one's skeletons; one cannot easily free oneself of words themselves finally freed from their daily duty to justify and to conceal. It takes more courage than one might imagine to destroy
the secret diaries, the letters, and the Polaroids, the videotapes
and audiotapes, the locks of pubic hair, the unlaundered items
of intimate apparel, to obliterate forever the reliclike force of
these things that, almost alone of our possessions, decisively
answer the question "Can it really be that I am like this?" A
record of the self at Mardi Gras, or of the self in its true and
untrammeled existence? Either way, these dangerous treasures
—hidden from those near and dear beneath the lingerie, in the
darkest reaches of the file cabinet, under lock and key at the
local bank—constitute a record of that with which one cannot
part.

And yet for Sabbath there was a puzzle, an inconsistency,
that he couldn't fathom, a suspicion that he couldn't elude.
What obligation was she fulfilling, and to whom, by leaving
her sex diary to be discovered? Against which of her men was
she protesting? Against Matija? Against Sabbath? Which of us
did you intend to slay? Not me! Surely not me! You *loved* me!

"I want to see your hands up in the air!"

The words boomed at him out of nowhere, and then he was
fixed in the spotlight as though he were alone among the tombstones to perform a one-man show, Sabbath star of the cemetery, vaudevillian to the ghosts, front-line entertainer to the

troops of the dead. Sabbath bowed. There should have been music, behind him the slyly carnal old swing music, ushering Sabbath onto the stage there should have been life's most reliable pleasure, the innocent amusement of the B. G. sextet's "Ain't Misbehavin'," Slam Stewart playing the bass and the bass playing Slam . . . Instead there was a disembodied voice politely requesting that he identify himself.

Sweeping up from his bow, Sabbath announced, "It is I, Necrophilio, the nocturnal emission."

"I would not do that dip again, sir. I want to see those hands in the *air*."

The patrol car illuminating Sabbath's theater was manned by a second trooper, who now climbed out with a gun drawn. A trainee. Matthew would be riding alone unless he was breaking somebody in. "When he breaks them in," Drenka would boast, "he always wants them to do all the driving. Fresh from the academy, kids on probation for a whole year—and it's Matthew who they used to break them in. Matthew says, 'There are some good kids who really want to do the job and do it well. There are some assholes, too. Bad guys with a don't-give-a-shit attitude, whatever they can get away with, and so on. But to do a good job, to do what you're supposed to do, to keep your motor vehicle activity up and get your cases in on time, to keep your car the way it's supposed to be kept . . .' That's what Matthew teaches them. He just rode with somebody for three months, and the boy gave Matthew a tie clip. A gold tie clip. He said, 'Matt's my best buddy ever.'"

The trainee had him covered but Sabbath did nothing to resist arrest. He had only to start to run, and a trainee, rightly or wrongly, would more than likely drill him right through the head. But when Matthew made it to the bottom of the hill, all the trainee did was slap the cuffs on Sabbath and assist him into the back of the car. He was a young black man about Matthew's age and he remained absolutely silent, uttered not a syllable of disgust or indignation because of what Sabbath looked like or how he was dressed or what he had done. He helped Sabbath onto the backseat, mindful to see that the flag did not slip from his shoulders, and gently recentered on Sabbath's bald skull the God Bless America yarmulke, which had fallen forward onto his forehead as he ducked into the car.

Whether this betokened an excess of kindness or of contempt the prisoner couldn't decide.

The trainee did the driving. Matthew was no longer in tears, but from the backseat Sabbath could see something uncontrollable working the muscles of his broad neck.

"How's my partner?" the trainee asked as they started down the mountain.

Matthew gave no reply.

He is going to kill me. He is going to do it. Rid of life. It's happening at last.

"And where are we going?" asked Sabbath.

"We're taking you in, sir," the trainee replied.

"May I ask what the charges might be?"

"The charges?" Matthew erupted. "The *charges*?"

"Breathe, Matt," the trainee said, "just do the breathing you taught me."

"If I may say so," Sabbath offered overprecisely, in a tone that he knew to have driven at least Roseanna crazy, "his sense of effrontery is lodged in a fundamental misapprehension—"

"Be still," the trainee suggested.

"I only want to say that something was happening that he cannot possibly understand. The serious side of it he has no way of assessing."

"*Serious!*" cried Matthew, and pounded the dashboard with his fist.

"Let's take him in, Matt, and that's it. That's the job—let's just do it."

"I am not using words to confound anyone. I do not exaggerate," said Sabbath. "I do not say correct or savory. I do not say seemly or even natural. I say serious. Sensationally serious. Unspeakably serious. Solemnly, recklessly, blissfully *serious*."

"It's rash of you, sir, to go on like this."

"I'm a rash guy. It's inexplicable to me, too. It's displaced virtually everything else in my life. It seems to be the whole aim of my being."

"And that's how come we're taking you in, sir."

"I thought you were taking me in so I could tell the judge how I depraved Matthew's mother."

"Look, you've caused my partner a lot of pain," the trainee said, his voice still impressively subdued. "You've caused his family a lot of pain. I have to tell you that you are now saying things that are causing *me* a lot of pain."

"Yes. That's what I hear from people all the time, people continuously telling me that the great thing I was called to do in life was cause pain. The world is just flying along pain-free—happy-go-lucky humanity off on one long fun-filled holiday—and then Sabbath is set down in life, and overnight the place is transformed into a loony bin of tears. Why *is* that? Can someone explain it to me?"

"Stop!" cried Matthew. "Stop the car!"

"Matty, get the bastard *in.*"

"Stop the fucking *car*, Billy! We're not *taking* him in!"

Sabbath straightaway leaned forward in the seat—*lurched* forward without his hands to steady him. "Take me in, Billy. Don't listen to Matty, he's not being objective—he's let himself get personally involved. Take me in so I can purge myself publicly of my crimes and accept the punishment that's coming to me."

There were deep woods to either side of the road where the police car crept onto the shoulder. Billy stopped the car and turned off the lights.

The dark domain of that night again. And now, thought Sabbath, the feature attraction, the thing that matters most, the unforeseen culmination for which he had battled all his life. He had not realized how very long he'd been longing to be put to death. He hadn't committed suicide, because he was waiting to be murdered.

Matthew leaped from the car and around to the back, where he opened the door and pulled Sabbath out. Then he undid the handcuffs. That was all. He undid the handcuffs and said, "If you, you sick freak bastard, if ever you mention my mother's name to anyone, or anything *about* my mother, to *anyone—to anyone at any time anywhere*—I'm coming after you!" With his eyes just inches from Sabbath's, he began again to cry. "You hear me, old man? *You hear me?*"

"But why wait when you can have your satisfaction now? I start for the woods and you shoot. Attempted escape. Billy here'll back you up. Won't you, Bill? 'We let the old guy take a leak and he tried to run away.'"

"You sick fuck!" screamed Matthew. "You filthy sick son of

a bitch!" and, flinging open the front passenger door, he violently pitched himself back into the car.

"But I'm going free! I've reveled in the revolting thing one time too many! And I'm going free! I'm a ghoul! I'm a ghoul! After causing all this pain, the ghoul is running free! *Matthew!*" But the cruiser had driven, off, leaving Sabbath ankle-deep in the pudding of the springtime mud, blindly engulfed by the alien, inland woods, by the rainmaking trees and the rainwashed boulders—and with no one to kill him except himself.

And he couldn't do it. He could not fucking die. How could he leave? How could he go? Everything he hated was here.

CHRONOLOGY

NOTE ON THE TEXTS

NOTES

Chronology

Born Philip Roth on March 19 in Newark, New Jersey,
        second child of Herman Roth and Bess Finkel. (Bess
        Finkel, the second child of five, was born in 1904 in Eliza-
        beth, New Jersey, to Philip and Dora Finkel, Jewish im-
        migrants from near Kiev. Herman Roth was born in 1901
        in Newark, New Jersey, the middle child of seven born to
        Sender and Bertha Roth, Jewish immigrants from Polish
        Galicia. They were married in Newark on February 21,
        1926, and shortly afterward opened a small family-run
        shoe store. Their son Sanford ["Sandy"] was born De-
        cember 26, 1927. Following the bankruptcy of the shoe
        store and a briefly held position as city marshal, Herman
        Roth took a job as agent with the Newark district office
        of the Metropolitan Life Insurance Company, and would
        remain with the company until his retirement as district
        manager in 1966.) Family moves into second-floor flat of
        two-and-a-half-family house (with five-room apartments
        on each of the first two floors and a three-room apart-
        ment on the top floor) at 81 Summit Avenue in Newark.
        Summit Avenue was a lower-middle-class residential street
        in the Weequahic section, a twenty-minute bus ride from
        commercial downtown Newark and less than a block
        from Chancellor Avenue School and from Weequahic
        High School, then considered the state's best academic
        public high school. These were the two schools that
        Sandy and Philip attended. Between 1910 and 1920, Wee-
        quahic had been developed as a new city neighborhood at
        the southwest corner of Newark, some three miles from
        the edge of industrial Newark and from the international
        shipping facilities at Port Newark on Newark Bay. In the
        first half of the twentieth century Newark was a prosper-
        ous working-class city of approximately 420,000, the ma-
        jority of its citizens of German, Italian, Slavic, and Irish
        extraction. Blacks and Jews composed two of the smallest
        groups in the city. From the 1930s to the 1950s, the Jews
        lived mainly in the predominantly Jewish Weequahic
        section.

1938   Philip enters kindergarten at Chancellor Avenue School
            in January.

1942   Roth family moves to second-floor flat of two-and-a-half-
            family house at 359 Leslie Street, three blocks west of
            Summit Avenue, still within the Weequahic neighborhood
            but nearer to semi-industrial boundary with Irvington.

1946   Philip graduates from elementary school in January, having
            skipped a year. Brother graduates from high school and
            chooses to enter U.S. Navy for two years rather than be
            drafted into the peacetime army.

1947   Family moves to first-floor flat of two-and-a-half-family
            house at 385 Leslie Street, just a few doors from commer-
            cial Chancellor Avenue, the neighborhood's main artery.
            Philip turns from reading sports fiction by John R. Tunis
            and adventure fiction by Howard Pease to reading the
            left-leaning historical novels of Howard Fast.

1948   Brother is discharged from navy and, with the aid of G.I.
            Bill, enrolls as commercial art student at Pratt Institute,
            Brooklyn. Philip takes strong interest in politics during
            the four-way U.S. presidential election in which the Re-
            publican Dewey loses to the Democrat Truman despite a
            segregationist Dixiecrat Party and a left-wing Progressive
            Party drawing away traditionally Democratic voters.

1950   Graduates from high school in January. Works as stock
            clerk at S. Klein department store in downtown Newark.
            Reads Thomas Wolfe; discovers Sherwood Anderson,
            Ring Lardner, Erskine Caldwell, and Theodore Dreiser.
            In September enters Newark College of Rutgers as pre-
            law student while continuing to live at home. (Newark
            Rutgers was at this time a newly formed college housed in
            two small converted downtown buildings, one formerly a
            bank, the other formerly a brewery.)

1951   Still a pre-law student, transfers in September to Bucknell
            University in Lewisburg, Pennsylvania. Brother graduates
            from Pratt Institute and moves to New York City to work
            for advertising agency. Parents move to Moorestown,
            New Jersey, approximately seventy miles southwest of
            Newark; father takes job as manager of Metropolitan
            Life's south Jersey district after having previously man-
            aged several north Jersey district offices.

1952   Roth decides to study English literature. With two friends, founds Bucknell literary magazine, *Et Cetera*, and becomes its first editor. Writes first short stories. Strongly influenced in his literary studies by English professor Mildred Martin, under whose tutelage he reads extensively, and with whom he will maintain lifelong friendship.

1954   Is elected to Phi Beta Kappa and graduates from Bucknell magna cum laude in English. Accepts scholarship to study English at the University of Chicago graduate school, beginning in September. Reads Saul Bellow's *The Adventures of Augie March*, and under its influence explores Chicago.

1955   In June receives M.A. with Honors in English. In September, rather than wait to be drafted, enlists in U.S. Army for two years. Suffers spinal injury during basic training at Fort Dix. In November, is assigned to Public Information Office at Walter Reed Army Hospital, Washington, D.C. Begins to write short stories "The Conversion of the Jews" and "Epstein." *Epoch*, a Cornell University literary quarterly, publishes "The Contest for Aaron Gold," which is reprinted in Martha Foley's *Best American Short Stories 1956*.

1956   Is hospitalized in June for complications from spinal injury. After two-month hospital stay receives honorable discharge for medical reasons and a disability pension. In September returns to University of Chicago as instructor in the liberal arts college, teaching freshman composition. Begins course work for Ph.D. but drops out after one term. Meets Ted Solotaroff, who is also a graduate student, and they become friends.

1957   Publishes in *Commentary* "You Can't Tell a Man by the Song He Sings." Writes novella "Goodbye, Columbus." Meets Saul Bellow at University of Chicago when Bellow is a classroom guest of Roth's friend and colleague, the writer Richard Stern. Begins to review movies and television for *The New Republic* after magazine publishes "Positive Thinking on Pennsylvania Avenue," a humor piece satirizing President Eisenhower's religious beliefs.

1958   Publishes "The Conversion of the Jews" and "Epstein" in *The Paris Review*; "Epstein" wins *Paris Review* Aga Khan Prize, presented to Roth in Paris in July. Spends first summer abroad, mainly in Paris. Houghton Mifflin awards Roth the Houghton Mifflin Literary Fellowship to publish the novella and five stories in one volume; George Starbuck, a poet and friend from Chicago, is his editor. Resigns from teaching position at University of Chicago. Moves to two-room basement apartment on Manhattan's Lower East Side. Becomes friendly with *Paris Review* editors George Plimpton and Robert Silvers and *Commentary* editor Martin Greenberg.

1959   Marries Margaret Martinson Williams. Publishes "Defender of the Faith" in *The New Yorker*, causing consternation among Jewish organizations and rabbis who attack magazine and condemn author as anti-Semitic; story collected in *Goodbye, Columbus* and included in *Best American Short Stories 1960* and *Prize Stories 1960: The O. Henry Awards*, where it wins second prize. *Goodbye, Columbus* is published in May. Roth receives Guggenheim fellowship and award from the American Academy of Arts and Letters. *Goodbye, Columbus* gains highly favorable reviews from Bellow, Alfred Kazin, Leslie Fiedler, and Irving Howe; influential rabbis denounce Roth in their sermons as "a self-hating Jew." Roth and wife leave U.S. to spend seven months in Italy, where he works on his first novel, *Letting Go*; he meets William Styron, who is living in Rome and who becomes a lifelong friend. Styron introduces Roth to his publisher, Donald Klopfer of Random House; when George Starbuck leaves Houghton Mifflin, Roth moves to Random House.

1960   *Goodbye, Columbus and Five Short Stories* wins National Book Award. The collection also wins Daroff Award of the Jewish Book Council of America. Roth returns to America to teach at the Writers' Workshop of the University of Iowa, Iowa City. Meets drama professor Howard Stein (later dean of the Columbia University Drama School), who becomes lifelong friend. Continues working on *Letting Go*. Travels in Midwest. Participates in *Esquire* magazine symposium at Stanford University; his speech "Writing American Fiction," published in *Commentary* in March 1961, is widely discussed. After a speaking engagement in Oregon, meets Bernard Malamud, whose fiction he admires.

1962   After two years at Iowa, accepts two-year position as writer-in-residence at Princeton. Separates from Margaret Roth. Moves to New York City and commutes to Princeton classes. (Lives at various Manhattan locations until 1970.) Meets Princeton sociologist Melvin Tumin, a Newark native who becomes a friend. Random House publishes *Letting Go*.

1963   Receives Ford Foundation grant to write plays in affiliation with American Place Theater in New York. Is legally separated from Margaret Roth. Becomes close friend of Aaron Asher, a University of Chicago graduate and editor at Meridian Books, original paperback publisher of *Goodbye, Columbus*. In June takes part in American Jewish Congress symposium in Tel Aviv, Israel, along with American writers Leslie Fiedler, Max Lerner, and literary critic David Boroff. Travels in Israel for a month.

1964   Teaches at State University of New York at Stony Brook, Long Island. Reviews plays by James Baldwin, LeRoi Jones, and Edward Albee for newly founded *New York Review of Books*. Spends a month at Yaddo, writers' retreat in Saratoga Springs, New York, that provides free room and board. (Will work at Yaddo for several months at a time throughout the 1960s.) Meets and establishes friendships there with novelist Alison Lurie and painter Julius Goldstein.

1965   Begins to teach comparative literature at University of Pennsylvania one semester each year more or less annually until the mid-1970s. Meets professor Joel Conarroe, who becomes a close friend. Begins work on *When She Was Good* after abandoning another novel, begun in 1962.

1966   Publishes section of *When She Was Good* in *Harper's*. Is increasingly troubled by Vietnam War and in ensuing years takes part in marches and demonstrations against it.

1967   Publishes *When She Was Good*. Begins work on *Portnoy's Complaint*, of which he publishes excerpts in *Esquire, Partisan Review*, and *New American Review*, where Ted Solotaroff is editor.

1968   Margaret Roth dies in an automobile accident. Roth spends two months at Yaddo completing *Portnoy's Complaint*.

1969   *Portnoy's Complaint* published in February. Within weeks
        becomes number-one fiction bestseller and a widely dis-
        cussed cultural phenomenon. Roth makes no public ap-
        pearances and retreats for several months to Yaddo. Rents
        house in Woodstock, New York, and meets the painter
        Philip Guston, who lives nearby. They remain close friends
        and see each other regularly until Guston's death in 1980.
        Renews friendship with Bernard Malamud, who like Roth
        is serving as a member of The Corporation of Yaddo.

1970   Spends March traveling in Thailand, Burma, Cambodia,
        and Hong Kong. Begins work on *My Life as a Man* and
        publishes excerpt in *Modern Occasions*. Is elected to Na-
        tional Institute of Arts and Letters and is its youngest
        member. Commutes to his classes at University of Penn-
        sylvania and lives mainly in Woodstock until 1972.

1971   Excerpts of *Our Gang*, satire of the Nixon administration,
        appear in *New York Review of Books* and *Modern Occa-
        sions*; the book is published by Random House in the fall.
        Continues work on *My Life as a Man*; writes *The Breast*
        and *The Great American Novel*. Begins teaching a Kafka
        course at University of Pennsylvania.

1972   *The Breast*, first book of three featuring protagonist David
        Kepesh, published by Holt, Rinehart, Winston, where
        Aaron Asher is his editor. Roth buys old farmhouse and
        forty acres in northwest Connecticut, one hundred miles
        from New York City, and moves there from Woodstock.
        In May travels to Venice, Vienna, and, for the first time,
        Prague. Meets his translators there, Luba and Rudolph
        Pilar, and they describe to him the impact of the political
        situation on Czech writers. In U.S., arranges to meet
        exiled Czech editor Antonin Liehm in New York; attends
        Liehm's weekly classes in Czech history, literature, and
        film at College of Staten Island, City University of New
        York. Through friendship with Liehm meets numerous
        Czech exiles, including film directors Ivan Passer and Jiří
        Weiss, who become friends. Is elected to the American
        Academy of Arts and Sciences.

1973   Publishes *The Great American Novel* and the essay
        "Looking at Kafka" in *New American Review*. Returns to
        Prague and meets novelists Milan Kundera, Ivan Klíma,
        Ludvik Vaculik, the poet Miroslav Holub, and other
        writers blacklisted and persecuted by the Soviet-backed

Communist regime; becomes friendly with Rita Klímová, a blacklisted translator and academic, who will serve as Czechoslovakia's first ambassador to U.S. following the 1989 "Velvet Revolution." (Will make annual spring trips to Prague to visit his writer friends until he is denied an entry visa in 1977.) Writes "Country Report" on Czechoslovakia for American PEN. Proposes paperback series, "Writers from the Other Europe," to Penguin Books USA; becomes general editor of the series, selecting titles, commissioning introductions, and overseeing publication of Eastern European writers relatively unknown to American readers. Beginning in 1974, series publishes fiction by Polish writers Jerzy Andrzejewski, Tadeusz Borowski, Tadeusz Konwicki, Witold Gombrowicz, and Bruno Schulz; Hungarian writers György Konrád and Géza Csáth; Yugoslav writer Danilo Kiš; and Czech writers Bohumil Hrabal, Milan Kundera, and Ludvik Vaculik; series ends in 1989. "Watergate Edition" of *Our Gang* published, which includes a new preface by Roth.

1974   Roth publishes *My Life as a Man*. Visits Budapest as well as Prague and meets Budapest writers through Hungarian PEN and the *Hungarian Quarterly*. In Prague meets Vaclav Havel. Through friend Professor Zdenek Strybyrny, visits and becomes friend of the niece of Franz Kafka, Vera Saudkova, who shows him Kafka family photographs and family belongings; subsequently becomes friendly in London with Marianne Steiner, daughter of Kafka's sister Valli. Also through Strybyrny meets the widow of Jiří Weil; upon his return to America arranges for translation and publication of Weil's novel *Life with a Star* as well as publication of several Weil short stories in *American Poetry Review*, for which he provides an introduction. In Princeton meets Joanna Rostropowicz Clark, wife of friend Blair Clark; she becomes close friend and introduces Roth to contemporary Polish writing and to Polish writers visiting America, including Konwicki and Kazimierz Brandys. Publishes "Imagining Jews" in *New York Review of Books*; essay prompts letter from university professor, editor, writer, and former Jesuit Jack Miles. Correspondence ensues and the two establish a lasting intellectual friendship. In New York, meets teacher, editor, author, and journalist Bernard Avishai; they quickly establish a strong intellectual bond and become lifelong friends.

1975   Aaron Asher leaves Holt and becomes editor in chief at Farrar, Straus and Giroux; Roth moves to FSG with Asher for publication of *Reading Myself and Others*, a collection of interviews and critical essays. Meets British actress Claire Bloom.

1976   Interviews Isaac Bashevis Singer about Bruno Schulz for *New York Times Book Review* article to coincide with publication of Schulz's *Street of Crocodiles* in "Writers from the Other Europe" series. Moves with Claire Bloom to London, where they live six to seven months a year for the next twelve years. Spends the remaining months in Connecticut, where Bloom joins him when she is not acting in films, television, or stage productions. In London resumes an old friendship with British critic A. Alvarez and, a few years later, begins a friendship with American writer Michael Herr (author of *Dispatches*, which Roth admires) and with the American painter R. B. Kitaj. Also meets critic and biographer Hermione Lee, who becomes a friend, as does novelist Edna O'Brien. Begins regular visits to France to see Milan Kundera and another new friend, French writer-critic Alain Finkielkraut. Visits Israel for the first time since 1963 and returns there regularly, keeping a journal that eventually provides ideas and material for novels *The Counterlife* and *Operation Shylock*. Meets the writer Aharon Appelfeld in Jerusalem and they become close friends.

1977   Publishes *The Professor of Desire*, second book of Kepesh trilogy. Beginning in 1977 and continuing over the next few years, writes series of TV dramas for Claire Bloom: adaptations of *The Name-Day Party*, a short story by Chekhov; *Journey into the Whirlwind*, the gulag autobiography of Eugenia Ginzburg; and, with David Plante, *It Isn't Fair*, Plante's memoir of Jean Rhys. At request of Chichester Festival director, modernizes the David Magarshack translation of Chekhov's *The Cherry Orchard* for Claire Bloom's 1981 performance at the festival as Madame Ranyevskaya.

1979   *The Ghost Writer*, first novel featuring novelist Nathan Zuckerman as protagonist, is published in its entirety in *The New Yorker*, then published by Farrar, Straus and Giroux. Bucknell awards Roth his first honorary degree; eventually receives honorary degrees from Amherst,

Brown, Columbia, Dartmouth, Harvard, Pennsylvania, and Rutgers, among others.

1980   *A Philip Roth Reader* published, edited by Martin Green. Milan and Vera Kundera visit Connecticut on first trip to U.S.; Roth introduces Kundera to friend and *New Yorker* editor Veronica Geng, who also becomes Kundera's editor at the magazine. Conversation with Milan Kundera, in London and Connecticut, published in *New York Times Book Review*.

1981   Mother dies of a sudden heart attack in Elizabeth, New Jersey. *Zuckerman Unbound* published.

1982   Corresponds with Judith Thurman after reading her biography of Isak Dinesen, and they begin a friendship.

1983   Roth's physician and Litchfield County neighbor, Dr. C. H. Huvelle, retires from his Connecticut practice and the two become close friends.

1984   *The Anatomy Lesson* published. Aaron Asher leaves FSG and David Rieff becomes Roth's editor; the two soon become close friends. Conversation with Edna O'Brien in London published in *New York Times Book Review*. With BBC director Tristram Powell, adapts *The Ghost Writer* for television drama, featuring Claire Bloom; program is aired in U.S. and U.K. Meets University of Connecticut professor Ross Miller and the two forge strong literary friendship.

1985   *Zuckerman Bound*, a compilation of *The Ghost Writer*, *Zuckerman Unbound*, *The Anatomy Lesson*, with epilogue *The Prague Orgy*, published. Adapts *The Prague Orgy* for a British television production that is never realized.

1986   Spends several days in Turin with Primo Levi. Conversation with Levi published in *New York Times Book Review*, which also asks that Roth write a memoir about Bernard Malamud upon Malamud's death at age 72. *The Counterlife* published; wins National Book Critics Circle Award for fiction that year.

1987   Corresponds with exiled Romanian writer Norman Manea, who is living in Berlin, and encourages him to come to live in U.S; Manea arrives the next year, and the two become close friends.

1988   *The Facts* published. Travels to Jerusalem for Aharon Ap-
        pelfeld interview, which is published in *New York Times
        Book Review*. In Jerusalem, attends daily the trial of Ivan
        Demjanjuk, the alleged Treblinka guard "Ivan the Terri-
        ble." Returns to America to live year-round. Becomes
        Distinguished Professor of Literature at Hunter College
        of the City University of New York, where he will teach
        one semester each year until 1991.

1989   Father dies of brain tumor after yearlong illness. David
        Rieff leaves Farrar, Straus. For the first time since 1970,
        acquires a literary agent, Andrew Wylie of Wylie, Aitken,
        and Stone. Leaves FSG for Simon and Schuster. Writes a
        memoir of Philip Guston which is published in *Vanity
        Fair* and subsequently reprinted in Guston catalogs.

1990   Travels to post-Communist Prague for conversation with
        Ivan Klíma, published in *New York Review of Books*. *De-
        ception* published by Simon and Schuster. Roth marries
        Claire Bloom in New York.

1991   *Patrimony* published; wins National Book Critics Circle
        Award for biography. Renews strong friendship with Saul
        Bellow.

1992   Reads from *Patrimony* for nationwide reading tour, ex-
        tending into 1993. Publishes brief profile of Norman
        Manea in *New York Times Book Review*.

1993   *Operation Shylock* published; wins PEN/Faulkner Award
        for fiction. Separates from Claire Bloom. Writes *Dr. Hu-
        velle: A Biographical Sketch*, which he publishes privately
        as a 34-page booklet for local distribution.

1994   Divorces Claire Bloom.

1995   Returns to Houghton Mifflin, where John Sterling is his
        editor. *Sabbath's Theater* is published and wins National
        Book Award for fiction.

1997   John Sterling leaves Houghton Mifflin and Wendy Stroth-
        man becomes Roth's editor. *American Pastoral*, first
        book of the "American trilogy," is published and wins
        Pulitzer Prize for fiction.

1998   *I Married a Communist*, the second book of the trilogy,
        is published and wins Ambassador Book Award of the
        English-Speaking Union. In October Roth attends three-

day international literary program honoring his work in Aix-en-Provence. In November receives National Medal of Arts at the White House.

2000   Publishes *The Human Stain*, final book of American trilogy, which wins PEN/Faulkner Award in U.S., the W. H. Smith Award in the U.K., and the Prix Medicis for the best foreign book of the year in France. Publishes "Rereading Saul Bellow" in *The New Yorker*.

2001   Publishes *The Dying Animal*, final book of the Kepesh trilogy, and *Shop Talk*, a collection of interviews with and essays on Primo Levi, Aharon Appelfeld, I. B. Singer, Edna O'Brien, Milan Kundera, Ivan Klíma, Philip Guston, Bernard Malamud, and Saul Bellow, and an exchange with Mary McCarthy. Receives highest award of the American Academy of Arts and Letters, the Gold Medal in fiction, given every six years "for the entire work of the recipient," previously awarded to Willa Cather, Edith Wharton, John Dos Passos, William Faulkner, Saul Bellow, and Isaac Bashevis Singer, among others. Is awarded the Edward McDowell Medal; William Styron, chair of the selection committee, remarks at the presentation ceremony that Roth "has caused to be lodged in our collective consciousness a small, select company of human beings who are as arrestingly alive and as fully realized as any in modern fiction."

2002   Wins the National Book Foundation's Medal for Distinguished Contribution to American Letters.

2003   Receives honorary degrees at Harvard University and University of Pennsylvania. Roth's work now appears in 31 languages.

2004   Publishes novel *The Plot Against America*, which becomes a bestseller and wins the W. H. Smith Award for best book of the year in the U.K.; Roth is the first writer in the 46-year history of the prize to win it twice.

2005   *The Plot Against America* wins the Society of American Historians' James Fenimore Cooper Prize as the outstanding historical novel on an American theme for 2003–04. On October 23, Roth's childhood home at 81 Summit Avenue in Newark is marked with a plaque as a historic landmark and the nearby intersection is named Philip Roth Plaza.

2006   Publishes *Everyman* in May. Becomes fourth recipient of PEN's highest writing honor, the PEN/Nabokov Award. Receives Power of the Press Award from the New Jersey Library Association for Newark *Star-Ledger* eulogy to his close friend, Newark librarian and city historian Charles Cummings.

2007   Receives PEN/Faulkner Award for *Everyman*, the first author to be given the award three times. Wins the inaugural PEN/Saul Bellow Award for Achievement in American Fiction and Italy's first Grinzane-Masters Award, an award dedicated to the grand masters of literature. *Exit Ghost* is published.

2008   Roth's 75th birthday is marked by a celebration of his life and work at Columbia University. *Indignation* is published.

2009   Honored in program at Queens College, "A 50th Anniversary Celebration of the Work of Philip Roth." Receives the Charles Cummings Award from the Newark Preservation and Landmarks Committee, the sponsor of semi-annual tours of "Philip Roth's Newark." Publishes *The Humbling*. Wins the annual literary prize of the German newspaper *Die Welt*.

2010   Receives *Paris Review*'s Hadada Award in April. Publishes *Nemesis* in September.

Note on the Texts

This volume contains Philip Roth's novels *Operation Shylock* (1993) and *Sabbath's Theater* (1995).

Operation Shylock was published in New York by Simon & Schuster and in England by Jonathan Cape in 1993. A limited edition of the novel was brought out that year as well by the Franklin Library, which contained a short introduction by Roth also published as "A Bit of Jewish Mischief," *New York Times Book Review*, March 7, 1993; in the present volume, this introduction is included in the Notes. Because corrections were made to the text of the paperback edition when published in Random House's Vintage Books series in 1994, the text printed here of *Operation Shylock* is taken from the Vintage paperback edition.

Sabbath's Theater was published in Boston by Houghton Mifflin and in England by Jonathan Cape in 1995. A two-part pre-publication excerpt had appeared in *The New Yorker* as "The Ultimatum" (June 26 and July 3, 1995) and "Drenka's Men" (July 10, 1995). Corrections were made for the 1996 Vintage paperback edition, which contains the text of *Sabbath's Theater* printed here.

This volume presents the texts of the original printings chosen for inclusion here, but it does not attempt to reproduce nontextual features of their typographic design. The texts are presented without change, except for the correction of typographical errors. Spelling, punctuation, and capitalization are often expressive features and are not altered, even when inconsistent or irregular. The following is a list of typographical errors corrected, cited by page and line number: 518.7, de Carlo (and *passim*); 532.17, *tchotchkees*; 545.14, side-kicker. . . . and; 774.1, mother.

Notes

In the notes below, the reference numbers denote page and line of this volume (the line count includes chapter headings). Biblical quotations are keyed to the King James Version. Quotations from Shakespeare are keyed to The Riverside Shakespeare, ed. G. Blakemore Evans (Boston: Houghton Mifflin, 1974).

OPERATION SHYLOCK

1.1   OPERATION SHYLOCK]   A limited edition of the novel published by the Franklin Library contained the following prefatory note by Roth:

In January 1989 I was caught up in a Middle East crisis all my own, a personal upheaval that had the unmistakable signposts of the impossible, as opposed to those of the predictable, plausible reality to which I am as hopelessly addicted as any other human being. A man of my age, bearing an uncanny resemblance to me, turned up in Jerusalem shortly before I did and set about proselytizing for "Diasporism," a political program he'd devised advocating that the Jews of Israel return to their European countries of origin in order to avert "a second Holocaust," this one at the hands of the Arabs. Inasmuch as his imposturing constituted a crisis I was living rather than writing, it embodied a form of self-denunciation that I could not sanction, a satirizing of me so bizarre and unrealistic as to exceed by far the boundaries of amusing mischief I may myself have playfully perpetrated on my own existence in fiction.

Now, in life as in art, mischief can be a relief from all the prescriptions. The more scrupulously exacting the prescriptions, the greater the relief afforded by the mischief. Perhaps because of the abundance of prescriptions both internally and externally generated by Jewish history, perhaps because of the singular sort of care that living as a Jew has generally required, perhaps because of the exaggerated seriousness with which a thoughtful Jew is often burdened, Jewish mischief—as couched, say, in the inexhaustible jokes about their peculiarities that Jews themselves so much enjoy—flourishes, surprisingly enough, in even the most superdignified Jewish circles. The mischief subverts all the strategies that the Jewish predicament imposes, affords immeasurable if transitory relief not only because it is counterprohibitive but because it is counterparanoid as well, indifferent to threat, to enemies, to all the defenses.

As a writer, of course, I have myself been not merely labeled mischief maker but condemned by any number of affronted readers—among them some of the most superdignified Jews alive—as very much a dangerous operative in behalf of the "radical, primitive impulse" that Edgar Allan Poe accurately christened "the Imp of the Perverse." With my mischief, whose malice is alleged to outstrip its playfulness far too energetically, I have enraged a community whose members wish understandably to divest themselves of a slanderous reputation for the very wickedness that I have appeared to exhibit to a suspicious world all too eager to find Jews odious.

In their eyes I commit not amusing mischief but serious mischief, not responsible mischief but irresponsible mischief; with a crazy intensity that is unremitting, I enact a farce about issues that are anything but farcical, and trivially misrepresent things that all Jews are haunted by, including themselves as Jews. They have reminded me more than once that my impertinence imposes on even our gravest concerns a demeaning and most ridiculous shape. Because of this my mischief-making is something other than a relief. It is a menace and a scandal.

Well, having only barely outmatched the double who turned up in Jerusalem in 1989 to demythologize Israel and pathologize me—that criminal impersonator who usurped my biography as well as my name while all but calling himself the Messiah—I now understand a little more subjectively something of the disorienting extremes of distress with which my books are said to bedevil these readers. In him I confronted an impertinence as galling, enraging and, yes, personally menacing as my own impertinence could ever have seemed to them. With a crazy intensity that was unremitting and that did indeed, in my estimation, give our gravest concerns a demeaning and most ridiculous shape and trivially misrepresent all the things that Jews are haunted by, he drove me no less crazy than I had driven them, and maybe more so.

Though to this day I have never found out what was hidden in this stranger's trickery or what his secret was, my impossible adventure with an impostor who aspired to become as much a "co-personality" as he was a physical facsimile has, at this late date, forged an astonishing affinity between myself and the audience that has long considered me exactly what I considered him: deformed, deranged, craven, possessed, an alien wreck in a state of foaming madness—someone, in short, who isn't really human at all. Those whom I've offended should be happy to hear that I now have more than a faint idea of why they have wanted to kill me and of what, rightly and wrongly, they have been through.

5.7–10   The whole content . . . KIERKEGAARD] From *Repetition: An*

Essay in Experimental Psychology (1843), translated from the Danish by Walter Lowrie (1941).

7.12   the Mossad] HaMossad LeModi'in U'Letafkidim Meyuhadim (Institute for Intelligence and Special Duties), founded in 1951, conducts espionage, covert action, and counterterrorist operations outside of Israel and the occupied territories.

7.13   Demjanjuk case] Ukrainian-born John Demjanjuk (b. 1920) immigrated to the United States after World War II and became an American citizen. After he was accused of having been "Ivan the Terrible," an especially brutal guard at the Treblinka extermination camp, Demjanjuk was stripped of his American citizenship by a federal district court in Ohio and was extradited in February 1986 to Israel. An Israeli court convicted Demjanjuk of war crimes and sentenced him to death in 1988, but his conviction was overturned in 1993 when evidence from the former Soviet Union cast doubt on his identification as "Ivan the Terrible." He returned to the United States and had his citizenship restored, but in 2002 it was again revoked after a federal district court ruled that Demjanjuk had become a citizen under false pretenses by concealing his wartime service as a guard at the Sobibor and Majdanek extermination camps. In May 2009 Demjanjuk was deported to Germany to face war crimes charges; his trial began in Munich on November 30, 2009.

14.7–8   King David Hotel] Five-star hotel in Jerusalem opened 1931. See also note 119.19–20.

17.1   Bernie Avishai] Bernard Avishai (b. 1949), Canadian-born academic, editor, and writer, author of *The Tragedy of Zionism* (1985).

20.38–39   much-praised . . . Kafka] Most famously in Kafka's novella *The Metamorphosis* (1915), in which Gregor Samsa wakes up one morning to discover that he has been transformed into a monstrous bug.

21.35   Lech Walesa . . . Gdansk] Polish labor leader and statesman (b. 1943), head of the Solidarity union suppressed by Poland's Communist regime in December 1981, winner of the Nobel Prize for Peace (1983), and president of Poland (1990–95). Solidarity was founded in the Baltic port of Gdansk in September 1980.

22.30–31   Spain . . . Jews] Spain's Catholic monarchs, Ferdinand II of Aragon and Isabella I of Castile, issued an edict of expulsion against Spain's Jews in 1492.

23.23–25   authentic Jewish homeland . . . Hasidic Judaism] Rabbinic Judaism, which incorporated and codified the Oral Law of rabbinic scriptural interpretation, emerged after the fall of Jerusalem in 70 C.E. and the resulting dispersion of the Jews; Hasidism, an eighteenth-century movement emphasizing mysticism and spiritual enthusiasm, was founded in the Polish-

Lithuanian Commonwealth by Israel ben Eliezer (c. 1700–1760), known as the Baal Shem Tov (Master of the Good Name).

23.38–39   Shalom . . . Heine]   Shalom Aleichem, pen name (meaning "peace be unto you," a Hebrew greeting) of Yiddish writer Sholem Rabinovitch (1859–1916), best known for stories featuring his character Tevye the milkman; German Jewish poet Heinrich Heine (1797–1856).

24.15   *mishigas*]   Yiddish: craziness.

28.37   East Jerusalem]   The area of the city controlled by Jordan after the 1948 Arab-Israeli War and captured by Israel in the 1967 Six-Day War.

28.38   Old City]   Ancient walled area within East Jersualem that contains the Western Wall and Temple Mount, the Church of the Holy Sepulchre, and the Dome of the Rock and the al-Aqsa mosque.

30.21–22   that French . . . Kaye]   French actor Charles Boyer (1899–1978) spoke English in his roles with a cultured, seductive accent; Jewish comedian Danny Kaye (1913–1987) had a routine where he spoke nonsense with a mock-French accent.

30.25   Philippe Sollers]   Pen name of Philippe Joyaux (b. 1936), French novelist, critic, and editor, co-founder of *Tel Quel*, influential French literary and political journal (1960–82).

31.4   robbery . . . Jean Genet]   The early career as petty criminal and prostitute of French novelist, playwright, and activist Jean Genet (1910–1986) was the basis for books such as his autobiographical novels *The Miracle of the Rose* (1946) and *The Thief's Journal* (1949).

31.10   Pierre Roget]   English lexicographer Peter Mark Roget (1779–1869) published his English thesaurus in 1852.

35.39   Ramallah]   West Bank city six miles north of West Jerusalem.

36.2–3   Dizengoff Street]   Central boulevard in Tel Aviv, named for the city's first mayor.

37.9   Brandenburg Gate]   The only one remaining of a series of gates built in Prussian Berlin.

37.15–19   President Ceauşescu . . . selling Jews]   In 1969 Israel secretly negotiated an agreement with Romanian dictator Nicolae Ceauşescu (1918–1989) permitting the immigration of Romanian Jews to Israel in exchange for cash payments of $2,500 (later increased to $3,300) per immigrant. The payments continued until 1989; by then more than 40,000 Jews had immigrated in return for the payment delivery of an estimated $112 million into clandestine accounts controlled by Ceauşescu and the Romanian secret police.

37.25–26   Herzl's negotiations . . . Constantinople] The Hungarian-born founder of Zionism, Theodor Herzl (1860–1904), met with Ottoman sultan Abdul Hamid II (1842–1918) in 1901 in an unsuccessful attempt to secure territory for a Jewish homeland in Palestine, then under Ottoman rule.

38.15   *Der Spiegel*] "The Mirror" in German, a weekly news magazine based in Hamburg.

38.35–36   *Le Monde* to *Paris-Match*] Eminent left-of-center Parisian daily newspaper and glossy weekly magazine featuring celebrity profiles and gossip as well as lifestyle and news items.

40.28   KGB] Komitet Gosudarstvennoy Bezopasnosti (Committee for State Security), the Soviet intelligence and internal security organization, 1954–91.

40.36   DP camp] Before emigrating from Germany to the U.S., Demjanjuk lived in several Displaced Persons camps that were built to house war refugees.

41.28–29   Mishkenot Sha'ananim] Built in 1869 as an almshouse by British philanthropist Sir Moses Montefiore, since 1973 Mishkenot Sha'ananim has served as a guesthouse for internationally recognized artists visiting Israel.

43.4–7   Lebanon war . . . criminal murderers] Israel invaded Lebanon on June 6, 1982, beginning a campaign aimed at destroying the Palestine Liberation Organization (PLO), which had been using southern Lebanon as a base for attacking Israel since 1969. After defeating PLO and Syrian forces in the south, the Israel Defense Forces (IDF) reached the suburbs of Beirut on June 13 and began a prolonged siege of West Beirut that ended with the evacuation of thousands of PLO fighters in late August. During the invasion and siege Israel came under intense international criticism for thousands of civilian casualties caused by IDF air raids and artillery bombardments. On September 14 Bashir Gemayel, the president-elect of Lebanon and leader of the Christian Phalange movement that had been allied with Israel since 1976, was assassinated by a Syrian agent; two days later Phalangist militamen murdered several hundred Palestinians in the Sabra and Shatilla refugee camps in Beirut. (In 1983 an Israeli investigating commission found that Israel bore "indirect responsibility" for having failed to prevent the massacre.) Although Israel succeeded in expelling the PLO from southern Lebanon, it was unable to force the Syrian army to leave the country or to sign a peace treaty with the Lebanese government. By June 1985 the IDF had withdrawn to a six-mile-deep security zone along the Israel–Lebanon border first established in 1978 (the security zone was evacuated in 2000).

44.13–18   Transnistria . . . Bukovina] After German and Romanian forces overran western Ukraine in 1941, the Nazis gave administrative control over Transnistria, an area between the Dniester and Bug rivers, to Romanian military authorities (October 1941–March 1944); it was the site of two concentration camps and several ghettoes for Jews from Transnistria, Bukovina, and Bessarabia. Bukovina is a region on the northern side of the Carpathian mountains now in Romanian and Ukrainian territory. Bessarabia is a region between the Dneister and Prut rivers, once part of the principality of Moldavia. After a brief period of independence in 1918 as the Moldavian Democratic Republic, it united with the kingdom of Romania. It is now divided between Moldova and Ukraine.

46.16   Bruno Schulz]   Bruno Schulz (1892–1942) was one of the Eastern European writers included in the Penguin paperback series, *Writers from the Other Europe*. Roth conceived of the project and served as general editor from 1974–1989. It was influential in bringing certain Eastern European writers to prominence in the West.

46.21–22   Max Brod . . . circle]   Kafka's close friend and literary executor Max Brod (1884–1968) wrote the biography *Franz Kafka: A Life* (1937), from which the quote is taken.

48.16   St. Stephen's gate]   Also called Lion's Gate, one of eight gates in the walls of Jerusalem's Old City. It is supposedly built on the site where Christian martyr Stephen was stoned to death (see Acts 6:13–14) in 35 C.E.

49.13   Magrittishly]   In the manner of Belgian surrealist artist René Magritte (1898–1967).

49.23–24   Knesset and the museum]   The buildings of the Israeli parliament (Knesset) and the Israel Museum are located in the Givat Ram neighborhood in the western part of the city.

59.18   Ticho House]   Nineteenth-century mansion, one of the first houses built outside the Old City walls, and now a branch of the Israel Museum that includes a vegetarian restaurant. It was the residence of painter Anna Ticho (1894–1980) and her husband, the Moravian-born ophthalmologist Abraham Ticho (1883–1960), who ran a clinic at the house from 1924 until his death.

61.8–9   Love . . . *Dial*]   The story "The Love Vessel" was published in the first issue of *The Dial* (Fall 1959), a journal that took its name from the long-running literary magazine that had ceased publication thirty years earlier.

62.14–15   Marcel Marceau]   French mime (1923–2007).

62.23   nebbishly]   In Yiddish, a *nebbish* is a poor unfortunate, weak-willed and timid.

62.31   shlimazl]   A Yiddish word that combines *schlimm* (German for "bad") and *mazel* (Hebrew for "luck").

63.13   Swados]   Novelist, essayist, and editor Harvey Swados (1920–1972), author of *A Radical's America* (1962), *The Will* (1963), and *Standing Fast* (1970).

63.15   Podhoretz]   Critic Norman Podhoretz (b. 1930), editor of *Commentary* magazine from 1960 to 1995.

63.16–17   Gilman . . . *Good*]   Critic Richard Gilman (1925–2006), reviewing Roth's *When She Was Good* in *The New Republic* (June 24, 1967), called the novel "a flawed but energetic melodrama on the highest level of ladies' magazine fiction."

63.19   Professor Epstein]   Critic Joseph Epstein (b. 1937), whose essay "What Does Philip Roth Want?" was published in *Commentary* in 1984.

63.20   *Ms.*]   Feminist magazine founded in 1971.

63.21   Wolcott]   Critic James Wolcott (b. 1952).

63.33–34   Capote . . . mafia]   In interviews given during his later career, writer Truman Capote (1924–1984) would often invoke a "Jewish mafia," which he claimed "control much of the literary scene" and ensure that "members of their particular clique rise to the top." He was a frequent guest on NBC's *The Tonight Show*, hosted by Johnny Carson.

69.7   Jung on 'synchronicity.']   In *Synchronicity: An Acausal Connecting Principle* (1952) by Swiss psychologist Carl Jung (1875–1961).

69.12   *The Secret of the Golden Flower*]   Taoist treatise translated from the Chinese by Jung's friend Richard Wilhelm (1873–1930) with Jung's encouragement and help. Jung also wrote a foreword and commentary to Wilhelm's translation.

70.23   schmatas]   Yiddish: rags.

70.32   Jonathan Pollard]   Jonathan Jay Pollard (b. 1954), a civilian analyst working at a U.S. naval intelligence center in Suitland, Maryland, met in the late spring of 1984 with an Israeli air force officer studying in the United States and offered to supply Israel with highly classified information. Pollard became an agent of Lakam (Bureau of Scientific Liaison), an intelligence unit within the Israeli ministry of defense, and eventually gave his handlers more than one million pages of documents, including detailed information about Soviet weapons, Arab military capabilities, and U.S. intelligence collection methods. Despite assurances that he would be "taken care of" if discovered, Pollard's Israeli contacts quickly left the country after he fell under suspicion; when Pollard and his wife sought asylum in the Israeli embassy in Washington, D.C. on November 21, 1985, they were refused entry, and he was arrested by the FBI. After pleading guilty to espionage charges, Pollard said that he was motivated by concern for the security of Israel, while admitting that he had accepted cash payments of $1,500 a month (later increased to $2,500), as well as thousands of dollars in travel expenses and jewelry. Pollard was sentenced to life imprisonment in 1987. The Israeli government initially described his spying as the result of an unauthorized operation, but subsequently granted him citizenship and has sought his release without success.

72.6   Ashkenazis] Yiddish-speaking Jews from Central and Eastern Europe ("Ashkenaz" means "Germany" in Hebrew), one of the major branches of Jewry.

72.13   pure commedia dell'arte] Largely improvisatory form developed in sixteenth-century Italy in which traveling troupes made use of stock characters given to exaggerated gestures and played by masked actors.

72.21–22   Oliver Sacks] British-born neurologist and author (b. 1933) whose widely read books based on unusual medical cases include *The Man Who Mistook His Wife for a Hat* (1985).

74.27–28   Kosinski's *The Painted Bird*] Novel (1965) by Polish-born Jewish writer Jerzy Kosinski (1933–1991) recounting a boy's horrific journey through Eastern Europe during World War II.

74.30–31   landscape . . . *Molloy*] In the novel *Molloy* (1951) by Samuel Beckett (1906–1989), the title character and the detective Moran wander through desolate landscapes that offer little comfort; both commit murders.

74.38–39   tale . . . incarceration?] Italian writer and chemist Primo Levi (1919–1987) wrote about his experiences in Auschwitz in *Se questo e un uomo* (*If This Is a Man*, 1947; English translation published in the United States as *Survival in Auschwitz*) and other works.

80.38   *Sarah Bernhardt*] Celebrated French actress (1844–1923).

81.18   Strindberg] Swedish playwright, poet, and novelist August Strindberg (1849–1912), author of *Miss Julie* (1888), *The Ghost Sonata* (1907), and many other works.

82.21   Near North, Rush Street] The Near North is a Chicago neighborhood south of North Avenue, between the Chicago River and Lake Michigan. Rush Street is the area's entertainment district.

95.6   the golem . . . Prague] According to legend, Rabbi Judah Loew (Liva) ben Bezalel (c. 1525–1609), a Talmudic scholar and astronomer from Prague, created the golem, a clay automaton, to protect the Jews.

100.37   Ohel-Moshe] Working-class neighborhood in Jerusalem.

101.8   the Rothschilds] Family of German Jews with family ties to other nations who have been prominent in investment banking and philanthropy in Europe since the late eighteenth century.

102.39–40   Dr. Jekyll . . . Second] The doubled selves of Robert Louis Stevenson's novella *Strange Case of Dr. Jekyll and Mr. Hyde* (1886) and Fyodor Dostoevsky's novella *The Double* (1846).

103.32   omphalos at Delphi] Delphi, an ancient Greek site sacred to Apollo, was the seat of the most famous oracle of antiquity; the *omphalos* (literally, "navel") there was a stone said to mark the center of the earth.

104.5   Paul Bunyan] Legendary giant lumberjack of North American folklore.

108.15   Nablus] West Bank city thirty miles north of Jerusalem.

109.24   Zabar's] Popular specialty-foods supermarket on Manhattan's Upper West Side.

110.21   Preston Roberts] Professor of literature and religion at the University of Chicago Divinity School (1948–68).

110.22   Herb Haber and Barry Targan and Art Geffen] Roth's friends from graduate school.

111.15   Shin Bet] Sherut HaBitachon HaKlali (General Security Service), often called Shin Bet (after its first two Hebrew initials) or Shabak (its Hebrew acronym). Founded in 1948, Shin Bet is responsible for internal security, counterespionage, and counterterrorism in Israel and the occupied territories, and the protection of Israeli delegations in foreign countries. Like the Mossad, it is a civilian agency that reports directly to the prime minister.

111.25   Kahanes and Sharons] American rabbi Meir Kahane (1932–1990) founded the militant Jewish Defense League in 1968 and immigrated in 1971 to Israel, where he founded the extreme right-wing Kach political party. Kahane was elected to the Knesset in 1984, but in 1988 his party was banned from participating in new elections because of its incitement of racism. He was assassinated in a Manhattan hotel in 1990 by an Egyptian immigrant. Ariel Sharon (b. 1928), a retired general, was minister of defense during the Israeli invasion of Lebanon in 1982. He was removed from office after an Israeli investigating commission found him "remiss in his duties" for not preventing the massacre in Beirut refugee camps of hundreds of Palestinians by Phalangist militia in September 1982. Sharon later served as prime minister (2001–6) of Israel. See note 43.4–7.

111.26   Yehoshuas and Ozes] Left-leaning Israeli writers: A. B. Yehoshua (b. 1936), author of nine novels, plays, and nonfiction including *Between Right and Right* (1980); novelist and essayist Amos Oz (b. 1939), whose books include the novel *A Perfect Peace* (1982) and the essay collection *The Slopes of Lebanon* (1987).

112.27   Saul Alinsky] Chicago-based labor activist and writer (1909–1972), author of *Reveille for Radicals* (1946) and *Rules for Radicals* (1971).

112.27   David Riesman] Influential sociologist (1909–2002), best known as one of the authors (with Nathan Glazer and Reuel Denney) of *The Lonely Crowd* (1950).

112.27–28   Meyer Schapiro] Art historian and critic (1904–1996), long-time professor at Columbia University, and a co-founder in 1954 of the magazine *Dissent*.

112.28   Leonard Bernstein] Conductor and composer (1918–1990), music director of the New York Philharmonic (1958–69), and composer of many works for orchestra and musical theater, including *On the Town* (1944), *Candide* (1956), and *West Side Story* (1957).

112.28   Bella Abzug] Outspoken feminist activist (1920–1998) and Democratic U.S. congresswoman from New York (1971–77).

112.28–29   Paul Goodman] Social critic, novelist, poet, and prolific writer (1911–1972) whose best-known book is *Growing Up Absurd* (1960).

112.29   Allen Ginsberg] Poet (1926–1997), one of the foremost members of the Beat Generation, author of *Howl* (1956), *Kaddish* (1961), and many other books.

113.13–14   The Golden *Calf*] In the book of Exodus, an idol made by Aaron and worshipped by the Israelites when Moses was at Mount Sinai receiving the Ten Commandments.

113.15   Samaria and Judea] Biblical Hebrew names for territory now comprising the West Bank.

113.37   Molotov cocktails] Homemade firebombs named after Vyacheslav Molotov (1890–1986), Soviet premier (1930–41) and foreign minister (1939–49, 1953–56).

119.6–7   Brenda Patimkin] In Roth's novella *Goodbye, Columbus* (1959), the girlfriend of protagonist Neil Klugman.

119.7   Anne Frank] Anne Frank (1929–1945) died of typhus at the Bergen-Belsen concentration camp. Her twenty-six-month diary, nearly all of which was written while she and her family were in hiding from the Nazis in Amsterdam, was first published posthumously in the Netherlands in 1947 as *Het Achterhuis* (*The Back House*) in a small printing. It was translated into some fifty languages, with sales in the millions for the American edition (1952) alone. Frances Goodrich and Albert Hackett adapted it into a successful and Pulitzer Prize–winning Broadway play (1955); it was later made into a film (1959).

119.7–8   Big Ten basketball] Collegiate basketball conference that has consistently been competitive in the NCAA championship tournament.

119.19–20   terrorist Begin] Menachem Begin (1913–1992), prime minister of Israel (1977–83), led the Zionist underground organization Irgun Zvai Leumi from 1943 to its disbanding in 1948. The Irgun's attacks against the British in Palestine included the 1946 bombing of the British military head-quarters at the King David Hotel that killed ninety-one people.

119.28–29   blowing off the limbs of Arab mayors] Bassam Shak'a (b. 1930), the mayor of Nablus, and Karim Khalaf (1935–1985), the mayor of Ra-mallah, were maimed on June 2, 1980, by car bombs planted by extremist Jewish settlers.

119.40   *Shoah*] The Nazi mass murder of European Jews (the word means "catastrophe" in Hebrew). The reference at 120.5 refers to the docu-mentary film (1985), running nine and a half hours, by the French Jewish filmmaker Claude Lanzmann (b. 1925).

120.6–7   *Holocaust*. . . Streep!] The four-part television miniseries *Holocaust* was broadcast on NBC on April 16–19, 1978, and subsequently in other countries. American actress Meryl Streep (b. 1949) plays Inga Helms-Weiss, a Christian woman who marries into the fictitious German Jewish Weiss family.

121.2   gangster Shamir] Yitzhak Shamir (b.1915), twice prime minister of Israel (1983–84, 1986–92), was a leader of Lehi, an underground organization that split away from the Irgun in 1940; it was known as the Stern Gang after its founder, Avraham Stern (1907–1942).

122.11   Law of the Return] Israeli law (1950) that declares the right of Jews to immigrate to Israel and claim citizenship.

122.13   Ingathering of the Exiles] *Kibbutz galuyot*, Hebrew phrase refer-ring to the arrival of Diaspora Jews in Israel.

122.29–30   smear campaign . . . Spinoza] Philosopher Baruch Spinoza (1632–1677) was excommunicated from his congregation in Amsterdam in 1656 because of his purported "evil opinions and acts."

122.32   B'nai B'rith] Jewish service organization founded in 1843.

123.7–8   the underground man] Anonymous protagonist and narrator of Dostoevsky's *Notes from Underground* (1864).

125.4   the Mandate] Period of British rule over Palestine (1922–48) as established by a League of Nations mandate after the breakup of the Ottoman Empire.

125.22   Sephardic boys] Jews who originated from North Africa and Spain. In contrast to Ashkenazim or "German Jews."

127.10   a Druze] A member of a religious sect that developed from Islam in the eleventh century and evolved to incorporate elements of Judaism, Christianity, and Gnosticism. Druze volunteers fought in the Israel Defense Forces during the 1948–49 war, and Druze men in Israel have been subject to compulsory military service since 1956.

130.28   schmucks] Yiddish: dopes, fools. Obscene: pricks.

130.35   Stockholm] City where the Nobel Prize in Literature is awarded.

131.13–14   Jewish Jesse . . . Chomskys] Civil-rights leader Jesse Jackson (b. 1941) and linguist and leftist polemicist Noam Chomsky (b. 1928) have been outspoken critics of Israeli policies.

132.1   Shi'ite Islam] Second largest branch of Islam, whose members believe that Ali, the son-in-law of the Prophet Muhammed, was his rightful successor.

136.40   Coolidge Hall] Since demolished, the former site of Harvard's Center for Middle Eastern Studies, among other programs.

137.2–4   WGBH . . . Netanyahu] From 1977 to 1991, journalist and media personality Christopher Lydon (b. 1940) hosted *The Ten O'Clock News* on WGBH, Boston's public television station. Benjamin Netanyahu (b. 1949) was the Israeli ambassador to the United Nations from 1984 to 1988 and became a frequent guest on American news programs; he has since served twice as the prime minister of Israel (1996–99, 2009–).

137.14–15   Newton] Prosperous Boston suburb with a large Jewish population.

138.34   agitprop] Soviet term for "agitation and propaganda."

141.18   Woody Allen . . . *Times*] "Am I Reading the Papers Correctly?" a *New York Times* editorial critical of Israel, published on January 28, 1988.

141.29   in Tunis] The headquarters of the PLO, 1982–91.

143.26   up with the bonnet!] Irving Berlin's "Easter Parade" (1933) begins "I could write a sonnet / About your Easter bonnet."

143.31   people . . . Jewish] Actor Cary Grant, born Archibald Alec Leach (1904–1986), was believed by some (such as the film critic Pauline Kael) to be of Jewish ancestry on his father's side.

143.33–34   Bing Crosby . . . Easter!] Bing Crosby sang both "White Christmas" (whistling part of it) and "Easter Parade" in the movie musical *Holiday Inn* (1942), featuring Berlin's music.

146.14   Abu Nidal] Palestinian terrorist (1937–2002).

150.6   mot juste] French: the precise word—the finding of which was Gustave Flaubert's aim as a writer.

150.14–16   Jesse Jackson . . . leader] Jackson was photographed with PLO leader Yasser Arafat (1929–2004) when they met in September 1979; actress Vanessa Redgrave (b. 1937), a supporter of the PLO, interviewed Arafat while working on the documentary *The Palestinians* (1977).

150.22   Gramsci] Italian Marxist theorist Antonio Gramsci (1891–1937), Italian Communist Party leader who was imprisoned by the Fascists in 1926. His *Prison Notebooks* were published posthumously after World War II.

150.23–24   Mitterrand . . . Pinter] American novelist William Styron (1925–2006), author of *The Confessions of Nat Turner* (1967) and *Sophie's Choice* (1979), and French president François Mitterand (1916–1996) were mutual admirers; Mitterand invited Styron to his first inauguration in 1981. Colombian novelist Gabriel García Márquez (b. 1927) was an enthusiastic supporter and friend of Cuban dictator Fidel Castro (b. 1926). English playwright Harold Pinter (1930–2008) hosted Daniel Ortega (b. 1945), Sandinista leader and Nicaraguan president, at his home in England and visited Nicaragua as a guest of the Sandinistas.

150.25   character . . . fate] Cf. *On the Universe* by Greek philosopher Heraclitus (c. 540–c. 480 B.C.E.), frag. 121: "A man's character is his fate."

152.20–21   Meir Kahane . . . Shimon Peres] Meir Kahane, see note 111.25; Shimon Peres (b. 1923) has held several government positions in Israel, including prime minister (1984–86, 1995–96) and president (2007–).

153.3   Israeli settlers] Israeli citizens who have settled in the West Bank and other occupied territories.

159.23   Jack Ruby] Nightclub owner Jack Ruby (1911–1967) fatally shot Lee Harvey Oswald on November 24, 1963, two days after Oswald was arrested for the assassination of President Kennedy.

162.31–32   your dialogue . . . himself] Roth's interview with Levi was published in the *New York Times Book Review* on October 12, 1986. Levi committed suicide on April 11, 1987.

164.9   Meema] Yiddish: aunt.

165.21   Studebakers] Make of American automobiles popular from the 1920s through the 1940s; the company manufactured its last car in 1966.

168.10   *shivah*] Week-long period of mourning conducted at the home of the deceased.

171.6   NBA] National Book Award.

172.9   *tuchas*] Yiddish: backside.

174.27   Dreyfus case] In October 1894, the French Jewish artillery officer Alfred Dreyfus (1859–1935) was wrongfully arrested on charges of treason and sentenced to life imprisonment. The intense controversy that followed resulted in the case being reopened, and in September 1899 Dreyfus was pardoned by President Emile Loubet. He was fully exonerated by a military commission on July 12, 1906, and one week later publicly decorated with the Legion d'Honneur.

175.19–20   your friend Styron] See note 150.23–24.

180.24   Ron . . . Segal] Well-known Jewish-American actors George Segal (b. 1934) and Ron Liebman (b. 1937).

182.30   Magnum . . . Minutes] *Magnum, P.I.* (1980–88), popular CBS television series starring Tom Selleck about a private investigator living in Hawaii; weekly CBS news magazine *60 Minutes* (1968–).

185.11–12   Eugenio . . . anti-Semite] Eugenio Pacelli (1876–1958), Pope Pius XII, was elected pope in 1939; he never publicly criticized the Nazi regime during World War II.

186.1–2   oversized pole . . . *Lysistrata*] In Aristophanes's sexually frank play (fifth century B.C.E.), the women of Athens resolve to withhold sex from their husbands until the Peloponnesian War is ended.

186.10   Mortimer Snerd] A dummy used by the ventriloquist Edgar Bergen (1903–1978).

188.1   Shave . . . *bits*] Simple call-and-response phrase: the first five notes are the call, "two bits" (twenty-five cents) the response.

192.38   Lenny . . . Mason] Two blunt, outspoken comedians: Lenny Bruce (1925–1966), convicted for obscenity in 1964, was posthumously pardoned; Jackie Mason (b. 1936), ordained as a rabbi, has starred in several one-man shows on Broadway.

193.13–17   in Mailer . . . Gilmore] Sergius O'Shaugnessy, protagonist of Mailer's novel *The Deer Park* (1955) and short story "The Time of Her Time" (1959); Stephen Rojack, narrator and hero of his novel *An American Dream* (1965); murderer Gary Gilmore (1940–1977), the subject of *The Executioner's Song* (1979). Louis "Lepke" Buchalter (1897–1944) was a Jewish labor racketeer and leader of the gang of hired killers popularly known as

"Murder, Incorporated," which he founded with fellow racketeer Jacob "Gurrah" Shapiro (1899–1947).

200.32–33   *Hellzapoppin'*] Popular Broadway musical comedy revue (1938) and film (1941).

200.38   Chancellor Kohl] Helmut Kohl (b. 1930), chancellor of the Federal Republic of Germany (1982–98).

201.6   England's green and pleasant land] Phrase from the preface to *Milton: A Poem* (1804–10) by William Blake (1757–1827), widely known because of the English hymn "Jerusalem" (1916) by Hubert Parry (1848–1918) a musical setting of the poem.

203.17–18   boy . . . Jodie Foster] John Hinckley, Jr. (b. 1955), who tried to kill President Ronald Reagan in 1981, was obsessed with actress Jodie Foster (b. 1963), who had played a child prostitute in *Taxi Driver* (1976). The film depicts the attempted assassination of a presidential candidate.

203.40–204.2   little couplet . . . I."] The epitaph for his wife attributed to English poet John Dryden (1631–1700).

205.39   Hare Krishna] Popular name for the International Society for Krishna Consciousness, founded by A. C. Bhaktivedanta Swami Prabhupada (1896–1977) in 1966. The group is known for their orange robes, shorn heads, and chanting of the "Hare Krishna" mantra in public.

210.3   the Phil Donahue show] Nationally syndicated talk-show (1970–96) hosted by the television personality Phil Donahue (b. 1935), a pioneer of the genre.

212.36   *goyische nachis*] Yiddish: Gentile pleasure (used ironically).

215.28–29   roman-fleuve] French term for a fictional narrative told over multiple volumes, such as Romain Rolland's *Jean-Christophe*.

216.3   underground with Persephone] Greek goddess who was abducted and taken to the underworld by Hades. Her grieving mother, Demeter, made the earth barren until it was arranged that Persephone be allowed to return for part of every year, starting in spring.

223.33   deus ex machina] Latin: God from a machine; a term in ancient drama indicating the sudden appearance and intervention of a god late in the play to resolve a seemingly intractable plot dilemma.

227.1   the *Guardian*] British left-wing newspaper.

229.29   Pirandellian effect] Italian playwright and novelist Luigi Pirandello (1867–1936) explored the uncertain relation between reality and artifice in works such as *Six Characters in Search of an Author* (1921).

231.22–23 Did . . . Die?] Six million is the generally accepted number of Jews killed in the Holocaust.

232.6–7 Masson . . . false] Jeffrey Moussaieff Masson (b. 1941), a non-practicing psychoanalyst who taught Sanskrit at Berkeley, argued in *The Assault on Truth: Freud's Suppression of the Seduction Theory* (1984) that Freud had deliberately dismissed the real sexual abuse of his female patients as fantasy in order to win acceptance for psychoanalysis.

232.12 Oppenheimer] J. Robert Oppenheimer (1904–1967), physicist who directed the design of the first atomic bombs at Los Alamos, New Mexico, 1943–45.

232.15 Elie Wiesel] Romanian-born Jewish writer (b. 1928), author of more than forty books, most notably *Night* (1958), an account of his experiences surviving the Holocaust.

232.35–36 Paget's disease] A degenerative bone condition.

232.36 Ted Koppel] Journalist (b. 1940) and longtime host of ABC's late-night news program *Nightline*; he was born in England to German Jewish parents who had fled the Nazis in 1938.

232.37 Mike Wallace] Television journalist (b. 1918), for decades a fixture of CBS's *60 Minutes* news magazine.

233.11–12 Wiesel, Singer, and Bellow] Wiesel was awarded the Nobel Prize for Peace in 1986; Saul Bellow (1915–2005) and Isaac Bashevis Singer (1902–1991) won the Nobel Prize in Literature in 1976 and 1978, respectively.

233.12 Graham Greene . . . it] English author Graham Greene (1904–1991) was often named as a likely recipient of the Nobel Prize but did not receive the award.

233.12 Isaac Stern] Ukrainian-born Jewish classical violinist and internationally popular recording artist (1920–2001).

233.15 Wannsee Conference] Meeting of SS leaders with other German officials held in the Berlin district of Wannsee on January 20, 1942, to coordinate plans for the deportation and murder of European Jews.

233.15 A. J. P. Taylor] English historian (1906–1990) whose controversial *The Origins of the Second World War* (1961) argued that Hitler did not invade Poland as part of a plan for wider European conquest.

233.17 Hilberg] Austrian-born historian and Holocaust scholar Raul Hilberg (1926–2007), author of *The Destruction of the European Jews* (1961) and *Perpetrators, Victims, Bystanders: The Jewish Catastrophe, 1933–1945* (1992).

233.40 Schoenberg] Austrian-born composer Arnold Schoenberg (1874–1951).

233.43   Pissarro]   French Impressionist artist (1830–1903).

234.1   Richard Wagner on the Jews]   See, for example, the anti-Semitic tract *The Jew in Music* (1850; expanded edition, 1869).

234.4   Herman Wouk]   Popular novelist Herman Wouk (b. 1915), whose novels include *The Caine Mutiny* (1951) and *Marjorie Morningstar* (1955).

234.11   Arthur Miller]   Playwright (1915–2005), author of *Death of a Salesman* (1949), *The Crucible* (1953), *After the Fall* (1964), and many other plays.

234.17   Boesky]   Investment banker Ivan Boesky (b. 1937) was convicted of securities fraud in connection with illegal insider trading in 1987 and sentenced to three years in prison and a $100 million fine.

234.24   Norman Lear]   Television producer, director, writer, and liberal activist (b. 1922), best known for creating and producing 1970s situation comedies such as *All in the Family*, *Sanford and Son*, *Maude*, and *Good Times*.

234.42–235.2   Miller . . . *Hot*]   Arthur Miller was married to Marilyn Monroe from 1956 to 1961; Monroe starred in director Billy Wilder's film *Some Like It Hot* (1959) opposite Tony Curtis and Jack Lemmon, and *The Misfits* (1961), starring Clark Gable, for which Miller wrote the screenplay.

236.6   a Farrakhan guy]   Member of the Nation of Islam, militant black nationalist organization led since 1978 by Louis Farrakhan (b. 1933).

237.3   extract money . . . government]   West Germany paid reparations to Israel under the terms of an agreement signed in September 1952 between the two governments.

241.9   *Gan Eden*]   Hebrew: Garden of Eden.

242.1   *Jerusalem Post*]   Israeli daily English-language newspaper founded in 1942.

242.8–12   defense minister . . . Beatings]   Yitzhak Rabin (1922–1995), then defense minister, visited Ramallah after Palestinians had been beaten there by Israeli soldiers in accordance with a policy announced by Rabin in January 1988 that "force, might, and beatings" rather than live ammunition would be used against Palestinian protestors.

242.13   "Hezbollah" and "Mubarak"]   Hezbollah ("Party of God" in Arabic), Lebanese militia, terrorist organization, and Shi'a Islamist political movement; Hosni Mubarak (b. 1928), president of Egypt (1981–).

242.36–37   Shevat . . . 1408]   The date "January 27, 1988" in Hebrew and Arabic.

244.24   making aliyah]   Immigrating to Israel (*aliyah* is a Hebrew word meaning "ascent").

244.30   Kinneret Lake]   The Sea of Galilee.

245.12   *hozer b'tshuva*]   Hebrew: returned to the answer; i.e., became a newly observant Jew.

246.27   Sandhurst]   The Royal Military Academy Sandhurst (RMAS) is the British Army officer-training center.

247.22–23   Sammy Davis, Jr. . . . Wall]   In the summer of 1969, American singer and actor Sammy Davis, Jr. (1925–1990), a convert to Judaism, visited Israel and prayed at the Western Wall.

251.34–35   Shylock . . . Keans to Irving]   English actor Edmund Kean (1789–1833) and his son Charles (1811–1868) both played Shylock, as did English actor Henry Irving (1838–1905), who wrote, "I look on Shylock . . . as the *type* of a persecuted race; almost the only gentleman in the play, and the most ill-used."

251.39   Crucifixion pageants at York]   The crucifixion was among the subjects dramatized by the Mystery Plays performed at York, England, in the fourteenth and fifteenth centuries.

252.25–27   Jew-hating dramas . . . Marlowe]   Playwright, poet, and actor Christopher Marlowe (1564–1593) wrote *The Jew of Malta* (1592), a play about a Jew's unrestrained revenge against the Maltese authorities.

252.31   *Judenrein*]   German: cleansed of Jews.

253.14   diary of Anne Frank]   See note 119.7.

253.35   André Gide's]   For most of his life, the French writer André Gide (1869–1951) kept a revealing diary, which was published in three volumes between 1939 and 1950. He was awarded the Nobel Prize in Literature in 1949.

254.23–24   *Achille Lauro* hijacking]   On October 7, 1985, four members of the Palestine Liberation Front (PLF) hijacked the Italian cruise liner *Achille Lauro* in the eastern Mediterranean and threatened to kill the ship's passengers if their demanded release of fifty Palestinian prisoners was not met. The next day the hijackers murdered Leon Klinghoffer (1916–1985), a disabled sixty-nine-year-old American passenger, and threw his body overboard. They then brought the ship to Port Said, where they surrendered on October 9 to Egyptian and PLO officials. Despite American demands for their arrest, President Mubarak granted the hijackers safe passage to Tunis on an Egyptair plane along with Abu Abbas (1948–2004), the leader of the PLF. President Reagan ordered that the airliner be intercepted, and U.S. Navy fighters

forced it to land at a NATO base in Sicily. The hijackers were tried and convicted in Italy, but the Italian government allowed Abu Abbas to leave the
country. He was captured in Iraq during the 2003 American invasion, but
died of a heart attack before being brought to trial.

255.22–23   made Anne Frank . . . work] In *The Ghost Writer* (1979).

263.7   Xanadu] Byword for an idealized luxurious place, from Cole-
ridge's poem "Kubla Khan" (written 1797, pub. 1816).

266.22–23   uprising . . . 1943] On August 2, 1943, Jewish prisoners,
forced to work for the SS in *Sonderkommandos* (special units), staged a revolt
at the Treblinka death camp using kerosene and small arms stolen from the
camp's arsenal. Of the hundreds who were able to escape about sixty survived
the war.

268.26   *Vachmanns*] In German, *Wachmann*: guard.

269.13   critical prefaces of Henry James] James wrote prefaces to accompany the New York Edition (1907–9) of his novels.

273.10   *landsmen*] Yiddish: fellow Jews coming from the same town or
region in Europe.

273.11–12   famous prison letters . . . Vanzetti] Nicola Sacco (1891–1927)
and Bartolomeo Vanzetti (1888–1927) were anarchist Italian immigrants convicted of murder and armed robbery in 1920. They were executed in 1927 despite international protests that their guilt had not been proven.

279.9   Chmielnicki] Cossack leader Bohdan Chmielnitzski (c. 1595–1657),
at whose instigation at least one hundred thousand Jews were massacred in
1648 and 1649.

279.10–11   national hero . . . Garibaldi] Jan Hus, Czech religious reformer (1369?–1415) condemned to death as a heretic and burnt at the stake;
Giuseppe Garibaldi (1807–1882), Italian nationalist and soldier who was one
of the primary figures in the struggle for Italian unification.

279.17   Volodymyr] Ukrainian form of the name of Vladimir the Great
(c. 956–1015), grand prince of Kiev and the first Christian ruler of Kievan Rus.

279.23   Bandera . . . Petlura] Stepan Bandera (1909–1959) joined the
Organization of Ukrainian Nationalists in 1929 and became the leader of its
militant faction (OUN-B) in 1940. He collaborated with the German army
before the invasion of the Soviet Union, but was imprisoned in Germany
from July 1941 to September 1944 because of his support for an independent
Ukraine; during this period, many of his followers in Ukraine collaborated
with the Germans in the mass killing of Jews. Bandera was assassinated by the
KGB in Munich in 1959. Symon Petliura (1879–1926) commanded the Ukrain-

ian national army during the civil war in Ukraine (1919–20), during which his troops killed thousands of Jews. Petliura was assassinated in Paris in 1926 by Shalom Schwartzbard (1886–1938), a Jewish anarchist seeking to avenge the deaths of family members during the 1919 pogroms. Schwartzbard was acquitted of murder by a French court after a trial during which the prosecution accused him of being a Soviet agent.

280.6   Canarsie]   Brooklyn neighborhood near Coney Island and the Atlantic Ocean.

280.27–28   Hitler . . . Bessarabia]   See note 44.13–18.

281.38–40   Pipik . . . forever]   Cf. the closing of Psalm 23: "Surely goodness will follow me all the days of my life, and I shall dwell in the house of the Lord forever."

284.26–27   Talmud Torah]   Hebrew School, instructing Jewish boys in preparation for Bar Mitzvah at age thirteen.

287.3   shtetl-born]   Immigrants from the small rural Jewish towns of Eastern Europe.

288.6–9   Popkin . . . Oswald]   Richard H. Popkin (1923–2005), a philosophy professor at the University of California, San Diego, put forth this argument in his book *The Second Oswald* (1966).

295.21   Edith Wharton's]   American novelist and short-story writer (1862–1937), best known for the novels *The House of Mirth* (1905) and *The Age of Innocence* (1920).

295.27   *Nostromo*]   Novel (1904) by Joseph Conrad (1857–1924).

295.35   *The Bellarosa Connection*]   Novel (1989) by Saul Bellow.

296.16   Nineveh's]   Ancient Assyrian city near the Tigris river.

296.22   Rorschachish]   Swiss psychiatrist Hermann Rorschach (1884–1922) developed the Rorschach test, which analyzes a person's perception of inkblots.

298.8   Chaim Weizmann Institute]   The Weizmann Institute of Science in Rehovat, Israel, established in 1933 and renamed in 1949 after its founder, Chaim Weizmann, chemist and statesman (1874–1952), who served as the first president (1949–52) of Israel.

298.18   Kibbutz]   Hebrew: A collective community in Israel. In the first decade of the twentieth century, Eastern European Jews began settling in Palestine en masse. Kibbutzim were originally small agricultural communities that were socialist in organization and Zionist in political outlook.

298.25 shrine of the Holocaust] Yad Vashem, complex of museums, libraries, and memorial sites dedicated to the Holocaust.

298.27 Billy Rose's art exhibit] The Billy Rose Art Garden, designed by Japanese American artist Isamu Noguchi (1904–1988), is part of the Israel Museum in Jerusalem. It is named for its founder, the theater producer and lyricist Billy Rose (1899–1966).

304.39 Second Temple] The rebuilt temple in Jerusalem that succeeded Solomon's temple, destroyed in 586 B.C.E. when the Jews were sent into Babylonian exile. The Second Temple, dedicated in 515 B.C.E., was razed in 70 C.E. when the Romans sacked Jerusalem.

305.17 Vilna Gaon] Elijah ben Solomon (1720–1797), Lithuanian rabbi, revered scholar, and leader of non-Hasidic European Jewry. "Gaon" was the Hebrew term given to Talmudic scholars who headed Yeshivas.

305.18 the Midrash] Body of rabbinical commentary and scriptural exegesis.

305.34 Chofetz Chaim] "Desirer of Life" in Hebrew, the popular name for the Polish rabbi Israel Meir HaCohen Kagan (1838–1933); also the title of his most famous treatise (1873), concerning proper speech and the avoidance of slander.

309.26 Eretz Yisroel] Hebrew: land of Israel.

310.5 *pisherkehs*] Yiddish: little squirts.

310.5 *Ha'aretz*] Israeli daily newspaper, founded in 1918.

310.17 bill of attainder] Legislative act that exacts punishment without a trial.

312.2 hysterical aphonia] Loss of voice due to emotional stress.

313.24–25 the government . . . visa] Born Maier Suchowljansky (1902–1983) in Russia, Meyer Lansky immigrated to the United States as a child, became a gangster in New York City, and helped form a national crime syndicate in the 1930s. Fearing that he was about to be indicted for tax evasion, he fled to Israel in 1970, but after American authorities requested extradition, he was declared a "threat to the state" and expelled in 1972.

314.12–13 Mr. Vanunu . . . nuclear secrets] Modechai Vanunu (b. 1954) worked as a technician at the Israeli nuclear research center at Dimona from 1976 to 1985. After leaving Dimona, Vanunu traveled to Australia and England, where he gave the *Sunday Times* detailed information about the Israeli nuclear weapons program, along with photographs he had secretly taken inside the Dimona complex. Although the Mossad succeeded in using a female agent to lure Vanunu to Rome, where he was abducted and returned to Israel to stand trial, they were unable to prevent his revelations from being published by the *Sunday Times* in October 1986. Vanunu was sentenced to eighteen years in prison in 1988 and was released in 2004.

317.25   Oliver North] A lieutenant colonel in the Marines, North (b. 1943) served on the National Security Council staff from 1981 to 1986 and was a central figure in the Iran-Contra affair, involving the secret sale of weapons to Iran in an attempt to obtain the release of Americans held hostage in Lebanon, and the use of funds from the arms sales to illegally funnel supplies and funds to the Contra rebels seeking to overthrow the Sandinista government in Nicaragua.

320.16   Ambassador Pickering] American diplomat Thomas R. Pickering (b. 1931) served as ambassador to Israel (1985–88).

323.11–12   Gush Emunim] "Bloc of the Faithful," religious Zionist movement founded in 1974 that established Jewish settlements on the West Bank and opposed the return of any of the territory occupied by Israel in 1967.

325.1   UJA] United Jewish Appeal.

328.5   Slough of Despond] Bog in which Christian, the protagonist of John Bunyan's *The Pilgrim's Progress* (1678), sinks under the weight of his sins.

340.34   Charles Manson] Leader of a cultlike "family," Manson (b. 1934) ordered his followers to go on a killing spree in Los Angeles in the summer of 1969.

343.14   Céline-like way] Louis-Ferdinand Céline (1894–1961), French writer whose first novel and best-known work, *Journey to the End of the Night* (1932), is the violent and sexually candid story of its nihilistic hero, Bardamu.

347.30–31   Miami Beach's Fontainebleau] Designed by architect Morris Lapidus, the Fontainebleau Hotel in Miami Beach opened in 1954, and set a standard for glitzy elegance and ebullient conspicuous consumption.

348.3   kasha . . . fish] Traditional Jewish side dish mixing toasted buckwheat groats with egg noodles; fish patties of ground deboned whitefish.

348.38–39   "Our revels . . . air"] See Prospero's speech in Shakespeare, *The Tempest*, IV.i.148–50.

349.17   Negev] Desert region of southern Israel.

349.22   Beersheba] Largest city in the Negev, populated by large number of Jews who emigrated from Arab countries after 1948.

352.7   put a contract . . . Rushdie]   Iran's Supreme Leader, the Ayatollah Ruholla Khomeini (1900–1989), declared in a 1989 fatwa that British author Salman Rushdie (b. 1947) should be put to death because of alleged
blasphemy in his novel *The Satanic Verses* (1988).

354.25   Mr. Yagur and Mr. Eitan]   Yosef Yagur, the scientific attaché at
the Israeli consulate in New York, became Jonathan Pollard's handler in the
fall of 1984. Rafi Eitan (b. 1926), the director of Lakam, was the senior Israeli
official in charge of the Pollard operation and met with Pollard in Paris and
in Israel. (A former officer of the Mossad and Shin Bet, Eitan led the team
that captured Adolf Eichmann in 1960.)

355.11   the book about baseball]   *The Great American Novel* (1973).

355.13   a bit like reading *Finnegans Wake*]   James Joyce's notoriously difficult novel (1939).

357.11   *tsuras*]   Yiddish: trouble, aggravation.

359.14   Ted Solotaroff]   Literary critic and editor (1928–2008), author of
The Red Hot Vacuum (1970) and *A Few Good Voices in My Head* (1987) and
editor of the *North American Review*.

359.17–19   parking garage . . . Deep Throat]   Bob Woodward (b. 1943)
and Carl Bernstein (b. 1944) were the two *Washington Post* reporters who investigated the involvement of senior officials in President Nixon's reelection
campaign in the burglary at the Democratic National Committee Headquarters at the Watergate Hotel in Washington, D.C. During their investigation
Woodward met in an underground parking garage with an informant identified only as "Deep Throat" (until 2005, when he was revealed to have been
FBI associate director Mark Felt [1913–2008]).

360.6–7   chained . . . shadow]   See Plato *Republic* 7.514a–516b, the
"parable of the cave" where people confuse shadows projected on the wall of
a cave with real things.

361.22–23   pound of my flesh]   The payment Shylock demands from Antonio for his defaulted loan in *The Merchant of Venice*.

361.35   Mazel tov]   Hebrew: congratulations.

364.8   shtupped]   Yiddish: stuffed. Obscene: fucked.

365.22–23   remember . . . Kosinski!]   Kosinski's (see note 74.27–28) reputation suffered in the 1980s after he was accused of employing ghostwriters
and of misrepresenting his past. He committed suicide in 1991.

366.3   *tzaddik*]   Hebrew: righteous one. Also the Hasidic term of respect
for their rabbi.

SABBATH'S THEATER

373.22–23   Henson . . . Street]   Puppeteer, director, and writer Jim
Henson (1936–1990), whose Muppets have been a main feature of the PBS
children's program *Sesame Street* since its debut in 1969.

373.28   Hollywood Walk of Fame]   Stretch of sidewalk along Hollywood
Boulevard and Vine Street in Los Angles embedded with stars honoring
celebrities and fictional characters.

373.29   Bob Hope]   English-born comedian and movie star (1903–2003).

375.32–33   in 1948 . . . Union]   The pursuit of policies independent of
the Soviet Union by Josip Tito (1892–1980), Communist leader of totalitarian
Yugoslavia from 1945 to 1980, caused Yugoslavia's expulsion in 1948 from the
Cominform, a Soviet-dominated organization of Communist parties from
Eastern Europe, Italy, and France. Tito responded by ordering a purge of
suspect Soviet sympathizers that resulted in the imprisonment of more than
twelve thousand people in the concentration camp on Goli Otok.

376.29   *Drug*]   Serbo-Croatian: comrade.

382.18   Tintoretto's painting]   *The Origin of the Milky Way* (c. 1575; National Gallery, London), painting by Venetian artist Jacopo Tintoretto (1518–
1594).

382.40   *chumitz*]   All things forbidden at Passover, such as leavened
bread.

384.16   Army Air Corps]   The U.S. Army Air Corps (1926–41) and the
U.S. Army Air Forces (1941–47) were the predecessors of the U.S. Air Force.

389.32   *The Cherry Orchard*]   Play (1904) by Anton Chekhov (1860–
1904).

389.38–39   GI Bill]   Officially called the Servicemen's Readjustment Act
(1944), the G.I. Bill guaranteed access to college education and provided tu-
ition funding for veterans.

389.39   Madame Ranyevskaya]   Aristocratic matriarch of a failing estate in
The Cherry Orchard.

399.23   Monmouth County]   County in north-central New Jersey, the
northernmost county of the New Jersey shore.

402.18   Charles Bovary]   Cuckolded husband in Gustave Flaubert's
Madame Bovary (1857).

404.29–30   Uncircumcised . . . thus!]   See Othello's final words before
his suicide in Shakespeare's *Othello*, V.ii.351–56: "Set you down this; / And say
besides, that in Aleppo once, / Where a malignant and a turban'd Turk /

Beat a Venetian and traduc'd the state, / I took by th' throat the circumcised dog, / And smote him—thus."

406.3 Rotarians] Members of Rotary International, a fraternal organization of service clubs for businessmen and professionals founded in 1905.

420.2–4 Paunch . . . Satan] In Shakespeare's *I Henry IV*, Prince Hal refers to Falstaff as a "huge hill of flesh" (II.iv.243) and "Sir John Paunch" (II.ii.66). Hal calls Falstaff a "white-bearded Satan" at II.iv.462–63.

421.9 "Honeysuckle Rose,"] Song (1928) with music by Fats Waller (1904–1943) and lyrics by Andy Razaf (1895–1973).

421.19–20 Goodman's boys . . . the Basie band] For the Carnegie Hall concert the Goodman Orchestra was joined by members of the Count Basie Orchestra, including tenor saxophonist Lester Young (1909–1959), trumpeter Buck Clayton (1911–1991), guitarist Freddie Green (1911–1987), bassist Walter Page (1900–1957), and Basie (1904–1984) himself on piano.

421.27 That's James] Bandleader and trumpeter Harry James (1916–1983).

423.6 The trio . . . Soul."] At its inception in 1935, the Benny Goodman Trio featured Goodman (1909–1986) on clarinet, Teddy Wilson (1912–1986) on piano, and Gene Krupa (1909–1973) on drums; the group became the Benny Goodman Quartet a year later with the addition of Lionel Hampton (1908–2002) on vibes. For the Carnegie Hall concert, before inviting Hampton on stage, the Trio performed "Body and Soul" (1930), music by Johnny Green (1908–1989), lyrics by Edward Heyman (1907–1981), Robert Sour (1905–1985), and Frank Eyton (1894–1962).

423.23 painting by Otto Dix] The works of German Expressionist artist Otto Dix (1891–1967) often depict sexual violence.

423.28 "The Man . . . Shostakovich] Teddy Wilson, who had classical training, played piano on the Goodman Quartet's Carnegie Hall performance of "The Man I Love" (1927), music by George Gershwin (1898–1937), lyrics by Ira Gershwin; Dmitri Shostakovich (1906–1975), Russian modernist composer.

424.24 'Sugarfoot Stomp.'] Arrangement (1925) of trumpeter and bandleader King Oliver's (1885–1938) "Dippermouth Blues" for Fletcher Henderson's (1897–1952) orchestra.

424.26 the lindy] A precursor of the jitterbug, a partnered dance that combined hand-to-hand and solo dancing, named for transatlantic aviator Charles Lindbergh.

425.3 Elman's] Trumpet player and bandleader Harry "Ziggy" Elman (1914–1968).

425.4 "Bei Mir Bist du Sheyn"] "You Are Beautiful to Me": Yiddish song written by Jacob Jacobs (1890–1977) and Sholem Secunda (1894–1974) for the 1932 musical *If I Could I Would*. An English adaptation by Sammy Cahn and Saul Chaplin was recorded by the Andrews Sisters in 1937 and was their first hit.

426.33–34   *Ad majorem Dei gloriam*]   Latin: to the greater glory of God.

431.1   Borden]   Dairy company and food conglomerate.

437.15   objet trouvé]   French: found object.

442.34   Il catalogo]   "Madamina, il catalogo è questo" is an aria from Mozart's opera *Don Giovanni* (1787), act I, in which Leporello, Don Giovanni's servant, tells Donna Elvira of his master's sexual conquests from Spain to Turkey.

448.10–13   Ophelia . . . Miranda and Rosalind]   Young female characters in *Hamlet*, *The Tempest*, and *As You Like It*, respectively.

448.14   Forest of Arden]   Setting of *As You Like It*.

449.13   AA]   Alcoholics Anonymous.

451.8   step meeting]   AA members following the organization's Twelve Step recovery program meet regularly for mutual support.

453.1–2   how-to books . . . dying]   The *Meditations* of Roman emperor Marcus Aurelius (121–180) is an expression of his Stoic philosophy.

453.4–17   "Thus far . . . person . . ."]   From *Western Attitudes Toward Death from the Middle Ages to the Present* (1974) by the French historian Philippe Ariès (1914–1984).

462.39   Batista's Cuba . . . casino]   Cuban general and president Fulgencio Batista (1901–1973) ruled Cuba from 1933 to 1944 and 1952 to 1959; under his regime, American organized-crime syndicates controlled much of the gambling and prostitution on the island.

463.8   B.A.]   Buenos Aires.

464.40   Miltown]   Meprobamate, a tranquilizer.

466.30   bouzouki music]   Greek folk music played with a bouzouki, a long-necked, flat-bodied string instrument.

469.19   Parker House rolls]   A slightly sweet doughy roll invented a century ago at the Parker House hotel in Boston.

473.2–4   razor . . . *Miss Julie*]   August Strindberg's play (1888) ends with the title character walking through a doorway with a razor before what is almost certainly her suicide.

473.29–31   Amenhotep . . . Osiris] Amenhotep III, Egyptian pharaoh who ruled in the fourteenth century B.C.E.; Osiris, god of the underworld in Egyptian myth.

488.35   Tom Brokaw] American TV journalist (b. 1940) who anchored the NBC Nightly News from 1982 to 2004.

491.12–13   wound up in a whorehouse . . . *Sanctuary*] In William Faulkner's novel *Sanctuary* (1931), the impotent criminal Popeye rapes Temple Drake, the daughter of a prominent judge, with a corncob and takes her to live in a Memphis brothel.

491.22   Lautrec] French artist Henri de Toulouse-Lautrec (1864–1901).

492.7   Altman's] Upscale New York department store, founded in 1865, that closed in 1989.

495.31   Sheepshead Bay] Bay in Brooklyn, east of Coney Island.

503.2   Dogpatch] Fictional rural town of boisterous hillbillies that was the setting for *Li'l Abner*, comic strip (1934–77) by Al Capp (1909–1979).

503.4   Russian pale] Empress Catherine II ("The Great") of Russia established the Pale of Settlement in 1791 to contain the Russian Empire's expanding Jewish population.

505.36   gold star] Small banner bearing a gold star displayed in homes where a family member had been killed in the war.

507.38   I wasn't living with Doris Day] Actress and singer Doris Day (b. 1922) personified an image of American wholesomeness through her movie roles in the 1950s and early 1960s.

508.10   Army Benrus] Watch supplied to the army by the Benrus Watch Company.

508.17   laid tefillin] Tefillin (phylacteries), two black leather boxes containing Torah verses that are fastened with leather straps to the left arm and to the forehead by Jewish men when they recite their morning prayers.

514.6   Dalton School] Elite private school on Manhattan's Upper East Side.

514.9   K. Chopin . . . Woolf] Novelists likely to be assigned at school: Kate Chopin (1850–1904), author of *The Awakening* (1899); Toni Morrison (b. 1933), author of *Beloved* (1987); Amy Tan (b. 1952), author of *The Joy Luck Club* (1989); Virginia Woolf (1882–1941), author of *To the Lighthouse* (1927) and *A Room of One's Own* (1929).

514.10–11   *The Yearling . . . Tales*] *The Yearling* (1938), novel by Marjorie Kinnan Rawlings (1896–1953); *Fairy Tales* (1835–37) by Danish writer Hans Christian Andersen (1805–1875).

516.22–23   O'Neill . . . Conrad]   Playwright Eugene O'Neill (1888–1953) and novelist Joseph Conrad (1857–1924) wrote works that drew on their experiences at sea.

516.27   Rascal Knockoff]   A play on Raskolnikov, protagonist of Dostoyevsky's *Crime and Punishment* (1866).

518.9–11   Mishima . . . Benjamin]   Prominent writers and artists who committed suicide: Japanese writer Yukio Mishima (1925–1970); American painter Mark Rothko (1903–1970); American writer Ernest Hemingway (1899–1961); American poet John Berryman (1914–1972); Hungarian-born English writer Arthur Koestler (1905–1983); Italian writer Cesare Pavese (1908–1950); Jerzy Kosinski (see note 74.27–28); Armenian-born painter Arshile Gorky (1904–1948); Primo Levi (see notes 74.38–39 and 162.31–32); American poet Hart Crane (1899–1932); German Jewish political theorist and literary critic Walter Benjamin (1892–1940).

518.12–14   Faulkner . . . Gardner]   The alcoholism of novelist William Faulkner (1897–1962) contributed to his death from a heart attack; actress Ava Gardner (1922–1990) was known for her beauty, tempestuous marriages with celebrities such as Mickey Rooney and Frank Sinatra, and hard-drinking lifestyle.

518.17   Yvonne De Carlo]   Stage name of Margaret Yvonne Middleton (1922–2007), Canadian-born actress whose films include *Salome Where She Danced* (1945) and *The Ten Commandments* (1956).

518.19   *A Room of One's Own*]   Feminist essay (1929) by Virginia Woolf; its title is derived from her contention that a "woman must have money and a room of her own if she is to write fiction."

518.38   Punch]   Anarchic English puppet, a trickster figure related to Pulcinella in Italian *commedia dell'arte*.

519.15   Quimper]   Glazed pottery often decorated with pastoral scenes, named for the French town where it was first manufactured.

519.21–22   Tiptree . . . Little Scarlet]   Made from a tiny variety of strawberry, "Little Scarlet" is a brand of expensive strawberry preserves sold by Wilkin & Sons, a company based in Tiptree, England.

520.39   *alte kocker's*]   Literally "old shitter" in Yiddish: old-timer, old fart.

524.26   "Meru"]   This sonnet is the last of the twelve "Supernatural Songs" in Yeats's collection *A Full Moon in March* (1935). In Hindu cosmology,

Mount Meru (or Sumeru) is the physical center of the universe and its summit the axis on which all creation turns.

525.15–16   "We free ourselves . . . to the void."]   Yeats to the English poet Thomas Sturge Moore (1870–1944), April 17, 1929, collected in *W. B. Yeats and T. Sturge Moore: Their Correspondence, 1901–1937*, edited by Ursula Bridge (1953).

525.26   the Prado, the National Gallery, the Uffizi]   Art museums in Madrid, London, and Florence, respectively.

527.31   Merlin's]   Wizard of Arthurian legend.

527.32   *agápe mou*]   Greek: my love.

528.9–10   Eldridge Cleaver]   A leader of the Black Panther Party, Cleaver (1935–1988) was the author of the autobiography *Soul on Ice* (1968), written in prison.

528.10–12   *John Kennedy . . . Warburgs*]   *President Kennedy: Portrait of Power,* a history of the Kennedy presidency (1993) by journalist Richard Reeves (b. 1936); popular memoir (1993) about the African American sisters Sarah L. Delany (1889–1999) and Annie Elizabeth Delany (1891–1995), written with Amy Hill Heath; study (1993) of a twentieth-century German Jewish dynasty prominent in investment banking, philanthropy, and the arts by Ron Chernow (b. 1949).

530.27   General Noriega]   Panamanian dictator (b. 1934) who was ousted from power by the 1989 American invasion of his country. Brought to Miami, Noriega was convicted in a federal court of cocaine trafficking, racketeering, and money laundering, and sentenced to forty years in prison.

531.35   *treyf*]   Yiddish: unclean, not kosher.

531.38   *davening*]   Yiddish: praying.

532.10   Bergdorf]   Bergdorf Goodman, luxury department store with flagship store on New York's Fifth Avenue.

533.12   Vesuvius had preserved Pompeii]   The eruption of Mount Vesuvius, volcano east of Naples, buried the Roman city of Pompeii in 79 C.E.

534.9–11   El Greco . . . background]   Crete-born Spanish artist El Greco (1541–1614) made paintings and altarpieces with stylized figures and a vivid, nearly expressionist color palette. He lived much of his life in the Spanish city of Toledo.

535.30   Voltaren]   Anti-inflammatory drug.

535.30   *Volare!*]   Italian: to fly. Also the usual title given for "Nel blu dipinto di blu" (1958), international hit by Italian singer Domenico Modugno (1928–1994).

535.30–32   Via Veneto . . . Trastevere] Street and neighborhood in Rome.

536.19   *El momento de verdad*] Spanish: moment of truth, said of the time when the matador prepares to kill the bull.

540.20   NOW] National Organization for Women.

540.21   to Mussolini] Italian Fascist dictator Benito Mussolini (1883–1945) and his mistress, Clara Petacci, were captured and shot by partisans near Lake Como on April 28, 1945, and their corpses were strung up by their heels in Milan's Piazzale Loreto the following day.

540.22–24   that woman . . . husband] In a case that attracted national attention, Lorena Gallo Bobbitt (b. 1970) severed the penis of her sleeping husband, John Wayne Bobbitt (b. 1967), on June 23, 1993, in Manassas, Virginia. At her trial for malicious wounding, she testified that he had raped her earlier that night and described a history of domestic abuse in their relationship. She was found not guilty by reason of temporary insanity. John Wayne Bobbitt was acquitted of charges of marital sexual assault in 1994.

540.30   *bris*] Hebrew: circumcision and naming ceremony.

540.40   Exodus 21:24] "Eye for eye, tooth for tooth, hand for hand, foot for foot."

541.4   *A Doll's House*] Play (1879) by Norwegian playwright Henrik Ibsen (1828–1906).

541.21   Bill W.] William Griffith Wilson (1895–1971), the co-founder of Alcoholics Anonymous.

541.32   Sierra Club] Environmental organization founded in 1892 by naturalist and conservationist John Muir (1838–1914).

541.33–35   Joan Baez . . . Agnew] Folk singer and political activist Joan Baez (b. 1941); Republican politician Spiro Agnew (1918–1996), vice president of the United States, 1969–73.

542.7–10   'Who . . . hand.'] Lady Macbeth's two quotations appear at V.i.39–40 and V.i.51–52 in Shakespeare's *Macbeth*.

543.1   Louis to knock out Schmeling] Heavyweight champion Joe Louis (1914–1981) knocked out German boxer Max Schmeling (1905–2005) two minutes and four seconds into the first round of an internationally broadcast fight held at Yankee Stadium in New York City on June 22, 1938. A rematch of a 1936 non-championship bout in which Schmeling had knocked out Louis in the 12th round, the second fight was touted as a symbolic battle between Nazi Germany and the United States by both sides.

544.4 Rip Van Winkle] Story (1819) by Washington Irving (1783–1859) about a man who wakes up after a twenty-year slumber.

544.16 Con Ed] Consolidated Edison, New York utility company.

547.12 Colet] French poet Louise Colet (1810–1876), Flaubert's mistress.

547.16 Zelda] Writer and painter Zelda Fitzgerald (1900–1948), wife of F. Scott Fitzgerald.

547.16–17 Hughes . . . Plath] American poet Sylvia Plath (1932–1963) married English poet Ted Hughes (1930–1998) in 1956 and settled in England. After the couple separated in the fall of 1962, Plath lived with their two children in London through the winter, writing the poems gathered posthumously in *Ariel* (1965). Plath committed suicide on February 11, 1963.

548.23 Nietzsche's . . . *Evil*] *Beyond Good and Evil* (1886) by German philosopher Friedrich Nietzsche (1844–1900) was an attack on Christianity and conventional morality.

550.4–6 Neither . . . man] Parody of Polonius's advice to Hamlet ("Neither a borrower nor a lender be . . .") in *Hamlet*, I.iii.75–80.

550.13 Bo Jackson] Professional athlete (b. 1962) who had simultaneous careers as a running back in the National Football League and an outfielder and designated hitter in Major League Baseball.

550.19 Freie Bibliothek u. Lesehall] German: free library and reading hall.

551.23 Sonja Henie] Norwegian figure skater, Olympic gold medalist, and actress (1912–1969).

551.23–24 Ann-Margret] Swedish-born actress, singer, and sex symbol (b. 1941) with starring roles in films including *Viva Las Vegas* (1964) and *Carnal Knowledge* (1971).

551.24 Grace Kelly] Actress (1929–1982) whose films include *Rear Window* (1954) and *The Country Girl* (1954). After marrying Prince Rainier, she became Princess Grace of Monaco.

552.21 Mixmaster] Popular kitchen appliance, an electric mixing machine.

554.8–9 Toreador . . . for!] Parody of the familiar "Toreador Song" aria from Georges Bizet's opera *Carmen* (1875).

556.18 *tsimmes*] Yiddish (slang): a big deal made out of nothing.

561.16–17 the Grand Guignol] Parisian theater (1897–1962) featuring sensational and grotesque spectacles.

563.8–9 Fats Waller . . . letter."] In 1935 Fats Waller recorded "I'm Gonna Sit Right Down and Write Myself a Letter," song with music by Fred E. Ahlert (1892–1953) and music by Joe Young (1889–1939).

570.7 opening of "Ode to Autumn"] Keats's poem (1819) begins "Season of mists and mellow fruitfulness, / Close bosom-friend of the maturing sun."

570.20–571.6 twenty-five years . . . Aristophanes] Writers and notable works banned or censored for their purported obscenity: *The Story of O* (1954) by Pauline Réage, pseudonym of Anne Desclos (1907–1998); *Tropic of Cancer* (1934) and other works by Henry Miller (1891–1980); *Lady Chatterley's Lover* (1928) by D. H. Lawrence (1885–1930); *Ulysses* (1922) by James Joyce (1882–1941); *Memoirs of a Woman of Pleasure* (1748–49), original title of novel more commonly known as *Fanny Hill*, by John Cleland (1710–1789); the often bowdlerized poetry of John Wilmot, 2nd Earl of Rochester (1647–1680); and the writings of French author François Rabelais (1494–1553), Roman poet Ovid (43 B.C.E.–17 or 18 C.E.), and Greek comic dramatist Aristophanes (446–386 B.C.E.).

573.2 molly-bloomed!] Molly Bloom is the wife of fictional character of protagonist Leopold Bloom in James Joyce's *Ulysses* (1922), which concludes with a soliloquy in which she rhapsodizes about her first sexual experience.

573.15–16 "When Hearts Were Young and Gay"] *Our Hearts Were Young and Gay*, movie (1944) based on bestselling book (1942) by Cornelia Otis Skinner (1899–1979) and Emily Kimbrough about their trip to Europe in the 1920s after graduating from Bryn Mawr College.

578.7–9 "Sometimes . . . Berigan] Berigan (1908–1942) played trumpet on the 1935 hit recording of "Sometimes I'm Happy" by Benny Goodman and His Orchestra.

578.14–15 "Stardust" . . . Carmichael] Songwriter and singer Hoagy Carmichael (1899–1981) first recorded an instrumental version of "Stardust" (as "Star Dust") in 1927. Mitchell Parrish (1900–1993) added lyrics in 1929.

578.15–16 Suivant . . . nom] From French version of "Stardust": Following the silence of the night / Repeat your name. . . .

579.18–20 "Roll 'Em" . . . blues in F] Jess Stacy (1904–1995) played piano on the Benny Goodman Orchestra's 1937 recording of "Roll 'Em" by composer and arranger Mary Lou Williams (1910–1981). Boogie-woogie, a subgenre of blues that uses a driving bass line of continuous eighth notes, was wildly popular in the late 1930s.

580.2–3 "Sweet Leilani"] In 1937 the Goodman Trio was recorded playing "Sweet Leilani," a 1934 song written by Harry Owens (1902–1986) and popularized by its appearance in the 1937 movie *Waikiki Wedding*.

580.3–6   Martha Tilton . . . arranger]   After singer Helen Ward (1913–1998) left Goodman's band in 1936, Martha Tilton (1915–2006) replaced her; drummer Dave Tough (1907–1948) played with Goodman's band after Gene Krupa formed his own band in 1938; tenor saxophonist Bud Freeman (1906–1991) briefly played with Goodman's band between stints with the Jimmy Dorsey Orchestra and his own band; arranger and tenor saxophonist Jimmy Mundy (1907–1983) had worked as an arranger for Earl Hines's band before joining Goodman's band.

582.4   Gene Tierney's in *Laura*]   *Laura* (1944), film starring Tierney (1920–1991) as a beautiful woman whose presumed murder is investigated by a detective who becomes obsessed with her.

586.13   Capisco]   Italian: I understand.

586.27   at Nuremberg]   The trial (November 1945–October 1946) of twenty-two Nazi political and military leaders for war crimes by an international tribunal at Nuremberg ended with twelve defendants sentenced to death, seven sentenced to prison, and the acquittal of three defendants.

587.23   ancient Attica]   Athenian Greece.

587.33–34   *patriotism* . . . scoundrel]   Cf. Samuel Johnson as quoted in James Boswell, *Life of Johnson* (1791), entry for April 7, 1775: "Patriotism is the last refuge of a scoundrel."

587.35   Virgil to your Dante]   Virgil led Dante through hell in *Inferno*.

588.39–40   bludgeonings of fate]   Cf. "Invictus" (1875) by English poet William Ernest Henley (1849–1903): "In the fell clutch of circumstance / I have not winced nor cried aloud. / Under the bludgeonings of chance / My head is bloody, but unbowed."

590.28   "Running Wild,"]   Song (1922) by A. H. Gibbs, Joe Grey, and Leo Wood, first recorded by the Goodman Quartet in August 1938.

592.27–28   Put out . . . light]   *Othello*, V.ii.7, from Othello's speech over the sleeping Desdemona shortly before he murders her.

593.8–9   what they did . . . box]   In the film *The Bridge on the River Kwai* (1957), Alec Guinness (1914–2000) plays a British officer at a Japanese prisoner-of-war camp in Thailand who is placed in a metal box ("The Oven") after refusing to perform manual labor for his captors.

594.32   Petrushka]   A Russian folk tale about a puppet come to life.

595.22   Akim Tamiroff]   Russian-born actor (1899–1972) of Armenian descent whose films include *The Great McGinty* (1940) and *For Whom the Bell Tolls* (1943)

595.38–596.4   I heard . . . hair]   The final stanza of Yeats's poem "For Anne Gregory," collected in *The Winding Stair and Other Poems* (1933).

596.9   Tojo and Hirohito]   Japanese general Hideki Tojo (1884–1948), Japan's prime minister from 1941 to 1944; Japanese emperor Hirohito (1901–1989).

596.13   "The Sheik of Araby."]   Song (1921) with music by Ted Snyder, lyrics by Harry B. Smith and Francis Wheeler, recorded by the Goodman Quartet in August 1938.

596.18–19   Koreans . . . thirty-five years]   Japan occupied Korea from 1910 to 1945.

596.19–20   Ask the Manchurians . . . Ask the Chinese]   Japanese troops seized control of Manchuria in northeast China in autumn 1931, and in 1932 Japan established and recognized a puppet Manchurian state, Manchukuo. In 1933 its army advanced as far as Tianjin and forced the Chinese to establish a demilitarized zone on the southern side of the Great Wall and acknowledge Japanese control of the territory on the northern side. A full-scale, though undeclared, war between China and Japan broke out in 1937; by October 1938 Japan occupied almost all of eastern China. Fighting among Chinese Nationalist, Chinese Communist, and Japanese forces continued until the Japanese surrender to the Allies in August 1945.

619.10–11   "Night and Day"]   1932 song by Cole Porter (1891–1964).

621.18   "The great god Pan is dead,"]   In *Morals*, Plutarch recounts a legend that in the reign of Tiberius an Egyptian pilot on a ship sailing from Greece toward Italy heard the cry "The great god Pan is dead," and was told to tell the news at the port of Palodes. When he did, his announcement was met with wailing and lamentation. Later Christian commentators said that the pilot heard the cry at the moment of the Crucifixion, and that it signified the cessation of all pagan oracles.

622.30   *chuppa*]   Hebrew: wedding canopy.

623.3   *zebu*]   Type of domesticated cattle originating in South Asia.

623.27   Elohim]   One of the names of God in Hebrew.

628.13   Shirley MacLaine]   Actress (b. 1934) known for her New Age beliefs.

634.19–20   Erik Erikson . . . stage]   "Intimacy-versus-isolation" is one of the "eight stages of man" outlined in *Childhood and Society* (1950) by psychoanalyst Erik Erikson (1902–1994).

637.12   "When . . . In,"]   New Orleans jazz-band favorite.

639.18   Tobacco Road]   Novel (1932) about Georgia sharecroppers by Er-
skine Caldwell (1903–1987).

639.29–30   "Live . . . plates]   The motto of New Hampshire, "Live
Free or Die," appears on the state's license plates.

640.18   Rue St. Denis]   Street in Paris notorious for its prostitutes.

641.2–3   like Vronsky and Anna]   Adulterous couple in Tolstoy's *Anna
Karenina*, who leave Russia to journey together to Italy.

641.30–32   "Pray . . . Methinks]   *King Lear*, IV.iv.58–63, spoken by Lear.

642.1   nuncle]   The Fool calls Lear "nuncle" with affectionate ridicule.

642.12–14   "O look . . . kneel."]   Cordelia to Lear in *King Lear*,
IV.iv.56–58.

642.28   "You . . . grave,"]   Lear's dismissive reply to Cordelia at *King
Lear*, IV.iv.44.

643.32   APO]   Army Post Office.

648.11–12   "'Pray . . . foolish.'"]   *King Lear*, IV.iv.84.

648.15–16   Thou'lt . . . never]   *King Lear*, V.iii.308–9: Lear's words
when he realizes Cordelia is dead.

650.22   Diogenes in his tub?]   The Greek Cynic philosopher Diogenes
(412?–323 B.C.E.) is reputed to have lived in a tub.

650.29   Two-Ton Tony Galento]   Heavyweight boxer and entertainer
(1910–1979).

650.30   Man Mountain Dean]   Pseudonym of Georgia-born wrestler and
entertainer Frank S. Leavitt (1890–1953).

652.19–20   Mammy Yokum]   Character in the *L'il Abner* comic strip (see
note 503.2).

654.9–10   "*Bolbotish.*"]   Yiddish: master of the house (adjectival form).

654.12   Pandemonium]   In John Milton's *Paradise Lost* (1667), the capital of Hell.

659.5   Galahad]   Arthurian knight identified with gallantry.

660.38   shmegeggy]   Yiddish: foolish person.

661.24–25   Charlotte Moorman . . . cello bare-breasted]   In 1967,
avant-garde cellist Charlotte Moorman (1933–1991) gave a public performance
in New York City of Nam June Paik's *Opéra Sextronique* playing naked from

the waist up, as the composer had instructed. The performance was stopped and Moorman was arrested. She received a suspended sentence for indecent exposure.

661.26   *Nation*] Left-wing magazine.

662.33   *Ulysses* case] In 1933, U.S. district judge John Woolsey ruled in New York City that *Ulysses* (1922) was not obscene and could be legally brought into the country. His decision was later upheld on appeal to the U.S. circuit court and cleared the way for Random House to publish an American edition of the novel the following year.

662.34   'Miracle' case] Accusations of sacrilege in the short film "The Miracle" (1948; released in the United States in 1950 in the two-part anthology film *Ways of Love*), directed by Roberto Rossellini, led to the censorship of the film by the New York State Board of Regents. In *Joseph Burstyn, Inc v. Wilson* (1952), the Supreme Court ruled 9–0 that the suppression of the film violated the First Amendment.

663.1   *farshtunkeneh*] Yiddish: stinking.

664.40   St. John's] Catholic university in Queens.

665.1–2   Cardinal Spellman] Francis Spellman (1889–1967), Roman Catholic archbishop of New York, 1939–67.

667.21   *zaydeh*] Yiddish: grandfather.

667.30   Savonarola] Girolamo Savonarola (1452–1498), Florentine monk, reformer, and moral scourge.

668.6   like Lear, "Let copulation thrive!"] *King Lear*, IV.vi.107.

668.25   *chazerei*] Yiddish: junk (literally "pig food").

669.2   When I hear . . . device] Cf. Hanns Johst, *Schlageter* (1933), "When I hear the word 'culture' . . . I reach for my pistol," a remark often attributed to Hermann Göring.

669.30–31   Bataan death march] Forced sixty-five-mile march of some eighty-five thousand American and Filipino prisoners-of-war after the fall of Bataan in April 1942. Brutal treatment of the prisoners by the Japanese, including beatings, starvation, medical neglect, and summary execution, resulted in the deaths of an estimated ten thousand men during the march.

670.20   Peter Jennings] Canadian-born journalist and ABC network anchorman (1938–2005), host of *World News Tonight*.

671.9   Zeroes] World War II Japanese fighter planes.

672.27–28   New Jersey's Colette] French novelist (1873–1954), author of

Cheri (1920) and the pseudonymously published "Claudine" tetralogy, who wrote candidly about sex and erotic relationships.

673.38   *schmutzig*] Yiddish: dirty.

676.12–14   Kant . . . law."] *The Metaphysic of Morals* (1797), ch. II.

678.36–37   and no I said no I will no] Cf. the end of Molly Bloom's soliloquy in the final chapter of James Joyce's *Ulysses* (1922): "yes I said yes I will Yes" (see also note 573.2).

679.23   Little King in the old comic strip] *The Little King*, pantomime comic strip (1931–1975) created by cartoonist Otto Soglow (1900–1975).

680.6   "China Boy."] Song (1922) by Dick Winfree and Phil Boutelje, a staple of the Benny Goodman Trio.

680.24   Rodolphe] Rodolphe Boulanger, one of Emma Bovary's two lovers in Flaubert's *Madame Bovary.*

689.8   *meshuggeneh*] Yiddish: crazy.

689.34   Lawrence's gamekeeper] In *Lady Chatterley's Lover* (1928), Constance Chatterley has an affair with her estate's gamekeeper, Oliver Mellors.

690.2   Linda Lovelace] Stage name of Linda Susan Boreman (1949–2002), star of the pornographic movie *Deep Throat* (1972).

693.8   Payne Whitney] Psychiatric clinic at New York Hospital.

696.13   sugar] Diabetes.

698.13   *schvartze*] Yiddish: black.

704.25–26   make straight . . . crooked] Ecclesiastes 7:13.

706.4   Cheshvan] Hebrew month usually falling in October–November.

711.15   pebbles to place on the stones] An act of remembrance to indicate that a grave is attended.

718.34   Mrs. Nussbaum . . . *Allen* show] Pansy Nussbaum, a Jewish housewife from the Bronx, was one of the characters on the "Allen's Alley" segment of the popular radio program of comedian Fred Allen (1894–1956).

719.29   *shicker*] Yiddish: drunk.

720.10–11   came over . . . on and off] Jewish law forbids work of any kind from sundown Friday to sundown Saturday.

723.12–13   shaving on Saturday] Prohibited by Jewish law.

727.14   H. V. Kaltenborn] Radio commentator and journalist (1878–

1965) whose broadcasts were heard in millions of American households in the 1930s and 1940s.

728.12   *Vu den?*]   Yiddish: what else?

733.28   Willie Pep]   Featherweight boxing champion (1922–2006), born Guglielmo Papaleo.

741.26   Hopalong Cassidy]   Cowboy hero of fiction and movies created by Clarence Mulford (1883–1956).

741.28   Baal Shem Tov]   See note 23.23–25.

743.20   USO]   United Service Organizations, privately funded organization providing entertainment and support for soldiers.

744.34   Saraka]   A laxative manufactured by the Schering Corporation.

747.9   B.4 bag]   Army-issued canvas luggage.

748.12   v-mail]   Printed correspondence forms that were microfilmed and sent overseas, then enlarged and delivered.

748.26   "When Irish eyes are smiling"]   *Irish Eyes Are Smiling* (1944), movie biography (1944) of popular Irish American composer Ernest R. Ball (1878–1927).

748.40   Bob Hopes . . . home"]   Hope's first book, published in 1944.

751.26   Paul Stuart]   Conservative, expensive clothing line with its flagship store on Madison Avenue in New York City.

752.21–22   until LeMay . . . Command]   Major General Curtis LeMay (1906–1990) took over XXI Bomber Command, the B-29 force based in the Marianas, in January 1945.

756.28   Dioklecijan]   Born in Dalmatia, Roman emperor Diocletian (244–311) returned there after abdicating in 305 and built himself a palace in Split on the Adriatic coast.

756.31   *Aqua femina*]   Latin: water woman.

759.8   Cookman . . . away]   Cookman Avenue, the main shopping street in Asbury Park, was devastated by race riots in 1970.

759.17   *shmatte*]   Yiddish: rag.

765.13   Shit from Shinola]   From the common put-down, "You don't know shit from Shinola." Shinola was a boot polish.

768.3–4   *Came . . . Red Book*]   Alcoholics Anonymous publications *Came to Believe* (1973), *Twenty-four Hours a Day* (1975), and *The Little Red*

Book: An Interpretation of the Twelve Steps of the Alcoholics Anonymous Program (1957)

769.3   *forshpeis*]   Yiddish: appetizer.

770.38–771.2   Aquinas . . . that pin]   Opponents of medieval Scholastic philosophers such as Thomas Aquinas (c. 1225–1274) charged that they made tedious arguments about matters as absurd and trivial as the number of angels that could dance on the head of a pin.

777.11   Duncan]   King of Scotland murdered by Macbeth.

779.20   Martin Buber]   Jewish philosopher and theologian (1878–1965) who popularized Hasidism in *Tales of Rabbi Nachman of Breslov* (1906) and *Legends of the Bal Shem Tov* (1908). In 1923, the philosophical work *I and Thou* established his international reputation.

780.1–2   old . . . Tiresias]   In Greek mythology and literature, the blind prophet Tiresias is often depicted as a very old man.

784.4–6   B.G. sextet's . . . Slam]   The Benny Goodman Sextet's version of the 1929 Fats Waller standard included Leroy "Slam" Stewart (1914–1987) on bass, who would bow the instrument while humming the tune.

THE LIBRARY OF AMERICA SERIES

The Library of America fosters appreciation and pride in America's literary heritage by publishing, and keeping permanently in print, authoritative editions of America's best and most significant writing. An independent nonprofit organization, it was founded in 1979 with seed money from the National Endowment for the Humanities and the Ford Foundation.

To subscribe to the series or to order individual copies,
please visit www.loa.org or call (800) 964.5778.

This book is set in 10 point Linotron Galliard,
a face designed for photocomposition by Matthew Carter
and based on the sixteenth-century face Granjon. The paper
is acid-free lightweight opaque and meets the requirements
for permanence of the American National Standards Institute.
The binding material is Brillianta, a woven rayon cloth made
by Van Heek-Scholco Textielfabrieken, Holland. Compo-
sition by Dedicated Business Services. Printing by
Malloy Incorporated. Binding by Dekker Book-
binding. Designed by Bruce Campbell.

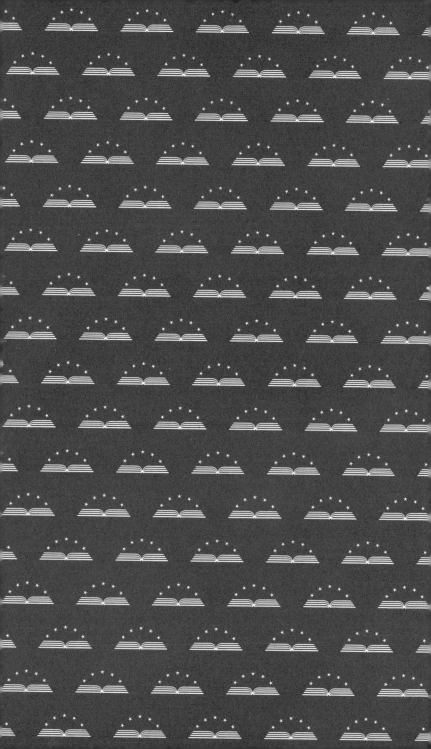